# 美国内战前女作家
爱丽丝·凯瑞 研究

MEIGUO NEIZHANQIAN NÜZUOJIA
AILISI KAIRUI YANJIU

杨林贵
丹尼斯·博索德(美) 主编

东北师范大学出版社　长　春

图书在版编目（CIP）数据

美国内战前女作家爱丽丝·凯瑞研究/杨林贵，(美)博索德主编. —2版. —长春：东北师范大学出版社，2015.4（2024.1重印）
ISBN 978 - 7 - 5602 - 9058 - 4

Ⅰ.①美… Ⅱ.①杨… ②博… Ⅲ.①凯瑞，A.—文学研究—文集 Ⅳ.①I712.065-53

中国版本图书馆CIP数据核字(2015)第 030123 号

□策划编辑：魏芳华
□责任编辑：曲　颖　王丽娜　　□封面设计：张　然
□责任校对：刘　芳　　　　　　□责任印制：刘兆辉

东北师范大学出版社出版发行
长春净月经济开发区金宝街 118 号（邮政编码：130117）
网址：http：//www.nenup.com
东北师范大学出版社激光照排中心制版
河北省廊坊市永清县晔盛亚胶印有限公司
河北省廊坊市永清县燃气工业园榕花路 3 号（065600）
2015 年 4 月第 2 版　　2024 年 1 月第 2 次印刷
幅面尺寸：155mm×230mm　印张：29　字数：426 千

定价：79.50 元

序

（一）

最近30年来，美国文学在发生着巨大变化。文学界对后现代主义进行着新的界定，对美国经典作品进行着重新考虑与衡量，过去被认为不能登上大雅之堂的通俗文化产品在以咄咄逼人的姿态，不仅出现在文坛上，而且正在迈进大学的文学课堂。这些包括通俗文学作品、科幻小说、"邦克与铁心"（Punk and Hardcore）文学作品、"X代"（Generation X）文学作品、同性恋作品、女性主义文学作品以及如雨后春笋般出现的多种族、多文化类作品等。人们发现，新时代正在努力建立自己的新文坛，推出自己的新思想、新概念、新成果。一种日渐强劲的打破偶像的暗流在明显地浮上台面，一种离经叛道、走出新路的态势正在各个文学领域内形成气候。不论在内容或是技巧方面，美国作家都在以前所未有的精气神向传统提出挑战，表达自己欲以全新的创作直面新世界、新生活的决心。毫无疑问，这些新事态都和20世纪60年代民权运动之后几十年来文化与思想界所感到的自由与开放气氛有着密切联系。

我国外国文学研究界对此早有察觉，并作出了相应的反应。不少介绍和评论文章在谈及此事，翻译与出版界也在注视着事态的进展。例如译文出版社翻译和出版美国学者哈罗德·布鲁姆（Harold Bloom, 1930—）的《西方经典》（The Western Canon: The Books and School of the Ages）一书，就是比较突出的例子之一。现在即将面世的"爱丽丝·凯瑞研究"文集则是这方面研究的另外一个可喜成果。由杨林贵教授主编的这部论文集对美国文学史上曾被忽略的一个作家——爱丽丝·凯瑞（Alice Cary, 1820—1871）进行了透彻的研究与介绍，不仅填补了我国外国文学及美国文学研究领域的一个空白，而且为这些领域的研究者们作出了极重要的提示，即要以全新的目光重新审视外国文学和美国文学领域内的作家与作品，一味沿袭传统做法不仅会失于偏颇，而且会脱离这些国家的文学创作实际。这是很不可取的。

（二）

文学领域活动的特点之一是它既拥立声名，也推翻权威，既让人名留青史，也让人从人世彻底"蒸发"。这种"成败"有时是永久性的，有时则具有相对的时间性。美国作家亨利·大卫·梭罗（Henry David Thoreau，1817—1862）从文坛"蒸发"了几十年，英国诗人约翰·堂恩（John Donne，1572—1631）从人们的视野"消逝"了长达两个世纪之久。但是，历史和时间是公平的。此二人到20世纪又都成为文学界介绍与研究的热点。历史和时间作判决自有其公正的标准，这就是，看一个人对人类的智慧金字塔是否作出了某种可以令人称道的贡献，看此人是否在福克纳（William Faulkner，1896—1962）说的"一块石头"（或曰永恒的巨石）上留下过他"抓挠的手印"。爱丽丝·凯瑞所以能从"默默无闻"的泥沼中历经近百年而脱出身，这是历史和时间看到了她的手印的缘故。杨林贵教授主编的"爱丽丝·凯瑞研究"文集让读者仔细看清了这个手印的内容。这部论文集涵盖了爱丽丝·凯瑞的生平、创作活动及其主题与技巧特点等诸多方面，为读者了解和鉴赏这位女作家提供了丰富的资料与指导意见。

爱丽丝·凯瑞生活在美国争取文化独立的时期，文学史上传统称之为浪漫主义的时期。在19世纪上半叶，美国文学界的不少人大声疾呼"美国文化独立"。爱丽丝·凯瑞是在这种大氛围下成长和进行文学创作的。她的作品具有浓郁的美国味。她反映美国西部边地移民的生活，揭露其黑暗面，鞭挞美国资本主义发展为美国所带来的种种弊病。她以典型的美国人的反叛精神，逆潮流而动，不用当时流行的"歌特"派浪漫主义手法，而采取现实主义甚至写真主义的技巧，仔细审视和描绘发展中的美国，真实地记录它的历史面貌。在她生活的时代，霍桑（Nathaniel Hawthorne，1804—1864）、麦尔维尔（Herman Melville，1819—1892）、埃德加·艾伦·坡（Edgar

Allan Poe，1809—1849）及狄金森（Emily Dickinson，1830—1881）等人也在根据自己的体验，以自己独特的方式，客观地反映着有关发展中的美国的心态，他们的作品常常显示出不同于当时文化文学界主流思想的倾向。这或许是他们当中一些人"曾被埋没、之后再被发现"的原因所在。爱丽丝·凯瑞的作品在一些方面与这些人的作品似乎有些相近之处。

爱丽丝·凯瑞的一个突出之处在于，她在挖掘和表现本身某些经历时，表现了她的时代的精神。从广义上说，作家大多在写自己，凯瑞也不例外，她的一些作品显然是以其生活体验为底本的。当个人经历的本质恰和公众经历的本质相吻合时，"伟大"就会出现在世人面前。这样的人会成为著名作家，他们的作品会成为著名作品。这样的作家和作品有时会即刻被发现，如艾略特；有时也需等待一段时间，如《了不起的盖茨比》；也有需要等待很长时间的，如爱丽丝·凯瑞。

爱丽斯·凯瑞的个人经历包含着什么样的"真理"与她时代的、公众的经历所包含的"真理"相吻合呢？杨林贵先生在其主编的论文集的"导言"、"绪论"和12个章节里在这方面为我们提供了充分而详细的信息，如凯瑞的性别意识、女权主义、对城市喧嚣的反感、她的特异的自然观和生态美学思想等。这些我们没有必要在这里一一赘述了。只需说一点：由于爱丽丝·凯瑞的思想中有不少因素具有独特的、超前的性质，而具有这种思想特点的人又通常很容易遭到误解或忽略，这位女作家在文学史上遭到忽略的命运也就不可避免了。

（三）

杨林贵教授熟悉美国文学发展状况，找出新的研究课题，率领一队学者辛勤耕耘，为我们献上本文集。这部文集除让我们了解这个文坛"新"秀之外，还在不少方面给了我们深刻的启示。

它给我们的启示之一是，从事美国文学研究的人们要时刻注视和反映美国文学创作的实际。经历过几个世纪发展的美国文坛，可以说是人才济济，佳作比比皆是，值得我们挖掘与研究的宝藏很多。在这个意义上，"爱丽丝·凯瑞研究"文集很可能是我国美国文学研究新动向的标示之一。

  这部文集给予我们的另一个启示是，要走出自己的路。做学问意味着在荒野里走出新路。真正意义上的学者是率先挖掘新领域、引出新思维的人。他拒绝因循保守，率由旧章，不沿袭任何"八股"，不崇拜任何权威，不以任何方式限制自己的想象力和独创性。本文集在相当程度上为我们研究者提供了一个可琢磨的新模式。

  杨先生主编的文集是一部很优秀的研究成果，很值得我们大家认真一读。

常耀信
2011 年 12 月于天津

目录
Contents

论 述 / 1

导 言:大背景下的小作家 / 3

1 爱丽丝·凯瑞研究绪论 / 9

2 女性现实主义文学的先驱——从凯瑞小说中的死亡和忧郁谈起 / 34

3 凯瑞独具一格的美国哥特文学 / 51

4 让死亡不那么可怕——凯瑞《苜蓿角》的地域美学特征 / 72

5 浑然一体 物我交融——透过《维尔德明斯一家》看爱丽丝·凯瑞的生态美学思想 / 87

6 凯瑞短篇小说集《苜蓿角》中的悲剧意识 / 94

7 凯瑞的死亡叙事——解析《苜蓿角,或曰西部邻里旧事》/ 102

Contents

8 凯瑞短篇小说对残障人物的感伤关照 / 110

9 《外祖父》中的男性身份与情感闭锁 / 125

10 悲凉不屈的歌者——凯瑞诗歌集 / 144

11 华尔街与苜蓿角——《录事巴托比》和《克里斯多弗舅舅家》对工薪奴役与家庭虐待的描写 / 158

12 普救派,福音派与虐童——凯瑞在《彼得·哈瑞斯》和《克里斯多弗舅舅家》中对儿童抚养的宗教批判 / 184

著者简介 / 206

附　录 / 209

致　谢 / 454

Contents

Foreword: Alice Cary in Context / 3

1 Alice Cary and Cary Studies: An Introduction / 9
  Lingui Yang and Dennis Berthold

  Part I. Alice Cary and Aesthetic Approaches

2 Toward a Feminist Realism: Death and Melancholy in Alice Cary's Stories / 34
  Lingui Yang
3 Alice Cary's American Gothic / 51
  Dennis Berthold
4 "Making Death Less Terrible": Alice Cary's Regionalist Aesthetics in *Clovernook* / 72
  John A. Staunton
5 Cary's Eco-Aesthetics as Seen in *The Wildermings* / 87
  Xueying Qiao
6 Tragic Consciousness in Cary's *Clovernook* / 94
  Peixi Huang

  Part II. Narratives in "Minor" Genres: Cary's Short Stories and Sketches

7 Alice Cary's Death Narrative in the *Clovernook* / 102
  Sheng Li
8 The Sentimental Disabled Body in Alice Cary's Short Stories / 110
  Laura Cheshier
9 Masculinity and Emotional Isolation in *My Grandfather* / 125
  Jane M. Galliher

Part III. Alice Cary's Poetry and Other Topics

10 Melancholic Singer: Alice Cary's Sentimental Poetry / 144
    Yunhua Gao

11 Wall Street and Clovernook in *Bartleby, the Scrivener* and *Uncle Christopher's*: Sites of Wage Slavery and Domestic Abuse / 158
    Elizabeth Schultz

12 Universalism, Evangelicals, and Child Abuse: Cary's Religious Critique of Childrearing in *Peter Harris* and *Uncle Christopher's* / 184
    Jane M. Galliher

Notes on Contributors / 206

Appendix: Chinese Translation of *Clovernook: or, Recollections of Our Neighborhood in the West* / 209

Acknowledgements /454

论述

导言：大背景下的小作家

一个作家的文名可大可小，可能显赫也可能湮没，但其独特的声音是不会彻底消亡的，因为那文字传达的声音承载着作者个人身份信息和时代印记，而对于当代生活的个性化书写往往在不同时代得到不同的解读。从狭义的文化人类学角度讲，它以文字形式的记载抗衡人类记忆缺陷的同时，隐含了作者、读者、文本背后深层的文化关系。这就需要我们走出用纯"美学"的标准来评判一个作家的传统做法，因此牵涉西方后结构主义之后的文论中强调的、称为"背景"的东西。文字能指与所指之间的鸿沟，部分地存在于创作背景与接受背景的差异之中。虽然"文字制品"一旦问世，便成了独立的存在，而对于其内涵的理解却不再局限于文本之内；后世可能从书写文本中寻找到部分真相，而更多的意义存在于文本内外的文化语境。这语境既有共时性又有历时性，既涉及文本产生的时代文化特征，又涉及读者接触文本时的社会政治状态和文化认知特点。本书将要介绍和研究的就是一位曾经在文坛发过声、被湮没、又被发掘出来的女作家——爱丽丝·凯瑞。我们不仅研究她在19世纪中期美国文学中的地位，更研究其作品在后现代语境下的意义。

应该讲，爱丽丝·凯瑞这样一位小作家能够进入我们的视野同样得益于后现代批评话语对于阅读界限的破除，特别是20世纪中期以来女性主义、马克思主义、文化唯物主义等理论对于文本价值的重新界定。在这样的语境下，不仅莎士比亚这样的经典作家的文本及其意义的稳定性被打破，一些名不见经传的作家也得到重新挖掘，其作品得到重新认识。很多这样的"次要"作家，特别是女性作家的作品得以进入当今文化教育的课堂。凯瑞的作品已经进入21世纪出版的文学读本，如《希思美国文学选读》、《美国文学传统》等。而最早将凯瑞作品呈现给当代读者的是朱蒂斯·菲特利1987年出版的《苜蓿角及其他故事合集》。此乃凯瑞成为文学研究话题的大背景。我们在这样的大背景下认识她的创作应当有益于了解或者重新审视美国文学中的一些问题（如地域文学的历史以及女性作家在美国文学版图上的位置），也能帮助我们更好地分析美国文化传统，辩证地看待这个国家社会文化的变迁史。

笔者十余年前在读博士学位时首次接触到凯瑞的作品，就是读的菲特利主编的这本凯瑞短篇小说选。当时还自不量力地写成所谓研究论文，未曾想得到了美国文学专家（也是本书的合作者）丹尼斯·博索德教授的褒奖。后来我们合作于2000年：在美国得克萨斯召开的一个学术会议上共同组织了一个凯瑞研究专题研讨。本人因为主要研究方向不在美国文学，此后没再接触凯瑞话题，直到三年前应邀到上海讲学，和东华大学的年轻学者谈起凯瑞，他们表示出极大兴趣。因为国内还没有凯瑞作品出版，大家首先想到的是翻译她的作品。我们选的是1852年出版的 *Clovernook：or, Recollections of Our Neighborhood in the West*（《苜蓿角，或曰西部邻里旧事》）。但是我们认为只是翻译一部作品远远不够，有必要更深入地介绍和研究凯瑞。我们不仅要为普通读者提供一个译本，还力争在研究中呈现关于凯瑞作品的较全面的认识，虽然这些认识可能还很幼稚粗浅。我们更希望能抛砖引玉，为进一步研究凯瑞提供一点参考，也希望本书能够引起国内外美国文学文化研究者的注意。所以，本书中章节使用中英两种文字；同时，为方便读者阅读，每章配有中英文摘要。本书的设计和写作得到所有参与者的积极合作，特别是得到了博索德教授的支持，形成现在的格局。

本书除了绪论，包括三个主要部分，共12章，分析了凯瑞作品所涉及的特定的美学范畴，探讨了对于她的创作的界定的具体问题，论述了她的小说的一些叙事特征，阐释了她的小说和诗歌中的特定主题和主题元素。绪论介绍了凯瑞的生平和创作，并对该作家的现有研究状况作了评述，认为研究这样一位作家有利于认识她在美国文学文化史上的地位，更有利于从更广阔的美国社会文化背景中认识19世纪美国文学的发展。从第二章开始专题论述凯瑞创作的特点，探索用传统的美学范畴以及后现代的理论话语研究凯瑞作品的可行性。第二章探讨凯瑞如何把后世才成熟起来的女性主义的写作手法融入现实主义的写作模式。本章以《两姐妹》等以描写年轻女性人物死亡为主的短篇为例，研究贯穿凯瑞小说作品的忧郁基调，论证了凯瑞的女性现实主义将忧郁作为一种表现方式，认为凯瑞以一种新的表现模式，挑战了当时盛行的男性主导的文学观及其表现方式中的浪漫色调。这种艺术观预示了后世的女权主义艺术表现理论。第三章研究凯瑞的几个具有哥特小说特点的短篇。在这些短篇里，死亡和愧疚感缠绕着叙事者，冲击着人物情感和宗教信仰。凯瑞多样的哥特主题和传统的写作手法共同作用，超越了现实主义，也超越了怪诞离奇；既受到爱伦·坡哥特小说的影响，又在怪诞气氛的营造上独具匠心。本章强调凯瑞独特的哥特小说不仅营造了离奇的气氛，而且说明了哥特式的恐怖是19世纪美国生活的重要组成部分。凯瑞创作的独树一帜还体现在伦理层面上，而且以移情作用为主要审美工具来阐发她的道德观。第四章分析凯瑞在其《苜蓿角》系列中所呈现的伦理和美学意义上的离经叛道。故事集巧妙地诘问并刻意改写了她发表作品的《女士宝典》这类杂志所宣扬的道德观并挑战其性别权威性话语，进而提出了以移情和直面死亡为出发点的逆反主体构成模式。凯瑞认识世界的方式和她的艺术表现方式一样具有独特性，这和她早年在家乡农村的生活经历有关。当年的俄亥俄在美国版图进一步扩张之前还属于西部边陲，对这一地区的开发正并入美国人信心满满地征服自然、改造自然的快车道。然而，凯瑞对自然的认识不同于她那个时代的一般看法。她不仅通过人物之口表达了对城市的喧嚣的反感，而且表现了特异的自然观。第五章以凯瑞的短篇小说集中的《维尔德明斯一家》为例，探讨她的作品中体现的生态美学思想，认为凯瑞以自觉的生态意识来透视人与自然的关系。她的作品透露了这样的思想：自然是一个独立的主体，人类在融入自然中寻求心灵慰藉，人类的死亡是一个自然过程等。因此，不难理解为什么她的作品中充满了死亡的阴影。这阴郁的气氛既是她多数作品的主色调，又被她升华为一种表现方式。第六章从亚里士多德悲剧美学概念出发，分析凯瑞小说体现的悲剧意识。这些作品对死亡和忧郁的描写使读者产生怜悯和恐惧，既引起读者的注意，也让读者产生共鸣。凯瑞作品所特有的恐怖描写往往因特定的乡村意象的描画而加深强化，使作品隐藏着一种冷峻的、阴郁的美，成为一种特别的悲剧感受。

　　第二部分的三章集中讨论凯瑞作品的叙事特征及其小说的一些主题倾向。第七章简略概括了故事集《苜蓿角，或曰西部邻里旧事》中独特的死亡叙事，其特征体现在死亡现实的残酷性、死亡结局的宿命性、死亡救赎的虚幻性和死亡关怀的颠覆性四个方面。整部作品对西部边疆生活的描写颇具黑暗现实主义特色，从而为读者呈现了较为真实的西部早期生活面貌。如上所述，凯瑞的现实主义一反当时主流作家为城市中产阶级的乐观向上精神所唱的赞歌，而是特别关注那些无权无势，受到社会忽视甚至歧视的小人物。第八章聚焦凯瑞作品对残障人物的关注。本章在感伤主义文学、地域文学和现实主义文学的范畴内认识凯瑞对弱势群体给予的文学关照的复杂性。凯瑞用以吸引读者的不是对创痛的同情，而是使读者渴望共鸣、沟通并融入同情对象。凯瑞关注的不仅仅是无助的妇女和儿童的遭遇，也关注男性角色如何成了压制性的社会结构的牺牲品。所以，第九章涉及了极具前沿性的性别意识问题，认为凯瑞作品中的性别意识甚至超前于结构主义理论。她的短篇《外祖父》正是显示这种男性牺牲行为的代表作品。凯瑞描绘了处于矛盾状态下的外祖父，像故事中的其他男性一样，长期屈从于社会对于男性的期望，从而陷入情感的自我闭锁。凯瑞对男性角色的关注揭示了父权制作为一种压制性的权力结构，对压迫者和被压迫者而言都是残缺的，而且是有危害的。

  本书的第三部分除了分析凯瑞诗歌的特征，还通过比较分析研究凯瑞作品揭示的资本主义社会中的工薪奴役、家庭虐待、儿童虐待等社会问题。第十章指出凯瑞诗作以哥特式描写为主要形式，以对死亡和爱情主题的表达为内核。两个主题相互交织，互为补充，构成了作家独特的死亡观和世界观。本章以凯瑞早期诗歌为研究对象，并联系作家的早期个人生活，分析了诗人是如何在人生过程中以诗歌作为精神寄托，在生活中思索死亡，并在死亡的阴影中追寻爱情的艰难求索。诚然，凯瑞不论在诗歌中还是在小说中都对死亡主题情有独钟。然而，她的作品昭示的思想是：死亡虽是个自然过程，却不是自然造成的，虽有天灾的影响，却更是人为的祸殃——社会制度及其意识形态制造的恶果。而天灾人祸的直接受害者就是挣扎在社会底层的弱势群体。因此，和死亡主题并行的是凯瑞作品一贯对受到摧残和虐待的人群的关注。第十一章比较分析了凯瑞的《克里斯多弗舅舅家》和赫尔曼·梅尔维尔的《录事巴托比》。两篇小说都揭露了美国19世纪中叶资本主义经济崛起时期扭曲的基督教民主制度所带来的后果。凯瑞和梅尔维尔的作品不仅向读者展示了建立在工业基础之上的资本主义经济如何将家园变为工厂,使家人沦为工薪奴隶,两部作品还表明,受新兴资本主义所造成的不平等和阶级压迫影响的主要是一些弱势群体——妇女、儿童、贫民和无话语权之人。他们遭受苦难,忍受孤独,甚至夭折。同样,主导意识形态在维护不公平的社会制度时加重了对弱势人群的危害。最后一章挖掘凯瑞作品所揭露的虐童现象的社会意识根源。凯瑞的作品中常见的主题之一就是批判虐童行为,尤其是打着宗教名义实施的虐童行为。在《克里斯多弗舅舅家》和《彼得·哈瑞斯》两篇作品中,这种虐童行为导致了儿童的死亡。此外,《彼得·哈瑞斯》还以隐喻方式揭露了不公正的种族意识,因而具有更重要的意义。应当指出,凯瑞的种族平等思想受到基督教普救派的影响,因此具有其源于宗教特性的局限性,但是,普救派在关于种族问题的认识在美国内战前后还是比其他基督教教派更为积极开明。尽管凯瑞的作品尚无法全面摒弃偏见,但她同情并主张保护那些她认为无力保护自己的人们。在这个意义上,她的作品对弱势群体的关注不论对于她的时代还是对于后殖民时代生活都具有积极意义。

《苜蓿角》中文翻译也是本书的重要组成部分,希望帮助没有机会接触凯瑞作品原文的读者了解她的创作提供方便。这里引用本书绪论的一段概括,权作对故事集的总结:

《苜蓿角》所有故事各自成篇,却又都围绕生活在一个村子的人物,讲述他们的家长里短,有青年男女的情感纠葛,儿童和老人的不幸,单亲母亲的凄凉,日常生活的挣扎与无奈,挥之不去的死亡和阴郁。苜蓿角这地方村舍农田、阡陌交通,似有恬静自然的诗情画意,早年开疆破土的艰难困苦留给柔弱的女孩的记忆却不都是烂漫温馨的。尤其联系到女性人物的处境,更是一派苦涩辛酸。凯瑞特别擅长描写儿童成长经历,常常进入人物内心世界,然而他们的生活不是无忧无虑的。故事中不乏幽魂怨鬼,却没有魑魅魍魉充斥的妖邪之气,也不似爱伦·坡哥特式小说那么古灵古怪和阴森恐怖。

绪论中还有关于集子中的 35 个故事的概述。当然,要欣赏这些故事还请读者关注《苜蓿角》译文或者原文。要说明的是,翻译能够顺利完成是参与翻译的人员共同辛勤努力的结果。译文是否得当,还请有心的读者和专家评判。虽然在翻译和校订过程中我们尽量避免疏漏，但不妥之处肯定在所难免。这样讲不是为了推卸责任，而是恳请广大读者尤其是专家学者批评指正，以期改进。

最后，各章中和译文中的所有问题和责任应由本人承担。

杨林贵
2011 年 11 月

1 爱丽丝·凯瑞研究绪论

Alice Cary and Cary Studies: An Introduction

杨林贵　Dennis Berthold

摘要：爱丽丝·凯瑞（1820—1871）是19世纪为数不多的以写作为生的女作家之一。美国内战前夕活跃在纽约文坛，起初以诗歌成名，后以其关于当时西部生活的系列短篇小说和速写而名声大噪。虽然凯瑞作品在她生前极受欢迎，经济上也很成功，但去世后名声淹没，她的作品近百年很少重印。因此20世纪初学术界对美国文学的兴趣开始以来也很少有人提到凯瑞，少数学术著作提及凯瑞的创作也仅限于出现在脚注中。这种情况到80年代妇女研究的兴起才有了改观。当今，她的生平和创作已被收入多种参考书，作品被收入多种美国女性作家文集。例如，《苜蓿角》第二系列（1853）中的《克里斯多弗舅舅家》被收入广泛使用的美国文学教材《希斯美国文学选读》；《维尔德明斯一家》被收入《美国哥特小说选集》（1999）以及《美国文学传统》（第10版，2002）。目前为止还没有专门研究凯瑞的著作出版；近年已经有博士研究项目专门研究她的作品；有多篇研究论文以及专著章节发表。

作为引论，本章概要总结了20世纪80年代以来关于凯瑞的主要研究成果。这些成果研究凯瑞对女性心理、青春期情感、性别角色以及劳动世界的洞悉，更涉及与凯瑞创作相关的、更广阔的美国社会文化背景，部分地说明了凯瑞对19世纪美国文学的贡献，有利于给这位女作家在美国文学文化史上确定地位。作为一位地域现实主义的开拓者,凯瑞以其对工业化转型时期美国边疆生活的速写,为我们呈现了常常被东部作家忽视的美国乡村生活的生动详尽的图景。从另外一个角度看,凯瑞在当时受欢迎的程度给我们研究 19 世纪中期美国人的文学趣味和阅读习惯提供了极有价值的参考。

Abstract: Alice Cary (1820—1871) was one of the few women who made a living by writing in the 19th century. She first made a name as a poet in Cincinnati, Ohio, and published series of sketches and stories about life in the western frontier after she moved to New York in the 1850s. Although Cary was a popular and financially successful writer during her lifetime, her reputation faded quickly after her death, and her works were seldom reprinted. Consequently, she dropped out of the critical conversation during the great renewal of academic interest in American literature during the early twentieth century, and not until the rise of women's studies during the 1980s was she more than a footnote in literary scholarship. Today she is included in many reference works and anthologies devoted to American women writers, and her stunning story *Uncle Christopher's* from *Clovernook Second Series* (1853) is included in the widely used *Heath Anthology of American Literature*. No one has written a monograph devoted to Cary, and only one dissertation focuses exclusively on her work. Several excellent articles and one outstanding collection of her writing have been published.

In addition to an introduction to Cary's life and works, this chapter provides an overview of available publications on Cary since the 1980s. These studies focus on her short fiction that is gaining a new generation of readers who appreciate her insights into female psychology, adolescent emotions, gender roles, and the world of work. As a pioneering realist and chronicler of life on the urban frontier, she offers detailed descriptive accounts of American scenes often ignored by Eastern writers, and by her popularity provides valuable perspective on the tastes and reading habits of mid-nineteenth-century Americans.

1891年，美国辛辛那提的一位教育家、文学鉴赏家、历史学家写道："世界将会承认这样一位乡村女子——她无缘于图书资料、正规教育、贵人提携、经济来源、母仪亲情，而又要供养弟弟妹妹，受着繁重家事的拖累，却在这样的岁月里成就了一番写作生涯。"[①]这位传奇式的乡村女子就是活跃在美国内战前夕纽约文坛的爱丽丝·凯瑞（1820—1871）。

凯瑞生前以诗歌成名，诗风颇为儒雅，多以感伤情怀畅叙衷肠，极受当时读者喜爱，得到同时代作家爱伦·坡的赏识。有幸读到她的诗作的当今读者仍能深受感染。她的散文和小说作品风格独特，20世纪中期以来得到文学史家和美国文学学者的重视，如同埋没多年的珍宝重得拂拭，在女权主义以及其他后现代语境下更成了可以雕琢把玩的璞玉。如著名女性主义文学学者菲特利（Judith Fetterley）1987年重新整理出版了凯瑞的短篇小说合集，在美国文学界产生了影响，受到了广大读者的喜爱和学者的关注。凯瑞的作品还进入了很多大学的文学课堂，开始有文学学者和博士研究生以此为读本和研究题目。她的短篇记事以白描的手法记叙了早年俄亥俄拓荒时期的生活图景，是现实主义拓荒文学的早期代表，可以认定为此类题材的发端之作，预示了半个多世纪后成熟起来的美国"现实主义区域文学"[②]。我们在此除了对凯瑞的生平创作作一些简单勾勒，还将评述对于该作家的研究现状。

---

① Venable, W H. *Beginnings of Literary Culture in the Ohio Valley*. Cincinnati, Ohio: Robert Clarke, 1891: 485.
② 凯瑞作品在主题、题材以及表现手法上给现实主义区域文学代表作家（如弗里曼（Mary Wilkins Freeman）和贾兰德（Hamlin Garland））提供了样板。

从农村到城市：凯瑞的文学梦想与成功之路

爱丽丝·凯瑞，1820年4月26日出生于俄亥俄州辛辛那提市北面8英里的罕米尔顿县，当年属于美国西部边陲。① 其祖父克里斯多夫·凯瑞因为在革命战争中效过力，美国独立后在这片西部边疆得到了一块土地，其父母（罗伯特·凯瑞和伊丽莎白·凯瑞）靠经营农场维持生计，共生养了9个子女，爱丽丝排行老四。爱丽丝13岁时，年长她两岁的姐姐罗达得肺结核去世了，年仅3岁的小妹妹露希也不幸夭折。仅仅两年后，母亲又因多年的劳累而病逝。母亲故去，父亲续弦，青少年阶段的爱丽丝不得不承担更多家庭负担，帮助照顾年幼的弟弟妹妹。可见，凯瑞早年的生活虽然有温馨的回忆，但更多的是苦涩的故事，因而进入她作品的常常是哀伤的回忆。她18岁时公开发表的第一首诗《伤心小孩》（The Child of Sorrow）就是记录当时痛失亲人的心境。这首诗歌得到爱伦·坡等有名的作家和批评家的赞誉。她后来的诗歌《小家伙》（My Little One）和短篇《两姐妹》（The Sisters）分别追念这两位早逝的姐妹。

就这样，凯瑞从记录真诚的感受开始进入创作世界，又以真实记录拓荒时期的生活而笔耕不断，在当时以男作家为主导的写作圈子里闯出一片天地。然而，她的写作受到诸多条件的限制，这使她意识到，必须走出村庄，才能成就梦想。

由于农庄地处偏僻，少年爱丽丝只能断断续续地跑到远处的市镇上点学，主要是从母亲那里接受了有限的教育。凯瑞父母的生活信念是追逐所谓的美国梦，即通过努力工作获得物质生活的提高，对孩子的成长往往忽略或者根本无暇顾及，这在凯瑞记忆中留下了矛盾的印象。

虽然凯瑞在对外公开谈到母亲时往往带有溢美之辞，但在她的作品中孩子的世界里母爱完全是一个空白。1855年凯瑞在给《女士宝典》（Ladies Repository）编辑的信中提到母亲时讲，母亲是爱尔

---

① 美国西部的概念随着领土的扩张和开发疆域的扩大不断变化，直到其疆域从大西洋海岸到太平洋海岸东西贯通，这个概念成为历史，西部边陲对于美国文化的形成和发展影响深远。美国西部边疆的概念在北美十三州独立后还刚刚从大西洋海岸跨过阿巴拉契亚山脉，向西到达密西西比河流域。

兰后裔,很有头脑,生活打理得井井有条,她比周围的所有女人都更聪明、更纯洁、更勤劳,也更有爱心;但凯瑞只字未提母亲对孩子的爱心。凯瑞15岁没了母亲,但耐人寻味的是,凯瑞没有像痛惋其姐妹那样做诗哀悼其母亲。凯瑞的小说及速写集中描写的母亲形象,虽然不是负面人物,但也乏善可陈。她们往往是没有母性的干活机器,只知道终日劳作,对孩子漠不关心,甚至常常视若冤家,对他们的身心成长不闻不问,对他们的合理要求推诿搪塞,更谈不上主动发现孩子的特殊天分,鼓励和引导孩子才能的发展。小说中的孩子缺少母爱,虽然母亲在世,但仍然感觉像是孤儿,正如《两姐妹》中的主人公所讲,"我们孤苦伶仃"。

凯瑞讲,母亲比村里的其他女人更有知识,因为母亲曾经受过一定教育。她读过的书主要是历史、政治和宗教方面的,对人物传记和道德杂文感兴趣,虽也读过诗歌,但对虚构作品没有兴致。凯瑞的父亲14岁时跟随退伍的祖父从新罕布什尔州迁到俄亥俄州,受了点中小学教育。据凯瑞姐妹回忆,父亲年少时也喜欢读传奇故事和诗歌,但家境的贫穷和拓荒生活的艰辛早就吞噬了他那点早年的闲情逸致。

虽然凯瑞的父母算不上目不识丁,但孩子的教育问题对他们来说似乎无所谓。家里面的书籍也是少得可怜。凯瑞早年所读限于《圣经》、圣歌,探险家路易斯和克拉克的《日志》,苏珊·罗森的小说《夏洛特圣堂》,英国诗人托马斯·格雷和亚历山大·蒲伯的诗歌,以及波士顿出版的普救派报纸《号角》。然而从她的作品中我们可以看出她熟稔一些文学经典。她在小说中频繁引经据典,除了《圣经》外,出自莎士比亚、托马斯·莫尔、格雷、弥尔顿、浪漫诗人华兹华斯和柯勒律治等名家的引文比比皆是。这些应该是后来通过自学所得,特别是搬到纽约之后的恶补。

青少年时期由于艰难的生活处境,正规教育和业余读书对凯瑞来说都是奢侈。特别是在凯瑞17岁时父亲再婚,她不仅受到继母的敌视,而且独自挑起了家庭重担,读书写作就更加艰难。继母不仅本人对文学不感兴趣,也阻止凯瑞姐妹读书写作,怕写作影响她们做家务。凯瑞只好转入地下,在夜里偷偷写作,不得不把手稿藏在楼梯下的小储藏间。秉烛夜读和写作被发现后,连蜡烛的使用都受到了限制。两年后父亲与新婚妻子在农场的另外一处地方另筑新巢,把老房子的日常事务和照顾四个未成年弟妹的重担全部留给凯瑞，凯瑞本人担当起了"母亲"的角色。这时虽然家庭生活负担加重了，但有了一定的自由空间，她可以更自由地追逐童年时的文学梦想了。

　　凯瑞早年开始的文学梦想更多地受逝去的罗达的启发。凯瑞和姐姐罗达的关系是影响她创作的最重要因素。提到这种关系时她本人写道："可爱的姐姐与我同劳动、同玩耍、同学习。我们从未有一天分开过……正当她成熟为女人之季——她还不到16岁——死亡就将我们拆散，这变故令我情绪低落甚至悲伤到不能自拔。时至今日她都是每天早晨醒来时第一个进入我脑海的人，也是晚上入睡前最后一个告别的人。"（凯瑞1855年致《女士宝典》编辑的信）凯瑞在《两姐妹》中表达了她对姐姐的景仰和怀念，其中记叙了罗达的讲故事天赋和对凯瑞的影响。罗达精彩的故事往往能讲上一路，走在放学回家的路上，快要到家时，每每要停下来坐在树下才能把故事讲完。凯瑞被姐姐那引人入胜的讲述吸引，学着讲自己的故事。也是在姐姐的鼓动下，她开始尝试诗歌写作。因此，对于凯瑞来说，姐姐既是闺中密友，又是文学梦想的启蒙者。凯瑞又影响了妹妹芙波（1824—1871），并引导她也走上创作道路。姐妹俩在城里相依为命、共同创作，合作发表了诗歌集，共同完成了从西部乡村邻家女孩到都市作家的蜕变。

　　凯瑞18岁时开始发表诗歌作品。她的《伤心小孩》1838年在辛辛那提普救派教会办的报纸《前哨》上发表。此后约十年间，她连续在当地的报纸和期刊上发表作品，在辛辛那提小有名气。但对她走上专业创作道路、靠写作为生，以至最终成为闻名全国的作家起到决定作用的，不能不说是贵人的赏识，尽管谈不上特别提携。她的第一个贵人是著名编辑、作家、批评家格里斯沃尔德。[①] 1848年他写信要求把凯瑞姐妹的作品收入他编辑的《美国女诗人大全》（*The Female Poets of America*），使凯瑞的读者面和影响扩大到全

[①] 格里斯沃尔德（Rufus W. Griswold，1815—1857）在当时的文学圈已经建立起很高的名望。他编撰的《美国诗人诗歌大全》很有影响，不断增订再版。很多作家希望作品能够入选本集。格里斯沃尔德与爱伦·坡的恩怨成为美国文学史的一个话题。

美国。在同年 12 月出版的文集引言中，格里斯沃尔德提到他两三年前从西部的报纸上开始注意到了凯瑞姐妹的创作。"大全"中收入的凯瑞诗歌还得到了爱伦·坡的高度评价。1849 年 2 月的《南方文学信使》杂志发表了爱伦·坡对《美国女诗人大全》的书评，其中他特别提到凯瑞的诗《记忆之画》（Pictures of Memory），称其为"集子中确定无疑的最好的诗篇"。格里斯沃尔德一直是凯瑞文学事业的坚定支持者，1849 年为凯瑞姐妹筹划出版了诗集《爱丽丝和芙波·凯瑞诗集》（Poems of Alice and Phoebe Cary），并写了序言。

  凯瑞的第二个贵人贝利（Gamaliel Bailey）是提倡废奴的报纸《国民时代》（National Era，1847—1860）的创办人和主编。他不仅为凯瑞作品在全美国的传播作出了贡献，而且让凯瑞有了相对稳定的收入。凯瑞经远房亲戚、身为编辑的加拉格尔（William D. Gallagher）介绍结识了在辛辛那提寄居的贝利。贝利于 1847 年在华盛顿创办了《国民时代》，斯托夫人的《汤姆叔叔的小屋》就是在该报连载首发（1851—1852）的。凯瑞 1847 年开始在此报上发表短篇小说并有了可靠的稿费收入，使她能更专注于创作。另外，在《国民时代》发表作品也使她的文名远播，从而结识了文学圈子里的其他名人，如著名诗人惠蒂尔（John Greenleaf Whittier）。1847 年 9 月惠蒂尔撰文称赞凯瑞的创作，此后两人结下了终生友谊。凯瑞与报刊的关系的变化带来的不仅仅是经济条件的改善，也反映了她写作成熟和事业成功的过程。从最早免费为本地教会报纸写诗，到与东部的进步刊物签订长期稿约，乃至搬到纽约后应邀为主流期刊撰稿，印证了她三十多年为了圆文学梦而不断探寻的足迹。

  为了在文学上有更大的发展，1850 年刚刚而立的凯瑞只身从西部乡下东移迁居到正在演变成美国文学中心的纽约城，开始"北漂"生涯，在文人齐俱的大都会靠着笔耕进行打拼，竟然能购房置地，站稳脚跟。到 1855 年，她已经有足够经济实力，在东二十一街购买了一处房产，除了接来妹妹芙波和最小的妹妹艾尔弥娜和她共住，还雇了两个女仆帮助做家务。芙波一直受凯瑞的庇护，虽然在生活中姐妹相依相伴，互相支撑，但某种意义上讲凯瑞对妹妹起到的一直是母亲的角色。多年艰苦生活的磨砺让凯瑞早就习惯了照顾别人，因此有这样一个依靠她的亲人在身边对彼此都是慰藉。妹妹芙波一直伴她度过纽约的岁月。写作是凯瑞最大的乐趣。应该讲，投入写作既是她的精神寄托，又是谋生的手段。为此，她很少外出度假。

凯瑞的社交生活也是和文学有关，以文会友。凯瑞姐妹的晚餐会在纽约文人圈内很有名气，每星期日在家里定期举办，持续了15年之久。常来捧场的不乏当时的文坛名人，如著名报人、纽约《论坛》主编格里利（Horace Greeley），女权运动领袖斯坦顿（Elizabeth Cady Stanton），著名诗人惠蒂尔，诗人、编辑、出版商菲尔兹（James T. Fields），杂文家汉弥尔顿（Gail Hamilton），诗人、杂文家萨拉·惠特曼（Sara Helen Whitman），演说家安娜·狄金森（Anna Dickinson），政治改革家、文学家欧文（Robert Dale Owen，早期英国社会主义者罗伯特·欧文（Robert Owen）之子），新闻家、废奴政治活动家、编辑加里森（William Lloyd Garrison），娱乐表演家、实业家巴纳姆（Phineas T. Barnum）等。据记载，赫尔曼·麦尔维尔也曾于1865年光顾沙龙，还给凯瑞兴致勃勃地讲他的航海经历。① 凯瑞姐妹和当时的进步知识分子交往频繁，同情支持平权运动、废奴运动等进步运动。因为在文学上的成就，凯瑞1869年被推举为第一个职业妇女组织——纽约"妇女俱乐部"主席。

凯瑞终身未婚。据她的传记作者，也是崇拜者埃姆斯（Mary Ames）回忆，凯瑞离开家乡前夕曾经遭遇一段痛苦的恋情，但没有其他佐证材料可以证实。在她的半自传性质的《苜蓿角》系列中受伤害的女孩子身上似乎可以隐隐约约地看到少女凯瑞的影子。1850年凯瑞与格里斯沃尔德曾一度频繁鸿雁往来，但无果而终。除了这段短暂情事，没有其他情感经历的确切记录。凯瑞迁居纽约后，按当时的婚嫁标准已是大龄。除了写作，凯瑞把时间和精力都投入了供养弟弟妹妹上。凯瑞于1871年2月12日去世，被葬在纽约布鲁克林的格林伍德公墓。

---

① 见 Judith Fetterly. *Provisions: A Reader From 19th-Century American Women*. Bloomington: Indiana UP, 1985: 218.

"苜蓿之乡的歌鸟"：凯瑞作品中的乡土记忆

惠蒂尔在一首诗中称凯瑞是来自西部"苜蓿之乡的歌鸟"。① 凯瑞的主要作品记录了她对早年西部生活的记忆，所刻画的人和事有浓厚的地域和乡土气息。凯瑞的创作从诗歌开始，也是因为诗歌而成名。她生前出版了五卷诗集，除了最早的一卷和妹妹芙波的合集外，还有四本个人诗集问世，分别是：《天琴座及其他杂诗》（*Lyra and Other Poems*，1852），《诗选集》（*Collected Poems*，1855），《民谣、抒情诗及圣歌》（*Ballads, Lyrics and Hymns*，1866），及《情人日记》（*A Lover's Diary*，1868）。两本儿童读物《苜蓿角儿童》（*Clovernook Children*，1854），《雪果：献给年轻人》（*Snowberries*，1867）。她的诗歌作品抒发普通人群的日常情感，特别是生活的考验和谋生的焦虑，常常带有强烈的宗教式的悲悯。

凯瑞有三部小说单独出版：《夏甲，今日故事》（*Hagar, a Story of To-Day*，1852），《婚而不配》（*Married, Not Mated*，1856），《主教之子》（*The Bishop's Son*，1867）。另有两部在报刊连载：《霍利伍德》（*Holly-Wood*，1854），《生来为奴》（*The Born Thrall*，在《革命》期刊连载，未完成）。此外，凯瑞还在其他报刊发表一系列"鬼怪故事"以及描写在俄亥俄与纽约之间旅行经历的多篇杂文。代表她主要成就的是她的速写作品。凯瑞前后发表了三部速写集：《苜蓿角，或曰西部邻里旧事》（*Clovernook: or, Recollections of Our Neighborhood in the West*，1852），《苜蓿角第二系列》（*Clovernook, Second Series*，1853），以及《乡村生活图

---

① 惠蒂尔的诗 *The Singer* 赞美凯瑞姐妹，特别提到凯瑞作品对于家乡"苜蓿之地"景物的刻画。诗的最后两节是这样的：

　　Yet ere the summer eve grew long,
　　Her modest lips were sweet with song;
　　A memory haunted all her words
　　Of clover fields and singing birds.

　　Her dark, dilating eyes expressed
　　The broad horizons of the west;
　　Her speech dropped prairie flowers; the gold
　　Of harvest wheat about her rolled.

景》(Pictures of Country Life, 1859)。

虽然当代批评家对她的小说评价不高，但普遍看好她的三部短篇速写集。菲特利认为仅凭这几部集子所创造的独特类型就"足以在我们（美国）的文学史中占有一席之地"（《苜蓿角速写及其他故事选集》"引论"）。凯瑞的《苜蓿角》系列短篇，以家乡的人和事为内容，叙事以人物为核心，因此故事结构往往具有开放性，甚至不完整性，在当时的文坛独树一帜。故事的组合方式和格调颇似乔伊斯的《都柏林人》，叙事结构和主题的探索更为萨拉·朱维特在《尖尖的杉树之乡》(Country of the Pointed Firs, 1899) 以及舍伍德·安德森的《俄亥俄州的温斯堡》(Winesburg, Ohio, 1917) 中的同类作品尝试的成功埋下伏笔。

凯瑞的首部短篇速写集于1852年出版，并一炮打响，开始走红。《苜蓿角》所有故事各自成篇却又都围绕生活在一个村子的人物，讲述他们的家长里短，有青年男女的情感纠葛，儿童和老人的不幸，单亲母亲的凄凉，日常生活的挣扎与无奈，挥之不去的死亡和阴郁。苜蓿角这地方村舍农田、阡陌交通，似有恬静自然的诗情画意，早年开疆破土的艰难困苦留给柔弱的女孩的记忆却不都是烂漫温馨的，尤其联系到女性人物的处境，更是一派苦涩辛酸。凯瑞特别擅长描写儿童成长经历，常常进入人物的内心世界，然而他们的生活不是无忧无虑的。故事中不乏幽魂怨鬼和阴郁气氛，却没有魑魅魍魉充斥的妖邪之气，也不似爱伦·坡哥特式小说那么古灵古怪和阴森恐怖。

正如凯瑞在"前言"中所讲，《苜蓿角》第一系列的35个故事讲述了农耕阶层的日常生活细节，并展示其"人性诸端"。开篇便讲述外祖父濒死之前大家的种种反应，记叙了幼年时期的叙述人初次接触死亡的感悟和乡村人处理此类事件的细节。接下来的一篇《光影之间》更像是一曲散文体的挽歌，小伙伴、小妹妹7岁夭折，令叙述人懊悔，并发出宗教意味的感慨。下面几篇都是伤心故事，死亡和忧郁成了核心主题和基调。作品中涉及一系列儿童以及女性人物——有孤苦的"怪妇人"，英年早逝的19岁的萨拉·沃辛顿，受冤而死的维尔德明斯小姐。特别是《维尔德明斯一家》中竟讲述了两个年轻女子的神秘早逝：一个是"没犯过多大的错，却受了极大的冤屈"，另一个死不瞑目。故事中有描写幽魂出没的场景，主人公的身世和死亡充满了神秘色彩,难怪本篇被收入美国哥特小说集。第7篇略有一点幽默色彩:两个农妇——希尔太太和特鲁斯特太太——谈论乡间的家长里短中透露了邻里生活现实,隐含之意不无反讽。第8—10篇都是关于戴尔叔叔的,既有戴尔叔叔年轻时和印第安人打交道的传奇,又有老来无靠的无奈,还有老牛吃嫩草的"艳遇"。戴尔叔叔娶的小寡妇带来个小孩,却没人愿意和小孩玩耍,5岁就夭折了。

接下来的两篇讲述了两个宗教家庭的变故,包括两对青年的婚恋,但既没有浪漫情调,也不是叙事的主线。作者的白描手法似乎着意要给乡村爱情做"去浪漫化"处理。其中的关于家长对待孩子的描写倒是值得留意和玩味。汤普金斯先生"从不想与孩子们平等地说话,以为那样有失身份。所以他很少开口,也从不笑,因为那样可能会显得他想要说话似的"。而汤普金斯太太在跟孩子们说话的时候,"总好像他们应该为索取东西而受到狠狠的责备,或者,事实上,只是因为他们来到这个世界上就应该受到责备"。女儿苏珊精心准备了参加晚会的裙子,非但得不到母亲的认可,反而被兜头浇了冷水。叙述人说道:"她母亲却浇灭了她所有的希望。"在两个关于教士家庭的悲喜剧之后,《苜蓿角》又回到悲情路线。

《苜蓿角》的主调仍是悲剧色彩的,虽然青年男女的爱情插曲时常点缀上一点玫瑰色,但总体上更像是莎士比亚的"社会问题剧",呈现的是社会习俗对弱势群体遭蹂躏的平淡处理和冷漠态度。第13—15篇是两个爱情悲剧加一个虐待儿童的故事。小彼得·哈瑞斯寄居叔叔家,遭到嘲笑和虐待,又在学校受体罚后,抑郁而死。《安妮·希顿》中主人公卖掉自己的传家宝供男友上了大学,却遭遇始乱终弃的结局。《玛格丽特·费兹》是另外一个女主角被抛弃的"爱情"悲剧。那个让玛格丽特期盼许多年的青年牧师最终另寻高枝,却不忘在烦透了娇生惯养的妻子之后,又常到玛格丽特那里寻求安慰。虽然主人公最后麻木了,甚至不愿表达哀怨,但故事末尾,叙事人不忘加一句补白:"她自己内心的伤痛藏着不让别人知道。"接下去的两篇讲述了城里姑娘莉迪娅到苜蓿角的萨姆奈尔家做客,最终迷恋这里的神秘气氛以及她中意的神秘青年。虽然故事以婚姻结局,但并不突出谈情说爱或者任何浪漫过程,而是用神秘猎人的鬼怪故事作为框架,富于哥特小说气氛。

至此，经过神秘爱情的过渡，苜蓿角故事重又回到悲剧。这次的悲剧主角是一位起初好高骛远、自暴自弃，却在最终自食其力时遭遇不幸的男青年。第 18—27 篇讲述理查德·克莱维尔的人生轨迹。理查德读书和学医都半途而废，早早结婚，但无力养活和他一样无所事事的妻子，很快便离婚了。两岁的孩子被同样不靠谱的妻子带走，照顾不周，很快从世上消失了，"可怜的小宝宝，名字从未登记过，连墓碑上都没写名字"。认识乡村女教师后，理查德重新鼓起生活的勇气，事业也有了起色。但某种冥冥的力量不肯让他品味刚有的幸福感。为了躲避邻里的冷眼，理查德和女教师离乡出走，半路淋雨，竟然不治身亡。悲剧的部分原因似乎仍然与社会习俗有关。

从第 28 篇《两姐妹》起至集子收篇是带有自传性质的 8 篇故事，主要人物是苜蓿角村哈德利家的艾丽和丽贝卡。她们分明是凯瑞和姐姐罗达的化身。姐妹俩形影不离，姐姐激发、鼓励妹妹的文学兴趣，直到姐姐丽贝卡在关于她和死去的校长暧昧的谣传中，香消玉殒，抑郁而亡。艾丽"现在是年龄最大的孩子了。她不算年轻了，正值青春大好年华。妹妹们都迅速地长成了大姑娘，在她的眼中，她们都非常亲，但是仍然不能填补坟墓中的亲人在她心中的位置。照料幼小弟妹的重担落在她的肩上，她的性情生来忧郁，后来却习惯性地经常表现出忧伤、不满、痛苦的情绪"。人物和作者生活经历的重叠让我们有理由相信艾丽就是爱丽丝。但是，我们无法确知是否艾丽的感情生活就是爱丽丝·凯瑞早年遭遇的写照。和其他女性人物一样，艾丽感情遭到玩弄。那位柳树谷的主人汉姆斯塔德先生用种种暗示勾起艾丽极大的幻想，但是这位从城里来的绅士、派头十足的上流人士最终没有选择土里土气的村姑，而是和一位优雅的城市女子出双入对。艾丽只能不断重复"伊人已陌路，万事皆成空"的诗句。不管故事是否包含埃姆斯在凯瑞传记中所提的伤心恋情的影子，《苜蓿角》叙述人是同情女主角的。叙述人声音在故事结尾的再次出现，似乎提醒我们这故事的真实性："我要写的就是平凡人生的故事，我写完了；至于艾丽的将来，关于自制和谦虚的用处，也无须赘言了。她的额头满是忧伤；她忙着家务时尽量保持心里平静，但没人想象得到那内心流血的创痛，只有死亡才能完全平复这创痛。有时她受了落日余晖启发，把思绪写成随意的韵文；而当她动人的描述搅起情感的喷泉,没人会质疑那颗心灵及其情感赖以产生的生活。"

"苜蓿之乡的歌鸟"唱的不是浪漫欢歌,而更多的是苦痛、幽怨、哀愁、忧郁的曲调。凯瑞用白描手法如实记叙转型时期美国西部农村的生活现实,描绘了一系列乡村人物,有开疆的功臣和大家长戴尔叔叔,喋喋不休的贝茨太太,拘谨的艾丽,勤劳的哈德利太太等等,构成生动的苜蓿角人物图谱。《苜蓿角》第一集大获成功。凯瑞在此基础上很快完成了第二系列的创作,于次年出版。第二系列继续了第一系列的白描风格,绝不理想化、浪漫化乡村生活。另外,虽然只有14个故事,但每个故事都有较长篇幅,人物心理刻画也更有深度。例如,《克里斯多弗舅舅家》生动记叙了一个冷酷无情、毫无温暖的农庄家庭;又如,《夏洛特·瑞安》讲述了苜蓿角人物走出乡村的心理撞击以及女主角搬到城里后灵魂的失落。1854年凯瑞给她的儿童故事集也冠以"苜蓿角",足见她的苜蓿角故事的成功程度。1859年凯瑞的《乡村生活图景》虽然又回到苜蓿角场景,但已经不及最初的两个系列那么受欢迎了。

凯瑞与19世纪美国文学:凯瑞研究述评

凯瑞的作品在她生前极受欢迎,经济上也很成功,特别是最早的两个《苜蓿角》系列在她去世后多年还在重印,而且在全美国出版了多种版本。但是从20世纪初起,特别是现代主义兴起之后,凯瑞的农村叙事似乎被遗忘了。因此20世纪初学术界对美国文学开始产生兴趣以来也很少有人提到凯瑞,少数学术著作即使提及凯瑞的创作也仅限于脚注中。这种情况到80年代妇女研究的兴起才有了改观,特别是菲特利主编的《苜蓿角及其他故事合集》出版,为广大读者和研究者了解凯瑞作了开拓性贡献。近年来对凯瑞叙事作品的关注增多,她又赢得了新一代读者的欣赏。当今,她的生平和创作已被收入多种参考书,作品被收入多种美国女性作家文集,例如:《苜蓿角》第二系列(1853)中的《克里斯多弗舅舅家》被收入广泛使用的美国文学教材《希思美国文学选读》;《苜蓿角》第二系列中的《维尔德明斯一家》被收入《美国哥特小说选集》(1999)以及《美国文学传统》(第10版,2002)。

同时，对凯瑞的研究方兴未艾。有多篇研究论文及专著章节研究凯瑞。美国大学近年来已经有博士研究项目专门研究她的作品。下面概要总结20世纪80年代以来关于凯瑞的主要研究成果。这些成果部分地说明了凯瑞对19世纪美国文学的贡献，有利于给这位女作家在美国文学文化史上确定地位。除了前文提到的菲特利对凯瑞三部速写作品的高度评价，或许我们还会从现有其他研究中，了解到和凯瑞创作相关的更广阔的美国社会文化背景，也能更深入地欣赏凯瑞对女性心理、青春期情感、性别角色以及劳动世界的洞悉。作为一位地域现实主义的开拓者，凯瑞以其对工业化转型时期美国边疆生活的速写，为我们呈现了常常被东部作家忽视的美国乡村生活的生动详尽的图景。从另外一个角度看，凯瑞在当时受欢迎的程度给我们研究19世纪中期美国人的文学趣味和阅读习惯提供了极有价值的参考。

第一个严肃对待凯瑞的知名学者是克罗尼（Annette Kolodny）。克罗尼在其1984年的著作 *The Land Before Her*：*Fantasy and Experience of the American Frontiers*, 1630—1860 中用了相当篇幅讨论苜蓿角速写集。该书研究女性作家在美国文学文化演进过程中的作用，把凯瑞作为勾勒边疆风貌和文化形态的代表人物之一。他指出，凯瑞的速写强调中西部农村生活图景，那里有富足的农业资源，田垄交错的祥和农耕景象，和柯克兰（Caroline Kirkland）的城市中产阶级创作形成鲜明对比。凯瑞的速写杂糅了对城市化进程的关注和对田园生活的怀旧。克罗尼重点分析了凯瑞《苜蓿角》（1853）第二系列中的一个故事，认为《威瑟比太太的缝纫派对》突出了这个主题。叙述人领悟到城市及其习惯方式对乡村生活构成威胁，对于首次进城的高度热情很快变成了极度沮丧。尘土飞扬的街道、拥挤的人群、恼人的喧嚣，还有臭气熏天的屠宰场让她对所谓的城市生活的进步产生反感。然而，此次纽约之旅还是给她带来了一些影响，回到乡村后，她与新丈夫一起建起一个酷似新英格兰地区或者纽约西部风格的家园，与西部边陲的风格迥异，犹似凯瑞的父亲按照城里的式样不断翻新的老房子。结果西部倒是越来越像东部了，变成一个城乡结合的所在，构造了乡村与城市元素相得益彰的别致的图景。克罗尼从凯瑞的生平角度研究她的速写，认为凯瑞的"回忆"启用的"角色面具"正是年少时期的作者本人（186），正是这个叙述者的声音让作品颇具现实主义色彩，真实地记录了19世纪中叶席卷西部的变革。

目前为止，综合研究凯瑞最具代表性的成果是菲特利为其主编的《苜蓿角及其他故事合集》所作的引论。菲特利的选本是目前最好的凯瑞短篇小说合集，对于不论普通读者还是研究者都是很好的开篇读本。这个选集收录了凯瑞各个时期创作的短篇，首篇是《梦境与象征》，最初发表在1847年《国民时代》杂志，末篇是《名医》，首发于1866年《大西洋月刊》。全书共收16篇，多半选自两集《苜蓿角》。菲特利写凯瑞生平时，收集了有限的有关凯瑞的案卷和书信，参考了已经出版的传记，很多地方对凯瑞第一个传记作者埃姆斯的评述亦步亦趋。评价凯瑞姐姐罗达之死对于她创作和生活的影响时，菲特利写道：这是个"悲剧性事件"（Ⅷ），给凯瑞小说以"深沉的悲凉感"，令凯瑞产生"人生不过是某种不可见的整体的一个碎片而已"（ⅩⅩⅣ）的看法。这种"深沉的忧郁贯穿《苜蓿角》首集"（ⅩⅩⅧ）；对于死亡、鬼魂的描述在前六篇故事中更是俯拾皆是。菲特利认为《苜蓿角》第二系列较第一系列内容更丰富，也更有艺术含量，但同时承认第二系列叙述人与叙述客体的疏离让故事叙述较第一系列少了切实感；之后的两个集子《苜蓿角儿童》以及《乡村生活图景》较前两部缺乏统一性以及叙事的复杂性。不过菲特利收录的凯瑞后期发表在通俗杂志上的几篇小说很有早期作品的力道。菲特利选集中加了注释、版本背景说明，以及简要书目，为读者和研究者更好地理解凯瑞短篇小说成就作出了重要的开拓性贡献。

菲特利最有影响的关于凯瑞研究的成就是她发表在期刊上的这篇论文"Entitled to More than 'Peculiar Praise': The Extravagance of Alice Cary's *Clovernook*"（*Legacy*，1993）。这篇文章超越了传记批评，借鉴了其他研究者的成果，如Joanne Dobson和Nancy Miller的弗洛伊德式的解读，认为19世纪女性作家渴望表达情感和愿望。另外，菲特利不仅把凯瑞作品置于其时代背景下，更关注凯瑞的叙事技巧。通过深入的比较研究，菲特利归纳了一幅凯瑞女性叙事人的特征：这些"乡土代言人"专为往往被城市读者所忽视的"农耕阶层"说话。《苜蓿角》第一系列在不起眼的人物身上体现了凯瑞的叙事意识，例如小彼得·哈里斯，虽是寄居人家，备受歧视，却有鸿鹄之志，风度大气。通过对小彼得这样的乡土代言人的志向的强化描写,凯瑞避免了"按照性别区分其小说人物功能"(105)的做法,从而让女性叙述人代表并同情故事中的男男女女。菲特利深刻分析了凯瑞叙述人的作用。凯瑞让叙述人和叙述主体关系密切,以至于"模糊了作者和叙事人,以及叙事人和叙事主体之间的界线"(106),这样反倒给故事更大的权威性。第一人称视角还使叙事超乎年龄限制,易于进入"女性主体内心世界"(106),让叙述人认同于所描写的地域,认同于那里的居民。例如,在《维尔德明斯一家》中,叙述人观察其叙事主体的同时还要后者有所反应。注意到小木屋中的陌生来客的同时,她希望得到他们的回馈,这个相互认可的过程进而转移到叙事人和读者之间,叙事人让读者既关注所描述的奇怪的家庭,也关注叙述人本身。通过强调这种叙述同情关系,凯瑞为其叙事主体,其叙述人,以及作者本人寻求认可,以此关系为基础营建一个"细节诗学"。例如,《汤普金斯一家》中描写渴望参加晚会的汤普金斯小姐精心准备的围裙却被撕破了,围绕围裙被撕破前后的描写,笔法可谓细致精微,生动入微地展示了人物的内在渴求。然而,当这种奢求触及人物所处的阶层这条线时,如在《玛格莱特·费兹》等故事中,凯瑞既批判自觉高人一等的贵族派头,又批判乡下人欲与其为伍的虚妄臆想。第二系列中的《夏洛特·瑞安》是个半自传性质的小说,主人公夏洛特在寻求认可的过程中饱受挫折(116)。描写小说主人公受挫的经历似乎有意遮掩凯瑞本人寻求认可的远大抱负。凯瑞的抱负是真真切切的:她只身来到纽约打拼,创立了一番事业,成为经济和精神上独立的女性,还成了成功的作家,她跨越了阶层、地域以及性别的种种樊篱和障碍,文学成就获得了当之无愧的认可。

菲特利的批评方法对90年代以来的凯瑞研究有深远影响,为其他学者所借鉴。凯瑞对女性和小人物的关注是女权主义文学批评研究关心的中心话题之一。托马斯·菲克的论文"Maternal Iconography and Nation Building in Alice Cary's *Mrs. Walden's Confidant*"(*Studies in American Fiction*,1997)运用女权主义理论把菲特利提倡的凯瑞研究向前推进了一步。论文专门对《乡村生活图景》中的《瓦尔登太太的知己》(*Mrs. Walden's Confidant*)作了深入研究。故事发生在俄亥俄州的一个无名小镇,时间是7月4日美国独立日,描写了一个闷闷不乐、心灰意懒、自艾自怜的妻子和母亲如何蜕变为一位积极、知足、自尊的家庭和社区成员。主人公萨丽·瓦尔登丈夫遇雷击差点一命归西,萨丽开始承担起家庭责任,改善家居环境,和丈夫一起在家庭农场上忙碌,把女儿嫁给事业有成的村医。菲克认为这是一个极具象征意味的故事,象征"妇女通过放弃麻木的受害感有能力在国民生活中占据一席之地"(141),担当起"共和国母亲"式的责任。这是一篇具有"极其深厚的女权主义意味"的故事(135)。瓦尔登这个名字出典于亨利·梭罗的经典《瓦尔登湖》并"为梭罗的警世名言提供了例证:改造别人之前要先改造自己⋯⋯而故事是从女性视角证明这一点的"(138)。菲克强调,这个故事是一个国民生活的"性别化了的寓言"。虽然萨丽的新生是有其局限的,但她走出了凯瑞笔下女主角共有的忧郁状态,从而汇入美国生活的主流,纳入积极进取与个人成功的主导神话。

在男权主导的时代,女性作家的题材和方法的选择,正像职业选择一样,受到更多限制。她们只能在主导话语划定的规则内作一些有限发挥。詹妮特·奥顿在"Parental Guidance: Disciplinary Intimacy and the Rise of Women's Regionalism"(2001)中将凯瑞的《苜蓿角》故事置于美国期刊出版实践及其政策的语境中进行研究。凯瑞《苜蓿角》中的故事许多都是先在期刊上发表的,当时的期刊青睐说教性的振奋人心的作品,凯瑞这样的女作家愿意唯命是从。期刊政策给女作家分配了家长的角色。奥顿认为,女作家承担了用新鲜话题讲述新兴地区故事来教育读者的角色。凯瑞的话题便是乡俗村情。要在男性主导的期刊发表作品,女作家必须寓教于乐,所以"女性地域作家发展了一种运用自身和某一地方的联系来寓教于乐的文学样式,以期确立权威性"(68)。凯瑞《苜蓿角》前言同时强调其自身经历和其卑微的也是"最率性的忠实"(69)。凯瑞的故事以质朴、诚实、信任、实在取代浪漫和虚构。奥顿以《老克里斯多弗》(*Old Christopher*, 1855)以及《拜访威廉舅舅家》(*About My Visit to Uncle William's*, 1853)为例,把凯瑞和另外两个当时美国期刊的主要撰稿人斯托夫人以及罗斯·库克作了比较。奥顿的结论是,所有这些女作家所面临的两难处境是,要在担当起现实主义写作的阳刚角色的同时,保持她们道德激励的阴柔传统。

凯瑞对于女性写作传统的贡献更在于她对速写体裁的发展。艾利卡·克里格在"Rustic Matters: Placing the Rural Community Narratives of Alice Cary, Susan Fenimore Cooper, and Caroline Kirkland in the Context of the Nineteenth-Century Women's Sketch-writing Tradition"（2001）一文中认定凯瑞是速写体裁发展的关键人物。速写是妇女作家开创的写作传统，肇始于英国女作家玛莉·米特福德（1787—1855）的《我们村：乡土人物速写》（*Our Village: Sketches of Rural Character*，1824—1832）系列。凯利是美国女作家运用这一体裁的先锋人物之一，其他以此见长的美国作家还有卡罗琳·柯克兰（其 1839 年的 *A New Home，Who'll Follow* 具有代表性）以及苏珊·库珀（代表性作品有 1850 年的 *Rural Hours*）。这些"乡村速写"使用简单直白的新闻体的散文，描写普通的事件，采用女性视角，关注地方历史，以及强调与城市中日益盛行的推崇个人主义的资本主义截然相反的乡村生活价值观。《苜蓿角》中反映的这一写作传统的特点包括如下几方面：①非线性叙事结构；②对单个社区的细节描写；③公社式的价值体系；④乡土环境。凯瑞、库珀以及柯克兰作品都描述田园式的、处于荒蛮与文明之间的"中间景象"，但和其他两位相比，凯瑞更加原生态地处理农村现实，毫无保留地为更加严酷的生活环境写真。凯瑞从"处于劣势的穷困的乡野视角"（202）出发，来描写"农耕阶层"的困苦及其对人物产生的麻醉作用。大自然不时给处于贫乏熬人的日常生活中的人们提供点解脱，这样《苜蓿角》速写集的总体结构给乡村生活赋予了基本上乐观的，甚至是进取向上的观点。这一点克罗尼早有论述，但克里格文章中作了更加充分的发挥。克里格论文的注释还提到新兴的生态文化批评方法对于研究凯瑞作品的意义，更提供了大量的关于速写体裁的参考书目。

除了体裁和写作风格，凯瑞对美国地域文学的发展也作出了贡献。菲特利与玛乔里·普赖斯合著的《地方书写：地域特色、妇女与美国文学文化》（*Writing Out of Place: Regionalism, Women, and American Literary Culture*）论证了凯瑞在地域文学发展史上的地位，而以往的地域文学批评往往忽略凯瑞的贡献。在对妇女写作与地域小说的兴起作了广泛研究的基础上，该书认定凯瑞在内战前 10 年的作品为美国地域文学传统的滥觞，并认为《苜蓿角》前言是"地域小说的肇始宣言"（173）。凯瑞的写作以其真诚率直、乡味纯正、亲身体验、感同身受等特点有别于仅仅用地方特色作包装的所谓地域主义。她的小说给地域文学赋予个性、新奇，甚至怪异因素，一些后世作家如萨拉·朱丽特和维拉·凯瑟的作品传承了这些特点。应当说明的是，美国地域文学传统有更早的渊源，可以追溯到1800年玛莉雅·埃奇沃思的《莱克兰特城堡》中的地域主题和地方人物，其他作家如华盛顿·欧文、利迪娅·希格尼（1791—1865，美国19世纪早期红极一时的诗人）、斯托夫人、卡罗琳·塞奇威克，以及西南幽默作家乔治·华盛顿·哈里斯等都对地域写作的流行有所贡献。菲特利和普赖斯书中所举的例子印证了前面讲到的奥顿和克里格的论文中的关于凯瑞独特的农村视角的论断，认为凯瑞把玛莉·米特福德的英国"乡村速写"风格和约翰·尼尔（1793—1876，美国作家、文艺批评家，著有《新英格兰人乔纳森兄弟》）的美国乡村速写体裁向前推进了一步。凯瑞的贡献是赋予其速写以心理深度，这极大影响了后世作家，如罗斯·库克、玛莉·弗里曼以及凯特·肖平。凯瑞以其对"农耕阶层"的同情笔调以及对这个阶层的"日常琐事"的昭示给这种写作形式增添了分量。她的速写给这个人群描绘了幅幅感性、生动而又复杂的群体画像，讲述他们的真切的生活、希望、恐惧，并赋予应有的关注和同情。凯瑞很好地控制了速写这种较灵活的写作体裁，细节拿捏得当，完成了为其叙事主体赢得尊重的艰巨的任务，靠的是一种"移情诗学"。这种移情诗学给她的小说注入了情感以及对普通人日常生活的感性体验。她的移情诗学不仅体现在题材和人物的选择上，还贯穿于她的叙事手段上。通过一个"叙事认同"过程，即通过创造亲身经历所描述情景的叙事人的做法，凯瑞"久久不让我们离开'苜蓿角'，就是让我们学会见苜蓿角所见，闻不可闻之事，最后认识到微不足道之重要"（174）。早期的地域写作往往是为了某种目的而只是利用乡土人物，这样就把乡土人物和城市读者拉开了距离。而凯瑞让我们参与到她的人物的生活当中，更通过一种"细节诗学"——菲特利在前文探讨了这种技巧——揭示人物的感性与知性的深度。这本研究著作针对《苜蓿角》第一系列的几个故事作了简短而富有洞见的分析，如《我的外祖父》、《两姐妹》以及《维尔德明斯一家》等。更重要的是这本书的作者重新认定了凯瑞在文学史上的地位，把她放到了更高的位置。

凯瑞《苜蓿角》第二系列中的《克里斯多弗舅舅》是目前为止

受到关注最多的一篇。它被收进《希思美国文学选》（Heath Anthology of American Literature）便是最好的证明。伊丽莎白·舒尔茨的论文"Bartleby, the Scrivener and Uncle Christopher's: Sites of Wage Slavery and Domestic Abuse"（收入本书）把凯瑞的这篇力作和麦尔维尔的小说作了比较研究，把它的重要性提升到和麦尔维尔的杰作《录事巴托比》（和凯瑞《苜蓿角》第二系列同年发表）相提并论。舒尔茨分析认为两篇小说中对于阶级和性别不平等的处理异曲同工，有很多相似之处。凯瑞作品中的10岁男孩马克和麦尔维尔作品中的同样受压迫的誊写员代表的是被上升时期的资本主义所囚禁并最终摧残致死的"工薪奴隶"人群。舒尔茨比较了两篇的场景、人物、情节、主题思想、意识形态、意象以及其他主题元素（如静默）。该研究还认为凯瑞的重要性超越了俄亥俄河谷乡野的地域界限，延伸到工业化的东北地区的血汗工厂和产业办公间，因此小说显示出凯瑞关注到了地域性乃至全国性的社会问题。

除了上述公开出版的研究成果，已有三篇博士论文包含对凯瑞的研究。其中一篇还专门研究凯瑞，昭示会有更多的博士研究选择凯瑞。温迪·里普利于1996年在乔治·华盛顿大学完成的"Women Working at Writing: Achieving Professional Status in Nineteenth Century America, 1850—1875"是首篇分析凯瑞作品的博士论文。论文以凯瑞的小说《夏甲》（1852）为例说明妇女作家如何"重新设计和拼合不同文学体裁，以适应她们的职业写作需要"，同时以这种方式给自己授予和男性作家同等级别的作为职业作家应有的权力。里普利把凯瑞当成对女性作家的"警告"：一个追逐文学上的成功而把自己逼上绝境的作者代表。诚然，凯瑞在全国性期刊上发表作品，获得约翰·惠蒂尔的高度评价，曾经激励了一代妇女向往当职业作家。凯瑞给她们提供了一个新样板，开拓出一条书写她们所熟知的地区生活的正常渠道，还可以真名实姓地把自己展示给读者。通过沙龙形式在纽约城维持一个文学圈子，担任妇女俱乐部（首个妇女文学协会）首任主席（虽然非出自本人意愿），凯瑞帮助妇女们组织起来形成一股受人尊敬的全国性文学力量。她本人的写作在东部与西部、城市与乡村之间架起桥梁，同时给妇女写作的职业水准建立了新标杆，为后来的女作家，如萨拉·朱伊特，搭建起坚实的职业平台。

约翰·士丹顿的博士论文"Character, Community, and the Form of Ethics in Four American Regionalists: Alice Cary, Kate Chopin, Walker Percy, Larry Brown"（1999）以凯瑞作品为例研究地域作家是如何显现伦理立场的，从而让读者重新认识乡村以及其他被边缘化的社区的道德状况。论文辟专章研究凯瑞："Making Death Less Terrible: Alice Cary's Regionalist Aesthetics in *Clovernook Sketches*"分析了凯瑞如何运用叙述与描写手段来减弱死亡的恐惧，却让其人物对个体的孤寂感保留接受态度。她的伦理前提，用她的《两姐妹》中的话讲便是"我们都孤苦无依"，这个"我们"既包括小说人物，也包括读者。叙述人声音反复出现，鲜明的意象再加上现在时叙事与过去行动的交织，这些都把读者的注意力导向凯瑞笔下普通人的生活状态，同情他们生活的艰辛。士丹顿对凯瑞早期为《女士宝典》撰稿的分析特别有价值。士丹顿认为，凯瑞含蓄地挑战了杂志的父权伦理以及传统的忠信观。对《苜蓿角》第一系列中的《两姐妹》、《彼得·哈瑞斯》、《安妮·希顿》，对第二系列中的《克里斯多弗舅舅家》以及《威廉姆斯舅舅家》的分析支撑这种观点。例如，《外祖父》中叙事人的现在和过去意识交融一起，令死亡"不那么可怖"，尽管故事中也有吓人的细节。对于凯瑞来说，死亡是不可逃避的变故，是我们都得接受的宿命。而无法接受这种变故的人，例如《苜蓿角》第二系列中的威廉舅舅，注定要感受到极强烈的恐惧。士丹顿分析了从凯瑞最早发表的作品到后期在《哈勃月刊》上发表的短篇小说，结合叙事理论、伦理意识，讨论凯瑞短篇小说的主题和技巧的融合。

研究凯瑞的最新博士论文是简·嘉利赫的"The Family of God: Universalism and Domesticity in Alice Cary's Fiction"（2009），这也是第一篇专门的凯瑞研究论文。研究没有采用地域研究、叙事学、体裁分析、女权主义等方法，而是探讨凯瑞创作的宗教背景，强调基督教的普救派对凯瑞小说、速写以及系列故事的重要性。普救派本是基督教抗议派的一个分支，其信条把普遍得救的信念与启蒙理性以及当代社会意识熔为一炉。此教派的官方报纸《号角》是凯瑞父母订阅的唯一出版物。嘉利赫认为，很强的普救派观点渗透于凯瑞的故事及小说作品中，这些作品因为不符合地域研究及女权主义研究方法的主导原则，往往被论者所忽视。嘉利赫研究凯瑞故事与小说的版本间性，指出凯瑞写作面貌的多重纹理，因此既承认凯瑞有感伤主义及保守主义倾向，又高度评价她的现实主义、阶级意识以及对传统的性别角色的批判。凯瑞对妇女的刻画使用出自哥特小说、童话故事甚至伤感小说的象喻性典故，用以批判基督教福音会教派的信条、超验主义以及其他领域的僵化教条，同时提倡社区服务和个人身份，这是凯瑞的首部小说《夏甲》的一个鲜明主题。嘉利赫对《瓦尔登太太的知己》的解读方法与菲克有所不同。嘉利赫把本篇跟《苜蓿角》第二系列中的《两次拜访》作了互文解读，认为凯瑞女主角的一个理想的生活目标就是主内。同样，凯瑞也解剖诸如"纯爷们"、"斯文家长"、"英雄匠人"之类的男性理想，并将其置换成了推崇性别身份流动性和个人牺牲的普救派典型。嘉利赫讨论了《外祖父》、《克里斯多弗舅舅家》以及凯瑞后期小说《主教之子》中的例子。凯瑞作品的儿童刻画不是简单地把他们当成阶级压迫的受害者，而是进一步颠覆流行文学中将儿童浪漫化的模式化做法，借以批判福音派以及自由派对儿童抚养问题的不顾社会阶层差异的态度。凯瑞在《克里斯多弗舅舅家》、《婚而不配》及《雪果：献给年轻人》中显露了对童工和虐童现象的抗议。她还以其不折不扣的现实主义描写颠覆了把儿童当成救赎人物的想法，虽然读者还是会被她笔下的小彼得·哈瑞斯之死深深打动。《威瑟比太太的缝纫派对》、《婚而不配》及《古迹遗风》等作品拿儿童作为比喻，代表了非洲裔美国人和土著美国人。如此，凯瑞又成了奴隶制和种族歧视的批判者，这反映了她的普救范围的扩展，涵盖了"救主大家庭"的所有成员。嘉利赫把凯瑞单个作品放在全部创作的大背景下研究，展示了自由宗教信仰对现实主义的影响，并揭示了宗教桎梏为生活所制造的紧张局面。

如上所述，虽然有论者认为凯瑞在文学体裁、题材选择等方面具有独特的和开创性的贡献，但是应该承认，所有研究对凯瑞作品的挖掘还都无法给这样一位作家作出准确定位。女权主义者、普救派基督徒、社会批评家、感伤主义者、现实主义者——这些是研究者们已经给凯瑞作的一些定性，然而多数研究者认为凯瑞最难定性，有必要综合她的全部创作作更深入的研究。目前，凯瑞研究的数量与对本阶段男性大作家的研究相比可谓少得可怜，即使和其他女作家也无法相比。但我们摘要介绍的现有成果足以证明，凯瑞研究的深度、范围以及复杂性都在提高。以后的研究会覆盖更多凯瑞作品，作整体研究，而不是拆分开来孤立研究。正如凯瑞希望她的人物得到关注一样，只有当她的作品得到全面关注，读者才能充分欣赏她的成就，更好地认识她在美国小说发展史上的地位。本书各章从不同方面，运用跨学科的理论方法，分析了凯瑞作品的美学特征、独特的叙事手法，也尝试对凯瑞的创作给予评价和定位，希望对现有研究作出有效补充。我们也期待后来者在这方面作更深入全面的研究。

参考书目：

Primary Bibliography：

Poems by Alice and Phoebe Cary (1850).

Clovernook：or，Recollections of Our Neighborhood in the West (1852).

Hagar：A Story of To-Day (1852).

Lyra and Other Poems (1852).

Clovernook：or，Recollections of Our Neighborhood in the West，Second Series (1853). *Clovernook Children* (1854).

Poems by Alice Cary (1855).

Pictures of Country Life (1859).

Early and Late Poems of Alice and Phoebe Cary (1887).

Secondary Bibliography：

Ames, Mary Clemmer. *A Memorial of Alice and Phoebe Cary with Some of Their Later Poems*. Boston：Houghton Mifflin，1874.

Auten, Janet Gebhart. "Parental Guidance：Disciplinary Intimacy and the Rise of Women's Regionalism". //Aleta Feinsod Cane, Susan Alves, ed. "*The Only Efficient Instrument*"：

American Women Writers and the Periodical, 1837—1916. Iowa City: University of Iowa Press, 2001: 66—77.

Bayless, Joy. *Rufus Wilmot Griswold*. Nashville: Vanderbilt University Press, 1943.

Fetterley, Judith, ed. *Clovernook Sketches and Other Stories*. New Brunswick: Rutgers UP, 1987.

"Entitled to More than 'Peculiar Praise': The Extravagance of Alice Cary's *Clovernook*". Legacy 10.2, 1993: 103—119.

Fetterley, Judith, Marjorie Pryse. *Writing Out of Place: Regionalism, Women, and American Literary Culture*. Urbana: University of Illinois Press, 2003.

Fick, Thomas H. "Maternal Iconography and Nation Building in Alice Cary's *Mrs Walden's Confidant*". Studies in American Fiction 25: 2 (Autumn) 1997: 131—146.

Galliher, Jane M. "The Family of God: Universalism and Domesticity in Alice Cary's Fiction". Doctoral Dissertation: Texas A&M University, 2009.

Griswold, Rufus W. "Alice and Phoebe Cary". *The Female Poets of America with Additions by R H Stoddard*. New York: James Miller, 1877: 372—379.

Kolodny, Annette. "Alice Cary and Caroline Soule". *The Land Before Her: Fantasy and Experience of the American Frontiers*, 1630—1860. Chapel Hill: University of North Carolina Press, 1984: 178—199.

Kreger, Erika M. "Rustic Matters: Placing the Rural Community Narratives of Alice Cary, Susan Fenimore Cooper, and Caroline Kirkland in the Context of the Nineteenth-Century Women's Sketch Writing Tradition". // Rochelle Johnson, Daniel Patterson, ed. *Susan Fenimore Cooper: New Essays on Rural Hours and Other Works*. Athens, GA: University of Georgia Press, 2001: 193—214.

Ripley, Wendy. "Women Working at Writing: Achieving Professional Status in Nineteenth Century America, 1850—1875."

Doctoral Dissertation: George Washington University, 1996.

Schultz, Elizabeth, "*Bartleby, the Scrivener* and *Uncle Christopher's*: Sites of Wage Slavery and Domestic Abuse". // *Melville and Women*, 82—97. Kent, OH: Kent State UP, 2006.

Staunton, John Anthony. "Character, Community, and the Form of Ethics in Four American Regionalists: Alice Cary, Kate Chopin, Walker Percy, Larry Brown". Doctoral Dissertation: Fordham University, 1999.

2 女性现实主义文学的先驱
——从凯瑞小说中的死亡和忧郁谈起

Toward a Feminist Realism: Death and Melancholy in Alice Cary's Stories

杨林贵

Abstract: By focusing on several stories about the life and death of young female characters, and especially Rebecca in *Clovernook: or, Recollections of Our Neighborhood in the West*, this chapter examines how Cary deromanticizes the masculine model of representation. Cary's pre-feminist realism emphasizes the melancholic as a means of representation as she adopts it as a venue to assert a claim for an egalitarian perspective. This assertion anticipates feminist assumptions on women's artistic expression.

Cary's peculiar way of feminine realistic narrative has added much to her contemporary debates over the doctrine of domesticity, thus changing the landscape of the antebellum women's writing. Cary presents the gloomy reality as it appears to the lower-class girl persona in her "sketches," a form that would not be considered "literary" in the tradition of the dominant romance by the sentimentalist writers. Cary's writing resists the romanticizing approach to life by depicting a social reality of lower-class struggles. Cary's deromanticization of the domestic ideal not only makes a difference between her writing and those by other women writers of her time, but also challenges the patriarchal way of literary representation.

摘要：本章以几篇描写关于年轻女性人物死亡的短篇为例，研究贯穿凯瑞小说作品的忧郁基调，认为凯瑞以一种新的表现模式，挑战了当时盛行的男性主导的文学观及其表现方式中的浪漫色调。通过对小说《两姐妹》等对丽贝卡描写的分析，论证了凯瑞的女性现实主义将忧郁作为一种表现方式。凯瑞以忧郁为其思想载体来宣扬艺术与现实的平等观。这种艺术观预示了某些后世的女权主义艺术表现理论。

凯瑞以独特的女性现实主义叙事方式参与了关于家庭生活信条的论辩，并因此改变了美国南北战争前女性创作的格局。一反当时盛行的将家庭生活理想化的做法，凯瑞真实地呈现了下层社会女孩所遭遇的阴郁的现实，反映了下阶层群体的心声。从同时代的感伤主义女性作家以及浪漫主义男性作家所运用的主流浪漫传统的角度看来，凯瑞的速写甚至称不上是文学作品。凯瑞通过描写下层社会苦苦挣扎的社会现实抵制感伤主义文学对于生活的理想化。她偏爱描写日常生活，去除了家庭生活理想化描写的浪漫色彩，这不仅使她的作品与同时代女性作家作品得以区分，而且更为有力地挑战了父权制文学表现模式，点明了在浪漫表现模式中受到压制的忧郁的文化意义。

"*All things are beautiful in their time. Even Death, whom the poets have for ages made hideous...*"

(Cary, Conclusion to *Clovernook*, *Second Series*: 361)

As stated in this quote, Alice Cary has discovered the beauty of death, which is not only at odds with the traditional aesthetic values set by male writers for ages but against the grains of female writings of her time. It is intriguing, however, that Cary made a name for herself as well as a living with her publications in a time when writing was not supposed to be a career choice for women. To be sure, the melancholic tone throughout her fictions challenges the romantic view of the world with a new mode of expression. This chapter will examine how Cary deromanticizes the masculine model of representation by rediscovering the abysses of melancholy. By focusing on several stories about the life and death of young female characters, and especially Rebecca in *Clovernook: or, Recollections of Our Neighborhood in the West*[①], this study will demonstrate that Cary's feminine, if not feminist[②], realism emphasizes the melancholic as a means of representation, and will argue that Cary uses it as an ideological platform to claim an egalitarian perspective for art and reality. I will further suggest that Cary's use of melancholy as a venue of representation anticipates Kristeva's feminist assumptions on women's artistic expression, and that Cary's realistic presentations cut an edge of class consciousness for the Kristevan feminism.

In an age of romanticist myth of subjectivity with its assertion for middle class individuality and domestic sentimentality as the dominating trends of literary creation, how did Alice Cary's plain-styled low life sketches fare? Can Alice Cary be counted in the nineteenth-century American literary world, which was allegedly controlled by a "mob of scribbling women" (Hawthorne)? Do her writings carry any feminist sway? And is her feminism the same as that of her contemporary female writers who took domestic sentimentality as their feminist weapon? These are questions her

---

① In three stories—*The Sisters*, *William Martin's Remorse*, and *Mrs. Grey's Two Visits* (in the first series of *Clovernook*), Cary describes the love story of Rebecca, who is considered by critics as the shadow figure of Cary's sister Rhoda. *The Sisters* and part of *Mrs. Grey's Two Visits* are also collected in Judith Fetterley's collection of Cary, 49—66.

② It is not easy to simply attach a feminist label to Cary. Rather, I would use feminism as a means of discourse, adopting its recognition of difference in the human experience of life. I will show, however, some feminist elements in Cary when she is viewed from such twentieth-century feminist perspectives as those of Luce Irigaray, Hélène Cixous, and Julia Kristeva.

critics cannot avoid, and yet are difficult to answer.

In her otherwise qualified critique of twentieth-century criticisms of the antebellum women writers, Lora Romero fails to mention Alice Cary as a woman writer of that "women-dominated" literary realm. ① This failure might be because the female writers she discusses are most of the middle class who are thought by other critics to have taken the ideology of domesticity as a vehicle of resistance to the patriarchal society. However, Cary's appearance in such a study as demonstrating that the "apparently conventional and monolithic popular doctrine of domesticity" was "contentious and internally contested" (Romero: 11—12) must be helpful to a better understanding of the actual situation of the nineteenth-century American literature. Actually, Cary does not even fit in the "monolithic" picture of the "dominating" group of female writers.

Cary's peculiar way of feminine realistic narrative, I would argue, has added much to the contentiousness of the doctrine of domesticity, thus changing the landscape of the antebellum women's writing. Instead of sentimentally depicting the domestic sphere as an avenue of self-control, which unfortunately confirms the idealization of domesticity and femininity as the male writers did, Cary presents

---

① In her book, Romero discusses some resisting women writers who challenge the patriarchal order by portraying strong female characters who exerts the female power in the domestic sphere. These well-educated feminist writers—advocators of "first wave feminism" —resorted to romanticized story of "historical" renowned women who were believed to have ever controlled in the feminine way. In these feminists' romance, a literary category which was said to be the best form women would be able to vile with male writers, the royal, aristocratic, or gentle women in foreign lands and in the ancient rival with their men for power, creating the illusion of women's "good old days," a time when they allegedly became in power through "feminine" means. Thus, we have Lydia Maria Child's romance of ancient Greece *Philothea* (1836) working on performing women, Eliza Buckminster Lee's Parthenia (1858) fictionalizing the struggle between men and women, and Louisa Mary Alcott's *Behind a Mask: A Woman's Power* (1866) representing the ideal traditional womanhood as it was in the aristocratic English household (19—25).

the gloomy reality as it appears to the lower-class girl persona in her "sketches" —a form that would not be considered "literary" in the tradition of the dominating romance the sentimentalist female writers as well as the Romanticist male writers in Cary's time employed, nor even in the formalist critical tradition. While the romantic, sentimental writings express the leisure of the status quo, Cary's writing gives voices to the "subaltern communities" —the poor, the suppressed, women, children, and all in all, the powerless Other. Cary consciously resists the romantic version of individual autonomy from the social by depicting a social reality of the lower-class struggles. While the bourgeois sentimentality imposes an idealized vision upon life, Cary's realistic fiction represents life and the social world as they are. Her preference for the commonplace everyday life does not attempt to transcend ordinary experience. Further, Cary's deromanticizing the domestic ideal not only makes a difference between her writing and that of her contemporary women equivalents, but also—and most importantly—more strongly challenges the patriarchal way of literary representation. Julia Kristeva distinguishes the feminine "poetic language" or the "semiotic" from the masculine Symbolic, emphasizing the multiplicity in cultural meaning that the semiotic allows. ① However, while Kristeva only suggests displacing the Symbolic within the limits it allows, Cary makes manifest the existence of melancholy, which is one of the cultural meanings that the masculine Symbolic has suppressed in the romantic mode of representation.

Defending herself against some contemporary critics who complained that her first series of *Clovernook* stories are "of too

---

① Arguing against Freudian patriarchal model of desire, Kristeva not merely considers melancholia as a feminine trait but also regards it as a positive experience from which women address their difference from the masculine representation of them in the hegemonic system. Judith Butler includes an analysis of Kristeva in chapter 3 of *Gender Trouble*: *Feminism and the Subversion of Identity* (79—93).

sombre a tone,"① Cary articulates her aesthetic manifesto of melancholy. She refuses to attempt "any descriptions of the gay world" that other writers of her sex practiced to "amuse or instruct society" (Cary, *Clovernook Second Series*: 363). The amuse-instruct aesthetic had been the key principle of the long tradition of male writing since Spenser rewrote the Aristotelian poetics in the English world. Cary argues that female writers' participation in duplicating this tradition necessitates them to write of only the "sunny side" (363) of life so as to falsify their experience and vision. Their romanticized vision and emphasis of sentimentality and femininity-virtue, beauty, and chastity would be the primary imperatives of it—as the male system of desires coincide with the "means of phallocratic model." (Irigaray: 85). Thus, her female counterparts' separating and abstracting the "common lot" (363) from the reality comply with the male system of writing. In contrast, Cary would "*unpretending* [ly]" write the "reminiscences of what occurred in and about the little village" in which *The Sisters* story is set. Therefore, against the idealistic portrayal of reality in that tradition and her contemporary version of it, the Romantic sentimentality, Cary gestures toward a realism that purports to capture the actual circumstances around her life. This is a suffering life of the deprived women, abused children, and the poor—the "humbler classes" she had shared experiences with. Instead of beautifying it or moralizing it to amuse or/and instruct, she endeavors to "exhibit in their customary lights and shadows" (363). She feels an urge to speak for the "bruised and crushed hearts and desolate spirits" (Cary, *Clovernook*: 298). To Cary, the hearts are not only crushed, but are dead so that her suffering persona reacts masochistically to afflictions that harsh environment imposes upon her innocent mind. The dark realism is thus characterized with

---

① Fetterley notes a "suitable form of defying both critics and conventions." See her "Introduction" to *Clovernook Sketches and Other Stories*, xxxiv.

and deeply embedded in melancholia, the feminine experience of life in the Kristevan sense of feminine melancholy, as noted earlier, since it explores the gloomy spheres of her female characters, both circumstantial and psychological. Cary's realism if we may add is a way to represent the "unpresentable" in the male system of representation.① Thus, Fetterley finds a profound sense of melancholy in Cary's stories:

> A profound sense of melancholy pervades the first volume of Clovernook sketches. Each of the first six stories centers around dying and death; moreover many others take place in October or November, a season Cary inevitably associates with mourning. (XXVII)

With this realism of melancholy has Cary set out to write stories about her girl characters in the first series of *Clovernook*. In the second piece of the series, the narrator mentions the death of a seven-year-old girl in a remorseful tone. This elegiac narrative is followed with stories about the death of two young girl lovers, Sarah Worthington and Mary Wildermings, both hurt and ill, starred albeit in different trajectories. While Sarah died at age 19 because of a heart-broken love with a young doctor, Mary, a "fair young girl who died, more sinned against than sinning" (*Clovernook*: 49) as the narrator quotes Shakespeare (*King Lear*: 3.2). She has "been heard to sing sad lullabies under the waning moon sometimes, and at other times ha [s] been seen sitting by her sunken grave, and

---

① While Hélène Cixous advocates women write women, and write of the "dark continent" (884) that the masculine order would not represent, or the "two unrepresentable things: death and the feminine sex" (885) in the twentieth century, Cary already practiced that in the nineteenth-century. Furthermore, although some transcendentalist writers wrote of death, in their romantic vision of death, it is given some transcendental meaning which aims to defeat the ugly reality. Cary's death narrative is rather death itself without edifying it to enable it to carry any meaning of spiritual salvation. This point will be illustrated later in a discussion of the text of Cary's stories.

braiding roses in her hair, as for a bridal" (49). The Wildermings girl is soon joined in her graveyard by another girl, who has a mysterious identity and has just moved to the village. Visiting the haunted place later, the narrator found that "close by the grave of Mary Wildermings was that of the stranger child" (55—56).

Melancholy is not only the dominant sense Cary's stories give, but the key word to describe her girl characters, alive or dead. The mood seems endemic and transmits from tragic fate of the dead girls to those who are still alive. In the thirteenth story, the titular protagonist Annie Heaton has "deep-blue melancholy eyes" and "long, heavy tresses of jetty black hair" as her "peculiar cast of countenance...[makes] her seem the saddest" even when she smiles (121). The melancholic girl's life seems to be brightened with hope in the coming of a poor student Mills. She supports his academic pursuit with her only valuable belonging, the silver watch, her grandmother bequeathed her on death bed However, getting a job upon leaving the school, Mills abandons her. He now flirts with her younger sister Mary, saying that Annie's bright-colored dress is "positively shocking," which breaks the "last illusion of her dream" (186) so that she lives on hopelessly and aimlessly.

The disillusion of a love relation with a man characterizes several other stories of abandoned girls, including Margaret Fields, Ellie Hadly, and Rebecca Hadly. Margaret is "never mirthful, even before the fountain of sorrow [has] been struck open in her heart, by that hand that no love can turn away, but now she [is] more quiet, and pensive almost to melancholy" (158). But no sooner than Margaret's dreams brightened and hopes awakened with a relationship with a young clergyman, he falls in love with the more beautiful Florence, a town-living church minister's daughter. However, when "he is no longer very young, the pastor of a wealthy church in the city," he still comes back to Margaret for comfort, "listening to the cheerfulness and wisdom that drop from the lips which perhaps he remembers to have kissed" (162); whereas, Margaret "has herself a wound concealed" (163). Similarly, Ellie Hadly's rosy dreams that the gentlemanly Mr. Harmstead has evoked with his encouraging gestures and praises have been battered by "glimpses of a stately woman by his side, the countenance beautiful, but its expression proud and half pitying" (339). As Cary ends the story as the conclusion of the whole series, when she passes Willowdale, Mr. Harmstead's old place, "she repeats the line of England's gloomy bard—so simple, yet containing so much—Thou art nothing—all are nothing now" (342).

All the misfortune of Cary's sorrowful girl characters is crystallized in the fate of Rebacca in the second half of the series. The three stories—*The Sisters*, *The Remorse of William Martin*, *Mrs. Grey's Two Visits*—centered in the character of Rebecca starts with a narrative of the melancholic girl, Ellie, and ends with her mourning of her dead sister, Rebecca. Even death incurs no transcendent meanings but dark shadows in the heart: Cary writes, "there are no tears in her large melancholy eyes, for she knew not what death was; but she was oppressed with a vague fear, and kept out of the house all the time" (300). Actually, melancholy as connected with death in the sketch is not only the tone of narrative, but a discourse through which the author Cary transfers her own melancholic perspective of life to the reality of her girl characters. We may not agree with Sigmund Freud's sex-orientation and gendering tendency in his psychoanalysis of melancholia. But, his generalization of melancholia as the result of the "internalization of a lost object of love"[①] is helpful in a biographical reading of Cary's melancholy narrative. Cary's sisters of the story are really of herself

---

[①] Freud, "Mourning and Melancholia", quoted in Judith Butler, *Gender Trouble*: *Feminism and the Subversion of Identity*, 61. Melancholy is significant to Cary's "ego formation" as is revealed in her reflections of her sister to be quoted in this discussion.

and her own sister. Cary's sister, Rhoda's death has impacted her life perspectives, and has been memorialized in this story. Cary described her relationship to Rhoda in a letter like this:

> A beloved sister shared with me in work, and play, and study; we were never separated for a day...Just as she came into womanhood she was not yet sixteen death separated us, and that event turned my disposition, naturally melancholy, into almost morbid gloom. (quoted in Fetterley, XIII)

Hence, in the story we see that young as she is, Ellie is sad, "sad even in childhood so that" a calm but constant melancholy [veils] the sunshine of her life (270). The only wonderful times for the sisters are when they tell stories in the woods. Nevertheless, these times are short and interrupted by Rebecca's mentioning of Mary Wildermings's death and by her prediction of her own death before she is sixteen, which anticipates her own actual death later in the story, casting a gloomy atmosphere—the "winter" is soon coming.

In terms of melancholy, Cary may be either of the sisters of the story or a combination of both so that she can deplore the perceptive depth of melancholia; and the deeper the melancholy is, the higher she develops her creative capacity. Cary's peculiar relationship with her sister, Rhoda, explains both the sources of Cary's melancholy and the "fluidity" between the artistic world and the reality. As suggested by Cary's autobiographical journal quoted earlier in the paper, the early death of her elder sister had devastating effect on Cary's perspectives of life, leaving her a deep sense of gloom. But to retain this feeling in writing, Cary transforms the sister relations of the actual circumstances of her life into that of the story. We thus see in the story the melancholic girl, Ellie, is endowed with poetic sensitivity, which unfortunately comes to capture the dark reality of the death of her only important person—her sister, Rebecca. Ellie, the younger one in the story, is Alice Cary in melancholic disposition; whereas, Rebecca, the elder in the story, who has less romantic illusions, represents another side of Alice Cary whose optimistic childhood longings had long been worn out in harsh circumstances.

In Cary's imagined recreation as well as in real life, the younger sister lives to embrace the "beauty" of the death in her art as a memorial testimony of Rhoda on one level. On another level, furthermore, the early death of the elder sister also signifies that Alice Cary died in heart with the death of her dear sister, a death of a naive, dreamy mind for the loss of the most loved one. Isn't the death of a happy heart, i. e. , "psychic death," a gloomier thing than a physical death? It absolutely is for Cary. As revealed in her reflections on her earlier life, Cary was thrown into "almost morbid gloom" upon Rhoda's death. In a similar sentiment, she has nearly touched the bottom of the melancholic sea with such treatment of the heart's death in the story.

Fortunately, Cary fumbles her way out of the depth of melancholia and finds her own way of expression by attributing a poet's capacity, together with its psychological trait, melancholy—which is peculiar to feminine creativity in Kristevan terms—to the younger sister who lives both in the story and in real life. In this sense, the transposition of artistic and real-life positions, or a kind of empathy, demonstrates Cary's power of artistic expression. Her writing motif is deeply rooted in her feminine experience—melancholia—and at the same time, this artistic creativity locates its representing form in melancholy, establishing melancholy as the vehicle of articulating one's personal experience of life. To be sure, Cary already employed the "Semiotic language," which Kristeva identifies as women's language a hundred years later, to represent the "unrepresentable," or the multiple, or all the suppressed in the "Father's Law" with its Symbolic mode of expression. In other words, Cary uses melancholia as the psychological and expressional norm of women. Kristeva links melancholy to artistic production, which will best be illustrated the case of Cary's *Sisters*. For Kristeva melancholy is a "voluptuous sadness" that seems tied to the sublimated production of art.① Further, Kristeva also associates melancholy with motherhood. Cary's action of writing—giving birth to her works—can be taken as an expression of maternal experience. In that sense, she is the mother of the sisters of the story and of the mother of herself: "she is her own mother" (Kristeva, *Desire*: 239). In the sister story, the sisters' conversations of becoming poets reverberate with this notion of the production of art, and are part of their expression of themselves in the sister bond in the story as with Cary's "beautiful relations" with her sister. They love each other "with a love that was more than love" (*Clovernook*: 270). When the younger sister comes into a mournful mood, then the elder would kiss her, saying "Dear Ellie, you will be a poet" (271). And so Rebecca coaxes Ellie to "read the verses she had written yester eve, or the last Sabbath." The narrative goes on:

> Creditable they were, no doubt, but love and an unschooled judgment exaggerated their merits; still, pleased, each with herself and the other, they toward sunset crossed the homeward meadows, as if they came in inspiration from the holiest mount of song. (271)

The homosocial relations between the sisters negate the masculine system of the Symbolic, which highlights romantic representations of heteroerotic relationships. In that system, Rebecca's early adolescence would be a best site for romantic explorations. She is "fifteen years, seven months, and five days," having just "[come] into womanhood," an age of rosy dreams and romantic adventures, and the age at which Cary's sister Rhoda died. She is certainly older than the "classic" romantic heroine, Juliet, supposedly being in prime days of romantic ventures. However, under Cary's pen, Rebecca has "a less dreamy" (270) temperament and serves as the protector of her younger sister, the role of a father

---

① In addition, the "highest form of that sublimation seems to center on the suffering that is its origin" (Butler, 161 n-32).

or a brother as Cary herself performed in life.

Cary's stories do not fall into the established tradition of romance in other ways. The few successful love stories in the series are not only unnoticeable but also undermined by Cary's narrative approach. To label them as successful is because both end with a possible marriage. However, the process of wooing and courting is void of nothing romantic even when there is such a process. Even though it hints at some romance, it is insignificant in the whole account of a religious relation, or an at-the-edge-of-bankruptcy farm, a gothic mystery. Sally Whitfield's secular union with the young clergyman in *Deacon Whitfield's Folks* is buried in the description of the complicated relations among the local church authorities. Susan in *About the Tompkinses* has to hide her motivation to attend a party and acts with the morale of her low-class family. Giving weight to the family's status in the neighborhood, the story does offer details of Susan's emotion, which is most of the time one of frustration. As a result, readers of the story might be left in a fog when the news of her relation with the farm helper Maurice is indicated by the young man in his report to his employer. Maurice asks Mr. Tompkins if the family does not let an unused cottage, he and Susan will take it (116). Lydia's encounter with the mysterious Archibald Sumner in *Lydia Heath at the Sumners* is presented only as a continuation of *The Phantom Hunter* story, the protagonist of which is the more mysterious figure of the young man's uncle, Jonathan Sumner, a phantom hunter.

The narrative of Rebecca's sore experience is more against the grains of romance than the non-romantic "happy" ending of those successful girls. In this story, Cary's representation of melancholy finds more profound expression in her treatment of the Rebecca seemingly rosy story, as the depiction of star-crossed lovers does not include a romantic core. While her narrative somewhat hints towards some romantic element, romantic love is not the focus of the story anyway. Perhaps romance is not what Cary wants to depict, or at least she does not fall into the romantic model of representation, indeed. The supposed "romance" of Rebecca and the young schoolmaster cannot be confirmed in the story. The "love" affair is reported by Rebecca's mother's friend, Mrs. Grey, who receives reports from yet others that

> Rebecca and the schoolmaster were engaged to be married; that they were in the habit of meeting each other in the woods, by the school house; and that Rebecca went to see him after he was dead, and wept and moaned at such a rate, that they heard her all over the house. (295)

Curiously, there is not any direct description of the relationship except for this report and for a tenuous hint in the middle of the story when Rebecca answers Ellie's question if the schoolmaster is ugly. There, Rebecca's reply does not even show the kind of sentiment that a girl in love has in romantic stories. Then upon the report, the narrator's voice comes in, saying: "Now, if all this had been true, there would have been no actual wrong in it." (295) There is even no description of Rebecca's reactions upon her supposed lover's death. Furthermore, Rebecca's own death is not for love or an obsessive and excessive mourning of her lost "sweetheart," nor of a suicide, like Juliet, to follow her love to the grave, becoming a love martyr as lovers in traditional love models do.

Indeed, the romance cannot be real in that Rebecca shows much indifference to romantic topics. The paralyzing atmosphere of the country life has deprived her of dreamy illusions. Her indifference to romantic affairs reflects in one aspect the cruelty of her living environment as Cary depicts in her Clovernook sketches. The deprived, particularly children or especially young girls have to suffer in their supposed happy years. Actually, the impossibility of the romance very much lies in Rebecca's loss of romantic sentiment, resulting from the crushing surroundings that keep a close gaze on young people's adolescent life. In such an environment, Rebecca's romantic heart seems to have already died. In a story in the second Clovernook series, *Charlotte Ryan*, Cary writes of another girl's frustrated, crushed dream of romance. Charlotte's vainly waiting for Mr. Sully Dinsmore ends up with tears after an entire lonely, chilly day on a hill, and with the loss of a happy heart— "the heart, which, once gone, never come [s] back" (281). Even if "the fresh young feeling, the capacity to enjoy," or any sparkling of romantic love, had not died, they would have been extinguished by the assailing gossips busy people—like Mrs. Grey—spreads. And even if Rebecca still had romantic sentiment, the sprout of love could not survive the harsh parental interference. Although Mrs. Hadly, Rebecca's mother, does not even want to communicate with her daughter about this reported affair, she resolves to punish Rebecca because she regards "the dreamy and poetic dispositions of her children as great misfortunes; something worse in fact—something to be ashamed of" (*Clovernook*: 295—296). Rebecca is consequently punished for an untested rumor. This punishment is directly responsible for her death. She seems to have died of the punishment her mother imposes upon her for her "deviant" behaviors with the schoolmaster, which have been informed by Mrs. Grey. Rebecca does not seem to know why she is punished nor does she even ask for reasons for her mother's refusal to allow her to the promised tour to town. She silently accepts the punishment and takes hard labor with a desolate heart.

 Her silence in face of unfair treatment is in the same vein with her indifference to romantic dreams. And here the story has really reached the abyss of melancholy in Rebecca's masochist reaction to the unfair punishment—the highest degree of melancholia so to speak. According to Kristeva, the melancholy—the "voluptuous sadness" of melancholy—is tied to masochism. In other words, suffering is the source of melancholy. Rebecca is only one of the many suffering figures in Cary's stories, and yet she represents the extreme type. She is actually punishing herself by indifferently accepting the punishment. Rebecca,

> calm and unquestioning, resumed her work-day dress and her accustomed labors. All day her thoughts were colored with saddest memories. She had little appetite for dinner, and less

for supper, but forebore to speak of the headache with which she suffered, performing every task which usually fell to herself and Ellie, alone. (297)

With a crushed heart, hard labor, and the unquenched thirst to see Ellie, who has left for a week, Rebecca finally collapses. The heart dies first, then the existence of the body does not really matter to the innocent girl. This is how Alice Cary conveys her perception of masochism. And with the plainest form—sketches—she earnestly presents things as they are, rather than beautifying them as her contemporary writers did.

Therefore, different from her contemporary "feminists," Cary consciously assumes a plain, unornamented, "unpretending" style of narrative, true to her aesthetic manifesto as in her "Conclusion" to the *Clovernook Second Series*. Her way of realism distinguishes her from the female literary culture of her time by presenting the unrepresentable—death and melancholy, to answer the first question at the beginning of the paper. In the twentieth-century sense of feminism, especially that of the revisionist feminism, we may well say that Cary's version of "feminism" has gone much ahead of her contemporary feminist attempts, and anticipates the feminism of the twentieth century, to answer the rest.

Works Cited

Butler, Judith. *Gender Trouble: Feminism and the Subversion of Identity*. London: Routledge, 1990.

Cary, Alice. *Clovernook: or, Recollections of Our Neighborhood in the West*. New York: Redfield, 1852.

Clovernook: or, Recollections of Our Neighborhood in the West, Second Series. New York: Redfield, 1853.

Cixous, Hélène. *The Laugh of the Medusa*. Keith Cohen, Paula Cohen, trans. Signs 1.4 (Summer), 1976: 875—893.

Fetterley, Judith, ed. *Clovernook: or, Recollections of Our*

Neighbor in the West, *Sketches and Other Stories*. New Brunswick: Rutgers UP, 1985.

Irigaray, Luce. *The Sex Which Is Not One*. Ithaca: Cornell UP, 1985.

Kristeva, Julia. *Desire in Language: A Semiotic Approach to Literature and Art*. Leon S. Roudiez, ed. Thomas Gorz, others, trans. New York: Columbia UP, 1980.

"Motherhood According to Belline." // *Revolution in Poetic Language*. Margaret Walker, trans. New York: Columbia UP, 1984.

Romero, Lora. *Home Fronts: Domesticity and Its Critics in the Antebellum United States*. Durham: Duke UP, 1997.

3 凯瑞独具一格的美国哥特文学

Alice Cary's American Gothic

Dennis Berthold

Abstract: Although usually identified as a regional realist, Alice Cary had an early interest in Gothic fiction, notably Anne Radcliffe's *The Italian* (1797). She knew Edgar Allan Poe's works both from her own reading and through her relationship with Rufus Griswold, Poe's literary executor and first editor, and she surely knew of Poe's favorable review of her poetry in the *Southern Literary Messenger*. She quotes *Annabel Lee* in *The Sisters* and repeatedly describes early deaths set against dark autumnal landscapes to create an "undercurrent of meaning" just as Poe advocated in his review of Nathaniel Hawthorne's tales. The Gothic is most evident in her first five *Clovernook* sketches and *Uncle Christopher's*, where death and guilt plague the haunted narrator and destabilize both sentiment and religious affirmation.

Cary's Gothicism is best understood through Sigmund Freud's concept of the unheimlich, usually translated as "uncanny" but resonating more fully with Fred Botting's concept of "homely gothic," or the transformation of everyday life into something strange, unfamiliar, eerie, and possibly threatening, like the household pet in Poe's *The Black Cat*. Such defamiliarization creates the uncanny mood of *Uncle Christopher's*, where the narrator feels dislocated and alienated from her own cousins, who seem more like robots than humans. As though recounting a bad dream, Cary's young narrator describes a world of domestic abuse and brutal patriarchy with a chilling objectivity and dispassion. Numerous Gothic motifs and conventions simultaneously advance realism and the uncanny, as when the narrator of *My Grandfather* sees her grandfather for the last time and experiences feelings of mortality, or when a childhood friend's smiling corpse provokes irrational feelings of guilt in the narrator of *Light and Shade*. In *The Strange Lady* a son's successful growth to manhood pales beside the "awful reality" of his mother's death, and in *The Pride of Sarah Worthington* Gothic motifs of ruin, isolation, and cold penetrate the narrator's adult consciousness and prevent her from exorcising her guilt over the death of a childhood friend. *The Wildermings*, Cary's most thoroughly Gothic sketch, employs explicit Gothic imagery not only to create an uncanny atmosphere but to show that, as Teresa Goddu has argued, Gothic horrors are part and parcel of life in nineteenth-century America.

摘要：爱丽丝·凯瑞虽然通常被认为是现实主义区域文学作家，但是她早期曾对哥特式小说颇有兴趣，特别是安妮·拉德克利夫的《意大利人》（1797）。通过自己的阅读以及与鲁弗斯·格里斯沃尔德（爱伦·坡的文学执行者和第一位编辑）的关系，她熟悉了坡的作品，而且肯定知晓坡曾经在《南方文学信使》上对她的诗歌作出好评。在她的短篇小说《两姐妹》中，她曾引用了《安娜贝尔·李》中的词句，并且多次描述了秋日暗淡的景象以及生命的早逝，来制造一种"意义的暗流"，而这正是坡在评论纳撒尼尔·霍桑的小说时所倡导的。哥特因素在她《苜蓿角》的前五篇短篇小说和短篇《克里斯多弗叔叔》中体现得最为明显。在这些短篇里，死亡和愧疚感缠绕着叙事者，冲击着人物情感和宗教信仰。

弗洛伊德的 unheimlich 的概念非常有助于我们理解凯瑞作品中的哥特元素。unheimlich 通常被译为"怪异"，但其含义更接近于弗雷德·博廷的"家居哥特"的概念，即将日常生活中的事物转换为奇怪、陌生、神秘、可怕的很可能带来威胁的事物，例如坡的《黑猫》中的那只猫。正是这种陌生化技巧在《克里斯多弗叔叔》中营造出了诡异的气氛。故事的叙述者感到自己被表亲们厌恶、疏远，这些表亲的行为更像是机器人，而不是人类。如同讲述一场噩梦一般，年轻的叙述者异常冷静客观、不动声色地描述了一个充满了家庭虐待和野蛮家长制的世界。当《外祖父》中的叙述者见了外祖父最后一面，体会到生命逝去的感受时，或者当《光影之间》中一个儿时玩伴面带微笑的尸体激起了叙述者内心难以遏止的负疚感时，多样的哥特主题和传统的写作手法共同作用，超越了现实主义，也超越了怪诞离奇。在《怪妇人》中，儿子的长大成人在母亲死亡的"可怕现实"面前黯然失色。在《萨拉·沃辛顿的自尊》中，毁灭、孤独、冷漠等哥特主题渗透了叙述者的成人意识，使她在面对儿时伙伴的死亡时无法消除内心的负疚感。《维尔德明斯一家》则是凯瑞最彻底的哥特小说，故事中出现了清晰的鬼魅形象，不仅营造了离奇的气氛，而且说明了哥特式的恐怖是19世纪美国生活的重要组成部分。

In the back of the first edition of *Clovernook* (1852) readers found eighteen pages of advertisements for additional volumes available from Redfield, the company that published *Clovernook*.[①] Publisher's advertisements were customary in the nineteenth century and can still be found in paperback editions today. Behind them lies an implicit commercial assumption: if you liked the book you just

---

[①] Alice Cary. *Clovernook*: *or Recollections of Our Neighborhood in the West*, 4th ed. New York: Redfield, 1852. All citations are to this edition and are included in the text.

finished reading, you might also like some of these from our backlist. Most of the authors and titles listed in the back pages of *Clovernook* are unknown today, and range from popular novels by Caroline Chesebro and the emerging genre of illustrated histories to children's books, a manual on drawing instruction, and collections of Scottish legends, religious essays, and Hungarian folk tales. Such a hodgepodge of choices might suggest that Redfield had no clear idea of *Clovernook's* audience. But one advertisement—for *The Works of Edgar Allan Poe*—stands out for its resonance with the Gothicism that predominates in the first five stories and continues, less obviously, throughout the book. No critic has attended to this feature of Cary's writing, yet it is one key to her popularity and the renewed interest in her work today. *The Wildermings* and *Uncle Christopher's* are perhaps her most Gothic sketches and have been included in at least two widely used anthologies of American literature, whereas her more realistic stories have been neglected. [1] These stories and others reveal Cary's affinities with the Gothic tradition and expose the darker sources of inspiration that help explain the uncanny aura in many of her tales, as well as some of the specific imagery that frames them. They demonstrate her debt to literary tradition, not just personal experience or regional values, and they inject a complicating strain in her feminist themes, for the

---

[1] *The Heath Anthology of American Literature*, ed. Paul Lauter et al., 1st edition, Volume 1 (Lexington, Massachusetts: D.C. Heath and Company, 1990) was the first major anthology to include "Uncle Christopher's." The 3rd edition added "My Grandfather," which was removed from later editions. *The American Tradition in Literature*, ed. George Perkins and Barbara Perkins, 10th edition, Volume 1 (New York: McGraw-Hill, 2002) was the first major anthology to include "The Wildermings," which is also reprinted in such specialized anthologies as *American Gothic: An Anthology 1787—1916*, ed. Charles L. Crow (Oxford, UK: Blackwell Publishers, Inc., 1999) and *Women's Work: An Anthology of American Literature*, ed. Barbara Perkins, Robyn Warhol-Down, and George Perkins (Australia: McGraw-Hill, 1994). I have found no anthologies that reprint any other Clovernook sketches, although this is a very dynamic publishing market and editions change rapidly.

Gothic, as we know from *The Fall of the House of Usher* (1843) if not *The Castle of Otranto* (1769), typically pits fragile heroines against abusive and domineering villains and often makes death the price of feminine triumph, not just a sad fact of life on the Ohio frontier. As important as realism, regionalism, and feminism are to Cary's project, recognizing her Gothicism extends her imaginative reach, provides psychological depth, reveals her mastery of metaphor, symbol, and motif, and introduces the melancholy strain that pervades all of the sketches in *Clovernook*.

Currently we know little about Cary's early reading and literary influences. Mary Clemmer Ames's 1873 biography remains the best source, and she lists a pathetic and predictably small collection of books available to Cary's family: the Bible, a hymn book, a history of the Jews, Lewis and Clark's travels, Poe's *Essays*, and *Charlotte Temple*.① Ames also lists "a mutilated novel called the 'Black Penitents' with the last pages missing, which Alice regretted her whole life" (21). Had Ames done a little research, she would have discovered that the "mutilated novel" was *The Italian, or the Confessional of the Black Penitents, A Romance* (1797), by the popular English Gothicist Anne Radcliffe. One of the most famous and durable thrillers of all time, The Italian has all the elements of the classic Gothic novel: a wicked mother who thwarts her son's marriage by kidnapping Ellena, his betrothed; a mysterious apparition that utters grave warnings to Ellena's earnest lover; a Catholic priest who sends Ellena to a lonely convent where she is imprisoned by a cruel Abbess; Ellena's harrowing escape from the convent, followed by several trials before the Catholic Inquisition; and the usual complicated family relationships that are only unraveled at the end. Although the novel ends happily, its descriptions leave the reader with descriptions of unbridled lust, murderous violence, eerie specters, and pervasive uncertainty and unease. Since Cary

---

① *A Memorial of Alice and Phoebe Cary, with Some of Their Later Poems*. New York: Hurd and Houghton, 1873: 21. Further references in text.

apparently never finished the book, she must have associated a state of unresolved anxiety with the Gothic, a mood perfected in the stories of Edgar Allan Poe and evident in several *Clovernook* tales.

Along with Radcliffe, Poe too evidently exercised an influence on Cary. No one has explored the Cary-Poe relationship, yet it is clear that their association went beyond the mere presence of an advertisement in *Clovernook*. Poe's professional acquaintance and literary executor was Rufus W. Griswold, the influential editor who encouraged Alice and Phoebe Cary's careers by including their poetry in *The Female Poets of America* (1849). After Poe's death in 1849 Griswold wrote a slanderous obituary that blackened Poe's name for a century, yet he duplicitously capitalized on Poe's misplaced trust by editing his works for Redfield—the volume advertised in the back of *Clovernook*. At the same time Griswold, although married, enjoyed a romantic correspondence with Alice who was, in the words of Griswold's biographer, "swept off her feet by the attentions of her mentor," and the two came very close to marriage.[①] Cary may even have moved to New York to be near Griswold, and in one letter contemplating such a move she told him, quite passionately, "But I Love with a love that is more than love" (Bayless, 214), a nearly exact quotation from Poe's *Annabel Lee* ("But we loved with a love that was more than love"). Although Griswold soon divorced his wife and married a wealthy New Yorker, he and Cary stayed on good terms and in 1856, when he moved into smaller quarters, he loaned her Samuel S. Osgood's 1845 portrait of Poe to hang in her parlor (Bayless, 192). Clearly, Griswold and Cary knew Poe's works well and must have discussed them at length around the time Cary was writing *Clovernook*, for Cary repeats the line from *Annabel Lee* in the opening paragraph of *The Sisters* (270).

---

① Joy Bayless. *Rufus Wilmot Griswold, Poe's Literary Executor*. Nashville, Tennessee: Vanderbilt University Press, 1943: 215. Further references in text.

Cary's admiration for Poe was, surprisingly, reciprocated. In February 1849 Poe reviewed *The Female Poets of America in The Southern Literary Messenger* and lavished uncharacteristic praise upon it that any aspiring author would have cherished:

> We are proud to be able to say, moreover, in respect to another of the ladies referred to above, that one of her poems is *decidedly the noblest poem in the collection*—although the most distinguished poetesses in the land have here included their most praiseworthy compositions. Our allusion is to Miss Alice Carey's [sic] *Pictures of Memory*. Let our readers see it and judge for themselves. We speak deliberately: in all the higher elements of poetry, in true imagination, in the power of exciting the only real poetical effect—elevation of *the soul*, in contradistinction from mere excitement of the intellect or heart—the poem in question is the noblest in the book. ①

Such an encomium from the infamous "tomahawk man" of American literary criticism was not only rare; it was prized, especially when it appeared in a well-regarded journal like the *Southern Literary Messenger*. True, Poe often treated women writers more generously than men, and there is more than a faint whiff of condescension in his use of the word "poetess." But even if we ascribe his praise to a well-meaning but patronizing sexism, within his universe of "female poets" Alice Cary stood out as one of the few to achieve his own high standards for poetry as announced in "The Poetic Principle": "I need scarcely observe that a poem deserves its title only inasmuch as it excites, by elevating the soul."② In the same essay he considers Alfred, Lord Tennyson "the noblest poet that ever lived" because he is "the most ethereal—in

---

① The Edgar Allan Poe Society of Baltimore, http://www.eapoe.org/works/criticism/slm49g01.htm, 2011-06-25.

② G R Thompson, ed. *Edgar Allan Poe: Essays and Reviews*. New York: The Library of America, 1984: 71. Further references in text.

other words, the most elevating and the most pure" (92). In Poe's aesthetic vocabulary, "elevation," "soul," and "noblest" are words of praise that know no gender, and he applied them with equal force to Tennyson and Cary.

Poe's Gothicism at its best, as in *The Black Cat* or *The Cask of Amontillado*, grounds itself in the stress and anxiety of daily life and explores the repressed feelings that suddenly burst forth in acts of violence that appear unmotivated or inexplicable. It relies less on the fantastic or supernatural than what the narrator in *The Black Cat* calls "a homely narrative" and "a series of mere household events" related as "nothing more than an ordinary succession of very natural causes and effects."① Despite its strange coincidences and grotesque conclusion, nothing in *The Black Cat* demands a supernatural explanation. The story recounts utterly plausible and realistic occurrences familiar to most readers: alcoholism, poverty, wife and animal abuse, compulsive behavior and the guilt that follows, and the pervasive presence and fear of death. In both stories there are plot elements that remain mysterious, such as the appearance of the second cat in the first story or the injury Fortunato inflicted on Montresor in the second tale, and they force readers to dig deeper into the souls of the narrators and venture into the dark recesses of abnormal psychology. But neither detail requires a supernatural explanation. A writer for the *Philadelphia Ledger*, quoted in the Poe advertisement in *Clovernook*, noticed this quality: "There is an air of reality in all his narrations—a dwelling upon particulars, and a faculty of interesting you in them such as is possessed by few writers except those who are giving their own individual experiences" (np). It is precisely this "air of reality" that characterizes Cary's Gothic and gives it a peculiarly American tone that distinguishes it from Ann Radcliffe's outlandish plots or even the baroque sexual inversions and

---

① Patrick F, ed. Quinn. *Edgar Allan Poe: Poetry and Tales*. New York: The Library of America, 1984: 597. Further references in text.

domestic complications of Emily Bronte's *Wuthering Heights* (1847). Teresa A. Goddu's pathbreaking study *Gothic America* situates the best-known American Gothic writers within their social and political milieus to demonstrate how "American Gothic literature criticizes America's national myth of new-world innocence by voicing the cultural contradictions that undermine the nation's claim to purity and equality."① The violence and conflict associated with Indians, slavery, race, market capitalism, women's rights, and similar historical people and events drive the plots and characters in such Gothic writers as Charles Brockden Brown, John Neal, Poe, Nathaniel Hawthorne, Harriet Jacobs, and Louisa May Alcott, and dissociate it from the British romance tradition that relied more on the fantastic and supernatural. Goddu's approach explains how realism and Gothicism co-exist in American literature and provides a sound theoretical framework for linking Poe and Cary as twin practitioners of a distinctively American Gothic literature.

Understanding the blend of realism and Gothicism in Cary's works profits from the insights in Sigmund Freud's essay on *The Uncanny*, whose German title, *Das Unheimliche* (1919) better represents his meaning.② "Heimlich" literally translates as "homely," which in American usage invariably means "plain" or even "ugly," but in more traditional British usage means "of the home," "domestic," "familiar," or intimate (OED). "Unhomely" sounds ungrammatical to the American ear, and is virtually a nonce word in British English—the OED added it in 1989 with only three occurrences, all between 1871 and 1892. If "unhomely" were a common word in English, however, it would mean something alien to domesticity and would involve a process whereby the familiar

---

① *Gothic America: Narrative, History, and Nation.* New York: Columbia University Press, 1997: 10.
② See, for example, Fred Botting, "Homely Gothic," in *Gothic* (London: Routledge, 1996: 113—134).

becomes unfamiliar, as a household pet becomes an agent of retribution (*The Black Cat*), or a friend becomes a murderer (*The Cask of Amontillado*), or one's cousins turn out to be robotic strangers (*Uncle Christopher's*). The terror and anxiety evident in the American Gothic most often comes from the familiar made strange, the domestic made foreign, the heimlich made unheimlich. Translated as "uncanny," it also connotes the known—a "canny" person is a knowledgeable person—transformed into the unknown. This process of "defamiliarization" is an essential Gothic technique mastered by such twentieth-century American Gothicists as Shirley Jackson and Stephen King, and is a staple of contemporary horror movies, where ordinary people morph into monsters and commonplace activities descend into violence. The uncanny, then, especially when applied with all of its connotations, is an essential feature of American Gothic, and Alice Cary may well be one of its earliest practitioners.

Although I want to concentrate on the first five sketches in the 1852 *Clovernook*, a good example of Cary's unheimlich Gothic occurs in *Uncle Christopher's*, a well-regarded story from the second series (1853). The story is narrated by a young woman who accompanies her father on a winter visit to the farm of Uncle Christopher Wright and his family. When she enters the house to meet these relatives for the first time, her surreal description of them alienates her as much as any Gothic heroine entering a dark, lonely castle:

The group consisted of eight persons—one man and seven women; the women so closely resembling each other, that one could not tell them apart; not even the mother from daughters—for she appeared as young as the oldest of them—except by her cap and spectacles. All the seven were very slender, very straight, and very tall; all had dark complexions, black eyes, low foreheads, straight noses, and projecting teeth; and all were dressed precisely alike, in gowns of brown flannel, and coarse leather boots, with blue woolen stockings, and small capes, of red and yellow calico. The six daughters were all marriageable; at least the youngest of them was. They had staid, almost severe, expressions of countenances, and scarcely spoke during the evening. By one corner of the great fireplace they huddled together, each busy with knitting, and all occupied with long blue stockings, advanced in nearly similar degrees toward completion. (175)

The seven women are less human beings than automatons, slaves of patriarchy and the means of production like the paper mill workers in Herman Melville's *The Tartarus of Maids*. They have no individuality, no identity, no purpose except to serve their father, Uncle Christopher, and to knit stockings endlessly, mechanically, meaninglessly, silently, just like Melville's identical young women. All but one qualifies as an "old maid," a woman past her prime for marriage, effectively destroying their opportunities to escape the paternal prison and fulfill their own desires. Their silence and severity mark them as victims of a system of domestic economy as rigid and dehumanizing as the abbeys and inquisitorial trials in The Italian, and the reality of their situation—Cary repeats the stocking motif to emphasize the women's incessant labor—implies no relief from their plight. Cary manipulates her narrative to shift almost imperceptibly from a routine tale describing a casual domestic visit to an uncanny vision of life-in-death, blending realism and Gothicism to expose the horrors of patriarchy, religious zeal, and rural isolation. Although Cary's stated aim in *Clovernook* was to show "sympathy for the poor and humble" (Preface, Ⅵ), she remains sufficiently candid to expose the abject consequences of such conditions. As Elizabeth Schultz finds in her comparison of *Uncle Christopher's* to Melville's *Bartleby, the Scrivener*, in the stocking scene and others "Cary subversively alludes to democratic America where the press of tyrannous laws was apparent in the South's chattel slavery and the deadening influence upon humanity in the North's wage slavery, class inequities, and domestic abuse,"① all themes that Goddu finds essential to the American Gothic. No wonder that Judith Fetterley, who values Cary's realistic depictions of social classes, women, domesticity, and daily life, nevertheless finds in *Uncle Christopher's* "Cary's dual interest in realism and romance...it might be taken for a bad dream, were it not from start to finish so chillingly realistic."②

Traditional Gothic motifs combine with the uncanny to run throughout *Clovernook* and simultaneously advance realism and Gothicism like the undercurrent of meaning Poe admired in Hawthorne's tales. For example, Fetterley notes how "a profound sense of melancholy pervades the first volume of Clovernook sketches. Each of the first six stories centers around dying and death; moreover many others take place in October or November, a season Cary inevitably associates with mourning."③ These are the months of harvest and nominally connote plenty and security, but Cary renders such comforting implications uncanny by making autumn the season of mortality, following Poe's practice in his well-known poem *Ulalume*:

> It was night, in the lonesome October
> Of my most immemorial year;
> It was hard by the dim lake of Auber,
> In the misty mid region of Weir;
> It was down by the dank tarn of Auber,
> In the ghoul-haunted woodland of Weir. (*Poetry and Tales*, 89)

---

① "Wall Street and Clovernook in 'Bartleby, the Scrivener' and 'Uncle Christopher's': Sites of Wage Slavery and Domestic Abuse," in Elizabeth Schultz and Haskell S. Springer, eds., Melville and Women. Kent, OH: Kent State University Press, 2006: 83.

② *Heath Anthology of American Literature*, volume B, 5th edition. Boston: Houghton Mifflin Company, 2006: 2802.

③ Judith Fetterley, ed. *Clovernook Sketches and Other Stories*. New Brunswick: Rutgers University press, 1987: xxviii. Further references in text.

Poe's setting is deliberately vague and unrealistic and prepares readers to expect that an October visit to a "dank tarn" will naturally lead to a "ghoul-haunted woodland." Cary, however, situates her Gothic motifs in detailed and realistic settings, rendering them uncanny and destabilizing reader expectations. In *My Grandfather*, the opening story in *Clovernook*, the narrator recounts her first "consciousness of death" when she was a child, and like Poe's persona in *Ulalume* she remembers "the twilight, as though it were yesterday—gray, and dim, and cold, for it was late in October, when the shadow first came over my heart, that no subsequent sunshine has ever swept entirely away" (13). Cary's narrator is the one haunted, not the woodland or the autumnal setting. Even her grandfather's mill, normally an image of prosperity, is "an especial object of terror" to her (18), yet it offers more comfort than her grandfather's "cold forbidding presence" (19). Cary indulges the grotesque when the girl steals a peek at the dying old man's face:

[I] was transfixed; the rings beneath the eyes, which had always been deeply marked, were not almost black, and the blue eyes within looked glassy and cold, and terrible. The expression of agony on the lips (for his disease was one of a most painful nature) gave place to a sort of smile, and the hand, twisted among the gray locks, was withdrawn and extended to welcome my parents, as the door closed. That was a fearful moment; I was near the dark steep edges of the grave; I felt, for the first time, that I was mortal too, and I was afraid. (21)

Realistic details lead to the girl's innermost thoughts as Cary turns to analogy— "the dark steep edges of the grave" —to convey the sense of mystery and vulnerability that attends a child's first experience with death. The Gothic imagery defamiliarizes her grandfather physically and his last words, "child, you trouble me" (24), alienate him from both the narrator and the reader. It is a profoundly *unheimlich* comment because it is so inappropriate, so unexpected, so cruel. After his funeral Cary uses details borrowed from Poe's *The Fall of the House of Usher* to confirm the reality and horror of death: the granddaughter views "the unsmiling corpse" (an inversion of Madeline Usher's "suspiciously lingering smile" [*Poetry and Prose*, 329]) and watches as the lid of the coffin is screwed down, just as does Poe's narrator. For these American writers realistic details open an avenue for Gothic reflection and undermine religious and sentimental reactions to death, even the narrator's faint glimmer of hope in the last sentence: "Death is less terrible to me now" (26). Cary's Christianity, more evident in her poetry than her fiction, requires a moral that the story does not support, and makes hers a tentative Gothicism more like Hawthorne's than Poe's, but a powerful sally into the Gothic darkness nonetheless.

Light and Shade, the second story in *Clovernook* about a ten-year-old girl who refuses to play with a seven-year-old friend and then feels responsible when the younger girl dies, employs Gothic motifs similar to *My Grandfather*: shadows, a narrator who knows that "the edges of the grave are steep" (28), a November setting, when "the woods were all dreary and withered" (29), a smiling corpse in a coffin (33), and the narrator's irrational guilt for a friend's premature death. By rejecting the comforts of Roman Catholicism, the narrator assumes the Protestant burden of responsibility for her acts, even her "childish misdemeanor" of scorning a playmate: "Fasting, nor prayer, nor penitence, nor scourge, may ever wholly lay the ghosts of bad actions. When we least expect them, they open the doors of our most secret chambers, and come in" (31). Both the idea and the imagery recall Hawthorne stories such as *The Haunted Mind* (1835), where the narrator enters the psychic borderland between dream and reality to find his bedchamber peopled by a procession of ghostly figures. *Light and Shade* has a clearer psychological emphasis than *My Grandfather* and it emboldens Cary to conclude on a more Gothic note, one that enforces the moral and emotional consequences of early exposure to death: "Away in the distance lies [my friend's] brief existence, bordering my own, like a beam of beautiful light; but from her grave stretches a shadow that would reach me in the uttermost parts of the world" (33). John Staunton finds "Death is the interstice in which [Cary's] characters see the forces that have been at work in their lives, both to nourish and inhibit their growth, and it confronts them with the need to seek out the help of others."[①] At this particular stage in the narrator's young life, there is still much help needed.

The third story, *The Strange Lady*, ends with religious affirmation, but not before it presents motifs similar to those in the first two stories while adding bats, owls, a "desolate and ruinous cabin" (34), and a "pale lady" (35) who lives alone with her child for nine years until, during a dark autumn storm, he returns to the cabin to find his mother on her deathbed: "He kissed her lips; and, when she returned not his kisses, he knew she was dead." (37) In one final paragraph Cary moderates this "awful reality" (37) by assuring readers that the community cares for the boy and helps him grow into a man who loves others, but this is merely asserted, not shown, and is at odds with the events in *Uncle Christopher's*, where a Christian zealot forces a young ward to his death. In a letter to Griswold written in the spring of 1850, Cary wrote "I am sometimes passionately fervent in piety, and sometimes rebellious as the fallen" (Bayless, 215). This is the tension I find between her Christian faith and her Gothic sensibility, and the opening stories in *Clovernook* set this tone and make any easy acceptance of religious orthodoxy difficult. The confrontation with death may be the beginning of ethics, as Staunton says (64), but whether one accepts

---

① John Anthony Staunton. "Character, Community, and the Form of Ethics in Four American Regionalists: Alice Cary, Kate Chopin, Walker Percy, Larry Brown." Dissertation, Fordham University, 1999: 30. Further citations in text.

a specifically Christian or even spiritual ethic remains uncertain, as it does in so many Poe and Hawthorne stories.

The fourth story, *The Pride of Sarah Worthington*, is similar to *Light and Shade* in the narrator's recollection of childhood guilt after one night "late in December" when she teases her proud playmate, Sarah Worthington, about her fondness for an older man (44). Some years later, when she reads Sarah's obituary in the newspaper, she feels intense regret for exposing Sarah's secret and never letting her know it was wrong. The story is the narrator's attempt to expiate her childish, ignorant deed, to exorcise "the phantoms that come up from the grave … and folding back the shroud, cry out to the dust for forgiveness. In vain! There is no green hollow in the wilderness, no blank sands of the desert, that to me would not be haunted" (41). Neither art nor religion comforts her, and when she recalls "an old ruinous church" she is clearly dredging up a haunting symbol of her tenuous faith (42—43). Rather than leading to thoughts of salvation, the church leads to further thoughts of the unbridgeable gulf between the dead and the living and the futility of worship: "Nor loud denunciation, nor soft admonition, nor trembling hymn, provokes the sleeping dust." (43) Cary's almost imperceptible shifts between present and past in this story mark the narrator's difficulty in confronting her "phantoms" and making a straightforward confession, either to herself or to the reader. The Gothic motifs of ruin, isolation, darkness, and cold penetrate the narrator's adult consciousness and refuse to assuage her of her guilty conscience.

The fifth story in *Clovernook*, *The Wildermings*, is Cary's most Gothic work, yet its power depends less on traditional Gothic imagery than its ambiguity and eerie effect on the narrator. When "a family consisting of three persons—an old lady, a young man, and a child some fourteen years of age" (48) —moves into a vacant cottage beyond the local graveyard, the narrator feels joy at seeing smoke curling once more from the chimney, a conventional emblem of domestic well-being. After one brief visit to welcome the newcomers, she soon discovers that this is no typical family, and that in fact the relationships of all three are unclear. She later refers to the "old lady" as a "mother," but whose mother she never surmises, and she never sees this "mother" unless she is also "the housekeeper, or one that I took to be her" who appears at the end (48, 51, 55). When the narrator realizes that the young man visits the graveyard at twilight and plays the flute over the grave of Mary Wildermings, "a fair young girl who died, more sinned against than sinning" (49), we realize, without any explicit comment from Cary, that the young man is the child's unwed father and has returned with the child and his mother to absolve his guilt for leaving Mary without benefit of marriage.① The phrase "more sinned against than sinning" comes from *King Lear* III. ii. 60, and in the Victorian era typically denominated a "fallen woman," seduced and abandoned by her lover and, though guilty of a moral crime, worthy of sympathy. It's unclear how the child came into her father's custody or where he went, but it's likely that he has returned to the scene of his transgression because his daughter is dying from a strange illness that links her to her mother. On the narrator's second visit to the cottage, hoping to comfort the sick child, she finds to her "horror" the child dead with her eyes "still unclosed." As the "housekeeper" explains, "the child would never in life close her eyes—her mother, they say, died in watching for one who never came, and the baby

---

① Fetterley says "we never find out the source of the mystery surrounding the new neighbors in *The Wildermings*," which is literally true. See "Entitled to More than 'Peculiar Praise': The Extravagance of Alice Cary's *Clovernook*", *Legacy* 10: 2 (1993): 106. I have attempted to give the story a more gothic reading by exposing its dark undercurrents and the implications of its confused, even repressed, narration. Always an acute reader of Cary, Fetterley stresses in this article Cary's "poetics of detail," which I believe enhance rather than obscure her gothic strain.

was watchful and sleepless from the first" (55). Such a bizarre connection between mother and daughter qualifies as uncanny because it is so different from the usual traits that identify children and parents, a characteristic that even the village doctor, who has been treating the child but has never seen her sleep, considers "strange" (54). The relationships and behavior among all the characters in this story, including the narrator, are ambiguous, secretive, and non-rational, in short—Gothic. The pluralized title implies that this is a tale of an entire family, and while other relationships are possible—the young man could be Mary's brother, for example—the subterranean theme of sexual transgression and remorse runs deeply through the tale and, certainly, the narrator's immature consciousness. Fetterley, although giving the story a more realistic reading than I do, finds "an uncanny resemblance" between the narrator and the child, a perception that places Cary squarely in the emerging tradition of nineteenth-century Gothic with its emphasis on doubles, alter egos, and that most unheimlich figure of all, the doppelgänger. [1]

The Wildermings employs abundant and explicit Gothic imagery—the isolated cottage, a graveyard where ghosts are said to walk, the eerie sound of a flute coming from the graveyard at twilight, the mysterious deaths of Mary and her daughter, and the narrator's horrifying glimpse of the child's corpse with its eyes still open, an image that has become a staple of contemporary horror films. But it is the story's intense focus on the narrator's reactions that gives it a more profound and far-reaching psychological significance than any other tale in *Clovernook* and confirms the craft and power of Cary's Gothic. As if following Poe's theories of

---

[1] "Introduction," *Clovernook Sketches and Other Stories*. New Brunswick: Rutgers University Press, 1987: xxix. See Botting, 113—134, for the rise of the double in Victorian Gothic literature.

writing, Cary creates in the opening five tales of *Clovernook* just enough traditional Gothic motifs to create horror, the grand "effect" that Poe considered essential to any successful tale, and intersperses them with a deceptively calm realism that, in contrast, makes the Gothic elements all the more shocking.① It is like opening the door to a familiar room in your own home and finding a pool of fresh blood on the floor. Further, by using the subjective point of view of a young woman remembering childhood events, and thus plunging into her own distant memories to achieve self-understanding, Cary goes beyond Poe, who is never autobiographical, to show how the Gothic is present in everyone's life, even in the lives of ordinary Americans in the pastoral village of Clovernook. What William Dean Howells called "the more smiling aspects of life, which are the more American," mask the anxieties that lie beneath America's optimistic and prosperous surface.② Realistic writers such as Cary appropriate and revitalize Gothic conventions to expose the repressed guilt, fear, and violence that underlie the American dream and reveal them as essential features of daily existence. As Charles Crow explains in the preface to his anthology of American Gothic tales, "Gothic literature can tell the story of those who are rejected, oppressed, or who have failed" and while Americans "want to believe in wholesome families, the Gothic can expose what many may know about, and never acknowledge: the hatred that can exist alongside of love, the reality of child abuse, even incest" (2). These types of characters and conflicts contribute to the uncanny mood of the five opening stories and surface in more realistic form in *The Moods of Seth Milford and*

---

① I am thinking of *The Philosophy of Composition* and Poe's reviews of Hawthorne's *Twice-Told Tales*, reprinted in *Essays and Reviews*: 13—25 and 568—588.

② "The Editor's Easy Chair," *Harper's New Monthly Magazine*, 73 (September 1886): 641. Accessed August 24, 2011, at the Cornell University *Making of America* website: http://digital.library.cornell.edu/cgi/t/text/pageviewer-idx?

His Sisters, *Annie Heaton*, *Peter Harris*, *Margaret Fields*, and the long sequence on Richard Claverel. Traditional Gothic motifs recur in the paired ghost stories *The Phantom Hunter* and *Lydia Heath at the Sumners*, which parodies Gothic heroines as Jane Austen did in *Northanger Abbey* (1818), and the final cluster of *Clovernook* tales, the autobiographical sketches analyzing the emotional bonds between Ellie and Rebecca Hadly, evoke the uncanny in their insistence on intangible connections between the two sisters, Rebecca's mysterious premature death, and Ellie's lifelong sense of loss.

Ames's biography opens with a ghost story that Cary related to her friend Ada Carnahan in 1869. The Cary family had just completed a new house across a ravine from their previous home. One afternoon while they were still living in the old house, the family looked out and saw Cary's thirteen-year-old sister, Rhoda, holding the baby, Lucy, in the open door of the new house. As the family watched, Rhoda, who had actually been upstairs watching Lucy, came down and joined them in observing the apparition. They continued to watch as the woman with the child began to "slowly sink, sink, sink into the ground, until she disappeared from sight" (18). Rhoda died a year later in November, followed by Lucy in December. Cary continued:

> Lucy has been seen many times since by different members of the family in the same house, always in a red frock, like one she was very fond of wearing...Since the apparition in the door, never for one year has our family been free from the shadow of death. Ever since, some one of us has been dying. (18)

Cary, not given to supernatural explanations and striving to write detailed, credible accounts of life in early Ohio, understands that ordinary people really do experience apparitions, visions, and other unexplained events because she did so herself. This distinguishes her Gothicism from Poe's as well as the British tradition that demanded exotic landscapes, castles, demons, witches, spells, and other supernatural elements to thrill the reader. Cary, a pioneer in creating a distinctively American Gothic, realized that such fantasies only detract from the uncanny reality of life in America, where hopes for a new life often outrun the inevitable harshness and loneliness of the pastoral frontier. In *Clovernook*, Cary recasts the Gothic mode to express these contradictory emotions in unadorned yet complex plots, images, and motifs that combine personal experience with the durable and malleable tradition of Gothic fiction.

4　让死亡不那么可怕
——凯瑞《苜蓿角》的地域美学特征

"Making Death Less Terrible": Alice Cary's Regionalist Aesthetics in *Clovernook*

John A. Staunton

Abstract: By the mid-1850s, Alice Cary's name was, in the words of one magazine editor, "synonymous with 'The West,'" by which he meant both the subtitle of his own magazine and the region itself. Indeed, several of Cary's *Clovernook* stories as well as her frequent poetry first appeared in the pages of the *Ladies' Repository and Gatherings of the West*, an Ohio magazine established under the auspices of the Methodist Church's Western Book Concern in Cincinnati. Examining several didactic images of gender and subject-identity formation from this magazine over against Cary's own work in her Clovernook stories reveals the discursive domain that Alice Cary engages ethically and aesthetically in her Clovernook series. Cary's deliberate re-writing of the ethos and challenge to the gendered authority of the *Ladies' Repository* become clear when we look to the formal and thematic rendering of *Peter Harris* and *Annie Heaton*, two early Clovernook stories that first appeared in the magazine. The *Ladies' Repository* actively and openly sought out prose and verse that would do the cultural work of upholding the virtues of piety and of the domestic sphere; these stories, however, work against the legalistic glorification of the domestic sphere and its presumed natural piety by showing the dark conclusions of lives lived uncritically and uncompassionately by people who do only what the law enjoins—but not everything one can—for widows and orphans and the other overlooked people of society.

The cycle of stories that pulls the curtain closed on Alice Cary's first series of *Clovernook*, likewise seems to put this legalistic ethic to the test. The fortunes of Rebecca and Ellie Hadly at first seem to embody the sentimental prospects for the mid-nineteenth-century American woman of artistic inclination: one dies of a broken heart and the other embraces a solitary life of sadness and studied introspection. Indeed, Cary seems deliberately and ironically to invoke for her readers the scenes of proper love and education in the engravings that frequent the *Ladies' Repository*. In a volume of regional sketches and short, interrelated fictions that begins and ends with views of death from the perspective of young women left behind in their grief to fashion viable bonds of community, Cary's *Clovernook*; or, *Recollections of Our Neighborhood in the West* (1852) subtly interrogates the discourse of gendered subjectivity and authority promoted by such magazines as the *Ladies' Repository* and offers a counter model of subject formation born out of empathy and confrontations with death.

摘要：正如一位杂志编辑所言，爱丽丝·凯瑞的名字在19世纪50年代中期的美国，"已然成了西部的同义语"，这句话里的西部既指他自己杂志的副标题，也指美国西部地区。的确，凯瑞的几个苜蓿角故事和她的许多诗作首先发表在《女士宝典及西部集锦》杂志上，该杂志由辛辛那提的卫理公会西部图书公司赞助创立。把该杂志有关性别和主体身份构成的说教色彩与凯瑞在《苜蓿角》故事集的作品相对比不难发现凯瑞在其《苜蓿角》系列中所呈现的伦理和美学意义上的离经叛道。凯瑞有意改写《女士宝典》的道德观并挑战其性别权威性,这一点在她对《彼得·哈瑞斯》和《安妮·希顿》这两个首先发表在该杂志的《苜蓿角》故事的形式和主题的诠释中是显而易见的。当时的《女士宝典》杂志积极征求宣扬虔诚和家庭生活美德的文章和诗歌;然而,这些小说跟那些颂扬所谓的闺阁忠悌的中规中矩的赞歌唱了反调,展示的是寡妇、孤儿以及遭到社会漠视的人群的灰暗终场。这些人过的是漠然索味的人生,从来都是循规蹈矩,不会为了展现自身能力而越雷池。

同样,爱丽丝·凯瑞《苜蓿角》第一部末尾几篇故事再次质疑这种中规中矩的伦理。丽贝卡和艾丽·哈德利的命运首先似乎体现了19世纪中期有艺术气质女性的感伤的人生:两个人物一个伤心而逝,另一个则孤苦无依,潜心自省。凯瑞呈现给读者的似乎是常见于《女士宝典》杂志版画的画面,表现的是适度的爱恋和教养,却是刻意以讽刺的方式呈现的。《苜蓿角》(1852)是一本以地域速写和情节相互关联的短篇小说构成的故事集,开头和结尾都从痛失亲人的年轻女性的视角对死亡发表看法,借以构筑了故事的群体纽带;故事集巧妙地诘问了基于性别差异的主体性话语及《女士宝典》这类杂志所宣扬的权威意识,并提出了以移情和直面死亡为出发点的逆反主体构成模式。

I.

"Orphaned as we are, we have need to be kind to each other—ready, with loving and helping hands and encouraging words, for the darkness and silence are hard by where no sweet care can do us any good."

—Alice Cary, *Clovernook*

4 让死亡不那么可怕——凯瑞《苜蓿角》的地域美学特征

Figure 1. *The Verb "To Love"* —*They Love* [Engraving]. Ladies' Repository 11.4 (April 1851)

The image and text above frame the discursive domain Alice Cary engages ethically and aesthetically in her Clovernook sketches, and they have a particular resonance for the first series of *Clovernook*: *or*, *Recollections of Our Neighborhood in the West* (1852) —a volume of regionalist sketches and short fiction that begins and ends with views of death from the perspective of young women left behind in their grief to fashion viable bonds of community. The engraving, which appeared in the 1851 volume of a mid-century Ohio magazine closely connected with the work of Alice Cary, offers in image and the verbal declension of its title—*The Verb "To Love"*:*"They Love"* —a fashioning of an empathetic community in the face of loss very much in tune with Cary's own project in her fiction. By the mid-1850s, Cary's name was, in the words of the *Ladies' Repository* editor (and much to his chagrin), "synonymous with 'The West,'"① by which he means both the subtitle of the magazine and the region itself. The magazine was begun in 1841 under the auspices of the Methodist Church's Western Book Concern in Cincinnati "to promote the healthful cultivation of the female mind, and to draw it from trifles into its appropriate sphere of privilege." According to the first editor, L. L. Hamline, it is "with this wise intention [that the magazine's] publication was conceived, and has at length been authorized by the suffrage of worthy, discreet men" ("Reading": 7).

Ten years after the inaugural 1841 issue, the two images below (Figure 2, *Education of Nature* and Figure 3, *Education of the World*) together with the image above provide a visual rhetoric for the field of this gendered ethical pedagogy and female cultivation. The subject hailed by the editorial discourse of the magazine, depicted first as a child and later as a young girl, regards herself in both images in a mirror, but the seemingly innocent lure of the reflection and beauty of the representation is countered and corrected by the moralistic titling of each engraving lest *Ladies' Repository* readers fall prey to their own beauty.

---

① The importance of Cary's place within the magazine is borne out by the extended profile a later editor, the Rev. D. W. Clark, makes of Cary and her work in his *Literary Women of America* (LR [August 1855]). While acknowledging Cary's place of prominence among his contributors—and among his readers' favorites—and drawing attention to her sketches in particular as marking the strength of Cary's regional vision, Clark then fails to mention a single one. Instead he dwells on what he considers to be the two or three examples of her poetic faults and excesses. Clark's reading at best reveals a curious bias against the very tropes of sentimentalism which mark nearly every other poem in his magazine; at worst he forwards a gross misreading of what Cary is attempting rhetorically and stylistically in *The Maiden of Tlascala*, the work which dominates Clark's criticism.

Figure 2. *Education of Nature* [Engraving]. *Ladies' Repository* 11.1 (January 1851)

Figure 3. *Education of the World* [Engraving]. *Ladies' Repository* 11.1 (January 1851)

These striking visual representations offer back to mid-century readers a lesson in proper-reflection: women must beware their own image and self-representation and learn to doubt what their own eyes show them about themselves. If we return to our opening image—the April 1851 engraving of *The Verb "To Love"* —the secret impulse to seek the beauty of one's own reflection which marks the education of "nature" and "the world," is transformed. Here the central female subject gazes not on her own image but on other subjects, each female, and all of whom are looked over by a ghostly portrait of the (presumed) absent mother. Taken together, the reading suggested by these three 1851 images is the didactic lesson that mirrors or representations of life—particular representations of the subjective lives of young women—can lie, distort, or mislead by offering back to us only ourselves and not the social world in which we should seek to act. *The Verb "To Love"* further creates a tableau of viewing which resists this self-seeking trap and "mirrors" sentiment differently. The recursive circuit of affection here offers a sort of "trickle down" sentiment which is potentially positive. And to read it through the filter of Cary's somber reminder about the "orphaned" status of us all, is to see embodied the sort of kindness Cary's narrator calls for when the "darkness and silence are hard by."

But the context of these three engravings invites questions to trouble this moral and invite a more nuanced view of Cary's own ethical and aesthetic enterprise during this same era, when two of the stories in the first series of *Clovernook*—*Peter Harris* and *Annie Heaton*—as well as several additional poems and sketches would appear exclusively in the *Ladies' Repository* prior to the 1852 release of *Clovernook*. The community of sympathy frozen in tableau by the engraving *The Verb "To Love"* exists of course in an imagined space, an allegorical or symbolic location staged for our edification. We even see what appears to be the theatrical apparatus of curtains and pillars, quite literally framing the open visual field. The ethical suggestion is that the circuit of love need not venture beyond this close-knit exchange of sentiment and feeling.

By way of contrast, the cycle of stories which pulls the curtain closed on Alice Cary's first series of *Clovernook*, seems to put this ethic to the test. The fortunes of Rebecca and Ellie Hadly at first seem to embody the sentimental prospects for the mid-nineteenth-century American woman of artistic inclination: one dies of a broken heart and the other embraces a solitary life of sadness and studied introspection. Indeed, Cary seems deliberately and ironically to invoke for her readers those scenes of proper love and education engraved in the *Ladies' Repository*. Rebecca and Ellie love "each other with a love that was more than love" (270). The final story in the first series of *Clovernook*, *The End of the History*, closes with Ellie Hadly casting a passing glance at the abandoned homestead of her lost love while en route to the church graveyard where her sister Rebecca lies buried. In this recursive circuit of grief, Ellie "repeats the line from England's gloomy bard—so simple, yet containing so much— 'Thou art nothing—all are nothing now'" (342). The invocation of Bryon's "Thyrza" here shows Ellie fully immersed in a self-conscious romantic idealism verging toward the sentimental— that is, seeking some sort of empathetic connection to sustain her in the absence of her sister.

Similarly, in *Mrs. Grey's Two Visits*, the third story[①] in the "Hadly cycle," Rebecca Hadly spends her last night of life thinking of her sister Ellie, "alone, and far away." She recalls "the schoolmaster and his solitary grave" (298) and she takes stock of her attempts to fashion for herself a life that might fuse the call of art with the demands of community. The dead schoolmaster and her absent sister represent the loss of the two people who could understand the artistic aims of the young Rebecca. Rebecca's own mother pits the aesthetic dreams of her daughter against a rigid and

---

① The story comprises the second half of what appears as the single story *The Sisters* in Judith Fetterley's edition of *Clovernook Sketches* (Rutgers UP, 1984). The omitted text consists almost entirely of the story, *The Remorse of William Martin*, which falls between *The Sisters* and *Mrs. Grey's Two Visits* in *Clovernook*. *The Remorse of William Martin* primarily gives the details of the schoolmaster's death at the hands of the young Billy Martin, whose remorse apparently does not prevent him from going unpunished for his assault on the schoolmaster nor from steadfastly and unrequitedly courting Ellie Hadly in the final three stories of the "Hadly cycle."

censorious view of ethics. She regards "the dreamy and poetic dispositions of her children as great misfortunes; something worse in fact—something to be ashamed of." Rebecca's condition and thoughts spur the narrator to comment on the lives of her characters who struggle to mark out for themselves something of their own while enduring the "severe and strict morality" of a mother who believes that violations against propriety (as she deems Rebecca's poetic aspirations and youthful infatuation with the schoolmaster to be) "should not go unpunished" (295). In her editorial aside to the Hadly sisters' condition, Cary's narrator presents one of the paradigmatic appeals of *Clovernook*, which powerfully focuses the attention of the reader out of his or her own condition and onto the condition of another. "Orphaned as we are," the narrator says, "we have need to be kind to each other—ready, with loving and helping hands and encouraging words, for the darkness and the silence are hard by where no sweet care can do us any good" (299).

As with the engravings above and throughout many of Cary's Clovernook stories, men remain conspicuously out of sight from the representations of women, but despite their visible discretion, they are noticeably present among the contributors to the magazine, authoring and *authorizing* the vision of the regional and female subject produced throughout its pages. The origins of the magazine as a vehicle of what recent critics have called "home literacy"① as well as the *Ladies' Repository's* early regional promotion of what it

---

① See, for instance, Sarah Robbins,"Periodizing Authorship, Characterizing Genre: Catharine Maria Sedgwick's Benevolent Literacy Narratives", *American Literature* 76.1, (March) 2004: 1—29 and Jennifer Phegley, "Literary Piracy, Nationalism, and Women Readers in *Harper's New Monthly Magazine*, 1850—1855", *American Periodicals* 14.1, 2004: 63—90. Cary's work does not quite fit Robbins' categories of the "benevolent" or "domestic literacy narrative," however. Typically, sites of literacy learning in Cary's stories are either folded into scenes of schooling (themselves often the occasion for, frequently ill-starred, romance) or else are located in homes violently deranged by the abuse and misuse of literacy (i.e., *Uncle William's* and *Uncle Christopher's* in the 1853 *Clovernook*).

terms "female education," are important factors in envisioning the horizons for writing and learning available to Cary in her youth outside Cincinnati. We will return to these images, but for now I offer them as a way to demonstrate how the editorial control of gender- and *gendered*-learning and the contrasting images of female self-recognition suggested by them reveal something of the aesthetic and ethical positions Cary negotiated in fashioning her own regionalist vision within mid-century discourses of gender, education, and literary value that were often at cross-purposes to her own.

II.

Cary's deliberate re-writing of the ethos and challenge to the gendered authority of the *Ladies' Repository* become clearer if we look to the formal and thematic rendering of two early Clovernook stories that first appeared in the *Ladies' Repository*. The *Ladies' Repository* actively and openly sought out prose and verse that would do the cultural work of upholding the virtues of piety and of the domestic sphere. But in stories such as *Peter Harris* and *Annie Heaton*, Cary works against the legalistic glorification of the domestic sphere and its presumed natural piety by showing the dark conclusions of lives lived uncritically and uncompassionately in accordance with these principles of doing only all that the law enjoins—but not everything one can—for widows and orphans and the other overlooked people of society.

The first of these stories anticipates Cary's ethical reminder of the orphaned status of us all, which she later offers more explicitly in the Hadly stories. Published in the March 1851 issue of the *Ladies' Repository*, *Peter Harris* is the story of a boy deliberately orphaned by his own father. The story relates the boy's abandonment by his father, his forced relocation to his relations' home, and his subsequent (and rather rapid) death there. The plot, in fact, is little more than this outline. But Cary gives fearful presence to the abstract and legalistic language of the *Ladies' Repository* to show where it may lead. What gives the story its force is the utter hopelessness of a boy whose only crime is to have had the effrontery after he has been abandoned by his own father to confess that he would like a great many things in life.① The boy's relations laugh at this desire and quickly put it in check. For example, the aunt, "a pious woman" (not unlike Rebecca Hadly's mother in *The Sisters* and *Mrs. Grey's Two Visits*), immediately questions Peter on his arrival in a manner that already includes her expected answers, eliminating any volition and agency from his responses. "You would like to be grateful," she says, and then elaborates the meaning of this word for the boy: "You must feel as if the consecration of all your energies to your uncle and me could never repay us"(*LR* [March 1851]: 103; *Clovernook*: 141). In the aunt, Cary ironically repurposes the engravings of January 1851 to present a version of the morally self-satisfied reader of the *Ladies' Repository*, she who might devour the pages of her bible without apparently digesting their lessons. Ruled by the desire to maintain propriety rather than to foster charity, such a "Christian" woman, the narrator reveals, must *know* that she will be obeyed. So she quickly continues her interrogation of Peter about his gratitude: "You will feel so, will you not?" (103/141). Again the question here harbors more directive than inquiry or conversation; it is designed to ensure the knowledge and power only of the one who asks it.

As with the description of the orphaned condition of Rebecca Hadly, Cary's narrator here encourages us to identify not with the voice of propriety but with the perspective of the overlooked. Accordingly, the narrator informs us that "Peter was quite at a loss. He knew no more than he knew what grateful was, what his

---

① For a slightly different take on the educational implications of this story, see my discussion in John A. Staunton, *Deranging English/Education* (NCTE 2008).

energies were, or how to consecrate them to his uncle and her; but he said he would try." (103/141) The indirect discourse of the narration forces us to give voice internally to Peter, thereby making his condition ours. Not surprisingly, then, Peter's answer seems humble and reasonable, especially for one nearly deserted by his own father in a strange town. But the aunt's rejoinder comes with all the conviction and violence of the falsely pious: "There must be no *try* about it. You must do it, or be whipped every day, till you do." (103/141) Given this opening, Peter's rapid decline and death as a result of the neglect of his family and his teachers is hardly surprising.

What is surprising in the story, however, is the extent to which Cary delineates the patterns of abuse that terrorize the young boy. By her casual recounting of its apparent ordinariness, Cary makes the abuse present and frighteningly real. Beginning with Peter's father, who, as he gives up on Peter to seek his fortunes further west, informs him that he will amount to nothing, Peter's life is filled with those who delight in administering verbal and physical torture to the child. That this abuse comes from the very systems that the *Ladies' Repository* says should care for children— the extended family and the school (Peter does not live long enough in the story to see the church) —is a particularly daring narrative move for Cary to make in a magazine that claims in one of its editorial self-congratulatory moments to uphold those institutions as virtuous, "doing all that the law can do." Cary's story challenges the presumption of the *Ladies' Repository* to be an organ for imparting piety and developing ethical wisdom solely because of its institutional affiliation or because of its stated intent to provide its readers only pious bits. The fate of Peter Harris—in the hands of just such readers of moral magazines as Mrs. Harris—presents a clear challenge to the very magazine that publishes the story. For the story suggests that if the *Ladies' Repository* is to be a truly religious and morally just publication, it must be prepared to direct its critical gaze inward, as the prophetic scriptures of presumably even Mrs. Harris' bible repeatedly advise, to see whether its pronouncements of the good and moral life have managed to become written on the hearts of both its editors and readers.

The very publication of the story would seem to suggest just such a willingness for self-scrutiny, but the appearance of another story, *Annie Heaton*, the same year raises another possibility, that the editors are somehow simply not aware of Cary's subversion. Where *Peter Harris* exposes the dangers of living by the word of piousness without critically engaging the reasons for such piety, Cary's story in the May 1851 issue of the *Ladies' Repository* critiques the empty industriousness of middle-class life and values that may characterizes readers. *Annie Heaton* tells the story of a young woman's frustration of her romantic and societal dreams by her stingy and moralistic parents. The parents, Cary's narrator tells us in characteristic understatement, were less accustomed to distribute than acquire. The father of Annie Heaton, we are told, "worked for love of gain, but also for mere love of work." What at first seems laudatory (working for the love of work), quickly turns to criticism, for the narrator finishes her characterization of Joseph Heaton by informing her readers that this industriousness and frugality also leads the farmer to abhor "those who do not work as he does" (*LR* [May 1851]: 169; *Clovernook*: 118). We know further that if he reads, then, like the overbearing and controlling Uncle Christopher and Uncle William in the second series of *Clovernook* stories, he reads *only* the bible or his newspaper or nothing at all. This limited scope, Cary suggests, is a recipe for a mangled moral vision. The magazines and newspapers that call for morally sound subject matter risk precisely this fate unless they proceed in their objectives less narrowly and come to view moral lives with a broader understanding of what terms like compassion and community can mean.

Even when mothers are present in Cary's stories, the prospects for young women are as limited as when men like Joseph Heaton are in control. As we see with Mrs. Hadly in *The Sisters* or Aunt Rachel in *Uncle Christopher's*, mothers have either lost, or refuse to assume, the ability to be effective guides to female selfhood. Aunt Rachel can only model for her daughters a fearful and deferential silence to male authority, as she and they spend night after night knitting one blue stocking after another to satisfy some precept of Christopher. Mrs. Hadly constantly lives her life according to a model of propriety which stifles the self-expression so vital to her daughters' lives that the mother becomes, Cary's narrator tells us, "scarcely aware of their existence." The effect, as the narrator reveals in both stories, is the same as if the children had no mothers at all, and so the children must create their own bonds of community if they are to survive.

Recalling the opening discussion of this essay, we can see that such children are orphaned indeed, but we also no doubt recognize that the bonds they attempt to forge in their mothers' physical or emotional absence are difficult to sustain. Because the circumstances for its need are presumably so unusual and shameful to the regional community of Clovernook—a mother who forgets her own children is hardly someone a community would want to valorize—the nature of the bond is difficult for Cary's narrator to articulate without making a wholesale indictment of her neighbors. The community lacks the language to offer the encouraging words that the narrator of the Hadly stories reminds us are so vital to protect us from "the darkness and silence…where no sweet care can do us any good." The bond between the Hadly siblings involves the psychologically real though seemingly impossible condition of being orphaned while still having a mother and father; and more immediately, with Rebecca's death the bond no longer exists. The narrator can only attempt to account for the quality of this love, then, by using it to define itself; the sisters loved "each other with a love that was more than love." The very inarticulateness of this bond is as strong as the desire of the "motherless" child who seeks it but who has no guide or model to point her to it. In fact, the three-fold repetition of the word "love" reinforces the presence of the bond, without however explicitly defining it. That presence, as tenuous as it is, Cary suggests, is still more sustaining to individual regional lives than an "absent" mother, and it is a presence which haunts the pages of Alice Cary's *Clovernook* stories, seeking sources of renewal for a community ever in the making.

5 浑然一体 物我交融
——透过《维尔德明斯一家》看爱丽丝·凯瑞的生态美学思想

Cary's Eco-Aesthetics as Seen in *The Wildermings*

乔雪瑛

摘要：《苜蓿角》是美国19世纪女作家爱丽丝·凯瑞的短篇小说集，书中很多地方都体现了凯瑞的生态美学思想，即人类是自然界的一部分；融入自然、返璞归真，是荡涤灵魂、平复心灵的一剂良药。本文试以该作品中的短篇《维尔德明斯一家》为例，初探凯瑞作品中体现的生态美学思想。凯瑞在该短篇中再现了人类与自然的交融关系：自然是作为一个独立主体存在的，人类在融入自然中寻求心灵慰藉，人类的死亡当视做自然过程等。总体而言，凯瑞以自觉的生态意识来透视人与自然的关系，人与自然的和谐共处，生与死的辩证并存及过程的必然性，这都体现出爱丽丝·凯瑞的生态美学思想。

Abstract: This essay studies Alice Cary's *The Wildermings* in her collection of stories *Clovernook; or, Recollections of Our Neighbourhood in the West* from an ecocritical perspective. As an American woman writer living in the 19th century, Cary views nature as a whole and man as part of it in her literary world. In *The Wildermings* as well as many other stories, she expresses her consciousness of the intrinsic value of nature by celebrating a poetics of human connectedness to and interaction with nature, thereby weaving a tapestry of the desire for a direct and intimate link with nature where humanity may find spiritual consolation. Her view of death as a necessary natural process, through which the suffered are finally released from endless suffering, also helps readers see their everyday lives in an ecologically refreshing way.

20世纪70年代末80年代初,美国文学研究领域将生态批评视角引入了文学研究。时至今日,生态批评得到了迅速发展,并已形成了相当的规模。在全球环境危机日益加重、人类中心主义盛行的背景之下,生态文学批评表达了对生态环境的忧患意识。生态批评学者在文学研究视域中挖掘当代环境危机的根源,探寻人与自然和谐共处的生态构想,为文学研究带来了新的视角。生态批评虽然至今没有一个明确界定的理论边界,但是无疑已成为一个充满活力的重要研究领域。生态批评研究的核心问题之一就是文学作品中体现的人与自然的关系,即作品对自然的再现方式,自然在作品情节中的角色,以及作品体现的价值观是否与生态伦理相一致。①

在这个全球环境不断恶化、生态危机日益加剧的时代,翻开爱丽丝·凯瑞的《苜蓿角》,一阵自然清风扑面而来。短篇小说集《苜蓿角》中的作品体现了文明与自然之间对立交融的关系,表达了回归自然、返璞归真的生态美学思想。这些作品所呈现的作者对人与自然的关系的理解以及作者的死亡观,都蕴涵着深刻的生态智慧。人类将自己融于自然,与天地万物和谐共处,共存共荣,是荡涤灵魂罪恶、平复心灵创伤的一剂良药,这是凯瑞作品中随处可见、俯拾皆是的朴素思想,在生态危机日益严重的今天也给我们提供了有益的启示。本文将以其中一个短篇《维尔德明斯一家》为例,来探讨凯瑞的生态美学思想。

《苜蓿角》以19世纪美国乡村为背景,讲述了发生在"苜蓿角"这个地方的一个个小故事,刻画了一群朴实无华的乡邻,记叙了他们的喜怒哀乐、生离死别,地方色彩浓郁,同时字里行间又浮现着淡淡的忧愁,仿佛是对过往的怀念和感伤。如同《苜蓿角》中的许

---

① 王宁."后理论时代"西方理论思潮的走向[J].外国文学,2005(3):30—39.

多其他作品一样，短篇小说《维尔德明斯一家》同样让人流连于一种隐逸、淡然的叙述带来的朦胧优美的意境，迷醉于远离尘嚣的宁静和尚未被文明侵蚀的纯美。

这篇短篇小说是以叙述者"我"的所见所闻展开的，用第一人称的细腻笔触，通过"我"的思想和感触来透视周围的乡邻和田园生活。邻里新搬来了一户人家，叙述者前去造访，发现新邻居并不算热情，闲聊两句便告辞了。两周后，叙述者听说那个邻居小姑娘死了，人们将她埋葬在墓地。如果这一点点故事也能算做情节的话，那么也仅此而已了。小说没有高潮，没有冲突，一切变化都是平静、缓慢地发生，没有什么跌宕起伏。

然而在平淡隐抑的叙述和乏善可陈的情节之外，我们分明能够感到作者与众不同的生态美学思想表达。首当其冲的便是作者的自然观。人与自然的关系历来是中外文学作品中取之不尽、用之不竭的一个主题，也是生态批评的重要研究问题之一。在许多文学作品中，甚至一些传世经典中，大自然成为人类征服和主宰的对象，处于消极被动的地位和失语的状态。在其他许多文学作品中，大自然即使不缺席，也往往沦为人物抒发胸臆的背景或展示英雄气概的陪衬。

国际知名生态批评家布伊尔指出，作家对自然的审美应该是自身的感知过程，而不是套用任何给定的模式；应该旨在展现自然本身的美，而不是用来表现人的思想。[①] 在谈到生态审美的自然性原则时，王诺教授认为，生态的审美是"活生生的感受过程"："生态的审美首先是对自然的审美，但这种自然审美既不是将具体的审美经验抽象成形而上的理性认识，也不是通过具体的审美对象来表达或对应审美者的思想情绪或人格力量。较之传统的审美，生态的审美突出的是自然审美对象，而不是突出审美者。审美者感知自然，与审美对象建立的是交互主体性的关系，而不是主体与客体的关系。生态的审美旨在具体地感受和表现自然本身的美"（19）。凯瑞作品中的自然描写的重点在自然本身，并不刻意赋予它某种意义或象征，也不用它来表现人物的思想或情感，更不是为了烘托人物或创造意境而存在。凯瑞笔下的大自然是人们的精神家园和心灵栖息地，是

---

① 转引自：王诺. 生态批评的美学原则 [J]. 南京师范大学文学院学报，2010 (2)：18—25.

一个独立的主体，时而淳朴清丽，时而雄浑壮美，气象万千，充满活力，蕴涵着生命和希望。阅读爱丽丝·凯瑞，就不能不被她笔下四时变换、五色斑斓的大自然所感染。

大自然在这篇短篇小说中扮演着重要角色，不可或缺。与情节的简单、弱化形成鲜明对比的是作品中有关自然的描写。作者洋洋洒洒、不吝笔墨、极尽铺陈地描写了村庄及周围的景色，小到一簇花、一丛草，大到茂密的树林、苍莽的山峦，大自然的各种美在这里得到了极致的呈现。作者之意并不在于将自然万物对应于人的内心，或为人物寻找心灵的寄托，作者之意在于极致地呈现自然本身的美以及人陶醉于其中而流连忘返的感受。自然在这里不再是情节的陪衬和烘托，仿佛成了故事理所当然的主角，而情节倒像是融在了自然描写里。甚至可以说，作者仿佛借助于情节的发展将各个地方的景色展示在读者眼前。

在一个夏日的美丽黄昏，叙述者"我"初次探访新邻居。走在路上，"我"情不自禁地坐在山谷中的一处古旧的断桥边，长久地聆听着鹅卵石上流水的潺潺声，凝视着阳光穿过树叶投下的斑块，就这样静静地坐着，直至暮色降临。凯瑞的叙述貌似肆意挥洒、不受题目约束，这段描写也似有离题之嫌，因为在出发之前，叙述者"我"对于新邻居充满了喜悦和好奇，似乎应该急不可待地直接赶往邻居家才是。在叙述者去往邻居家的路上，作者却荡开一笔，洋洋洒洒、收放自如地描写了叙述者在山间的行迹以及周围的自然景色，仿佛此行只是一次郊游，不带任何目的。虽然作者未作任何交代，但是读者不难体会到，叙述者"我"所以会在探访新邻居的路上忽然停了下来，静静地坐着直到暮色笼罩，无疑是因为大自然的美景吸引了"我"，使"我"陶醉其中，几乎忘记此行的目的。大自然在这里充实了"我"的心灵，平复了"我"的心情，使"我"以近乎单纯透明的心态去探访新邻居。

凯瑞描写和再现大自然的方式也有独到之处。大自然在她笔下不是静态的，而是灵动鲜活的，是作为有生命的独立主体而存在的。那广阔的田野、静谧的树林、天空舒卷的云、山间呼啸的风、颤动的枝叶以及潺潺的流水，在读者眼前展现出一幅幅生机勃勃、生生不息的自然画卷，给读者留下清新自然、栩栩如生的印象。日暮时分，土拨鼠开始不停地拱着"我"脚下的土，白色的蛾子扑扇着厚厚的翅膀在"我"四周飞舞，蝙蝠拍打着翅膀四处乱飞，几乎要撞到"我"的脸上。就在"我"流连于自然美景中忘记此行所为何事

5 浑然一体 物我交融——透过《维尔德明斯一家》看爱丽丝·凯瑞的生态美学思想

之时,是猫头鹰凄厉的叫声回荡在山谷,提醒了"我"继续前行。大自然在凯瑞的笔下就是这么灵动,充满生机。

在这灵动而充满生机的大自然中,人扮演的是充分融入的角色,而不是入侵者,甚或征服者。这里没有麦尔维尔笔下对代表神秘大自然力量的白鲸的追踪和杀戮,也没有海明威经典中血腥的狩猎场面或老人与海孤注一掷的搏斗。在这里,人与自然不是对立的两个主体,没有紧张的对立关系;相反,人是自然界的一分子,生活在自然中,融入自然中,从自然中汲取养分,寻求心灵慰藉。在这里,自然是人们的精神家园、心灵庇护所和灵魂栖息地。

王诺教授在论述生态审美的交融性原则时指出,"生态的审美不是站在高处远远地观望,而是全身心地投入自然……甚至需要忘掉自我,与自然融为一体"(22)。也就是说,只有全身心地投入自然中,忘我地感受自然,才能摆脱理性的束缚,回归人的自然天性,在一种平静而喜悦的心情中忘却自我,感受与自然的交融。这种人与自然的和谐和交融在《维尔德明斯一家》中得到了清晰的呈现。走在初次拜访新邻居的路上,"我"情不自禁地沉醉在夏日黄昏美丽的广阔自然空间里,"我"的感受已与自然融为一体,浑然不觉此行的目的。这一段貌似离题的描述实质上生动地体现了人与自然融为一体的审美体验。

在19世纪初期的美国乡村,现代工业文明对自然的侵蚀和破坏还远未开始。绿油油的草场、野草丛生的小径、光秃秃的土山、荒凉的山脊、简陋的村舍、寂静的墓园,这些就是村人们生活于其间的环境。与后现代作品中描写的人类的异化和自然对人类的灾难性的报复等场景不同,这里貌似荒芜却充满了生机,在草木繁茂的季节,四处一片鸟语花香。晨曦清透,暮色苍茫,自然之美以万千的变化随时随处展示着。生活在其中的"我"也是平和的,没有生活在现代文明中的压抑和焦虑。

凯瑞运用通感和移情展示了人与自然的息息相通。作者开篇提到了一件很小的往事。在首蓿角的那片小树林里,曾经有一棵高大的老橡树。它因为太高大,以至于叙述者"我"总觉得它旁边的树木都在被它痛苦地压抑着,因而希望它能被齐根伐倒。可是当有一天这棵老橡树真的被伐木工砍倒之后,"我"曾经梦想的欣喜心情被懊悔和悲伤替代了,因为没有了这棵大树,小树林将荣耀不再。

给这篇情节叙述简单、自然描写铺陈的短篇起到画龙点睛作用的,是作者对死亡的哲思。死亡是生命的终点,是一切感知的尽头。

在文学作品中，死亡向来与生活一起构成了完整的文学表现对象。对死的阐释必将影响和折射对生的理解。在凯瑞的作品中，死亡是个不断出现的主题，但作者笔下的死亡并不是对生的断然否定，也不是对生命的漠视，而是一个再自然不过的过程。人死后，肉体回归泥土，这是人对自然的归复，是天人合一的永恒。这一思想直接体现在作者对死亡及墓地的描述中。

死亡这一主题在美国浪漫主义作家笔下反复出现，并不鲜见。凯瑞的创作曾深受艾德加·爱伦·坡的赏识。但是在对死亡这个主题的表现上，凯瑞的描写与坡在短篇小说中刻意展现的哥特式的阴森恐怖截然不同。在《维尔德明斯一家》中，作者讲述了两个美丽的年轻女孩的早逝。她们早逝的原因并不十分清楚，甚至带有一点神秘的色彩，但是在谈及她们的死亡时，作者的字里行间并没有带出任何离奇的阴森恐怖的气氛。相反，美丽的玛丽·维尔德明斯的早逝以及流浪汉约翰·海恩的死，都常常被村人提及，仿佛他们的生和死都是首蓿角生活中不可或缺的一页。

玛丽·维尔德明斯的身世作者并未交代，只是含糊地说她生前并未犯下什么罪恶，倒是受过一些伤害。根据"我"的叙述，村人相传在夜晚有时能够听到她唱着摇篮曲，有时又能看到她坐在坟旁，将玫瑰编入自己的发辫，像是在为婚礼作准备。同样是描写年轻生命的死亡和幽魂的出没，但是凯瑞并没有刻意营造阴森恐怖的气氛，对所谓鬼魂的叙述也不在于显现村人的迷信。在这里，读者更加容易感受到的是死亡对一个受过伤害的弱小生命的安抚和慰藉。

对于与死亡直接相关的墓地的描述，也体现了凯瑞的生死观。墓园在整个短篇的叙述中都呈现出静谧、肃穆的景象，没有文学作品或通俗读物中常见的鬼魅凄凉的恐怖气氛。虽然村人们常常提到在夜晚曾看到一些魂灵在墓园周围四处游荡，这曾一度使得叙述者"我"感到害怕，但是"我"并未由于恐惧而避开墓地。相反，在探访邻人回来的路上，夜色笼罩了四周，"我"在墓地边停了下来，倚在墓园的门上开始思考生与死的玄秘。

籍叙述者之口，凯瑞讲出了自己的死亡观，即死亡不仅是生命的另一种状态，而且是更加本真、轻松、纯洁的状态。由于死亡的来临，恶人不再制造麻烦，疲倦的人得以安息，意志薄弱的人无须再抵制诱惑，痛苦的心灵不再哀伤。生命的结束使生命摆脱了软弱、贪婪、衰老、无能等种种缺憾；坟墓作为庇护，使人放下人生的重负，冲洗掉世间的罪恶，进入一个宁静祥和的世界。

这个短篇虽然用了很多篇幅讲述村中的那片墓地以及与之相关的人和事，且以早逝的玛丽·维尔德明斯作为小说的题目，但是其核心内容应该是讲述新搬来的一户邻居中的一个14岁女孩的生与死。生前，村人对女孩及其家人的了解不多，死后，人们将她静静埋葬，没有戏剧性的情节，没有大起大落的波澜。凯瑞将女孩的生与死轻轻地几笔带过，着墨不多，但是寥寥数语的背后透出作者对生与死的审美情感和价值判断。从生到死的一切经历，都是生命必经的一个个环节，没有大惊小怪，作者处理得很淡然，虽然不免有一丝悲凉和忧郁，但从另一个层面来说也是一种旷达自在。作品中的人物也并未因为死的必然而寻求生的狂欢。

　　在短篇的结尾，小说的题目似乎首次与邻居女孩交汇。玛丽·维尔德明斯和这个邻居女孩都是年轻美丽的姑娘，她们的早逝与她们短暂的一生都没有什么值得纪念的或意义重大的事件发生。女孩的坟墓就在玛丽的墓旁，两个坟墓都没有墓碑，也没有名字，但周围都种满了茂密的紫罗兰，静静盛开着蓝白相间的花。不管在世间曾经历过多少痛苦，她们都安息了。凯瑞如此不动声色地描写生命的离去，那看似淡然的结尾和低调的叙述，在读者心中激起一种涌动的情绪。

　　在新的世纪，人类面临的生态困境使得生态批评成为文学批评领域关注的焦点之一。透过《维尔德明斯一家》这篇短篇我们不难看到，凯瑞以自觉的生态意识表现了人与自然的关系。人与自然的和谐共处，天地万物的共存共荣，生与死的辩证并存及过程的必然性，都体现出爱丽丝·凯瑞的生态美学思想。对这些思想的深刻认识和借鉴，也是人类通往全面和谐之路。

参考文献：

　　王宁．"后理论时代"西方理论思潮的走向［J］．外国文学，2005（03）．

　　王诺．生态批评的美学原则［J］．南京师范大学文学院学报，2010（02）：18—25．

6 凯瑞短篇小说集《苜蓿角》中的悲剧意识

Tragic Consciousness in Cary's *Clovernook*

黄培希

摘要：亚里士多德指出，怜悯和恐惧是一种痛苦的情绪，而悲剧引起的怜悯和恐惧之情却是一种特别的快感，给观众以感情的满足。爱丽丝·凯瑞的短篇小说中悲剧意识具有一定的自觉性和自发性。这不仅与悲剧产生的艺术效果有关，和作者的身世也有一定的联系。爱丽丝·凯瑞的悲剧意识体现在死亡和忧郁等方面。这些主题的描写使读者产生怜悯和恐惧，既引起读者的注意，也让读者产生共鸣。小说悲剧主题所产生的恐怖是凯瑞作品所特有的，恐怖往往因特定的乡村意象的描画而加深强化，使作品隐藏着一种冷峻的、阴郁的美，成为一种特别的悲剧感受。凯瑞以死亡和忧郁为主题的悲剧艺术创作不仅产生特殊的悲剧效果，更通过两种悲剧内容传递生命的永恒，以及忧郁背后的光明等可贵的积极信息。

Abstract：Aristotle points out that pity and fear are painful emotions. However, these emotions as caused by tragedy can bring a special kind of pleasure, or a sense of emotional satisfaction, to the audience. Tragedy in Alice Cary's short stories is empathetic, as the author demonstrates her knowledge of what her characters are feeling, to some extent, blurring the line between her personal experience and that of her characters. The tragic sense in Alice Cary's stories is embodied in the motifs of death and melancholy, both involving readers' pity and fear so as to draw their attention as well as their sympathy. The fear depicted in the tragic stories is typical of Cary's works. However, this sense of fear is strengthened with the description of the particular rural scenes, which are often saturated in gloominess, forming a melancholic atmosphere for the tragic characters throughout the stories. This artistic creation of tragedy centered in death and melancholy not only engenders a special tragic artistic effect but conveys eternity of life and positive signals of brightness hidden in such negative feelings.

爱丽丝·凯瑞（Alice Cary, 1820—1871）出生于美国的拓荒时期，童年生活在美国中西部广袤的乡村土地上，长大后到城市中闯荡，经历几多磨难成就了她的写作事业。她的短篇小说集《苜蓿角》便是她在喧嚣的城市中，以城里人为读者对象，以一片宁静、广阔、近乎恐怖的村落和生活在村落中的街坊邻居为背景完成的一部叙事写实力作。作者将自己的思想情感融入乡村人物和时空之中，使作品带有浓郁的乡土气息。然而，在这样一部田园牧歌式的作品中却流露出强烈的悲剧感。作者通过讲述具有悲剧色彩的死亡故事和忧郁环境的描写，深深地打动着每个读者。

一、悲剧意识的起因

短篇小说集《苜蓿角》所流露出的悲剧意识具有一定的自觉性和自发性。自觉的悲剧意识源于悲剧作品所能产生的艺术效果。亚里士多德认为，悲剧的效果在于它能够使观众产生恐惧和怜悯的快感（63）。1850年，凯瑞只身从乡下来到纽约，面对看惯了花花世界的城里读者，如何让自己乡村题材的作品引起他们的兴趣，让他们对那片土地、那里的人和事产生好奇，这一问题很可能让她想到悲剧。为了达到引人注目、扣人心弦、惊心动魄的艺术效果，她常常在作品中有意识地营造情境让读者产生恐惧和怜悯，给读者带来一种特别的求知快感和情感上的满足，使读者对作品产生强烈的需求，并从中受到启发和教育。从这个意义上讲，小说的悲剧意识是自觉的。同时，凯瑞小说的悲剧意识也有其自发因素。这与凯瑞个人的生平有着一定的联系。据她的传记作者埃姆斯（Mary Ames）记载：凯瑞一共有兄妹九个，她排行老四。三姐罗达（Rhoda，1818—1833）和她关系非常密切，影响最大，可就是在15岁那年罗达死了；同一年，年仅四岁的可爱的妹妹露西（Lucy，1829—1833）也夭折了；两年后妈妈病逝，这一连串失去亲人的变故，使她的童年充满哀伤的回忆，直至成年也难以挥去。尤其难忘的是这些亲人就埋葬在家门前的山冈上。为此，在她和妹妹芙波（Phoebe，1824—1871）的诗中，有很多关于坟墓的词句和诗行，还招致了很多严厉批判。批评家们指责她们的诗中充满了坟墓。对此，埃姆斯为她们姐妹辩解道："试想一位刚刚丧失亲人，孤独无依的女孩，每天踯躅于山冈的墓地旁，那里长眠着自己的妈妈和姐妹，她早期的诗歌又怎能摆脱死亡的阴影，怎能没有悲痛，没有感伤呢？"（Mary Clemmer：22）对她们来说，这是现实中失去亲人的自然表白，在小说的创作中便是悲剧意识的自然流露。

二、悲剧意识的体现

凯瑞的悲剧意识在短篇小说集中主要体现在两个方面：一方面，她的许多短篇小说以死亡为主题作为描写对象，令人产生怜悯和恐惧。另一方面，作者又常常以忧郁为主题给人带来哀伤和惆怅。在这两大悲剧主题中，悲剧意识都有所体现。

1. 死亡的悲剧主题

凯瑞的短篇小说集《苜蓿角》共有短篇速写故事35篇，多数篇章都涉及人物的死亡，讲述悲剧故事。小说中不少篇章讲述了孩子的夭折，作品通过对这些儿童死亡的描写，激起了读者对故事主人公的同情和怜悯。恰如作者在文中所说，"生命阴影中摇曳闪烁的点点亮光中，最明亮的就是爱之光了，最甜美的莫过于对儿童的关爱"（Cary：28）。既然对儿童的关爱是最甜美的事情，那么，儿童的死亡，或者失去孩子便是最为悲痛的事情了，显然作者选择对儿童死亡的描写加深了悲剧的效果。小说开篇叙述外公的逝世，第二篇便是讲述了小妹妹的死。这是一曲充满忧伤的散文体的挽歌，叙述人为自己没有能够带上她一起玩耍，导致了终身的遗憾。小妹妹美丽宛若天使，温顺犹如羔羊。当大伙儿拒绝带她一起玩耍时，她泪水涟涟，却不放声大哭，眼睁睁无可奈何地望着大孩子们离去。然而，这么一个天使般的小姑娘，却因病夭折了，临别前还请求"我"下次带上她一起玩。这种儿童的纯真和她的逝去给读者留下了极强的反差。为此，作者说："从她的坟墓中投射出一道阴影，无论我到天涯海角它都找得到我。"（Cary：33）这种阴影成了萦绕作者的心头，终生难以抹去的永远的伤痛。整篇文章，充满了哀怨，充满了伤痕，充满了遗憾、自责和怜惜，具有浓重的悲剧气氛。

作者除了通过孩子的夭折引起读者怜悯外，还通过描写其他人物的死烘托令人恐惧的氛围，产生悲剧的效果。在小说集的第5篇《维尔德明斯一家》一文中，作者以死亡为线索，讲述了一家新搬来的邻居的故事。文章巧妙地利用死亡，不时地将坟墓、鬼魂，以及和自己有关鬼魂的种种猜测结合在一起，成功地将读者引向一个既紧张又神往的情境之中。作者在文中提到了四个人的死：约翰·海因、维尔德明斯和一个14岁的女孩以及她的妈妈。作者通过对这些人的死及他们的坟墓的描写，首先营造了一个令人恐惧的氛围；再以暮光中墓角传来的笛声，引出了"夜晚循笛声，墓地探实情"的经历。自然，这笛声不是鬼吹出的，可读者怀着紧张的心弦跟着她前去看个究竟。同时，作者还描述了一个林中树阴下一坐就几个小时的年轻姑娘。这位姑娘的行为似人非人，似鬼非鬼，简直就是一个活死人：她对人生无所热爱，对死亡无所畏惧，没有哭泣，没有欢笑；她临死前没有痛苦，而是一脸安详，眼睛在死后也一直睁得大大的。而她的妈妈一生痴情地守望自己的心上人而早已告别人世。这一连串的死亡故事和墓场环境，既扣人心弦，令人紧张，同时，又令人心情十分沉重。

然而，在小说集中虽有人物神秘早逝，甚至有的死不瞑目，凯瑞有关死亡的描写却没有"魑魅魍魉充斥的妖邪之气，也不似爱伦·坡哥特式小说那么古灵古怪和阴森恐怖"（引自爱丽丝·凯瑞研究绪论）。凯瑞通过死亡所营造的令人产生恐惧的情境之中隐藏着一种冷峻的、忧郁的美。这与她笔下的环境描写不无关系。凯瑞的笔下充满弯月、山丘、橡树和各种当地的野生花草；还有红色烟囱中袅袅升起的青烟，暮色中美丽的夏日以及枯草丛中突然从睡眠中被惊醒而闪电般逃离的兔子。这些乡村环境中特定的意象和那个环境中发生的死亡故事形成一定的反差。作者常常置读者于美好的事物之中，却又"突转"将其带入事物的反面——死亡。这些特定意象和死亡这一"苦难"的对比加强了死亡所产生的悲剧效果，同时使作品显得死亡气氛浓重但不血腥，环境忧郁却不恐怖。小说在一个以死亡为线索，以寻鬼为目的的片段中曾写道："赶到了小山的顶上，我看见前方不远处，有一个黑影渐渐地消失在视线之中。"很显然，作者并没有将黑影描述成恐怖的恶魔，而是给人一种令人神往，追随莫及，飘然而去的仙子的形象。作者正是通过这样将特定意象和死亡巧妙结合而产生其特定的悲剧效果。请看下面一段描写：

> 墓地看上去是那么静谧而肃穆！我向里面望去，心里有点害怕。我将墓地门上的插销打开又插上，看看这是否就是我听到的那种声音。就在这时，一只惊觉的兔子自草丛下蹿出，蹿过静静的土堆，逃到了树林中安全的地方。事实上，它吓了我一大跳。我只看到墓地的草被踩出了一条细细的小径，一直通向玛丽的坟墓。除此之外，我什么都没看到。（Cary：54）

作者在这段描写中将恐惧和美感摆在了读者的面前。在作者的笔下，墓地是一片庄严、安详之地。草丛中的兔子既吓人一跳，令人惊悚万状，又让人觉得可爱，欣然神往。就在读者要陶醉在这冷峻、忧郁而又十分美丽的山岭上的时候，作者却将其视线又带到了坟墓。在冷峻、悲凉的氛围中读者感受到了苜蓿角的美。

2. 忧郁的悲剧主题

凯瑞除了以死亡展示悲剧的主题外，其作品中充满了忧郁的悲剧色彩。忧郁的悲剧主题，与其生死观和认知思想影响不无关系。简·嘉利赫（Jane Galliher）认为，基督教的普救派对凯瑞小说、速写以及系列故事具有重要的影响。普救派认为人人都有得救的机会，不管人种、阶级，甚至罪犯也有最终得救的机会。得救意味着能见到上帝的普救之光。但一些信仰不够完善之人得救之前要经历一段地狱般的磨难，只是磨难短暂。这是乐观的普救派的一般观念。凯瑞作品中借鉴了普救派的普救之光思想，发扬了人生磨难观点。凯瑞在《苜蓿角》的开篇写道："万物变化是大自然的法则。新旧不断交替。往年落英缤纷的枝条业已枯萎，覆盖其上的是今年娇艳欲滴的鲜花。"（Cary：13）这种视世事变迁，新老更替，花开花落乃自然之法则的思想其实就是"佛家"的思想，暗示世事无常，沧海桑田，飘忽不定，也颇有中国古代"易"的意味。而她在第二篇中的"人生百事多被阴影笼罩，亮光时而在各处摇曳片刻，而后很快淡出"（Cary：27）这句陈述是继"世事无常"这一思想之后，有"人生苦海无边"之意。凯瑞认为普救之光短暂，而苦海无边。在这一点上，凯瑞的生死观超出了乐观的普救派一般观念，她的观点和佛家"苦海无边"的思想更相契合。小说《苜蓿角》着墨最多的就是这悲苦的境地，很好地体现了她的这一认知世界。从这些思想中，我们不难解读其对人生世事悲观层面的深刻认识。通过如此种种论调，我们不难解释为什么在作品中往往负面的描写比较突出。这种负面的描写主要表现在作品描写的基调是悲观的，景物色彩多黯淡。以《光影之间》一篇为例，除了文章开头人生百事多为阴影所笼罩的表述外，作者集中描写了自己的懊悔和遗憾——那是一种藏在心头的永远挥不去的阴影。正因如此，作者认为人生的光只是一种瞬间的美好和期待，犹如人生的幸福之短暂而苦难之永恒，而主导人生的却是阴影。因此，虽然《光影之间》这一标题似乎是说光与影可以交换轮替，体现了作者所主张的世事无常的思想，但从具体的描写中可以看出阴影还是占据了人生的主导地位。由此可见其作品忧郁的悲剧主题。这些忧郁的主题使得作品多描写人生惨事，如死亡、失恋、失意等。

在这样的主题下，其叙事的基调和色彩自然也充满了忧郁的气息。因此，文中大量描写了月色、树阴、黑夜、乌云、破瓦残垣的农舍、庄严肃穆的埋葬着许多人的大教堂以及许多有着不祥预兆的动物，如猫头鹰、蝙蝠等。就连季节的描写也多集中在秋天。秋是丰收的季节，有喜悦也有快乐，但转瞬即逝，更多的是绵绵的秋雨和阴霾，深秋的阴冷和肃杀。这些意象的出现，烘托了气氛，突出了忧郁这一悲剧主题。

三、悲剧意识的意义

在悲剧定义中，亚里斯多德强调悲剧应当"借引起怜悯和恐惧来使这种情感得到陶冶"（转引自《西方文艺理论名著教程》：56）。引起怜悯和恐惧之情是悲剧独特的快感。陶冶人们的思想感情，产生好的影响和作用，正是凯瑞创作这部作品的初衷。在小说《苜蓿角》的序言中，凯瑞写道："我国的乡村生活一直不是画家、诗人、言情作家特别青睐的题材。或许有的觉得农村生活缺乏美的元素；或许有的感觉其缺乏激情，平淡索然；也可能有的认为其过于切近稔熟。"（Ⅴ）作者首先承认了自己的作品在选材上可能存在上述的问题。然而，作者认为在这一片一度荒凉的土地上，在这里的人们的朴实行为中，在每天所发生的事件中蕴藏着充满人性而有趣的东西。作者担心自己对作品的努力可能不会引起城里人的兴趣，因为"城里人虽具怜悯之心，却对贫贱之人鲜有同情之意"（Ⅵ）。对此，作者除了有着许多文学大师们所没有的乡村经历和忠实的描写之外，悲剧的手法也是作品获得成功的重要因素。悲剧手法的运用使作品打动了城里冷漠的读者，引起他们的兴趣使他们对作品的人物产生怜悯。恐惧和怜悯，正如亚里士多德所说，是一种痛苦的情绪，而悲剧引起的怜悯和恐惧之情却是一种"特别的快感"，是一种求知的快感，可以强化心灵，"把人引到最高尚的方向"（转引自《西方文艺理论名著教程》：57）。在凯瑞以死亡为悲剧内容的描写中，一方面作品使读者对西部生活产生一种自然的、真实的认识。同时通过对死亡的理解使人们认识到人性中生命的永恒。

同样，凯瑞以忧郁为悲剧主题的描写，让读者沉浸于这样的一种氛围之中。在怜悯和恐惧氛围中，读者的情感受到了熏陶。让读者深刻地认识到人生无常，光明短暂，而黑暗常常袭来，并在现实中作好应对黑暗的心理准备，同时珍惜光明。由此可见，凯瑞《苜蓿角》的悲剧主题，无论是死亡的描写还是忧郁氛围的营造，不是将读者引向黑暗与消沉，相反，作者在向读者传递积极的信息。那就是以黑暗预示光明的价值，以死亡创造生命的永恒。可见，贯穿凯瑞小说的是一种超越了宗教观的自觉的悲剧意识。小说的"悲观色彩"或者一种悲情主义，不是消极意义上的悲观主义，相反，恰恰是凯瑞有意突出的内容，借以打动读者。因此，这一悲剧内容的突出是作者有意识的创作意图。从此意义上讲，作品中悲剧手法的运用是积极向上的。

综上所述，凯瑞短篇小说集《苜蓿角》的创作中具有强烈悲剧意识。作品的悲剧意识与作者的创作动机和作者的生平有着密切的关系，具有一定的自觉性和自发性。我们在作品中能够读到大量的死亡和忧郁为主题的描写。这是作品悲剧意识在内容上的体现。作者通过对儿童死亡的描写引起人们的深刻怜悯和同情，而对其他人物的死亡的描写让读者感到恐惧。作者的认知世界使得作品忧郁的成分占据了上风，让读者大部分的时间沉浸于具有悲剧效果的氛围之中。然而，凯瑞的悲剧所产生的效果往往因特定的乡村环境中的意象的巧妙运用而加强，使得读者在死亡面前感受不到血腥恐怖，反而让人觉得存在着一种冷峻的和忧郁的美，从而形成了独具特点的凯瑞式悲剧。凯瑞悲剧手法的运用，是积极向上的。读者在悲剧描写中反省与自责，产生怜悯和教育，从而避免或者减少错误，更好地适应现实的悲情生活。作者在作品中对忧郁氛围的描写和烘托，使读者更能从中感受到光明的宝贵，因而小说以忧郁为悲剧主题的描写预示着光明的价值，以死亡为悲剧主题的描写让读者领悟生命的永恒。

参考文献：

Ames, Mary Clemmer. *A Memorial of Alice and Phoebe Cary with Some of Their Later Poems*. Boston: Houghton Mifflin, 1874.

Alice, Cary. *Clovernook: or, Recollections of Our Neighborhood in the West*. New York: Redfield Clinton Hall, 1852.

胡经之，王岳川，李衍柱. 西方文艺理论名著教程［M］. 北京：北京大学出版社，2003.

刘海平，王守仁，张冲. 新编美国文学史：第一卷［M］. 上海：上海教育出版社，2000.

亚里士多德. 诗学［M］. 陈忠梅，译注. 北京：商务印书馆，1999.

7 凯瑞的死亡叙事
——解析《苜蓿角，或曰西部邻里旧事》

Alice Cary's Death Narrative in the *Clovernook*

李 盛

摘要：爱丽丝·凯瑞是19世纪中期美国文坛一个非常独特的女作家。当时浪漫主义为代表的文学思潮大行其道，与凯瑞同时代的作家总是试图按照其审美需要美化现实，甚至不惜歪曲真实的生活经历，对于死亡，往往表现出上流社会所特有的多愁善感。凯瑞始终坚持按照生活本来的面目呈现下层社会老弱妇孺等弱者所面临的残酷生活现实，在她的故事集《苜蓿角，或曰西部邻里旧事》里，凯瑞以其独特的死亡叙事，勾勒出当时西部边疆生活的颇为艰辛的一面，从而为读者呈现了较为真实的西部早期生活面貌。凯瑞以其颇具黑暗现实主义色彩的死亡叙事开创了后世的现实主义文学的先河。本章从死亡现实的残酷性、死亡结局的宿命性、死亡救赎的虚幻性和死亡关怀的颠覆性四个方面论述凯瑞颇具现实主义特色的死亡叙事。

Abstract：Alice Cary is a very unique woman writer in the mid-19th century American literary landscape. As romanticism was still the mainstream, many Cary's contemporary writers tended to beautify reality to suit the aesthetic need, even at the cost of distorting real life experience. In dealing with the topic of death, their works are characteristic of upper-class sentimentalism. Cary, on the contrary, adheres to presenting the cruel reality of life

7 凯瑞的死亡叙事——解析《苜蓿角，或曰西部邻里旧事》

for the powerless. In her collection of stories, *Clovernook, or, Recollections of Our Neighborhood in the West*, Cary sketches the tough side of life in the then-frontier west and thus presents a realistic picture of the early western life. With her realistic narrative of death, Cary foresees the upcoming tide of realism. This chapter to explores Cary's death narrative from four aspects: the cruelty of death reality, the predestination of death finale, the vanity of death redemption, and the subversion of death as a kind of humane care.

引 语：

19世纪中期是美国文学史上的一个转折时期，浪漫文学依然大行其道，现实主义文学也已悄然萌动。在这个特殊的时期，爱丽丝·凯瑞的《苜蓿角，或曰西部邻里旧事》故事集问世。凯瑞以其带有黑暗现实主义色彩的死亡叙事揭示了当时西部边疆生活的真实面貌。（Burt：196）她始终坚持按照生活本来面目再现西部边疆的生活，呈现下层社会老弱妇孺等弱者所面临的残酷生活现实，而同时代作家的作品却试图按照其审美需要美化现实，甚至不惜歪曲真实的生活经历。在19世纪的美国文坛，凯瑞颇具黑暗现实主义色彩的死亡叙事挑战了当时浪漫主义依然居于主流的文学传统，开创了后世的现实主义文学的先河。

在论述凯瑞独特的死亡叙事之前，有必要谈及凯瑞的死亡叙事与传统的死亡叙事的关系。孔子曾说，"未知生，焉知死"（《论语·先进·第十一》），这句话恰到好处地诠释了中国传统的死亡意识，因而中国文学传统的死亡叙事对死亡怀着一种忐忑的、莫测高深的敬畏，将之神秘化；西方文学传统的死亡叙事从不回避死亡，而是"向死而生"（陈民：18），认真地研究探索死亡及其之于人生的意义，将之视为人生自然而然的一部分；爱丽丝·凯瑞充分继承并挖掘了死亡的叙事功能，并进一步把死亡叙事发展为其作品的叙事核心，奠定了其黑色现实主义的基调。本文具体论述凯瑞的死亡叙事特色。

一、死亡现实的残酷性

凯瑞生活在 19 世纪中期的美国西部，当时的西部仍属于边疆地区，生活条件无疑是恶劣的，很多人没能成年就夭折了。当时的西部缺医少药的情况从理查德·克莱维尔行医一事可以一窥端倪。理查德·克莱维尔是个不学无术、好逸恶劳的浪荡子，只是跟着乡村医生游荡了一段日子竟然也能挂牌行医，而且口碑不错。不过这位理查德·克莱维尔医生自己后来也"被在这个国家普遍流行的疾病所击倒，忽冷忽热，最终演变成最恶性的那种发烧"（Cary：268）。理查德·克莱维尔从开始行医到自己最终病亡的经历看似荒诞，但从侧面间接反映了当时西部的医疗状况：由于缺医少药，今天看来很普通的病症，如感冒发烧等，对当时的西部边疆的居民来说都往往是致命的。《苜蓿角》故事集里有许多这样不幸而亡的人物，如怪妇人、小彼得、小学校长……这些当时西部的早期居民不仅要承受劳作的艰辛，往往还要同时面对世俗伦理的压制和迫害。艾丽的姐姐丽贝卡的早亡就是一个典型的例子。丽贝卡与小学校长之间的感情其实是属于少男少女之间的青春懵懂，原本无可厚非，但在以丽贝卡母亲哈德利太太为代表的世俗的眼里，原本少男少女之间美好的感情却成了大逆不道的行为。

> 她打定主意不能对这样无法无天的行为听之任之。作为女人，她正值壮年，做事果断，有着非常严格的道德观念，一向把孩子们喜欢幻想、非常感性的性情当成很大的不幸；这种性情在现实中会更糟糕——是可耻的。孩子们青春成长中几乎没有从她这里得到任何鼓励；的确，她几乎没有觉察到孩子的存在。（Cary：295—296）

故事集中怪妇人、小彼得和小学校长等人物的死亡无一不昭示着死亡现实的残酷。在自然条件和世俗伦理的双重压迫下，死亡成了生活的常态。在这种死亡现实中，人祸猛于天灾，以丽贝卡为例，她的死更多地源于世俗伦理的残酷压制。

年轻人之间的彼此爱慕之情在村里喜欢蜚短流长的人嘴里又被添油加醋了。许多上了年纪的，甚至也包括一些中年人往往会犯的一个错误，就是总把年轻人之间的单纯的乐趣看成不检点，把所有男女之间的情爱都看成恶事，他们忘记了自己也曾像他们现在说的那样年少轻狂，忘记了他们也有过各自不同的婚恋。(Cary：295)

在人祸横行的时候，自然充当了帮凶的角色，总是在人祸发展到极致时，不失时机地收割脆弱的生命。面对残酷的死亡现实，凯瑞同时代的作品多表现出上流社会所特有的多愁善感。与同时代的作家不同，凯瑞并没有试图粉饰太平，在她的作品中，她直面妇孺等弱者的死亡，丝毫不矫揉造作地揭示残酷的死亡现实，较为生动地还原了当时西部下层人民真实的生活面貌。

二、死亡救赎的虚幻性

基督教认为人生来就带有原罪，人生下来就要赎罪，主张人在今生多施善行赎罪，则死后可以升入天堂永享荣耀；死被描述成上帝的拣选，是荣归天家，因而死变得并不可怕，反而是荣耀的。凯瑞父母信奉基督教普救教派，普救教派信奉所有信徒死后都可以直接升入天堂，死后的世界没有地狱。因此，在普救教徒看来，死亡意味着解脱和救赎，死亡只是进入天堂、获得永生之福的一个过程。人生来对死亡都有本能的恐惧，而有了荣归天家的感召，基督教就解除了人们对于死亡本能的恐惧，从而劝导他们信主而得救赎。而在凯瑞作品中荣归天家的宗教说教呈现出其荒谬的本质。若是真的荣归天家，那么死亡场景的描述应该是快乐的、乐观的，凯瑞笔下的临终场景却十分阴郁和沉重，丝毫不见教义中宣扬的救赎应有的平安喜乐，例如，关于怪妇人临终的一段描述：

夜晚的黑暗似乎从未如此可怕。窗外藤蔓敲打着窗子，暴雨击打着屋顶，他害怕了。妈妈！他喊道，开始声音还很轻，到后来喊得越来越响，但是母亲没有任何回答，他把手搭到她额头，感觉又冷又湿，他吻她的唇，她没有回应，他明白母亲死了。(Cary：37)

再如，描写丽贝卡的一段：

这个世界到处都是伤痕累累满心凄苦的心灵；悲凉的呻吟随着阳光四处蔓延，哪怕是再欢快的笑声里也潜伏着呻吟；痛苦的枕头，无眠的房间遍布这个世界；既然蛇虫盘踞其间，那么这世上就没有不败的花朵；既然罪恶让这个世界坟冢遍布，天使白色的翅膀也为诅咒所遮蔽，那么我们就不再有安宁之日了。(Cary: 298—299)

这样的叙事手法似乎已经表明了死亡救赎只是一种自欺欺人的虚幻，只是一个残酷冰冷的现实。至少在凯瑞笔下，死亡并没有给故事中的死者带来真正的解脱和救赎，而只是一种荼毒生者的精神鸦片而已。在此，凯瑞以其犀利的笔锋揭示了一个残酷的事实：死亡救赎只是一种永远也无法兑现的虚幻。揭示了在死亡救赎这一虚幻外衣掩盖下的真相：既暴露了宗教对于当时西部残酷生活现实的无奈，也表达了作者对于死亡之于生者和死者意义的拷问。

三、死亡结局的宿命性

西方传统死亡观基于基督教教义，即人来到世间，其生命是有限的，人要在世间完成自身的救赎，在死后才能得到拣选升入天堂，因而死亡是必然的，是一种宿命，这也正是西方传统死亡叙事所认同和推崇的。然而在凯瑞的死亡叙事中，死亡结局的宿命性更具现实意义。对于出身于西部乡村的凯瑞来说，她非常了解西部乡村生活的艰辛，非常了解乡村下层弱势群体，尤其了解年轻女性的真实生活状态，她们不仅要和他人一样应对劳作的艰辛，往往还要独自面对世俗伦理的压制和迫害。对于她们，凯瑞给予了深深的同情，但凯瑞自身思想也存在着矛盾：在主张男女平等的同时，她也认同当时社会主流对女性的家庭生活定位，即为人妻、为人母是女性最崇高和最为满足的生活角色。囿于当时的时代背景和自身思想的局限，凯瑞没能为她的女主人公指明出路，因而她笔下的女性人物的命运就注定了悲剧性的结局，联系到死亡救赎的虚幻性，指望死后升入天堂得到幸福的想法也随之破灭，所以，在整个故事集中，她笔下的女主人公总是默默承受，直至最后死亡。对于凯瑞笔下的人物来说，在当时的社会现实背景下，死亡结局是一种无望的宿命，是一个毫无逆转的悲剧性现实。

四、死亡关怀的颠覆性

死亡叙事体现文学对于人的终极关怀，西方文学传统的死亡叙事倡导人们向死而生，鼓励他们积极地面对，乐观地生活，其实质体现了文学对生者的人文关怀；而凯瑞作品中则饱含了对生活弱者、生命脆弱的感伤。凯瑞小说中死亡的主角多为妇女和儿童，对于这些处于弱势的人群凯瑞给予了深深的同情。

凯瑞写道："我们如此孤立无援，所以我们需要善待彼此，要随时伸出爱心和援助的手给他人以鼓励，因为我们所要面临的黑暗和沉默不是一般的关心所能挽救的。"（299）在此，凯瑞提到了一个表示集体的词"我们"和人类所面临的存在性的孤独。这种充满感伤的意识危机与其说是源自对自我存在的最终消亡的焦虑，倒不如说是源自对与给予自我生命意义的人的注定分离的确切认识，不管这种分离是暂时的还是永远的。（Dobson：267）

由此可见，在凯瑞的思维中，"我们"是一个孤独的群体。这个世界充满了以死亡为代表的黑暗和沉默，面对着死亡。我们更加需要善待彼此，关怀彼此，纵然注定要彼此分别，也要彼此珍爱，哪怕天人永隔。正是基于这样的思维，在凯瑞的笔下，这些昔日的亲朋故交虽死犹生。她们的鬼魂常常出现在叙事人的面前，给人感觉不像是在另外一个世界。因而，凯瑞的死亡叙事更多的是对弱者悲剧死亡的同情，是对逝者亡灵的终极关怀。这是一种与倡导向死而生的西方传统死亡叙事截然不同的死亡关怀。传统的死亡叙事强调对生者的关怀，鼓励他们向死而生，而凯瑞的死亡叙事跨越了生死的阻隔，把文学的终极关怀延伸到逝者，令他们虽死犹生。这种视死若生的死亡关怀是对西方文学传统死亡叙事的延伸和颠覆。与这种独特的死亡关怀相适应，凯瑞作品多采用倒叙和插叙等回顾性视角，叙事者总是站在现在回看悲凉的往事。凯瑞一方面用写实笔触褫夺了死亡的种种幻象，还原了死亡的本来面目；另一方面，又以感伤的情怀为那些生前不曾得到应有关怀的逝者的灵魂带去一抹人性的光辉。

亲戚或余悲，
他人亦已歌。

> 死去何所道，
> 托体同山阿。
>
> （陶渊明：210）

死者之于生者的意义在于对生命意义的拷问，而生者之于死者的意义或许就存在于生者对于逝者的追思和哀悼。故事集里的这些逝者正是借助凯瑞极富同情的笔端，在凯瑞对西部往事的追忆中超越了死亡，得到了永生。他们活在凯瑞对西部往事的记忆里，不曾忘却；他们自然也活在《苜蓿角》故事集里，因为那是他们的故事。

结　语：

死亡叙事不仅已经成为凯瑞作品的叙事核心，而且成为凯瑞刻画人物，推动情节发展，达成其展现西部边疆人民生活真实面貌的一种叙事手段。因而，凯瑞的死亡叙事是全方位的。死亡不仅表现在故事中具体事件上，还表现为一种具有多种叙事功能的叙事手段，通过对死亡氛围的描述展现现实的残酷，也因此奠定了凯瑞的黑色现实主义的基调。在此，凯瑞继承了霍桑和麦尔维尔为代表的美国后浪漫主义叙事，在霍桑等人的作品中对生命的态度由乐观转为怀疑，田园牧歌式的生活也逐渐为恶的势力、感伤的情绪和死亡的威胁笼罩着（陈民：26）。凯瑞的作品中气氛更加阴郁，死亡肆意收割着脆弱的生命而留给生者无尽的哀伤。凯瑞以这样阴郁充满死亡气息的现实主义叙事揭示了西部下层社会人民的真实生活面貌，从而反抗了过度乐观理想化的浪漫主义文学传统，进而颠覆了西方文学传统的死亡叙事，并因此开创了美国现实主义文学的先河。《苜蓿角，或曰西部邻里旧事》可以说是一部以死亡为主题写下的关于乡村弱者死亡的悲情故事。

参考书目：

Burt, Daniel S, ed. *The Chronology of American Literature： Literary Achievements from the Colonial Era to Modern Times*. New York：Houghton Mifflin Books，2004：196.

Cary, Alice. *Clovernook： or, Recollections of Our Neighborhood in the West*. New York：Redfield，1852.

Dobson, Joanne. "Reclaiming Sentimental Literature". *American Literature*, 69.2, 1997: 263—288.

James, Edward T, Janet W James, ed. *Notable American Women: A Biographical Dictionary*. Cambridge: Harvard University Press, 1971: 297.

陈民. 西方文学中死亡叙事的审美风貌 [M]. 南京: 南京师范大学, 2005.

陶渊明. 陶渊明集. 汪榕培, 英译; 熊郅祁, 今译. 大中华文库. 北京: 中华书局, 2003.

8 凯瑞短篇小说对残障人物的感伤关照

The Sentimental Disabled Body in Alice Cary's Short Stories

Laura Cheshier

Abstract: Alice Cary provides nineteenth-century America with sophisticated short stories that blend sentimentalism with regional and realistic prose to reveal the complexity of sympathy, otherness, and identity in the domestic sphere. She incorporates the figure of the sentimental disabled body into both *The Great Doctor* and *The Sisters*, creating objects of sympathy that pull other characters and the reader into the disabled body's pain. Cary's objects of sympathy reveal the need for reform, and their experiences with sympathy can be as bleak as their experiences with actual suffering. For Cary, sympathy empowers change less often than it excludes the sufferer from community and encourages difference and self-repression. Instead of making her readers sympathetic to others, Cary's storytelling causes the reader to long for empathy, sameness, and inclusion into community.

Cary's sentimental disabled figures cannot act for themselves but move others to action that is, finally, insufficient to alleviate suffering, which creates emotional distance between the disabled person and the sympathetic community and underscores the often overlooked need for inclusion and empathy. Sympathizers may move others to feel and to act, but not to rescue. In *The Great Doctor*, Hobert's suffering empowers others to act, but their actions are inevitably inadequate to avert disaster. Sympathy fails to save Hobert from death and reveals that the only way to alleviate peoples' suffering is to accept them into a loving community instead of othering them. Sympathy by itself leaves the disabled body open for exploitation, and while it might point to necessary social change, empathy, the ability to share the disabled person's feelings, would better alleviate the sufferer's burdens. In *The Sisters*, Cary shows how isolation from others can cause the disabling that leads to death. When two close sisters Rebecca and Ellie distance themselves from each other and then allow an unjust othering of Rebecca from the family, they create the space in which Rebecca becomes a sentimental disabled body and that evokes only an impotent sympathy in others. This cannot save her from death, which proves that sympathy kills communication, relationships, and people, and it calls for a social empathy to replace the faulty familial model of merely sympathizing with another's pain.

摘要：爱丽丝·凯瑞为19世纪美国文学贡献了颇为成熟的短篇小说集，这些作品融感伤主义文学、地域文学和现实主义文学于一体，以揭示家庭中同情、异化和认同的复杂性。她把多愁善感的残障人物纳入《了不起的医生》和《两姐妹》这两部作品中，创作出吸引其他故事人物和读者关注残障身体之痛的同情对象。凯瑞的同情对象揭示了变革的需求，他们的同情体验与他们的实际苦难一样凄凉。对于凯瑞来说，同情催生变化，但同情更将受难者排除于群体之外并引发差别感和自我压抑。凯瑞的叙事促使读者渴望共鸣、一致和融入群体，而不是令读者同情他人。

凯瑞的感伤性残障人物无法为自身而行动，只能感动他人去采取行动，这样最终不足以消减苦难，这就造成了残障人物与同情群体之间的情感距离，并突显了往往被忽视的渴望接纳和共鸣的需求。富有同情心的人可以促使他人去感知，去行动，但不是去救援。在《了不起的医生》里，霍伯特的苦难促使他人去行动，但他们的行动必然不足以避免灾难。同情没能使霍伯特免于死亡并揭示出唯一消减人们苦难的方法是接纳他们进入有爱心的群体，而不是将其打入另类。仅仅是同情易使残障的身体受到利用；而共鸣，即分享残障人物情感的能力，可能会在表明必要的社会变化的同时，更好地减轻受难者的负担。在《两姐妹》中，凯瑞表明了孤立能够造成最终引发死亡的残障。一向亲密无间的两姐妹丽贝卡和艾丽彼此间产生了距离感，接着丽贝卡受到了家庭不公正的排斥，她们彼此的隔阂促使丽贝卡变成了一个多愁善感的残障之身，由此引发的他人的同情是于事无补的。这样的同情无法使丽贝卡免于死亡，这说明了同情阻断了沟通，切断了关系，扼杀了人们，进而呼唤用社会共鸣来替代仅对别人的痛苦表达同情的漏洞百出的家庭模式。

Most critics familiar with Alice Cary's poetry and short stories consider her to be a realist and a regionalist. Typically, realism would separate Cary from sentimentalists by a wide berth; however, Rosemary Garland Thomson's article, "Crippled Girls and Lame Old Women: Sentimental Spectacles of Sympathy in Nineteenth-Century American Women's Writing" defines a common sentimental figure that is present in Cary's fiction. Thompson avers that, since the nineteenth-century middle class woman was bound by strict gender roles, the only way for her to promote herself was through promotion of social change for those in similar positions (142). Sentimental writers found that disabled characters could evoke sympathy, moving other characters to a power position from which they could aid the less fortunate (132). Thomson asserts that "disability operates as the manifestation of suffering" (138), making the disabled figure an easy marker for areas needing reform. This type of sentimental reform requires "a victim and a rescuer" (135). Janet Gebhart Auten claims that there is "a pattern for reading regional sketches: an initial sympathy with human suffering should lead to connection and then understanding" (68). However, Cary's objects of sympathy are not only signs of needed reform; their experiences with sympathy are often as bleak as their experiences with actual suffering. Cary uses the disabled figure to show that sympathy empowers change less often than it excludes the object of sympathy from community and encourages difference and self-repression. Instead of making her readers sympathetic to others, Cary's storytelling evokes empathy, sameness, and inclusion into community.

Cary's short stories contain sentimental disabled figures who, unable to act for themselves, empower others to action that is insufficient to alleviate suffering. This is clearly evident in *The Great Doctor*, a story Cary published in *The Atlantic Monthlyin* 1866 and one Judith Fetterley included in *Clovernook Sketches and Other Stories*. Hobert Walker, a farmer (presumably from Clovernook) elopes with his young love Jenny to the Wabash valley in Indiana to start a farm, but after a few years during which they do well and form a loving familial community, Hobert becomes sick. He tries to hide his illness from Jenny, and she tries to hide her concern, but she is unable to hide her worry from the reader, who has learned to read Cary's fiction through the details in the text, for as Fetterley notes, "Cary makes of her fiction an instrument capable of recording and legitimizing the 'small things' which constitute the language her narrator and characters devise to signal their desire" (*Entitled*: 109). Jenny performs an act of hospitality, bringing out new cups for tea, which is coupled with her feeling insecure and her desire for their life to be as common as it was before. Jenny puts out the good tablecloth and the new cups because it "seemed to her as if

Hobert were some visitor coming, —not her husband. A shadowy feeling of insecurity touched her; the commonness of custom was gone" (247). Jenny's hospitality removes Hobert from the comfort of the habitual family tea, and this isolation only continues as his sickness lengthens, and he is kept in his sick-room apart from the rest of the house.

According to an established pattern in nineteenth-century writing, Cary establishes a sentimental disabled figure who moves others to act and attempt a rescue. When the decision is made that all the family's money will be spent to get Hobert into the medical care of the "great" Dr. Killmany of New Orleans, the larger community comes together in seeming empathy to bestow gifts on Hobert and to wish him well (255). However, Cary makes sure to stress the difference between the actions of the community and its words, for their sympathetic goodbyes were merely "calculated to convey the impression that the leave-taking was a mere matter of form, and only for a day" (255). Hobert's friends are hiding their true feelings, just as his family already has, and are isolating him further. Cary uses this sympathetic community to illustrate the emotional distance between the object of sympathy and those empowered to act for him, which underscores the often overlooked need for inclusion and empathy.

Cary's literary realism uses the pattern of the sentimental disabled figure to move others to feel and to act, but not to rescue. Just as the sympathy encountered in his hometown was intended for Hobert's good, so does Hobert find a seemingly beneficent sympathy when he arrives in New Orleans. Hobert finds Dr. Shepard instead of Dr. Killmany and enjoys a deeper and more beautiful sympathy than that he left behind in Indiana:

Dr. Shepard, who had just administered some cordial, was bending over him in the most kindly and sympathetic manner. …he carried about him an atmosphere of sweetness and healing that comforted and assured without words and without medicine. ... Perhaps—who shall say not? —it was the blessings of the poor, to whom he most generously ministered, which gave to his manner that graciousness and charm which no words can convey, and to his touch that magnetism which is at once life-giving and love-inspiring. (257)

Instead of initially othering Hobert as Jenny and his neighbors did by pretending that nothing was wrong, Dr. Shepard's sympathy leads to an open communication. Hobert even finds "himself opening his heart to this new doctor, as he had never opened it to anybody in his whole life" (257), and he divulges to him his life's story. Unlike the sympathy exhibited by his family and friends, Dr. Shepard's deeper sympathy leads to his honest communication of Hobert's illness. Dr. Shepard diagnoses him for free, advising Hobert that surgery would be fatal and that he should return to his family, yet Dr. Shepard is not truly capable of sharing the suffering of his patient. His sympathetic manner allows Hobert to open up to him, but it does not allow him to open up to Hobert in return. He gives a proper diagnosis and waives the fee, which is a charitable act. However, he is incapable of moving beyond a sympathetic otherness and is therefore unable to help shoulder the burdens of Hobert's sufferings or to accept partial responsibility for the decisions that Hobert must face. Hobert is unequipped for medical decision-making, yet upon sensing Hobert's unwillingness to accept his condition, Dr. Shepard distances himself from Hobert, declaring, "I must not say more to discourage you" (259). Hobert, therefore, ignores Dr. Shepard's advice and takes a chance with the "great doctor" of the title. Ironically, Dr. Killmany lives up to his name by viciously misdiagnosing Hobert for a surgery he cannot survive, taking his money, and having him transported and left onboard a departing steamboat the *Arrow of Light*. The sympathetic Dr. Shepard eases Hobert as he dies but was impotent to keep him out of the hands of a charlatan in the first place.

In *The Great Doctor*, Cary follows an established sentimental technique to place the disabled figure in a position where he is unable to help himself, but Cary denies her disabled figures rescuers. Their suffering empowers other characters to act, but their actions are inevitably incompetent to avert disaster. In this sense, Cary establishes her sentimental disabled figures in a pessimistic light in which sympathy fails to save them from death and instead reveals that the only way to alleviate a disabled figure's suffering is to accept them into a loving community instead of othering them. Indeed, Cary ends *The Great Doctor* with the obliteration of Hobert as a subject; his death objectifies him entirely, and when Dr. Shepard and the Captain of the *Arrow* speak of the tragedy they have witnessed they imagine themselves in the position of the great doctor, not of the dead Hobert:

"[I] f I had performed the operation, under the circumstances, I should think myself his murderer."

"And if you had taken his money, you would perhaps think yourself a thief, too! At any rate, I should think you one," was the answer of the captain. (264)

Depicting sympathy as a failure that leaves the disabled body open for exploitation, Cary uses the sentimental disabled figure to show that while sympathy might point to necessary social change, physical suffering could be eased or alleviated by an empathetic connection, in which the ability to share the disabled person's feelings makes his burdens easier to bear.

A dangerous use of sympathy in relation to sentimental disabled figures can also be seen in *The Sisters* from *Clovernook* (1852). Cary illustrates in this story the progression of a character from existence in an empathetic community to isolated sympathetic victimization. Ellie and Rebecca, the sisters of the title, begin their tale in a happy communion with each other, full of the regionalist empathy that Fetterley defines as "the capacity to understand how someone else might feel" ("*Not*": 26). The narrator reveals to the reader that "they were never from their first years separated for a single day" (49). More than physical proximity is implied in their common love of literature and their love for each other, symbolized by "their arms about each other, and their dark, heavy locks blown together by the wind" (49—50). Our title sisters are so empathetic that it is difficult to distinguish where one ends and the other begins, and after a day of working, dreaming, and reading outside, they would walk home, both feeling "pleased, each with herself and the other...as if they came in inspiration from the holiest mount of song" (50). In "Entitled to More than 'Peculiar Praise': The Extravagance of Alice Cary's *Clovernook*", Fetterley explains the sisters' importance to each other as their ability to recognize the value in the other's self and the other's desires: "Rebecca and Ellie Hadly create a world apart from the rest of the family in which each one feels pleased with herself and with the other as special and thus they are both recognized and recognizing" (110). Their empathetic connection, however, is not open to all. In fact, our narrator notes that "they began very early to be dissatisfied, and to think that beyond their little world was one full of sunshine and pleasure" (50). They isolate themselves from the larger world, imagining themselves objects of sympathy, and they exacerbate their alienation by going "apart from the others in the family" (50). Through this isolation Cary sets her heroine up to become a sentimental disabled figure who, as Thomson tells us, is differentiated from other characters (135). While isolation does not physically disable, it does allow a state from which future disabling will not be remedied.

Cary further diminishes empathetic relationship and employs sentimentality by giving Rebecca a premonition of her own premature death. Difference now exists between Rebecca and every other character, even her most-beloved sister, and instead of being able to talk about Rebecca's death with Rebecca's same "sad smile," "tears come to [Ellie's] eyes" and "half crying" she tries to bribe her sister with a new apron to stop this conversation (50). The differentiation of sympathy fractures the sentimental figure's connection with others. Rebecca does not accept the bribe but does maintain silence on this subject, which inevitably destroys the sisters' empathetic community. Rebecca has become a sympathetic figure to her sister, and "though the sisters never talked of death any more, there lay thereafter on the hearts of both an oppression—the consciousness of thinking often of what the lips must not speak" (51). Sympathy has created isolation and self-repression.

Rebecca has already been isolated from her mother's affections and empathetic understanding because Mrs. Hadly regards "the dreamy and poetic dispositions of her children as a great misfortune; something worse in fact—something to be ashamed of" (62). Mrs. Hadly's shame of her poetic daughters is a shame of her daughters' sense of themselves as special. Fetterley writes that "Cary's characters experience the press of tyranny not only from parents, to whom law and custom give authority over children, but also from a class system which ensures that some people will get more than others and which identifies certain desires as being out of bounds for certain persons" (*Entitled*: 110). This distance, caused by Mrs. Hadly's shame of her daughters' poetic ambitions, is exacerbated by Mrs. Grey reporting that the town believes Rebecca to have been engaged to her schoolteacher, to have been secretly meeting him after school, and to have been heard weeping and moaning beside his body before his funeral. If this report were true, then Rebecca's dangerous love of poetry would have flourished into an inappropriate sense of her value and an inappropriate acting out of her own entitled desires. A mother ashamed of a daughter's love of poetry is more deeply ashamed of her daughter's open desire for a man. Mrs. Hadly feels the already present distance from her daughter increase at this moment, setting Rebecca up to be a more sympathetic figure and setting herself up to be the means of

Rebecca's disabling.

After a "week went by, and not one word said Mrs. Hadly in reference to the information she had received, or of the odious light in which she regarded it" (62), the day arrives in which Ellie and Rebecca are to be driven to town for new dresses and bonnets. Mrs. Hadly blindsides Rebecca with her announcement, allowing the girls to dress, be merry, enter the wagon, and watch their father untie the reins from a cherry tree before exiting the house to pronounce, "stop, ...Rebecca is not going to town to-day" (63). Rebecca, already isolated from all other characters, obeys her mother "without question or hesitancy" (63). As a sentimental figure and an object of sympathy, she is unable to act for herself, even though she does not know why she is being punished. Thomson states that "suffering demands alleviation. Sympathy licenses a moral mandate to assuage suffering, a mandate that confers both status and agency on the sympathizer" (132). Thus a sympathetic Ellie accepts Rebecca's punishment for herself and responds for Rebecca, "I will stay, too, mother" (63). As with Cary's other sympathizers, however, Ellie is unsuccessful, and Mrs. Hadly finalizes Rebecca's place as a sentimental figure and establishes difference between the sisters by telling Ellie to "go to town and get you a new dress and bonnet; Rebecca don't deserve any" (63). Rebecca, as the self-repressive sentimental disabled figure must, accepts her fate "calm [ly] and unquestioning [ly]" (63); she has "little appetite for dinner, and less for supper, but foreb [ears] to speak of the headache with which she suffered, performing every task which usually fell to herself and Ellie, alone" (63). Now Rebecca truly fills the role of the sentimental disabled figure who is distanced from others, incapable of voicing her own needs or helping herself, and is left an object of sympathy who must suffer from her headache in silence. Discussing Mrs. Walden's transformation from an inactive to an active wife/mother in his article

"Maternal Iconography and Nation Building in Alice Cary's *Mrs. Walden's Confidant*," a Clovernook story Cary included in *Pictures of Country Life* (1859), Thomas Fick uncovers what may be the reason that Rebecca is thoroughly silenced and disabled by her mother. Fick notes that "self-criticism and rebirth are in this way conjoined and an important emotional precedent set: accepting that one has done wrong establishes one's active past agency and opens space for future action" (138). Unlike Mrs. Walden, who realizes that her failures as a mother were caused by wrong actions that are reversible, Rebecca is merely labeled by her mother as undeserving of new clothes without any explanation of what actions led to the label. Her mother's silence keeps Rebecca from telling her side of the story—a silence that kills.

Cary uses the tools of the sentimental tradition, but she divorces her sentimental disabled figures from the context of the family. Gillian Brown states that "the sentimental family reconciles the self with others, secures the notion of selfhood in relations with others that involve objectification, nurture, discipline, and appropriation of the self by others" (161—162). Rebecca has been objectified by her sister and her mother, but she has not been nurtured by them; instead, she has been silenced and disabled. Indeed, Rebecca reveals her isolation and need of nurture by the end of this day of unexplained punishment when she sees the wagon return and runs to the gate because "she so much felt the need of the words and the endearments of sympathy" (63). Here Cary proves how very ineffective sympathy is in relieving the suffering of the disabled, for Ellie has stayed in town with her aunt and will not be home for another week. Rebecca, with no empathetic community with which to share her anguish, spends a sleepless night with "one hand [pressed] against her head" (64), thinking of herself, Ellie far away, and the schoolmaster in his grave. Rebecca now faces a serious problem. Her sister's removal and her mother's cruel misunderstanding have divorced her from her family, which will threaten her ability to maintain a stable self. If, as Brown asserts, "identity always entails relation" (162), Rebecca is a sentimental disabled figure whose sister's sympathy has failed twice—once by her leaving Rebecca and again by her not returning immediately.

Cary illustrates Rebecca's loss of identity by turning from her story and silencing Rebecca's voice and perspective for the remainder of the text. The narrator interjects her presence in the text at this point and directly addresses the audience. The story continues after the direct address from the third person, but the narrator follows Ellie's actions and Rebecca only appears in the story as a dead body. Fetterley writes, "If the inability to speak marks the rustic subject's failure to present her (or his) case for entitlement to the world, then finding a way to tell one's story serves as a crucial stage in the negotiation for recognition of one's entitlement to more than peculiar praise" (*Entitled*: 117). This story clearly proves that sympathy kills communication, relationships, and people and calls the reader to establish a social empathy that replaces the faulty familial model of merely sympathizing with another's pain.

At this point, Cary's narrator interrupts the story to interject that "the world is full of bruised and crushed hearts and desolate spirits" (64), reminding the reader that sentimental figures abound in our fallen world. In fact, the implication is that we all are or have the potential to become sentimental, disabled figures. Auten insists that there is a distinction between the direct address of most Victorian narrators and the narrators in regional fiction: "While cozy relationships between narrators and readers were common in Victorian fiction, the regional narrator assumes a particular, familial intimacy in order to instruct readers by pulling them into place with her." (71) Cary's narrator pulls the reader into relationship with her by denying the reader's own family. The narrator's advice is that "orphaned as we are, we have to be kind to each other" (64). The narrator does not offer sympathy as a solution to despair, but recognizes that suffering is inevitable; she offers kindness, or empathetic community, as our only reconciliation with a fallen world. She writes of all humanity as a community of orphans from a Heavenly Father, who should be "ready, with loving and helping hands and encouraging words, for the darkness and the silence are hard by where no sweet care can do us any good" (64). Cary's narrator may invoke a true, pure, heavenly empathy at this moment in the text because of Cary's own relationship with a sister whose death broke their community before she was fully able to understand its importance in her life. Laura Rogers notes that two of Cary's sisters died in 1833, and that Judith Fetterley considers the loss of Rhoda, the sister two years older than Alice, as an event even more important than her mother's death two years later. Rogers adds that "it was Rhoda who encouraged Alice's early attempts at poetry and spent time with Alice telling and listening to stories" (26—27). Knowing how difficult it is to find empathetic community and inspiration on earth, Cary has her narrator encourage readers to create this kind of loving relationship in their own lives. The silence and isolation of the characters in *The Sisters*, while never malicious, are deathlike. Finally, the narrator foreshadows and seals Rebecca's sentimental fate with the declaration that a "few bitter drops may poison the fountain of life" (64). False blame has the power to cause a headache that the disabled sufferer will have no strength to overcome.

The reader knows from this foreshadowing and from Rebecca's earlier mystical premonition of her own death that Rebecca will die. The premonition, like Hobert's diagnosis of an incurable disease, partially absolves Rebecca's mother of Rebecca's death. Cary incorporates an element of fate in these texts that establishes suffering and death as inevitable aspects of life, what Rogers calls "the dark and melancholy tone of her work, work in which children suffer deprivation and death and women suffer unhappy and loveless marriages and limited lives" (29). After the narrator's interjection, the reader shifts to Ellie's perspective. Ellie, carrying a new bonnet and a new dress in becoming styles, is glad to see her father. He, however, is sad to inform her that "Rebecca [is] very sick" (65). The reader simply desires that Ellie will make it home in time to see Rebecca alive. Her father promises to hurry home, hoping that Rebecca will be better and declaring that Rebecca wants to see Ellie, but at home Ellie is met by neighbors who tell them to go in. Mrs. Hadly is unseen, Mr. Hadly brushes away tears in silence, and Ellie weeps out loud. She gives her dress and bonnet, the articles that solidified the distinction between her sister and herself, to Mrs. Grey and goes in to kiss Rebecca's lips, but Rebecca is already dead. Indeed, Rebecca's death is only partially what the reader feels sorry for. It is not sad that Rebecca dies, but that, like Hobert, she dies isolated from those who love her. Sympathy can do her no good, and empathetic sameness of feeling can now never be regained.

Alice Cary provided nineteenth-century America with sophisticated short stories that blended aspects of sentimentalism with her regional and realistic prose that reveal the complexity of sympathy, otherness, and identity in the domestic sphere. She uses the sentimental disabled figure to evoke sympathy in other characters as well as in the reader, but she proves what a truly impotent thing that sympathy is. She also shows moments of empathy between characters, which give hope that a community between people could be sustained and could sustain those in it. Creating sentimental, disabled figures to show unsuccessful rescues, Cary establishes that contact and inclusion in community can console suffering, even if physical disability cannot be ultimately relieved. She shows that sentimental sympathy produces a difference between the subject and object of sympathy, and that while this difference can come between the closest of family or strangers, it is harmful to everyone. Alice Cary's short stories reveal that living in empathetic community can avert the isolation and impotence of sympathy by providing fellow sufferers who share the emotional burdens of a realistic world of suffering.

Works Cited

Auten, Janet Gebhart. "Parental Guidance: Disciplinary Intimacy and the Rise of Women's Regionalism". Aleta Feinsod Cane, Susan Alves. *"The Only Efficient Instrument": American Women Writers and the Periodical*, 1837—1916. Iowa City: U of Iowa P, 2001: 66—77.

Brown, Gillian. *Domestic Individualism: Imagining the Self in Nineteenth-Century America*. Berkeley: U of California P, 1990.

Cary, Alice. *Clovernook Sketches and Other Stories*. Judith Fetterley, ed. New Brunswick: Rutgers University Press, 1987.

Fetterley, Judith. "Entitled to More than 'Peculiar Praise': The Extravagance of Alice Cary's *Clovernook*". *Legacy: A Journal of American Women Writers*, 1993: 103—119.

"'Not in the Least American': Nineteenth-Century Literary Regionalismas UnAmerican Literature". Karen L. Kilcup, ed. *Nineteenth-Century American Women Writers: A Critical Reader*. Malden: Blackwell, 1998: 15—32.

Fick, Thomas H. Maternal Iconography and Nation Building in Alice Cary's *Mrs. Walden's Confidant*". *Studies in American Fiction*, 1997 (25): 131—146.

Rogers, Laura. "Alice Cary (1820—1871)". *Nineteenth-Century American Women Writers: A Bio-Bibliographical Critical Sourcebook*. Denise D Knight, Emmanuel S Nelson, ed. Westport, CT: Greenwood, 1997: 26—31.

Thomson, Rosemarie Garland. "Crippled Girls and Lame Old Women: Sentimental Spectacles of Sympathy in Nineteenth-Century American Women's Writing". *Nineteenth-Century American Women Writers: A Critical Reader*. Karen L Kilcup, ed. Malden: Blackwell, 1998: 128—145.

9 《外祖父》中的男性身份与情感闭锁

Masculinity and Emotional Isolation in *My Grandfather*

Jane M. Galliher

Abstract: Although Alice Cary's depiction of women has been one of the most explored areas of her work, very little attention has been directed toward her presentation of manhood. While Judith Fetterley and Marjorie Pryse focus on Cary's male characters, most of their discussion concerns patriarchal culture's effect upon the female narrator and how she grows to become an artist. Critics have yet to focus upon how Cary presents the challenges faced by men in forming their own identities, yet it is a rich topic that reveals a strikingly modern sense of gender and in some cases even anticipates modern constructivist theories. Cary's fiction shows the effects of the masculine archetypes in American society discussed by David Leverenz and Anthony Rotundo, archetypes that are particularly evident in *My Grandfather*, which opens the first series of Clovernook sketches. Cary shows how the concepts of manhood predominant in American society and the social behaviors expected of men were often destructive forces in the very lives of the men whom these conceptions seemingly empowered. Cary does not portray men uniformly as villainous patriarchs; to the contrary, the men of Cary's fiction are often victims of their own beliefs about masculine identity. *My Grandfather* clearly exemplifies this message of masculine victimization. Cary paints an ambivalent picture of the grandfather, a man who is both admirable and profoundly flawed. Like the other men in the story, he faces isolation because he internalizes the social expectations placed upon men. Ultimately, Cary's fiction holds that any oppressive power structure, particularly the power structure of patriarchy, which is bolstered by fictions concerning identity, is as crippling and dangerous to the "oppressor" as it is to the oppressed. For Cary, humans can only be free and live up to their full potential when they are unencumbered by social stereotypes that dictate behaviors that imperil their souls and force them to remain alienated from emotional investment in others.

摘要：爱丽丝·凯瑞对于妇女形象的刻画已经成为评论家的关注焦点之一，但是人们对其作品中所呈现的男性人物鲜有研究。朱蒂斯·菲特利与玛乔里·普赖斯锁定凯瑞作品中的男性角色，集中笔墨于男性文化如何对女性叙事者产生影响，以及如何促使爱丽丝成长为艺术家的生活历程。文学批评家着眼于凯瑞如何刻画男性在培养其雄性身份时所面临的种种挑战，此论题揭示了极具前沿性的性别意识问题，其中的某些内容还预示了现代结构主义理论。

大卫·莱维雷斯与安东尼·罗土多探讨凯瑞的小说旨在展示美国社会中的雄性原型影响。雄性原型在速写集《苜蓿角》的开篇《外祖父》一章中表现得尤为显著。凯瑞描述了在美国社会中男性如何成为主宰力量的理念，而社会所期待的男性行为通常会成为固守那些理念的男性生活的破坏性力量。凯瑞并没有刻板地将男性刻画为邪恶的父权代表，与之相反，凯瑞小说中的男性往往成为自己寻求雄性身份的牺牲品。

《外祖父》正是显示这种男性牺牲行为的代表作品。凯

9 《外祖父》中的男性身份与情感闭锁

瑞描绘了处于矛盾状态下的外祖父——一位既令人尊敬，又有各种缺点的男性形象。像故事中的其他男性一样，他屈从于社会对于男性的期望而自我闭锁。最后，就支撑小说的个体身份这方面而言，凯瑞的小说揭示了任何压制性的权力结构，尤其是父权权力结构，对压迫者和被压迫者而言都是残缺而且危险的。在凯瑞看来，只有人类不再屈从刻板的社会观念，不再忍受危及他们灵魂的行为，不再对他人保持自我感情束缚之时，才能够真正获得自由，彻底发挥他们的潜能。

Although Cary's depiction of women has been one of the most explored areas of her work, very little attention has been directed toward her presentation of manhood. In fact, the only commentary concerning Cary's exploration of this topic consists of brief moments in Judith Fetterley and Marjorie Pryse's discussion of *Uncle Christopher's* and *My Grandfather*, and these observations are made within a feminist framework that concentrates upon the effects of patriarchy on the female narrator in each story. Cary criticism has yet to gain an in-depth discussion of Cary's presentation of manliness; nonetheless, the study of manliness in Cary's works is a rich ground for study in that her characterization of males reveals a strikingly modern sense of gender, which in some cases even anticipates modern constructivist theories.

Borrowing from feminist scholars such as Simone de Beauvoir—who famously quipped "one is not born, but rather, becomes a woman" (232) —several historians of masculinity and manhood have noted that "masculinity, like femininity, is a fictional construction" and that "masculinity involves diverse and continually changing sexualities" (Murphy: 1). This illusionary nature of "true" manliness is especially evident in the nineteenth century, when the definition of manhood was contested and in transition. Growing up in post-Revolutionary America, Cary witnessed the evolution of the many definitions of "ideal manhood" proffered by different segments of the American population, and in her works she exposes the falsity of these definitions and their punitive nature on men and the social structures they inhabit.

Following the American Revolution, both American society and its writers were in the process of redefining what being a man meant in the newly established country, and this effort involved navigating the lingering influence of Puritan and European standards of manliness as well as the new emphasis on independent action and capitalistic pursuit resulting from the post-revolutionary climate of the country. This was a time of crisis for defining American manhood, and Cary, like other writers of her time, was trying to navigate these competing models in order to posit her own definition of manhood. *My Grandfather*, the opening sketch of *Clovernook*, first series, displays Cary's negotiation of this shifting definition as she exposes the inherent psychological and sociological dangers of these dominant models of masculinity.

The Evolution of Ideal American Manhood in Early America

The late eighteenth and early nineteenth century was a pivotal time for redefining manhood in the United States. The dominant concept of "ideal manhood" —in other words the stereotype by which society at large evaluated a man's quality—underwent a distinct evolution as it moved from a community-based sense of masculinity to a market place masculinity based on individual interest and competition. Masculinity scholar E. Anthony Rotundo describes early American concepts of manliness as originating among New England Puritans. Although during this time period, the Puritans "rarely used words like manhood and masculinity" (terms which didn't come into vogue until the late nineteenth century), the community did have distinct expectations and standards by which to evaluate the worth of men (10). A man's worth was largely measured by the fulfillment of duty to his family and community and "he could expect to answer to his community if he failed badly" in these duties (12). Puritans also believed that men were ordained by God to be leaders in their homes, but the role of the community was to ensure that the men did not become tyrants. In fact, although the men were granted leadership in their individual homes, they were expected to submit to the demands and needs of the community: "The ideal man, then, was pleasant, mild-mannered and devoted to the good of the community." (Rotundo: 13) He embodied many qualities, including sympathy and submissiveness that would later be considered feminine or womanly.

Nonetheless, according to Rotundo, the New England Puritans had already laid the groundwork for separate spheres ideology. Although the Puritans presented a more androgynous vision of what an ideal man and an ideal woman should be, the social expectations were that certain characteristics came more naturally to men than to women, and vice versa: "Ambition, assertiveness, and a lust for power and fame were thought to be 'manly' passions. A taste for luxury, submissiveness, and a love of idle pleasures were considered 'effeminate' passions." (11) Men were also considered to have greater reasoning power than women (11). These beliefs naturally lent themselves to the theory that men were better suited to carry on the public duties of the home and community. However, the differences between the sexes were not as seemingly codified as they would become in the nineteenth century. Although Puritan women's opportunities were more limited than that of their male counterparts, women still participated in many activities such as trade and warfare. Men, on the other hand, were discouraged from actions of selfish ambition and encouraged to submit to the authority of the community, even while some acts of assertiveness and ambition were tolerated for the good of the community. It was this flexibility in the expected code of behavior among New Englanders that opened the doors to the American Revolution and eventually to the ideal of the "Self-Made Man" (14—15).

By the latter half of the eighteenth century, the American ideal of manliness was increasingly influenced by the growing success of trade, The Great Awakening, and migration to the western frontiers. These influences, combined with the Puritan acceptance of assertiveness for the good of the community, allowed men to "throw off their belief in the virtue of submission" and prepare "for revolution" (Rotundo: 15). During the revolutionary period, "a man was one who resisted arbitrary authority, who refused submission" (Rotundo: 16). However, according to Michael Kimmel, men still justified their newly declared independence as duty to the community by freeing the newly founded country from the "tyranny of a despotic father" (18).

Two other specific ideals of manhood also faced impending change following the Revolutionary period. David Leverenz describes two competing paradigms of manhood during the colonial period: the patrician paradigm and the artisan paradigm. Inherited from European culture the patrician paradigm is based upon the aristocratic ideal of manhood and rooted in inherited wealth and land ownership. The access to education, economic privilege, and physical resources allowed the patrician male access to political and social power, and being esteemed as a man rather than a boy depended upon a man's use of these advantages for the benefit of his family and community (McCurdy: 525—526). The patrician model of masculinity was also firmly rooted in the concept of aristocratic privilege which demanded deference from the lower classes (Leverenz: 74). However, during the American Revolution, this masculine ideal came under fire. Royall Tyler, offered in his play *The Contrast*, the first American drama produced professionally, a satire of the patrician paradigm in the character Billy Dimple as "a flamboyant fop," a man of luxuries and excesses, who seeks to seduce innocent virgins with false promises of marriage (Kimmel: 15—16). Although the model of the Genteel Patriarch still had considerable influence well into the nineteenth century, characterizations like that of Tyler were not uncommon among the American public.

In contrast, the artisan paradigm is an ideal rooted in the craft guild tradition of Europe. The artisan model demanded men to be virtuous, loyal, and honest. The artisan was "stiffly formal in his manners with women" and derived his sense of worth from what he could make with his hands: "On the family farm or in his urban crafts shop, he was an honest toiler, unafraid of hard work, proud of his craftsmanship and self-reliance." (Kimmel: 16) American writers like Tyler, in his character Colonel Manly, tried to appropriate this model as an American ideal; however, in the fierce capitalistic environment following the American Revolution, this model was gradually supplanted by what would become the dominant model of American masculinity, the "Self-Made Man" (Kimmel: 16—17).

Rooted primarily in communal values rather than strict individualism, ideal manhood during these early periods also differed sharply from later models of masculinity in its promotion of male sentiment and sociability. Mary Chapman and Glen Hendler claim that during this period, "sensibility" —the ability to feel and experience others' emotions—was considered a "biological fact," a sort of sixth sense that all people, including men, had and which was just "as essential to human nature as sight, hearing, taste, touch, and smell" (4). This belief in sensibility greatly shaped the behavior and social codes of American men. Chapman and Hendler describe a male "cult of sentiment" which emerged from the belief in human sensibility and "constructed the figure of the 'man of feeling' as a male body feminized by affect, a sort of emotional cross-dresser" (3). Writers like Henry MacKenzie, Laurence Sterne, Samuel Richardson, J. W. Goethe, and Adam Smith felt that "sensibility was an ideology...encompassing the republican discourses of both manly virtue and benevolent motherhood" (Chapman and

Hendler 3), and the influence of this philosophy was evident not only in middle-class men, but also in the behaviors of powerful political figures. George Washington publicly wept when resigning his commission (Chapman and Hendler: 2), and Alexander Hamilton wrote letters to a male friend declaring his love comparing his emotions to that of a jealous lover (Crain: 5—6). As strange as these declarations may seem to modern readers, such sentiments and behaviors were common in the eighteenth century, and the dominant versions of manhood during this period reflected a more fluid and flexible range than would later become the rule. Male friendships during this century were often characterized by similar declarations of love and emotional and physical intimacy such as caressing and sleeping in beds together (Crain: 16). Men even wrote and read sentimental novels and were instrumental in establishing this genre. Sentimental novels, like Charles Brockden Brown's *Clara Howard*, and sentimental poetry by writers such as Whittier and Longfellow enjoyed widespread popularity, and according to P. Gabrielle Forman and Tara Penry, other canonical "masculine" writers such as Frederick Douglass and Herman Melville at times relied on sentimentalism in their works (Foreman: 149; Penry: 227).

The Rise of the Self-Made Man

Nonetheless, the masculine ideal that came to be the dominant model for American manhood among nineteenth century middle-class Americans was the idea of the "Self-Made Man." Leverenz notes that the image of the "Self-Made Man" or entrepreneurial paradigm of American manhood first appears in Cotton Mather's early eighteenth century account of Governor William Phips, whom Mather praises for his ability to "[quell] mutinies on his ships and how he dominated people on ship and shore" (87). Later, in the late eighteenth century, the model of the Self Made Man began to take more definite shape in the writings of Benjamin Franklin, who in his "rags-toriches" autobiography emphasized the possibilities of upward class mobility (Leverenz: 74), but the model of the Self Made Man did not become widely accepted until the nineteenth century. While earlier models of manhood were "rooted in the life of the community and the qualities of a man's character" the standard for manhood shifted "from a doctrine of 'usefulness' and 'service' to the preoccupation with the 'self'" (Kimmel: 18). Perhaps the most important cause of this change was the "market revolution" taking place in the newly founded country. The government began constructing a national system of transportation, which made trade more profitable. In the years between 1800—1840, the quantity of exported American goods tripled, the percentage of people working outside of farms grew from 17 to 37 percent, and the banking system expanded from "eighty-nine banks in 1811 to 246 five years later and 788 by 1837" (Kimmel: 22). This economic success also fueled westward expansion providing even more opportunities for individual economic gain for the adventurous. Young men no longer had to depend upon inherited wealth or trade guilds for economic success. They could earn financial independence through trade and exploration. Thus, manhood for a large part of the American population came to be defined by how well a man succeeded in financial endeavors, and the public increasingly began to believe that financial success depended more upon a man's hard work than his ancestry. However, this new hope was not without cost.

The linking of masculine identity to success in the marketplace produced considerable anxiety since such success was neither stable nor assured, and manhood had to be "proved constantly" (Kimmel: 22—23). This anxiety in turn produced an atmosphere of competition that undermined sociability among males and a change in accepted patterns of behavior. Competitive actions that would have seemed immoral and "unmanly" in previous generations became more expected and tolerated. Kimmel describes this loss of communalism in the face of competition: "Gone were the casual intimacies of boyhood. Gone too was a view that other men—coworkers and friends—could act as moral constraints on excessive behavior. Instead, other men were potential economic rivals" (55). With other men reduced to merely competition, the "Self-Made Man" also became increasingly homophobic and close same sex relationships came to be considered as "unmanly" (Kimmel: 55—56). The ideal of the Self-Made Man greatly contributed to the ideology of separate spheres. The life of the Self-Made Man was one of competition and ambition. Boys were instructed early in the expected behaviors of this new manhood (Kimmel: 55), and interaction with one's mother (and by extension all women) threatened to "feminize" boys and men (Kimmel: 56). Further, as men's success began to be determined more by their financial success than their family involvement, men began working longer hours and became increasingly detached from domestic responsibilities (Rotundo: 27).

By the end of the nineteenth century, this model of manhood dominated American culture, and its influence is felt even today. However, it was not the only model of manhood. Earlier Puritan, patrician, and artisan conceptions still wielded considerable power and influence (Kimmel: 39). Also, newer ideas based on conceptions of natural men and liberal spirituality also circulated in nineteenth century America, and individual men and writers often composed alternate versions of manhood by borrowing from various conceptions and philosophies. For example, while Emerson ultimately rejects the focus on monetary success which was the core feature of the Self-Made Man, he borrowed the individualistic emphasis of the paradigm. Despite the growing widespread adoption of the Self-Made man as an ideal, by mid-nineteenth century it was still unclear just what version of ideal manhood would emerge as the dominant discourse on manhood (Kimmel: 39).

This crisis of manhood would have been especially evident to Cary as she grew up along the outskirts of Cincinnati. At Cary's birth, the region was still considered the Western frontier. Tales of men such as Daniel Boone and Davy Crockett were idealized in the cultural imagination; however, by Cary's adulthood, the area had seen a large influx of both population and industry. These changes are particularly evident when one compares the landscape she describes in *Clovernook*, the community of her childhood, and *Clovernook, Second Series*, the community of her young adulthood. While the first series describes stubble fields, harvest, and even Native Americans, the second series discusses the view of smoke stacks, pig sties, and the birth of suburbia. These drastic changes also brought with them the market place masculinity of the Self-Made Man, an ideology Cary criticizes in its extreme versions. Instead, she stresses individual development in regard to how people, both males and females, contributed to the community at large rather than merely how well individuals provided for their own needs and the needs of their immediate families. Further, Cary does not uphold one single pre-existing model for ideal masculine behavior. Cary criticizes what she sees as shortcomings in many different models of manhood, yet she also presents most of her male characters as having admirable traits. Her works reveal that the concepts of manhood and the social behaviors expected of men were often destructive forces in the very lives of the men that these conceptions seemingly empowered. Men are not uniformly villainous patriarchs; they are victims of their own beliefs about masculine identity. *My Grandfather* clearly exemplifies this message of masculine victimization.

Emotional Distance in *My Grandfather*

My Grandfather opens with the narrator, a young woman, describing an evening at home with her parents and two brothers. During the course of the evening, Oliver Hillhouse, a miller employed by the narrator's grandfather, arrives at the house with word that the grandfather is dying. The narrator and her parents then depart to visit the grandfather. After arriving at the grandfather's house, the narrator is relegated to the care of her Aunt Cary, who leads her to the mill, where they meet up with Oliver, who reveals to Cary that he is sad to see her father's passing since he was a good man; however, Oliver is more upset about his status after his employer's death. Oliver and Cary are in love, but Oliver has heard her father say that he will not allow Cary to marry any man who is not a man of property and that her father will make her promise to agree to this stipulation if he should die. Upon returning to the house, the narrator watches while people enter her grandfather's chamber and receive last words. Finally, the narrator, hoping that her grandfather will speak to her enters his chamber. She holds his hand and kisses his forehead, but he only states, "Child, you trouble me" (24). After the grandfather's death, the family learns that Oliver has been named the heir to the entire estate on the condition that he marries Cary. The two marry and take charge of both Cary's and Oliver's mother. The narrative ends with the narrator declaring that during her life she still remembers the sorrow surrounding her grandfather's death but that death is "less terrible to [her] now" (26).

Fetterley and Pryse view the sketch as an introduction to the stories, but moreover they hold that the story is about the way in which patriarchal society dismisses the significance of the female narrator as she seeks to find her own individual voice. The narrator, according to Fetterley and Pryse, is "insignificant" in the life of her family. The critics describe the narrator's initial interaction with her brothers and parents as "playing outside while the rest of the family," particularly the male members, resides in the "circle of significance" (175). Fetterley and Pryse also note that grandfather, too, fails to acknowledge the narrator:

 Death removes the possibility that he will ever recognize or mark her; death requires her to acknowledge that she will never get his attention. Out of such loss, however, she develops the capacity to signify and the determination to be herself one who notices. (176)

Accordingly, the grandfather's final words to his granddaughter symbolize the rejection of her female identity, but the narrator's early rejection at the hands of her family, especially the male members, helps her to develop her voice as Fetterley and Pryse notice. Her silence has enabled her to notice things that others miss, including herself (176), and "marking her own significance is understandably the first act of a consciousness that would wish to mark the significance of others who have also been considered insignificant" (175). In telling her story, the narrator recognizes that she is a significant person, and in doing so she becomes a champion for others who are oppressed.

While Fetterley and Pryse's focus on the narrator's initiation into artistic life is interesting and makes some valid observations about the narrator's position in the family, the story reveals much more than merely the patriarchal oppression of a young woman. In some respects the story actually affirms the virtue of the patrician model of manhood. The grandfather's position in the family and the community reflects an almost aristocratic sense of identity. Further, like the patrician described by Leverenz, the grandfather bases his concept of manhood upon land ownership. This emphasis is evident in his directions regarding who his daughter is allowed to marry. Oliver reveals these expectations to Cary when explaining why he believes they will not be able to marry: "Almost the last thing your father said to me was, that you should never marry any who had not a house and twenty acres of land; if he has not, he will exact that promise of you, and I cannot ask you not to make it, nor would you refuse him if I did" (22). Cary's father clearly wants to make sure she marries the "right" man, and for her father, a true man is a man with property. However, the father does not allow his mandate to ruin his daughter's happiness. In a departure from the class conscious model of the patrician, which emphasizes the superiority of the aristocracy and deference from the "lower classes," the grandfather in this story accepts his worker as an heir, an equal, and since the grandfather has only daughters, he decides to leave his fortune to the man with whom his daughter is in love. The grandfather also embodies the sense of communal responsibility and ethics required by the patrician paradigm. He is a "good man, strictly honest, and upright in all his dealings, and respected, almost reverenced, by everybody" (19). This reverence is easy for the reader to imagine given the grandfather's care for the community. Even on his death bed, he has ordered that his mill continue working because in his words his neighbors "could not do without bread because he was sick" (16). The narrator also reveals an anecdote that shows the extent of the grandfather's care for his fellow community members:

> I remember once, when young Winters, the tenant of Deacon Granger's farm, who paid a great deal too much for his ground, as I have heard my father say, came to mill with some withered wheat, my grandfather filled up the sacks out of his own flour, while Tommy was in the house at dinner. That was a good deed, but Tommy Winters never suspected how his wheat happened to turn out so well. (16)

As a sort of aristocratic figure in the community, the grandfather embodies a sense of nobility. His charity is so complete, in fact, that he does not even shame Winters by telling him of the good deed done on his behalf. Instead, the grandfather quietly substitutes flour from his private store when he encounters a young man who is struggling financially with his farm.

Nonetheless, Cary ultimately paints an ambivalent picture of the grandfather. Although he is admired by his community and acts compassionately with his family and neighbors, he is cold and distant with those he cares about. Along with the patrician ideal of manhood the grandfather's conception of manhood is influenced by a frontier model of self-made manhood, which required men to distance themselves from "emotional" femininity. This distancing required self control of the "passions," a control that was not expected of women and very young children (Rotundo: 22). Consequently, the narrator does not directly feel love from her grandfather. She describes him as "a stern man who" was uncompromising and unbending, " and she recounts hiding in the mill" to escape from his cold forbidding presence (19). When the narrator attempts to comfort and be comforted by her grandfather during his last moments, he rejects her and leaves her emotionally abandoned to experience alone the "sorrow" of her first encounter with the death of a loved one. While Fetterley and Pryse focus on how the narrator overcomes the emotional neglect she faces at the hands of her family, Cary also seems to be pointing out a type of victimhood in the grandfather. Unlike the narrator, he is incapable of verbalizing his affection. The closest the grandfather comes to showing his granddaughter affection occurs when he gives her an apple:

> He was a stern man—even his kindness was uncompromising and unbending, and I remember of his making toward me no manifestation of fondness, such as grandchildren usually receive, save once, when he gave me a bright red apple, without speaking a word till my timid thanks brought out his "Save your thanks for something better." The apple gave me no pleasure, and I even slipt into the mill to escape from his cold forbidding presence. (19)

Fetterley and Pryse dismiss the tenderness of this event entirely. Focusing on his rebuke for her acknowledgement of the gift, they determine that the narrator will never receive recognition from the grandfather (175), but these critics entirely overlook the fact that this act was an act of recognition. The grandfather has singled her out and offered her a gift, albeit a small gift. However, he is unable to verbalize this recognition of his granddaughter and thus his perceived coldness drives her to run away. This inability to express himself forever distances him from those he cares about. Not only does the narrator feel emotionally cut off from her grandfather, so too do all the other people he cares about. He is not even able to reveal to Oliver and Cary his ultimate plan to preserve their happiness, so his final moments with them are tainted by fear and dread, since both Oliver and Cary seem to focus more on the prospect of being separated from one another than on their love for the patriarch, and the grandfather is left to die isolated from the fellowship of the community.

Similarly, the other males, to varying extents, face difficulty in expressing their emotions. The narrator's father seems unable to express affection for those he loves. His interaction with his family, like that of the grandfather, is close to non-existent. The only family members he verbally acknowledges are his two sons:

My brother is reading in a newspaper...he reads loud and very clearly—it is an improbable story of a wild man... "I would not read such foolish stories," says my father... little Harry, who is playing on the floor, upsets his block-house, and my father, clapping his hands together, exclaims, "This is the house that Jack built!" and adds, patting Harry on the head, "Where is my little boy? this is not he, this is a little carpenter; you must make your houses stronger, little carpenter!" But Harry insists that he is the veritable little Harry, and no carpenter, and hides his tearful eyes in the lap of my mother, who assures him that he is her own little boy, and soothes his childish grief by buttoning on his neck the ruffle she has just completed; and off he scampers again, building a new house, the roof of which he makes very steep, and calls it grandfather's house, at which all laugh heartily. (15—16)

The father's only words for his older son are words of rebuke aimed at molding him into a man. By condemning the older son's interest in "silly stories," the father perpetuates the system of silence the males of this story face, which contrasts sharply to the son's reading about the possibilities of "wild" men who live uncontrolled and uncensored lives. The father's teasing of Harry, the younger son, also seems intended to push the child out of the realm of boyhood. While his interaction with his younger son is warmer than his interaction with the older son, the father foretells the child's future manhood by assigning him the adult role of a "carpenter" as a replacement for a childhood playing with blocks. Oliver Hillhouse also seems affected by the social expectation of emotional control in men. Although he is able at one point in the story to verbally express his love for Cary, the narrator comments that the discussion between the two seems to be the first time that Oliver has ever breached the topic with Cary, and he has only done so to say farewell. Oliver's emotional restraint is also evident at the funeral when the reader compares his behavior to that of the women present. At the funeral, Oliver holds his hands folded over his chest shedding only one or two dignified tears while the women at the funeral appear "pale," sobbing, and with their faces buried in their hands (25). Oliver's closed posture signifies the emotional distance he endures while the women are able to find community and some degree of comfort in their social act of mourning.

In fact, of all the males in the sketch, the only one who seems to be so far unaffected by the code of emotional restraint is the narrator's younger brother Harry whose youth still keeps him in the realm of the feminine mother. Harry's emotional outburst and the subsequent soothing by his mother suggest the true loss that men suffer in the story. Without emotional access to the comfort of others, Cary's males are forced to bear their grief by themselves rather than overcome it and experience the simple joys of life. Eventually, little Harry will grow up to join the emotional isolation that characterizes his father, his older brother, and Oliver Hillhouse. The ultimate tragedy of the story is that the men must inevitably face emotional isolation. While females are free to voice their emotions and make intimate connections, the males, restrained by expected codes of behavior, never really connect with others. Thus they are excluded from full participation in the larger family of humanity that Cary believed was essential to a full and rewarding life.

While critics of Cary have concerned themselves mainly with a feminist viewpoint that emphasizes the experiences and oppression of women in the face of patriarchy, these critics have ignored the heart of Cary's message. Cary's fiction holds that any oppressive power structure, particularly the power structure of patriarchy, which is bolstered by Cary's fictions concerning identity, is as crippling and dangerous to the "oppressor" as it is to the oppressed. For Cary, humans can only be free and live up to their full potential when they are unencumbered by social stereotypes that dictate the behavior of people at the expense of their souls and force them to remain alienated from emotional investment in others.

Works Cited

Cary, Alice. *Clovernook: or, Recollections of Our Neighborhood in the West*. New York: Redfield, 1851.

Mary Chapman, Glenn Hendler, eds. Introduction. *Sentimental Men: Masculinity and the Politics of Affect in American Culture*. Berkeley: U of California P, 1999: 1—16.

Crain, Caleb. *American Sympathy: Men, Friendship, and Literature in the New Nation*. New Haven: Yale UP, 2001.

DeBeauvoir, Simone. *The Second Sex*. New York: Knopf, 1953.

Emerson, Ralph Waldo. "Self Reliance". *The Essential Writings of Ralph Waldo Emerson*. New York: Modern Library, 2000: 132—153.

Fetterley Judith, Marorie Pryse. *Writing Out of Place: Regionalism, Women, and American Literary Culture*. Urbana:

U of Illinois P, 2003.

Forman, Gabrielle. "Sentimental Abolition in Douglass's Decade: Revision, Erotic Conversion, and the Politics of Witnessing in *The Heroic Slave and My Bondage and My Freedom*". Mary Chapman, Glenn Hendler, eds. *Sentimental Men: Masculinity and the Politics of Affect in American Culture*. Berkeley: U of California P, 1999: 149—162.

Kimmel, Michael. *Manhood in America: A Cultural History*. New York: Simon and Schuster, 1996.

Leverenz, David. *Manhood and the American Renaissance*. Ithaca: Cornell UP, 1989.

McCurdy, John Gilbert. "Your Affectionate Brother: Complimentary Manhoods in the Letters of John and Timothy Pickering". *Early American Studies*, 2006: 512—545.

Murphy, Peter F. Introduction. *Fictions of Masculinity: Crossing Cultures, Crossing Sexualities*. Peter F Murphy, ed. New York: New York UP, 1994: 1—17.

Penry, Tara. "Sentimental and Romantic Masculinities in Moby Dick and Pierre". Mary Chapman, Glenn Hendler, eds. *Sentimental Men: Masculinity and the Politics of Affect in American Culture*. Berkeley: U of California P, 1999: 226—243.

Rotundo, E Anthony. *American Manhood: Transformations in Masculinity from the Revolution to the Modern Era*. New York: Basic Books, 1993.

10 悲凉不屈的歌者
——凯瑞诗歌集

Melancholic Singer: Alice Cary's Sentimental Poetry

高蕴华

摘要: 爱丽丝·凯瑞是美国19世纪中期的女性作家。她以大量生动描述西部乡村生活的作品闻名于美国文坛。除了随笔之外,她创作了大量诗歌作品。其诗作以哥特式描写为主要形式,以对死亡和爱情主题的表达为内核。两个主题相互交织,互为补充,构成了作家独特的死亡观和世界观。这种特点的形成与诗人的个人生活经历有极大的关联。本文以诗人的早期诗集《爱丽丝和芙波·凯瑞诗集》为研究对象,并与作家的早期个人生活相联系,分析了诗人如何在人生过程中以诗歌作为精神寄托,在生活中思索死亡,并在死亡的阴影中追寻爱情。

Abstract: As a woman writer from the antebellum American frontier, Alice Cary was well-known for her vivid description of country life in the Old West in her short stories. In addition to the regional stories, she published several collections of poetry in her life time. Her poems were characterized by the Gothic atmosphere. The essence of her poems was a mixture of death and love, demonstrating a unique perspective in a poetic meditation upon death. The formation of her uniqueness is closely connected with her early experiences in the west. Focusing on Cary's early poems as in *Poems of Alice and Phoebe Cary* and on the poet's early life, this chapter analyzes how Cary's poetry reflect on death and reveal a quest for love under the shade of death.

爱丽丝·凯瑞（Alice Cary，1820—1871），是美国 19 世纪中叶美国女作家。她出身贫寒，但是在艰难的生活环境中笔耕不辍，而且将写作作为她一生的追求。早在 1838 年，她的第一组诗歌就见诸报端，勤奋和出于对写作的挚爱，使得她之后 22 年短暂的生命中，出版了五部诗集，三部小说和三部速写集。因此，她无愧于"诗歌圣殿里的朝拜者"（Griswold：1）这一美誉。爱丽丝的诗歌颇受著名编辑、作家、批评家格里斯沃尔德的青睐，1848 年，由于他的大力举荐，爱丽丝和妹妹芙波（Phobe Cary 1824—1871）的诗歌被收录到《美国女诗人大全》中，她们得以跻身于美国诗坛，而她们的影响也由俄亥俄州的辛辛那提扩大到了整个美国。在爱丽丝·凯瑞诸多作品中，最耐人寻味的当属《爱丽丝和芙波·凯瑞诗集》（*Poems of Alice and Phoebe Cary*）。此部诗集承蒙格里斯沃尔德筹措书款并慷慨作序，最终于 1849 年结集出版。

该部诗集是由两姐妹联袂完成，它汇集了两人的精心之作。它还是一部带有自传性质的诗歌集，该诗集中的诗歌直接或间接反映了凯瑞的生活经历、感情体验和人生感悟。对读者而言，它不仅成为了解凯瑞早期个人生活和感情经历的实情记录，也可以为研究凯瑞后期众多作品打开一扇大门。该诗集共收录诗歌 134 首。其中前 89 首为爱丽丝的作品，其诗歌大多数是以个人经历为蓝本，记录了作者家乡的风土人情和由此引发的诗人对于人生的种种思考。其内容极其宽泛，其中：有对伟人的缅怀，如《济慈》（1）、《汉尼拔哀悼其兄歌》（2）、《克里奥佩特拉之死》（32）、《怜悯之爱》（36）等；有对于贫苦乡民的同情，如《孤女》（10）、《无家可归者》（11）、《孤儿谣》（85）等；有对天主的崇敬，如《巴勒斯坦》（8）、《我知主在彼处》(30)、《信徒赞歌》(32)等。诗人在创作时，也将笔触伸向了对于人生的思索和死亡的探究，如《异乡客墓志铭》(18)、《死亡》(51)、《亡灵渡夫》(78)。作为一名年轻的女性，凯瑞对人世间的情与爱也有种种梦想，她笔端流露出对纯洁爱情的向往，而对人间真情的探究发人深思。读者会发现，年轻的诗人不仅仅只有抑郁哀婉之情，在细细品读她的作品后，还可以感受到诗人灵魂深处的热情幽默与坚忍不拔。以上诸多特点中最为独特的是凯瑞对于死亡的达观态度和对感情的真挚告白，然而这两个方面并不是各自为伍，而是相互交织，相互作用，从而构成了爱丽丝·凯瑞的独特诗风。这一风格贯穿了她的整个写作生涯。读者也可以感受到凯瑞如何在生活中饮啜无处不在的死亡痛苦，如何在死神的感召下品味永恒的宁静，在身形孤寂的阴影中捕捉爱情，探索未来。

人生苦短恨悠悠

用这样的诗句总结凯瑞的前半生丝毫不为过。凯瑞出生于美国西部的农村家庭，她早年所受到的正规教育和来自家庭的文学熏陶十分有限。与同为女性的英国作家弗吉尼亚·伍尔芙（Virginia Woolf, 1882—1941）相比，她有着先天的缺憾与不足。少年凯瑞生活十分贫困。其父母只是普通的农民，爱丽丝和其姊妹在文学上的启蒙只是来自于母亲的些许影响。她们所阅读的书籍远远不及家庭生活优渥、拥有大量藏书的伍尔芙。甚至于在凯瑞的生母不幸去世后，父亲续娶的继母严厉禁止她们从事任何"她认为浪费时间的事情"。但是出于对文学的痴迷，爱丽丝和她的姐妹们只能在深夜里用碎布做成捻子，偷偷点燃油灯进行阅读和写作。几年之后，她们的继母去世，众姊妹的阅读条件才得到了一些改观，正是在这样的艰难环境中，养成了爱丽丝这种忧郁敏感的性格。年少时的困顿生活，亲人们，尤其是长姊幼妹的相继离去，在诗人的心中留下了不可磨灭的阴影和精神缺憾。在诗集的89首诗中，涉及死亡的有38首之多，其中直接以死亡为标题的有《死亡》(51)、《魂灵》(75)、

《孩童之死》(80)、《何乡栖逝者》(89) 等 8 首。这些诗以死亡为标题，刻画了不同人物在面临死亡时的种种遭遇。其余 30 余首或吊古怀今，如《汉尼拔哀悼其兄歌》(2)、《克里奥佩特拉之死》(7) 等（在《克里奥佩特拉之死》中，作者发出了这样的疑问："她的陵寝可曾奏响胜利之歌，可曾有祈祷与赞歌送这亡灵一程？"(line 5—8, stanza 3)；或哀悼故人，如作者为其逝去的姐姐罗达和早夭的妹妹露西所写的悼亡诗；或触景生情，感慨人世苍茫。在诗歌集中随处可见欧洲哥特式作品风格的影子，作品中亦出现了大量与死亡相关联的意向，例如第 14 首《爱尔达》中出现了缠绕着藤蔓的双手，从墓穴中吹出的冷风，午夜乌鸦的哀鸣等等，为整首诗营造了凄凉萧瑟的氛围；在《异乡客墓志铭》一诗中，诗人刻画了一个被遗弃的怨妇对陌生的主人公倾诉自己的悲惨遭遇，打算在自己的墓碑上留下"她心碎而死"(line 1, stanza 2) 这样的铭文告知后来人。

但是在上述诗中，作者为我们描绘的绝大多数死亡场景并不阴森可怕，更谈不上诡谲恐怖——也许诗人的本意并非刻意地营造那种令人恐怖的气氛。与那种哥特式作品中大肆渲染的阴暗场景不同的是，在她的笔下，不论是命运乖舛的孤儿（如《孤女》(10)中生活惨淡的女孩，她说道"墓冢长廊之尽头，有枕将我安然等候"(line 7—8, stanza 3)；《无家可归者》(11) 中，流离失所的人有这样一番慨叹："孤夜为伴，我将宁静之坟茔默默期盼"(line 7—8, stanza 3)；还是《孤儿爱之梦》(16) 中渴望爱情的牧羊少年，《爱尔达》(14) 中早逝的长发美人爱尔达；还是其他与死亡相关联的诗句中《生命天使》(34) 中的最后一节中，作者写道："生命风暴频频来袭，实难招架，哦，大地啊，拥我入怀，让这颗燃烧的心，渐渐冷却，永远安歇在您幽暗宁静的臂弯。"(line 1—4, stanza 9)，读者不仅没有读到如爱伦·坡（Edgar Allen Poe, 1809—1849）的恐怖小说里那番读之心生畏惧、令人却步的话语，反而可以感受到作者在谈及死亡时流露出的淡淡喜悦之情。在作者笔下，死亡不复是一种令人可怖的事情，反而成为对于凡尘世俗的解脱。在《亡灵渡夫》(78) 一诗中，主人公表达了急于与亲人相见的心情。为了渡河，她还与死神进行了一番交涉。因死神在上一年拒绝了诗人，两者相约来年再见。诗人写道："在银色的沙滩，我等候在肃穆的人生之岸，将船夫声声儿唤。"（line1—4, stanza 8）主人公一心渡河的那种急切的心情令人动容。因为诗中提到的河不是一般的河，而是冥河。这里的"船夫"即在冥河上引领世间的亡灵通向冥界的摆渡人。① 摆渡人在西方文学中是一个让人闻之色变的形象，他残酷无情，毫不徇私，虽然是长者形象，但根本谈不上亲善。然而诗人在切切呼唤之后欣喜地说："听到了，温柔的船夫，他听到了我的呼唤！"（line 1, stanza 5）用"sweet"这样美好的词语来描述让世人避之不及的亡灵渡夫，凯瑞尚属首例。此外，诗人在提及死亡的同时，反复使用了诸如"宁静"、"和平"、"永恒"等字眼，使得那些原本听上去阴森可怕的，诸如"坟墓"、"墓冢"、"坟茔"等与死亡有关的词语，也都一扫其固有的阴霾之气，沾染上了一些祥和、欢喜之气象。在她的诗中，死亡非但不是爱情的坟墓，反而是孤儿找到情之所依的最佳方式。死亡不仅使无家可归者觅到栖身之所——坟冢，更使那些离别多年的亲人重新团聚的梦想成真。也许，在幼年经历了过多的生离死别之后，诗人反倒认为死亡是人类的最终归宿。众生在上帝的指引下，不分贵贱，重新团聚后终将归于沉寂。这一关于死亡的观念在凯瑞后来的诗歌中得到进一步升华，例如在《歌谣、抒情诗、圣歌集》中的一首《临终颂歌》（*Dying Hymn*）就是描述在信仰引导下拥抱

---

① 传说冥界有四条河，其中两条河上有船夫，其一为卡戎（Charon）冥河渡神，厄瑞波斯与尼克斯之子。希腊神话中，卡戎（Charon，又叫卡隆）是冥王哈得斯的船夫，通常被描绘成长满胡须的人或老者。他不仅在冥河上摆渡，还肩负着分辨来到冥河岸边的是死者的亡灵还是不应进入地府的活人的任务，因此他也是分辨之神。其二为菲雷机亚斯（Phlegyas），菲雷机亚斯是军神阿瑞斯之子，塞萨利国王（Thessaly），他女儿科洛尼斯（Coronis，医神阿斯克勒皮俄斯的母亲）与太阳神阿波罗相恋，却因太阳神的信差白羽乌鸦胡乱说话，让太阳神误以为科洛尼斯红杏出墙而射杀她，后太阳神得知实情后就把白羽乌鸦变黑并剥夺了他说话的能力（乌鸦座）。菲雷机亚斯一怒之下，放火焚烧了太阳神在德尔菲（Delphi）的神庙，他也因此被太阳神处死，死后他成为在恨河斯梯克斯（Styx）上摆渡的船夫。根据此诗上下文，船夫应当为卡戎。

死亡和灵魂飞升的。①

两情相悦待何时

　　虽然屡遭感情的折磨所带来的巨大伤痛，使得凯瑞不断思索死亡，继而得出死亡是解脱，坟墓即家园的理念。她能够在坦然等待死神的眷顾中直面惨淡的少年时期也部分仰仗了这一理念。通常人们在大彻大悟了这一点后，往往采取消极避世的做法。古今中外，概莫如是。中国唐代诗人王维（701—761）就采取了遁世的做法。他在经历了生与死的考验后，感到生死无常，而后寄情山水，不问世事，希冀得到精神与肉体上的双重解脱。与凯瑞同时代的女诗人艾米莉·迪金森（Emily Dickenson，1830—1886）则表现得更为突

---

① 凯瑞的《临终颂歌》（*Dying Hymn*）发表于诗集 *Ballads, Lyrics, and Hymns*（1866：326）。此诗至今广为流传，特别是在互联网上被广泛引用。尤其其中四行（My soul is full of whispered song/My blindness is my sight/The shadows that I feared so long/Are full of life and light）于黑暗处见光明的哲思已经超出宗教信仰，另外因其语言之简洁凝练，成为关于死亡的经典诗句。

试译全诗如下：

Earth, with its dark and dreadful ills	大地，连同它的阴暗、可怕的苦难
Recedes, and fades away;	向后退去，消失无踪；
Lift up your heads, ye heavenly hills!	举起你们的头啊，天堂的山峦！
Ye gates of death, give way!	死亡之门噢，快快遁形！
My soul is full of whispered song	我的心里回响起曾经低吟过的歌声，
My blindness is my sight;	我眼前的景象令我目眩；
The shadows that I feared so long	我曾经长期惧怕的暗影
Are full of life and light.	现在充满活力，光辉一片。
The while my pulses faintly beat,	我的脉搏开始变弱变细，
My faith doth so abound;	我的信仰却更加强劲；
I feel grow firm beneath my feet	我感觉到永恒的绿色大地
The green, immortal ground.	在我脚下变得坚实。
That faith to me a courage gives	我的信仰给我勇气，
Low as the grave to go;	径直走，走向深深的墓坑；
I know that my Redeemer lives,	我知道救主万世永恒，
That I shall live I know.	因此我也将获新生。
The palace walls I almost see	天堂之墙已依稀在望，
Where dwells my Lord and King;	那里住着我的主啊我的王；
Oh, grave, where is thy victory?	坟墓噢，怎不见你的胜利！
Oh, death, where is thy sting?	死亡噢，你的蜇刺又在何方？

出。在发出了"死亡即永恒"（Death is eternity）的慨叹时，诗人将自己与世隔绝，过着离群索居的生活，连作品也是本着自娱自乐、打发时间的宗旨而作。与那些消极避世的人相比，爱丽丝更为坚韧勇敢。她并没有因为生活艰难、人生苦短就埋葬了自己的感情，放弃了对生活的追求。她也没有消极等待与死亡的不期而遇，而是在生活的荆棘中艰难地开辟道路，努力追求自己的幸福生活。凯瑞在家乡生活时不仅要承担繁重的家务，还要照顾年幼的弟妹。在闲暇时的写作不仅是她的精神支柱，也成为她的经济来源。离开家乡前往纽约后她努力工作，在纽约购置房产，扶助妹妹。在此期间，她一直在承受疾病带来的折磨。虽然在诗作上，她表现得阴郁顿挫，但是在生活中，她是个勇于承担责任、百折不挠的强者。

在诸多描写生死，慨叹离别的诗歌之中，有一首诗歌十分独特。它是女诗人为数不多的笔调活泼、轻松欢快的诗作。诗名为"我该对他说我爱他"（4）全诗共有六节，它在韵律上与其他的诗歌并没有大的差异，即采取"aabb"的尾韵形式。然而形式上的因循并没有破坏其内容的丰富性。从这首诗和其他几首爱情诗中，读者既可以看到凯瑞羞涩多情的一面，也可以看到另外一个充满热情，幽默风趣的凯瑞。

郭沫若在阅读了德国作家歌德的爱情小说《少年维特之烦恼》后叹道："哪个少年不多情，哪个少女不怀春。"处在青春年少时的凯瑞自然也对爱情有着种种期待和幻想。她将自己的梦想变成诗句跃然纸上。由于诗集中收录的诗歌均未标出具体的写作年份，但是依照诗集诗歌的排列顺序来看，它排在了整本诗集的第四位，由此可以推断出这首诗应当是诗人的早期作品。《我该对他说我爱他》讲述了一位陷入爱河，但因为种种原因而分手的少女的内心独白。在第一节中，少女表达了自己对心上人的倾慕之情，她想表白，但是又担心遭致对方的挖苦。"他天生傲慢又自负，会把纯真的表白挖苦"（line 2）；而造成这一切的源头就是少女的贫寒出身。"芳草地和金色的玉米田里也曾留下过我的足迹，却从未离开过生养我的这片土地。"（line 3—4）"从未生就一张伶俐嘴，只会细语与轻言，但有婉转鸟鸣来相随，胜过泠泠佳音在耳畔。"（line 1—2, stanza 3）少女在情人面前感到些许的尴尬，部分因为家庭出身，部分是因为自己讷于言辞。但是令人尴尬的事情并不止于此，因为"若是他那傲慢的母亲知晓我对他的爱,纵然略闻一二也会用难以转述的恶言把我来对待"(line 3—4, stanza 3)贫富的差距,家庭的不同成为少女迈向幸福之路的巨大障碍。

尽管受到心上人的轻慢,也可能会因为表白爱情遭到男方母亲的羞辱,少女还是继续走她的爱情之路。少女的天真单纯由此可见一斑。

当得知情人将要与她约会,为了掩人耳目,又不失去"散步途中邂逅的良机"(line 3, stanza 4),她早早地离开自己姐姐的怀抱,转而捕捉他的身影。少女和爱人共同漫步,她苦于不能表白,但又想得到爱人,她进行了大胆的假设:"窃玉偷香的亲吻该有多甜蜜!"(line 4, stanza 4)。动情的少女被恋人无情拒绝之后,由最初的羞涩转变为对爱情大胆的追求。

在凯瑞的爱情诗中,不乏为了爱情而大胆宣言的诗句。《孤儿爱之梦》中,孤儿为了和心上人常相厮守,他说道:"两颗灵魂相逢,必将感知天堂的清风!"(59—60)。尽管最终他的愿望落空,天地间只剩下他一人徘徊,但仍无损于他对恋人的纯真情感。《异乡客墓志铭》中惹得那位异乡客泪流满面的"罪魁"就是爱情。在该诗的第三节,诗人写道:"不知为何,重重心事惹来泪满襟。"(line 11—12, stanza 3)她对那位异乡人的遭遇感同身受,并给予了极大的同情。诗人接着写道:"一声叹息,一滴清泪,片语只言,已道尽她心中的秘密无限。"(line 20—21, stanza 3)

爱情如此痛苦,又如此甜蜜,它不仅影响了人们的生活,也会让人在梦中牵挂。《我该对他说我爱他》一诗中的当事人在爱情梦想被情人无情地打碎后,少女没有沉沦,也没有悲怆到难以自拔的地步。相反,她做了一个大胆绮丽的梦。在梦中"我与他并肩伫立在牧师前,他赠予的白色花冠缠绕在发间;耳边传来亲昵的呼唤声,比姐妹友人更动听!"(line 1—3, stanza 6)。然而,梦终究是梦,醒后只能发出"美梦如斯唯愿长眠不复醒"(line 4, stanza 6)的哀叹!

重新回到现实中的少女对这段不了情依然不能释怀,她声明自己的爱情纯真,并无觊觎财产的企图。"理查得·铂西拥有的广厦良田不曾将我心房走。我独独爱上了他的激情与温柔手。海边洞穴,荒漠木屋,抑或是瀚海孤帐,作我居所心亦足。"(line 1—4, stanza 6)读到此,读者眼前宛若出现了一位既憨厚多情,又热情大胆的少女形象。让读者在莞尔之时,也不由得在心中升起了对她的怜惜之情。

诗人在这首爱情诗中加入了自己对爱情的向往和对生活的领悟。即使在像这样行文欢快的爱情诗中,也出现了海边洞穴、荒漠木屋、瀚海孤帐这样带有浓厚悲戚风格的词语,可见,凯瑞从事的写作这一感情寄托,一如她本人的人生经历,已经深深烙上了挥之不去的悲凉色彩。

这一风格不仅在凯瑞的诗歌作品中有所体现,在她的随笔作品中也可以体会到这种情感。在反映作家个人生活的随笔《苜蓿角》中,对于这种感情的描写也处处可见。在第一篇《外祖父》中,作者将第一次感受死亡阴影的小女孩的心理刻画得淋漓尽致,濒临死亡的老人,古旧的磨坊,干枯的树叶,翩翩飞舞的黄色蝴蝶,无一不传递着死亡的信息。作家写道:"有多少坟茔被芳草覆盖,有多少青丝变为华发;有多少意气风发、挥斥方遒的青年,而今步履蹒跚,韶华不再;有多少只手急切地伸出去采撷玫瑰,缩回手时却是鲜血淋漓,扎满蒺藜;最可悲的是,有多少颗心因此而碎了!"然而所有这些苦痛都是必然的。作家在开篇就以沉静的口吻作了交代:"变化是大自然的法则。新旧不断交替。"世上所有由岁月带来的苦痛都是合理的,可以被人们安之若素地接受。因此,在第二篇《光影之间》作家又给读者描绘了另外一幅美丽的图景:

> 但是在黑夜与荒凉之中,同样也积蓄了力量,尽情展示出其美妙的一面,这美妙装点着生命,使其跨过一道道金门,接受火的洗礼。朝圣者,鼓足勇气,前方就是休憩胜地,它如同花冠上的点点露珠发出熠熠光亮,点亮前进的路;慢慢接近圣塔,那些枯萎的花蕾顿时绽放出美丽的花朵。姑娘们,心中虽满怀希望,却饱受失望的折磨,以致身心交瘁!整理好飘落在苍白面颊上的绺绺发丝,安心等待明天的到来;疲倦、憔悴和郁郁寡欢的人们,耐心、平静、充满希望,等待明天的来临——就像孩子一样,在黑暗中受到惊吓,脸上挂满泪水进入梦乡,醒来后发现在母亲温暖的怀中,我们都一样——活着的人、垂死之人及醒着的人,安心等待明天的来临。

对于作家而言,这种希望不是别的,就是"爱"。她写道:"生命阴影中摇曳闪烁的点点亮光中,最明亮的就是爱之光了。"作为游走在人生边缘的凯瑞,内心深处无疑渴望着爱之光辉最终会照射在她的身上。然而这种爱迟迟没有出现。作家既有对生命的眷恋,又有死亡的期盼。这两种紧密糅合的情感贯穿了诗人的一生。它们在不断交锋,又不断和解,最终奠定了凯瑞独特的诗风。

参考书目:

Cary, Alice. *Ballads, Lyrics, and Hymns*. New York: Hurd and Houghton, 1866.

Griswold, Rufus Wilmot. *Female Poets of America*. New York: James Miller, 1874.

Poems by Alice and Phoebe Cary. Philadelphia: Moss & Brother, 1850.

附录1 爱丽丝及芙波·凯瑞诗歌集目录

1. Keats……15
2. Hannibal's Lament for His Brother……19
3. The Wreck……22
4. I Would Tell Him That I Love Him……26
5. The Spectre Woman……28
6. The Past and Present……30
7. Death of Cleopatra……32
8. Palestine……33
9. Napoleon at the Death of Duroc……35
10. The Orphan Girl……37
11. The Homeless……39
12. A Norland Ballad……39
13. Morna……43
14. Alda……45
15. The Pirate……47
16. The Orphan's Dream of Love……49
17. The Blue Scarf……52
18. The Stranger's Epitaph……55

19. The Betrayal……58
20. Annuary……60
21. The Children……62
22. To Mary……64
23. The Lover's Vision……65
24. Melody……67
25. To Lucy……69
26. An Evening Tale……71
27. Sailor's Song……73
28. The Old Homestead……75
29. Lights of Genius……77
30. I Know Thou Aret Free……78
31. A Good Man……79
32. Hymn of the True Man……80
33. Hymn to the Student of Nature……82
34. Life's Angels……83
35. The Pilgrim……85
36. Pitied Love……88
37. Alone by the Tomb……91
38. Two Visions……93
39. Lost Dillie……96
40. Pictures of Memory……97
41. The Two Missionaries……98
42. Leila……100
43. The Handmaid……101
44. The Poor……102
45. Heaven on Earth……104
46. Far Away……105
47. The Better Land……106
48. First Love……107
49. The Mill Maid……108
50. Love……110
51. Death……111

52. The Charmed Bird……112
53. Pride……113
54. Missive……114
55. One Departed……115
56. Musing by Three Graves……117
57. To the Evening Zphyr……122
58. The Sailor's Story……126
59. A Lock of Hair……130
60. Visions of Light……132
61. A Legend of St. Mary's ……134
62. The Novice of St. Mary's……137
63. Helva……139
64. The Time to Be……140
65. Eloquence……142
66. To Elma……144
67. To Flora……145
68. Myrrha……147
69. To Myrrha……148
70. To the Spirit of Truth……149
71. To……151
72. The Two Lovers……152
73. Abjuration……154
74. Old Stories……156
75. Spectres……158
76. Lucifer……159
77. Be Active……161
78. Death's Ferryman……162
79. Watching……164
80. On the Death of a Child……166
81. Cradle Song……167
82. Seko……169
83. The Deserted Fylgia……171
84. Music……173

85. Orphan's Song……174
86. Bridges……175
87. Book of Light……176
88. The Child of Nature……177
89. Where Rest the Dead? ……178

附录2　文中引用索引

Death of Cleopatra

Did songs and victories roll?
And were there fervent prayer and hymn
Said for the parting soul? (Page 32)

The Stranger's Epitaph

"She perished of a broken heart" (Page 55)

The Orphan Girl

"Down on the pavement of the tomb,
There waits a quiet pillow." (Page 37)

The Homeless

"And I sit with the midnight around me,
And long for the peace of the tomb" (Page 38)

Life's Angels

Borne down and weary with life's storms,
O Earth, receive me to thy breast;
Unlock thy dim and pulseless arms,
And cool this burning heart to rest. (Page 84)

Death's Ferryman

BOATMAN, thrice I've called thee o'er,
Waiting on life's solemn shore,
Tracing, in the silver sand,

Letters till thy boat should land. (Page 162)

Hear, sweet boatman, hear my call! (Page 163)

The Orphan's Dream of Love
Two kindred spirits, when they meet,
Must surely taste the bliss of heaven! 59—60 (Page 51)
...
But sometimes, though we scarce know why,
The heart is full, and tears will come. (Page 55)
...
A sigh, a tear, a broken word,
Have left her secret more than guessed. (Page 56)

11 华尔街与苜蓿角
——《录事巴托比》和《克里斯多弗舅舅家》对工薪奴役与家庭虐待的描写

Wall Street and Clovernook in *Bartleby, the Scrivener* and *Uncle Christopher's*: Sites of Wage Slavery and Domestic Abuse[①]

Elizabeth Schultz

Abstract: Although both were written in 1853, Alice Cary's *Uncle Christopher's* and Herman Melville's *Bartleby, the Scrivener* superficially seem to have little in common. A young woman narrates Cary's story, set in Clovernook, a rural community in America's Midwest; an elderly lawyer narrates Melville's story which is set on Wall Street. However, both stories reveal the effects of a lapsed Christian democracy in an aggressively emerging capitalistic economy during mid-nineteenth-century America. Cary and Melville demonstrate how a capitalistic economy, dependent on industry, transformed domestic settings into factories and individuals into wage slaves. They demonstrate that the class inequities and oppression resulting from this new capitalism primarily affect the powerless—women and children, the poor and the

---

① This essay was first published in *Melville and Women*, Elizabeth Schultz, Haskell S. Springer, ed. (Kent, OH: Kent State University Press, 2006: 82—97). Reprinted courtesy of Kent State University Press.

11 华尔街与苜蓿角——《录事巴托比》和《克里斯多弗舅舅家》对工薪奴役与家庭虐待的描写

silenced—and lead to misery, isolation, and early death. In their conclusions, both stories suggest the cruel abandonment of the central character—a feminized man-child. Rather than ending sentimentally, however, Cary's and Melville's stories remind readers of the loss of loving and respectful relationships between parents and children and between men and women at home and at work.

摘要： 爱丽丝·凯瑞的《克里斯多弗舅舅家》和赫尔曼·梅尔维尔的《录事巴托比》两篇短篇小说同在1853年问世。凯瑞的小说是一位年轻女子讲述的以苜蓿角为背景的美国中西部乡村邻里故事。梅尔维尔的小说则借助一位年长的律师之口叙述发生在华尔街上的故事。表面上看来，两部作品没有什么相同之处。然而，两篇小说却共同揭露了美国19世纪中叶资本主义经济崛起时期扭曲的基督教民主制度所带来的后果。凯瑞和梅尔维尔的作品不仅向读者展示了建立在工业基础之上的资本主义经济如何将家园变为工厂，使家人沦为工薪奴隶；两部作品还表明，受新兴资本主义所造成的不平等和阶级压迫影响的主要是一些弱势群体——妇女、儿童、贫民和无话语权之人。他们遭受苦难，忍受孤独，甚至夭折。两部作品得出的共同结论是：小说的主人翁——女性化的男童遭到无情的抛弃！但是两篇小说不是以感伤作结，而是让读者认识到，在新兴资本主义制度下，无论在家庭还是工作场所，父母和孩子、男人和女人之间缺失了关爱与尊重。

Wall Street, the urban setting for Herman Melville's *Bartleby, the Scrivener*, and Clovernook, the rural setting for Alice Cary's *Uncle Christopher's*, are separated only geographically. Published in 1853, both stories reveal the effects of power on the powerless—women and children, the poor and the silenced—in a lapsed Christian democracy and in an aggressively emerging capitalistic economy. Although a decade later Melville and Cary would become friends in New York,① at the time of the stories' publication, Cary had only recently moved from rural Ohio to the city, whereas Melville was still living in the Berkshires in rural Massachusetts.

Examining Melville's story in relation to Cary's suggests their emphatically shared concern with class inequities and with wage slavery engendered by capitalistic production; such examination also reveals that Melville, no less than Cary, recognizes the degradations of domestic abuse. Such a comparison provides a catalyst for considering gender as a significant issue in *Bartleby* and for understanding Melville's scrivener's position, in particular, as similar to that of both women and children in antebellum American culture. Although Melville's recognition of the oppression to which industrialization and the market economy in the antebellum period subjected women does not become fully apparent until his account of women operatives in *The Paradise of Bachelors and the Tartarus of Maids*, written in 1854, the year following *Bartleby*'s publication, *Bartleby*, read in relation to Cary's story with attention to gender, can be perceived as anticipating his later revelations regarding the debilitating conditions for working women.

A comparison of *Bartleby* and *Uncle Christopher's* also provides a catalyst for interpreting and appreciating Cary as a writer whose

---

① Although Cary moved with her sister Phoebe from Ohio to New York in 1850, there is no evidence that she and Melville, who visited New York regularly during the 1850s, met during this decade. However, Melville moved his family to New York in 1863, and as Charles Hemstreet, editor of *Literary New York*, recorded in his memoirs, Melville attended the Carys' popular Sunday-evening salon in 1865, where he felt relaxed enough in their company to give a thrilling account of his seafaring days. See Jay Leyda, *The Melville Log*, Ⅱ (New York: Gordian Press, 1969: 676—677); Laurie Robertson-Lorant, *Melville: A Biography* (New York: Clarkson Potter Publishers, 1996: 485—486); Judith Fetterly, *Provisions: A Reader From 19th-Century American Women* (Bloomington: Indiana UP, 1985: 218). It is also worth noting that the house Melville acquired for his family in 1863, which had formerly belonged to his brother whom he had visited regularly prior to his purchasing it, was on East Twenty-Sixth St., while the Cary home was on East Twentieth St., making them fairly close neighbors.

social concerns extended beyond the rural and midwestern locale of her stories. It could be argued that in *Uncle Christopher's* she appeals explicitly to an elite, urban audience with values resembling those of the lawyer-narrator of *Bartleby*. As Judith Fetterley maintains, citing from Cary's preface to *Clovernook*, her story collection in which *Uncle Christopher's* appeared, "The readers Cary imagines for her work are not the inhabitants of her region, on whose sympathy she might rely, but are rather 'the inhabitants of cities, where, however much there may be of pity there is surely little of sympathy for the poor and humble, and perhaps still less of faith in their capacity for those finer feelings which are too often deemed the blossoms of high and fashionable culture'" (Fetterley, *Legacy*: 105). For Bartleby, the scrivener, as well as for *Uncle Christopher's* "poor and humble" characters, who have a feminine capacity for "finer feelings," but who are caught in a changing economic and social system, mid-nineteenth-century society had finally little sympathy and no faith in their capabilities and desires.

While *Bartleby* illuminates the impact of changes in modes of production in the nation's largest city and in the urban workplace, *Uncle Christopher's* suggests their national ubiquity by indicating how they played out in Ohio, in rural areas, and in domestic arenas in antebellum America. Cary's preface to *Clovernook* argues that "there is surely as much in the simple manners, and the little histories every day reveals, to interest us in humanity, as there *can* be in those old empires where the press of tyrannous laws and the deadening influence of hereditary acquiescence necessarily destroy the best life of society" (3). While explicitly referring to feudal Europe, Cary subversively alludes to democratic America where the press of tyrannous laws was apparent in the South's chattel slavery and the deadening influence upon humanity in the North's wage slavery, class inequities, and domestic abuse. ①

　　Critics frequently note that the subtitle for *Bartleby*— "A Story of Wall Street" —alerts the reader from the story's beginning to the importance of its setting in the nation's financial capitol in New York as well as in buildings whose inhabitants are oppressively surrounded by walls. The lawyer/narrator describes his quarters as having windows at either end, offering close-up views of walls: one set looks onto a white wall, "deficient in what landscape painters call 'life,'" while the other "commanded an unobstructed view of a lofty brick wall, black by age and everlasting shade" and, given the proximity of neighboring buildings, appeared to open into "a huge square cistern" (14). In the law office, Bartleby's desk is separated from the other desks in the office, screened off from his employer's, and placed before a small side window which gives "no view at all" (19); to his employer's consternation, he takes to standing here, as if mirroring his surroundings, in a "dead-wall revery" (29, 31). Although the lawyer believes these arrangements allow Bartleby a combination of "privacy and society" (19), it is apparent to the reader that, apparent from his employer, Bartleby's only society must be found with himself alone. From the opening description of the law chambers to the closing description of New York's Halls of Justice and House of Detention—known as the Tombs, walls function in Melville's story to immobilize and isolate, to oppress and imprison individuals. *Uncle Christopher's* also opens with a painterly description of a still life, one monolithically white:

　　The night was intensely cold, but not dismal, for all the hills and meadows, all the steep roofs of the farm-houses, and the black roof of the barns, were white as snow could make

---

① Fetterley, citing the implications of this same passage, writes that "Cary's characters experience the press of tyranny not only from parents, to whom law and custom give authority over children, but also from a class system which ensures that some people will get more than others and which identifies certain desires as being out of bounds for certain persons" (*Legacy*: 110).

them. The haystacks looked like high, smooth heaps of snow, and the fences, in their zigzag course across the fields, seemed made of snow too, and half the trees had their limbs encrusted with the pure white. (67) ... All the shawls and muffs in Christendom could not avail against such a night—so still, clear, and intensely cold. The very stars seemed sharpened against the ice, and the white moonbeams slanted earthward, and pierced our faces like thorns—...yet the wind did not blow, even so much as to stir one flake of snow from the bent boughs. (68—69)

Although the setting soon shifts to the interior of Uncle Christopher's house, the freezing cold does not abate—its immobilizing persistence has a physical as well as an emotional effect—and life for some indeed proves dismal. On entering her uncle's house, the narrator finds herself in a large room "with a low ceiling, and bare floor, and so open about the windows and doors, that the slightest movement of the air without would keep the candle flame in motion, and chill those who were not sitting nearest the fire" (72—73). This is a house whose occupants move in darkness and in cold, with the light from its few candles and the warmth of its fire absorbed by its patriarch, Uncle Christopher. Abandoned by her father in this house, the narrator can only express her dismay: "I felt as if I were to be imprisoned." (75) Both the lawyer's office and Uncle Christopher's farmhouse, evoking sterility and confinement, prepare the reader for narratives where paralysis and oppression prevail.

Michael Paul Rogin, Michael Gilmore, and David Kuebrich have argued cogently that the lawyer's office in *Bartleby* reflects the changing modes of production in antebellum America, from a household system characterized by master-apprentice relationships, to a capitalistic enterprise characterized by hierarchical, impersonal relationships in which profit and property became dominant goals (Rogin: 192—201, Gilmore: 134—135, Kuebrich: 385). Rogin, noting that the "lawyer's title, Master in Chancery, evokes the personal ties of dependence between master and apprentice," points out that antebellum employers and their supporters defended "workplaces as families" although the "routinization of work undermined the familially based set of master-apprentice relations" (194, 196). Melville's lawyer-narrator, perhaps acknowledging the absence of such familial associations which distinguished America's earlier office arrangements in his own workplace, recognizes that an office's lack of those "humanizing domestic associations" can lead a man to commit murder (36). Yet his social anxieties and ambitions repeatedly undermine his concern to introduce such "humanizing domestic associations" into the office, and ultimately lead—if not to murder—then to Bartleby's untimely death. Although the workplace in *Uncle Christopher's* is a family farm, there is a complete dearth of any such "humanizing domestic associations." By demonstrating the devastation caused by substituting productivity for nurturing relationships in this setting, Cary harshly indicts the demand for industrial and capitalistic procedures.

The lawyer identifies himself as "an elderly man" (13), "somewhere not far from sixty" (15), and Uncle Christopher is described as "a tall muscular man of sixty or thereabouts" (71). These two men of similar age were socialized in an earlier, less industrialized time, but, as their narratives reveal, their behavior indicates their response to a class-conscious and capitalistic culture. From the second paragraph of *Bartleby*, the lawyer informs the reader, by emphasizing the first-person pronoun, that he is master and owner of the workplace: "it is fit I make some mention of myself, my employés, my business, my chambers, and general surroundings" (13). Cary indicates Uncle Christopher's position on his farm from her story's title, emphasizing both his prominence and, through the title's open-ended possessive, the comprehensiveness of his ownership—the farm and all on it, both human and non-human, are ostensibly his property. His surname, Wright, suggests that he is, in the O. E. D. 's definition, "an artificer or handicraftsman, especially a constructive workman." But as Cary emphasizes repeatedly throughout her story, not only is he the rightful master by legal, theological, and social right but he has also ordained himself the righteous judge of and for all who exist on his property. In his immediate family's eyes and in his own eyes, he establishes the rites of the household; his is the right, and he is always right.

Throughout both stories, the lawyer and Uncle Christopher are represented as fathers, employers, and respectable men of society. In describing the treatment of the employees/family members by the employer/patriarch in the office/household, Melville and Cary reveal the full dysfunctionality in American relationships—among family members and between classes.① Managing others through a combination of implacable logic, sarcasm, and threats, neither the lawyer nor Uncle Christopher shows any knowledge of those beneath him in the hierarchy of relationships, and, more disturbingly, neither—until it is too late—shows any compassion.

Both men profess religious convictions, but their hypocrisy rapidly proves transparent and opprobrious. Melville's lawyer attends church on Sunday, but it appears he does so primarily "to hear a celebrated preacher," and he cannot resist dropping by his office on the way (26); he recalls Christ's injunction that "ye love one another," but with cynical logic and to his own satisfaction goes on to establish that only "self-love" prompts charity (36). Cary's narrator with grim satire explains that Uncle Christopher "was one of those infatuated men who fancy themselves 'called' to be teachers of religion, though he had neither talents, education, nor anything

---

① Fetterley maintains that throughout the *Clovernook* stories Cary "identifies the primacy of class as an operative category in supposedly democratic America". She notes, in particular, that "In asserting the primacy of class as the organizing principle of social relations in America, … Cary organizes the family as well, parents and children occupying in effect different classes" (*Legacy*: 103).

else to warrant such a notion, except a faculty for joining pompous and half scriptural phrases, from January to December" (73). The actions of both the lawyer and Uncle Christopher, motivated by narcissism, class-consciousness, and capitalistic goals, speak louder than their sanctimonious words, which serve mainly to promote their reputations.

The lawyer's apparent paternalistic attention to his employees' eating habits and his concern that Turkey be well clothed and that Bartleby not be reduced to vagrancy indicate that their employer attempts to maintain relationships in his office characteristic of earlier modes of production; it thus is possible to support Edwin Haviland Miller's position that on occasion the lawyer "acts as a nurturing parent to his clerks" (263). This parental position is contradicted, however, when he expresses his delight at Bartleby's appearing "long famished for something to copy," at his "paus [ing] for digestion" in his work, and at his seeming "to gorge himself on my documents" (19). His ostensible paternal intent also seems primarily a concern for respectability. He reproves Turkey for his "indecorous manner" (15) and thinks well of Nippers for being "not deficient in a gentlemanly sort of deportment," for being "always dressed in a gentlemanly sort of way" (17). He wants his clerks to present themselves in respectable clothes so as to "reflect credit upon my chambers" (17). Complaining that Nippers consorts with "ambiguous looking fellows in seedy coats," he presents Turkey, whose coats he calls "execrable," and whose "hat is not to be handled," with one of his own cast-off garments, one that he still deems "a highly-respectable looking coat" (17). However, he subsequently can't resist a condescending evaluation of Turkey in this second-hand apparel, in judging him as "insolent" and one "whom prosperity harmed" (18), though he fails to recognize the degree to which these judgments may apply to himself.

Early in his story the lawyer reveals his values through his idolatry of John Jacob Astor, whom Stephen Zelnick assesses as notorious "for monopoly power, for the destruction of the values of the community, for political corruption, for the emergence of an arrogant new aristocracy of wealth, for large-scale theft cloaked by the shrewd manipulation of the law, ... and for the restructured social relations that reduced a significant portion of Americans to wage slavery and economic dependence" (75). The narrator "loves" the sound of Astor's name because it "rings like unto bullion," and he himself claims to have made "a snug business among rich men's bonds and mortgages and title-deeds" (14), a business which has, to his smug pleasure, permitted him to use the wealth of others to secure his own wealth and to separate himself from social responsibilities. He not only acknowledges the superior class and authority of Astor, but he is also susceptible to the opinions of his readers, with whom he identifies in the opening paragraph as "good-natured gentlemen" (13), as well as to the degrading effect Bartleby's bizarre appearance in his chambers might have on his "professional reputation" (38) and to the fearful possibility "of [his] being exposed in the papers" (40). Robert K. Martin summarizes Melville's lawyer's position succinctly: He is "too convinced of his own generosity to see the evil and inhumanity of the system in which he participates. His situation illustrates the sterility of a law divorced from morality. His dilemma is that of the 'good boss' whose integrity is inevitably compromised. He is a jailer who can never understand that even good treatment of a prisoner cannot alleviate the fundamental fact of imprisonment" (105).

Melville's respectable lawyer, perhaps because of his urban location, appears more sensitive to the judgment of others and the matter of class than does the more isolated, rural Uncle Christopher, for whom his own patriarchal authority is primary, with class being secondary. Given that the narrator of *Uncle Christopher's*, a young, unmarried woman, has a father who pressures and manipulates her into leaving her comfortable home to journey out into the frozen landscape to visit her uncle and then abandons her at his farm, the patriarch is condemned from the beginning of Cary's story. The narrator rapidly discovers on her arrival that Uncle Christopher's attitude toward his six daughters, like herself, all unmarried, and toward his two young wards, Mark and Andrew, is not that of a nurturing parent, but of a repressive task-master and social arbiter. Using her representation of Uncle Christopher to question a self-absorbed, individualism in relation to domestic ideology as well as the impact of rising class-consciousness and changing modes of production in rural America, Cary indicates that this self-reliant man is his own sole authority: "As a matter of form, Uncle Christopher always said, I will do so or so, 'Providence permitting;' but he felt competent to do anything and everything on his own account" (76). Though his wife may regard him "not only as the man of the house, but also as the man of all the world" (75) and worship his "gift," the narrator reveals the narcissism behind his heinous sadism.

As a parent, guardian, and host, Uncle Christopher provides the bare minimum. Cary's narrator describes meals at Uncle Christopher's as occasions for him to dominate: "To the coarse fare before us we all helped ourselves in silence, except of the bread, and that was placed under the management of Uncle Christopher, and with the same knife he used in eating, slices were cut as they were required" (77). Mark, the youngest of Uncle Christopher's wards, returning late to the farm, finds that "the supper was served and removed, and not even the tea was kept by the fire for him. It was long after dark when he came, cold and hungry—but nobody made room at the hearth, and nobody inquired...what he had seen or heard during the day" (85).

The boys are dressed poorly, while the women are all dressed plainly and "precisely alike, in gowns of brown flannel, and coarse leather boots, with blue woollen stockings, and small capes, of red and yellow calico" (71). The narrator's description of Uncle Christopher's care for his own clothes and appearance, however, testifies to his personal vanity and fashion-consciousness: he was "dressed in what might be termed [a] stylish homespun coat, trousers, and waistcoat, of snuff-colored cloth. His cravat was of red-and-white-checked gingham" (71). Although he greets the narrator by informing her that "ear-rings and finger-rings, and crisping pins" are "abominable" (72), he himself is much given to personal affectations, keeping a "long grizzly beard, which he wore in full" and combing his hair "straight from his forehead, and turn [ing it] over in one even curl on the back of the neck" (71). Although he judges women's pursuit of fashion as "foolish" and "unprofitable" (72), "much time and some money he spent in [the] vindication" (72—73) of his own mode of dress. If the lawyer signifies his authority in his office by his plaster-of-paris bust of Cicero, Uncle Christopher signifies it in his household not only by "monopoliz [ing] a good portion of the light, and all the warmth" but also by the "stout hickory stick" which he holds phallically between his knees (71—72).

Both men, representatives of earlier business arrangements, have agreed to take on young apprentices although Melville and Cary imply that these traditional arrangements are subverted through the masters' commitment to aggrandizing their own profit and status. Thus the twelve-year-old Ginger Nut, whose father, "a carman, ambitious of seeing his son on the bench instead of a cart... [sent him to the narrator's] office as student at law, errand boy, and cleaner and sweeper, at the rate of one dollar a week" (18), receives no instruction whatsoever from the lawyer. Instead, on his own, Ginger Nut learns to become an independent "cake and apple purveyor" to the other scriveners. Andrew and Mark, Uncle Christopher's wards, the former, "a relation from...Indiana, who, for feeding and milking Uncle Christopher's cows morning and evening, and [tending to] the general oversight of affairs, ... enjoyed the privilege of attending the district school" and the latter, his grandson, regarded as "a wicked and troublesome boy, [who was being] subjected to the chastening influences of a righteous discipline" (76) become wage slaves in his household and learn only misery.

The lawyer claims he would have enjoyed Bartleby's being "cheerfully industrious" as he goes about the "dull, wearisome, lethargic" business of copying, but Bartleby, preferring not to be a happy wage slave, performs "silently, palely, mechanically" (20). Silence is emphatically maintained in Uncle Christopher's shop. As he "talked, and talked, and talked" (73), he determines when others may or may not speak. The narrator comments repeatedly on the prevalence of silence in this household and the absence of laughter. Declaring imperiously that "Much speech in woman is as the crackling of thorns under a pot" (72) and that "It is better to dwell in the corner of the housetop, than with a brawling woman" (75), Uncle Christopher enforces silence from the women in his family in particular. His command to his wife—Woman, fret not thy gizzard!" (81) —in response to her momentary lapse into sympathetic self-expression—might be considered were comic it not so vicious. In this household, words are not spoken, but recited mechanically, and the mew of a kitten is regarded as an interruption. Uncle Christopher's voice thus becomes even more than dominant here. The narrator, who finds that "the shut mouths and narrow foreheads of the seven women grew hateful," ultimately breaks the silence imposed upon them all by telling their story and the story of this household.

To a degree, as indicated above, the lawyer accommodates his scriveners in managing his workplace. In consideration of Turkey's age, the same as his own, he retains him in service. It can also be argued that he paternally runs his office according to the humors of his two copyists, permitting Nippers' morning dyspepsia to balance Turkey's afternoon alcoholic paroxysms. However, Melville demonstrates that the lawyer keeps his distance from his employees, removing himself from them by screening himself from Bartleby, by referring to his three long-time employees only by their nicknames, and by reducing Turkey to servility at the thought of his possible dismissal. Pleading his case by observing that he and the lawyer are the same age, Turkey introduces his claim three times with the phrase, "With submission, sir" (16), indicating his sensitivity to his employer's need to feel empowered as well as his own powerlessness. The lawyer confirms his conviction of his own superiority, control, and ownership of his employees by evaluating them in the degree that they are "valuable" (15) or "useful" (17, 23) to him.

As critics also frequently note, by accommodating his scriveners' humors, he guarantees the mechanical production of efficient, rapid, and uniform copies. In describing this procedure, the lawyer indicates that he runs his office with mechanical and military efficiency: "Their fits relieved each other like guards. When Nippers' was on, Turkey's was off, and vice versa." With self-satisfaction, he concludes that "This was a good natural arrangement" (18). Although his methods cause his office to malfunction, the lawyer fails to note that nothing at all "natural" exists in any of the arrangements in his work place, and despite his ostensible attempts to accommodate his workers, he manages only to create a malfunctioning human machine in his office, transforming the labor of two men into that of one and depriving them both of individual dignity.

There is no degree of accommodation in the factory into which Uncle Christopher has converted his home. As patriarch and boss, he is, until the story's conclusion, a hard-driving, single-minded proto-capitalist, unlike the lawyer who occasionally expresses concern for his scriveners. Unstinting routinization, mechanization, uniformity, and silence, however, determine the lives of the inhabitants at Uncle Christopher's. Despite his proclamations of his competence and self-reliance, it is apparent that the women and children tend to the entire work of the household: we read that "in the genial warmth [of the fireplace] sat Uncle Christopher, doing nothing" (76), or "the family rose before daylight, and moved about by the tallow candles, and prepared breakfast, while Uncle Christopher sat in the great arm-chair, and Mark and Andrew fed the cattle by the light of a lantern" (84). The toll this work takes on the women of the household is evident as it consumes their individuality and humanity; on her arrival at the farm the narrator notes that they

> ...so closely resembl [ed] each other, that one could not tell them apart; not even the mother from the daughters...All seven were very slender, very straight, and very tall; all had dark complexions, black eyes, low foreheads, straight noses, and projecting teeth; ...They had staid, almost severe, expressions of countenances, and scarcely spoke during the evening. By one corner of the great fireplace they huddled together, each busy with knitting, and all occupied with long blue stockings, advanced in nearly similar degrees toward completion. (71)

While the indolent Uncle Christopher delivers "a homily on the beauty of industry" (78) the morning after her arrival, the narrator observes the women in his family take up their tasks, "untwist [ing] seven skeins of blue yarn, which they wound into seven blue balls, and each at the same time beg [inning] the knitting of seven blue stockings" (79). The seven women at Uncle Christopher's become parts of a smoothly functioning machine.

With the exception of Mrs. Wright and her youngest daughter, these women are denied any trace of individuality: they have neither names nor voices, with Uncle Christopher addressing his daughters in the collective as "maidens" or "the daughters of our house."

11　华尔街与首蓿角——《录事巴托比》和《克里斯多弗舅舅家》对工薪奴役与家庭虐待的描写

Embodying all the primary virtues of the Cult of True Womanhood—piety, purity, submission, and domesticity, they become in Uncle Christopher's house, not the angels who inhabit the houses of other antebellum writers, but caricatures of womanhood. In this household, those who dare to express themselves are suppressed into conformity: Andrew, dismayed by Mark's ill treatment, reverts to a mechanical reading of dictionary definitions; Mrs. Wright conceals her instinct for kindness in "obsequious servility" (81) to her lord and master. The narrator, a guest in this stultifying household, feels pressured into working "diligently all the day, though [she] fail [s] to see the use or beauty of the work on which [she] was engaged" (79). Thus, as she notes, life here becomes a commitment to silent, mechanical, and uniform production: "There was no variableness in the order of things at Uncle Christopher's, but all went regularly forward without even a casual observation, and to see one day, was to see the entire experience in the family." (75)

All the cogs do not run smoothly, however, in the machinery of the lawyer's office and of Uncle Christopher's factory-household. The lawyer's office, in which two men do the job of one, clearly is not a model of efficiency. However, Bartleby and Mark, new additions to their workforces, reveal the more serious flaws of these proto-capitalistic sites to the reader. Bartleby ultimately prefers not to work and not to speak to the lawyer. Mark tells the narrator that he does not like his grandfather (82), and as she observes, "he was, for the most part, sulky and sullen, and did reluctantly that which he had to do, and no more" (83—84). Though Bartleby is described as "a young man" (19) and Mark as a boy of ten or twelve, Bartleby seems boyish, while Mark seems old for his years. Cary's narrator, while repeatedly emphasizing the importance of play, laughter, and love in a child's life, informs the reader that Mark is forced into early manhood: he is described as acting "manfully" (70, 81); he is "thoughtful beyond his years" (74); and "in all ways he was expected to have the wisdom of a man—to rise as early, and sit up as late, endure the heat and cold as well, and perform nearly as much labor" (83). Slight in stature, both Bartleby and Mark border on physical starvation. Bartleby must feed himself, but has little money for food, and in the last stages of his life, when food is placed before him, chooses to eat nothing at all,① whereas Mark is consistently deprived of nourishment.

Initially both Bartleby and Mark seem determined to belong to the company team. They want to be considered respectable and to rise socially. In first meeting Bartleby, the lawyer notices that he was "pallidly neat, pitiably respectable, incurably forlorn" (19).② Bartleby's persistent defiance, to his employer's surprise, remains devoid of "uneasiness, anger, impatience or impertinence" (21). Whether understood in political, psychological, or philosophical terms, whether interpreted as a statement of self-assertion or passive resistance in the guise of deference, Bartleby's deferential "I prefer not to," as much as Turkey's "With submission, sir," emanates from polite society. Acknowledging that Bartleby was "an eminently decorous person," the lawyer can't imagine that his scrivener would "violate the proprieties" of Sunday by working

---

① Gillian Brown argues that Bartleby's refusal to eat is comparable to the behavior of an anorexic: "almost always a woman…, [s] he maintains in her body the fantasy of domesticity Bartleby enacts: a perfect self-enclosure. While anorexia hardly seems an ideal condition, it is the fulfillment of the ideal of domestic privacy, a state in which complete separation from the demands and supplies of the world is attained." "The Empire of Agoraphobia" in *Herman Melville: A Collection of Critical Essays*, Myra Jehlen ed. (Englewood Cliffs: Prentice Hall, 1994: 145).

② Remembering "the bright silks and sparkling faces I had seen that day, in gala trim, swan—like sailing down the Mississippi of Broadway" a vision of wealth and style testifying to capitalistic success, the narrator expresses his own melancholy and alienation from society, thus momentarily identifying with Bartleby and concluding, "For both I and Bartleby were sons of Adam" (28). It is noteworthy, however, that although the sons of Adam, generically, are all men, of his immediate offspring, one was Cain.

(27) —although he has no apparent qualms about doing so himself. However, as if to assure himself of Bartleby's respectability, the lawyer actually scrutinizes and itemizes his scrivener's pitiable attempts to keep up appearances: "Rolled away under his desk, I found a blanket; under the empty grate, a blacking box and brush; on a chair, a tin basin, with soap and a ragged towel." (27) Rooting more deeply among Bartleby's belongings, and justifying his voyeuristic actions by asserting, "the desk is mine, and its contents too" (28), the lawyer finds a savings' bank. Evidence of the scrivener's determination to survive economically and perhaps of his desire to rise socially, the bank would provide him the means for improving his "pitiably respectable" appearance. Yet, the lawyer will later refer deprecatingly to Bartleby's belongings as "his beggarly traps" (33). Bartleby's endeavors to maintain a standard of social respectability, the lawyer scorns by sarcastically referring to his "cadaverously gentlemanly *nonchalance*" (27), and when the gaoler at the Tombs suspects that Bartleby is "a gentleman forger," he is quick to disassociate himself from Bartleby, superciliously asserting that he "was never socially acquainted with any forgers" (44). Although the professional copyist engaged in legal occupation in the nineteenth century, as one who imitated original documents, he might be associated with forgery. In this sense, the lawyer, in dismisses Bartleby from his social register and from society at large, denies a relationship with all of his scriveners as well.

While Bartleby at least initially manifests a commitment to maintain the appearance of respectability and to participate in a society organized by production, Mark actively attempts to pull himself up by his economic bootstraps into social respectability, with results as pitiable and futile as the scrivener's. Knowing that "money buys new things" (75), he struggles through chores and through small sales to earn a little, but he loses his earnings, once because of his own naiveté to some older boys and once because of his uncle's taking it from him as a fatuous and arbitrary moral lesson.

Mark's disappointment in losing his hard-earned cash, as he explains to the sympathetic narrator, derives from the specific fact that "once he had enough money to buy ever so many clothes" (83). Appreciative of the linen the narrator hems, which he notes is "fine and pretty" (85), and acutely sensitive to his own "homely and ill-fitting garments" (83), he grieves that he cannot leave his present status because of his lack of appropriate and respectable dress. In this rural setting, although Mark may express "those finer feelings which are deemed the blossoms of high and fashionable culture," that his desires are literally so dependent on fashion suggests their desperation and limitation. Unlike Cary's narrator, who has created art from her restricted surroundings, he cannot perceive this as an option.

Dependent on their economic and social superiors, both Bartleby and Mark are suppressed in their position of social inferiors; consequently emotional starvation shapes their psyches as physical starvation shapes their physiques. Though Bartleby does not suffer the sadistic extremes of physical cruelty from his boss that Mark does from his grandfather—isolation outside in freezing temperatures, deprivation of food, whippings, incessant verbal abuse and humiliation, he is, like Mark, subjected to psychological cruelty. Both Bartleby and Mark must know that they are evaluated in relation to property rather than as human beings. Thus, the lawyer not only perceives his scrivener as "a valuable acquisition" (26) and "a millstone" (32), but he also tries to buy him off (33) and seeks to dislodge him by demanding, "What earthly right have you to stay here? Do you pay any rent? Do you pay my taxes? Or is this property yours?" (35). Mark, too, is conscious that his failure to produce income is directly responsible for his suffering. Because his earlier naiveté resulted in the loss of his earnings, he was punished by being sent to his grandfather. When he subsequently demonstrates his ability to earn money, however, his grandfather, instead of praising him, claims Mark's money for his own self-promoting and sanctimonious projects.

Melville and Cary also represent Bartleby and Mark in positions similar to those of women in antebellum America, thus challenging gender construction as well as domestic ideology. Melville's sisters, Augusta and Helen; his wife, Lizzie; and for some of his later writings, his daughters, Fanny and Bessie, toiled to produce legible copy from his manuscripts. Melville, consequently, was familiar with the plaints of the women scriveners in his own household, engaged in the endless reproduction of his words, a point Elizabeth Renker discusses in her study, *Strike Through the Mask: Herman Melville and the Scene of Writing*.① Even though, as Renker's argument implies, he might have understood the lawyer's frustrations with Bartleby's resistance, he writes in sympathy with the working women in *Pierre, or the Ambiguities*, his novel of 1852,② and of the women operatives in "The Paradise of Bachelors and the Tartarus of Maids," his story of 1855. In a single explicit reference in *Bartleby* to the lawyer's cleaning woman who lives in the attic over his chambers (26),③ Melville also indicates his sensitivity to women's lives and work and to the limitations imposed on lower-class women in his day. Reduced to subservient positions as domestics, poor women without families become nameless drudges and, like Bartleby, eke out solitary existences in their

---

① Elizabeth Renker notes that *Bartleby* was copied by Augusta. More significantly she discusses the stress that copying duties placed upon the Melville women, citing a letter from Lizzie to her stepmother, dated August 3, 1851: "I cannot write any more it makes me terribly nervous I don't know as you can read this I have scribbled it so." *Strike Through the Mask: Herman Melville and the Scene of Writing*. Baltimore and London: Johns Hopkins UP, 1996: 64—65.

② When Pierre moves to the city, in financial destitution, he becomes dependent upon the services of three women—Delly, Isabel, and Lucy—even as they are dependent on him.

③ She may be connected to those antebellum women discussed by Sandra M. Gilbert and Susan Gubar in *The Madwoman in the Attic: The Woman Writer in the Nineteenth-Century Literary Imagination*. New Haven and London: Yale UP, 1979.

workplaces.

Both Patricia Barber in her neglected 1977 essay, *What If Bartleby Were a Woman?* and Gillian Brown in her 1987 essay, *The Empire of Agoraphobia* provocatively feminize Melville's scrivener, allowing readers to perceive him in the housebound context of antebellum American womanhood. Barber associates the passivity of Bartleby's resistance with a general concept of femininity① whereas Brown explicitly identifies his immobility with a nineteenth-century agoraphobia, associated with women's private sphere: "Reproducing the enclosure and stillness of home in the deportment of the individual, agoraphobia approximates domesticity, often proclaimed the nineteenth-century antidote to commercialism. ... Bartleby presents an extreme version of such a model: in his 'long-continued motionlessness' he achieves an 'austere reserve,' the ideal of domesticity within Wall Street." (142) The silence that Bartleby maintains in the lawyer's presence may be interpreted as a response to the oppression of his work and of his environment as well as to the absence of communication in the office; it also mirrors the silence imposed upon women in antebellum patriarchal households such as Uncle Christopher's.

In addition, Bartleby's habitual tidiness, in conjunction with his endeavor to set up housekeeping in the lawyer's office, displays the domestic inclinations expected by the dictates of the Cult of True Womanhood. When the lawyer inadvertently discovers Bartleby in "a strangely tattered dishabille" (26) at the door of his office, and apparently in charge and at home, he feels himself "unmanned" (27) and unable to answer Bartleby's mildness with the vigor—and

---

① Barber asks her readers to imagine Bartleby as a woman secretary in a modern office and, subsequently, writes her essay with "Miss Bartleby" in mind. See "What If Bartleby Were a Woman?" in *The Authority of Experience: Essays in Feminist Criticism*, eds. Arlyn Diamond and Lee R. Edwards (Amherst: U of Massachusetts P, 1977: 212—223).

possibly the violence—that he might use in responding to another man. This evident gender anxiety leads him not only to speculation about the possibility of Bartleby's appearing "in a state approaching to nudity" (27)① but also to his proprietary and voyeuristic investigation into his scrivener's paltry belongings. His masculinity thus threatened, the lawyer responds with gestures signifying his determination to categorize humanity by gender as well as by class and to dominate those his class consciousness authorizes him to deem beneath him—women and his employees. Although Melville would deconstruct gender categories in his creation of Bartleby, his narrator, in his anxiety, vigorously reconstructs them.

Mark's determination to progress socially and economically, in resembling that of other young men, differentiates him from the passivity of Uncle Christopher's daughters.② He is, however, aligned with the "finer feelings" of sentiment a feminine gender attribute entirely repressed in them. Like Bartleby, he also exacerbates the desire of a powerful male to manage and control his life. Ostensibly attempting to eradicate the feminine in him and to make a "man" of him, Uncle Christopher literally seeks to freeze the boy's sensitivities; he treats Mark's frostbitten fingers and toes, cracked and bleeding from his ostracism in the barn, by sending him back out into the snow; he requires the destruction of the kitten Mark had tenderly placed in an old hat by the kitchen fire by demanding that he throw the creature into an old stone well. As

---

① Although Barber also calls attention to the erotic undertones in the story (217, 219), she completely skirts the issue of homosexuality, indeed giving a decided homophobic cast to her essay: "If little of this erotic quality seems apparent in the tale of the male Bartleby, there are, I think, two explanations—one, that the lawyer' propriety and language tend to lead us away from seeing that element, and two, the more important, that we simply do not expect to find a man having an erotic feeling for another man, no matter how familiar we are with Melville's scene of Ishmael and Queequeg in bed" (221—222).

② Fetterley asserts that in *Clovernook*, "Being male or female does not give one more or less chance of escaping rustic circumstances" (*Entitled to More*: 105).

Bartleby sabotages his boss' demands through feminine passivity and silence, Mark sabotages his master's demands, but through feminine action and sentiment. He saves the kitten with fierce resolve; acting maternally, he contrives the means of placing the creature, more defenseless and small than he, on a secure ledge in the well and shares his meager helpings of bread with it. Mark also circumvents his grandfather's insistence on ostracism and his command for silence. With Andrew and with the narrator, whose empathy and affection for the boys dissolves class and gender differences, and unlike the forlorn Bartleby, he discovers the "delight of communicating... his little joys and sorrows" (82), of sociability among those he trusts as they work together over domestic chores.

In challenging an oppressive economic, class, and gender system, both Bartleby's and Mark's protests are ineffectual in so far as their own lives are concerned.① Melville and Cary leave the nature of their deaths open-ended, allowing readers to consider the possibility that Bartleby and Mark finally choose suicide as the sole means by which they can ameliorate their situations. Betrayed by their surrogate fathers, their employers, and the men in their lives, they reject them unconditionally and die in the process. Bartleby dies in the cistern-like Tombs, "[s] trangely huddled at the base of the wall, his knees drawn up, and lying on his side, his head touching the cold stones" (44). Mark, rather than the kitten, dies at the bottom of the stony farmhouse well. Only in their deaths do the men responsible for their well-being, cross class and gender lines, to reach out in gestures of love: the narrator touches Bartleby as he lies

---

① Martin argues that "Bartleby the wage slave of meaningless work can only triumph by destroying himself" (105), and Rogin notes that "Bartleby punishes the lawyer by punishing himself" (195). Brown sees that "[i] n the logic of anorexia's perfection of agoraphobia," Bartleby's death is "the best method of self-preservation (148).

in what is clearly a fetal position, and Uncle Christopher "lifted the lifeless form of the boy into his arms, where he had never reposed before" (89).

When it is too late, when Bartleby and Mark are dead and imagistically infantilized, both Melville and Cary tug at the reader's sentimental chords. Through the sentimental words with which he concludes the scrivener's story— "Ah Bartleby! Ah humanity!" (45) —as well as through the penance of his telling the story itself, the lawyer may exorcise Bartleby's pale ghost and his own guilt. ① Cary's Uncle Christopher—now "softened and contrite" (89) —is described as more overtly repenting; yet, ever conscious of his appearance, he ostentatiously orders the costliest of coffins for the poor boy's burial. The turn toward sentimentality in the conclusions of both *Bartleby, the Scrivener* and *Uncle Christopher's* does not dispel the inequities and oppressions generated by the development of a capitalistic production system and its accompanying domestic ideology. It does, however, suggest both Melville's and Cary's anxieties for what has been lost and what possibly may be retrieved: loving and respectful relationships among men, between parents and children, and between men and women—at home and at work.

Works Cited

Barber, Patricia. "What If Bartleby Were a Woman?" // *The Authority of Experience: Essays in Feminist Criticism*. Arlyn Diamond, Lee R Edwards, eds. Amherst: U of Massachusetts

---

① Barbara Foley maintains in "From Wall Street to Astor Place: Historicizing Melville's *Bartleby*" (*American Literature*, 72.1 (March 2000]) that "The lawyer's irrational clinging to the scrivener— 'him whom I had so longed to be rid of' (39) —takes shape not only as a subliminal recognition of his felt moral implication in the scrivener's fate but also, we may speculate, as a covert expression of the author's own implication in the fates of those who died at Astor Place" (109).

P, 1977.

Brown, Gillian. "The Empire of Agoraphobia" in *Herman Melville: A Collection of Critical Essays*. Myra Jehlen, ed. Englewood Cliffs: Prentice-Hall, Inc, 1994.

Cary, Alice. *Uncle Christopher's* in *Clovernook Sketches and Other Stories*. Judith Fetterley, ed. New Brunswick and London: Rutgers UP, 1987.

Fetterley, Judith. "Entitled to More than 'Peculiar Praise': The Extravagance of Alice Cary's *Clovernook*". *Legacy*, 10.2, 1993.

"Preface to *Clovernook: or, Recollections of Our Neighborhood*" in *Clovernook Sketches and Other Stories*. New Brunswick and London: Rutgers UP, 1987.

Provisions: A Reader From 19th-Century American Women. Bloomington: Indiana UP, 1985.

Foley, Barbara. "From Wall Street to Astor Place". *American Literature*. 72.1 (March), 2000.

Gilmore, Michael. *American Romanticism and the Marketplace*. Chicago and London: U of Chicago P, 1985.

Kuebrich, David. "Melville's Doctrine of Assumptions: The Hidden Ideology of Capitalist Production in *Bartleby*". *NEQ*, 69.3 (September), 1996.

Gilbert, Sandra M, Susan Gubar. *The Madwoman in the Attic: The Woman Writer in the Nineteenth-Century Literary Imagination*. New Haven and London: Yale UP, 1979.

Leyda, Jay. *The Melville Log*, Vol. II. New York: Gordian Press, 1969.

Martin, Robert. *Hero, Captain, and Stranger: Male Friendship, Social Critique and Literary Form in the Sea Novels of Herman Melville*. Chapel Hill: U of North Carolina P, 1986.

Melville, Herman. "Bartleby, the Scrivener: A Story of Wall Street". //*Piazza Tales*. Harrison Hayford, Alma A MacDougall, G Thomas Tanselle, ed. Evanston and Chicago:

Northwestern UP and the Newberry Library, 1987.

Miller, Haviland Miller. *Melville: A Biography*. New York: George Braziller, Inc, 1975.

Renker, Elizabeth. *Strike Through the Mask: Herman Melville and the Scene of Writing*. Baltimore and London: Johns Hopkins UP, 1996.

Robertson-Lorant, Laurie. *Melville: A Biography*. New York: Clarkson Potter Publishers, 1996.

Rogin, Michael Paul. *Subversive Genealogy: The Politics and Art of Herman Melville*. New York: Alfred A Knopf, 1983.

Zelnick, Stephen. "Melville's 'Bartleby, The Scrivener': A Study in History, Ideology & Literature. *Marxist Perspectives*, 2 (Winter, 1979/1980).

12 普救派,福音派与虐童
——凯瑞在《彼得·哈瑞斯》和《克里斯多弗舅舅家》中对儿童抚养的宗教批判

Universalism, Evangelicals, and Child Abuse: Cary's Religious Critique of Childrearing in *Peter Harris* and *Uncle Christopher's*

Jane M. Galliher

Abstract: Cary's portrayal of children and childhood works both with and against the popular stereotypes of her time and is much more complex and nuanced than readers would typically guess upon first reading. Motivated by her Universalist belief in the fatherhood of God and "brotherhood" of all humans, Cary's works expose the dangers faced by nineteenth-century children—dangers that result, in part, from popular ideologies concerning the nature of childhood. One of the most obvious themes that appear in Cary's writing is her critique of child abuse, especially when it occurs in the name of religion. While evangelical families on the frontier typically practiced physical punishment to shape their children from "animalistic" and "immoral" creatures to upright Christians, Cary exposes these practices as religiously motivated child abuse. In both *Uncle Christopher's* and *Peter Harris* this abuse results in the death of a child. Cary also assesses the more liberal ideology of the angelic child that had begun to emerge in her lifetime. Despite

Cary's apparent acquiescence to the Romantic view of children as moral saviors or Christ-figures, Cary actually questions both the need and effectiveness of child sacrifice. Further, Cary exposes the dangerous class dichotomy that arose from this liberal ideology. While the middle and upper classes came to adopt the Romantic conception of childhood in regard to their own children, the children of the working class became demonized. In contrast, in sketches like *Peter Harris* Cary portrays working-class children as some of the noblest characters in her fiction. The sketch takes on larger significance as the title character becomes a metaphoric portrayal of racial injustice as well. In accord with Universalist beliefs on the equality of all races, Cary uses racialized references to Peter in order to express her disdain for slavery and ethnic prejudice and to expose the artificiality of the black/white race dichotomy. Further, Cary's inclusion of Peter as an actual family member (as opposed to merely an orphan who shows up on the family's doorstep) also points to her Universalist upbringing which held that all people, including black slaves, were part of the "brotherhood of man." While Cary's depictions may not be completely without prejudice, she does attempt to act upon her Universalist beliefs to sympathize with and protect those she views as defenseless.

摘要：凯瑞对于儿童以及孩童世界的描写与作者所处时代的流行看法既有吻合又有抵牾之处，远比读者在初次阅读时的泛泛揣测复杂微妙得多。在"天父"之下皆"兄弟"的普救思想指引下，凯瑞的作品展示了生活在19世纪的儿童所面临的危害——那危害从某种程度上而言，是流行的针对儿童天性的主导意识造成的。凯瑞的作品中常常出现的主题之一就是批判虐童行为，尤其是打着宗教名义实施的虐童行为。在拓荒地区信奉福音派的家庭通常实施体罚，以使孩子守规矩，并使他们摆脱"兽性"和"不道德"的天性,从而成长为正直的基督徒。凯瑞揭示出这些做法实际上是宗教动机下的虐童行为。在《克里斯多弗舅舅家》和《彼得·哈瑞斯》两篇作品中,这种虐童行为导致了儿童的死亡。凯瑞的作品也反映了在那个时代出现的视儿童为天使的自由派理念。尽管凯瑞似乎默认把儿童当成道德的救赎者或基督形象的浪漫观点,但实际上她对牺牲儿童的必要性和所起的作用提出了质疑。此外,凯瑞还揭示了由自由派思想提出的阶级二分法的危害性。中上阶层倾向于接纳自由派思想中关于他们后代的浪漫理念,而工人阶层的儿童则被妖魔化了。与之相反,在《彼得·哈瑞斯》这类速写作品中,凯瑞将最高贵的品质赋予劳动阶层的儿童。在对主人公的描写中,本篇速写以隐喻方式刻画了种族不公,因而具有更重要的意义。凯瑞遵循普救派的种族平等的信条,描写彼得时使用了种族化的指代,以表达她对奴隶制和种族偏见的不屑,同时揭示了黑白人种的二分方式绝不是天经地义的。此外,凯瑞将彼得当做真正的家庭成员,而不是放在家门口台阶上的孤儿。表明她曾接受过普救教派教育,相信全体人类,包括黑人奴隶,都是"人类兄弟大家庭"的成员。尽管凯瑞的作品尚无法全面摒弃偏见,她至少尝试推行她的普救思想,同情并主张保护那些她认为无力保护自己的人们。

The nineteenth century was a time of flux in American culture as Americans, faced with the industrial revolution and the subsequent urbanization of the country, were attempting to redefine gender and familial roles. One of the most significant cultural transformations taking place was that of the American concept of childhood, and during this period the legal and social status of children was undergoing radical alteration. Responding to these changes, Cary engages this cultural redefinition; however, not one Cary critic has really addressed Cary's presentation of children as a response to her historical context. In fact, analyses of Cary's depictions of children and childhood have most often been subsumed in a discussion of class. For example, Elizabeth Schultz, in her analysis of *Uncle Christopher's* states that Cary shares with Herman Melville "a concern with class inequalities and with wage slavery engendered by capitalistic production" (82). Judith Fetterley and Marjorie Pryse also conflate the issues of childhood and class declaring that in Cary's fiction, "parents form one class and children another" (299). In truth, Cary does display an awareness of class in her works as she populates her fiction with a variety of personages living in a socially stratified society. She reveals this preoccupation with class in the preface to her second collection of *Clovernook* sketches when she expresses concern about both the public's lack of "sympathy for the poor and humble" (Ⅵ) and the prejudicial stereotypes which characterize the rural farming classes as "different," "inferior," and "entitled to only... peculiar praise" (Ⅶ). In contrast, she states a desire for representing the rural farming class as they actually are rather than as conforming to the stereotypes presented by the "masters of literature" (Ⅵ). Nonetheless, reducing Cary's depictions of child abuse and neglect to class commentary, as critics like Fetterley and Pryse have done, undermines Cary's interest in her culture's redefinition of childhood and her concern over the mistreatment of children. Further, in interpreting family dynamics merely as class dynamics, these critics ignore the way in which the children in Cary's texts sometimes function metaphorically to enhance her religious ideals. Indeed, Cary's presentation of childhood is one of the most important aspects of her fiction because she portrays childhood in both a literal and a metaphoric fashion, particularly in the sketches *Peter Harris* and *Uncle Christopher's*. As a Universalist writer holding the belief that all people regardless of age, class, or race are a part of the family of God, Cary uses her portrayals of children to criticize both the evangelical attitudes toward childhood and the newly emergent liberal approaches to childrearing, and she also presents childhood as a metaphor for people of other races, whom she depicts as children of God—children who are in need of both protection and guidance.

At the heart of Cary's critique regarding the treatment of children is her belief in Christian Universalism. While most frontier children were typically raised in evangelical homes, Cary's early religious and moral education, according to Mary Clemmer Ames's biography, was provided by Universalist teachings. Therefore, Cary's religious alternative is not the evangelical Christianity at the heart of most sentimental works. The friction between evangelical and Universalist teaching and practices, especially during the first half of the nineteenth century, was quite pronounced. Having emerged from a liberalized form of Calvinism, Universalists publicly rejected and openly criticized the evangelical doctrines of Arminian theologians and preachers, who were characterized as irrational "soul hunters," and instead embraced the concept that a sovereign God, rather than a person's individual choice, led people to repentance (Bressler: 56).

Universalism was highly influenced by the Enlightenment's emphasis on rationalism: "Reason, Universalists argued, dictated that a benevolent God would redeem all of creation." (Bressler: 9) Drawing upon comparisons of "imperfect" human parents to a divine and perfect Father, Universalists reasoned that if human parents could not conceive of turning their own children into the torturous world of hell described by evangelicals and earlier Puritans, then God, as a perfect being and perfect Father, would never condemn any of his children to eternal suffering. This belief in both God's fatherhood and the universal salvation of all people was at the heart of Christian Universalist teaching. In addition to rejecting evangelicalism, Universalists also ridiculed Unitarianism. For modern scholars familiar with the Unitarian Universalist denomination, this tension between the denominations would be surprising, but it was not until 1961 that the two denominations actually united officially. In the nineteenth century, the two movements formed distinct organizations. While both the Unitarian and Universalist churches "shared significant elements of belief—and disbelief—they represented two quite different, even opposed, strains in American religious culture" (Bressler: 4). According to Bressler, Unitarian teachings emerged from liberal Arminian theology and rationalism that held that humans were created in the likeness of God and had the responsibility to maintain a moral life. In contrast, Universalists emphasized God's compelling and universal love which overwhelmed humanity and led individuals and communities into pious reverence for God and humanity. Thus, while Unitarians emphasized that humans were too much like God to be eternally condemned, Universalists emphasized that God was too perfect to allow humans to be condemned (Bressler: 5—7).

The emphasis upon communal piety mingled with the rationalist conclusion of universal salvation to outline the core beliefs of the Universalist denomination. The "Winchester Profession," the earliest coordinated statement of Universalist faith outlines the faith's principle beliefs:

We believe that the Holy Scriptures of the Old and New Testaments contain a revelation of the character of God and of the duty, interest and final destination of mankind.

We believe that there is one God, whose nature is love, revealed in one Lord Jesus Christ, by one Holy Spirit of Grace, who will finally restore the whole family of mankind to holiness and happiness.

We believe that holiness and true happiness are inseparably connected, and that believers ought to be careful to maintain order and practice good works; for these things are good and profitable unto men.

In addition to their principle belief in the eternal character of God and the final restoration of all mankind, the "Winchester Profession" also emphasizes the role of personal behavior and service. According to this statement of faith, people can only achieve true happiness when engaged in service to others. Further, this statement expands upon this connection using the repetition of "holiness" and "happiness" to hint at a utopian vision which involved human action and would aid the spirit in uniting the family of God. Later, AdinBallou, a nineteenth century Universalist reformer, added to this statement of belief outlining the principles of personal righteousness and social order inherent in Universalism. According to Ballou, personal righteousness is linked to the following attributes:

1. Reverence for the Divine and spiritual.
2. Self-denial for righteousness' sake.
3. Justice to all beings.
4. Truth in all manifestations of mind.
5. Love in all spiritual relations.
6. Purity in all things.
7. Patience in all right aims and pursuits.
8. Unceasing progress towards perfection.

This list is premised upon God's fatherhood and the "blood" connection of all humans regardless of race, class, gender, or creed. However, Universalists also viewed humans as naturally selfish. It was only through God's grace and universal salvation that God transformed "human affections and [turned] naturally self-centered human beings to the love of God and the greater creation" (Bressler: 9). Thus, Universalists emphasized the power of God to transform the obedient and thereby transform the society at large. Although the "Winchester Profession" and Ballou outline a utopian vision for a society in which Christians embrace this prescription for personal righteousness to create a society that is just, early Universalists did not emphasize social activism, but by the time of Cary's childhood and early adulthood, the denomination was increasingly coming to emphasize personal development through service to the community and moral activism. Universalists worked in a number of social causes including prison reform, abolition, women's rights, and universal education (Bressler: 77).

At her most obvious, Cary's depictions of children renounce the beliefs of Christian evangelicals who held that children were base, animalistic creatures in need of religious discipline and salvation. Although most modern readers would find such a negative view of infancy and childhood foreign or even monstrous, this unsympathetic portrayal of childhood was commonly understood as truth in the seventeenth and eighteenth centuries. Children were also seen as evil, tainted by original sin. The influence of evangelical and Calvinistic doctrines held that children were primarily unenlightened, sinful creatures in danger of damnation. Puritan Reverend Benjamin Wadsworth even described newborn infants as "filthy, guilty, odious, abominable...both by nature and practice" (Mintz: 11). To counter this belief in the damnation of children, families began religious instruction as soon as possible, and fathers, as divine representatives and the source of financial security in the family, served as the supreme religious and material authority over their children (Mintz: 15). The dominant colonial depiction of children also conceived of childhood as a period of "deficiency and incompleteness," in which infants were seen as "animalistic" because they could not speak or stand. Accordingly, a parent's job was to hurry children's progression to adulthood through early work and responsibility (Mintz: 3). These beliefs led to a number of restrictive and abusive practices aimed at ushering children into adulthood as quickly as possible (Mintz: 3); parents routinely beat children with sticks, whips, and other items, forced infants to wear corsets that made them sit upright, drugged babies with opiates, and participated in a number of other questionable practices (Russell: 35).

By the nineteenth century, childrearing practice had begun to become more humane, but this evolution still had not completely saturated the country. While in the urban North, Puritan and other evangelical influences were becoming displaced by more liberal religious beliefs and humanistic philosophies, the western frontier was undergoing a "revival" of evangelical fervor as non-formalist evangelicals like Baptists and Methodists took root (Johnson: 17). These evangelical teachings, spurred by dicta such as "Better whipt, than Damn'd," emphasized the use of physical punishment as a reformer of children's innate sinfulness (Heywood: 100). Apparently, evangelical parents overwhelmingly subscribed to this prescription for violence. Colin Heywood states that in the nineteenth century about seventy-five percent of children in the U.S. experienced being beaten with instruments ranging from wooden switches to horsewhips and that although such beatings were not typically a daily occurrence, neither were they rare occurrences (100).

In contrast, Universalists who urged a gentler approach to childrearing were one of the earliest American denominations to abjure corporal punishment. George S. Weaver, a prominent nineteenth century, Universalist advice writer labels "the rod" and other such implements of physical punishment as "an evil in the family" and states that instead of attempting to "break" children parents should seek to "make, or mould a child's spirit" and to "win" obedience from children through "a calm, even-handed system of kind and gentle government, in which the persuasive power of love, directed by wisdom, mingles as the chief element" (Weaver: 77—78). Cary, in keeping with her Universalist roots, shunned the rigid childrearing practices that were especially prominent on the frontier where she grew up. In fact, one of the most obvious themes that appears in her writing is her critique of child abuse, especially that which takes place in the name of religion. This type of religiously motivated child abuse is a recurrent and conspicuous feature in Cary's writing.

12 普救派，福音派与虐童——凯瑞在《彼得·哈瑞斯》和《克里斯多弗舅舅家》中对儿童抚养的宗教批判

In both *Uncle Christopher's* and *Peter Harris*, Cary reveals her dissatisfaction with the evangelical notions of childrearing, which in each story result in the death of a child. One of the most obviously "heaven minded" child abusers in Cary's fiction is Uncle Christopher. Although the centerpiece of *Uncle Christopher's* is Christopher's physical and emotional abuse of his grandson, critics have not addressed this abuse in terms of its religious significance. Fetterley and Pryse view the story as a sort of dialectic between the patriarchal declarations of Uncle Christopher, which demand silence and obedience from others, and the feminine voice of the narrator, who gains freedom through storytelling (39). In contrast, Schultz compares Uncle Christopher's farm to a factory and notes how the inhabitants of the household are like factory workers toiling to provide material production (91). Schultz also points out that Uncle Christopher, in addition to his lack of toil, treats himself to luxuries and vanities. He purchases for himself fine, stylish clothing, but mandates that his wife and daughters wear identical, drab brown flannel dresses, and he dresses his two wards, Mark and Andrew, poorly. For Schultz, the members of his household become merely "wage slaves" who must satisfy Uncle Christopher's desire for luxury and power (Schultz: 88).

Neither of these interpretations recognizes how much conservative childrearing practices, rooted primarily in evangelical Christian doctrine, enable Uncle Christopher's extreme behavior toward his grandson Mark. While many of Uncle Christopher's behaviors emerge from his attempts at emulating masculine stereotypes, understanding Christopher's evangelical notions about childhood can help the reader see how these conceptions not only interact with Uncle Christopher's masculine stereotypes but they also help to generate these stereotypes and enable his abusive behavior. The narrator's initial description reveals this interaction:

I soon discovered by his conversation, aided by the occasional explanatory whispers of his wife, that he was one of those infatuated men who fancy themselves "called" to be teachers of religion, though he had neither talents, education, nor anything else to warrant such a notion, except a faculty for joining pompous and half scriptural phrases, from January to December. (177)

Uncle Christopher's evangelical fervor and self-proclaimed calling to evangelize is emblematic of the growing movement of uneducated bi-vocational ministers on the frontier (Johnson: 17), and in this quotation, the reader learns of both the narrator's and Cary's disdain for the religious self-righteousness Uncle Christopher embodies. Nearly all that motivates him is his belief that he is God's representative on earth, especially in his home, and that his spiritual responsibility is to save others from the fires of hell—a task he accomplishes through physical abuse, constant preaching, and quoting scripture, both real and imagined. The reader first glimpses Uncle Christopher's abusive tendencies when the narrator meets Mark. The boy enters the house laughing, but his grandfather quickly silences him by quoting verse three of Proverbs 26: "A whip for the horse, a bridle for the ass, and a rod for the fool's back!" (179). Christopher views his grandson, who is an emotionally empathetic boy, as "wicked and troublesome" (180), and he declares his desire to "change the boy into a man" (181). To accomplish this task, Uncle Christopher feels perfectly justified to both threaten and enact physical violence upon the child. The grandfather believes that the use of extreme punishment—in the form of physical beatings, forcing the child to walk barefoot in the snow, and ordering the child to drown his pet kitten—will banish Mark's supposed "wickedness."

Cary chooses an interesting voice of wisdom in the narrator, who is both a child and female and who calls attention to the extreme notions of evangelical instruction that taught children were depraved and sinful while men were empowered by God to enforce His will in their families. Cary's choice of the child narrator in this sketch and others is also indicative of the Universalist belief that children could serve as teachers for adults. Universalists believed that children, like adults, were often prone to be governed by selfishness (Weaver: 110), and they tended to hold the Enlightenment view of children as a blank slate which developed through mirroring the character of their parents (Weaver: 106). Nonetheless, Universalist teachings also held that children had a role in helping parents achieve their potential and develop their character as they met the regular challenges and responsibilities of childrearing. Weaver describes the coming of a child to a family as a time of training for the parents:

> The birth of a child in a family is a good omen. It is sent as a teacher. It has a great moral mission. It must be guarded with *care*. It must be managed with *prudence*. It must be nurtured with *tenderness*. It must be provided for with *diligence*. It must be reared with unselfish *love*. It must be educated with *judgment*, and trained with moral *rectitude*. And this care, prudence, tenderness, diligence, love, judgment, and rectitude, are so many virtues which the little child is every day impressing upon the hearts of its parents with a steadily increasing force. (108)

Although Christopher has attempted to educate with judgment and prudence, he has failed to develop the other traits of care, love, diligence, tenderness, and rectitude. Uncle Christopher's failure to develop all the necessary traits of liberal Christian love in his childrearing has become dangerously imbalanced.

Children also had another important role within the family for

Universalists. Weaver writes,

 Children help to keep alive our own childhood. They will not let us forget that we were once children. They are reliving our lives before our eyes. Sad, sad, it is for a man when he forgets he was once a child. He becomes petrified, —a rock, cold, hard, unyielding. (Weaver: 104)

 Unlike Mark and the child narrator who make empathetic connection with others, the grandfather has become so "cold, hard, and unyielding" that he attempts to banish one of the truly spiritual qualities in Mark, his sympathy for living things—a character trait which Weaver lists as a central responsibility in Christian children. Weaver goes even so far as stating that children who do not show sympathy are not *Christian* children (104—105). Cary takes this teaching a step further to show that such disconnection from sympathetic connection endangers life itself. The grandfather's refusal to submit to his true appointed role within the family directly contributes to Mark's death. The spiritually pure boy cannot survive in a world that demands he give up his Christian sympathy. Further, Uncle Christopher in viewing Mark, the narrator, and all other children as "wicked," has forgotten his own childhood, and it is this "forgetfulness" that Cary reveals in Christopher that is truly "wicked." Instead of protecting his grandson, Uncle Christopher's "righteous discipline" kills the grandson by the close of the story.

 Similarly, the title character of *Peter Harris* is subjected to adults who desire to reform him spiritually. His aunt repeatedly refers to the child as the "heathen boy," and she and her husband see their role as "snatching" Peter "like a brand from the burning" (141). This phrase is a direct reference to God's promise in the third chapter of Zechariah. In the passage, God defends the high priest of Israel in the face of Satan's accusations. God states, "The Lord rebuke you, Satan! The Lord, who has chosen Jerusalem, rebuke you! Is not this man a burning stick snatched from the fire?" Then God goes on to have the priest's filthy garments replaced with clean white garments and promises that Joshua's sins (and the sins of Israel) will be forgiven. It is also interesting to note that John Wesley the famous Methodist evangelist often referred to himself as "a brand snatched from the burning" (Tyerman: 17). In choosing this reference, Cary makes a direct critique of the evangelical family. Uncle Jason and his wife have usurped the role of God in the life of their nephew. While the Biblical reference, and indeed Wesley's own claims, use the expression to demonstrate God's grace in the life of the sinner, the aunt and uncle have decided to assume that their actions rather than God's active love will save their nephew from the fires Hell. In their attempts to reform him, the aunt and uncle threaten to whip him "everyday" (141), force him to sleep on a pallet of haying the coachman's drafty apartment above the stable, and deny the child both the comfort of company and medicine when he is sick. Likewise, the school teacher's attempts to "reform" and "educate" Peter result in abuse. Because Peter cannot sit upright for hours at a time and he cannot read, the teacher denies the child playtime, feeds his lunch to a pig, "inflict [s] upon him a merciless beating" (145), and detains Peter after school so that he is forced to walk home after dark in a downpour (145). Like Uncle Christopher's efforts, however, these acts of discipline prove to be merely abuse and neglect and directly result in the child's death because the aunt, uncle, and school master lack the Christian traits of love, sympathy, and kindness.

While Americans of earlier periods tended to view children as incomplete, animalistic, and sinful, by the nineteenth century a number of influences contributed to a more positive view of childhood. Enlightenment writers such as John Locke stated that children were blank slates that needed to be taught and prepared for adult life rather than beaten into submission to avoid the fires of hell. Romantic writers represented childhood as a distinct period of life to be enjoyed and prolonged (Mintz: 77) and depicted children as "symbols of purity, spontaneity, and emotional expressiveness, who were free from adult inhibitions" (Mintz: 76). Further, because children were seen as morally pure, writers began portraying them as moral and religious redeemers (Brewer: 46). Cary's fiction responds to this stereotype of the pure and angelic child remarkably sympathetically, at least upon superficial examination. Very seldom does Cary actually present a child with a disagreeable or evil character. Most often children in Cary's fiction are oppressed by their parents or guardians while the child quietly endures abuse or neglect as is the case of Mark, Peter Harris, and numerous other child characters who appear in Cary's fiction. Cary also shows children who literally give up their lives and in death provide salvation for the adults around them. Nanny's death in Cary's novel *Hagar, A Story for Today* (1852) inspires Joseph Arnold to engage in a life of Christian service. Similarly, Mark's death initiates Uncle Christopher into the world of empathetic feeling. Despite this apparent acquiescence to Romantic view of children as moral saviors or Christ-figures, Cary actually questions both the need and effectiveness of such child sacrifices. Unlike many of the sentimental writers of her time, rather than merely presenting the Christ-like child, she emphasizes instead the moral debt and blindness of adults that directly contributes to child death.

Although she does demonstrate in numerous stories that children can and do die to provide redemptive examples of righteous behavior, she also depicts children who die and whose deaths seem to serve no redemptive value because the people around them refuse to change. Peter Harris's death is a prime example of this phenomenon. Peter dies alone on a bed of damp straw in a cold room above the stable, and the only person who acknowledges his death is the Harris family's coachman, John, who, aside from Peter himself and the brief appearance of the family maid, is the only character who shows any characteristics of Christian love. The sketch ends abruptly with the coachman's recognition that the boy will no longer have to suffer, and given the actions of the other characters, particularly the refusal of Peter's aunt to provide comfort, companionship, or even a dry, warm place to sleep in his sickness, the reader is left to assume that the rest of the characters in the story—those who truly need redemption—will simply continue their lives untouched by the tragedy that has transpired. Further, unlike the deaths of children in other nineteenth century novels such as *Uncle Tom's Cabin* or *Little Women*, novels that portray children dying from disease, many of Cary's child characters die as a direct result of abuse. While Little Eva's mother in Stowe's novel may not be particularly attentive to her child, she does not physically abuse the girl, but Peter's illness results directly from being denied food and being exposed to the elements. Further, Eva experiences her death surrounded by loved ones and dispenses words of love and spiritual guidance to the adults around her. In contrast, Peter (as well as many other Cary's child characters) dies cold, alone, silent, and almost unnoticed.

Part of the reason Peter's death goes unnoticed perhaps lies in the limitations of the evolving conception of childhood. Although the popular imagination was beginning to adopt a more Romantic stereotype of childhood, this angelic depiction was reserved mainly for the children of the middle and the upper classes. The nineteenth century was a time of transition, in which actual children's experiences varied widely across economic, racial, and regional boundaries. Historian Steven Mintz describes this reality: "At no point in American history was childhood as diverse as it was in the mid and late nineteenth century. " (134) While childhood for middle-class urban children, like Peter's cousins, came to be a protected time of play and education, working class children were ushered into the world of physical labor and deprivation. The first appearance of Peter and his cousins displays this dichotomy well. Peter's physical appearance reflects abject poverty that contrasts with his cousins' wealth:

> Sitting by the old man was a little pale-faced boy. His clothes, much too thin for the season, were patched with different colors, and ragged still. His hat was of white fur, and had as it seemed, originally been too large, but by means of scissors, needle and thread, and the rude ingenuity, probably of some female hand, had been made to assume a reduced size. He wore no coat or jacket, but, instead, a faded shawl was wrapped about his shoulders... and his little naked feet...dangled about in a most uncomfortable sort. (139)

Peter's condition stands in stark contrast to that of his cousins who "[trundle] hoops on the path" and are dressed "in bright jackets set off with black buttons, and velvet caps with heavy tassels" (139). While his cousins appear to emerge from a nineteenth-century Romantic painting, Peter appears pale, barefoot, and wearing threadbare clothes.

In order to fuel this kind of dichotomy in regard to the treatment of children, the public conception became divided. While the middle and upper classes came to adopt the Romantic conception of childhood in regard to their own children, the children of the working class became demonized. These children were not seen through the same interpretive lens as middle-class children. At the same time that the American middle-class began to conceive of their children as angelic, innocent beings, politicians, writers, and government officials held an overriding fear of working class children and "orphans" —a term that social leaders tended to apply to all poor children, regardless of whether the children's parents were alive or not (Lang: 14—15). Such poor working class children were viewed as not only morally corrupt, but they were also seen as a threat to social order (Lang: 15). In contrast, Cary's works portray working class children as some of the noblest characters in her fiction, and in the few accounts in which Cary presents morally tainted children, these children are always from the middle-class or upper-class.

Cary reveals the common perception of working class children like Peter upon his presentation to his aunt and uncle. They believe that because the child is poor and lacks a formal education, he must be both stupid and immoral. Mrs. Harris repeatedly questions Peter's morality and character, but when she asks her own son to teach Peter his evening prayers, Cary reveals the true state of affairs in the family:

> Calling her little son, who sat on the floor, sticking pins in the paws of her lap-dog, the lady told him to come and teach his poor little heathen cousin to say, "Now I lay me down to sleep;" but the boy said he did not know it, and continued at his work of torment. (141—142)

Although Mrs. Harris thinks that Peter's ignorance of the prayer indicates a moral deficiency, her own son does not know the prayer either. Further, Cary reveals the cruel personality of Peter's cousin, who sits torturing a small dog. Not only does the boy torture animals, but he also emotionally tortures people, as evidenced by his repeated taunts of Peter at the opening of the sketch. Cary's presentation of Peter and his cousins flatly refutes the stereotypes of the morally bankrupt and dangerous working-class child. In fact, Cary portrays that if any child is a dangerous influence on society, it is the spoiled middle-class child who has been pampered and doted on by its parents.

In addition to these commentaries on childhood itself, *Peter Harris* takes on larger significance as Cary uses the child as a metaphoric portrayal of racial injustice, the first time she does so in her fiction[①]. In accord with Universalist beliefs on the equality of all races, Cary uses racialized references to Peter to express her disdain for slavery and ethnic prejudice. Although Peter is a family member, he is traded like property. In fact, Peter's father states that he has come to his brother's house "to make him a present of the little 'wite-faced boy'" (140). Peter's father does not bother saying goodbye to his son or to introduce him to the members of his new home. The father simply abandons the son to the brother's coachman John stating " Here, John, or whatever your name is, take this boy into the house and tell Jason that his poor old brother… gives this little fellow to him" (140). The father never once acknowledges that the child has a name but seems to view Peter more as an asset to be given or, in this case, discarded. The child is further coded in his cousin's initial assessment of him. They first mistake him for an "Ingen" (139) and later make fun of him because Peter's name is identical to that of "the black boy that tended their cows" (140).

These racial references to Peter expose the artificiality of the black/white race dichotomy. Peter shares the same name as a local black man but is not a black. He may even look like an "Ingen" but he carries with him a nearly identical bloodline to those who taunt him. In fact, Peter is the blood relation to his abusers, just as many slaves in the South were actually the children or brothers of their masters. Cary's inclusion of Peter as an actual family member

---

① Cary uses a similar strategy in later works as well, most notably in her last novel, *Married Not Mated* (1856). The novel depicts the life of a deformed, white child named James, who is treated as a slave and then turns black upon his death.

(as opposed to merely an orphan who shows up on the family's doorstep) also points to her Universalist upbringing which held that all people, including black slaves, were part of the "brotherhood of man." Bressler indicates that although there was a minority of pro-slavery Universalists in the South, the majority of Universalists believed that slavery was a sin against God who was the father of all humans (89). Cary's empathetic portrayal of Peter as a small abused child and family member to his white masters emphasizes this Universalist ideal that all people were children of God and members of the same family deserving of rights, respect, and protection, but not necessarily equality. Ironically, in using the metaphor of childhood to represent the injustice of slavery, Cary also infantilizes African Americans. Whether intentional or not, she indirectly affirms at least some of the more paternalistic defenses of slavery, like those of George Fitzhugh, who claimed that slaves could not survive without masters, since slavery provided guidance and protection to the enslaved (222—234).

Cary's portrayal of children and childhood works both with and against the popular stereotypes of her time and is much more complex and nuanced than readers would typically guess upon first reading. This complex depiction of childhood reveals the way in which stereotypes of children, even the more idealized and Romantic stereotypes, have been used to oppress children. However, Cary also uses these same sympathetic, idealized portrayals of childhood not only to arouse sympathy on behalf of abused and oppressed children, but to create metaphors that question, however tentatively, the mistreatment of other races. While Cary's depictions may not be completely without prejudice, she does attempt to act upon her Universalist beliefs to sympathize with and protect those as she views as defenseless.

Works Cited

Ames, Mary Clemmer. *A Memorial of Alice and Phoebe Cary with Some of Their Later Poetry.* New York: Hurd and Houghton, 1873.

Ballou, Adin. *Practical Christian Socialism, A Conversationalist Exposition of the True System of Human Society.* New York: Fowlers and Wells, 1854.

Bressler, Anne Lee. *The Universalist Movement in America, 1770—1880.* New York: Oxford UP, 2001.

Brewer, Priscilla. "'Little Children': Images of Children in Early Nineteenth Century America". *Journal of American Culture* 7.4, 1984: 45—62.

Cary, Alice. *Clovernook: or, Recollections of Our Neighborhood in the West.* New York: Redfield, 1851.

Clovernook: or, Recollections of Our Neighborhood in the West, second series. New York: Redfield, 1853.

Hagar, A Story for Today. New York: Redfield, 1852.

Fetterley, Judith, Marjorie Pryse. *Writing Out of Place: Regionalism, Women, and American Literary Culture.* Urbana: U of Illinois P, 2003.

Fitzhugh, George. *Cannibals All! Or Slaves Without Masters.* 1857. C Van Woodward, ed. Boston: Harvard UP, 1988.

Heywood, Colin. *A History of Childhood: Children and Childhood in the West from Medieval to Modern Times.* Malden, MA: Polity, 2001.

The Holy Bible: New International Version. Grand Rapids: Zondervan, 1984.

Johnson, Curtis. "'Sectarian Nation': Religious Diversity in Antebellum America". *OAH Magazine of History*, 2008 (22):

14—18.

Lang, Amy Schrager. *The Syntax of Class: Writing Inequality in Nineteenth-Century America*. Ann Arbor: U of Michigan P, 2003.

Mintz, Steven. *Huck's Raft: A History of American Childhood*. Cambridge, MA: Belknap, 2004.

Russell, Hillary. "Training, Restraining, and Sustaining: Infant and Childcare in the Late Nineteenth Century". *Material History Bulletin*, 1985: 35—49.

Schultz, Elizabeth. "*Bartleby the Scrivener* and *Uncle Christopher's*: Sites of Wage Slavery and Domestic Abuse". *Melville and Women*, 2006: 82—97.

Stowe, Harriet Beecher. *Uncle Tom's Cabin*. 1851. Elizabeth Ammons, ed. New York: Norton, 1993.

Tackach, James. "Why Jim Does Not Escape to Illinois in Mark Twain's *The Adventures of Huckleberry Finn*". *Journal of the Illinois State Historical Society* 2004 (97): 216—225.

Tyerman, Luke. *The Life and Times of the Rev. John Wesley Founder of the Methodists*. Vol. 1. London: Hodder and Stoughton, 1871.

Weaver, George S. *The Christian Household: Embracing the Christian Home, Husband, Wife, Father, Mother, Child, Brother, and Sister*. Boston: A Thompson and B B Mussey, 1854.

"The Winchester Profession", 1803. *The Unitarian Universalist Historical Society*. Web 25 Jan 2009. < http://www25.uua.org/uuhs/duub/articles/winchester.html>.

著者简介

Notes on Contributors:

Lingui Yang（杨林贵） is Professor of English at Donghua University（东华大学）. He has also been on the English faculties of Texas A&M University and Skidmore College, where he has taught Shakespeare, British literature, and other literature and writing courses. His publications include articles in *Shakespeare Yearbook*, *Theatre Research International*, *Foreign Literature Studies*, and other journals and anthologies. Among his recent articles is "Cognition and Recognition: Hamlet's Power of Knowledge", anthologized in Bloom's Modern Critical Interpretations *Hamlet* (New Edition, 2009). He is the editor of several books on Shakespeare, most recently *Shakespeare and Asia* and *Evaluating Scholarly Research on Shakespeare* (both published by the Edwin Mellen Press, 2010).

Dennis Berthold is Professor of English at Texas A&M University with special interests in the Gothic, the sea, transnationalism and visual arts in nineteenth-century American literature and culture. He is the author of numerous essays on Nathaniel Hawthorne, Charles Brockden Brown, Herman Melville, and other American authors. His most recent book is *American Risorgimento: Herman Melville and the Cultural Politics of Italy* (2009).

John A. Staunton is Associate Professor of English Education and American Literature at Eastern Michigan University. He is the author of *Deranging English/Education: Teacher Inquiry, Literary Studies, and Hybrid Visions of "English" for 21ˢᵗ century Schools* (NCTE, 2008). His work on American regionalism has appeared in *Studies in American Fiction*, *Religion and Literature*, and *Larry Brown and the Blue Collar South*. His recent work—including classroom studies of students and teachers exploring local literature in a global age—explores the intersection of literary studies and literature pedagogy in the context of 21st century English teacher education.

Xueying Qiao（乔雪瑛） is an Associate Professor of English Language and Literature at Donghua University. Her primary academic interests focus on contemporary American literature and culture. She earned her Ph. D. from Nankai University in 2007. Her dissertation, "Tales Plainly Told: The Culture of Narcissism and Minimalism in Ann Beattie's Fiction", explores Ann Beattie's novels and short stories published in the 1970s and 1980s, and has been revised as a book, which is forthcoming. In addition, she also has interests in the cultures of English-speaking countries. Her recent book is *New Zealand: It's History, People and Culture* (Fudan University Press, 2009).

Peixi Huang（黄培希） is a lecturer of English as a Foreign Language at Donghua University, Shanghai, with special interests in Chinese poetry translation, British and American literature, and English pedagogy. He is the author of several essays on cultural studies and translation and is currently working on a book project on English translation of classic Chinese literature.

Sheng Li（李盛） is an Associate Professor of English as a Foreign Language at Donghua University. He has a Master's Degree in English Language and Literature. His primary interest is American young adult literature as one of his early studies, "Artistic Representation of Lost History: Interpretation of *Dragonwings*", explores Laurence Yep's narrative features. Sheng Li has published articles on American literature and EFL pedagogy. His recent interests include Asian American studies, narratology, filmology, and theatrical studies.

Laura Cheshier has a Master's Degree in English Literature from Baylor University and a Doctor of Philosophy Degree in English Literature from Texas A&M University. Her specialization is in the nineteenth-century British novel, and her dissertation was written on lovesickness and the nineteenth-century British novel. She has lectured on British literature and on technical writing at Texas A&M University.

Jane M. Galliher is an Assistant Professor of English at Blue Mountain College in North Central Mississippi. She earned her Ph. D. from Texas A&M University in 2009. Her dissertation, "The Family of God: Universalism and Domesticity in Alice Cary's Fiction", explores the influence of Cary's Christian Universalist beliefs upon her fictional characterizations of families. In addition to the study of Cary, Dr. Galliher also has interests in women's studies, gothic literature, regionalism, and nineteenth-century American literature.

Yunhua Gao (高蕴华) is a lecturer of English as a Foreign Language at Donghua University with special interests in American poetry, American drama, and Greek mythology. She has earned a Master's degree in American literature with a focus on Eugene O'Neill and has published studies in American poetry and English pedagogy. She is currently working on a comparative study of Ezra Pound and Confucian conception of education.

Elizabeth Schultz is Professor Emerita of English at the University of Kansas. In addition to numerous scholarly essays and poems, she has published books on Melville; an environmental memoir; essays for *The Nature of Kansas Lands*; two collections of poems, *Conversations* and *Her Voice*; and a collection of short stories. She also writes a regular column for the Kansas Land Trust newsletter. In 2007, she was a Distinguished Fulbright Lecturer in Beijing, and in 2008 she co-organized an international conference on ecocriticism in Beijing.

美国内战前女作家爱丽丝·凯瑞研究

附 录

《苜蓿角,或曰西部邻里旧事》

目　录

前言（杨林贵译） ………………………………………… 212
1. 外祖父（高蕴华译） …………………………………… 213
2. 光影之间（黄培希译） ………………………………… 224
3. 怪妇人（李盛译） ……………………………………… 229
4. 萨拉·沃辛顿的自尊（宁妍译） ……………………… 233
5. 维尔德明斯一家（乔雪瑛译） ………………………… 239
6. 塞斯·米尔福德兄妹的心情（颜海璐译） …………… 246
7. 希尔太太和特鲁斯特太太（张琳译） ………………… 254
8. 古迹遗风（赵晶译） …………………………………… 259
9. 戴尔叔叔的烦心事（赵晶译） ………………………… 264
10. 老夫孀妻（张琳译） ………………………………… 267
11. 惠特菲尔德执事一家（颜海璐译） ………………… 271
12. 汤普金斯一家（乔雪瑛译） ………………………… 279
13. 安妮·希顿（宁妍译） ……………………………… 289
14. 彼得·哈瑞斯（李盛译） …………………………… 306
15. 玛格丽特·费兹（黄培希译） ……………………… 312
16. 猎手魅影（高蕴华译） ……………………………… 325
17. 莉迪娅·希思做客于萨姆奈尔家（高蕴华译） …… 331
18. 克莱维尔一家（黄培希译） ………………………… 344
19. 学生哥（李盛译） …………………………………… 350
20. 羊群犬祸（宁妍译） ………………………………… 357
21. 愚蠢的婚姻（乔雪瑛译） …………………………… 363
22. 青年医生的生存之道（颜海璐译） ………………… 370
23. 对比鲜明的访客（张琳译） ………………………… 376
24. 崭新的开端（赵晶译） ……………………………… 383
25. 女教师（赵晶译） …………………………………… 389
26. 糖厂早春（张琳译） ………………………………… 395
27. 倒霉鬼的末日（颜海璐译） ………………………… 398
28. 两姐妹（乔雪瑛译） ………………………………… 401
29. 威廉·马丁的懊悔（宁妍译） ……………………… 407
30. 格雷太太的两次造访（李盛译） …………………… 415
31. 雨天（黄培希译） …………………………………… 425
32. 窘境（高蕴华译） …………………………………… 431
33. 派克斯夫人的派对（张琳译） ……………………… 437
34. 一个冬季的变迁（张琳译） ………………………… 444
35. 故事结局（赵晶译） ………………………………… 450

前　言

  我国的乡村生活一直不是画家、诗人、言情作家特别青睐的题材。或许有的人觉得农村生活缺乏美的元素；或许有的人感觉其缺乏激情，平淡索然；也可能有的人认为其过于切近稔熟。本人对东部及北部各州之乡村略有所察，对南方则毫无体验，而在大西部，拓荒者忙于伐木开垦，无暇吹笛弄簧。在本人家乡腹地，虽父辈初涉时一片荒野，而今人烟稠密。素朴风习蕴涵丰富内容，日常琐事潜藏人性诸端，趣味之丰，绝不逊于旧日帝国，彼时专断律法高压之下，世袭陋习窒息之中，生活情趣荡然无存。

  落笔之时，本无意结集成书，只想给曾经掠过本人成长轨迹的几许暗影与灿烂追录一笔。不期然间，竟然录得如此篇什，就此汇总付印。所记之事多无卓彰要义，居于所谓大世界的名士多不会留意此间琐碎。

  望着出版社不断送来的清样，却不时陷入遐想，担心本人着力描述之亲历不为城市读者关注。城里人虽具怜悯之心，却对贫贱之人鲜有同情之意，更不会相信他们具备高雅时髦的文化人才有的细腻感情。文学大师们虽有一时兴起，着墨于乡土生活，却缺乏亲身体验，极少例外。因此他们的描绘虽然非常精彩，却少见真实，或许他们的华丽笔法就是最具魅力之处。就本人而言，我承认不会虚构。本人不过一介穷困艺术家，谨以此速写集求教于大方之家，我相信他们至少能见证所述情景给人自然真实之感，如无确凿反证，当以真人真事视之。有鉴于此，愿本集记事得到应有关注，更希望能对读者有所教益。

苜蓿角，或曰西部乡里旧事

1. 外祖父

万物变化是大自然的法则，新旧不断交替。往年落英缤纷的枝条业已枯萎，覆盖其上的是今年娇艳欲滴的鲜花。就连像我这样默默无闻的生灵也有那么多的变化要向他人诉说啊！有多少坟茔被芳草覆盖，有多少青丝变为华发；有多少意气风发、挥斥方遒的青年，而今步履蹒跚，韶华不再；有多少只手急切地伸出去采撷玫瑰，缩回手时却是鲜血淋漓，扎满蒺藜；最可悲的是，有多少颗心因此而碎了！我还记得少年不识愁滋味的日子，还记得死亡的意识如何潜入我的心灵。我原本徜徉于一片被露水打湿的鲜花丛中，周围闪耀着如同成千上万只小蜜蜂的翅膀般可爱的光芒，忽而被逐入到一片广袤的平原，所有的事物在青天白日下露出了原本的面目——我们是如何从懵懂无知到直面生活的现实。

事情就像发生在昨天，我仍记得那是十月末的一个黄昏——天色阴暗，凄冷无边。阴霾第一次划过我的心灵，纵然日后再灿烂的阳光亦无法将其从我的心底彻底驱逐。透过我家农舍的窗户，太阳投射进一方光柱，我坐在阳光下，用蔷薇花绛红色的浆果穿珠珠。

在此之前，我也听说过死亡，但是我并不怎么害怕，就像我对恶魔和女巫的感觉一样，他们经常在月牙初上时，在童话的森林里，收集有毒的草药，或者用柳枝、野葡萄蔓、常春藤等制成的魔杖绊住无辜的路人。我不大愿意去关心他们的事情，我也觉得自己不会受到他们魔法的威胁。

也许在某些地方，某些人有时会死去，我对此一无所知。但是那个人肯定不会是我或者我认识的人。因为他们是那么健康，那么强壮，人人那么满怀期冀。他们的脚步怎么会变得蹒跚？他们的眼睛怎么能变得暗淡？他们的手臂怎么会变得虚弱并且放下手中的活计而撒手人寰呢？不，不——这绝对令人难以置信。

快活无知岁月里的快乐思绪不时泛起，轻柔地

像五月吹拂的阵阵清风
轻快地拾起阴霾
像绽放的水仙举起雪花片片

那阴霾沉积了这么多年！如今能把这些阴霾一扫而光真是畅快，自己仿佛重返童年，那番一直压抑的痛苦已然不再，而我前行的路旁那些孤寂的坟茔已开满鲜花——仿佛妈妈那深色的头发又拂过我的脸颊，就像她当年教我读书或祈祷时的样子；仿佛又看到了年近古稀、头发稀疏花白、望之令人歔欷的父亲当年意气风发参加比赛的样子；仿佛又看到了孩提时代的自己，戴着一顶新帽子和一条粉红色的绸带抑或是手拿着自己叫做"珊瑚"的用蔷薇花骨朵儿穿成的花串。就像在某本书里读到的那些贵妇人摆弄她们的珍珠那样，我一会儿把花串缠在脖子上，一会儿把它挂在额头上，一会儿又把它编到头发里。当秋风吹落樱桃树上那些残留的黄叶时，无端地生出一丝伤感。我挪到窗户边上，就着灯光，偷偷地向屋里张望：一切都那么安详，那么令人愉悦，壁炉里的原木上火焰跳跃，父亲在修补马辔。就在昨天，最受我们家钟爱的坐骑"旅行者"受到一头大象的惊吓，把马辔折成了两段。那头大象是路过我们这儿的。那时它身上披着一块巨大的白布，将要在日后进行的表演中供人观赏。妈妈正在给衣服缲边，也许是让我下一学期上学穿的；哥哥正在读一份报纸，我不知道是什么报纸，但是在报纸的一面，我看到了一头熊的图片。让我听听看——我把脸颊紧紧地贴在窗玻璃上。我完全能够听得清他在念什么，因为他读报纸时，声音又响亮又清楚。那是一个荒诞不经的故事——最近人们在一个遥远的小岛的树林里发现了野人。那野人似乎已经在那里住了很久，手指甲长得像鸟爪一样，头发乱糟糟地纠结在一起，一直垂到膝盖上；发出的声音介于人类的呼喊和动物的号叫之间。被人追捕的时候，他在丛林和灌木中敏捷矫健地奔跑，追捕者即使奋力驱策迅疾的骏马也追赶不上。有人第一次看到野人的时候，他正坐在地上用牙齿嗑噬坚果，胳膊上满是虬结的肌肉，让他看起来力气大得能勒死一打男人。但是一看到人，他就蹿进浓密的树林，发出一声可怕的长啸，那声音使得他的发现者们用双手捂住自己的耳朵。据说这种因为与世隔绝而变成野人并不是独一无二的个体，而是一个群落，他们中许多人的个头也许更大，也许更加可怕。但是他们是否有任何清晰易懂的语言，他们是否住在石洞里或者是中空的树干里，还有待更加大胆的人们在日后作进一步的探索。

哥哥放下了报纸，看了看熊的图片。"我才不会看这种愚蠢的故事呢。"爸爸说，他边说边把辔头凑到灯下，看看是不是完全缝好了。妈妈剪断了绲边的线。她既和蔼又温柔，不喜欢听哪怕是最细微的斥责，但是她一言不发。小哈利正坐在地上玩耍，搭建一座木头房子。爸爸拍着双手，叫道："这就是哈利建造的房子呀！"他又拍拍哈利的头接着说道："我那小家伙在哪里？这不是他，这是一个小木匠。你必须把房子盖得再结实些，小木匠！"然而哈利坚持说他就是那个真正的小哈利，才不是什么木匠，还泪水涟涟地把头埋在妈妈的腿里。妈妈安慰他，说他正是她的那个小儿子，为了安慰他那孩子气的伤心之情，还把她刚刚做好的领子围在他的脖子上。过了一会儿，他又蹦蹦跳跳地建起一座新房子。这座房子的顶部十分陡峭，他说这是外公的房子，惹得所有的人都开心地大笑起来。

在听完了野人的故事以后，我有一点点害怕，但是现在，听到大家欢快的笑声，我为自己的胆怯感到难为情，我跳到前面，坐在一截绿色的土梁下。这截土梁把院子斜着分了开来，别人告诉我那个地方原来是一道篱笆。难道这儿曾经生长过那些原本应该种植在花园里面的玫瑰、丁香和鸢尾花吗？我想——不，如果真的有过那样的篱笆，那也肯定是许久以前的事情了，我没有办法使自己相信这种变化的可能性，就一门心思地摆弄那些蔷薇花的花骨朵儿。我先把它们摆成字母，又把那些字母拼成名字。我一会儿摆成我的名字，一会儿摆成某个我喜欢的人的名字。天空中有一朵悠悠的云彩，起初还有粉色、红色和金色的光焰，现在慢慢褪去了色彩，斜斜地挂在西天。西天之下是一望无际的枯萎的树林——山毛榉树灰色的枝杈直直地插向云霄；猩红的枫树如火焰一般从巨大的深色的老橡树和银色的悬铃木中喷薄而出。灰色的沙沙作响的薄暮为更深沉的夜色和静默所取代。

我听见远处的山路上传来一阵急促的马蹄声，我想骑马者正从桥后茂密的树林里沿山而下。我竖起耳朵听，空空的马蹄声证实了我的猜测，忽而马蹄声越来越轻——他正在爬坡，并离我越来越远。现在我又能清楚地听到了——他快骑到我下方的山涧那儿啦。在夏天，蒲公英星星点点地开满了这个山涧，现在全都是些褐色的荨麻和干枯的杂草。这会儿他该过了山涧了——他要到哪里去呢？又有何公干呢？我要起身看看。一朵云拂过月亮，皎洁的月光投射在骑马者的身上。他勒了缰绳，急切地向这座房子张望。我当然认得他，红色长长的卷发一直垂到脖子上，还戴着一顶草帽。没错儿，那正是奥利弗·希尔豪斯，那个碾磨工，他是我住尖顶房子的外公三年前雇的——比我记事的时间还长呢！他叫住我，我大笑着蹦到他面前，高兴地叫着，双臂搂住马儿顾长的脖子，马儿一边咬着嚼子，一边用蹄子刨着路面，我问他："你怎么不进去呀？"

他微微一笑，笑容里有一丝不祥的意味。他递给我一卷纸，说道："把这个交给你妈妈。"说罢，他勒了下马缰，飞快地骑马走了。我马上就跑进房子交差："给你，妈妈，奥利弗·希尔豪斯让我把这个给你。"她双手颤抖地接了过去，我怯怯地在一旁等她把信读完。她流着泪，一言不发地把信递给我的父亲。

那夜的情景给我带来了一种刻骨铭心的恐惧感，伤心的痛哭和悲叹时不时地将我从梦中惊醒，自那之后，这情形使我永远无法彻底忘怀。清冷而鬼魅的月光倾泻在我枕上，壁炉里蟋蟀的鸣叫声多么凄切，我的窗户被吹过光秃秃的树枝的寒风拍打得吱呀作响，我倍觉凄惨。我平生头一次无法入眠，我多么渴望晨曦的到来啊。最后它终于来了，东方泛白，群星隐没，天边现出的那抹绯红和紫色的云霞现在被太阳金色的光辉扫走了。屋外阳光灿烂，屋内却仍是黑云密布。

我紧靠着妈妈，有她在，我就找到了安全的庇护之所，这种保护别无他处可以寻觅。

"我不在的时候你要乖一点儿，"她说，俯下身来吻了吻我的前额，"妈妈今天要出趟门，你那可怜的外公病得厉害。"

"我也要去。"我边说边紧紧地抓住她的手。我们很快就收拾停当。小哈利咕嘟着嘴，伸出小手，爸爸递给他一把折叠小刀让他玩。妈妈一次又一次地回头张望，只见他站在走廊上眼巴巴地看着我们，风吹动了他那黄色的卷发，遮住了他的眼睛和前额。我们要步行将近两英里——沿着公路向北走大约一英里，直到走进一条横亘其中的长满青草的马路后，再向东走大约一英里，接着又向北走。顺着一条狭窄的，两侧长着因年久而开始朽烂的樱桃树的小路，我们到了外公的房前，那座房子样式十分古老，山墙既高又陡，石砌的烟卤笨重低矮。房后是一座老磨房,磨房的门槛上斜搭着一块木板与院子地面连接,作为进出磨房的阶梯,磨房山墙上开凿了一个方形的敞开的窗户,通过窗户,人们就可以用绳子和滑轮把谷物拉上去。

对我而言,这座磨坊格外令人恐惧,只有当凯莉姨妈牵着我的手,只有当奥利弗·希尔豪斯乐呵呵的笑声一扫磨坊里的晦暗之气时,我才敢走进去。说实话,来这儿的人并不多,这里到处都是些黑糊糊的阁楼,古里古怪的粮仓,还有随处放着的梯子。猫咪静悄悄地在房梁上潜行,伺机抓捕老鼠或者燕子,如果有时燕子被逮住了,它们的泥巢就会从椽上耷拉下来,随后整个巢就会彻底坍塌。那时我常常在想凯莉姨妈待在这个破旧的地方害不害怕,这里成天到晚轰隆作响,巨大的布满灰尘的轮子慢慢地转了一圈又一圈,轮子下面那两匹可怜的马一刻也不得闲地拉磨。但是她不这么看,她似乎很喜欢这个磨坊,每次我来,她都会带着我四处参观这座复杂的磨坊。现在我已经解开了这个谜团,或者毋宁说我是从残存的回忆中领会了那个时候只有大人才能够理解的事情。

一片橡树和胡桃树林一直延伸到农场的尽头,在农场的房子、谷仓和磨坊(人们管它们叫增建物)的两边伸出两条暗色的边条,完全挡住了人们的视线,只有顺着通向南方的那条人迹罕至的路还能让人略微看到点什么,前来磨坊的人们主要走这条路。我的外公不仅给四乡八邻磨制面粉和制作玉米饼用的玉米粉,还给母牛制作"嚼谷"。

外公现在老了,他身材高大,有着运动员般的体型,略微有些驼背,稀疏的头发像雪一样白,深蓝色的眼睛中满是热情与睿智。多年来他身体一直硬朗,他也一直坚持有益的劳作,这次他突然病倒,毫无痊愈的可能。

"希望他的身体能好转。"妈妈边听着磨坊轮子转动的轰鸣声边说。她也许已经知道外公不会因为自己得病而允许任何人停止正常的工作,他说不能因为他一个人生病而没有面包吃,也没有必要让大家放下手中的活计,无所事事地等着他死。当大限到来的那一天他会叫他们来道别并接受他的祝福,但即使到那时,最让他高兴的事也莫过于能够看到大家都像平常一样织布或缝纫。他是一个固执的人——甚至于他的仁慈也是如此不容妥协,毫不变通。我记得有一次他给了我一个新鲜的红苹果,他一言不发直到我怯生生地道了谢,"把你的感谢省了吧,干点有用的事儿比什么都强。"那个苹果没有给我带来任何快乐,为了不看到严峻冷面的他,我甚至会溜进磨坊里。

然而他是一个好人,非常诚实,从不偷奸耍滑,因此他获得了每一个人近乎崇拜的尊敬。我记得我父亲曾经讲过,有一次,格兰格执事农场里的佃户——年轻的温特斯花了一大笔钱买下了一块地皮后带了些干瘪的麦子到外公的磨坊磨面,趁他回家吃饭的时节,外公用自家的麦面装满了温特斯的面袋子。这是件好事,但是托米·温特斯从来没有怀疑过他的麦子怎么会碰巧这么好。

当我们走近房子时,我觉得它比以前更加孤寂荒凉。我当时希望自己和小哈利一起待在家里就好了。我如此急于写下每一件事情,是想记住这一天。在小路上靠近排水沟的地方站着一头脾气乖张的母牛,它毛色发红,背上有一道白色印记。凯莉姨妈给它挤奶的时候我经常跟着去,但是看上去今天它还没有出过奶。在这头母牛旁边有一头黑白相间的小母牛,犄角又短又尖,眼睛上蒙着一块方板;还有两匹马,一匹是灰色,另外一匹是短尾巴的栗色马,它们正伸长脖子凑到花园里啃吃灌木。当我们走近时,它们向前跳跃了几步,其中一匹半戏耍、半生气地咬另一匹马的肩胛,之后它们又静悄悄地回去啃吃灌木,全然不顾从田野那边传来召唤它们的叫声。

一群火鸡正在门旁晒太阳,没有人过来驱赶它们。它们有黑色的,有带斑点的,有的高昂着头耷拉着尾巴,有的在啄着青草,有的发出"咕咕"的声音,有的站着,有的昂头走路,它们纷纷给我们让道。从烟囱中冒出的一丝轻烟悠然地打着卷儿飘进了树林。枯死的牵牛花蔓条从窗户上半耷拉下来,但是曾经管护过它们的手已经顾及不了那么多,它们只有任由自己变黑并褪去美丽的容颜。在那下面,白色的窗帘被拉上了一半,我的外婆胸前别着一块带有斑点的手绢,她那苍白的面容比以往越发苍白了,她正在向外张望,看到我们,她便迎了上来,看到妈妈那询问的眼神,她摇了摇头,默默地把我们带进了屋子。我们进来的房间有一块桌布大小的自制的地毯,它平铺在房子地板的中央,地板的其他部分擦洗得十分白净;天花板是用胡桃木做的;四周的墙用石灰涂成白色;一张非常老式的书桌和几把木头椅子就是这个屋子所有的家具。其中的一把椅子上放着一块皮制的垫子,它被放在了一边,外祖母既没有让我母亲坐,自己也没有坐在上面。我想她是为了让自己静下心来,才把她帽子边沿上的黑色缎带解了下来,这个过程没有读者想象中那么复杂,这个花边只有一截缎带,而且总是黑色的,戴上帽子后,她用缎带把头缠住并将两头绑起来后在额头上打一个结。凯莉姨妈,可以称得上是性情温和,她像平常一样高高兴兴地迎接我们,然后重新在壁炉旁舒舒服服地坐下来,继续完成她手中的活计——给一截白色流苏打网边。

我喜欢凯莉姨妈,因为她总是煞费苦心地让我高兴,让我看她做的杂拼花布,带着我去牧场和牛奶厂,还带我去磨坊,尽管我觉得她带我去磨坊有点出于私心,但是,在那时,对我而言,我总是发自内心地对她表示感谢:孩子们远比人们想象的知道得更多,想要的更多,感受也更多。

这一次她把我叫到她的跟前,试图教我学会她打网边的秘诀。她告诉我必须让我的父亲给我买一个小小的带抽屉的桌子,那样的话我就可以编织一块流苏给它做一个漂亮的桌布。在恍惚的刹那,我想我可以这么做,在我的脑子里已经盘算好了在哪里摆放它,应该往里面放什么东西,我甚至于在思考我是否该询问一下她,到底要织多少才够用。我钩织流苏的本事从来都没有得到任何长进,我也从来没有得到过什么带抽屉的小桌子,我现在觉得自己永远也没有得到它是有道理的。

现在我的父母被带进了另外一个房间,我压制不住自己想看一看房子里面情形的渴望,在他们进去后房门关闭的那一刹那,我偷偷地朝里面瞥了一眼。床前地面上铺着一块灰棕黄色的地毯,床上铺着一块蓝白双色的床罩,在床边放着一张高靠背的木质椅子,上面搭着一块毛巾,木椅下面有一个样式奇特的罐壶。尽管如此,我不知道我是怎么看到这些的,但是我完全记得它的样子,然而不一会儿,我的注意力还是完全被病人的脸庞吸引住了,他的脸正对着打开的门,苍白、乌青、恐怖。我颤抖着,被吓呆了。那些在眼睛下方纹路一向很深的眼纹,现在几乎变成黑色,蓝色的眼睛看上去像玻璃般透明,冷漠而可怕。当房门被关上的时候,我看到他做出痛苦情状的嘴唇(他得的是那种最让人疼痛的病)挤出一丝微笑,还松开了那只死死揪住白发的手,并伸出去迎接我父母的到来。那是一个令人恐惧的时刻,我濒临漆黑幽深的坟墓边缘,我平生第一次感到我也死了，我对此深感恐惧。

　　凯莉姨妈将她手中的活计放到一边，在窗棂的钉子上取下了一顶棕色的女式棉布太阳帽，在我看来，这顶帽子足足有半码宽，她将帽子系在我的头上，边仔细端详我的脸边拍手，"躲猫猫咯！"惹得我又是笑又是叫。她则为自己戴上了事先准备好的一顶帽子，那顶帽子是外婆的，挂在窗户的另一边，帽子和我的很相似，只是可能比我戴的那顶更大一些。她牵着我的手和我一起到磨坊去。我们进来时奥利弗正忙着。"我给你带来了一位小客人。"在凯莉姨妈作介绍的时候，他迎上前来。然后他让我们坐在粮袋上，同时摘下了草帽，把红色的卷发从他那低低的白皙的额头上拨开，露出局促不安的神情。

　　"对于这个季节来说，天气确实算是暖和的。"凯莉姨妈说道，我想她是为了打破沉寂。那个年轻男子简短地说了句"是的"，接着便问磨坊的轰隆声会不会打扰病床上的人，凯莉姨妈答复说："不会，我父亲说这是他的音乐。"

　　"一个好老头儿，"奥利弗说，"他也听不了多久了。"之后，他更加沉痛地说："每一件事情都会变。"凯莉姨妈默不作声，他接着说："我在这儿已经待了很久了。特别是在你们碰到这样的困扰的时候，要离开这儿让我感到十分难过。"

　　"噢？奥利弗，"凯莉姨妈说，"你的意思不是说想要离开吧？""我看不出来还有什么可以回旋的余地，"他回答道，"我无事可做，如果一年以前我离开的话可能会好些。""为什么？"凯莉姨妈问道。但是我觉得她知道为什么。奥利弗没有作正面回答，只是说："你父亲最近跟我交代说，一个没有房子、田产还不到20亩的人，你可不能嫁；现在没有的话，就要对你作出承诺。可我无法作出这样的承诺，就不能为难你，违背他的嘱托。我很久以前或许有可能拥有那样的地产，可是为了我的姐姐（她已经精神失常了）和我那瘸腿的弟弟，我得让他上学，好当上校长，因为他干不了活；还有我那失明的母亲。但是上帝饶恕我！我没什么好抱怨的，也不应该抱怨。过不了多久，凯莉，你也会宽恕我，会有比我富有，也比我强的人给你一切，给你我曾经希望给予你的一切，或许更多。"

　　那个时候，我还理解不了那段对话的意思，但是我觉得自己有点多余，我就去磨坊的其他地方，看面粉从雪白的筛粉机里筛出来，听轮子发出的轰隆声。等我回过头来时，看见奥利弗坐在粮堆上那个原本是我坐的地方，还用胳膊搂住凯莉姨妈的腰。这种样子我可不大喜欢。

巨大的悲哀就像风暴一样，将我们平常的情感一扫而空，我们将自己的心交付给仁慈的双手——世界的准则就是如此冷酷、虚空、了无意义。以前他们也许从未谈及爱情，现在他们如同谈论其他任何事情一样，平静地谈论爱情，希望却是如此渺茫，能有个好事多磨的结局也是不错的，然而未来充满了未知数。最后他们的声音越来越低，低得我都听不到他们在说些什么，但是我看到的是他们十分哀伤的表情，还有就是，凯莉姨妈把手放在奥利弗的手里，像妹妹一样。

"为什么面粉出不来了？"我说道，因为筛出的面粉越来越薄，越来越轻，最后几乎要停下来了。奥利弗站起身来，轻轻地笑了说道："这连给孩子买连衣裙都不够。"说着将一袋小麦倒进了送料斗，原来那里面几乎没有料了。寻思着除了我以外没有其他孩子，我想他的意思是不是打算给我买一件新的连衣裙，如果他真的那么做的话，我那带抽屉的小桌子里面立即就会有东西可放了。

"我们已经打扰希尔豪斯先生够久了，"凯莉姨妈捉住我的手说，"咱们回房去吧，好吗？"

我在想为什么她要说"希尔豪斯先生"，我以前可从来没有听她这叫过。看起来奥利弗也在想这件事，他用批评的口吻强调了自己的名字："我肯定你没有打扰希尔豪斯先生，但是如果你想走，我不能强留你。"

"我没想让你强留我，"凯莉姨妈说，"如果你不愿意的话，而且我很清楚你是不愿意的。"她把我抱到斜木板上，我们踩着弯曲的木板从上面走下来。

"凯莉。"从我们身后传来一个声音。她没有回答，也没有回头看，但是她似乎突然想对我表达爱意，尽管我对她而言有些太重了，她仍紧紧地把我抱起来，一次又一次地亲吻我，还说我像根羽毛一样轻，她边说边笑着，给人感觉她不难过，也不是无事可做。

我永远都无法解释清楚这一小小的插曲，只知道"获得真爱的道路永远不会永远一帆风顺"。我们回到房子半个小时之后，奥利弗的身影出现在门口，他说："凯莉小姐，能麻烦您给找个杯子，让我接一点水喝吗？"凯莉姨妈陪着他到了水井边，他们在那儿逗留了一会儿，等她回来的时候，脸上已经恢复了往常那种开朗活泼的神情。

那一天过得很慢，准备好了的饭菜，几乎没有被碰一下就又撤掉了。凯莉姨妈忙着钩织她的流苏，外祖母轻手轻脚地准备茶水和果汁。

到了日落时分，病人感觉舒服一些了，他表示要打开自己的房门，他还想看看我们在干些什么，听听我们的谈话。人们就照他的吩咐做了，他被独自留在房间里。我妈妈笑着说她希望外祖父能够就此好起来，但是父亲伤心地摇了摇头说："他希望我们不会留意他的离去。"外祖父持家总是做到粮满仓足，我相信他是个本性仁厚的人，但是他不显露出哪怕是丝毫的温情，也不愿意别人对他流露爱恋之意。与他的高调性格相去甚远的是，一直到他生命终结，他都喜欢开一些低调的玩笑。一次，凯莉姨妈给他送喝的，他说："你知道我对你将来的期望是什么，希望你当回事儿。"

我偷偷地溜到他的房门前希望他能对我说些什么，但是他什么都没有说。我走得更近一些，凑到他的床前，怯怯地握住他的手，他的手多么潮湿冰冷啊！他还是什么都没有说。我又爬到了椅子上，把他稀疏的头发向后拢了拢，吻了吻他的前额。"孩子，你烦死我了。"他说，这就是他对我说的最后几个字。

太阳越落越低，向狭小的窗户射出的光柱开始越过地毯，投到病人的房间里，照到床上，再爬到墙上。他别过脸去，似乎在看天花板上斑驳的光斑。天气变得压抑幽暗，却没有一丝云彩，橙色的光芒变成单调耀眼的红色，即将枯萎的和已经枯萎的树叶悄无声息地落到了地面上。那时一丝风都没有，鸟儿钻进了树丛，灰色的蛾子从灌木丛下面涌出来，拍打着逐渐微弱的灯光。几只蝙蝠从磨坊旁边的树洞飞了出来，漫无目的地飞速盘旋，它们的翅膀有一两次碰到了病人房间的窗户上。最后一缕阳光渐渐隐去，磨坊轮子的轰鸣声也归于沉寂。在磨坊轮子奏响的属于他的音乐声中，他就此长眠不醒。

葬礼在第二天举行。这是多么凄凉的时刻啊！小路上停满了各种货车、四轮马车和马匹，每个认识外祖父的人都前来给予了最后的致敬。"我们帮不上他什么大忙了，"他们说道，"不过我们觉得应该来。"紧靠着门有一辆小小的等候着前往墓地的棕色的马车，马车上停放着一具灵柩，这辆马车是他生前常常使用的。拉车的两匹马深深地垂下了头。我觉得它们看上去也明显地表露出了伤心之意。

那天天气不冷，老屋的房门和窗户全部敞开，屋外的人们可以听到牧师讲话。他说了什么我一点儿也记不起来。我只记得听到妈妈的啜泣声，看到外祖母将脸埋在手中，还看到凯莉姨妈僵直地坐着，脸色苍白却没有泪痕，奥利弗坐在她旁边，除了间或抬起手擦掉泪水外，他的双手一直交叉着放在胸前。

我没有哭泣，只是感到恐惧和陌生，感到与死者靠得太近了，希望这一天赶快过去。我使劲回想一些愉快的事情好将现实一扫而去，但是只是徒劳而已。我仍然记得在那个时候，那首回荡在空中的赞歌：

> "惊恐之心重振作，
> 哪怕头顶布乌云；
> 云遮自有云开日，
> 云开尔首福降临。
> 盲目无信终有误，
> 毋咎主上费精神；
> 主上自有常纲在，
> 自当明示慰凡心。"

在门旁铺着一块青石板，沿着石板种着一排灌木和其他树木，它们中有丁香，有玫瑰，还有梨树和桃树，那些都是外祖父在很久以前栽种的，在露天的石板上停放着一具棺椁，包裹尸首的白布被拿开后放在盖板上。我记得一阵狂风从树林里哀号而出，使得那排花木不断战栗摇摆，风势逐渐减弱，最终消弭于山峦之间，有三两片枯叶飘落在逝者的脸上，奥利弗轻轻地把它们取下来，还赶走了一只在附近翩翩飞舞的黄色蝴蝶。

朋友们不断哭泣，他们被人带领着走近毫无笑意的尸首，然后就一个接一个地离开了。有人把手放在亡者的前额，之后白布被重新盖上了。棺盖也上了螺丝。裹着一块单子的棺椁放在棕色的马车上，一列长长的队伍缓缓地向树林中的墓地走去，与人们诵读"尘归尘"声相伴的只有马车倾轧地面发出的阵阵吱呀声，落日的余晖投射在那里，枯死的树叶被风裹挟着越过平整的墓冢。

遗嘱宣读完毕，奥利弗发现自己继承了一笔财产——那座磨坊和半个农场——条件是他迎娶凯莉姨妈。他一定是娶了姨妈,因为尽管我不记得婚礼的事,但几乎一直记得我有个凯莉·希尔豪斯姨妈。奥利弗那精神紊乱的姐姐被送进了精神病院,她一直都在唱那些关于一个不忠的情人的歌曲,直到死神把她带到天国才拨开了她的双眼。那位母亲被带到家中和外祖母一起过着安逸的生活,她们坐在角落里谈神说鬼,神聊婚丧嫁娶,这样的日子过了好多年。她们的回忆终于趋于平静了,因为她们都去了那永远的家园。奥利弗那瘸腿的兄弟在学校教书,在闲暇时吹吹笛子,还读读莎士比亚的作品——那是他读过的全部书籍。

年复一年,时光带走了我的童年,也带走了我的天真和不知黑暗为何物的福分,却时常带来最初身临哀伤的痛苦回忆!

死亡于我已不再那么可怕。

2. 光影之间

人生百事多处于阴影之中,光亮时各处摇曳片刻,而后很快淡出——我们所挚爱的人不再对我们微笑,抑或定格为一幅静谧、平和而令人惧怕的笑容,我们无论怎样亲吻都不能令其尽展笑靥;眼睑由于疲倦而低垂下来,由此也遮住了我们心中的阳光。岁月流逝,这种黑暗越发深沉,充满幽怨之气。如同荆棘树上的花朵尽落,只留下光秃秃的树干,丑陋得难以入眼;又如那汩汩而出的泉水,初而浪花喷涌,极其清凉,然而水流渐渐变小,只剩下了黏液般的水泡,最后也干涸断流了。我们看到的群山,盛夏时节草木旺盛,郁郁葱葱,一派繁荣景象,而今现出座座坟丘,令人生厌。生活实际上极其严肃,就是一个谜,充满了焦虑和苦难,不安与倦怠,但是在黑夜与荒凉之中,同样也积蓄了力量,尽情展示出其美妙的一面,这美妙装点着生命,使其跨过一道道金门,接受火的洗礼。朝圣者鼓足勇气,前方就是休憩胜地,它如同花冠上的点点露珠发出熠熠光亮,点亮前进的路。慢慢接近圣塔,那些枯萎的花蕾顿时绽放出美丽的花朵。姑娘们,心中虽满怀希望,却饱受失望的折磨,以致身心交瘁!整理好飘落在苍白面颊上的绺绺发丝,安心等待明天的到来。疲倦、憔悴和郁郁寡欢的人们,耐心,平静,充满希望,等待明天的来临——就像孩子一样,在黑暗中受到惊吓,脸上挂满泪水进入梦乡,醒来后发现在母亲温暖的怀中。我们都一样——活着的人、垂死之人及醒着的人，安心等待明天的来临。

怀有这样的希望，就像浩瀚苍穹中高高在上遥远的星辰，它们亘古不变，照亮了我们的人生——这是一种众神心中的希望，这是使人忘掉所有倦怠的希望，这是像孩子般纯洁真诚的希望。怀有这样的希望是多么了不起的一件幸事啊。但是除此之外，还有其他一些尘世间的希望，使我们感到亲切、快乐。

生命阴影中摇曳闪烁的点点亮光中，最明亮的就是爱之光了，最甜美的可能莫过于对小孩子的关爱。我心中所想的不是对很多人的爱，而是对一个人的爱——一个至今给我带来的都是甜美的记忆的人。多年以来，萧瑟的秋雨已经打落了她坟墓上曾经盛开的花儿。那时我们都是小姑娘，但是她的面容娇美无比，死神因她的美貌而选了她。她的脸颊苍白无色，大眼睛乌黑闪亮，嘴角总挂着淡淡的微笑。她从来不开怀大笑，也从不愠怒。这一点使得我每每想起她来，内心就要受到深深的谴责。她走之后，我才知道自己有多么爱她。我满怀悔恨想抱住她，渴望她能在我额头印上宽恕之吻，我将把它当做最珍贵的王冠，可是她的坟墓太陡峭，我无法把她从黑暗中拉起。

现在已经是六月份了，鸟儿整天对着她啾啾鸣叫。但是她狭小房间的窗户被厚厚的尘土所覆盖，她根本听不见。白色的紫罗兰花儿点缀着她上面的绿色盖子，但是她的小手不再张开去采摘这些美丽的花儿。当晨曦洒下一缕瑰丽的霞光，呼喊她："醒醒，已经是白天了！"她却一动不动，金色的卷发垂下落到安静的枕头上，她还是一如既往地沉睡着。主啊，您还未取下荆棘王冠走向圣坛，就把小孩子们揽入怀中，祝福他们，而独把她攫为己有，就因为尘世中的她却有着您赐予的天使的美貌。

那时她七岁，我十岁。我总喜欢找大一两岁的孩子玩而不喜欢和她玩。她温顺耐心，我却任性霸道。我尽管很爱她，但时常招惹她，想办法阻挠她。当然我会用野花给她编花环或给她的布娃娃做身新衣服，我当时认为这些是补偿她了，现在想想这种补偿是多么不值得一提。我做好后给她，她总是非常高兴地收下，好像我从未做过苛刻或不友好的事情。

我大她三岁。我满脑子都是奇思怪想，她的小脑瓜是想不到的。我总认为她只是个小不点，绝不是我的玩伴。我最大的罪过莫过于我明知道她想和我一起玩,而我总偷偷溜走。有时,我的朋友和我打算到树林中漫步或是去一个我们喜欢去的地方,我们总设法说服她留在家中,向她允诺下次带她去或者允诺给她带些坚果或浆果,看见什么好东西我们都会给她带回来。每当我们这样惺惺作态地劝她,她都很听话,几无例外地留下来。我们知道她非常不愿意留下,但是她不会硬缠着我们带她。我们常常告诉她去她自己的玩具房,说那里有个好东西,或者说有人在屋里叫她,常常这样连哄带骗,偷偷甩掉她,自己去找乐子。

一天早晨(我多么清楚地记得那一天),那是十一月末的一天,树林里一片肃杀,万物凋谢。玉米剥叶机正在地里收割玉米穗子,然后割倒根茎,为耕地作准备。到处可见牛马耐心地站着。我们能听见满满的篮子被倒空发出的"咯咯"声。狗在长满杂草和残留的庄稼秸之间相互追逐,穿来走去,时而惊起野鸟或惊起野兔,狗便"汪汪"地叫着去追。当天的气温在那个时节中算是比较温和的,天际处笼罩着一层蓝色的雾霭,夏末常见的小溪上翩翩起舞的蓝色的、带斑点的、黄色的等各式各样的蝴蝶已经见不到了,河水也渐渐干涸,不再欢流。但我们并不在意这些——因为我们要去捡鹅卵石。

我们几次想摆脱掉珠儿(我们都这样叫她),都没有成功。她那天身体不好,比往常更想和我们在一起。小孩子并不容易糊弄。有一次她看见我们沿着绿色小径跑走,她在后面叫我们停下来,我们就跑了回来,对她说我们只是想看看到底能跑多快,但是她仍旧满脸狐疑。我们都坐下来,装出我们一整天都不打算动的样子。她穿梭在我们中间,让我们给她讲故事或是给她做个漂亮的东西,要不就带她去什么地方。最后我实在没有耐心了,生气地对她说:"我要是你,我就不待在别人不欢迎我的地方。"

她低下头,我看到自己占了上风,语气稍微缓和点,继续说着:"去你的玩具屋玩去,这才是个好孩子。"

"不,不,"珠儿说道,"我想待在这儿。"

"你想待在这儿是吧?那好,你就待在这儿吧,我们要去树林了。"

说到这里,我的语气一下子变得非常严厉。她哭了起来,说:"我想和你们一起去。"

"你刚才说你想待在这儿,现在你又想去。"

我非常清楚，她不过是想跟我们做同样的事情，所以我接着说："要是你想去树林，那就去好了，我们就待在家里。"

她在她那张未上漆的小椅子上坐下，拽着她那金色长发的发卷，脸上困惑极了。

"你要待在这里啦？"我说道。

我们把帽子放在围裙下边，这样就没有人怀疑我们的动机了，我们就这样离开了房间。因为没有得到大人的允许，所以我们还未走远，便回头看看，确认一下没有人发现我们逃走的事，却发现小珠儿跟在我们后面。我们一开始跑得很快，但是她跑得几乎和我们一样快，所以我们就停下来等她走近，我们吓唬她说我们要穿过一片玉米地，那里有很多狗，可能有二十只，具体数目我们也不清楚。实际上，我们认为到那里狗很可能会跑过来咬我们的，但我们跑得比她快，很快就跑远了，狗就撵不上我们了。如果这时狗咬住了她，我们就无能为力，没法帮她了，我们已经警告过她了。

她的嘴唇颤抖着，眼中已经汪满了泪水，她没有去擦，也没有大哭起来，她双手交叉握在胸前，眼中满是责备地看着我们，但是无可奈何，只得让我们走了。刚开始，我们兴奋不已，但是很快内心就开始自责起来，我回头看看，发现她还在原地站着。我内心有些动摇，几乎想让她和我们一起去了。如果真是那样的话，我会少掉多少痛苦啊。但是当时恶念占了上风，我们继续走了。

有些事情，本身很细小，微不足道，但是它们终生缠绕着我们，让我们不得安生，就像伊甸园的那条蛇一样，"我们每爬一圈都要受到诅咒"。

每当此时，即使采摘时觉得香甜无比的果子，到了嘴里也索然寡味，满巢的蜂蜜也无法让我们有丁点兴致。

我所写的这些幼稚的不端行为会让读者看清楚那些藏在脑海深处苍白而模糊的面孔，一排模糊的阴影一下子挡在光亮之前。斋戒、祈祷、忏悔或是惩罚都不能抹杀掉这些恶行。我们最不愿意想起它们时，它们却能推开我们内心最私密房间的大门，自己走进来。

田野里已割倒的黑色秸秆上仍挂着几朵枯萎的小花。小河边的野草杂乱地缠结在一起，泛出一片灰暗色。熟透的坚果随处可见，松鼠忙碌着储藏果子以备过冬。阵阵秋风吹起，刮得枯叶像天上的云朵般聚拢成一堆。我们或藏在树叶堆后，或大捧大捧地把叶子聚拢起来，迎着拂面而过的风儿把叶子使劲扬起，自得其乐，玩得不亦乐乎。

我们沿着小溪上上下下走着，河水在各处的蓝石头间泛起涟漪，我们在其中翻来翻去寻找奇石异卵。然后我们从树根上和朽木上剥下大片的黄绿色的苔藓，一则因为这些确实很漂亮，二则我们可以做珠儿玩具屋里的垫子。珠儿当时很孤单而且心里不高兴，我们不能完全置她于不顾，尤其是在那样天色已晚的时候把她留下来。

太阳已经西沉，我们的围裙里装满了苔藓、鹅卵石和其他此类的宝贝。大家又累又饿，就开始往家赶。牧场的牛群已经远远地走在我们的前面，收割庄稼的人也都牵着牛、撵着狗回去了。西边的天空上飘着一片狭长的火红的云彩，但是我们在归途中看到它慢慢消失。我们快到家时，看见一颗星星挂在天空，看起来清冷硕大，而且很遥远。

我们把苔藓铺在珠儿玩具屋的地板上，按照黄绿相间的色彩搭配铺得非常漂亮。我们想给她一个惊喜。而后才发现她的卧室里有一盏灯亮着，这引起了我们的注意。但是很快我们的好奇心变成了恐惧。房间有扇小方窗，白色平纹细布的窗帘被风吹起，从中我们看见一个陌生女人。她戴着一顶雪白的帽子，好像弯着腰俯在床边。我们知道那天早上珠儿身体不太好，我们一下子意识到这个情况——她现在病得很厉害。

她房间里很多人进进出出——脚步很轻很轻，时不时地有些人压低声音交谈几句，屋里到处弥漫着药品的难闻气味。过了好一会儿，我们才被说动进去看看她。最后我们都站在她床边，心里吓懵了，同时又感到十分愧疚。我依然记得当时她的脸烫得吓人。但是她还是笑得那么甜美，她伸出胳膊抱住我们说："你们回来了，我真高兴。你们说的那些狗真让我害怕了。"她搂住我的脖子，胳膊滚烫。她问我下次能带她去吗，我一口答应她—好起来就带她去，还告诉她我们给她带回来的苔藓，还答应她好起来后我会为她做一千件事。

她的病情日渐严重，我一刻也不离开那个房间。祖父去世时，我就已经明白了死亡是怎么一回事。磨坊旁边老房子的情景常常浮现在我的脑海。我害怕了，吃不下，睡不着，无法休息。她发了高烧，非常严重。而我总是俯身对着她，又加上过度疲劳，也被传染上了，不得不离开她。她跟我说的最后一句话是："等我好了，你也好了，你会带我去的，是吗？"我只隐约记得，但是不知道是谁，晚间时分走进来，轻轻地摸摸我，脸上的神情很吓人，告诉我她死了。又过了一两天，他们抬来棺材。我清楚地记得她的模样。她微笑着，跟她活着时一模一样，双手合拢放在胸前，就像我看过无数次的那样。

第二年春天来了之后，我才又一次走进小树林——是去把紫罗兰花的种子种到她的坟墓周围。我常常凝视着把她独自一人扔下使她那么难过的地方，但是她已经不在了。要是能收回那些绝情的话，我愿意付出任何代价——当时我还有什么样的代价不愿付出呢？

许多年过去了，我种植紫罗兰的坟墓已离我千里之遥。然而我仍时常想起，每次想起都会在心中投下一片阴影。她的生命如此短暂，但是她去世时犹如朝霞般绚烂。我一直徘徊直到午后，已经深刻地感受到了一整天的炙热和负担。遥远的地方有她短暂的存在，如同一道美丽的亮光；但是从她的坟墓中延伸出一道阴影，无论我到天涯海角，它都如影随形。

3．怪妇人

有一个幽静的小河谷，四周是起伏的丘陵，这里终年流水潺潺，云雾缭绕，雾气拂过草地，缠绕于枝条之间，在阳光和树影的映衬下忽明忽暗。就在这片景致之中有一座破败的小茅屋，里面曾经住过一个人，邻居们都叫她"怪妇人"，而她叫自己为克利福德太太。在这片美丽的景色中整个夏天草地上开满了各种各样的花朵，有金凤花、红色的银莲花和浅色的雏菊。黄樟树长满了山坡，特别是当东方玫瑰色的晨曦渐渐消失在明亮的天光之中的时候，黄樟树会随着林中百鸟的歌声而摇曳。

就在茅屋门口不远的地方，一堵灰色的石墙上牵牛花在阳光下垂下一串蓝色的铃铛，墙上的野蔷薇也努力地向上生长和绽放着。清亮的泉水流过满是青苔的墙边，荡起银色的涟漪，慢慢地消失在水波深处。

如今的这片河谷似乎已经不如当初那样美丽，尽管草木依旧，但是失落在其中的人性赋予了它格外的魅力。大地充满了哀怨，而当初天使用翅膀拨开天堂灿烂的云霞时不曾这样悲伤。就在这片不朽的废墟中，罪恶潜出了天堂，用它轻轻的脚步唤醒了坟墓可怕的回声。罪恶！罪恶！由于你这个世界暗淡无光，不复最初的光辉，而在这个世界美丽的边缘聚集的人们只有在闪耀的永恒之门旁才能释下心中的重负。

  我不明白，这是因为之前她突然来到此地，还是什么别的原因，但很明显克利福德太太身世颇有些神秘。当初她搬来这座小屋时，谁都不清楚她来自何方。她那时清秀而憔悴，一身重孝，一副心如止水的样子，也只有她那天真可爱的小儿子能为她带来一丝快慰，小家伙那时已经会回应母亲的微笑了。

  克利福德太太仅有为数不多的简单家具，一张床、几把椅子、一张桌子、一些坛坛罐罐和一个摇篮，这些就是她全部的家当了。除此之外就只有那一架子书了，有些已经破旧，有些有烫金的天鹅绒封皮。那些破旧的书上面用清秀的字体写着"玛丽·威尔福德"，而那些烫金天鹅绒封皮书上面的字体更为遒劲，"献给玛丽，L·C敬赠"。

  天气不错的时候，邻居们经常看到这位面色苍白的妇人坐在门前那棵榆树的树荫里。榆树垂下的柔软枝条轻叩着屋檐，屋檐上乳白色的鸽子正在暮色中晒着自己的羽毛，钢青色的燕子温驯地绕着屋檐盘旋鸣啭着。她常常就是这样拿着书抱着孩子坐在那里，一个小时接着一个小时，直到透过树冠洒下的明亮的阳光消失，直到脉脉含情的星星面颊绯红地站在夜的门槛。回到屋内，随着小家伙的笑声和快乐的咿呀童语渐渐沉寂下来，她会唱一些歌曲的片段，嗓音低沉而甜美，但总是透着深深的哀怨，就这样一直唱到孩子那双带着凹坑的胖胖的小手在睡梦中蜷缩起来。

  她家的小屋很少有光亮。夏天清冷的月光穿过敞开的屋门照入屋内，蝙蝠自在地飞进飞出，猫头鹰则从榆树上对着阵阵山风抱怨着，而山风并不为它哀婉的歌声所停息，在群山之间来回奔跑着——时而在浓密的树叶中欢笑，时而在山顶恸哭。冬天屋内炉火的余烬只能透过那扇小窗投射出一丝亮光。窗外从未修剪过的藤蔓和多花蔷薇纠缠在一起，爬满了墙壁，使小屋变得更加阴暗。

  邻里之间曾经一度流传着许多关于怪妇人的流言和猜测，但后来这些议论都渐渐消失了。邻居们的登门造访，无论是出于善意，还是好奇，最终都没有坚持下来，这是因为邻居们登门造访尽管得到极其温馨得体的款待，但是主人从未回访过他们。到后来除了给她家送奶的老太太之外再也没有人去打扰她了。送奶的老太太声称怪妇人向来对她彬彬有礼，而且能顺便看一眼那个小家伙，会让她一整天都很开心。

  孩子长大了些，于是邻居们经常看到戴着草帽的小家伙手里满是蒲公英和雏菊四处跑着。他妈妈就坐在榆树下，经常从书中抬起头来看看孩子有没有跑得太远，因为这孩子似乎比他妈妈更喜欢独处。再大一些他喜欢一个人坐着，看阳光下飞蛾跳舞，看燕子在屋顶盘旋。他最喜欢看天上的云朵和山林里的雾气了。他经常会躲到鸟迹罕至、不透阳光的地方。他深深的眼眸继承了他妈妈的忧郁，甚至笑容里也带着悲伤。至于是天性如此，是生活习惯使然，还是某种联系，我也说不清楚。这孩子不喜欢读书，尽管他一向听从他妈妈哪怕是一点点的想法，但是他妈妈也只能苦口婆心地劝他去学着读书。

  孩子渐渐长大，不再需要母亲从前那么多关爱，于是从前构成她生命之网的那些金线渐渐消失了踪迹；从前哄婴儿入睡的歌谣也已经想不起来了；从前爱看的那些书籍已经失去了往日的魅力，整天放在她腿上却不曾翻动过；她到榆树下坐坐的次数也没有从前那么多了，而且脚步更加踉跄。要不了多久时间就会改变山谷里那条黑暗的沟渠，疲惫的人在那里安息。

  自从克利福德太太搬到小屋来，九年已经过去了，她的孩子几乎不知道在他生活的这片山林世界之外还有一个更为严酷的世界。

  燕子飞走了，榆树的叶子也黄了，一片片悄然落下，转眼已是仲秋时节了。已经长成少年的孩子整天都泡在树林里，倾听坚果落下的声音，倾听山风单调的呻吟。山风吹起枯叶覆盖了满山的野花，天空布满了浓重的灰云。夜幕降临的时候雨点开始敲击小屋的屋顶，宛如一首欢快而有哀怨的乐曲。

  孩子此时已经从林子里回来了，坐在树下，闪亮的雨点不时打在他金色的卷发上，溅到他的脸颊上。他在琢磨着是星星被人从天空中抹去了，还是依然在暴雨之上的天空闪耀着。

  "我的孩子，我的孩子，你还不到妈妈这里来吗？"孩子的母亲轻声呼唤着自己的儿子，但声音比从前更低，更悲凉。于是他飞快地跑到母亲身边，母亲伸出瘦削冰冷的手理了理儿子被风吹乱的金色卷发，亲了儿子一次又一次，之后才说："我就要出远门了——可能就是今晚——再也不会回来看你了。我已经筋疲力尽了，要去哪里我也不清楚，我病了。我不能再拥抱你的时候，如果你爱上帝，上帝就会拥抱你的。"说到这里，她的头跌回到枕头上就一动不动了，虽然眼睛依然看着她的孩子，但是此时趴在母亲床头的孩子就像一根柔软的枝条猛然戳到了石头上。他此刻很难理解母亲话里的奥妙，但是出于本能他还是不寒而栗，就像每个人感受到死亡临近时候一样。

夜晚的黑暗似乎从未如此可怕。窗外藤蔓敲打着窗子，暴雨击打着屋顶，他害怕了。"妈妈！"他喊道，开始声音还很轻，到后来喊得越来越响，但是母亲没有任何回答。他把手搭到她额头，感觉又冷又湿，他吻她的唇，她没有回应，他明白母亲死了。

出于孩子的天性，他想抛开眼前残酷的现实。他想起了林中落下的坚果、笼罩山丘的白雾，想起了阳光和飞鸟。突然之间他想起了春天鸟巢失踪的那件事来。当时在林边上那座老桥拱下有一个鸟巢。每天他都跑去观察雏鸟成长，但是在一个阳光灿烂的午后，他发现鸟儿都不见了，鸟窝也塌了半边。他闷闷不乐地往回走，在一棵树下停住了脚步，随着枝条之间鸟儿翅膀的扇动，一阵鲜艳的花瓣雨落在他的脸上，接着听到一阵悦耳的鸟鸣，抬头向上看，树上正是他那群失踪的鸟儿。他把这件事讲给他母亲听，他记得她当时说："当我们的俗缘尽了，我们就离开那悲伤黑暗的拱顶来到天堂开满鲜花的枝头永远地歌唱。"伴着这神圣的回忆他酣然入睡。就这样母子俩都进入了梦乡——一个醒来时神性的永恒会降临她的眉梢，而另一个醒来时要体味这坎坷人世的哀痛。

怪妇人下葬的时候到场的人没有参加我祖父葬礼的人多。此时小克利福德已经是无家可归了，然而让"他所眷顾的人安息"的上帝会无形中庇护他的子女。怪妇人生前一人独居，沉默寡言，但让邻居们对她的孩子怀着一种莫名的温情。现在这孩子已经长大成人，一直得到众人的关怀。

4. 萨拉·沃辛顿的自尊

我从毗邻苜蓿角最近的城市所出版的一叠报纸中捡出一份，按照女士读报的习惯，先翻到列出所有国内新闻事件的版页。一则消息先吸引了我的注意力，萨拉·沃辛顿去世了。"她因一种令人痛苦的病症而离世，终年十九岁三个月零十一天。"我内心充满疑问，不愿意接受这个事实，于是我又反复看了几遍，的确是她，不会有错的。街道的名称，还有顺带提起的那些悲痛的家庭成员。所有的信息都证实了我第一眼看到而我内心不愿相信的消息是正确的。一个朋友的经历再次验证了诗歌里不断讲述的亘古不变的真理，即：

"有的人英年早逝，
但他们的内心依旧如夏天的尘埃般炙热，
心中充满激情。"

这则噩耗好比是晴天一声霹雳，把我们从美梦中唤醒，又回到活生生的现实中来。窗外，大雨倾盆，不断敲打着窗棂，小山坡上暴风雨在咆哮肆虐着，四周一片黑暗，朋友离去的消息使我们惊愕迷茫。几周前，或是几天前，我们还在一起，为她的身体健康、活力四射而愉悦欢欣；可现在，再也听不到她那轻柔悦耳的声音，再也看不到她那暖人心扉的笑脸。

最初的惊异和悲伤过后，我们紧接着又陷入了伤感的思绪中。我们与死者的最后一面是在什么时候呢？在何种场合呢？她都说过什么？她看上去怎么样？当时是清晨还是傍晚？我们聊天时的言语和说话方式是否友善？我们当时是沉默寡言，还是刻板严肃？在我们的记忆中，究竟有多少次我们本可以说一些温和体贴的话，而我们却偏偏没有？又有多少次我们本应该做一些友善的行为，而我们什么也没有做呢？如果去世的是我们的近亲，我们又该为自己的严厉、冷酷和无情怀有多深的懊悔呢？我们又将为自己有意夸大的过失和徒劳无功的悔恨饱受怎样的煎熬呢？

我们中的任何人都不可能忘记她那苍白的嘴唇说过的话，我们愿意用世界上任何东西来交换那句祝福："我原谅你了。"对我而言，我心中萦绕着一段比其他任何人更难以释怀的记忆。这段记忆反复再现，让我畏缩，不敢去深想。山峰、森林、溪流，已成了我和我最要好朋友之间的层层障碍。我有愧于我的朋友，但那错事并不是我深思熟虑后的有意行为，而是由于当年的年少无知和一时的头脑发热。我亲爱的朋友，我永远失去了你，可如果当初在你奄奄一息时，你能把手放在我的头上，亲口说原谅了我，并且祝福我的话，我现在内心那无法遏制的悲痛可能早就平息了。原本简单纯粹的祝福，由于我的过错，竟然成了我的诅咒。

在整个漫长的夏日里，我心里清楚她将离我们远去，但是我一拖再拖，没有告诉她这个情况。有时候，她感觉好一些，并谈起对未来的打算，而一向很依赖相信她的话的我，也会变得对未来怀有希望。这种令人兴奋的场合使我总是忘记告诉她真相。后来，她身体越来越虚弱，甚至不能像从前那样拥我入怀。她整天整夜地躺在床上，透过敞开的窗户遥望云朵和草坪。本能和直觉告诉我，她离开我们的日子已经为期不远了。这时，我更不愿意开口告诉她这个事实。我不想告诉她我之前的错误而加深她的痛苦。有时候，我的姊妹们会离开她的房间一小时，或是一整天，小孩子嘛，考虑事情会经常不周全。但是我一直待在她那里，为她端茶倒水，或者厚厚地包裹住她冰冷的手脚，或者整理铺平床单。对她深深的喜欢和欣赏使我不愿意离开她半步，但每每她感激我对她的照顾时，我都会跑到屋里哽咽哭泣。

随着时间一天天过去，秋天萧条的身影掠过夏日的脸庞。我最终还是没有向她坦白：我做了错事，我愧对你，我亲爱的朋友，我愧对苍天。我的看护工作告一段落，他们说最后萨拉的脸上洋溢着笑容，充满了活力和友爱，可这笑容似乎在谴责我的良心。

夜晚时分，坟墓中游荡出来的幽灵使我陷入混混沌沌的沉睡中；清晨，我又清醒过来，回想起年复一年的痛苦、悲伤和失望。我敞开胸膛，向大地呼喊，祈求原谅。可一切都是徒劳的。无论是荒野里青翠的山谷，还是沙漠里空旷的沙地，到处都有鬼魂出没。上天啊，难道是这个折磨人的鬼魂爬过坟墓的门槛，笼罩了纯洁的永恒之光，用咒语让我正值华年的身体患上霉病吗？难道那段记忆将永远不会从我的脑海中消失？难道那负罪感将永远不会从我的内心中淡忘掉吗？

但是我并不在意这些冥想。我心里很清楚她是我故事里的主角，她已经归于尘土。她评价我的时候不会说出任何不利于我的话语。我也因此一定会在今后成熟的岁月里有更好的表现，我也许已经学会注意控制粗暴的脾气和冲动不妥当的言辞，但是我担心与幼年时候相信纤细的树尖离天空很近的我相比较，现在的我离天堂之路是越来越远了。

"月光悄然潜入，
与黄昏的余晖融为一体。"

正值一年丰收的季节，空气中弥漫着刚刚割好的干草清香，沁人心脾，收割机整天都忙碌在一望无垠的田地里。无论是平坦的地面上，还是崎岖的山路上，到处都点缀着笔直繁茂的狭长条田地。这里星光闪耀，这里为疲倦的风提供了休憩的温床。树尖处繁星点点，窥探着大地，空气似乎也停止了流动，不再与婆娑而又沾满灰尘的树叶窃窃私语。

一轮满月悬挂在东山头上，硕大无比却又很暗淡，我们可以很清楚地看到月宫里背着荆棘的男人，还有我童年时代经常爱玩的捉迷藏，这些都使得我幼稚的幻想比以往更加明了了。

我想一下，我们一共有六个人，我的小侄子沃德，当时九岁；我的远房表亲罗伯特，他是个品德高尚的年轻人；还有萨拉·沃辛顿、艾丽、小亨利和我。我们是快乐的一伙人。我们的笑声传到高山，引起阵阵回音，然后飞过果园，飞过牧场，还穿越了浓密的树林。院子里到处都堆着绿油油的小草堆，满院飘着清香。而且这些草堆都成了绝佳的藏身之处，尤其是当桃树荫投落在草垛上及其四周时，黑黝黝一大片。沃德非常喜欢这些嬉闹游戏，而且他自我感觉他的藏身之地比堂兄罗伯特的更加隐蔽安全。一切的一切对我而言恍如昨日，永远都是一段鲜活的记忆，有时候就如同天使一般纯真美好。记忆中还有很多泉眼，总是用深色大石头封盖好。捉迷藏游戏、时间、场地、肆无忌惮的行为、略显幼稚的情感，对于每一个来到这个繁华世界的生命来说，都是隽永美好的。一座座簇新的坟墓墩上爬满了小草，看上去生机盎然，但模糊了我对过往的记忆。西面不远处有一座破损残败的教堂，我曾去过一两次。这座教堂属于那种一旦见过，就很难再从记忆中抹杀掉的东西。教堂的修建时间应该是很久很久以前，因为自从我能记事起，那座教堂的状况几乎也并不比现在好多少。四周橡树和核桃树的树荫投落在那些拓荒者的坟墓上，这些大革命时代前拓荒者的虔诚催生了修建这座教堂的粗糙技艺。

"砍掉柱杆，换上楣梁。"

活着的人已经几乎摒弃了这座教堂。成群的燕子从破碎的窗户玻璃飞进飞出，随意地在里面搭巢安家；厚重的双层门上数以千计的钉子早已变得锈迹斑斑，黑漆漆的；那些未上漆的木器也随着时间的流逝渐渐褪色泛白；有几处房檐板已经腐烂脱落。教堂没有采用钟楼和尖顶的设计，屋顶上爬满青苔，颇为陡峭，还保留着一两处有尖角的框架结构。这样的结构只有在乡村老式建筑中才能看到，也许是为了方便建筑工人。很早之前曾有个巡游四方的牧师路过这里。他在村子里停留了一段时间，以便为村民做一次礼拜。布道时间定在星期天的十一点钟，地点就在那所破旧的教堂。于是和他同住的孩子们把这个消息传给了方圆四五里的所有邻居。在指定的时间，人们渐渐地聚集在那里，十分安静。可那天罗伯特并没有露面。当时既没有大声的斥责，没有轻声的谴责，也没有诵读赞美诗来唤醒长眠的灵魂。

……

那晚，我们在皎洁的月光下嬉戏打闹，罗伯特当时是多么满怀希望、精力充沛啊。他和我们中最可爱的一个一起度过了那个夜晚，而且情绪一直很好，因为爱一个人使得我们学会去爱所有的人。我们中大多数人在从百合花丛中或是草堆后的藏身处退回到家门口时被捉到，并按我们小孩自己的规矩接受惩罚。甚至一向很稳重淑女的萨拉，那天晚上也变得无拘无束，当快要抓住罗伯特时，她跑得飞快，比罗伯特负责抓人的时候还快。她是个美丽的女孩，我一直称赞她庄重高贵，但她一直沉默寡言，不善于社交，还有点自私。我感觉在这个世界上除了她的小狗之外，她不喜欢任何东西。她对她的小狗是温柔备至，给予它全部的抚爱和温柔的话语。无论是母亲、兄长还是其他任何人都无法走进她的内心世界，得到她的认可。她谈论起亲戚时十分冷漠，就像在谈论素不相识的陌生人。有时候，她会抱着我，似乎喜欢我，但即使当时她的确表现出了脉脉温情，也很快会用冷淡代替。我们之间存在着无法逾越的冰海。

长久以来，我一直感叹着我们与生俱来的热情、友爱是否已经被不合时宜的冰霜所冲淡，或者这种温情一开始就这样淡如水。她既不谈论过去阳光灿烂的日子，也不谈及对未来怀有的希望，至于现在，她则表现得比家畜或者石头还要冷漠。小娃娃几乎可以向任何人撒娇，祈求怜爱，但从她那里讨不到任何关爱。她也会去满足他们的要求，不过却似完成一项任务，里面不掺杂任何温情。

我已经研究过她的个性，我的感觉是，除了对朋友的冷嘲热讽之外，她不会对任何事情引以为傲。

她有一头乌黑浓密的头发，时常梳成发辫。当她解开发辫时，头发散落下来，在肩头舞动，几乎垂到脚跟。我经常看到她把前额的头发甩到脑后，动作宛如王后般优雅，然后双手抱胸，在屋里踱来踱去，默默无语，仿佛在思考帝国的毁灭兴衰，这样的状态会一直持续到后半夜。

"神奇的睡眠，那令人舒适的鸟儿。"

我还清楚地记得大约在十二月底的一个晚上，当时很寂静也很寒冷，我们坐在炉火正旺的壁炉前东聊西谈了一个多小时。我悄然意识到她在整个聊天中没有说过她讨厌任何人或者任何事情，这对她来说可是少有的。她身材高挑儿，亭亭玉立，似乎有一种多年来拒绝任何机会、任何变化的气质。我又一次谈到她的美丽，我不知道是她的美丽还是冷漠使她充满魅力。我们喜欢追求得不到的东西。所有认识她的人都羡慕她，爱恋她，但是那些爱慕者的心弦总难逃被她无意伤害折磨的命运。那个晚上，我们一直在谈论她的爱慕者。是我提起这个话题的，我希望能探知她内心深处的真实想法。最后我鼓足勇气，试探地问道："有一个追求者，你还没有见过，如果你同意，明天我愿意很荣幸地把他介绍给你。说不定他就是那个百名追求者中命中注定会中奖的那位呢。"

"有可能，非常有可能，"萨拉一边回答道，语调中充满了讥讽，一边把手放在胸前，笑着说，"我觉得我开始感受到爱情的力量了。他在哪里？告诉我，现在，马上告诉我，我无法再等待下去了。"

"冷静一点，"我用同样的语调回敬道，"我可以告诉你他头发的颜色，他穿着的衣服，还有哪月哪天他会来迎娶你……"

"拖延是一种折磨。"她说着，脸色呈现出急切和热情。她突然跪倒，大叫着："恩底弥翁（月神），你在哪里？像日神那样，在小树林里打猎？我可以蹲下来，亲吻我的爱人？"

"你认识 D 律师吗？"我用询问的口气问道。

她停下了嬉笑，直挺挺地站着，反问道："谁说我认识他？"那种语气令我永生难忘。

我简略地解释了我的本意。她一脸庄重地坐好，离我有一点点距离，很简洁也很冷漠地说，她不怎么认识他。

"我们的一个年轻朋友在和 D 律师一起学习，"我说道，"他在第四大街的办公室工作。等我们去城里时，我们去拜访一下他？"

"不必了。"她的回答就这三个字，仅此而已。于是我以壁炉里的火越来越弱为理由，抓过枕头，佯装要睡觉，因为我意识到如果再继续对话下去，谈话将变得令人恼火。

萨拉一个人待在屋里。她取下头发上的梳子。这把发梳款式新颖，做工精致，价格不菲。她把梳子丢在地上，落在脚边。她又散开自己满头黑色的发辫，一身睡衣开始在屋子里走来走去。一两次转身时，梳子被她踩在脚下，但是她并没有蹲下来查看，也丝毫没有想注意避开的意思。炉火变得微弱起来，摇曳着，最终熄灭，煤炭上残留的灰烬泛着灰白色，凝结在玻璃上的冰霜也变得白灿灿的。当时的天气十分寒冷，但无论是茫茫黑暗还是冰冷刺骨的气氛对她都毫无作用。时钟指向十二点、一点、两点钟。她跪倒在窗前，手在玻璃上划出几道痕迹。她的脸颊紧紧贴在冰冷的玻璃上，热切地注视着窗外的马路。街道上的灯光全部熄灭了，冰冻的地面偶尔会有人走过。

她就这样一声不吭，静静地待着。看到她行为如此奇怪，我开始有些担心了。最终我试探性地和她搭话，好像我并没注意到她的举动，不清楚她整晚在做什么。

"请不要打搅我，"她说，"我在与天使说话。"

看到她既没死掉也没疯掉，我很满意，因为她总习惯说些奇怪的话。精神上的煎熬使我筋疲力尽，我很快酣然入睡。尽管我梦到自己和一个骷髅同床共眠，但我还是一觉睡到天亮。醒来的时候，我发现自己几乎淹没在萨拉浓密的头发中，她正蹲在我旁边，问候我早安，并说道："知道吗？我们要去拜访那个人，这次可能会决定我的命运"。

然而，还没等到预定的时间，她又编出了某个理由，我也没有提出质疑，就取消了拜访。后来也没有去拜访过，从来就没有去拜访过。

之后，我经常能碰到 D 先生，和他一起探讨生死的问题和有关爱情的话题。但是他谈论爱情时非常平静，就好像在谈论一个客户。

他四十岁左右，相貌堂堂，家资殷实，影响力非凡，彬彬有礼，而且意志坚定，无论是怎么样的希望、恐惧、仇恨或是爱情，都无法使其改变。如果他下定决心的话，无论是世界上最有魅力的女孩，还是最最悲惨的人，他那双深蓝的眼睛看上去都是一样的冷漠，一样的镇定自若。他一直单身，是个万人迷。但无论他是怎样的人，我已经明白了曾经困惑我的问题：

"好比水流冲击着沙石，
我的心在呻吟中失落。"

我的确这样。可怜的萨拉，我过去曾经责怪她，但现在我只是可怜她。

今天早上，我读了她的讣告。我无法想象她面色苍白，虚弱多病，直至死亡。她在人生的最后一刻想到了什么？说过什么？她的思绪是否穿越了茫茫山峰，而最终想到我？我脑海里多次想到她。当她一步步走向那些我们最后都将去往的寂静的宫殿时，她是否对亲戚间的关爱温情有了更深刻的认识呢？她是否比在世时对上帝安排在她身上的苦难有更清楚的认识呢？我不知道这答案，我只知道她的发髻再也不会散落在我的胸前，她的声音再也不会来唤醒我。

我不晓得她是安葬在一个庄严的纪念碑下，还是长眠在起伏的土墩下。但是我清楚一件事，她的枕边再也不会有人冷嘲热讽，她的心中再也不会冒出一些空洞索然无味的话。

"为了能酣然入睡，你需要躺在这样一张床上。"

5．维尔德明斯一家

邻居中新搬来一户人家，三口人，一个老妇人，一个年轻人，还有一个十四五岁的孩子。他们居住的地方与苜蓿角之间隔着一片小树林。我仍然清楚地记得，当我第一次看到青烟从那个高高的红色烟囱冒出来盘旋而上时，我是多么的高兴。那个村舍长期以来无人居住，看到有人住到了我们附近，我很是开心。或许，即将与他们相识的喜悦也并不比前者少。我们对于身边的人和事，往往会熟视无睹；只有当分别来临，我们才会知道他们对我们来说意味着什么。

附带提一下，在这片我提到过的小树林里，我记得有一棵橡树，

239

比旁边的树木高出许多。曾经千百次，我总有这样一种感觉，仿佛它的同伴们肯定会因为低人一等而郁闷不已，于是真的很希望能把它齐根伐倒。终于有一天，耳边传来了毁灭者响亮的砍伐声，问过之后才知道，伐木工接到指令，不再放过这棵大橡树。一开始，我急切地听着，那砍击声像是胜利的凯歌。随后，欣喜的心情逐渐消退，我开始惊讶地想，在这个树王倒下之后，小树林将会是什么样子。然后我想到，这片树林将荣耀不再。细想之下，已将盼它倒下的理由封存不提了，所以当一声巨响宣告了它的倒下，叫醒了山间沉睡的回声时，那一刻，我心中的悲伤难以言表。如果我能再一次看到它矗立林间该多好，哪怕就一次！但是我再也看不到了。时至今日，每当想起那棵高大的老橡树，阵阵懊悔仍会袭上心头。

但是，我的新邻居！我的喜悦之中混合着些许好奇。于是，一想到他们已安顿下来，我便仔细地打扮一番，前去拜访。

村舍离大路有一小段距离，由一条窄窄的小径相连。小径上满是野草，一边是一片绿油油的草场，另一边便是那片小树林。小径沿地势逐渐向上，一直通往一座小土山。小山上，子子孙孙一起，

"村野先人长眠于此"①

再往远处，便是那个村舍，还能看到它旁边那歪歪扭扭的柏树和白色的墓碑。对于墓地，我向来是不怕的。但是从幼时起，一看到这一片墓地，我总是会逃之夭夭，心里有着某种迷信的恐慌。我永远不能忘记，在约翰·海恩死后，劳拉·哈斯廷斯是如何看到一团亮光亮了一个冬夜。约翰是一个流浪汉，四处为家，一生从未伤害过任何人，除了他自己。他用愚蠢的放纵加速了自己的死亡。然而，人们不止一次地看到他的鬼魂，坐在他冰冷的坟堆上。坟堆下，他灵魂的躯壳日复一日地萎缩、消逝——至少，邻居中那些最年长、最虔诚的老人们是这样说的。那里还埋葬着玛丽·维尔德明斯，一

---

① 引自托马斯·格雷（Thomas Gray）的诗作《墓园挽歌》（"Elegy Written in a Country Churchyard"）。此处作者的引文是"The rude forefathers of the hamlet slept"，而格雷诗作的现行版本中这句诗多为"The rude forefathers of the hamlet sleep"，与作者的引用略有出入。

个美丽的年轻姑娘,没犯过多大的错,却受了极大的冤屈的人①。有时在月亏之夜,人们能听到她唱着悲伤的摇篮曲。另外一些时间,有人曾看到她坐在自己凹陷的坟墓旁边,将玫瑰编入自己的发辫,像是在为婚礼作准备。虽然我从未见过这些奇怪的事情,但是要说还有什么地方比那里更容易有罪恶之人那未能得到安息的灵魂出没,还真难以想象。那片小树林草木繁茂,鸟雀众多。树木沿着路边一直延伸下去,在荒凉的山脊处才渐渐稀疏零落。山脊上,野蔷薇爬满坟冢,遍布断篱,一如他处。高矮不齐的杂草丛中,随处可见小片的空地,留做新坟之用。

那是一个夏日的美丽黄昏。我走在野草丛生的小径上,穿过寂寞的墓地,去那间村舍作初次拜访。不知为什么,心里有种莫名的哀伤。在村舍与死亡之地之间的山谷里,有一个老旧的断桥。我记得我坐在桥边,长久地聆听着鹅卵石上水流的潺潺声,凝望着阳光穿过树叶投下来的金色斑块,直到它们消失殆尽。"夜晚已悄然来临,暮色苍茫,万物都包入她素色的衣裳"。②

就这样,我静静地坐着,没有一点声响。日暮时分,鼹鼠已开始了它盲目的工作,不断翻动着我脚下的土壤。白色的蛾子扑扇着厚厚的翅膀,从落满灰尘的野草下面飞上来,在我周围飞舞,扑入我的怀中。蝙蝠拍打着翅膀四处乱飞,几乎撞到我的脸上。

猫头鹰凄厉的叫声回荡在山谷,消失在远方的山上,提醒我继续前行。就在这时,我听到了美妙的诗句,来自那首挽歌,其中美妙的一节的最后两行提到了那只忧郁的猫头鹰。诗句如同我的心声一般,低沉而忧郁地回响着。我清楚地听到了这样的诗句——

"比如,徘徊在她神秘的树荫旁,
搅扰了古老而寂寞的她的领地。"③

---

① 原句"more sinned against than sinning"出自莎士比亚剧作《李尔王》第三幕第二场,意为"天下人皆负我,而非我负天下人"。
② 此处作者引自约翰·弥尔顿(John Milton)的诗作《失乐园》("Paradise Lost")。
③ 此处作者引自托马斯·格雷(Thomas Gray)的诗作《墓园挽歌》("Elegy Written in a Country Churchyard")。此处作者的引文是"Of such as wandering near her sacred bower, / Molest her ancient, solitary reign",而格雷诗作的现行版本中这两行诗句多为"Of, such as, wandering near her secret bower, / Molest her ancient, solitary reign",与作者的引用略有出入。

抬头望去，有人慢慢向我这边走来。他很年轻，容貌似乎也很俊朗，双臂交叉环抱在胸前，眼睛看着地上。他从我身边走过，根本没有注意到我。我想应该说他对我根本是视而不见。不过，这样一来我倒是能够更好地观察他，虽然我宁愿放弃这一特权，以换取他的一瞥。他让我很感兴趣，同时让我感到蒙受了耻辱，因为他竟如此漠然地从我身边走过。他脸色苍白，神情沮丧，额头上覆着一团浓密的黑发，从一侧太阳穴处分开，凌乱地披散在另一侧。

"好吧！"我说，看着他爬上了对面的小山，感觉他似乎在肆意漠视我对他的某种要求，虽然实际上我不可能对他有任何一丁点的要求。怀着糟糕的心情，我转过身，快步朝着那个村舍走去。

一个金发女孩正坐在窗前读书，见我到来，便起身相迎，仪态从容优雅，很有教养。但是在我拜访的过程中，她的态度算不上友好。她非常美丽，但那是一种雕像般的美。我没有见到这家的母亲。女孩告诉我，她母亲身体不舒服。当我请求不要去打扰她母亲时，女孩欣然默许。这里的每一样东西都显得文雅而高贵。但是我想知道的是，他们何时到来，准备待多久，那个年轻人与其他人又是什么关系。

看到桌上的长笛，我谈起了音乐，因为我猜这长笛应该属于那位缺席的先生。然而我什么也没了解到。暮色已深，我觉得有必要告辞了，虽然仍没看到那个年轻人。在我的想象中，他是如此的年轻英俊，并且，当然也是如此的讨人喜欢。

太阳不知何时已经落山，一轮明亮的满月也已升了起来，所以即使在穿越墓地的时候，我也并不害怕。不过，这次我比以前放慢了脚步。走到墓地门边的时候，我停了下来，开始思考可怕的生与死的玄秘。

斜倚在门上，这里的静谧浸入了我的灵魂。这个地方其实并不很荒凉，我这样想。在这里，恶人不再制造麻烦，疲倦的人也已安息。邪恶虽如长长的裙裾，附着在人生最美好的阶段，但在这里已被淡忘。宁静已伸出素手，将荆棘编就的花冠从哀伤的额头上取下。而那些曾经始终处于阴影中的心灵，虽曾忍受巨大痛苦，且不幸无人怜悯，但在这里也再无伤痛。最令人欣慰的是，即使是无法抵制诱惑的薄弱意志，也已被尸布覆盖，为其挡住了令人羞愧的怜悯的目光和傲慢的冷眼。我们需要感恩，只有这样，当人们本初的美好天性之上长出罪恶的霉菌时，上帝才不会彻底抛弃我们，而会在他难以捉摸的无限怜悯之中，为我们打开坟墓作为庇护。如果没有喷泉将我们猩红的罪恶冲洗成羊毛般洁白，如果死亡的黑夜不能毗邻永生的金色晨曦，如果安息的白色堡垒无法将地基陷入黑暗的深处，那么，将生活的重负彻底放下，就成为一种难以估量的优势，因为生命迟早会变成一种重负，最终沦为废墟间的回声。

墓地的一角，树木最为茂密。这里是玛丽·维尔德明斯的坟墓，与其他坟墓有一点距离。年复一年，坟头已下陷。在坟头的荒草里，蓝色的蓟子花开了又谢。

我的思绪很自然地想到了她。将目光转向她安息的地方，我看到了，或者自以为看到了一个人影。玛丽那未能安息的鬼魂的故事，我仍记得，所以起先我并未怀疑自己看到了她。独自一人，如此地接近一个若真若幻的身影，当我意识到这一点时，一阵奇怪的感觉不由袭来。

于是，我自语，这不过是幻觉。当我凝神细看时，一束微光一闪而过，我赶紧用手遮了一下眼睛。我朝着村舍望去，想确定是不是哪户人家的灯火。但是四周一片黑暗，一片云遮住了月亮。我不敢再看那个鬼魂出没的坟墓，赶紧推开墓地的门走了出去。虽然我的动作很轻，大门依然吱呀作响。这时除了我的心跳声，其他任何声音都会给我勇气。走开一小段距离之后，我扭头再次向墓地望去，但是浓重的阴影遮住了一切，即使那里有什么东西，我也不可能看到了。事实也正如此，我什么都没看到。

回到家后，我问管家是否还记得玛丽·维尔德明斯。管家是个说起话来滔滔不绝的人，我请她给我讲一讲玛丽是如何被埋在树林那边的墓地的。

"是的，我记得她。她被埋在小山上那块墓地的一角。她葬礼的那一天，大雨下了一整天。人们来到我家，我知道的，来拿杯子之类的东西，来把她坟墓里的水排出来。"她接着说："但是，有这么多活着的人，足够我们聊的，聊那些死人干什么？"

事实上，她是想让我聊聊我们的新邻居。而我没说，这让她有点恼火。可是，那晚墓地的一幕无疑更有吸引力，已将新邻居从我的脑海中挤了出去，否则的话，我可能会跟她说说的。于是，像管家一样，我又困惑又失望，便去睡了。那晚，我做了一些噩梦。不过,第二天倒是阳光明媚,我的思绪又回到了快乐的轨道上。

日子一天天地流过,转眼已是数周,我们既没看到过我们的新邻居,也没听说他们的什么事。对于我的拜访,他们没有回访。而他们不过是邻人,我也没有作进一步的表示。但是黄昏时分,每当我坐在门边的苹果树下,总能听到远处传来的悦耳的笛声。

"是从那个村舍传来的吗?"一天晚上管家问我,"我听着觉得好像是从墓地的一角传来的。"

她微微侧过头,手围在右耳上,急切地听了几分钟,进而肯定地表示,这笛声绝非凡人吹奏。我笑了。

"你听到过鬼魂吹笛子吗?"我说。

"笛子!"她愤慨地说,"这要是笛子,那你也是根笛子。为了让你明白你在瞎猜,我要去一下墓地。晚上也不怕,只要你愿意跟我去。"

"好的,"我说,"我们走吧。"

于是,在一弯月牙昏暗的光线下,我们一起上路了。渐渐地,音符变得更加低沉忧郁,逐渐消失殆尽。我催促着我那颤抖不已的同伴加快脚步,以免鬼魂也一同消失。她没说话,但显然在照我说的做,这让我立刻相信她刚才的说法是认真的。就在我们开始爬山的时候,她忽然停了下来,说:"在那里!听到了吗?"

我说我听到了一点声音,但是在周围有人居住的地方,这种声音并不足为奇,而现在时间也并不算晚。"这是给墓地的门插上插销的声音,"她郑重其事地说,"你既然还珍惜你不朽的灵魂,就别再往前走了。"

我徒劳地争辩道:"鬼魂没必要先打开插销。"可她坚持不再前行。于是,以一种前所未有的勇气,我独自一人继续走过去。

"你以为我不知道那声音吗?"她在我身后喊着,"我忘了什么也忘不了那种声音。噢,停下吧,先听我说!玛丽·维尔德明斯死的那天晚上……"我听到她在说。但是像她一样,我也听出了那是门的声音,所以即使有鬼故事可听,我也不愿停下来。后来我一直希望当时自己停了下来,因为在那之后我再也没能说服她讲那个故事。

登上山顶,在我前面不远处,我看到一个黑色的身影正在渐渐远去。但是因为我太专注于那个鬼魂了,以至于根本没注意那个人。后来,当我再次回想起当时的情景时,我才渐渐将以前我坐在桥上看到的那个人与这个身影联系起来。

墓地看上去是那么的静谧而肃穆。我向里面望去，心里有点害怕。我将墓地门上的插销打开又插上，看看这是否就是我听到的那种声音。就在这时，一只惊觉的兔子自草丛下蹿出，蹿过静静的土堆，逃到了树林中安全的地方。事实上，它吓了我一大跳。我只看到墓地的草被踩出了一条细细的小径，一直通向玛丽的坟墓。除此之外，我什么都没看到。

整个夏天，我有时会在树林里看到那个年轻女孩。我注意到，她不采花，也不跟小鸟一起唱歌，只是长时间地坐在浓密的树荫深处，动也不动。就连被风吹到脸颊和额头上的卷曲的发丝，她也不像别人那样撩开。她似乎不喜欢有人为伴，也不去寻求伴侣。只有一次，也是她最后一次走入小树林，我才注意到我认为是她哥哥的那个人在陪着她。那次，她没有像往常一样坐在树荫里，而是闲散地走着，时而倚在她的守护者的臂膊上。他几次撩开她额上的卷发，将头低下去，仿佛在吻她。

又过了几天，我有些不舒服，便叫来村里的医生。我们的话题很自然地扯到了那些生病的和死去的人那里。

"在我的病人里，"他说，"我最深切关注的莫过于那个村舍中的一个年轻女孩。真的，自从我知道她必死无疑之后，我就几乎不再考虑其他任何事情。一个奇怪的孩子，"他接着说，"她似乎不喜欢活着，也不惧怕死亡。她不哭，也不笑。虽然我近来常跟她在一起，却从没见她睡过觉。她的身体并无疼痛折磨，脸上的表情也始终很平静，那双忧郁的眼睛总是睁得大大的。"

在那之后的第二天晚上，虽然病还没好，但我还是顺路拜访了那间村舍，希望能为那个病中的女孩做些什么。她房间的雪白的窗帘已放了下来，一扇玻璃窗被推上去一些，里面很静——无声无息。门微微开着。我停了下来，听到里面传来一声低沉而压抑的呻吟。我不会听错的。我没有敲门，将门推开，走了进去。

一袭白单，将一个人从头到脚盖了起来。瞬间，我明白了可怕的事实——女孩死了。床头边坐着一个人，像石头般一动不动。这正是我常常想要见到的那个人。房间几近黑暗，他的脸埋在手里——然而，我认得他——是他那天在桥上从我的身边走过。

就在这时，他们的管家，或者说一个我认为是管家的女人走了进来。那个女人对他耳语几句，他便起身走了出去，所以我只模糊地看了他一眼。他离开之后，那个女人将尸体头上的白布掀了开来。我大吃一惊，因为我看到那双眼睛仍未闭上。看到我如此吃惊，她开了口，同时将一块餐巾叠起来，压在女孩的眼皮上。

"是很奇怪，不过这孩子活着的时候，也总不愿闭上眼睛——人们说她妈妈死的时候，仍在期盼着一个不会回来的人。这孩子从生下来就很警觉，而且不睡觉。"

接下来的两天一直阴雨连绵——先前的刺激和过早的出门，使我的病又犯了，所以我没去参加葬礼。然而，透过窗户，我看到人们正在为尸体的埋葬作着准备，就在树林边荒凉的小墓地中。我很吃惊。

接下来的两周里，我为去那个村舍吊唁作着准备。但当我到了那里，才发现人已走了——村舍一片寂静，空无一人。

回家的路上，我在那个鬼魂出没的墓地旁停了下来：在玛丽·维尔德明斯的坟墓旁，就是那个更为奇怪的孩子的墓。那里的荆棘和蓟草已被仔细地割除。两个坟墓都没有墓碑，也没有名字，但是周围都种着茂密的紫罗兰，盛开着蓝白相间的花。我所知道的只是，她们都已安息了。

6. 塞斯·米尔福德兄妹的心情

十月天空蓝色底边上笼罩着红色的薄雾，时不时可以听见依依不舍地徘徊在同伴身后的鸟儿捉摸不定的、不耐烦的啁啾声。最后的鸟群也已如同云彩一般飞越山峦消失在远方。森林还未退去秋日的光辉，绚烂至极。北风似乎仍然在呼唤逝去的夏日，掠过枫树长长的枝头，把所剩无几的颤抖的枝叶抖落到金色的垄沟中。山间的岔路口到处都是低矮的泛着红色光泽的桉树。褐色的、浓密的野葡萄藤上缀满了一簇簇黑色的果实，费力地攀爬在黄樟及榆树间。橡树依然高高耸立，笼罩着一层宏伟的绿色。

太阳爬上山头，愈变愈大，然后逐渐下山，慢慢地夜幕就降临了，将一层神圣的宁静洒向周围的一切，秋夜！

对于大多数人而言，秋天无疑是让人忧郁的季节，拂去夏日的光芒和美丽，留给世界的就如同当初的伊甸园，人类的堕落抹去了它的光辉，悲伤的雨露遮盖了天使的足迹。

在一片又高又平的田茬中，塞斯正在犁地，田茬两边与浓密的森林接壤处，一边是一片开放的草坪，另一边视野所到之处是一间农宅和一条乡间小路。空气中散发着泥土的清香，疲倦的马匹顺从地由主人牵引着来回犁地。

暮色日渐深沉，透过两边的树梢已然可以看见一轮新月的银色光圈。塞斯在离家最近的地头停了下来，从垄沟中拔出犁，搁在紧邻地里收割过后的残株边上，松开马长长的缰绳，卷起来，系在其中一匹马细长光滑的脖颈上，松开门闩，让牲口们独自悠闲地踱回家去。

双手环绕胸前，双眼低视脚下，年轻的庄稼汉无精打采地在篱笆上靠了一段时间，直到马群们行进到下一个栅栏，没法继续前进，不耐烦地发出一两声嘶叫声才打断了他的白日梦。塞斯拖着笨重的靴子在枯萎的长草丛中来回地走着，似乎是要洗掉身上从田沟中带来的潮湿的泥土。又一次地双手环绕胸前，塞斯把帽檐拉低了一点，盖住了他愠怒的眉宇，慢吞吞地机械地踱回家去，直到他被一声轻快活泼的问候打断。"塞斯，你好啊！"抬头望去，塞斯露出半是悲伤半是轻蔑的笑容，几乎不明白世上还有人如此快乐，不知道应该表示遗憾还是蔑视。问候塞斯的是一位年轻的农夫邻居，他脸色红润，无疑身体健康，本性善良，他有一对灰色的大眼睛，胡子已经开始有点变黄。年轻的农夫热情友好地握着这位异乎寻常的邻居的手，率直地因为擅自穿越田地而向塞斯道歉。因为显然此片土地是有主人的，而且不管公正与否，塞斯或多或少都被认为是有一点自私和挑剔，尤其对擅自闯入他的领地的人。显然，年轻人已经把最好的服饰穿上身，至于他的衣服式样看起来是否更适合娱乐场所，这位年轻人并没放在心上。他说，他要去一英里左右的地方去和死尸一起"熬夜"，他现在走的路显然可以缩短距离。

"谁死了？"塞斯询问，头一次表露出一点兴趣。"哼！"得知死者是谁后，"小伙子比我还年轻呢，不过死了也未尝不是一种幸福。"塞斯继续说道。

"是的，"快乐的农夫说，似乎没有听懂或者显然没有留意塞斯最后的话，"是的，他太年轻了，如果他能活到一月二十二号的话，他就可以自己独立了。晚安！"

塞斯目送着年轻人离去，一边朝家里走去一边半是大声地重复着——
"人类的第一次不服从，偷食了禁果
禁树上致命的味道
给世界带来了死亡，给人类带来了悲伤"

有些时候我们看上去似乎不得不盲目地到处漂流，最终如同花儿一般毁灭。尤其真实的是，经过认真但是徒劳的试图突破位于想象最远处以及上帝的永恒光芒间的黑暗的努力之后，我们的思绪回到凡身之上。此外，似乎人类注定将要从永恒到某一轮回，无法逃避，于是伤心之后，我们都抛弃了各自崇高的理想。我们太缺乏孩童的信念，太缺乏对"我们的上帝"简单的信任和依赖。

"善良的人都非宿命论者
邪恶的人因需要而作恶。"

我们的诗人如此吟诵。然而也有一些本身不坏的人最终选择相信难以捉摸的命运，这部分人归因于脾气不好——喜怒无常或者更有甚者病态的，或部分归结于长期以来因为强烈的渴望与能力不足的矛盾产生的烦躁情绪。

这类不幸人的代表之一就是塞斯·米尔福德。出生、成长与他如今所继承的这间农庄，从未远离他所生活的这片大山，然而内心拥有"永恒的渴求"。他天生羞怯无自信，没有受过完整的教育。他逐渐长大成人，对世事充满着不满，一刻不能停歇，可怜的人蔑视他在习惯和行为上都隶属的圈子。他不合群，尽管他拥有比社会上那些有着更高地位的、看不起他的人更有天赋的头脑思维。没人喜欢他，哪怕是和他一起住的他的两个亲姐妹。他供养她们，尽管不是十分富裕的生活，却也是尽他所能。他本来或许可以做得更好些，但是他的命运决定他只能如现在这般，不可能比现在更好了。

他的两个姐妹，玛丽和安妮，比他受过更好的教育，比他更老练，更有雄心，她们自己认为她们已经通过种种方式成功地提升了自己的地位，远高于她们笨拙、心地不良的兄弟。

塞斯敏感地意识到她们缺乏爱，并痛苦地意识到她们有时以他为耻，结果他不愿耗费丝毫力气去保持她们想要的状态。当春天来临的时候，他无精打采地播种，当夏日的艳阳转为秋日的丰收时，他本能地去收割庄稼，没有任何虔诚的祈祷吟诵，没有想过去打更多的谷子。

……

她们有理由抱怨她们兄弟的鼠目寸光以及奢侈的生活，但由于总是强调这一点，同时又夸大塞斯的缺点，她们逐渐对弟弟越来越冷淡，而塞斯本人懒得改变这一状况。他们很少碰面，通常是在吃饭的时候，大家几乎是沉默。

农场拥有大片的值钱的土地，但可悲的是由于没有得到重视而毫无利润可言。草坪中到处都是一片片的荆棘，篱笆是如此的残破，邻居家不受拘束的猪群牛群经常随意穿过来。即使是原先以出生高贵而引以自豪的田产，如今看上去也是

"往昔的愉快场所

今朝的烦恼处所，我们的房子"

护墙板上的油漆已经有些脱落了，有些烟囱摇摇欲坠，百叶窗已经破烂不堪，阳台上一半的栏杆已经消失，尽管还有些大柱子，院子里的篱笆东倒西歪，而且前门的铰链也已经脱落。然而杂草丛生的过道两旁的花圃以及窗上那些没有拉上的百叶窗上积满雪的帘子都预示着此处有人居住。刚刚从厨房烟囱飘出的大团的蓝色烟雾给这个地方以不同寻常的快活舒适的感觉。

玛丽在沏茶，在地窖里上上下下忙进忙出，边忙边唱。安妮去挤牛奶了。她们生活得很简朴。尽管在大多数情况下，正如我所描述的那样，姐弟之间常常保持沉默，没有任何表情。但是偶尔也有共有的好秉性融化彼此之间冰山的时候，那样的早晨或者晚上会在愉快中度过。

"告诉我们今天发生了什么意外以至于凯撒看上去如此悲伤？"当塞斯走向她以及边上的斑点奶牛时，安妮·米尔福德愉快地问道。没有留意到安妮的愉快问候，塞斯突然打开门，他没有像他应该做的那样把手穿过马缰，他折磨他的马，按照他所选择的路线行进，这条路线如此接近那头奶牛以至于它突然转了一个圈，因此把牛奶全部倒翻在安妮的干净衣服上。然而，安妮心情很好，所以没有发很大的火，她在塞斯身后喊道："快停下来，看看你干的好事——我正好在想到底什么颜色最映衬我的肤色。"

年轻人默不作声，闷闷不乐地走过去，看上去似乎没有留意到安妮的斥责声。他假装自己很忙的样子，直到安妮重新往桶里挤了些牛奶才走过去，像是偶然的样子，他在安妮手里接过桶提到屋子

里去。

"我觉得马上快要下雨了。"安妮边使劲挤牛奶边说道。塞斯回应说他也如此认为，这是当天他第一次和她说话。

当塞斯在平时总是放在门边石头台阶上的锡盆里洗完手和脸时，安妮也挤完奶，洗完手，把井栏边她的铮亮的锡盆龙头拧小。茶也沏好了，尽管女孩们已经竭尽所能利用贫乏的食物，这顿饭还是显然不能满足一个饥肠辘辘的男人的需求。

"好吧，塞斯，"玛丽说道，一边往他的茶杯里加了一勺糖，塞斯喜欢喝甜一点的茶，"我今天把你所有的旧靴子送给希尔上尉了，他想用它们来熏烟驱赶蚊子。"尽管很努力地想要控制，塞斯还是忍不住大笑，开始吃晚饭，刚才他还表示没心情吃饭呢。

"他和我们待了一会，"玛丽继续说道，"拿一些早期的逸闻趣事把我们逗得哈哈笑，那些事情都是他退伍不做国民军上尉之后发生的，他用他的制服换了一头小公牛。"

"噢，好大的落差啊，我可怜的同胞！"塞斯把自己的杯子递过去想再添点——他以前很少这么做。在这类轻松活泼的谈话中，晚饭时光很快过去了——一件如此小的事件改变了吃饭的氛围。当晚饭快要吃完的时候，塞斯拿起菜篮子，说他要去村庄看看能不能给家里添点储备。

"今天晚上就算了吧，"姐妹俩马上同时说，"你看上去很疲惫，明天再说吧，或者后天也行。"

然而，她们越是劝他不要去，他越是想要去——平时就是责备他整整一周他也不会去做——他还是出门了，说也许他可以去寻找一些无害的谈资，活跃一下明天晚饭的气氛。好多天来，他的脚步和心情没有如此轻松了。抬高那扇破门走了出去，他决定要去铁匠那里订购点新的铰链。

喝茶时谈论的事情被抛在了一边，夜晚愈变愈冷，灶台上有一小簇火苗在欢快地燃烧。当塞斯回来的时候，安妮坐在一张老式的工作桌旁，正在用灰色的羊毛纱线编一只袜子，玛丽则在读她最喜欢的小说。塞斯把装满东西的篮子放在桌子上，拿出一块半干的牛肉火腿，"明天晚饭的时候我想烤这个吃，这里还有一些蔓越莓，也可以炖着吃。"

玛丽说没问题，按照他说的办，好心地把摇椅让给他坐，他们三个一起坐了下来——安妮织袜子,玛丽看书,塞斯则在火前面前前后后地摇着他的摇椅,偶尔还对玛丽看的书作一些评论,直到门边樱桃树边的老公鸡鸣叫,九点了。

接着,他们三人把烟灰聚拢,讨论未来的修缮计划。院子里的木栅栏需要弄直,然后刷白,灌木需要修剪修剪,走道上要铺垫沙砾,百叶窗要修补并且油漆,女孩们编织的碎呢地毯要重新编织一下铺在饭厅,要雇一个人帮忙挤奶以及协助做一些农场的活。"然后,塞斯,你就会有更多的时间看书思考。"女孩们说。

对于他们而言未来看上去是如此的美好。通过交换观点、愿望,甚至是恐惧,彼此间的手握得更紧。看上去他们的计划执行起来是如此的简单。他们各自回去休息,对他们自己以及世界都无比满意。

第二天,塞斯又同往常一样出现在田茬里,但是面部表情比以往振奋不少,脚步更加扎实轻松,时不时停下来让他的马休息一下,随意吃点田边的荆棘,他自己则从口袋里拿出一本书,坐在草地边上开始他的阅读。看上去他的确很令人羡慕——他是他身边这大片田地的主人。

天色很阴沉,东风又冷又阴,树叶掉得很快,落叶沿着小树林堆成一堆一堆的。一阵强风吹来,树上的坚果纷纷掉落,疾风迫使家畜们躲到了围栏的角落里,山两旁的天色一直都是阴沉,让人感到十分不适。

给自己定了一些任务,日落后塞斯继续前后来回地犁地。最终他完成了他的任务,接下来和之前那晚一样,从垄沟中拔出犁,搁在紧邻地里收割过后的残株边上,松开马的缰绳,吹着一首歌的片段,塞斯轻快地往家走去。照看好他的马之后,他在胳膊下夹了一捆干草,打算回家喂奶牛。可是遗憾的是,当他走到院子里的时候,他发现奶牛不见了,天色渐晚,天上的乌云也预示着很快就会有一场暴雨。

我可以很快把它带回来,他想,晚饭很快就好了,于是他匆匆忙忙地朝草地走去,可是当他到那里的时候,天色是如此的黑暗,以至于他看不清很远的地方,他不得不一圈一圈地寻找它的下落。此时,他发现篱笆已经被吹倒在树林边上,塞斯猜想它无疑应该在树林里面,于是他继续搜寻,尽管此时黑暗已经变得越来越浓厚,冰冷的雨不断落下来,早晨的温暖使得塞斯并没有穿着外套去地里干活，因而尽管他的搜寻最终成功了，他自己也被淋得浑身湿透。最终还是从这头让人愤怒的奶牛身上挤出奶来，装满奶的桶也拎回了家，塞斯想当他打开门走进厨房，家里应该有温暖的火苗，晚饭也准备好了。可是让他惊讶和不悦的是，两者都没有。饭厅依然荒芜没有生机，不过客厅倒是通红的，有灯光和温暖。欢快的喋喋不休的说话声表明家里有陌生人。塞斯不悦地眉头紧锁，他姐姐们的朋友不是他的朋友，完全不属于同一个阶层，他既不认识他们也不想认识他们，而且在目前这种轻快下，他显然不用假装出现。家里没有佣人可以使唤换外套——他自己不知道去哪里找，于是他在没有生机的厨房坐下，全身又湿又冷，他尽量耐心地等客人的离去。

  这种情形令人很不舒服，他的心情很快变得不好，他想起他所知道的或者经历的所有不公正和怠慢——它们不止是一点点，他开始夸大那些让他苦恼的困难和障碍，直到人生看上去没有希望，没有值得继续活下去的事情。他的前面后面都是黑暗。时间变得让人难以忍受的冗长，最终，塞斯精疲力竭地回到他的房间，半是幼稚地希望他还是死了算了。

  愤怒、寒意使他刚开始的时候睡不着，再没有什么比失眠更可悲了。突然一阵强烈的头痛向他袭来，他在床上长时间地翻来滚去，从床的这边滚到那边。然而疲倦还是最终战胜了痛苦，接近早晨的时候他终于恍恍惚惚、断断续续地睡着了。这一觉一直睡到了大天亮，太阳早已升得老高。头疼依然，大脑迟钝、笨重，脸颊两旁因为发烧而泛出红晕。他让自己半躺着，拉起床头的窗帘，朝外望去。声音吵醒了他的忠诚的常常睡在主人窗户下面的小狗朱诺，朱诺直起身来，四肢趴在窗台上，摇晃着尾巴，渴望地看了他一会，发出"呜呜"声。他马上伸手去亲切地抚摸它，他用呆板沉重的目光望着它，它从窗台上跳下来，像往常一样蜷伏在地上，哀怨地狂吠。

  "不祥之兆。"塞斯自言自语道，随即又躺倒在他的枕头上，发出一阵阵呻吟声。

  与此同时，姑娘们都起床了，发现火还没有生，没法准备早饭。于是一个人去敲她们兄弟的房门，厉声叫他起来生火。而塞斯因为在熟睡中，既没听见当然也没法回答。等了一会儿，没有回应，她们很费力地自己生起火来，而且成功了。最终当早饭终于摆上桌子后，她们坐下抱怨，如果塞斯不愿意起来生火的话，她们也肯定不会叫他一起吃饭了。

她们这么做也并不高兴，相反的是，她们非常的不快。然而，她们觉得程序上这是必须要履行的职责，要不就会对不起她们受侮辱的尊严。

早饭时光在沉默中度过，姐妹俩收拾好桌子，塞斯依然一直没有过来。然而坐在饭厅的火炉前，重复着前一天晚上所谈论的事件，她们很快就完全把塞斯忘了。

大概过了一个小时左右，年轻人从他的房间里走出来，经过她们俩坐的房间，不过姐妹俩谁都没有抬头，或者说无论如何她们都没有注意到他，直到听到他在厨房里倒了一杯冷咖啡。其中一个说道："如果你在该起床的时候起来，你本该有早饭吃的。现在你没饭吃了。"

"我不想吃早饭。"塞斯回答。

"你突然变得很谦恭了。"她回答道，接下来就不再说话了。

拖着沉重的身子走了一会，感觉并没有怎么被注意到，他觉得他有必要回到自己的床上去。他又回到床上了，没人多注意他一眼。

"我猜想塞斯是不是生病了？"当他回自己房间去的时候，他的一个姐姐说道。

可是另外一个说以往他病了，他一定会想办法让她们俩知道的。于是她们的谈话又回到了轻松的事情上。她们愉快的音调和笑声穿过塞斯的房间，让他感到既伤心又刺耳。年轻的农夫觉得漫长的时间是如此令人厌倦。

他被口渴所折磨，但尽管发着烧，想到早晨那个刺耳的声音，他没让别人倒水给他，于是这也就自然加剧了他的痛苦。他躺在床上翻来覆去直到一天几乎结束，他的呻吟声被安妮听见，引起了她的注意。此刻的安妮不同于早晨的厉声斥责，她能够感觉到他可能需要关注。放下手中的活，安妮马上朝他的房间走去。

诧异惊慌于他在一天一夜内的可怕变化，她尽她的所能想要减轻他的痛苦。

她很快地拿来亚麻布，当他的脸和手完全浸在冷水中，他的枕头位置被调整了一下，塞斯觉得舒服多了。随之，安妮去准备沏茶，告诉他睡一小觉茶就会沏好了，然后她确保他马上会好起来。但是刚才片刻歇息的头痛此刻来得更强烈了，他的两颊迅速热得发烫。

"哦，但愿塞斯很快能够好起来！"玛丽去准备晚饭了。无疑现在她们会准备他最喜欢吃的食物。做好晚饭后，把塞斯的饭放在火炉旁，玛丽打开他的房门叫他起来，"你不会想到我们今天的晚饭有多棒！"

"哦，玛丽，"塞斯回答道，"我可能再也不能和你们一起吃晚饭了。"

他的话让玛丽几乎喘不过气来，匆忙跑到他的床前，双手环绕他的脖子，玛丽哭得像个小孩，祈求他原谅她以往所有的忽视，说她没给他足够的爱——夸大她自己的缺点，赞美放大塞斯所有的仁慈和他所有的忍耐，一遍遍地说道："噢，你必须好起来，塞斯，你必须好起来！"

他微弱地笑了一下，说他自己的缺点远远超过她的。但是如果他能够康复的话，他可能也不会做得更好，他的生命还长得很。

一周过去了，树上的树叶几乎全部掉落，躺在大片的沉重而潮湿中。大风围绕着这处老房子发出沉闷的悲叹声，天空布满乌云，秋天的雨下个不停，又阴冷又让人感到悲伤。草地的边缘处，田茬的边上，那把犁还是立在一周前的位置，犁刃上满是厚厚的黄锈。

在光秃秃的槐树下，在村庄墓地的一个角落，有一抔新土，边上是一条狭长的土墩。

愿上帝带给逝者和生者以和平！我，一个脆弱又容易犯错的人，没资格评判孰是孰非。

以上是我想要讲述的一个简单的关于一个卑微的人物的悲哀和痛苦遭遇。但愿它能教会你如何体贴关心那些陪伴你共同走过通往死亡的朝圣之旅的人，途中不要争吵，当我们记起我们所做的某件错事，感受到我们根本没办法让逝者抬起苍白的头颅，接受我们的忏悔和爱的祝福，还有什么比这更痛苦呢？

7. 希尔太太和特鲁斯特太太

七月份一个最热的下午，刚刚两点钟，希尔太太已经用过了正餐，戴上了她干净的帽子，穿好了围裙。这会儿正坐在北面的门廊上，为彼得·希尔先生缝制一件棉衬衫，棉布未经漂白，因为彼得·希尔先生在收获季节总是穿这样的棉衬衫。希尔太太是一位节俭的主妇。她已经缝了一会儿了，只是时不时地要停下来"嘘"的一声轰走一群群半大的小鸡。这些小鸡总是唧唧喳喳地在门口寻觅从桌布上掉落的面包屑。正在这时，一把蓝色的大棉布伞突然合上的声音使她放下了手中的活儿，并且大声招呼：

"啊，是特鲁斯特太太啊，您怎么想到来看我们啊！"

"哦，我已经好几次都想要来了。"客人说道，很快地在蓝色的石板上跺了跺她的小脚——这是位小个子的女士，她用细布手帕仔细地擦了擦脚，然后才大胆地踩在了希尔太太家的地面上。接着，她一边握手，一边又说："可有一阵子了，我记得上次是带着我们家简来的。你记得吗？那会儿她还是个婴儿呢，现在她都三岁了。"

"真的吗？"希尔太太说，她边去解开邻居头上戴的软帽的帽绳，边接着又说，"没错，二月份她就三岁了。"听到这句话，特鲁斯特太太连着叹了两口气，一次比一次重，尽管据我所知没有什么可能的原因会让她如此叹气，除非，我想到，也许时光的流逝使她想到了人生的短暂。

希尔太太将特鲁斯特太太的软帽放在了她的"备用床"上，又用一块小小的、淡蓝色的、专门为这样的情况准备的纱巾盖上。接着，从柜子抽屉里取出一把大大的火鸡羽毛做的扇子，递给了她的客人，说道："今天真暖和，是吧？"

"噢，太可怕了！太可怕了！天热得像烤箱一样，我整个夏天都多多少少地在忍受酷暑的折磨。可是这本来就是一个充满了苦难的世界。"特鲁斯特太太半闭着眼睛，似乎要挡住这可怕的现实。

"你也知道，晒干草需要这样阳光充足的天气，所以我们只能忍着了，"希尔太太答道，"另外，我大部分时候都能在房子附近找到个凉快的地方。我把针线活放在门廊这里，烤面包或者做晚餐时就做上一些，这样就不会中暑了。另外，我一天中总能做上不少呢！"

"这里的确是个凉快的好地方，被葡萄藤完全遮住了，"特鲁斯特太太说，又叹了一口气，"料理它们一定费了你不少工夫吧？"

"噢，不不，一点儿也不麻烦。你只要把它们种下去，它们早晨晒那么会儿太阳就能长得很好了。今年秋天我帮你留点种子，明年夏天你的门廊下就能跟我这里一样有浓密的绿荫了。"

"就算那样，对我也没什么用。"特鲁斯特太太说，"我一个星期从头到尾根本没时间坐下来。另外，藤蔓之类的东西我从来没种好过。你知道，有的人就是无论如何也种不好。"

希尔太太个子矮小，体态丰满，看起来可能会让人觉得她行动起来应该不怎么灵活，会觉得太热的天气让她行动不便。她生性乐观，是个乐天派。一到下雨天，她就会卷起裙子，穿上厚底鞋，跟平时一样蹒跚着东走西走看看，边走边自言自语："这下草可就长起来了。"或者："这雨能让萝卜长得快些。"或者说些其他让她能略感安慰的话。

特鲁斯特太太则又瘦又小，看起来似乎一年四季中应该没有行动不灵便的时候。但是，正如她自己常说的，她是个可怜又不幸的人。她常常顾影自怜，按理说这倒也不奇怪，因为据她自己说，没人关心她要承受多重的负担。

她们——这些贤妻良母们——是近邻，但是她们之间诸如饮茶这样的社交活动倒并不常有，这是因为特鲁斯特太太有时没法像其他人那样穿衣服，因为天气有时候太热，有时候又太冷，而且像上面说的那样，没人想要见她，她也确定自己不会愿意去一个别人不想她去的地方。另外，别的女人没有一个像她那样要打理一个那么简陋的大宅子。但是整个邻里之间都把她的房子称作大宅，所以特鲁斯特太太为此付出的辛苦倒也以某种方式得到了补偿。不过，正如她自己所言，家里倒也真的挺简陋，有一半的房间里都没布置，部分原因是他们用不上这些房间，还有就是他们也弄不到家具。所以，那座宅子就那么立在太阳底下，没装百叶窗，周围也没有树，特鲁斯特太太说她觉得可能以后也就保持这个样子了。她一直反对建这个宅子，可又毫无法子。但是，也有人说特鲁斯特先生曾经用他太太的围裙上的带子量他们房子的尺寸——但这也可能是诬陷。

特鲁斯特太太坐在那里为着泛泛的事情大发感慨的时候，希尔太太钉好了最后一粒扣子，把完工了的衣服上的线头抖了抖，似乎是举起来满意地看了看，然后叠了起来。

"看，你总是这样！"特鲁斯特太太说，"你都做好了半件衬衣，而我什么也没干成。我的手老出汗，所以没法儿拿针，再试也没用。"

"把你手里的活儿放一放吧，我们去园子里走走。"

于是希尔太太往头上搭了条毛巾，手里拿了个小铁盆子，两人就朝园子走去——特鲁斯特太太打着那把蓝色的伞遮着太阳，嘴里却说伞重得要死，还不如不打。园子里豌豆、萝卜、覆盆子、红醋栗，还有许多别的东西，都长势喜人。特鲁斯特太太说什么东西到了希尔太太这里都长势茂盛，而自己的园子里全长着杂草。"你这里还有蜜蜂，难道它们不会蜇到孩子，给你惹很多麻烦吗？我想是五月里吧，特鲁斯特（特鲁斯特太太总是这样称呼自己的丈夫）买了一个蜂房，事实上，他拿一头小牛犊换的——那可是头很不错又漂亮的牛犊——那些蜜蜂可从来没给我们带来一丁点儿的好处"——这个不幸的女人又在叹气了。

"的确，他们说，"希尔太太同情地说，"有些人是养不了蜜蜂，万一蜂王死了，它们就可能会发生纷争，那就养不好了。不过我们从来没遇到过这种倒霉的事情，而且去年我们除了自己家里用的，卖蜂蜜就卖了40美元。你们家的蜜蜂都陆续死掉了吗？还是怎么了，特鲁斯特太太？"

"天啊，"这位闷闷不乐的访客说道，"我的大儿子有一天被蜇到了，他一怒之下就把蜂箱给掀了，而我两三天后才发现，叫特鲁斯特去把蜂箱重新放好的时候，上上下下哪里都找不出一只蜜蜂了。"

"不会吧！这些固执的小家伙们！不过一定得小心点照顾它们，我也听说过它们无缘无故地就飞走了。"

这会儿盆子里已经装满了红醋栗，所以她们就回到了房子里。希尔太太坐在厨房的门槛上，开始准备下午茶的水果了。而特鲁斯特太太把椅子拉过来，说："你听到过威廉·麦克米肯家的蜜蜂的事吗？"

希尔太太从没听到过，又表示非常急于知道，就听到了下面的故事：

"他太太，你知道，就是那个叫萨莉·梅的，老话说——
　　'姓改了字母没改，
　　没有飞上枝头可落在了鸡窝'

"萨莉可是个讲究穿戴又奢侈的姑娘，每年她的帽子都要'重新收拾'两次，她有数不清的衣服、缎带和别的好东西。她妈妈事事都惯着她，以前总说萨莉拥有的一切都是她应得的，还说她有多重，就值多重的金子。萨莉以前哪都去，真的。任何的大场面都少不了她，女人们缝棉被的聚会她也总是帮着张罗。姑娘们要赶时髦就学她，因为她经常待在城里汉娜姨妈家里，也总带来些新的花样。你记得吧，以前她的衣服袖子总比别人的宽大些，然后她会在里面垫上垫肩——啊，天哪！她的奢侈说也说不完。

"她有件会变颜色的丝绸衣裳，黄蓝相间的，胸前还加了硬衬。以前有些人说，她一穿上这件衣服，连在地上走都是对她的亵渎。不过我倒从来没觉得她有丝毫的傲气或者狂妄。要是有谁生病了，没人会比她心肠更好。而且，她这个人总是那么温厚善良，干活儿的时候嘴里会一直哼着歌。我记得她嫁人之前老是唱同一首歌，第一句是：

'我的心上人有着乌黑明亮的眼睛。'

"他们说她指的是威廉·麦克米肯，还说她终归不大可能得到他——因为很多人觉得他们两个一点儿也不般配，因为他们的性情反差太大。威廉性格太过安静，绝对是个居家男子。可是尽管他有学问，有时候还在内河的汽船上工作，就家世来讲真没什么可夸耀的。"

希尔太太此时已经把红醋栗都拣好了，特鲁斯特太太也停了下来。希尔太太把茶壶装上水，然后往井边的架子上挂了条毛巾，随风飘动的毛巾告诉彼得该回来吃晚饭了。

"噢，要是你愿意，把椅子往厨房门口挪一点点好吗？"希尔太太说，"这样我就可以一边做饼干，一边听你讲了。"

她说着，走到门口这里来，把手里的面包屑撒在地上，还一边唤着："咕咕咕——唧唧唧——"听到声音，一大群鸡马上就围了过来。她弯下腰，抓了一只最肥的。一小时后，这只鸡就烤熟摆在了餐桌上。

"我的天，你这么容易就抓住了！"特鲁斯特太太叫道。

她好一会儿也没能平静下来接着刚才的话题讲。不过，她最后还是讲了下去——

"其实，像我刚才说的，大家都认为威廉·麦克米肯不会娶萨莉·梅。可怜的家伙，都说他完全变了个人。他能娶上一打老婆，可谁也不能代替萨莉。她会是他出色的妻子，尽管她是个野丫头。

"梅爸爸反对这桩婚事，他威胁说要把萨莉——自己的亲生女儿逐出家门，还要脱离父女关系。但是她犟得很，非要嫁给自己喜欢的人。她也做到了，尽管没从家里得到一根线，也没得到任何嫁妆。真的，她离家的时候，除了一箱蜜蜂，她父亲什么东西也没给她。他脾气非常暴躁，女儿结婚后就一直称她麦克米肯太太。可是萨莉好像并不介意，仍然精心料理着蜂箱，好像那些蜜蜂值一千美元似的。到了冬天，她就每天喂它们，如果有就喂枫糖，没有的话，就把黑砂糖放在小碟子里，或者馊了的剩菜。

"可是有一天一只蜜蜂蜇了她的手——我记得好像是右手——萨莉马上就说这是个恶兆。当天夜里她就梦到自己出去喂蜜蜂的时候，一块黑纱系在蜂箱上。她觉得那是死亡的标记，就告诉了丈夫，还告诉了我跟汉克斯太太。哦不，我不确定她是不是告诉汉克斯太太了，不过汉克斯太太的确从什么地方听说了此事。"

"是吗？"希尔太太边说边用围裙擦眼泪，"我真的现在才知道，可怜的麦克米肯太太去世了。"

"哎呀，她没有去世，"特鲁斯特太太答道，"她一直都好好的，只是觉得自己就快不行了。"不过特鲁斯特太太讲的故事带来的伤感让她自己没法干活，所以一下午过去了她也没干成什么——她一出来串门就干不成活儿了。

与此同时，希尔太太似乎没费什么事就做好了令人胃口大开的晚餐。彼得回来的正是时候，他从井里打了一桶水，拿了井边架子上的毛巾，自然又不需费力，也省得妻子麻烦。

"特鲁斯特永远也想不到这么做。"特鲁斯特太太说，说完又表示感叹："啊，算了！"似乎她的苦日子不久就会过去。

特鲁斯特太太品尝了甜滋滋的蜂蜜，想起了自己家翻掉的蜂箱，清脆的小红萝卜又让她想到家里满是杂草的园子。因此，总的说来，她今天来串门，她自己说，只是令她觉得自己很可怜，会让她接下来的整整一周都心情低落，就连她临走时希尔太太又拿给她的一小筐新鲜水果也没能让她心情好上一点点。

"彼得可以驾马车送你的。"希尔太太说。

"不了，"特鲁斯特太太说，拒绝得像是对方在施舍她，"上车下车的比走路还麻烦。"所以她就步履蹒跚地走回了家，嘴里说着："还是有的人生下来运气就好啊。"

8. 古迹遗风

苜蓿角的墓地只不过是个朴素简单的乡村墓地，没有诸如"幽幽境"或"安息谷"之类诗化的名字。在那块墓地里，有个长满青草的高土丘，朴素的大理石墓碑上铭刻着一个革命前辈的生辰卒日。墓志铭出自墓主人手笔，因为墓主是个意志坚定、一丝不苟的民主党人，所以尽管墓志铭简明朴素，但未曾忘记提及墓主十七岁就加入正规军,直至战争结束一直在军中服役的往事。戴尔叔叔为这段不同凡响的经历而感到格外自豪,他可受不了亲戚朋友把这段经历忘得一干二净。我猜想,戴尔叔叔会沾沾自得地以为常有疲惫的旅人会在他坟头大树的阴凉处休憩,读着铭文,想着这墓下埋着的一定不是什么凡尘俗骨。紧挨着他那盖满草皮的宽大高耸的安息之所有一个低矮的小墓穴,上面长满野玫瑰,却连块墓石都不见。

  光阴十载,墓上落满了树叶。荆棘藤上,两块墓碑间也满是树叶,树叶变黄,枯萎,然后随风飘逝,但从没看见有哪个孩子或孩子的孩子们为此洒过一滴眼泪。偶尔,会有人穿过墓碑间长长的蒿草地去看望他,这时人们总是平静地谈到他的乐善好施、慷慨大方,骄傲地说起他的自我牺牲和英勇行为。有时,人们从那些无名的小坟丘上采集些玫瑰花放到那个大墓前。

  戴尔叔叔和他的三兄弟属于最早在苜蓿角定居的人,因而现在欣欣向荣的小村中的众多家庭都跟戴尔叔叔家有点或亲或疏的关系,我们家就属于其中之一。尽管我叫他戴尔叔叔,并不表明我们有亲戚关系。而是如同认识他喜欢他的很多年轻人,因为受到他那温和开朗的性格感染而那么叫他,这样显得很亲近。

  我记得第一次见他的时候,觉得他很老。对于小孩子来说,长大成人似乎要迈过我们很难企及的界限,而我们与白发苍苍的老者之间的年龄差距远比我们想象的大。

  让我描述一下他的形象,只是恐怕我难以将我心目中的戴尔叔叔完完整整地呈现出来。我对这个形象虽历经多年,记忆仍然深切,只可惜我的拙笔不是生动的画笔。在我家小茅屋西边的常春藤遮顶的走廊上,有多少次夏日的午后,我坐在他的腿上,听他讲突袭和防御的故事,描述胜利和失败,讲述遭遇野兽的故事,听他描述草原熊熊的火光和水牛群在草原奔跑时发出的类似地震的隆隆声。我经常听他谈到他独自在荒野上度过的第一晚,后来他在那儿盖了自己的小木屋。一棵参天大树的树干着了火,火势迅速蔓延到树顶,火焰吞噬了无数枝干,火花四处飞落,借着风势如同一列闪亮的列车飞速前进照亮了整个森林。他和他的兄弟打算在那里安家立命,那里在当时可不是什么好住所,他们没有床睡觉,只用一堆树叶做床,而且他们可以用来御寒的衣被也少之又少。没有人站岗放哨,他们根本不敢睡觉，担心野兽和野人来袭。他们曾经有一两次竟真的看到灌木丛里透出的饥饿目光，但是他们不能确定到底是人还是野兽。因此他们手拿锋利的匕首或装满子弹的滑膛枪，或躺，或坐，彻夜保持警惕，可能只能对着狼群的号叫和豹子的低吼讲故事了。

两对又瘦又疲倦的小牛翻山越岭为他们驮来生活用品，到目的地后就被他们赶去吃草了。但他们到达早就选好的地点时天已经黑了，只能听到猫头鹰在昏暗的月光下不和谐的叫声。

在计划中即将建起的小木屋旁边的高地旁有几棵胡桃树，成为草原上的方向标，旁边那条通向附近要塞的小路也清晰可见。荒野上的景象大致差不多，但对于经验丰富的猎手来说，这样一个特殊所在是非常容易辨认的。

牛已经十分的疲倦，不必担心它们会跑远，它们在离营地最近的小树边吃了一会儿草，趴在树叶中睡去了。有一段时间你可以听到它们踩踏低矮的灌木丛的声音，或是用牙啃断榉木碧绿的枝叶，或是榆树的嫩枝，但是不久以后，它们就地卧倒，发出沉重的呼吸声。

拂晓时分，它们中的一头不见了，留下它的同伴，尽管戴尔叔叔警惕地搜寻了所有地方，但是仍然没有寻觅到它的踪迹。

我永远想象不到体格强壮的戴尔叔叔年轻时伐树、造屋、击杀野兽的样子。但那时造房子也不过是小事一桩，只不过是找一些笔直的小树，运来一些黏土泥灰（当然这活是牛来做的），然后找些壮汉砍树，砍个一天半日的。我只记得他是个头发稀疏的老头，手上青筋暴突，脸色苍白，看上去体力衰退，但是这一点我也说不清，因为他似乎生命力旺盛，尽管年已六十，仍然有一颗年轻的心。他心态年轻，又追求年轻的东西，这点从他在花甲之年却娶了一个年轻老婆这件事上可见一斑。

按当下标准他算不上时髦，但在着装和行为举止方面可是他那代人的典范。他的性格有一半可以在他的穿着上体现出来，他一生喜爱浅黄色和蓝色。他最后的愿望是，不要等老得不能再老了才结束生命之战斗，而且要和对手握手言和。他那古朴的服装样式总是让我兴致盎然：三角帽上打着缎带结，银护膝和鞋扣子，蓝色外套上亮闪闪的纽扣和浅黄色的臀部装饰，还有边角绣有雄鹰图案的大块丝手帕（他半生都是这套装束）。这些稍许填补了他思路接不上时的空白，因为他常常把脸靠在自己精心雕刻的手杖的金头上，故事讲了一半就没了下文。

有时我小心翼翼地把手放进他的口袋里，做出偷他皮夹子的样子，好让他从梦幻中清醒过来。那个皮夹子很古旧，是很久以前一个印第安姑娘精心缝制的。那个姑娘叫"柳花"，戴尔叔叔说因为她长得美、举止优雅才得此名字。她起初到他的小木屋是当间谍的，以卖草药为幌子，很老道地顺走了那个年代不可多得的物件，顺道还给看门狗沃里克下了毒。那个可怜的家伙不吃不喝，没精打采地哀鸣了一两天，然后舔舔主人的手，离开了主人和自己的狗窝，跑到树林中一个隐秘的地方刨开树叶和小木棍，把自己葬了。

后来柳花有悔过之意，沃里克的坟上就多了一层层的苔藓和一圈深红色的竹桃植物。不过，她的懊悔不能说不是受了两块丝手帕和做鹿皮鞋的那撮羊毛衬里的影响。戴尔叔叔感到这印第安姑娘来者不善，立即赶往整整十英里外的华盛顿堡买了一些小饰品准备送给柳花，好破财免灾。羊毛采自他自己的羊群，他相信他的雪白的羊毛是整个西部最漂亮的。礼物准备得正是时候。柳花在戴尔叔叔离家的时候来过小木屋，但觉得单枪匹马无法洗劫一空，便通知了自己的族人，定下了晚上进行劫掠的计划，这些都是她后来坦白的。戴尔叔叔黄昏才回来，由于是冬天，所以他又累又冷。临近午夜时，他被门前的动静惊醒。因为他睡在灶台旁的毛皮床上，所以他半起身把炉火的余烬归拢到一处，很快那个小屋就亮了起来。不断紧逼的脚步声使他的担忧得到证实，在那没有窗帘的小窗子上突现的黑影，看上去像一个张开的巨大黑翅膀，使他的忧惧进一步证实。在那一刻，他深刻理解了恐惧的本质。柳花带她的族人来到这里打的可是坏主意。她躲在窗外偷听里面的动静，风吹拂头发扫过窗户，形成了刚才的黑影。

抵抗是没用的，当然要逃跑或躲起来也不是完全没希望，但是戴尔叔叔不想用这招。他躲过了从窗户射进来的箭，迅速穿好衣服，凛然打开了门。这一突然的举动让门外的六七个歹徒猝不及防，有一两个举起了棒子。"柳花，美丽的柳花！"戴尔叔叔高声叫道。那个印第安姑娘从移民那里学过英语，也能结结巴巴地讲点英语。戴尔叔叔接着说他梦见她来了，还说令他高兴的是她果然来了，还带了她的兄弟前来，他恳请她进屋接受刚给她买的礼物。两条红色手帕完全征服了来者，这一群人很快就坐在火堆边的床上了，火烧得噼啪作响，人们分享着戴尔叔叔的面包和烤肉，也许还有一壶威士忌，但我不是很肯定是否有酒。黎明时分，带着或真或假的满意的笑容他们离开了，没造成任何伤害，只是带走了羊毛和红手帕，戴尔叔叔丝毫没有损失，相反还多了六七个朋友。

当柳花再来时，她的头发别着象征悲痛的铁杉树枝，戴着用桦木做成的项圈，牵着一条生龙活虎又黑又壮的狼狗，她说这狗比沃里克强多了，那死狗即使周围有上千个敌人也不叫一声。从那以后，她经常来，那个小钱包就是她示好的表示之一。钱包是用她的一缕头发和丛林里某树皮的金色纤维做成的。我从没问过戴尔叔叔他的钱包里通常装多少金块银币，我现在当然不能神吹，毕竟他既不是工人，也不是有远见的经济师或精明的领导。有一件事是肯定的，那时成百英亩的荒地成了美丽丰饶的耕地，六英里外的华盛顿堡也逐渐扩大，由于风景美，被称为"西部的皇后"。那个原始的小木屋，门坏了，窗塌了，但依然矗立着。周围是厚密的丛林，来这里的乡村小路已经不是过去牛群走过的路了，所以那幢老房子就孤零零地立在耕地的最远处。它的设计者和建造者永远也不会愿意听到它被推倒的消息，感觉好似对初恋情人不忍割舍的情怀。但是和初恋情人一样的命运，那幢房子也被人遗忘得差不多了：木板缝里杂草丛生，柳花和他的族人再也没到过那里。

这样的故事西部的老人们给孩子们讲得多了。在人类历史的长河中，拓荒者们总是能目睹一个伟大帝国的鼎盛辉煌，总可以讲述他们是如何在那些似乎很古老的帝国里亲手栽下文明的种子。又好比好奇的罗马贵族从堂皇的街市跑到台伯河畔，找到依然活着的西尔维亚，探寻牧羊人福斯特劳是如何行善，收养她的受到母狼哺育的双子。[①]

---

① 故事出自罗马神话，西尔维亚是罗马城奠基人罗慕洛斯之母。罗慕洛斯和双胞胎弟弟一出生就因为祖辈的王位争夺而遭到遗弃，弃婴得到一只母狼的喂养，后被牧羊人福斯特劳发现并收养。

9. 戴尔叔叔的烦心事

从没有人问过为什么贵族们依靠老百姓生活却比老百姓生活得好。戴尔叔叔过得很舒服，他所需的东西早有人给他悄悄准备好了。金融市场是否资金短缺对他根本没有影响。那个在前面章节里讲过的神秘的小钱包终年都藏着那么多钱。

在戴尔农庄的西面有一条类似公路的大路，旁边除了几棵树外是两幢居高临下的漂亮的大房子，那两幢房子不仅具有乡村房屋的舒适，还有豪华生活的精致气派。那里住着约翰·戴尔和约瑟夫·戴尔，我前面描写过的那个老战士的儿子们。他们住在继承来的大房子里，平静地收割着父辈在危险和困难时期就播种好的庄稼。他们住在那里，收获着果实，可他们的父亲居无定所。有时他住在一个儿子家，有时又到另一个儿子家住。但是似乎一个老人是不可能激起儿孙们的怜爱的，儿子们长大了，总是想要让自己过得最好，孙子们在父亲和祖父有分歧时肯定是站在父亲这一边的。

有时恐怕乌云会遮挡戴尔叔叔生活的阳光，但愿情况不总是这样。他一手握住拐杖头，另一只手再扣上去，把下巴抵到上头，眉头紧缩，瘪着嘴，满腹心事，一坐就是几个小时。我永远也不会忘记那个时刻。约瑟夫·戴尔太太留他在家摇摇篮，哄孩子：为什么祖父就不能干干照看孩子这么简单的活？有老人照看孩子，她自己可以做其他活。这活就是终年侍弄十七只鹅和一两只鸭子，依我看，这可不是什么好活，可是乡下的家庭妇女们硬是要自己把这活揽上身。这个贤良女人从小养成节俭的习惯，虽然现在生活不那么困难，仍然保持着勤俭持家的传统。她的十二张床上塞满了变得硬邦邦的鹅毛鸭毛，但她不在乎。她的橱子里堆的全是她用不着的蓝色的、红色的漂亮床罩，她在每年的七月十号左右把这些东西全拿出来，晾晒在院子里的篱笆上，让它们见见太阳，就像那些鹅和鸭子一样装点她自己的院子。略过这些怪僻不谈，她和她的男佣女佣以及她大点的孩子们总能顺利地赶着那些鹅和鸭子，穿过沟沟坎坎，把它们送回自己的窝里，这窝在她自己的房子外，一般叫做鹅屋，它上面盖着一件她母亲从前用做类似用途的老式长衫。约瑟夫·戴尔太太头发蓬乱，带着一顶刚合适的白色平纹布帽，开始做她自己的活了，这时孩子醒了，哭了起来。她还是接着干活，相信她的公公可以通过摇摇篮或者催眠般的轻声细语安抚住孩子，但这一切都没有用：哭声越来越响。这个生气的女人从腿下揪出那只脖子只拔了一部分毛的灰鹅,生气地大声嚷嚷:"让孩子自己哭死算了!"

过了一会儿她出现了,眉毛头发全是鹅毛,还有一缕挂在头发边上。她一声不吭地把孩子抱走了,冷冷地看了一眼那个善良的老人,这一眼不由得让人心生恐惧,老人忙道歉,说他做得不够好——在他看孩子时他自己睡着了,结果就成现在这样子了。他的儿媳妇语气冷淡地说:"我看也是。"然后这个女人还说他没有一次能够做好自己的事。这些话老人没有全听明白,但他还是气得把帽子拧来拧去,然后他起身去另一间屋子,他挺直身子,迈着大步,好像从没有得过痛风和风湿病似的。

两边吃午饭的时间通常很准时,当阳光直射进南门时,午餐时间就到了。但是今天约瑟夫·戴尔太太由于忙着自己的活计做饭晚了,约翰·戴尔太太由于要串门子早就吃过饭了。

戴尔叔叔平常最得意的是午餐,下午茶之前没谁会安排什么吃的平复一下他情绪的躁动。打过招呼,他独自坐在那里,心情不佳,他把头靠在他的手杖上一声不响,他恼火时就是这个样子。他明白,约翰·戴尔太太知道他没有吃饭,但是她不想给老人做饭,给自己添麻烦。

有时他会直接说出他的要求,但是今天他希望这些人能主动想到。他觉得自己就是一个既无用又麻烦的老头子,没人愿意自找麻烦养活他。偶尔当他抬起头时,他会看到墓地,他有时甚至希望自己已经躺在自己的墓里了。

与此同时,约翰·戴尔太太似乎没注意到他的存在,还在为串门子,与亲戚或邻居闲聊打发下午时光而忙活着。她系着一条崭新的整洁的方格布黑丝围裙,带着一顶有卷边和蓝带子的帽子,看上去非常不错。她手拿一个小包裹,让她可以在串门子时也可以做活计(是用来做两块桌布和床单的布料)。在时钟敲响一点时她准时出门,戴尔叔叔笑了,也许他认为这世界上还有和他儿媳妇一样可爱的女人,有时丰饶的庄稼和其他很多事也会让老人家开怀大笑。尽管她平时都温柔体贴,但今天她没有对老人说一声就出去了,也许她看见老人全神贯注地想心事,而老人也不愿意告诉她说她妯娌家乱糟糟的,根本不适合去串门子,毕竟他的儿媳妇没有告诉他要去干什么。稍微挪动了一下身子,他想看看自己判断得是否正确,果真约翰·戴尔太太出了门向南走，穿过了桥边的山谷，爬过了小山坡，推开了一个专为访客设的小门，来到了约瑟夫家，约瑟夫·戴尔太太满头满脸都是绒毛，企图哄睡那个最不爱睡觉的孩子。戴尔叔叔想，她去的可真不是时候，我应该告诉她让她别去的。但他想错了，女人们很快就笑成一团。玩笑了一会，约瑟夫·戴尔太太抱起了孩子，而她的妯娌忙着整理自己的衣服，鹅群自由自在地排队走向小溪边，那个女仆南希在厨房门口的门廊前打鸡蛋。这是个多么惬意的午后啊。

对于那个又孤单又饥饿的老人来说——看到没有人费心为他的饭食和快乐张罗，心里老大不高兴，因为一点点的轻蔑忽视往往会被夸大成生活的不幸。

很快他就厌烦了这样想来想去，由于想做点什么事散散心，或者是受自己哀惜心理的驱使，他慢慢地向早已荒废的小木屋走去。一开始他唉声叹气，因为他看到鸟儿在晃晃悠悠的烟囱、石头上筑巢，看到屋顶已经塌了，雨水打在木缝间，看到地板已经腐坏，霉菌爬满了墙。然后他考虑的是如何修葺，他需要一些木瓦，需要稍微整修一下烟囱和灶台，还需要新地板，一点灰泥和白涂料，重新安装窗玻璃，这样就能彻底修复这个房子，让它展露新颜甚至比新房子还要漂亮。为什么不呢？只要一个壮汉忙活一两天就够了，当然还要花点钱，事实上，他相信他自己做这件事问题也不大。他把拐杖放到一边，脱掉了自己的蓝外套，就像个二十岁的小伙子一样。他干劲十足地开始整理那些不牢靠的石头，拔除那些坏了的地板，似乎修整老房屋是早就计划好了的一样。他自己既是建筑师、泥瓦匠，又是木匠和装玻璃工。但是很快他就精疲力竭了，毕竟让一个六十来岁的人像一个二十岁的小伙子一样整理这些木材石料是不现实的。他突然决定不干了，就像他刚才心血来潮决定动手修房子一样突然。但是他的脸上没有丝毫遗憾惋惜，相反全是心满意足的神情，然后他精神勃勃地往回走，看上去比刚才年轻了二十岁。

在午后漫长的时光里，约翰·戴尔太太忙着做桌布和床单，约瑟夫·戴尔太太则忙着缝六个大袋子，用来把小麦装好送到磨房去，她们很自然地谈到令她们讨厌的人和事，大部分话题牵扯到他们公公的怪癖和小孩子气。当然她们并不是真想说公公的坏话，无论如何她们也不会这么做。当她们的话题一再被打断时，她们总是说：

"我一定要告诉你一件令我非常气愤的事。"紧接着发通牢骚——说什么他总是在茶杯里放很多糖,说什么当有客人来访时,公公总是霸着话题,不让别人说,或者他早晨起得太早,把大家都搅得睡不了安稳觉等等。

当然,戴尔叔叔从来没听到这样的闲话,但是他本能地感觉到她们会这样说,这一切又令他更加不舒服。

10. 老夫孺妻

日落时分,约翰·戴尔太太回家时发现"爷爷"(她就是这么称呼戴尔叔叔的)不在家。问了家里所有人他去哪里了,最后唯一清楚的就是有人最后看到他正登上一辆过路的马车,除此之外大家一无所知。一周过去了——十天——两周——一个月过去了,然后一天傍晚,戴尔叔叔乘着那辆他离开时乘的马车回来了,身体极佳,神采奕奕,打扮得也比平时更加一丝不苟。两家人都觉得似乎他在暗暗打算着什么,所以并没有十分热情地表示欢迎他的归来,尽管很明显大家都在强作笑颜。为了让他满意,大家表现得比平时更卖力,可是客气得过于拘谨了,倒使得每个人都明显地局促不安起来。

工人们宣布要开始修缮小屋时,没人敢随随便便去问他要做什么。孩子们爬上他的膝头,逗着问他的打算时,大人总是叫他们闭嘴,说他们太重了,祖父抱不动。

这并非因为众人缺乏好奇心。到底怎么了?戴尔叔叔已经有好多年没有表现出丝毫对此类事情的兴趣了,可现在他忙着修复这座老房子,每天都亲自参与其中,直到工程完工,而在此之前,他可好久都不习惯干体力活了。

房子修好了,他看着温暖舒适的小屋,心满意足,可是没人注意到他的感受,也没人像他那么觉得。事实上似乎大家对他的所作所为毫不在意,即使他说等他把家具运回来,小屋看起来会更不错,也没人表现出丝毫的关心。

这种沉默让他明显不安起来。他很希望有人来问他,甚至有意提供机会让人发问,可是这种机会没人要。他说,约翰跟约瑟夫可能都会欢迎他住到他们的大房子里去,可他宁愿住在小屋里也不愿跟他们两个中的任何一个同住。可他的尝试只是徒劳。直到最后他心生不满,开始坐卧不宁,有时候会坐在那里一连几个小时,头搭在拐杖上，一言不发。有时候又会从约翰家走到约瑟夫家，然后又从约瑟夫家走到约翰家，一天能走上六七个来回。可是，两个儿子没有一个愿意给他机会说出自己想说的事。

一天早晨，约翰正要上马车，他打算到苜蓿角去办点小事（他常常赶着两匹马出去就为了买回来六磅糖或者一块新鲜奶酪），戴尔叔叔说，语气中带有些许慌张："约翰，你今天能不能匀一两个小时的时间给我？"

"哦，可以，我想应该可以吧，"他答道，"不过你有什么事？"

"没什么要紧的，"戴尔叔叔回答，"我想把我那几件家什搬出来，给你媳妇腾点地方出来——就这些。"

"啊？"约翰吃了一惊，把缰绳拉得太紧了，两匹马开始把车子往后坐，撞上了一棵漂亮的小树，"你想搬到哪儿去？"

"自然是搬到小屋里去：那里挺适合我住的。"

"可你打算怎么过？——不是自己吧？"

"不，当然不是了，我需要个人来照顾我，料理家务，我已经有了一个年轻女人来做这些事情了。"

"你惹了大麻烦了！"约翰吃惊地喊道，落下了鞭子，结果让两匹马很快地往前跑了起来，不一会儿他就不见了影子，留下戴尔叔叔又是苦恼又是困惑。不过一天下来，他倒是清楚地把自己的打算告诉了大家：他要结婚了，娶一个二十五岁的漂亮的年轻女人。当然他渲染了她的美貌和她种种温和可爱的性格特点，但是似乎还有些什么是他应该很乐意讲而实际上又没有讲到的，因为好多次他在讲完了她某一个出众之处之后就会说"可是"，或者换一个别的含含糊糊的转折词，让人知道此事与他计划中的婚事有关，可想起来又让人不那么愉快。

婚事使他年轻了许多。他搭晚班的马车出发去迎娶新娘，不过走前没有听到任何"上帝保佑你"的祝福。事实上后来那些先前沉默不语的人谁也没真的管住自己的嘴。

约翰·戴尔太太跟约瑟夫·戴尔太太每天都会互相串门，串门的时候她们先是大发一通议论，接着又对事态的新发展展开无边无际的想象。她们不单单是不高兴而已，事实上她们愤慨极了。家里有人要做一件绝不会得到允许的蠢事，而且竟然压根没有跟他们进行任何商量。不过，我们必须略过这些紧张焦灼的心态和所有的闲言碎语，或者将它们留给读者自己去想象。两家人都几乎没做任何款待新娘的准备。约翰·戴尔太太想新娘可能会先去约瑟夫·戴尔太太那里，约瑟夫·戴尔太太也觉得约翰·戴尔太太家会是新娘先去拜访的地方。所以她们都为自己找好了借口。无论如何，老父亲指望的不过是一杯茶，加上一片黄油面包，至于年轻的妻子，可没人愿意为了她费工夫。

戴尔叔叔走了两三个星期，一天傍晚，约翰一家人坐在餐桌前吃晚饭时，孩子中的一个上气不接下气地进来，说爷爷已经到了，还带来了一个女人和一个小姑娘。儿子跟儿媳谁也没有迎上前去缓解他的尴尬。实际上我猜，他宁愿回到四十年前与英军的一个团会战，也不想面对眼前这一群人，还要把他的妻子引见给他们。不过现在也别无选择了，仪式在一种别扭的气氛中完成，那个蓝眼睛的小女人浑身发抖，不知不觉就来到了这里，而她从未见过如此奇特的地方。她把带来的小姑娘抱到膝盖上——小女孩五岁左右，脸色苍白，乌黑的眼睛透着悲伤。她抚平小女孩额前的黑发，一言不发。

年轻的妻子看起来一点也不像个新娘，戴尔太太也根本不愿见到她做新娘的样子。相反，她身穿朴素的丧服，样子可能有点过时。她没戴任何饰物，有一头浓密的栗色长发，白皙的前额笼罩着忧伤，头发虽然简单地盘了起来，还是在额前留出了密密的卷发。只有衣服袖口白色的褶边和高领的款式使得她显得不那么昏暗阴沉。

年轻的妻子拼命想要掩饰还是无法遮住眼中泛起的泪光，尤其当那个黑眼睛的小姑娘搂着她的脖子，软软地说"妈妈，你怎么哭了"时，她更加无法自制。所以尽管戴尔太太下决心要坚持到底，很明显她还是有些心软，有些动摇了。

年轻母亲的脸上涨得通红，一直强忍着的泪水这时也一滴滴地落在小女孩的头上，而小女孩靠在她的胸前，很快就睡着了。

戴尔叔叔把脸转过去，草草地说了几句日落如何如何的话，孩子们都来到他跟前，争相问："她是谁，爷爷？""她怎么哭了？"

戴尔叔叔没有回答最后一个问题，只是说给他们带来了一个新婶婶，要称她波莉婶婶。虽然这话是说给孩子们听的，可戴尔太太凭着女性的机智马上心领神会，也开始叫波莉婶婶，所以很快所有的人都开始自然又亲密地叫起爷爷和波莉婶婶来。

我还记得在他们在小屋里安顿下来后去拜访他们那次，一切都那么舒适亲切——地板上色彩鲜亮的碎呢地毯，放着《圣经》和《赞美诗》的普普通通的小桌子，敞开的小橱里面可以看到精心摆放给客人看的瓷器和金属餐具，还有戴尔叔叔垫的软软的椅子。此刻我还能清楚地记得每件东西，就像看着自己房里的家具一样。戴尔叔叔和波莉婶婶，他们的样子又浮现在我的眼前，一点儿没变——她温顺文雅，心无旁骛，只因她性格沉静，又是我所见过的人中心地最为善良的一个，不是在织毛衣就是缝缝补补，或者做着别的什么家务活，而戴尔叔叔总是坐在门边或壁炉边，视季节而定，大声地读着报纸或者讲些陈年旧事。

波莉婶婶并不十分聪明，事实上，丈夫的话她连一半也听不懂，但她虔诚地爱着，对丈夫一切的愿望都愉快而毫无保留地顺从。生活如静静的流水般滑过，我相信他们也一定是幸福的。

面对这样的新局面，以及年轻的小媳妇，约瑟夫·戴尔太太跟约翰·戴尔太太两人明显地妥协了，因为小媳妇已经完全赢得了所有人的心，尽管她们二人有时会说她不大像祖母（其实她们从没见过祖母），倒也觉得自己不该有所抱怨——当然她们完全没有理由这样。

但是那个小女孩从没得到过任何关爱之词，他们也从不叫她的小名，尽管这家的孩子并不多，但没人喜欢和她一起玩。这一点没人直言，大家只是心照不宣。所以那孩子就一个人在林子里晃荡，有时候也会在小溪边太阳底下坐上一整天，直至夏日逝去，秋日已往，冬雪也染白了群山。然后一切戛然而止，他们在深深的积雪下给她挖了个墓穴，此后她再也无须玩伴或是任何爱语了。春天的时候，她的墓前后都长出了紫罗兰，几乎要掩去她栖身的那一小抔黄土，花团锦簇的明丽景象堪比要继承一百个王位的继承人头上的王冠——这就是她唯一的纪念碑了。

孀居的妻子现在还住在那间刷成白色的小屋里，给窗边的玫瑰剪枝。一切都还保持着"祖父"喜欢的样子，仿佛他还坐在那个宽大的扶手椅上，给她讲着那些打仗拓荒的故事，他的一切都被奉为神物一般。结婚时穿的裙子精心地挂着，她只在去皂荚树下的那两座墓时才会穿上。但是她的丧服从未换下，——我想也永远不会换了，正如她仍然坚韧温顺的表情，只是其中更多了些悲恸。她是每个人的"波莉婶婶"，受人爱戴敬重。

11. 惠特菲尔德执事一家

要想完美地勾勒出苜蓿角社会各阶层的样貌，我就不能不提提本地教堂的一些事。在苜蓿角人的故事中那些事无疑是非常有趣而又重要的一部分。所以在此我应该专辟一章写写我们教堂里的头面人物，就如同更大场面里的达官贵人一样，小镇的种种变迁教会也是责无旁贷的。

收获的季节恰逢满月，一堆堆散发着甜香味的干草小山一样的堆满了草场，金色的麦浪随着阵阵山风起伏着。被剪去厚厚羊毛的羊群们似乎还不适应新状况，沿着山坡一路"咩咩"叫，小母牛们光滑的肚皮深深陷入大片的苜蓿丛中，在我看来一向耐心而又漂亮的公牛们在轭套里躬身低头，吃着收割的以及捆起来的干草：

"小公牛忘了吃草，
站在被篱笆切断了的小路上，
牛角指向了邻家的田地，
哞哞地叫唤它的同伴。"

尽管是收割的季节，而且如同所有丰产年，对于惠特菲尔德执事一家而言，也没有带来太多的喜悦。坐拥大笔财富，他自己不喜欢为财富所累，也不喜欢家人这样。他的这种持家之道与他太太的想法不谋而合。无论生病与否，她日复一日地辛勤劳作，如同一个饱受折磨的殉道者，丝毫没有想过要卸掉她身上的担子。这早已成为她命运的一部分，她欣然接受。然而孩子们有时会有点叛逆。劳动起来从来没有休息，哪怕是片刻的歇息，如果他们厌倦了某件事情，他们会被要求做另外一件，这就是所谓的充足的休息了。诚然，礼拜天的确不工作，但是也没的玩耍。《天路历程》、《圣贝克斯特的永恒的长眠》以及一两卷其他书就是执事家全部的藏书了，而且被视为在任何时间任何季节都足够有趣的书。一模一样的外套、裙子，一模一样的帽子给孩子们穿戴足够了，两三年内的确够了。如今，当孩子们察觉到他们的奇特穿着使他们成了人们注意力的焦点时，他们大多都感觉不舒服。但是他们的执事爸爸丝毫不受影响。有时惠特菲尔德夫人会以一种温和的方式，斗胆建议孩子爸爸修饰一下外表，执事一定会不变地回答说，他老爹从未穿过他这样的好衣服，而且对他老爹而言足够好的东西对他而言也是足够的好。于是这个好心的女子即使没有被劝服，也不说话了。

　　同样的情形也适用于家具，他们家的家具又少又简陋，他们也曾经做过一些维护。事实上，尽管他们最大的儿子已经二十岁了，在执事看来家具依然是如同以前一样簇新。他只作了一次革新，就是买了一张很时髦的沙发，在它那些微小而老式的同伴中间显得极不相称，倒有点明珠投暗的意味①。当执事宣布要买这张沙发的意图时，对家人而言，这简直太让人惊讶了——简直是震惊。农场里乳制品库存过多，已经接近收获季的晚期，执事说奶牛到开春前会狂吃猛嚼，他必须把它们中的两头卖掉"为你们的母亲"去换一张沙发——与其说是让妻子，还不如说是让孩子们明白他的惊人的智慧。

　　"什么！父亲，你刚才说换一张沙发？"萨莉·惠特菲尔德大叫，手中针织物掉到了腿上。

　　"是的，我刚才是这么说的，给你们母亲买了一张沙发。"他回答道。

　　"我并不想要什么沙发。"惠特菲尔德夫人开口道，转过去擦掉眼泪。就她的丈夫而言能够如此体贴周到，这很快融化了她的心灵。"塞缪尔，到底是什么让你有这想法呢？"

　　"我猜父亲怕是不小心打开酸苹果汁桶了，"杰瑞·惠特菲尔德低声和他的姐妹说。尽管声音很轻，还是被他们的妈妈听见了。她转向他，严肃地斥责："杰瑞·惠特菲尔德！"只是简单的几个字，不需要多说什么。

　　任何人都有慷慨的时候，惠特菲尔德执事也不例外，尽管这种事情二十年才发生一次。这次对话之后的几天，他坐着他的用来去市场的马车，穿上他最好的衣服，沉着严肃地向小镇方向前进。杰瑞赶着两头奶牛跟在他身后。

　　故事的开端就如同我之前所说的那样，现在是执事家收割的季节，因此额外劳动没有额外报酬的结果就使大家都普遍有点不满和不悦。

　　当父亲和儿子晚上从集市回来的时候，他们每个人都如同平时

---

① 出自莎士比亚戏剧作品《罗密欧与朱丽叶》第一幕第五场，与成语"明珠投暗"语义相同，意为格格不入，极不相称。文中用来形容新买来的沙发和原来使用多年的旧家具摆在一起极不相称。

一样带回一篮苹果,这当然是为第二天烘干作准备的——所有的时间都要很善用。于是这天晚上全家人,也就是说执事和他的妻子以及他们的儿子杰瑞、女儿萨莉一起坐在走廊上,沐浴着月光,把苹果切成片,然后准备烘干。

他们在一片沉默中干活,作为任务,这些事实上本来应该是上了年纪的人的活,不知不觉就成了年轻人的活。日夜躺在前门边上的花斑看门狗发出的低沉的吠声,让所有人都为之一动,"咔嗒"的门闩声加上迫近的急促的脚步声更是带来少有的骚动。

"晚上这个时候到底是谁来了?"执事大嚷道,带点惊慌,因为此刻已经是晚上八点了。

"我猜想可能有人病了或者过世了。"惠特菲尔德夫人说道。这个悬念只保持了一会,一声亲切的问候"我的邻居,你好啊"驱散了所有的恐惧。

来访者是怀特执事,一个矮小但是秉性很善良的人,他有一双蓝色的眼睛,每天都穿着时髦的外套,带着时髦的帽子,而且他晚上不需要切苹果。杰瑞很快地站起来给客人腾出椅子来,自己则坐到了一个巨大的斑纹南瓜上面,调皮地看了看萨莉,继续默不作声地工作,因为孩子们一直被教导不要擅自在长辈——也就是说上了年纪的人面前说话。这两个邻居什么都谈,从地里的所有庄稼,尤其是收割的小麦,到燕麦以及土豆的可能卖价,接下来就是他们所能想起来的这一带所发生的各种各样的变化,谁从东边来,谁又去了西边,谁结婚了,谁又去世了,直到萨莉开始思考她可能永远无法得知怀特执事到底是来干什么的。最后他终于吐露来此做何公干,这正事却成了他那一大堆闲磕的插曲,似乎只是微不足道的小事一桩,对他来说早已习以为常。虽然,这事起先就毫无疑问让他心绪不宁,他觉得一旦公布定会引起点轰动。明显让他失望懊丧的是,这事没能引起轰动,即使能有这效果,惠特菲尔德执事也不会显露一丝动容——不为所动可是他个性的亮点之一,他为此而特别引以为豪。

"你认为我们家人会去吗,杰瑞?"萨莉一边问道,一边帮助她的兄弟运走那一篮苹果皮。

"不,我想不会,"杰瑞说,随即以一种挖苦的音调补充道,"我很高兴他没有要我去——即使他叫我了,我也不会去的。"

读者们一定要了解苜蓿角教堂里那位老套的牧师，他对小镇人当中滋生出的那些荒唐事非常不满，于是他在引用"喔，你们这些毒蛇一般阴险的家伙"这一段《圣经》原文作了一场告别布道之后，抖抖脚下的尘土就离开了。

于是，有一个非常出名的帅气的牧师，精于社交礼仪，应邀前来接掌神职，他即将到来的就职宣言将在怀特执事家的晚宴上进行，于是怀特执事就亲自来邀请他的兄弟执事们。在过去的这些年中他私下里也接受了一些老牧师的嘟嘟嚷嚷的劝诫，这些无疑随着日出日落而宣告结束。乐意于自己的这种改变，他自然希望所有教徒也能如此。他希望把在他家里请客当成对那些可能心怀不满的人一种善意的表示，然而包括惠特菲尔德执事在内的一小部分依然顽固不化。

五点的晚餐会！这是他所听说过的最不可思议的事情。他通常四点吃完晚饭。

尽管老辈人出席餐会，却并无丝毫赞赏这类荒唐活动的意思，然而萨莉还是很自然地迫切地希望参加。她盼望发生的好事情莫过于此，她也很好奇到底有哪些人会去参加聚会，他们会穿什么样的衣服，他们的举止如何，这一切都加强了她想去参加聚会的念头。但是五天来她丝毫没有看到符合她愿望的迹象。于是她开始对结果感到绝望，然而抵抗不了聚会的诱惑，她一次次地试图使自己相信她能够去参加聚会。她在自己房间里无数次地审视自己的衣柜，在为数不多的一堆衣服中挑了一件白色的薄纱，她想只要在颈部加一条新的缎带就可以搞定，然而要得到一条新缎带可就难了。她不下千次地想了很多权宜之计，但是没有一样看上去是可行的。最终，当那个日子日益迫近的时候，她决定来一次大胆的冒险。正当她的父亲吃完晚饭准备离开家的时候，如同刚刚想到一样，她以一种愉快的语调对父亲说："噢，爸爸，我想问你要五十美分。"在某种程度上想要掩盖一下她提要求的感觉。

执事停下来一会，在门槛边坐下，故意装作脱鞋子，他从鞋子里倒出不少干草种子，重又穿上，紧紧系好，看都没看一直站在一旁用手指拉围裙褶缝的萨莉一眼，径直朝地里走去，根本不回答问题。

他也许没有听见我的话，她想。我会再问他要的，这个决定需要更大的勇气，因为她私底下认为他的确是听见她的话的，第二次拒绝可能不会再是沉默。但是当她的父亲回来时，她心里开始忧虑起来，整个晚上她都默不作声地坐在那里切苹果。当最后一满篮苹果都切好时，她大着胆子轻轻地提示她父亲关于刚才一直在占据她脑子的事情，她说："我们今天应该比平时做得更晚一些。"

长时间停顿后，执事说："我不觉得我们有必要做得晚一点。"

萨莉认为没有必要解释为什么，于是她说："噢，那是因为——"

"萨莉·惠特菲尔德！"他们的母亲叫道，充分表达了对她想要自由发言的斥责。

可怜的孩子感到又委屈又困惑，半是难过半是恼火地回到她的床上，最终还是睡着了。睡眠的确有极佳的恢复疗效，尤其是对年轻人而言，第二天早晨，她更加坚定了再次向她父亲提要求的念头。重要的一天终于到来了。在可能的最后时刻，萨莉说道："爸爸，难道你不打算把我问你要的钱给我吗？"

"你想要它来干什么，孩子？"他回答。

似乎受到了一点鼓励，她回答她的父亲她想要买一条穿去怀特执事家聚会的新丝带。

"真是一个相当不错的事由，"她的父亲说，"如果你在你的母亲和我在家里工作时，你却准备精心打扮，去参加五点的聚会，你不如不要一条新丝带而要一个新大脑好了。你最好祈求你自己是一个好女孩，而不是渴望要一条新丝带。"

萨莉似乎来了胆子，叫道："你很久以前答应过要给我买件礼物的，作为帮助你扬谷的回报。"

"难道你每天没有礼物吗？是谁提供你一日三餐？是谁给你买的新鞋和裙子？"

她认为这些算不上对她每天艰苦劳动的回报，但是她也没有继续往下说什么。

接下来的一整天她都心情沉重地干着活，然而到了晚饭时分她的父亲对她说："瞧，萨莉，看我今天给你带了什么礼物回来！"她的心里一下子像卸掉一些重量一般，宴会上的玫瑰花清晰明亮地出现在她眼前，但是随着他继续往下讲，玫瑰花一下子又痛苦地凋谢了。"这可不是蠢蠢的便宜货，而是一块很漂亮的砂岩，下午你可以用它来刷刷搅乳器以及牛奶桶，你想刷多亮就多亮。"

只觉心里堵得很，小女孩离开了桌子，坐到了厨房门边上的一棵樱桃树下，开始捡她脚下堆着的厚厚的苜蓿花，一直捡了五十朵。她数了一遍又一遍，想用它们做点其他事情。她是如此全神贯注以至于没有注意到她父亲的大镰刀已经挥向了她头顶的那棵大树枝，慢慢向她逼近。看到她阴沉的面容以及无所事事的样子，她父亲大声斥责她说："现在从我的视线里消失，要是你还是这副面孔就别回来见我！"

在离主道稍微远一点有一小片漂亮的榆树林，有着让人心情愉悦的树荫。她常去树林，没什么特别的目的，只是一种习惯。

无意中她带了一些苜蓿花花蕾在身边，让自己坐在一棵爬满了野葡萄藤的山毛榉树下，她开始把苜蓿花编成花环。她虽算不上漂亮，一双深沉浓黑的眸子，浓密的深棕色卷发，但年轻、健康。树林里朦胧、宁静，密集的树荫越来越延伸到厚厚的绿草上，天色日渐变暗，蜘蛛忙着在树枝间编织它淡淡的、细长的网，和金色的阳光纠缠在一起；鸟儿的歌声更加短促而低沉了，一开始很少，让人感到昏昏欲睡，接下来这旋律占据了整个树林。微风吹拂着她两颊的卷发，抚弄着她膝上的花环。此时此地似乎有一种让人软化和安抚的效果，然后，双手合十，哼着她所知晓的所有赞美诗，头靠在她坐着的那棵树的树干上，她慢慢地睡着了。风儿和鸟儿都没有打扰到她，直到最后一个尽管低沉但礼貌的声音叫她，吵醒了她的美梦。抬起头来看到眼前站着的年轻的乡村牧师时，她的脸一下子变得深红。

由于他的神圣职业的缘故，年轻的牧师温文尔雅地，同时带点欢快地为他的闯入向她道歉，告诉她他没有意识到这片美丽的森林有着一位更加美丽的人，他赶着参加与他负责教区的教友的首次见面，在路上他被这片异常美丽的树林所吸引而转变了方向，让自己的心灵和这美景相交融。"但是难道你不是住在附近这一带？我是否能在宴会上再次见到你？"他继续说道。

尽管萨莉尽全力克制，泪水还是浸满了双眼，她指了指山对面自己所住的那幢老式房子，说："我很想去，但是——"她并没有继续解释些什么，解开她的花环，撒在地上。

"地上的花朵会腐烂毁灭，"牧师说道，"年轻的女孩，我们的希望也常常如此。"随之似乎如同脑海里出现什么愉快的事情一般，他的调子更加轻快,"你经常来这里吗?"

"哦,我常常来,除了冬季和天气不好之外,因为一般没别人来这里,所以看见您我很吃惊,都没顾上请您到我的座位上,不过我现在请求您接受我的邀请。"

她正要起身,年轻人示意她坐着别动,"那我就和你坐一会儿,虽然我担心人家已经在等我了。"

我无从得知他们说了些什么,也猜不出来,但那一定是有趣的事情,因为怀特执事拉了不下二十次帘子,想看看牧师到底来了没有,这着实让怀特太太很是烦恼,虽然她没什么可急的,可那些满腹怨言的老妇人互相嘀咕,说这个新牧师也太时髦了一点。年轻的女士们早已失去耐心,她们的头发已经不再卷曲。听到一位打扮正经、带着善意表情的少女提示道:老彼得前一天从马上摔死了,牧师可能去给他的葬礼布道去了,闻此大家的情绪给兜头浇了盆冷水。她尤其强调的事实是他被抬进屋里后再也没说话。在这种不合时宜的消息之后,沉默一直持续到差五分五点的时候才被门口的一阵快速的脚步声所打破,出现在他们面前的是面带笑容的牧师。面对众多的询问,他回答道,他并没有去给葬礼布道,只是被一件偶然发生的事情所耽搁了,至于什么事情,他没有解释。然而,人们似乎对他的解释很满意,一切不愉快都过去了。晚餐对于怀特夫人而言无疑是很有面子的事情,那些来的客人无疑给这次晚饭带来不少荣光。一些老人认为他作为一个牧师有一点追求名利,但是年轻人都很仰慕他。整体而言,他给人们的印象远远比他所希望的好。

惠特菲尔德执事家的晚饭吃了大约一小时后萨莉才出现,让她父母感到惊讶的是,她的脸上并没有呈现出悲伤或失望的痕迹,与之相反的是,她看上去显得不同寻常的愉快。

尽管惠特菲尔德执事和他的妻子每年安息日都出席教堂活动,但他们从来没有逗留一下和新布道人握握手,不是因为他的天赋和雄辩没有打动他们的心灵,而是因为他们觉得表露谦恭就意味着他们默认自己有毛病,他们还没有准备好屈尊降贵。

年轻的牧师注意到了这些,然而他看上去丝毫没有被他们的冷淡所触怒,他最先到访的就包括惠特菲尔德执事家。我们的绅士惠特菲尔德执事擦了鞋,穿上最好的衣服,在客厅款待了他,而且喝完茶后惠特菲尔德夫人带着她的干净的帽子,穿着干净的长袍也露了一下面，但是萨莉不被允许去客厅，哪怕是去茶桌前也不允许。尽管早已年过十六，她在父母眼里还是一个不懂事的小女孩。

很快晚饭后，牧师准备离开，表示希望今后能够在教堂里见到惠特菲尔德执事全家。

接下去一个安息日，女孩并没有和父亲一起去教堂，再接下来一个星期也没有，整个夏天过去了，她一次都没有去教堂。

九月的一个早晨，执事和他妻子赶着马车去镇上，车上有两头牛犊，两桶苹果，还有一麻袋用来喂马的燕麦。

萨莉想要一件新裙子，一顶软帽，她说如果不给她买的话她就一直不去教堂，直到世界末日，旧的那顶她已经戴了很长一段时间了，这是事实。

晚饭后，杰瑞去村里向牧师借一本书，对他来说不管是诗歌、科学、浪漫故事或者历史都无所谓，只要是他有的。他觉得他内心渴望精神食粮，于是他决定去借一本。于是他麻利并且愉快地做完了家务。而萨莉，精心打扮了一下，穿着白色棉布裙，系上蓝色方格花布的围裙，坐下来做针线活。杰瑞很快就回来了，给她念他书上的文字，关于耶路撒冷及圣地的故事。然而杰瑞没读多久就被牧师的到来打断了，牧师很好心地又给他拿来一本书，他说他认为年轻人可能对这本书的兴趣会大于之前挑选的那一本。杰瑞觉得现在他似乎有了一个永远挖掘不尽的宝藏，退到门阶边，他坐到了那个满是斑点的南瓜上，整个下午都在那里读书，看完这本看那本。

秋天逐渐过去了，冬天和春天相继到来，又到了收获季的满月时分。年轻的牧师已经赢得包括惠特菲尔德执事和他的妻子在内的所有人的爱戴。他已经成了惠特菲尔德执事家的常客。然而他的名望慢慢地从这群人中延伸开去，他要去一个更广阔的地域发展——他已经被任命去打理隔壁城市里的一个富裕社区的教会事物。

村庄里的所有人都为他们所热爱的牧师的离去而感到遗憾，而萨莉的难过难以说清，她觉得——

"广袤的土地
命运注定把我们分开，把你的心留在了我的心扉
伴随着脉搏的双倍跳动。"

当离别的一天终于到来时，她清楚地知道她的心灵将要背叛自己，决意不去见这痛苦的最后一面，她戴上帽子，独自来到了橡树

林,悲伤的阴云笼罩过来压在她身上。她全神贯注于自己的思绪,泪眼朦胧,快到她常去的树荫处的时候才注意到那里早已有人。牧师比她先来。她很想转变方向,但是已经来不及了。

年轻人半是悲伤半是责备地给她让出布满苔藓的一半树桩,他们一年前坐在上面。"简直没想到你会试图避开我,你刚才看见我来了竟然想走开。"

"我是不想让自己受罪说再见。"女孩说,嘴唇颤抖着,眼中满是泪水。

"那你会让自己不受这份罪吗?对,直到死亡把我们俩分开。"

牧师质问之后就吻了她,而她并没有愤怒地把脸颊挪开。

萨莉怎么回答的我只能从接下来的情形中推断,因为当天晚上执事和年轻的牧师握了握手,他说:"我能大大方方给予的只有我的祝福。"

"我真是感激不尽啦,"牧师说,"可是你还能赐予我更大的祝福。"

"行了,孩儿他妈,"牧师走进客厅,坐在沙发上,把妻子拉到身边,用一种久违的爱意亲吻她瘦弱、苍白的脸颊,"我猜将来我们要开始过萨莉不在身边的日子了。"

12. 汤普金斯一家

与惠特菲尔德一家颇为相似的,是住在苜蓿角另一边的汤普金斯一家。汤普金斯家不像惠特菲尔德家那么体面,他们确实不太富裕,也不常参加聚会,他们的亲戚大多还不如他们。然而,这两家在许多方面都非常相像。正如这一篇里将要讲到的,两家常会遇到类似的经历。

外面天色已暗,寒冷彻骨。是呀,太阳落山已有一个小时了,鹅毛般的大雪纷纷扬扬地洒落。窗下,石楠的细枝已被压弯,越来越低。屋旁樱桃树的枝头落满了雪,看起来像一座座金字塔。窗沿上,一只大看家狗蜷伏着,抵御着寒冷,偶尔听到屋里孩子们的欢笑声,便发出几声"呜呜"的哀叫。在晴朗温暖的日子里,孩子们常常会跟它一起玩。孩子们共有三人,最大的是个女孩,十五岁了。她就着火光,正在默默地织着什么。石砌的大壁炉里,山核桃木正在熊熊燃烧。银汤匙花哨地一字排开,摆在敞开的壁橱里,后面是仔细摆放的瓷器。火光温暖而舒适，在火光的映衬下，银汤匙也在闪闪发光。另外两个是男孩，一个九岁，一个十一岁。除了个头略有差异，两个人几乎长得一模一样。他们长着浅黄色的头发，额前的头发在离他们大大的灰眼睛一寸的地方被齐齐剪去。这里的头发从来看不出长了或短了，因为每到月初，他们的妈妈便会把他们额前的头发梳得整整齐齐的，用一根线扎住，然后分毫不差地把多余的部分齐刷刷剪掉。他们的脸圆圆的，面色苍白，满是雀斑。胖胖的两腮鼓了出来，亮亮的，像是刚刚洗过一样。他们的手也是胖鼓鼓的，冻得通红。他们俩可以在房间里吵吵闹闹地互相追跑一个小时，把地毯四处的边都踢了起来，还不时地撞到他们的姐姐身上。姐姐继续默默地编织着，仿佛没注意到他们似的。等到玩腻了，他们就躺在炉火前，开始尖声喊叫起来。一个喊累了刚停下来，另一个便开始接着喊。

"我说，苏珊，给我点吃的吧。给我点东西，我说，我饿了，真的饿了。苏珊，给我点蛋糕吧——要不我就去告诉妈妈——看我告不告。"

"你们最好安静点，"到后来苏珊已被折腾得筋疲力尽，便会说道，"我听到你们的父亲进来了。"当她跟弟弟们说话时，她从不说"父亲"，而说"你们的父亲"，仿佛她比他们大很多，也明智很多，而且不必再受父亲权威的约束似的。但事实并非如此。她虽然身体已发育成熟，而且也不再像两个不守规矩的弟弟一样享有那么多优待了，但是在父母眼里，她仍不过是个孩子。

虽然如此，但是不可否认的是，在一些类似的事情上，她有时会行使一下自以为有的权力。如果弟弟们整晚都这样哭哭啼啼的话，她就会不给他们吃蛋糕。她会用父亲回来了吓唬他们，因为她很清楚，在父亲能听得到的情况下，他们是不会再缠磨的。

过了一会儿，落满雪的门阶上隐约传来一声沉重的脚步声。汤普金斯先生出现了。他脸色通红，表情异常的粗暴。当汤普金斯先生去拜访别人，去磨坊或是去参加集会时，他的态度总是无比的温和而友好。但是在家里，他总是摆出最严厉的架势，毫不妥协。只有当邻人偶然来访时，他才会稍微缓和一点。他从不想与孩子们平等地说话，以为那样有失身份。所以他很少开口，也从不笑，因为那样可能会显得他想要说话似的。对汤普金斯太太，有时他倒是会妥协一点点，因为不管他回不回应，她都会跟他说话。

汤普金斯先生脱下大衣，抖掉上面的雪。有些雪掉在了两个男孩仰起的脸上，有的掉在了苏珊的怀里，弄得她的针在织毛线时发出一阵刺耳的声音。抖完雪，他把大衣挂在炉火前的椅背上，以便烘干。然后摘下帽子，拿在手里使劲抖了抖，把帽子上仅存的一点皮毛上的雪抖了下来。汤普金斯先生从未戴过新帽子，至少在我的记忆里一直没有，虽然他妻子倒是常穿着不错的披肩和裙子。

这时，威廉和约翰仍在嚷着要蛋糕。但是汤普金斯先生一直没理他们。直到他在炉前坐了好一会儿，靴子上的雪融化后，都流成了一滩水，弄脏了蓝色石头砌成的壁炉边，他才准许了他们的请求——不是用语言，而是缓慢而严厉地将头转向苏珊，微微地扬了扬眉。看到这里，苏珊马上放下手中的活计，点上一根油蜡，走去地窖。为此，她不得不走出屋门，又绕过房子。结果，她很快便回来了，蜡烛已被风吹灭，围裙上也被撕开了一道口子。黑暗中，围裙被一个松动的醋桶箍钩到了。泪水涌进了她的眼里，半是出于愤怒，半是由于伤心，因为这条围裙是丝质的，是她专门为了第二天晚上去海伍德医生家参加朋友聚会而缝制的。当然，这围裙是用旧衣物改成的。虽然是用母亲棕色结婚礼服上的两块布拼成的，但是她已尽量作了修整。她把布料浸了水，趁湿熨平，然后又增加几处蝴蝶结作为装饰。顺便提一下，这几只蝴蝶结有些画蛇添足了，因为颜色很不协调，有些颜色很深，有些却已磨得发白。这几只发白的蝴蝶结，有一个夏天在汤普金斯太太的帽子上用过，还有两个夏天在苏珊的帽子上也用过，早已陈旧不堪。但是，这个可怜的孩子，她怎么会意识到这些呢！她看到玛丽·海伍德穿过一个有类似装饰的围裙，自然也想时髦一点。她并不习惯在家里穿着丝质的围裙，但是，由于这围裙是她在母亲不在的时候做的，所以她才斗胆穿一个晚上，假装要展示一下它的效果，来暗示即将到来的聚会。

在每一片邻里之间，必然会有一个家庭比其他人家更时髦，也更尊贵一些。在苜蓿角，这一家便是海伍德家。他们原先住在城里，不久前才举家搬到了这里的农场，紧邻着汤普金斯家的农场。他们搬到这里，与其说是为了孩子们能有自由的空气并得到锻炼——冠冕堂皇的出发点，不如说是因为家道中落。原本破旧的农庄，在加盖了新的厢房，修建了大院子，装上了百叶窗，又刷上了绿色和白色的新漆之后，很快便焕然一新，有了农舍般舒适的面貌。大门上装饰着一块银牌，上面刻着"海伍德医生"的名字，与门铃一起产生了这样的效果：在这周围的邻居中，还没有哪家可以炫耀这样不实用的装饰品的呢。

海伍德医生天生一副喜欢民主、长于社交的架势，可能还有事业成功的希望所带来的影响，很快便使自己成为一个颇受欢迎的人。他甚至还屈尊俯就，接受了本地区学校的邀请，定期到访，检查学生的习字簿和地理学习情况，听孩子们夸张地诵读彼得·帕雷的《第一部历史书》，神态庄严自若，就仿佛：

"从小就熟悉这些风俗"①

他还迷上了改良家畜，常去邻居们的牲口棚拜访，谈论自己种的麦子和土豆，还时不时地就耕作和收割的问题征求些意见。

但还是有一些人不满，坚称这家人为"大毒草"，因为海伍德太太的帽子上每天都插着花，还雇着一个黑人女仆在厨房帮忙，而且还有从城里来的客人。虽然人们也曾看到医生本人脱下西装穿着衬衣与打草的人在一起，但是不得不承认的是，他基本上从不沾手农活。但是，自从他兴师动众地建起他的新谷仓之后，人们的偏见基本上都消失了。他亲自邀请了所有的男人们和男孩子们来修建谷仓，还不断重复地打趣说，一个农夫不管有没有房子都得有个谷仓。在谷仓修建的最后，他还为人们准备了丰盛的晚餐——海伍德太太亲自赏脸跟大家一起喝咖啡，还邀请所有的男人带他们的妻子来做客，并为自己没能与邻居们熟识而感到抱歉。

这化解了不少怨气，但是，任何对已有传统的革新，都很可能遭到一些人的反对。这些人比我刚才谈及的人更明智一些。汤普金斯先生和太太就不愿也不会与那些坚持用仆人和门铃的人和解。海伍德太太曾打破规矩放下身段首先登门拜访，海伍德医生也曾一次次地去谷仓非正式地拜访汤普金斯先生，但都没用。

但是，苏珊没有她父母的那种顽固，因此，当她接到邀请函，请她出席玛丽·海伍德的生日聚会时，她迫不及待地想要去参加。最让她感到不安的是，她从父母那里没有得到任何鼓励。她父亲认

---

① 出自莎士比亚戏剧作品《哈姆雷特》第一幕第四场，原句为"though I am native here / And to the manner born"。

为整件事荒谬至极。她母亲虽然有时看上去有些妥协的迹象，但似乎仍认为她的尊严要求她在任何诱惑面前都不能动摇。所以，苏珊这个渴求的愿望被批准的可能性就越来越小了。到了本文开头部分的时候，时间已是"海伍德方丹戈舞"① 的前夜了——汤普金斯太太就喜欢这样描述这个即将到来的生日聚会。

一次又一次，苏珊偷偷摸摸地查看她那没几件衣服的衣橱，试穿着她所有夏天穿的旧连衣裙，看看哪件穿起来最好看。但是，由于这都是些褪了色的印花棉布裙子，所以很难作出选择。最后，她决定穿那件粉色的裙子。她把它从放冬天衣物的格子中取出来，熨平了，使它看上去尽可能漂亮一些。可是，她母亲浇灭了她所有的希望。她母亲仿佛一点也不知道这条裙子将要派什么用场似的，问她在这个时节拿出那条廉价的薄裙子要干什么。这个可怜的孩子无法鼓起勇气说她母亲明知故问，所以只好说她不过是想看看它什么样，然后就把它拿走，挂回了原来的地方。有那么一两天，她重又燃起了希望，便做了那条棕色的围裙。她很满意那条围裙，想象着再配上那条粉色的裙子看起来会怎样，直到它被撕开那道"狠心的裂口"② 的那一灾难时刻。

那时她仅存的希望是：如果她的母亲愿意让她穿上她礼拜日才穿的丝绸礼服就好了。确实，它不会很合身，但是没人会注意到的。她准备等母亲一回来就问一下，不管怎么说，总还是有一线成功的希望的。在这个希望的激励下，她又拿起了她的编织活，脑子里盘算着怎样提起这件事，努力忘却那件毁了的围裙。然而，快八点的时候，她的母亲回来了，脸色阴沉得像刚才她忙着盘算时外面的暴风雪一样。这时，令她难过的是，她的勇气全没了。母亲去了村里——汤普金斯家的房子离苜蓿角有大约一英里——去吊唁一个过世的人。

"哎，孩子妈，雪下得不是很大吗？"汤普金斯先生说，一晚上第一次打破了沉默。"噢，不，"善良的女人说，"时不时地会飞几片雪花，但我想现在还太暖和，不会下雪的。"苏珊想，这话暗含着对

---

① 方丹戈舞（fandango），一种西班牙舞蹈，节奏较快，男女共舞。
② "狠心的裂口"（envious rent），出自莎士比亚戏剧作品《裘力斯·恺撒》中布鲁图和安东尼的演讲部分，原文为"See what a rent the envious Casca made"。

她要外出的责备。

"我希望雪能在明天晚上之前停了。"苏珊说，手上编织的速度更快了。没人注意到她，过了一会儿，她便接着说："因为如果下雪的话我就不能去参加晚会了。"

"我想即使不下雪你也不能去。"汤普金斯太太说。苏珊舒了一口气。这时，在地毯上躺着的一个男孩站了起来，说："妈妈，苏珊把她的新围裙扯破了，真的。""我敢说，苏珊总是闯祸——是怎么回事，孩子？"母亲发着牢骚，从她手里拿过撕破的围裙，缝了起来。苏珊解释了事情的经过，但她母亲说："没事就别穿，如果不穿，就不会有这样的事了。"

没人知道她会絮叨到什么时候，中间只停下来一次，那是那个男孩子问她为什么没给他带回来一些好东西，她是这样回答的："好东西是要花钱的，你以为是长在灌木丛里的？你父亲和我得给你们买鞋，买衣服，买吃的东西，还得花钱供你们上学，我不知道还有些什么，然后才能轮到买好东西。"汤普金斯太太在跟孩子们说话的时候，总好像他们应该为索取东西而受到狠狠的责备，或者，事实上，只是因为他们来到这个世界上就应该受到责备。当孩子继续说沃尔特·海伍德有把刀子而他也想要一把时，她的情绪仍未缓和下来。

"沃尔特·海伍德，"她回答道，"他有而你没有的东西太多了，而且即使他有的东西你都有，你也成不了沃尔特·海伍德：人家是有钱人。"

汤普金斯先生和太太会抓住一切机会，给他们的孩子们灌输他们是多么的低下和卑鄙。一以贯之，她现在就在告诉她的小儿子，他成不了沃尔特·海伍德——仿佛他是个异类似的。

小家伙坐了下来，低下了头，心里很难过。最后，他问他的母亲他什么时候才能长大，也许在孩子气地想着到时候就能做一些了不起的事情了。"唉，孩子，"她说，"我也不比月亮上的人多知道多少。苏珊，带他去睡觉，现在是男孩子们该睡觉的时间了"。

于是，他被拽走了，一点也不情愿，也不知道自己什么时候能长大成人，而且他觉得，即使他长大了，他也成不了沃尔特·海伍德那样的人。

苏珊回来后，看到父母正在以不同寻常的热情谈论着刚刚去世的那个人何时举行葬礼,谁来布道,最后汤普金斯太太总结道:"尸体非常漂亮,看上去像活的一样。"

只要方圆四五英里之内有人死了,汤普金斯太太一定会去看看尸体,这是她的一个特别的嗜好。苏珊想她母亲的心肯定已被软化,便打算问问她能否去参加聚会。可就在这时,汤普金斯太太忽然转移了话题,用一种非常认真的口气说:"孩子爸,你听说了昨晚发生的抢劫大案了吗?"

"没有呀,孩子妈,我没听说。我一直在谷仓里忙活,簸了几蒲式耳①的燕麦。"语气中又带出明显的谴责。汤普金斯太太沉默了,知道他是冲着谁。汤普金斯先生问抢劫发生在哪里,性质怎样。

"在米勒先生家。"汤普金斯太太被得罪了,说完就又陷入了沉默。

"丢了什么了?"

"我想是一些火腿,还有些别的什么东西。"

"多少火腿?别的什么东西?"

"我没问有多少,还丢了一件细布衬衫。"

"他们有特别的怀疑对象吗?"

"是的。"

"谁呀?是这周围的人吗?"

"不算太远。"

"啊,是的!"然后汤普金斯先生似乎不再好奇了。于是,汤普金斯太太便把在这件事上她所知道的一股脑地讲了出来。

"我希望我所知道的是这件事的真相,"她说,"米勒太太亲口告诉我的。她说她觉得事情发生时她是醒着的。前半夜她有点牙疼,直到午夜都睡不着。后来她有点打盹儿了,她说她梦到所有的牛都跑进了院子,狗在试图把它们赶出去。然后,她说她觉得一头奶牛打开了熏制房的门。她吓坏了,以为奶牛要吃掉那天放在那里的一袋荞麦。然后她就惊醒了,她说当时狗正在狂叫,声音大得吓人。一开始她想起床,然后又觉得这很蠢——不过是邻居的狗或别的什么东西而已,于是她就静静地躺着,睡着了。当她早上起床之后,

---

① 蒲式耳:英制容量或重量单位,主要用于量度干货,尤其是农产品。在美国1蒲式耳燕麦相当于25.401公斤。

她说她看到熏制房的门开着，但是她想那很可能是被风吹开的，便没再想别的。直到她去切些火腿拿来做早餐的时候，才发现火腿都没了，那袋荞麦也不见了。看上去很有可能是有人对他们心怀不满，她说，因为特鲁斯特先生也把他的火腿放在那里熏制，却一块都没丢。"

"那就怪了，"汤普金斯先生说，"我们得锁上一把挂锁，下回他们就该抢我们了。米勒先生是很有胆量的，如果他没给熏制房加把锁的话，孩子妈，我一点也不吃惊。"

"最近有一家人搬进了希尔先生的旧房子。人们觉得这家人家不怎么地道，"汤普金斯太太说，"他们不干活，人们这样说，也没人知道他们是怎么生活的。但是我们都知道，他们必须得吃吧。有人认为他们是夜里搞到食物的。你把毛巾从晾衣绳上取下来了吗，苏珊？"

汤普金斯先生穿上他的厚大衣，从放锤子的壁炉架上取下锤子，出去把熏制房的门钉了起来，又把狗拴到地窖门前。他对狗很仁慈，把一个旧桶放倒，里面铺上一些稻草，给狗做了个窝。干完这些后，他给手表上了劲，放在耳边听了听，然后把它挂在镜子下面，就上床睡觉了。汤普金斯太太和好一小盆用来做早点的蛋糕面糊，用一条干净毛巾盖好，把盆放在炉边好让面发起来。然后，她对苏珊说现在到了小姑娘睡觉的时间了，说完她就去睡了。

苏珊仔细地考虑着第二天晚上的可能性——她能不能去，能去的话她妈妈会不会让她穿那条裙子，让穿的话穿上是否好看。想过之后，她便去了自己的厢房。

第二天早上，苏珊早早地起来，心情愉快。当她妈妈下楼时，她都快把早饭做好了。她希望这样可以使她多得到一点点宠爱。她开心地在屋里穿梭着，做着一切她被要求做的事，甚至没要求她的她也做。她哼唱着几句歌，跟在两个弟弟后面不停地跑来跑去，弟弟们则总是嚷着："苏珊，给我点东西。"

午饭像往常一样开始又结束了。汤普金斯太太准备去参加葬礼，并没说晚上有什么安排。她不在跟前的时候，苏珊把她所有的好东西都放在容易拿到的地方，把头发梳成她能想得到的最有品味的样式，又准备好了下午的茶点，以便没有事情可以耽搁她。她没心思吃晚饭，也等不下去了，便突然说道："妈，我可以去吗？"

"去哪，孩子？"

"去参加玛丽·海伍德的聚会：女孩子们都要去的，我也想去。"

"像你这样的孩子要是晚上也总跑出去参加各种各样的聚会，那就太好笑了！你觉得玛丽·海伍德要你去做什么？再说，我需要你在家做事。"

可怜的苏珊，即使讲出她此刻的感觉也是徒劳，这些感觉于事无补。一阵剧烈的头痛袭来，她坐了下来，继续她的编织。弟弟们总是不停地说："哎，苏珊，即使你把头发梳得这么漂亮，我也知道你去不了的。"

蛐蛐儿们在炉子下鸣唱着。大风刮来刮去，樱桃树的枝丫刮碰在窗玻璃上，吱吱作响。对苏珊来说，这是从未有过的孤独。她几乎忍不住希望自己死掉算了。忽然，院子里的狗紧绷着它的链子，狂吠起来。然后一切归于宁静，紧接着那狗叫得更疯狂了。门前传来一声跺脚声，还有响亮急促的敲门声。"进来。"汤普金斯先生说。

"紧跟着插销拔开了，

大门被风吹开了，

一个陌生人站在了门厅。"

是一个肤色黧黑的帅气小伙子，约摸二十来岁。他一只手拎着一个小背包，另一只手拿着一杆来复枪和一串死鸟。那杆枪很不错，擦得锃亮，还镀了银。他对着汤普金斯先生优雅地鞠了一躬，又向着苏珊更加优雅地鞠了一躬，然后便问汤普金斯先生是否是农场的主人，还问他是否愿意雇一个帮工。汤普金斯先生说他认为不需要，在冬天他没什么活儿要干，而且并不大雇得起，诸如此类的。但是汤普金斯太太在每件事上都会跟她丈夫唱反调。她说她觉得在她看来有很多活要做，所有的篱笆都已年久失修，这就够一个男人干上半年的了，然后很快就该熬制糖浆了，没别人的帮助，一个人可怎么干呢？

"我也不知道，不过你说得对，孩子妈，"丈夫说，"你有什么条件呢，年轻人？"

年轻人也不知道该提什么条件。他不是农夫，可是他愿意尽其所能，并愿意接受任何条件。所以双方达成一致意见，让他留下来干一个月。他把背包和枪放在一边，凑近炉火，一会儿便不再拘束了。他讲着旅途中的奇遇，聊着不同的国家，也说一说他自己。随着话题的不断深入，他说起自己是个法国人，来这个国家寻找发财的机会。他花光了钱，又发现自己的身体有点不好了，于是决定在这里逗留几个月，攒点钱的同时也养养身体。

他很会聊天，苏珊听着他那些海上陆上的故事，早已把玛丽·海伍德和她的聚会抛到脑后了。当他向她道晚安的时候，他称呼她为汤普金斯小姐。这一称呼带给她一种全新的颇有魅力的感觉，因为在此之前，所有的人都只是叫她苏珊或苏珊小姐。

第二天，莫里斯·道赫提先生，这便是他的名字，陪着汤普金斯先生去了磨坊，仍然带着他的来复枪，以便路上万一遇到什么猎物也好顺便打回来。在这一天里，苏珊找了点时间补好了她的围裙，还非常仔细地熨平了她的黑色法兰绒裙子。准备好茶点之后，她穿上这条裙子，把自己打扮得漂漂亮亮的，然后像往常一样坐下来开始做她的编织活儿。不过，这次她还在迫切地留心听着外面有没有磨坊马车车轮的隆隆声。最后那声音终于传来了。当马儿们被牵入马厩、一袋袋货物被放入谷仓之后，莫里斯出现了，手里拿着三只鸟，翅膀耷拉着，滴着血。他把这些鸟交给苏珊，告诉她最好的烹调方法。她把这活儿承担下来，作为他的早餐来准备。

她并不漂亮，身材矮小而丰满，但是她动作轻快，头脑聪明，且面色十分红润。当她说话的时候，特别是跟莫里斯说话时，她的脸颊会呈现出玫瑰色，看起来真的很好看。

早餐的时候，鸟肉端了上来。道赫提先生说他从未吃过味道烹制得这么好吃的鸟肉。他比海伍德医生更懂得如何去迎合汤普金斯夫妇，很快就赢得了他们的喜爱。所以，当他一个月的雇佣期到期的时候，他又被雇了三个月。

时光荏苒，篱笆都竖起来了，该修补的也修补好了，树桩都挖出来了，苹果树也都修剪过了，许多其他事情也都做完了。这使得汤普金斯先生感觉，两个人来照料他的农场，真比一个人要好得多。

他再也不愿孤军奋战了。既然他有了助手，他便打算在放糖的仓房边上盖一间小屋，这样一来熬糖的时候就方便多了。而且等莫里斯走了之后，还可以把它租给房客。年轻人十分热心地赞许了这一计划，工作便马上开始进行了。不过，莫里斯坚持要把小屋修得好一点。他说这个房子是他所建造的第一所房子，必须得值得他的付出，得请一位木匠来制作门窗，铺地板，再嵌入一两个壁橱，还得请一位泥瓦匠来建烟囱和壁炉。汤普金斯先生坚决反对,认为这都是些没用的开销,房子只不过是租给房客的。但是莫里斯竭力强调这房子应该舒适耐用,并最终实现了这一点。当小屋造好后,果真看起来方便又宜居,特别是当壁炉中点起火来熬糖的时候。

整个冬季,苏珊常被指派到小屋中去照看糖锅,莫里斯也常到汤普金斯家房子里来料理晚间的琐事。在火光的映照下,小屋非常明亮,莫里斯又如此殷勤地招待他的客人,以至于苏珊有时会冒险在这里一直待到他回来。一天黄昏,熬糖的工作已接近尾声,苏珊系上她的帽子,拿上一小篮苹果和蛋糕,想让莫里斯享用和消磨时间,便来到了小屋。

一路上她都在想,熬糖的工作很快就要结束了,莫里斯也要走了,她非常难过。她没问自己为什么难过,她只知道她从未像他在这里时那般快乐过,而且他走后,她将会非常孤独。

"唉呀,我的小森林女神这是怎么了?"在她放下篮子悲伤地转身要走的时候,莫里斯说,"你必须坐下来告诉我。"

她真的坐了下来,将脸扭过去一半,简单地说:"我在想我们可能,也许,再也不能在这里熬制糖浆了。"

"也许不能了,"莫里斯说,一只胳膊搂在她的脖子上,把她的脸颊扭到他的唇边,"但是难道我们不能不熬糖就只是住在这里吗?"

第二天早上吃过早饭,他告诉汤普金斯先生,如果他仍旧愿意出租那间小屋的话,他将和苏珊一起租住。

13. 安妮·希顿

十月下旬的一个夜晚,几近满月的月亮正渐渐隐退在树木枯萎凋败的小树林后。地面上到处都是成堆成堆的桉树叶,亮闪闪又红彤彤。那轻薄的枫叶随着风起风落,时而婆娑起舞,时而长久摇曳飘动,时而宛如一群群鸟儿在空中拍翅振翼飞来掠去。

那轮圆月正从西面缓缓落下,那片树林边缘有大片低洼潮湿的草地。沿着小树林东面的斜坡有一条杂草丛生的狭长公路,径直通向临近的一个集市。斜坡附近的低洼处有一间破旧的小农舍。这间农舍建在这里一定是看中了这里的泉眼,里面的泉水清新甘甜,四季常流。泉水流经一家砖瓦修葺成的十分宽敞的奶牛场,陡峭的屋顶上爬满青苔,厚重的大门上配有铁链和挂锁。泉水使得为附近集市提供所需的优质黄油的生产加工大大便捷起来。

房子的建造简单粗糙，后侧由天然的原木搭建而成。前面的客厅则选用直木修建，两层楼高，又高又窄的房门暗红色中泛着褐色。两侧的窗户修葺得四四方方，窗套的颜色和大门的颜色相近。前面有一条低矮的门廊，两侧各倚靠一棵苹果树支撑，这办法一举两得，既可以充当门柱又能遮阴避暑。门廊上盘绕着枯萎的牵牛花藤蔓，绚丽湛蓝的花朵早已败落，藤蔓叶子也已经枯萎，变得脆生生的，但这可以见证主人曾经精心呵护过这些牵牛花，试图让这些美丽的点缀使他们粗陋寒酸的住处洋溢着家园应有的温馨舒适。

一条公路将农舍与几乎在其正对面的大型谷仓分隔开。谷仓的四周堆满了马兰、干草等，这充分说明农舍的主人富庶并且上进。但那些瘦骨嶙峋、鬃毛蓬乱的小马，还有成群饥饿的牛群则表明主人的帮手勤于储备草料却不经常喂养牲畜。果园里灌木杂乱丛生，一角有个苹果榨汁房，冬天的时候可用来存放那辆四轮车，车上配有牛套，还堆放着犁具、锄头、镰刀以及各种各样的农具。这里还存放着所有报废的家具。有一个共同的特点是，所有家庭都非常虔诚地保存着这些东西。这个苹果榨汁房里总是塞满了这样的东西，一个地方悬挂着一张没有椅面的椅子，另一个地方挂着一个有点过时的破马鞍。马鞍破旧到根本无法修补的程度，它已经在那里放了十到十五个年头。这样的东西带给我的感受我只能意会，不能言传。横梁上悬挂着千奇百怪的破旧陶器，毫无疑问是为了炫耀；还有小孩子的鞋子、男人的靴子，由于时间太久而变得硬邦邦的，上面还长满了霉菌；还有各式各样的帽子。每年，主人会查看一两次所有的物品，再小心地摆放好。主人常常说，这些东西物尽所用，值得珍藏起来。事实上，古董爱好者们会发现这里很值得一游。

约瑟夫·希顿是这儿的主人，他拥有这里的谷仓、牛群、马群、苹果榨汁房以及那栋农舍。他是一个名副其实热爱劳动的人，因为他干活不仅仅是为了享受收获时的乐趣，还出于对劳作的热爱。从早到晚，从冬到夏，他都在忙碌个不停。在他的眼里，任何没有像他一样勤奋工作的人，无论男女老少，都是社会上多余的寄生虫，无论从哪个角度考虑都是他唾弃鄙视的可耻小人。

希顿太太是他的好帮手，这个女人很符合他的心意。结婚时，她带来的嫁妆就只有奶牛和马鞍，而他拥有土地产权，他们仍居住在这块土地上。她心中充满了感激之情，我不知道是否因为她念及这些，还是因为她丈夫身上超乎寻常的智慧使她折服，抑或两者兼而有之，她对丈夫一直是服从恭顺的，甚至觉得服侍丈夫是她的殊荣。希顿先生通常不直接说出自己的想法，他没有这样的习惯，但是希顿太太那双冷峻的蓝眼睛可以轻松地读懂他的心意，语言对于他们来说的确是多此一举。每当她看到希顿先生又系上那个黑领结，穿上褐色的马甲，观察到他有去拉马车的迹象，她就知道他又要进城，就让他捎带一些必要的家用小东西，然而每次只能指望他买回一小部分东西，因为每当好的记忆力意味着花费更多的钱时，希顿先生总是会习惯性地忘记一些东西。

每晚八点钟左右，希顿先生就会放下手头的《圣经》或者报纸，事实上，他就只阅读这两样东西。这时候，希顿太太就会放下手头的活计，默默地压好炉子里的残灰余烬。全家人上床休息的时间到了。所以，不足为奇的是，在这样的家庭长大的小孩子会感觉，父母的在场对他们来说是一种约束限制，从某种程度上讲，他们处在父母的监管下，遏制住了所有像欢乐、悲伤这样的自然情感，从少年时代就学会了虚伪、伪善的一面，而这些小孩子如果能早记事的话，他们可能躺在摇篮的时候就已经学会了这一点。

偶尔有时候希顿家里传出点嬉笑声，希顿夫妇会变得出离愤怒，感觉他们作为父母的尊严被践踏，他们的权威受到了挑战、扭曲。这时候，他们会制订出更为严厉的规矩，至少执行两个礼拜，以便使叛逆的孩子变得服服帖帖。

每天，日出之前，人们就要穿好土褐色的劳动服，越过满地露水的东面高山去劳作。房门的敲打声吵醒了所有美梦，也催促所有人重新回到枯燥无趣的劳作中。这样辛苦的日子日复一日持续下去，即使遥想将来也看不到劳作会有所减轻的迹象，也没有丝毫获得酬谢的希望。如果他们厌倦了这种枯燥的日常生活，他们会被责怪说他们给父母惹了很多麻烦和忧虑，他们是不想以这种方式来报答含辛茹苦养育他们的父母。

我们活在这个世上，要遭受种种不幸和煎熬，这些苦难以不固定的形式存在，也无固定的称谓。约瑟夫·希顿的三个孩子塞缪尔、安妮、玛丽就是活生生的见证人。但是这个家庭还有另外一个成员，人人都称他为包扎工，因为他是一个小学徒，他的真名叫做米尔斯·霍华德，他也见证了所有的一切。

本章开始时提到的正缓缓退幕的月亮宣告着他快乐的一天即将来临。从这天起，他将是个自由人。这也难怪他那晚睡不着觉，他太兴奋了。也许，他睡不着还有另外一个原因。他叹了一口气。在他做包扎工的最后一晚，随着月亮的渐渐隐去，他有点希望这一天不要来得这么早。

其实他并不是唯一一个在注视月亮慢慢消失在密林里的人。这么多年来，每逢秋天，他总会采集一些熟透了的坚果和红红的山楂，一股脑倒进安妮或玛丽的衣兜里。不管他是否更喜欢两个女孩中的一个，他总是把这些小东西送给他第一个碰到的女孩。但是如果先遇到的是安妮，他总是说："送给你和玛丽的。"可如果遇到的是玛丽，他很少提到安妮的名字。安妮就住在隔壁房间，她那双宝蓝色的眼睛一直在看着月亮渐渐沉下去。她不像

"一个神圣的隐居者，
　　总是处于半睡半醒之间"

她说话虽然声音低，可音质非常清晰。她用手碰了碰自己妹妹白皙的肩膀，喊了两三次"玛丽"，玛丽迷迷糊糊回答道："安妮，你叫我了吗？早上了吗？"

"还没呢，对不起，我吵醒你了，可我睡不着。我也不知道为什么，我想也许你也没睡着呢。"她说。她的姿势很不舒服，脑袋几乎从枕头上滑落下来，长长的黑发松散着，垂落到地上。有时候当我们内心烦躁不安时，我发现可以通过让自己身体不舒服的方式来减轻心里的痛苦。她现在就是这种心情。她并没有改变自己的睡姿，而是继续说下去，好像在自言自语："我多么希望月亮沉下去啊，对我而言，月光总让人倍感孤独寂寞。"她把薄棉窗帘拉到一边，月光如水般倾泻下来，洒落在姐妹俩的脸上。姐妹俩并不是很漂亮，但是青春和健康就是一种美丽。

姐姐安妮，身材瘦弱，长长的头发黝黑稠密，宝蓝色的眼睛时常流露出忧郁的神情。那独特的神情使她即使在微笑时看上去也像是世界上最忧伤的女孩。她十分恬静温柔，大多人都认为这是由于她对生活没有什么奢望，很满足。而事实上，她对周围的东西不感兴趣，她知道即使努力也不会改变什么。她是个有梦想的人，在她平静淡定的外表下涌动着澎湃的激情。她很少说出自己的想法，而当她讲出来时，她看上去十分诚挚，眼角有些湿润，脸上挂着淡淡

的忧伤的笑容。她这样的表情似乎是在安慰自己，她比自己看起来要坚强。

仅看她的眼睛，就可以知道她现在已经一反过去掩饰自己的习惯，而流露出她真实的一面。她说道：

希望愿望长久以来被压抑着，
压抑着并长久地珍藏在心里。

通过倾听一些成功的奋斗历程，感受着字里行间的修辞，朗诵着这些可以形象地描述自己内心情感的言辞，安妮找到了自己的快乐。有时候安妮过分渲染了自己所处的不幸，和想象中的苦难搏斗。有时候，夕阳西下时的绚烂辉煌，秋日树林的五彩斑斓，田野里的欢歌笑语，都会激发她对生活的热爱，她会在祈祷中倾吐自己的想法。有时候她会处于不同的心境中，那时候绮丽的世界对她来说似乎是一种嘲弄。如果她祈求的话，她就会十分迫切地希望能马上得到答复。她张开双臂，双手似乎已经推开了天堂之门。

玛丽比安妮小几岁，天性活泼浪漫，一双黑亮的眼睛现出淘气的神情，美丽又富有光泽的小卷发上时常插上一些大红色的花朵或是亮晶晶的金银花果子来装饰，鲜明的色彩对比令人心情愉悦。她喜欢艳丽的服装，还有点爱撒娇。如果她这些喜好得到满足，她就会展示出她天性中快乐无忧的一面。事实上，她有意充分利用周围的条件。如果环境与她的想法相反，她总是把欢笑暂时隐藏起来。她不敢经常肆意大笑，她知道这在家里是绝对不允许的。但她控制不住这种天性，经常在父亲面前靠衣橱、大门或者窗帘的遮掩来逃避父亲密切关注的眼神。她晓得利用一切对她有价值的东西。她经常引用圣歌里面虔诚的语句来表达不敢用自己语言描述的事情，她说的时候表情很虔诚，声音也毕恭毕敬。当包扎工在附近的时候，她喜欢用一连串的语言来展示自己的活力，而包扎工总是通过眼神或者手势让她明白他很欣赏她的机智，甚至有时候安妮也会露出微笑。姐妹两人在性格和脾气上有天壤之别，总而言之，如若让她们生活在有益于各自天性发展的环境里，这两个人都不会很依赖对方才能获取幸福快乐。

姐妹两人躺在那里，银色的月光洒落在她们身上。安妮乌黑的头发散落在枕头上，而玛丽白皙的小手压在自己有些湿润的头发下，显示出女人特有的优雅圆润和丰满之美。

她们谈论着梦想。玛丽梦到有个陌生男子走进她的房间，当时她没有穿鞋，便急急忙忙跑去取鞋子，却一下子撞翻了父亲的大椅子，父亲大发雷霆，把她关在熏肉房里。这个恐怖的梦把她吓醒了。"并且，"她继续很生动地说，"我梦见包扎工离开了。他离开时，向我要这绺卷发。"她从脑门拉下一绺卷发，用手指缠绕着，"这是一个奇怪的梦，是吧？"

"我也说不清楚，"安妮有点不高兴了，问道，"但是你为什么叫他包扎工呢？我很肯定，他总是叫你的大名啊。"

"才不是哪，他从不叫我的名字。如果爸爸不在场的话，他总是喊我小吉卜赛、小可爱，诸如此类的称呼。"

"我还不知道他给你起了这么多好听的名字。"

"嗯，是啊。"安妮又有点不高兴了。姐妹俩又陷入了沉默。后来，玛丽意识到了她刚才的话惹得姐姐不开心了，就先主动打破了沉默，很友好地问："安妮，你在想什么呢？"

"我看着这墙上的月光，很微弱惨淡，一点点减弱，直至最后消失在无尽的黑暗中。我在想，这多么像我内心深处的希望，闪烁了一会儿，然后就淹没在永恒的黑暗里。"

"你千万不要这么想。即使你的希望像这月光一样，你要记住这只是消失了一会儿而已。明晚，月光会重新照耀回来，比以往更亮，因为月亮现在还不是满月。你心眼好，人又聪明。"

安妮的心中又涌出了满满的希望，就像那满满的泉水，一句友好的话语就可以使她心潮澎湃起来。她把脸埋在枕头上。月亮沉了下去。最后，安妮抬起头时，月光已不在墙上摇曳了，屋子里一片黑暗。安妮双手紧紧抱住胸部，就好像在抱着什么东西一样，即使黑暗的力量也不能将其夺走。她说："玛丽，你是对的，我希望如此。"

这些话对玛丽来说如释重负，姐姐原谅她了。她在心里反复搜寻出一些善意的言语来弥补自己的错误。她知道她曾有意地伤害了姐姐那颗极为敏感的心。虽然没有开口承认自己的过错，但她决定作出补偿。或许，她自己还没意识到这一点。早上的时候，她弯着腰，把安妮前额稠密的头发整理好，梳成一个简单的发髻。安妮一向是这样的头型，她边做边称赞头发的美丽优雅。当她梳好头发时，突然不由自主地说："今天米尔斯要离开我们了。我们会变得非常孤单。但是安妮,他会经常给我们写信的,是吧?"

"他说他会的,但是也许当他离开一段时间后,他就会忘记我们。他要离开很久,你知道的,也许五年。我敢肯定五年的时间足以让他遗忘我们。"

"也许时间是很长,不过那时候如果他忘了我,我会看不上他的。我希望等他回来时,我还是那个爱笑的女孩。我可能不会比现在聪明多少,可是我很高兴再见到他。我希望时间能飞转起来,今天就是他回来的日子。让我想想,五年后,我就二十一岁了,就像他现在这么大。"

"而我,"安妮似乎有点不好的预感,叹了口气说,"我那时候二十五岁了。"

天渐渐泛白,随着惯例的召唤声,姐妹俩起床了。安妮默默无语,而玛丽笑着朗诵着:

"亲爱的!这就是我的命吗?
我现在很无忧无虑——
向早餐的屋子前进,
但也不再有准备好的早餐。"

当玛丽走过已经是自由身的小学徒的屋子时,她压低了声音轻声说:"再见了,包扎工。早上好,米尔斯·霍华德先生。祝福你一切都顺利。"当她笑着跑向安妮时,她又加上一句:"我希望我已经告诉他为父亲祈祷,父亲对他一向很好。"

"你说什么?"希顿先生问道。他正站在楼梯下那把铁灰色的椅子边梳头。

"我是说,"玛丽轻松地回答说,"早点起床真好。"她急忙从他的身边走过,然后像以前一样把脸藏在窗帘后面。等笑容平静下来,她又探出头,欣赏美丽的清晨。

希顿太太能在很短的时间内准备好早饭,这一点她一向引以为荣。希顿先生总是自己冲泡咖啡。喇叭一响,开饭时间到了。那喇叭总是挂在门廊尽头的同一颗钉子上。塞缪尔每当吃饭时和周末就把帽子挂在那上面。他是一个非常严谨刻板的人。包扎工在早饭厅露面了,说话时神采奕奕,好像自己孤身一人,无亲无友,去外面闯荡世界是一件稀松平常的小事。事实上,他根本都没考虑这件事。那天他没有套上以往那件工作服,这肯定会使他不由自主地意识到他今天的身份与以往大不一样了。他穿着一身意味着已经自由的衣服，布料是自己纺的，在村里的裁缝那里定做的，布料粗糙厚重，颜色灰中略带点蓝。他穿在身上很不合体，本该显露出来的身材和气质荡然无存。尽管他这身打扮，还拿着要带上的一根结实的胡桃木拐杖，一个蓝红相间的棉布手绢打成的包裹，里面装着几件衣衫，但是希顿夫妇并没有提到任何和他离开有关的话题，只有几个孩子静静地交换着眼神，好像在表示尽管他们一言不发，但他们心里头惦记着这事情。

米尔斯早饭似乎吃得特别香，频繁地递过杯子要求再续一杯咖啡，而他以往从未喝过第二杯。玛丽的脸上没有一丝笑意，安妮也一副没有食欲的样子。在旁人眼中，穿戴一新的米尔斯一定会招致一阵笑声，可对希顿一家人来说，这又是另一种感觉。他们一直在回想这个年轻人的诚实品行以及他为他们这个家所作出的慷慨无私的贡献。他们一起度过一段艰辛的日子，而这些艰难困苦经常被他的开朗幽默和善意的鼓励所化解。他们一直吃睡在一起，他清楚并分享他们的痛苦，而从今以后，这一切将不再有。

离别时，即使是对一个我们并没有什么特殊好感的人，我们心中也会涌出几分伤感。我们会发现，我们彼此之间已经达成一定的默契，虽然直到离别那一刻我们才意识到这一点。有时候我们会饶有兴致地看着匆匆而过的路人，但同时又会涌起几分伤痛，因为今生今世，我们可能不会再次相逢。可是等到我们要和心爱的人天各一方时，尤其是和那种世上为数不多的我们彼此都深爱的人分别时，这种心痛的感觉就会加深百倍千倍。这些时刻就好比是"一颗行星遮住了太阳"，阴影笼罩着大地。这段时间，我们会封闭自己的情感，我们会停止构筑希望的高墙，因为草地不再熠熠生辉，花朵不再鲜艳夺目，唯有新的友爱温情可以驱除阴霾，重洒明媚的阳光。

"我希望，"向米尔斯告别的时候到了，"年轻人，我希望你将来不会犯法进监狱，希顿家的人从没有过进监狱的，永远也不会。"这是希顿先生有生以来时间最长的一次演说。说完之后，他拿起那把一直放在最体面的屋角的斧头，向小树林走去。他不想把时间浪费在毫无意义的仪式上。

现在轮到希顿夫人上场告别了。她握住米尔斯伸过来的手，尽管她的手可能刚刚碰过帚柄，说她希望他能牢记约瑟夫·希顿先生的忠告。塞缪尔一把抓住米尔斯，似乎想把自己的力量传递给他一些。他诚挚的"再见，上帝保佑你"就是对米尔斯的衷心祝福。

可怜的玛丽，她心里本来准备好了无数的祝福，祝愿他幸福快乐，可她一个字也说不出来。她转过身去，脸埋在手里，放声大哭起来。米尔斯嘴唇颤动着低声说："玛丽，你是个好姑娘，愿上帝保佑你！"

尽管安妮看到母亲冷淡的蓝眼睛里流露出的不满，她还是戴上了帽子，说要送米尔斯一程，送到榆树那儿。他们静静地走着，一路上默默无言，可实际上他们俩都有满腹话想要倾诉。直到快到了榆树那里，他们才开始说起话来。站在稀疏斑驳的树荫下，米尔斯把安妮的小手攥在自己的手心里，说道："这些年我的生活是很艰辛，也许有时候我曾经认为生活比现在回想的还要艰辛百倍，可我现在觉得以前在那栋我曾认为是破旧不堪的老房子里度过的时光是多么的开心快乐。嗯，有一点我可以肯定，只要和你在一起，我都会无比开心幸福。"

"你现在是这么说，"这个小女孩有些伤感又有几分抱怨地说，"等你离开一段时间后，你就会慢慢淡忘我的。没有人会长久地记得我，或是爱上我，他们也没必要这样做。我既不活泼可爱，又不多才多艺，在任何方面都不引人注目。"说着说着，安妮眼圈开始变红，眼泪在眼眶里打转。她扭身打算离开，可米尔斯一下子把她搂在怀里，亲吻着她的额头和脸颊，并告诉她，她不该这么怀疑他的忠诚，她冤枉他了。他说，她是他生活的全部，他会为她努力工作生活，不会辜负她的。五年后——五年的时间会一晃而过，那时候他就会回来，他们将会开心幸福地生活。

"你会偶尔想起我吗？"

"我会经常想着你的，我知道，安妮，你也会经常想着我的。当生活把我们折磨得疲倦不堪时，当前途似乎黯淡无光时，就想想我们未来的美好生活吧。"

"我会时时牵挂你，永远深爱你，并永远为你祈祷的，米尔斯，这你是知道的，"安妮说，"你很清楚这一点的。"说着，她把一个小包放进他的手心，并叮嘱他到了目的地后再打开，"这至少会勾起你对我的思念。"

米尔斯把小包放在胸前，热情地亲吻那现在无法拒绝的火热双唇。米尔斯颤抖地说完"愿上帝保佑你"之后，便转身离去。榆树稀疏的树荫下，一个心碎的女孩在望着那渐渐远去的越来越模糊的背影。

一次，并且只有一次，米尔斯驻足回头张望，看到她仍然站在他离开的地方。他马上扭头疾走，很快就被蜿蜒的小路遮挡，消失在她的视野之外。

"我亲爱的姐姐，"安妮回到家时，玛丽跑过来迎她，说道，"别哭了，看到你流泪的样子，我会很难过的！"她用手臂搂着安妮的脖子，用尽了一切办法来安慰鼓励姐姐。不管安妮内心是否真的感到宽慰鼓舞，至少她看上去好多了。那天之后，安妮像以往一样忙着家务活。虽然她脸上比以往多了些忧郁的笑容，但她的步伐倦怠了许多，消瘦的脸庞愈发苍白。时间一天天地过去了。森林里，树叶都已凋落，光秃秃的树枝在寒冷的天空的映衬下愈发凄冷孤寂；牛群在草场周围瑟瑟发抖；寒风在门口的苹果树边日日夜夜呼啸着。远村近寨都飘起了雪花，凄冷乏味的冬天开始了。

榆木块在火炉里噼噼啪啪地燃烧着，红彤彤的。希顿夫人忙着编织衣服，希顿先生在修理马具和农耕用具，为来年春天作好准备。他时常说他们现在要比以前更辛苦地劳作。包扎工过去帮了他们大忙，现在他们必须完全靠自己。希顿夫妇总是辛苦地劳作着，以免日后无路可走而犯法进监狱。

塞缪尔已是十九岁的小伙子了。冬天时，他和玛丽一起去社区的学校学习。这样一来，所有的家务活自然而然地都落到了安妮的肩上。对安妮来说，她根本没有读书学习的时间，也没有假期。希顿先生总是说，安妮比妈妈懂的多，却连妈妈一半儿的活都做不好，书本知识解决不了吃饱肚子的问题。塞缪尔天性慷慨大度，他打算上学，也就是说，每年冬天去学校学习三个月，一直到他年满二十一岁为止。到那时，如果教育真的有用处的话，他希望他可以自立门户了。可塞缪尔总是在九个月的辛苦劳作后把之前三个月学到的知识抛到脑后。结果呢，每年冬天，他都在重复学习同样的知识。尽管希顿的孩子们在短暂有限的学习时间里只接受了一点点教育，但他们还是掌握了相当多的知识，因为除了粗糙的食物外，他们从不满足。希顿的孩子天生聪颖，勤于观察思考，他们能利用每次机会来学习知识，他们或者可以说是自学成才。

这期间一直没有米尔斯的消息。一天,希顿先生要去镇里跑一趟。镇子里有家邮局。安妮踌躇再三,鼓足了勇气问他是否可以帮忙去邮局打听一下有没有她的信。希顿先生当时在忙着用块碎玻璃片磨斧头柄。他一声不吭,甚至看都没看安妮一眼。安妮等了好一会儿也没听到答复,就又问了一遍,她想知道父亲是否听到了她的请求,如果听到了,他又是否能照她说的那样去邮局看看那里会不会有她的信。但希顿先生还是没给出任何答复,安妮只好继续耐心地等下去。三个小时过去了,希顿先生一直还在忙着弄那把斧头柄,从一端到另一端,反复磨来磨去。后来,他不小心被碎玻璃片扎破了手指,于是他拿起帽子,匆忙走出房间。安妮倒是多少有点庆幸这个小插曲,不然的话,希顿先生还不知要磨蹭到多久。她喊道:"爸爸,等一下,我去拿绷带和纱布给您包扎伤口。看看,您的手在流血呢。"但希顿先生并没理会这善意的请求。他急匆匆地走向马厩去牵马。安妮想到希顿先生已经出发了,她的心跳开始加快。

一个小时后,当安妮还在琢磨父亲是否快要回来时,希顿先生走了进来——他还没出去呢。他拿起报纸,从第一则报道开始读起。很显然,他打算按照老习惯把报纸通读一遍。时钟的指针指向了四点,安妮暗自在想:晚饭前是没有时间去镇里了,我早点准备好晚饭,也许他吃过后就会出发。想到这儿,安妮重新安排了一下自己的一部分家务活。这时候,玛丽放学回来了,小脸红扑扑地跑过来询问父亲是否去过了邮局。

"没哪,"安妮回答说,"他还没出发呢。"接着安妮描述了一下父亲那令人恼火的举动。

"我注意到邮局那儿有封信,是寄给你的。"

"你怎么知道邮局有我的来信?"

"因为我觉得那里有封信,我想亲眼看到它。嗯,家里现在缺啥东西吗?"她跑到厨房,乱翻着家里的瓶瓶罐罐,还大声嚷着:"哈哈,发酵粉没了,茶叶也就剩一点点了。妈妈去哪了?"她又跑到牛奶场,嚷道:"妈妈,爸爸要去镇里,家里没有发酵粉和茶叶了,我去告诉爸爸,让他买一些回来?"

"嗯,"希顿夫人说,"这些东西好像很快就要用完了。让你爸爸买四盎司的茶叶、十美分的发酵粉回来。"

"我才不管买多少呢,"玛丽心里想着,她跑回来对希顿先生说,

"妈妈说，如果你去镇里的话，捎点茶叶和发酵粉回来。"

"如果需要的话，妈妈会自己来讲的。"希顿先生说完，又继续读他的报纸。

"是妈妈让我来告诉你的，"玛丽努力控制着自己烦躁的情绪，又接着说，"不知道家里的茶叶够不够今晚上用的。"

希顿先生喜欢喝茶，玛丽使出最后一招杀手锏就退了出来，因为她意识到如果她一直盯着他的话，他是不会作出任何举动的。希顿先生又磨蹭了一会儿，等到晚饭都要准备好时才出发。夜幕早已降临，可希顿先生还没回来。她们已经等了两个小时，点心都变得凉冰冰、硬邦邦的了。每个人，尤其是安妮，都失去了耐性。最后希顿先生终于回来了，他先花了好长时间照料他的马，然后把大衣搁在一旁，坐在火炉前摊开手烤火。被催了两三遍之后，他终于坐到了饭桌前。安妮和玛丽互相探询地看着，但谁都没有开口询问她俩内心急切想知道的事。晚饭就这样在一片沉寂中结束。

安妮心想：如果他手头有我的信的话，他一定会把信给我的。可他并没有这样做，我确信他手头没有信。但玛丽实在忍不住一肚子的疑问，边从桌子上拿起糖碗，边问道："爸爸，你去邮局了吗？"希顿先生沉默了一分钟，说他去过了，然后就没了下文。临上床睡觉前，希顿先生站起身来，拿过大衣，伸手在衣兜里摸索着。两个女孩子踮起脚，但最终都大失所望——希顿先生从口袋里拿出茶叶包和发酵粉包，又坐回到椅子上。姐妹俩彻底失望了，静静地坐在火炉前。已经深夜了，希顿夫人收拾好了炉火的灰烬。

"孩子们，快点去睡觉，"希顿先生说道，"别浪费晚上的蜡烛和明早的清晨时光。"然后希顿夫妇回屋睡觉去了。

"哎，玛丽，"安妮等他们离开后说道，"你说过会有信的。"

"我感觉肯定有信，"玛丽说，"我觉得爸爸从衣兜里取茶叶时，差点就把信递给你了。我敢肯定他手里攥着什么东西。"说着，她一把抓过大衣，伸手先摸了一个衣兜，又去摸另一个。安妮依旧是一脸忧郁的笑容，注视着玛丽的一举一动。这时候玛丽显然找到了一封信。她把信拿到烛光下，兴奋地大叫起来："有邮戳，安妮·希顿的信。"

"让我看看，"安妮急切地嚷着，"是的，的确是他的来信。哦，这么整洁的笔迹，不可能是他的来信。"

"快打开看看。"玛丽急切地说。

但安妮在烛光中翻来覆去地看着信封，仔细地查看信封上的每一处，好像在享受这种折磨似的。玛丽调整了烛光，拉一把凳子坐在安妮跟前。安妮打开信封，开始读信：

"最最亲爱的安妮，我现在在大学里一间很舒适的小房间里。你知道吧，我当了学生。我面前有张桌子，上面堆满了书籍、卷子、誊写好的和没有誊写好的稿子。壁炉里的炉火燃烧得正旺，我对现在的生活很满意，也很快乐。今天所有的幸福快乐，我要感谢一个人。哦，安妮，还记得分手时你送给我的那个小包裹吗？我该如何报答你啊？我现在不想谈分开的两个月里我所经历过的种种艰辛，这会使你担心难过。那段时间，我一直没打开小包裹。我每天都盯着看，猜想里面会是什么东西，这些猜想让我非常开心。最后，一天晚上，我打开了小包裹。当我发现里面放的是唯有身处困境时才会用到的东西时，我是既高兴，又难过。尽管我感到惭愧万分，我还是用了你省吃俭用送给我的珍贵的礼物。亲爱的安妮，我怎能不把我今天的一切归功于你呢？我一直保存着信封，等我回去时，我打算在里面装上相同数目的钱带给你，作为结婚的礼物，这也是善良体贴的你赠送给我的礼物。这学期的勤奋努力使得我有资格去教一段时间书，之后我就可以自食其力了。我对未来有一些美好的规划设想，当然每一个想法都和你密切相关。所有付出的努力都是为了将来，都是为了我们共同的将来。你经常想起我吗，还是偶尔想到我？呵呵，我不想这样盘问你，冤枉你。我知道你肯定会时常想起我的。保持一颗充满希望的心，时间、忠诚和努力会为我们创造一切的。玛丽还是原来那个整天快乐无忧的小女孩吗？我希望是这样。请转告她让她代我好好地爱你。塞缪尔想念我没有？有没有提过我？有些特别的纪念品会使他想起我，比如说那个装有小玩意的抽屉，还有苹果酒压榨房。还有希顿先生，他肯定没有进监狱吧。原谅我，安妮，有些人有些事情我很难释怀的。上周的礼拜上，那个年轻英俊的牧师——我想玛丽一定会爱上他的——做了一段关于谅解方面的论述，我深受启发。他的言语真挚诚恳，这说明他对学说的真理性坚信不疑。他说，《圣经》里也没有规定要我们去原谅我们的敌人，甚至耶稣基督本人也只是为他敌人的愚昧无知而祷告。他说：'原谅他们，因为他们并不知道他们做了什么。'这些想法对我而言既古怪又新奇。由于没有深入研究宗教神学，我内心迷惑不解，等待着解脱。忘掉这个小插曲吧。我本来不想说，但是我知道如果你抛弃对我的爱，无论今生还是来世，我都不会原谅你的。夜深了，我只能写到这儿了，我不是为节省蜡烛，而是必须保证一定的睡眠。我一定会在梦中和你相会的。"

　　信的结尾还说了一些温柔体贴又热情洋溢的话语，并承诺会经常通信联络，恳求安妮及时回信，又保证他会海枯石烂，永不变心。

　　那天晚上，安妮·希顿的心情比以往任何时候都要轻松愉快，以至于第二天，以及之后的许多天，她一直保持着这样的一种心态。这份礼物使安妮的前途看上去光明灿烂，使她达成了心愿。那个人就是她的一切。安妮沿用了她外婆的名字，因为这个原因，那位善良的老太太去世前郑重其事地把她已过世丈夫的银表赠送给她最喜爱的外孙女安妮。这款银表的确不是最流行的款式，尽管如此，它还是价值不菲的。安妮在不同的年龄时，心里无数次盘算过如何好好利用这笔遗物，但还没有一次将其付诸实践。当她看到包扎工孤零零地一人离开而在这个世界上又无亲无故时，女人的直觉立刻告诉她，这块手表对他会大有用处。凭借着这块手表——尽管这是一件微不足道的小事——他却争取到了今日这样幸运的位置。女人的爱情就是最美的王冠，可以掩饰千般不足，万般缺陷，可以使忧郁的眼睛变得明亮，可以使苍白的笑容变得甜美。我们的家里需要处处充满爱，我们的生命中需要处处充满爱，我们的世界或者我们想象中的天堂也需要处处充满爱。

　　夏天的一个傍晚，这里上演了一个庸俗的故事。姐妹俩坐在同一棵苹果树下的门廊上乘凉，一个在很费劲地朗读尤金·阿拉姆的趣味故事，另一个在把彩色丝带编织成的花结系在精心编织出的纯白色荷叶边上。为了看看效果，她时不时地把荷叶边围在脖子上，脸上会露出微笑。这个举动暗示了她在假装聆听这个故事，而并没有真正融入到故事情节中去。这时候，一辆从远处驶来的马车吸引了姐妹俩的注意力。马车最终停在了门口，装饰得十分华丽气派。来客中的一位是个中年男士，戴着眼镜，看上去自信十足；另一位是个略有些跛足的女士，脸色苍白，穿着一袭黑色连衣裙，戴着颇为夸张的又大又沉的耳环。原来是希顿夫人的亲戚来了，他们住在东部城市，生活富庶，被称作时髦的上流人士。他们过来看望住在附近小镇里的亲戚。他们喜欢在乡间驾着马车，享受一下那里新鲜的面包和牛奶，看看他们的穷亲戚现在的生活水平提高了多少。

希顿夫人并没有因他们的出现而感到一丝的骄傲自豪，只是非常礼貌客气地招待了他们。她摆出了最好的桌布，打开了蜜酒坛。希顿先生也在最短的时间内向他们传递了这样的信息：他们丰衣足食，无须去偷去抢。眼镜男士回应说："是啊，是啊，我们也是这样认为的。"跛足女士也回应说："是啊，的确是啊。"希顿夫人接着说他们虽说不像有的人家那么富有，但的确是丰衣足食。眼镜男士频频点头附和"是啊，是啊"，跛足女士也不断重复着说："当然了，的确是这样。"

安妮觉得他们的来访多少有些傲慢无礼，尽管她说不清楚为什么会有这样的感觉。他们说话的腔调、一举一动，甚至他们的服装，都在暗示着他们隶属于不同的社会阶层，他们的社会地位远远高于希顿一家。她对自己的生活不满意，当然对他们的态度也不满意。她们友善的提议在她听来就像他们在恩赐一样，她对这些提议也不大理会。"他们不会喜欢我的，我也不会喜欢他们。我不会费力去讨好他们的。"因而，她一直与他们保持距离，在一边自言自语着：

"有土地的地方就有人在耕耘不息，

或是种上种子，或是鲜花，

而对我而言，无须如此。"

他们认为安妮反应迟钝，很适合她现在的生活，可玛丽活泼可爱，富有活力，她在这里没有更好的发展机会是一种遗憾。在他们的拜访接近尾声时，他们提出想邀请玛丽去他们家做客。玛丽当时自然是喜出望外。希顿先生说："玛丽在家里干不了什么活，没有她在家的话，安妮可以做更多的活呢。"希顿夫人也表示同意，说："是的，她不在家，安妮会做得更好的。"玛丽自己也说："一个还是两个在家，没有太大区别的。"于是，他们就这样一拍即合定下来玛丽将要和他们一起离开。他们尽可能地为玛丽作了简单的准备。安妮擦了擦眼泪，仔细地看了看自己衣橱中为数不多的几件衣服，选出一套她认为最体面的，说："穿这套吧，我不需要这衣服了，我现在不会离家出门的。"

无论是在西面的树林中，还是在破旧的老房子里，丝丝缕缕的光束中到处都看得到肆意飞舞的尘埃。安妮一个人形单影只。树影越来越暗淡,夜晚越来越幽暗,但她的思绪更为黑暗和渺茫。这时,塞缪尔的出现打断了她胡乱的思绪。塞缪尔脸色惨白,跌跌撞撞地跑了进来。他的一只手用手绢包扎着,搭放在另一只手上,鲜血已经浸透出来,血迹斑斑的。"天啊,塞缪尔,塞缪尔?"安妮大叫着跑过去,把他搀扶到屋里,"怎么回事,发生什么事啦?"

塞缪尔刚才在丰收的田野里收割庄稼,一不小心,镰刀差点砍断了他两根手指头。他当时只能用自己的手帕包扎一下,就回家了。他在大门口看到了停在那里的色彩鲜艳的马车,就不由自主地停下了脚步。塞缪尔天性害羞,很容易尴尬不安,如今看看自己寒酸破旧的草帽,补丁摞补丁的裤子,他更加自惭形秽。他顺手拿过几把稻草放下当做枕头,就躺在野蔷薇花丛下等着客人离开。客人们直到晚上才离开,可以想象得出,等塞缪尔走进屋里的时候,他由于失血过多,差点虚脱过去。乡村医生赶了过来,给他做了手指切除手术。第二天早上,塞缪尔一直在发高烧。第三天病情变得更加严重危险了。六周以来,安妮和他形影不离,一直在照看着他。后来,塞缪尔一点点恢复了健康,安妮自己却由于劳累和过度透支体力而病倒了。可是她的病榻前冷冷清清,没有人来嘘寒问暖。她的母亲的确也想尽力照料她,可她不得不时时料理家里的琐碎杂活,以至于无法抽身照看女儿。"安妮,如果你需要什么,"她说道,"你就喊我过来。我一直待在这里也没什么用。"可怜的安妮经常是自己一躺就是几个小时。

安妮经常说,她的人生毫无目的,她的生活索然无趣。三个月后,她的身体开始渐渐恢复,六个月的时候,她已经基本恢复健康,但她失去了那一头乌黑的长发,还有些弱视。有时候,米尔斯温情脉脉的来信会使她开心振奋。年复一年,米尔斯不再时常提起对未来的打算,谈起来也不如以前那样明确了。他已经大学毕业,开始从商,前景比预想的要好得多。时间一点点向前推移,在夏去秋来之季,米尔斯终于要回来了。玛丽也要回来了。美好的重逢已是指日可待!安妮尽管天生多疑而且常常沮丧悲观,但是心中还是重新燃起了希望之火。

玛丽先到了家。五年前那个淳朴的乡村女孩如今已经出落得楚楚动人,几乎认不出了。她衣着光鲜,彬彬有礼,一头秀发垂在纤瘦优雅的肩头,白皙圆润的手臂上手镯闪闪发光。

"安妮，别这样紧抱我。"玛丽刚一到家，就很冷淡也有几分傲慢地挣脱了安妮的拥抱。从那一刻起，她不需要说类似的话来责怪安妮了。

安妮想：一周左右，米尔斯就要回来了，他可以给我慰藉。漫长的一周终于过去了，安妮也熬过了长长的等待。米尔斯马上就要回来了，可他还是当年那个在老榆树下与她恋恋不舍地分手的米尔斯吗？她的梦想会实现吗？从他们重逢开始，米尔斯对她的态度就是温和亲切，极为和蔼的，但不让人满意。他总说对她感恩备至，永远心存感激，但很少提到未来的打算，也没有提出任何明确的计划。事实上，他大多数时间里都泡在那个景色怡人、秋意盎然的小树林里，和她的妹妹玩耍嬉戏。他根本没有时间认真地思考这个问题。

一天，安妮看到他俩肩并肩坐在果树下，就戴上帽子去找他们。她蹑手蹑脚地靠过去，本想吓吓他俩。可当她走近时，她看到米尔斯一边玩弄着玛丽光洁优雅的卷发，一边说："玛丽，要是安妮能像你一样就好了。安妮太呆板严肃了。我想她觉得自己已经不再像以前那样漂亮。玛丽，希望你有时间能教教她如何着装打扮，她穿的花里胡哨的衣服太扎眼了。"

安妮不想再听下去了。她最后的梦想也破灭了。玛丽的探亲行将结束。当安妮听到米尔斯说要陪玛丽一起回去时，她一点也不诧异。米尔斯临走时把一个信封放了她的手里，她的心剧烈地跳了一阵儿。然而希望向她抛来了嘲笑。这个信封和五年前分手时装有离别礼物的信封一模一样。但是，天啊，里面只装着一张价值相当的钞票和一封信。在信里，米尔斯反复表达了对她过去解囊相助的感激之情，以及对未来的种种美好的祝福和祝愿——真是无情的嘲讽。

就这样，安妮·希顿一天天地生活下去，毫无目标，浑浑噩噩。很少有人认识她，也再没有人爱过她。那年秋天，以及之后每年的秋天，安妮都会看着一缕缕月光悄悄地透过窗户，将银辉洒落在对面的墙壁上，最后慢慢消失在茫茫黑暗里。这时她总是在想：我的希望，就好比这月光，从无到有，又一点点幻灭掉。

14. 彼得·哈瑞斯

那是仲秋时节的一天。一缕青色的雾气飘荡在枯萎的树林上空。那边一片枫树伫立在地平线上,亮黄色的叶子望去就像一片金色的云。这边有一颗橡树俯视着周围的同类,仍然泛着绿色的叶子染上了几簇深红;矮小的桉树亮红色的叶片紧贴在一起,满山闪耀着,就像一座座火红的金字塔。马车驶出果园和田地慢悠悠地朝家里驶去,车上高高堆起的有颜色鲜亮的苹果,还有金黄色的玉米。谷仓里满是新收获的干草。到处是一片丰收的景象。

就在这个天气适宜的秋日的傍晚,在满是尘土的大路上,有一个其貌不扬的汉子驾着一辆简陋马车在赶路。从他的衣着看起来仿佛一个人在毫无准备的情况下赶上了一个突如其来的霜降的早晨。他稍许花白的头发上戴着一顶裘皮帽子,明显是哪个男孩子的帽子。他的大衣对他来说明显太大了,用的是一种适宜夏天的面料,衣服穿得太久已经磨得发亮了,从式样上看,不大可能是给他做的。他的裤子又太短了,是一条蓝白相间的格子呢裤子。他脚上穿的鞋很笨重,其中一只靠脚尖的地方割掉了一部分,可能是收割庄稼时弄的。他根本没穿什么袜子,从他脚面皮革一样的颜色可以看出,他从来就没穿过袜子。他驾车的那匹马又瘦又难看,身上的毛乱乱的,看样子多年干活已经耗尽了体力,而且它走路老往一边偏,很可能一只眼睛已经瞎了。可是它的主人倒似乎享受赶车的乐趣,挥舞着从荆棘上砍来的一根大枝条赶着它朝前走。

赶车的老人身边坐着一个脸色有些苍白的男孩。孩子穿的衣服太单薄了,上面尽管有不同颜色的补丁还是破烂不堪。他的帽子是白色裘皮做的,看起来好像原本是顶很大的帽子,但是通过剪刀、针线,还有一双很可能出自一位女士的巧手,帽子改小了。他身上没穿大衣或夹克,但用了一条褪色的披肩围在肩膀上,披肩的两端在胸前交叉而过,然后在背后用紧紧的结系在一起。他坐的座位对他来说太高了,坐起来很不舒服。他一双光着的小脚悬在半空中随着马车的行进而摇晃着,非常难受。

"哎,孩子,"老人说,这是他一路上第一次开口打破沉默,边说着边让那匹筋疲力尽的马在一条两旁都是榆树的林荫道边停了下来,这条林荫道一直通向离大路不远的一处高地上的一栋白色的房子,"哎,孩子,这就是你叔叔杰森的家。这以后也就是你的家了,你要在这安顿下来了。"他边说边把孩子从车上抱下来,"身子这么弱，脸色这么苍白，但是我能为你做的都做了，即使你像你父亲那样聪明，那样健谈，也不过如此。是的，这里是我给你找的一个不错的能活命的地儿了。"说着就抓着孩子的手沿着林荫道走去，他走得很快，小家伙要跑着才跟得上。路上有两个小男孩正在玩滚铁圈，身上穿着颜色鲜亮带黑色纽扣的夹克，头上戴着天鹅绒的帽子，一边还缀着重重的流苏。看到有陌生人来，其中一个对坐在一边指导，看着他们滚铁圈的人喊："约翰！嗨，约翰！快看呀！那边来了个老头领着一个野小子！"

"小点声！"约翰说着走上来，把说话的孩子推到一边，"我看你自己倒更像个野孩子！""你好，孩子！"他伸出手拉住这个陌生孩子的手。

那个小老头问约翰杰森·哈瑞斯在不在家。听到杰森在家，他说他是杰森的兄弟，但是没杰森那么走运，现在来这里想把这个"脸色苍白的小子"送给他。

差不多走到房子跟前了，老头停下来说："约翰，或者不管你叫什么，你把这孩子带进去，告诉杰森他可怜的哥哥要去闯落基山当猎人了，把这个小家伙就交给他了。"他把瑟瑟发抖的孩子托付给约翰，转身就走，爬上马车，扬鞭而去。

可怜的小男孩！在这么大而舒适的房子里面他感到很不自在。他从来没见过这么好的房子，这么鲜亮的地毯和窗帘。他的新叔叔为人傲慢，让他战战兢兢，所以叔叔问他话的时候，他几乎不知道该怎么回答。

"你叫什么啊，小子？"

小男孩顺从地回答他叫彼得·哈瑞斯。

听到他的名字，那两个穿鲜艳夹克的男孩狂笑起来，边笑边说给他们家放牛的那个黑小子才叫彼得。

"哎，小子，"这个叔叔板着面孔继续说，"既然我孩子都笑你的名字，以后我们就叫你'皮特'。你多大了，皮特？"

听到这话，那两个孩子笑得更起劲了，其中一个对另一个唱起来："彼得，彼得！吃南瓜的家伙！"

彼得把双手交叉背在身后说他八岁了。

"皮特，我想你从来没上过学，大概从来不知道什么是学校吧？"

"是的，先生，"彼得回答说，"我从来没上过学，但是我知道什么是学校,而且我也应该去上学。"

"我想,"叔叔说,"你会喜欢上很多东西的。"

彼得回答:"我会喜欢很多东西的。"这下子一家人都笑翻了。

"别,"哈瑞斯太太此时尽力克制住自己的笑,用一种好像自己从来没笑过的口气说道,"别像那小子那么蠢。"

彼得不清楚自己到底哪里蠢了,但是想自己一定表现得很蠢,就哭起来。

"山核桃木烧起来的火就是暖!"哈瑞斯太太边说边拨弄着炉火的余烬。但是彼得没有感受到一丝亲情的温馨,他坐得离壁炉很远,又冷又怕,不停地颤抖,用他那条褪色的披肩擦去脸上的泪水。

"你一举一动怎么那么蠢?"哈瑞斯太太接着问道,她这人外表倒是十足的淑女,"坐在这里哭得跟牛犊子似的!"说到这里,她转向丈夫说:"我倒是希望你心里能好受些。你把这孩子弄哭了。我肯定你应该为有机会拯救这孩子于水火而心存感激(她可是个非常虔诚的女人)。"说完,她把彼得叫到跟前说:"我想你这个小乡巴佬从来就没什么教养。"

彼得努力控制自己不哭,回答说他不知道什么是教养。

"哦,那么你会对你叔叔和我心存感激的,不是吗?"

彼得说他不懂什么是感激。

"可怜的土包子!我想你也不懂,"这位婶婶说,"你要感到就是把你全部的精力都奉献给你叔叔和我也报答不了我们的恩情。你会这样感觉的,对吗?"

说到这里彼得已经茫然不知所措了。他根本就不懂什么是感激,什么是他的精力以及怎样把这些奉献给他叔叔和婶婶,但是他说他会努力的。

"这不是努力,而是必须做到,要么就用鞭子抽到你做为止。"婶婶说完就叫她的小儿子过来,她儿子正坐在地板上用别针戳她的宠物狗的爪子,太太于是就叫他过来教他可怜的土包子堂兄弟学着说:"现在我要躺下睡了。"

但是她儿子说他不会教,就继续折磨那只狗去了。在又深入教导了一阵子之后,哈瑞斯太太叫来莎莉,她家的女仆,让她带彼得到约翰的房间,彼得以后就住那里。

"我带他过去之前,需要给他弄点晚饭吗?"女仆问。

"没有必要，"哈瑞斯太太说，"这孩子毫无疑问已经吃了一肚子水果，不会饿的。"她又冲着彼得说："你不再需要吃什么了，对吧？"

彼得说他没吃过饭，现在正饿肚子呢。

"我准许了，"他婶婶说，"孩子吃东西不知道多少的。你给他弄一块儿面包——很小的一块儿，不要放奶油。我觉得奶油对孩子不好——尤其是小男孩。"

莎莉把孩子带到厨房，从新鲜的吐司面包上切了一大块儿，在上面放足了奶油，然后把面包递给彼得，对他说："我觉得面包上涂匀了奶油才好，你说呢？"说着把蜡烛从桌子上拿起来，用一只手护着，免得给风吹灭了。他们一路走到约翰的房间，这是一间在马厩上面非常小而且别扭的房间，但是房间的一个角落里有明亮的炉火。约翰说他的稻草床很宽，够他们两个人睡了，说着还把两把椅子拉来一把给彼得，彼得就这样坐在炉火前啃着奶油面包，觉得这里像家一样温馨。

约翰这人心肠非常好，他给了彼得很长的一根麻线搓成的绳子和一个红红的苹果。之后从口袋里掏出几张小纸片，好像是他零零星星从报纸上剪下来的。他没有蜡烛照亮，就把炉火拨亮，然后坐在靠近壁炉的量谷机上，用一种逗他这位小客人开心的语调读起来：

"一大群野水牛从西部一个城市经过，它们赶起来像家里的牛一样温顺。"

于是他问彼得见过野水牛没有，告诉彼得这是一种野牛，西部森林和大草原一带有这种野牛，通常一群有 20 到 50 头。接着他又拿起另一份剪报，读起来：

"我们一般喜欢馅饼饼皮薄一点，但是前几天见过一个女人做馅饼，到后来居然没有足够的饼皮来包住里面的馅儿了。这饼皮用得也太少了。"

读到这里彼得大笑起来，约翰也笑起来，笑得就像他从来没看过这则故事一样开心，他还说这可真是他听说过的用得最少的饼皮了。展开另一卷剪报，他接着读道：

"对这世上所有的老处女来说，她们的名字都叫黎贞，当中最老的那个毫无疑问是 Miss Ann Thrope。改革派现在想竭力促成一段姻缘，并且他们觉得这事有一定成功的希望，让她和一个叫 Ben Evolence 的结为夫妻。但是 Ma Levolence 极力反对，因此人们担心两人可能永远无法共结连理。"①

约翰说他曾经认识好多老处女,她们都不叫黎贞,他又接着读起来:

"有一个男的因为偷了只表被看守看押起来,他看到看守脱岗了,就这样看守戴着那块表逃了。""有一个叫马科斯的家伙骑了一头小驴,这驴太犟,他气急了就朝后面跳了下去,用力太猛把脑子甩了出来,于是自己成了一头大叫驴。"

就这样又读了几段,约翰抬起头看到彼得已经坐在椅子上睡熟了,就收起剪报,抱起孩子小心翼翼地把他放在床上。

十一月下旬的一天上午,彼得穿着他的小堂兄扔了不要的衣服,胳膊上挎着一只红蓝相间的篮子,里面放着一个苹果派和一本入门课本,他要去离家一英里多的学区小学去读书。班上的女生和男生都死盯着这位"新来的学者"。彼得天性就胆小,这种形势让他几乎说不出话来。这时,班主任,一个个子高高面孔黝黑的男人,把他叫到讲桌跟前,问他问题:

"我想你来我们学校是来学习英式教育基础知识的。"

彼得知道他来上学是要学些东西的,他颤抖着回答:"是的,先生。"

"是的,先生,如果您觉得可以的话。"老师强调说。于是彼得又说:"是的,先生,如果您觉得可以的话。"

"你住哪里?"

"住在杰森叔叔家,如果您觉得可以的话。"

"哎呀,你小子真太笨了。如果时机适当,你才必须说'如果您觉得可以的话'。你叫什么?"

"我叫彼得·哈瑞斯,如果您觉得可以的话,如果时机适当。"

"这小子真是笨到家了!"班主任于是说。班上的男生和女生都用课本挡着脸一起偷笑。

"过来,过来!这样好了!班主任边说边看了一眼全班,一脸严肃地皱着眉头。接着他从讲桌上拿起戒尺,在彼得头上晃来晃去吓唬他,他告诉彼得所有学习不用心的学生都要挨戒尺打。然后他叫

---

① 这个笑话是个文字游戏,Miss Ann Thrope 即 misanthrope,恨世者;Ben Evolence 即 benevolence,仁善;Ma Levolence 即 malevolence,恶念。

彼得回自己的座位看书。

学校的座位是一种高高的没有靠背的木板凳，彼得觉得这样一坐就四个小时太单调了，尤其是他连 a 和 b 都分不清，根本没法学。过了一会儿，老师叫他去背书，结果一个字母都不认识，老师叫他在一只高高的凳子上站十分钟，并且要班上所有的学生都用手指着他，班主任把表放在讲台上计时。时间到了之后，老师叫他回座位，看看他这回会不会学了。但是结果还是一样，所以男孩子都出去玩的时候，他被关在教室里不许出去玩。

中午到了，老师告诉彼得不愿学习的男生不许吃饭，之后就从他红蓝相间的小篮子里拿走了那块苹果派丢给一头正好在门边游荡的猪，那些没挨罚的男生非常开心地笑起来。即使后来清扫教室满屋灰尘，老师也不让彼得离开座位，还派了一个大一点的男生站在门口看着他，而老师自己去吃午饭了。

下午课程上了一半，又累又饿的彼得渐渐趴到课本上，这时班主任说："彼得·哈瑞斯，你胸口难受吗？从你的姿势我断定你胸口有病。你给我坐直了，先生！如果我再看到你趴下，我就抽你的后背让你直起来。"

彼得的确坐直了一会儿，但最后还是忘记了，又变成了原来的姿势。班主任就把他叫过去，问他到底该不该打。"我没兴趣惩戒你，"他说，"但是这是我的职责。"他命令彼得脱掉大衣，然后毫不留情地抽了他一顿。

傍晚放学的时候，刮起一阵南风，天空布满了黑云，看样子很快就要下雨了，但是彼得在放学后还被留了半个小时，所以让他回家时天差不多已经黑了，已经有雨点落下来了。他到家时，全身都在滴水。约翰把炉火烧得旺旺的，把量谷机拿过来叫彼得坐下把衣服烤干，然后他到厨房给彼得弄些晚饭。他回来时端了一盘暖暖的吐司，说是莎莉好心送的，但是彼得仍旧坐在量谷机上，身上升腾着一团蒸汽，彼得说他头特别疼——他不饿，就想睡觉。

那天夜里风雨交加，狂风号叫着，大雨打透了屋顶，后来稻草床也差不多湿透了。第二天早上彼得头更疼了，喉咙也疼，而且还发高烧。约翰把能想到的法子都用上了，并且尽可能守在床前，但是他要干活，不时要离开他，于是可怜的孩子有时候一连好几个小时就一个人躺在那里痛苦呻吟。

当哈瑞斯太太得知孩子的病情，表示地太湿了没法过来看他，但是会给他送条毯子过来，至于药，她觉得孩子不需要吃药，尤其是对小男孩来说。

就这样一周过去了。北风凛冽，屋门在风中颤动，一棵老榆树的树枝整夜不停地来回敲击着窗棂。

有时会有些许雪花从屋顶或缝隙中飘落到小彼得的脸上，但是他苍白的小手软软地握在一起并没有抬起手拂去脸上的雪花。壁炉里的火烧得很旺。约翰早把床拖到壁炉跟前，他就坐在量谷机上把头靠在床尾，沉沉睡去。壁炉里火越来越暗，对面墙上炉火的影子也越来越模糊，直至最后完全消失。

夜里没有什么动静打扰这位疲惫的守护者，他就这样一直睡到晨光透过没有窗帘遮挡的窗子漫进屋内，他起身奔向床前，悄无声息地弯下腰看了一会儿，之后转过身，抹掉眼里的泪水，边把余火重新拨亮边说:"可怜的小彼得！他以后再也不会生病了。"

15. 玛格丽特·费兹

我曾读过一个关于画家布莱克的故事。故事说，有时候他在专心画画时，一个想象中的人物或是时常想起但是可能很多年都未见过的一张脸会一下子插在画布和画笔之间，迫使他去画那幅脑海中的肖像或诸如此类的东西，直到画好才能接着工作。我今天早上就遇到了这样的情形：我本来正在画着其他景物，而我下面要讲的故事拦在中间，因此我最好还是先完成这个令人苦恼的任务。

西部有许多美丽的山谷，有一个离苜蓿角不远。那儿有一座老式的茅舍，在细长的枫树、盘根错节的橡树和平滑的榆树间半隐半现——这些树是森林成长的见证，夏天时会在下面的草地上投下凉爽的树荫，让那些赤脚玩耍的孩子高兴不已。他们无忧无虑地在草地上玩，在那里采摘圆圆的三叶草的花儿，红的、黄的，颜色不一；筑起游戏场所，四周用细草围住，还找来碎瓷片来装饰一番。

这所房屋和周围的所有房屋一样，现在正慢慢朽坏，真让人痛心。但是从随处可见的残迹中仍看得出当初繁华富足时期的风貌。房屋挡风板的油漆已经剥落了；百叶窗已经坏了，无法拴上，每次暴风雨来临时都被吹得前倒后仰；栅栏倒在地上。到处都是一派萧瑟破落的残迹。蓝蓟花在草场怒放，几朵散落的玫瑰花和未加剪枝的丁香花告诉人们过去花园的位置。

但是我的故事跟现在的这个地方没关系。我必须往前追溯。十年前，这间房舍四周所有的一切亮丽、漂亮得难以想象。玛格丽特是这个家的阳光，是这家中最亮丽、最美的人。当然，按照普通人对美的理解，她还不算漂亮，她没有普通人所羡慕的那样曼妙的身姿，也不那么引人注目。但是她的眼睛里透出无限的温柔和深刻的思想，脸上显出智慧和优雅的高贵气质。本来她家里有两个孩子，但是那时她成了唯一的一个。孩提的花蕾正含苞欲放，但是一片乌云袭来，遮掩了她步入成年的所有的光彩。那时我经常在上学的路上看到她，自从她的玩伴走了之后，她常常坐在门边几棵老树的树荫下，双手无所事事地放在腿上，眼睛盯着地面。她从来都是郁郁寡欢的，早在很久以前痛苦之源还没有敲开她的心灵大门，那时没有任何人会夺走她的爱。但是现在她更加文静，脸上总是闷闷不乐甚至忧郁的表情。她的母亲已卧病在床好多年了，性情焦躁不安，爱发牢骚，总是不满意别人做的事情，照顾她这样的病人绝没有快乐可言。玛格丽特哪怕离开半小时都不行。母亲想喝水，只能由玛格丽特端才行，但是水端来后，不是嫌热就是嫌凉，要么倒得太多，或者太少——这时母亲总要拿那个已经故去的孩子和眼前的这个作比，这多少让玛格丽特苦不堪言。

玛格丽特必须读书给她听，而且要按时读，都是一些玛格丽特一点兴趣也没有的书。费兹太太特别热衷神学讨论，但是她只能接受和她根深蒂固的观点一致的讨论。异己者必须消灭，这一点毋庸置疑，因为在这样的幼稚观点上白白浪费时间是没用的。即使玛格丽特这样按时间读完那些乏味的作品后，也得不到半句好言好语或是谢意——她读得太快了或是太慢了，都让她可怜的母亲乐趣索然。她待在家里就只能是闷闷不乐，根本不像那个去了天堂的孩子——离开家，根本不用想着家里疾病缠身、饱受折磨的病人。玛格丽特没有去世了的亲人那样开心。可怜的玛格丽特，难怪她那么闷闷不乐！

夏天来了，转眼玛格丽特十七岁生日到了。玛格丽特独自一人坐在母亲房间的窗边，床上的病人整个上午都一直喋喋不休地数落个不停，此刻睡着了。这个女孩异常伤心，她一直凝望着群山那边村庄墓地边的小树林，只能看到一条暗黑色的线。那里柳树依依，素朴的墓碑周围的紫罗兰正迅速凋谢。她常看着那个地方，不是觉得那是个可怕的足以让人望而退却的归宿，而是把它看做一个能够获得彻底而永久的安宁之地。极度疲倦和极度孤独的人都会非常喜欢这个地方。她说，失去的人哪，我不会把你召回到面前来，再次经受痛苦、挣扎、憧憬、恐惧、挫折、失败、死亡。我们无力匹敌这些——从我们生来就与我们作对的力量袭扰我们。我宁愿打开你黑暗房间的大门，用裹着你躯体的沉静的白色永远地蒙上我的眼睛。

年轻美丽的人怎么会有这些奇怪的想法？她很年轻，我记得没有哪张脸比她的更可爱；在我看来，我一点也不觉得奇怪。她的父亲整日忙着照料数量日益增加的羊群，收割庄稼及扩大打谷场的事情，完全把自己的孩子忽略掉了。她的母亲是个疾病缠身且麻烦的人，从来不会轻言细语和她说话，从来没有温柔地喊过她。妹妹死后连姊妹之情也无法感受了。而那更强烈的、能使人留恋尘世的最强烈的情感尚未掠过她的心田。很快她就会听到她从未听过的收割庄稼的农夫唱的欢快的曲子，感受到如阳光照耀下的浮云轻抚着她所带来的温暖和快乐。爱情已经在她的天空升腾起来，崭新漂亮的饰物就要把她的世界装饰一新了。她坐在那里，阳光照在山谷中，把山头镀得金光闪闪，阳光在草场上跳跃闪烁，在她眼前的窗台上舞动，照着她栗色的长发。这些都是构成人生的欢乐或痛苦的元素。一个微笑或一句甜美的话语会让我们鼓起劲来完成一天的工作和任务，它要胜过夏天凉爽的空气，超过宽阔的屋顶下的阴凉地，甚至胜过美味珍馐、美酒琼浆。一个责备的眼神、一次不幸的事件、一种悲哀的信念会使人像中风一样瘫软无力，心像长了霉菌一样麻木。即使秋天连绵不断的雨水冷冷地打在花枝上，它对风景的破坏程度也远赶不上这些中任何一个对人的伤害厉害。

玛格丽特坐着的窗下有个人正在挖地，空气中弥漫着清新、特别而又充满生机的气息。他在轻轻哼着一支老歌：

"快活，快活，整天都快活

干活——干活赛过闲玩乐。

像我这样干活又唱歌

胜过叹气闲坐不干活。"

这一下子把她吸引住了。她边继续干一直忙着的活计，边说：

"老人家，你说得很对，能唱就唱吧，不知什么时候无忧无虑的曲子就唱到头了。"他把一些土垄到花根处，可以保护它们不被霜打。由于长期劳累，饱经风霜，额头已布满皱纹，抹一把额头上的花白头发，他接着干活、唱歌：

"唱歌干活真快活
下有甲壳虫，头上有黄雀
更有光辉围绕天天笑
因为唱歌工作胜过闲玩乐。"

玛格丽特笑了，又继续干起活来，说："啊，是的，是比玩要要强。"看到这个园丁这么乐呵呵地干活，她的情绪也欢快起来。不一会儿，园丁的儿子来了。他对儿子说："过来，接着挖。"他从那口袋中拿出火柴和火石点燃烟斗，坐下来抽口烟。年轻人接着干刚才的活。虽然他学着父亲的样子，但是两个人一点也不一样。这个小伙子瘦而结实，黄色的卷发盖住了眼睛，手像一根根错位的骨头，外面包着一层棕色的皮，还长着几颗疣子。灰色的眼睛微微泛黄，面庞有点像深黑色的玫瑰花色。身上仅有的衣服是带小点的白棉布上衣和蓝棉布裤子。他没穿鞋，所以他用力用锹挖土时老是碰伤自己的脚，不时地发出气恼的骂声，然后满脸不高兴地皱着眉四周张望着。此时，老人倚在花园的栅栏上，闭上眼睛，似乎非常享受烟斗散发出的烟草的芳香。儿子说："有些人过得倒自在，去他的。"他偷偷地走到他父亲身边，把锹竖在土里，用手轻轻推了一下，锹倒了，把烟斗从吸烟者的口中打落在地。老人吓了一跳，一下子从无限惬意的梦境中回到现实中来。他责备地看看小伙子，又心疼地看看打碎的烟斗。他拿起锹，非常起劲地干起活来。歌声比刚才还好听："干活比玩要要强。"

这孩子对干活好像一点也不喜欢，这下解脱了出来。于是他悄悄溜到窗户下，拿起笛子吹起一支简单的曲子，很明显是给上面那位漂亮的小姐听的。

小姐倚着窗户，声音甜美，她说："埃兹拉，这首曲子很好听，我刚才听乔赛亚唱过了，他的声音有些颤，人也疲劳了，但是他的歌声要比你的欢快。如果你能替他一个小时，我相信你一定会这样的，那你的歌声就会和他的一样欢乐。"小姐这样和气，少年好像被她说动了。他一句话没说，又溜了回去。他抓过老人疲倦的双手中的铁锹，跟老人道了歉，兴致勃勃地干起活来，没有再说他发泄不满常用的口头禅"去他的"。

这时老人蹒跚着往小屋走去，玛格丽特说："乔赛亚，你刚才唱得很好听，这是你的工钱。"她从窗户递给他一个新烟斗，乔赛亚觉得这个烟斗很漂亮，他有些困惑又很钦佩。他说："教堂里没有哪个人能有玛格丽特小姐一半好，一半漂亮。"她笑着说："你可不要这样夸奖我。我听说过比我睿智的人都会被夸奖宠坏呢。我给你礼物只是因为你说了那么多好听的话。"

老头往自己的茅舍走去，心里感到非常幸福。一则因为有了个新烟斗，二则因为他的儿子一下子变得那么好——他心里想，肯定是哪个神灵给了他点播。那个脾气暴躁而又头脑简单的男孩在花园里卖力地干活，心情却很愉快。这样的状态他还真有点不习惯。他时不时地抬起头看看窗户。玛格丽特正忙着缝纫，嘴里还哼着乔赛亚唱的词——"干活要比玩耍好"。她可能知道窗下的那个男孩在忙着，但是她太专注了，没有注意到村里年轻的牧师从这里经过。他经常在这一带散步。埃兹拉很想吸引她的注意力，哪怕把她的注意力转移到其他东西上他也要做。他折了一枝芸香扔进窗户，说道："玛格丽特小姐，看那儿。"她顺着他指的方向看去，发现有人在看她，脸一下子变得绯红。费兹家的房子在一条马路上，这虽然不是交通要道，但是几条路的交会口。那些路远的农民贪图方便经常从此经过，久而久之，便踩成了一条最常走的大路了。这路一头通向村子，一头通向村子以西半英里的城市。这条路整天灰尘弥漫，以南四分之一英里处有一幢时尚的红砖大房子。房子室内装饰着白色窗帘，房子的油漆考究，这一带绝无仅有。这是拉尔夫·米德尔顿的家。他是大革命时代的贵族后裔，仍有很浓重的贵族情结。整个郡中数他的马车最豪华，当然买得起马车的不过两三户人家罢了。他的马匹最精良，牛群最肥壮。他是整个地区公认的名人，甚至教堂执事怀特和海伍德医生都以能认识他为荣。

我常常想起，那时放学回家都要穿过田野去看他家果园的鹿群。我们家当时只养得起两头棕色的牛犊、一群绵羊和几只羊羔。现在我明白了当时我有些自卑又有些伤心的情感。我对米德尔顿家的崇敬之情无以复加。时隔这么久了，我还是很坦白地承认当时的这种心情，而我现在也明白了其实只有诚实正直的人才配得上有我们这种感情。当然尽管我很崇拜他家，但是和大部分同学一样，并不卑躬屈膝。我们倒乐意跟黑人詹姆斯聊天。詹姆斯经常骑着栗色小马去田野里放牧奶牛，晚上再把它们赶回来。有时他会把威利·米德尔顿放在他前面的马鞍上。我羡慕他们，但是绝没有到奴颜婢膝的地步。我仍记得我的几个小伙伴当时的情形：如果碰巧家里晚饭有些好吃的，那他们宁愿自己饿着肚子，希望晚上拿给威利·米德尔顿吃，而威利·米德尔顿拿过来喂给他的狗弗罗拉吃，有时甚至直接扔在地上扬长而去。

有时我们也看到他家的女儿弗罗伦斯·米德尔顿坐在果园的树下看书。她是个美人，可能我小时候幼稚地认为金色的长卷发、温柔的蓝眼睛、白皙的面庞就是美人的标志。她穿的衣服总是非常雅致好看。她不用劳作，不会晒黑年轻的面颊，不会磨硬她胖乎乎的小手。她手上戴着两枚蓝宝石戒指，熠熠发光。哪一枚都足以买下附近任何一处小房产。我认为她的脾气肯定特别好，特别和善。因为她有时会让我们这样一群粗俗吵闹的人到她身边，让我们看看她的花园（在我们眼里，这花园简直就像仙境般漂亮）。她给我们摘花，告诉我们花的名字，自然我们记也记不住，只是觉得这些花名又长又奇怪，好像是些外国名。我不知道她是怎样对待别人的，但是在我们面前，她总是一种自信能给人带来愉悦的样子。

我们当时没有一个人觉得玛格丽特·费兹好看，但是我现在回忆起来还是觉得两个人中她要漂亮些。她头发棕褐，梳得整整齐齐，从额头处一分为二，黑黑的大眼睛总露出温和的目光，宛如天使般的柔和，总是水汪汪的。但是她总穿着朴素的白棉布衣服，没有一件有弗罗伦斯那么时尚，穿着跟我们差不多。在乔赛亚的老婆因风湿病或牙疼得厉害而无法干活后，我们还看见她去他的小木屋，给他做面包或撒些面包屑喂鸡。她既好看又和善。她准时上教堂做礼拜，而让我们感到遗憾的是，我们从未见过弗罗伦斯。每个安息日，她都跟父亲坐马车去城里。我们听说那里教堂的长椅都垫着垫子，坐着很舒服。走廊上铺着地毯，窗户都染成彩色的，使得透过窗户射进来的光线比日落时穿过云层的霞光还要漂亮。

玛格丽特常坐在窗边。她在那里给她整天唠唠叨叨的母亲读书，坐在那里也能听见母亲在其他房间叫她的声音，从那里可以清楚地看见村子教堂白色的塔尖。教堂的牧师最近刚来到这个教区。这段时间，她母亲一直疾病缠身，脾气格外暴躁，她就没有去教堂这个常去之地了。埃兹拉把枝条扔到她腿上，她抬头看看，这是她第一次见到这个年轻的牧师。她说："这人长得真不错，是吧？"他一只手未戴手套，塞在金边书页的小册子里，另一只手拿着一朵红蓟花，慢慢走过去，目光不止一次地投向这所漂亮的房子。姑娘发出的感慨既是说给自己听的，也是说给埃兹拉听的。埃兹拉倚着铁锹，先是羡慕地看着这个年轻人，而后又看看姑娘。小伙子似乎感到他自己与教士之间的天壤之别，不由自主地发出感叹："去他的，该死。"他突然心潮起伏，扔下铁锹，看了玛格丽特一眼，快步朝牧师走去。在离牧师几步远的地方他放慢了脚步，像个奸细一样嫉妒地审视着他，似乎还希望自己不被发现。埃兹拉内心很自私。如果好处只他一个人得的话，他干起活来就不惜力气，但是他不愿意为父母干什么事。他嗜钱如命，唯此能制服他天生的懒惰。

有时他一连几个小时躺着晒太阳，无所事事，胡思乱想，而且总是躺在从玛格丽特窗口能看得见的地方，其用意由此可以猜得一二。他如同飞蛾爱上了天上的星星一般。在小木屋他睡觉的房间，他凿下紧挨着床头的墙壁上的石灰，挖了一个能藏下他的钱包的地方。他的钱包其实是一只灰色旧长袜的袜头，那里面藏着他为数不多的全部收入：从帮怀特执事送玉米得来的第一个先令到帮米德尔顿找到走失的牛而获得的亮闪闪的金币。埃兹拉细细地打量着这个年轻的牧师，然后径直走到简陋的小房间里，拿出他的钱包，仔细数数，偷笑了一声，又把钱放回去，然后在房间里踱来踱去。他整夜未睡——一会儿数数钱，一会儿不安地走来走去。天还没亮，他一手拿着那个奇特的钱包，一手拿着做午饭的面包，向城里走去。可怜的小伙子，他要做一件非常愚蠢的事。他在玛格丽特窗户下停了一下，虔诚地向上看看，然后唱起欢快的歌来，大步流星地向前走去。

时光流逝，藤蔓和玫瑰花叶在前一天晚上遭到霜打而变得僵硬，明亮的旭日升起，又一次把它们晒黑。尽管大自然正由盛而衰，玛格丽特的心里却出现了新的光亮，雾霭使得夏天蔚蓝的天空变得有些暗淡，但是似乎把世界装扮得更加美丽。

年轻的牧师已经习惯散步到费兹家这里。有时他继续走下去，一直走到前面茂密的小树林。玛格丽特所希望的只是看他一眼，知道他一切都好，知道他想着她，这成了她阴暗世界里一缕绚烂的阳光。她偶尔也陪他走走，在她眼中，这些是多么美好的时光，她多么珍爱他随意为她采摘的花儿，有时在隐蔽的角落里，他们还能找到耐寒怒放的花儿。他说的每一句话——不管多么平凡简单，有时讲讲日落或者大海，有时讲讲他们生活的尘世间或者高高在上的天堂——她都记在心上。他暗示说真有那么个静谧的世界，或者诸如此类的事情，但是这些东西在她心中都比不上他说的话更亲切。他的每一个微笑，他说话时洪亮而富于变化的声音，她都牢牢地记在心上。不管他的话题是严肃还是轻松，令人忧伤还是振奋人心，她都清楚地记得，而且日后还会经常想起。

玛格丽特心中一直渴望有人能理解她，能对她好些。她思想单纯，不会耍心眼。这也就难怪她会无比信任地把手放在这个牧师手中，一如信任以前为她做洗礼、在她前额行亲吻礼的白头发老牧师一样。藤蔓伸出卷须紧紧抓住最近的东西来支撑自己，花儿绽放，花蕾迎接太阳的亲吻，在风儿的吹拂下呈现红色，而人类的心同样也愿意依托善行的影响。

一天晚上，这个年轻人比平时都健谈，他谈到了自己的情况，谈到了他的过去，过去的生活充满了悲伤。这深深搅乱了她的心，泪水顺着脸颊流下，红润的脸庞都变白了。他亲吻了她一下，这初吻使她脸上又复红润起来，看起来比以往更漂亮。他们要分别了，相互都依依不舍，彼此没说什么，而至少其中一个是心潮澎湃。这时一辆车从长满青草的草地上驶来，沉闷的车轮声引起了他们的注意。不一会儿，米德尔顿先生的马车驶了过来。车夫衣服上的纽扣闪闪发亮，帽子的条带非常醒目，他表情非常傲慢。米德尔顿先生坐在马车的角落里倚着手杖的金黄色杖头，面带和善的笑容。弗罗伦斯戴着顶可爱的帽子，卷发被风刮得飘了起来，她看上去非常兴奋，脸上的笑容异常迷人。她手戴儿童手套，愉悦地给了玛格丽特一个飞吻，打招呼示意。其实他们打招呼只限于最起码的礼貌而已。

马车走后,这个年轻人极为兴奋地赞叹道:"漂亮,她真漂亮,是吧?"玛格丽特附和道:"的确漂亮。"但是声音中已经没有了先前的热情,脸颊上的那片红晕也消失了。她极力想抑制住泪水,但是泪水盈满眼眶——这次只有风把它们拭去了。牧师的眼睛一直看着慢慢消失的马车。

沉默了一会儿,玛格丽特尽力克制她的心情,轻轻地问:"你刚才说什么?"

牧师机械地回答说:"没什么。"他突然道了声"晚安",迅速地往家走去。姑娘一个人站在那儿,站在越来越重的阴影中,好像人们看到洁白的双翼从伊甸园里慢慢收起一样。她在回忆他们被打断的对话:"亲爱的,让我们忘掉过去,奔向未来。"这是他说的最后一句话。他们曾因为有了这个希望而激动不已。这个希望成了她的精神支柱——这是个微弱的信念支撑——因为他们之间的鸿沟已经加大。青春充满了活力,睡神最喜欢不流泪的眼睛,但是他有时也会喜欢泪水滂沱的眼睛。玛格丽特怀着这样的梦想,心中又燃起了新的希望,宛如四月雨水打湿的水仙花一般。

一整天她都在期待傍晚的来临,回想着最后一次见面时他说的那些甜言蜜语,想着他的表情,尽力不去想分别时他那冷淡而又突兀的声音。日落时,她坐在门口的大树下,不是去欣赏夕阳的美丽光芒,也不是在等待夜星闪烁的光辉,她在倾听着越走越近的脚步的回声,但是她始终未能听到想听的声音。

她异常仔细地打扮了一番。尽管还是平常朴素的棉布衣裙,但是棘刺花的亮叶在她栗色的辫子中闪亮,橙红相间的披肩包裹着她纤巧的双臂,脖子上和腕上的蓝色丝带露在外面。

风儿时时刮来,片片黄叶落在她腿上。时不时有鸟儿飞来,停留在离她很近的地面上。但是姑娘既没注意到风,也没注意到落叶或小鸟跳来跳去。她热切地朝着村子教堂的方向看着,教堂的尖顶在紫红色的云彩映衬下显得更白了。一个过路人的脚步声传来,她的心会怦怦跳个不停,就是突然下场暴雨也不会让她的心跳得这么响,这么快。一会儿,她的眼睛一直盯着的方向慢慢走来一个一袭黑衣的人,她的脸突然热得发烫起来。她认出了那是牧师。她的心跳得宛如死亡的钟声——恐惧的阴影遮住了她整个脑海——她不知道原因：他会怎样打招呼呢？亲切，难过，还是冷淡？一定是亲切了，否则的话他就不会来了。想到这些，她站起身来，走上前去迎接他，这时他已经快走到路口了。她想：他虽然低着头，但过一会儿他会看见我的，那时他就会加快步伐的。他看见她了吗？她的心无助地往下沉，告诉她"是的"。但是他穿过小路，朝另一个方向走去，一个她永远无法接受的方向。她是走向前去还是回家去呢？她犹豫了很久，什么也没做，只是呆呆地站在那里，像是被变成了一块石头一样。眼睛只是盯着他渐渐消失的背影。他自始至终也没有回过身来看她一眼。他选择的那条路是条灰尘扬天的大路，没有这条绿草覆盖僻静的小径舒适宜人。但是拉尔夫·米德尔顿家的花园紧邻着那条扬尘的灰路，漂亮的弗罗伦斯黄昏时分经常在花园里散步。还需要其他什么解释呢？时间一天天过去，日落依旧迷人，但是在玛格丽特眼里已经不再好看。她独自一人，踯躅着。十天或十二天之后的一个傍晚，她像以前有他在身边那样坐在茂密的树林边上长满苔藓的原木上，仰起头来看天上的云彩或星星。她正悲伤地凝神沉思，他忽然走来，让她感到很惊讶。他走到她身边，脸上挂着笑容，比以前更熟练地朝她伸出手，随即在她身边长着苔藓的原木上坐下。他兴致勃勃地讲了很多事情，但是和他以前讲话的态度大相径庭了。现在他有些像一位亲切、友善、亲密的哥哥，仅此而已。他谈到了将来，但没有说"亲爱的，让我们忘记过去，奔向未来"，没有任何这方面的意思，只是说他何时会有一个家，就像玛格丽特梦寐以求的美好的家一样。他期望的最大的快乐莫过于她经常能到那里去。"你消瘦了些，亲爱的朋友。"他说，恩赐般地拍拍她的面颊。"你太自我封闭了。我多希望你能放下些尊严，屈尊去和那边谦逊的邻居多接触接触。"她并未抬头，但是能感觉到他在指米德尔顿的房子的方向。他真是太刻薄了，但是她一言未发。这个背叛者还继续说着，好像他的话是疗伤的灵药而不是刺人的荆棘。"真的，费兹小姐，弗罗伦斯是世界上最迷人的人了。我相信如果你了解她，你肯定会喜欢她。她完全符合我的审美标准。""毫无疑问，她有你所说的那么好。"她说，"无论我付出多少，我都无法赢回爱情。我最好还是什么都不做，这样还能安生些。""费兹小姐千万不能这样看低自己，"这个年轻人回答道，"弗罗伦斯几乎每天晚上都会提到黑眼睛的姑娘,希望能说服她和我们一起去散步。"在此之前,他总习惯称呼她玛格丽特,称弗罗伦斯为米德尔顿小姐。

夜幕迅速降临,夜色也越来越浓,可怜的姑娘很高兴夜晚终于来临,这时她感觉到面颊上血色全无,眼眶里充满了泪水。上帝啊,请您大慈大悲,宽恕他的罪行吧,他这样满不在乎地拨动着别人的心弦。

两人陷入一片寂静,场面越来越尴尬。这时一个熟悉的声音传来:"终于找到你了。"是埃兹拉。他站在两人面前,笨拙地弯腰示意,又忍不住地感叹起来:"去他的。"然后他非常直截了当地告诉玛格丽特他一直在找她,他母亲,或像他经常称呼的老太太,风湿病犯得厉害,她希望玛格丽特能到她的小屋去,她最后的希望是看到她甜美的笑容。

过了一会儿,玛格丽特穿过田野,前往树林旁边的一间小木屋,窗户里闪烁着微弱的灯光。埃兹拉走在她身边,没有说话,但是很高兴,感觉好像赢得一百个情人般的大奖一样快乐。玛格丽特一直在想心事,根本没有跟他说话,甚至都没有注意到他。她的心情无法用言语来表达。她想着,

"朋友的情绪千万种,
首感无言皆苦痛。
而后陌路,各寻归宿,
难同归,永殊途。"①

牧师独自坐在那儿,他是否看到了姑娘远去的身影?月亮苍白又带责备的面容从树枝中间看着他,他是否谴责自己轻率地放弃一个年轻的生命?唉,一点也没有!"我从未说过我爱她。"他说,即使内心有一点点歉疚,他还是感觉到良心很安宁。至于很多不通过言语表达出来的情感,他说:"如果她误解了,怎么能怪我呢?"拉尔夫·米德尔顿家厅堂里绚烂的灯光、醉人的音乐及迷人的笑容让他那样陶醉,他很快就把自己和玛格丽特的分分合合、短暂的对话、此后的思索等等诸如此类的事情全都抛到九霄云外了。

---

① 引自朗费罗的诗。

"命运连接着奇异的两端，
绞刑架旁边就立着祭坛。"

玛格丽特独自一人坐在生命沙漏即将漏完的老太太床边，听她咕咕哝哝地说着，心中忧伤不已。她进门后，埃兹拉就早早地回到了自己的房间，但是她知道他并没有睡觉，因为她头顶上的地板不停地吱嘎作响，木箱子一会儿开一会儿关的声音不时传来。将近午夜时分，他悄悄溜进她在的房间，做出各种动作、手势，试图让她注意到他的出现，她感觉到他在旁边，但是她一直在床边前前后后地摇晃着，看着病人痛苦的表情，一直听她抱怨并安慰她，因此好几个小时过去了，玛格丽特也没注意到他。最后，他终于忍不住爆发了，"去他的，你就不能看看人家的新东西吗？"

"当然可以，埃兹拉，你买了新东西了吗？"玛格丽特笑着说，随后她转过头去，看到埃兹拉完全改变了形象。这实在出乎她的意料，脸上由刚才的微笑一下子变成了哈哈大笑。"这些东西是用我旧袜子里的钱买来的，"小伙子说着，挺直了身体，做了个鬼脸，"我觉得就连牧师也会看中的。"

"那一定的。"玛格丽特回答说。她看见他身上穿的这身新衣服是模仿年轻的牧师曾穿的那身。他一只手里还拿着一本镶金边的小册子，他把两个长手指夹到书页当中。可怜的糊涂小伙子！他和村子里的牧师长得一点也不像。那年整个秋天一直到冬天下雪，他始终穿着那身新衣服，手里拿着那本小册子，走在那条小路上，希望玛格丽特能看见他。他有时会在门口停下来，讲讲他听到的最近有关弗罗伦斯和牧师结婚的消息，最后总是语气肯定地说人们都说他们很快就会结婚。

到去年为止，年轻的教士来到玛格丽特·费兹和弗罗伦斯·米德尔顿居住的村庄已经整整十年了。两个女人都活着，只不过弗罗伦斯早已经更改姓氏，前面加上夫人的称呼。而我们的女主人公还仍然叫玛格丽特·费兹。她哭泣过的村庄墓地又多了两座坟墓，一个里面埋葬着一生都忙着为自己敛财的人，但是他走时并没有带走一针一线；另一个病人活着时整日唠叨不停，而今也缄默不语了。他们去世后，玛格丽特成了这片产业的继承人。产业从她手中慢慢流失，如今已经走向衰落，真令人感伤。但是富丽堂皇的教堂、为穷人子女和孤儿盖的朴实却坚固的校舍记载着她的诸多善行。她心中曾有过多么美好的希望，但是希望完全破灭，然而她并不悲观厌世，而是放下这个希望，仍然坚定地带着十字架，温顺地转向另一条道路，为他人尽义务。

　　她白皙的面庞几乎没有红润
　　正如冷冷的圣洁的星光不露一点红色，
　　仁慈博爱的圣人给予她温情
　　借给她一生美丽的梦想。

　　因此，她一天天变得宁静安详
　　爱着人，被人爱着，而热情不能撼动
　　年轻的心，它被包裹着
　　在救世主爱的柔软的衣钵里。

　　当年年轻的牧师如今已不再年轻了，他现在是城里一座有钱的教堂的大司祭，他的妻子成了人们所说的贵妇人。但是他常常离开那热闹喧嚣的大马路，离开他尊贵富贵的府第，前往他早期工作的寒酸之地。他说，他需要经常换换空气，需要体验不同的情感。他经常去一家干净整洁的小村舍，藤蔓爬满了窗户和屋檐，使得房子在其中半隐半现，小屋虽然很简陋，但是对于隐居在那里的人来说，足够生活了。他时常在那里品尝一碗香甜的牛奶，吃上几片可口美味的白面包，倾听他曾亲吻过的嘴唇中说出的乐观智慧的话语，总是不无伤感地说："多希望弗罗伦斯能多像你一点。"

　　至于埃兹拉，我并不清楚他现在的生死，也许他仍在人世间，辛苦劳作，这是他的命运。也许大家都乐意知道，从前他不高兴的时候总是骂骂咧咧地发泄他的不满，而今他这方面已经改变——一部分原因是玛格丽特送给了他一个红色的真丝钱包，非常漂亮，里面放满了金光闪闪的钱币，这一直是他梦寐以求的。袜子钱包就此弃之不用。尽管现在他身着上等黑色呢绒外衣，"穿得像个勇士"，但是这个钱包更让他喜欢。另一个原因是他到附近的私人马戏团去游玩，其中有一头非常凶猛难管的野兽出人意料地被他制得服服帖帖，他随即被聘做了饲养员。他身穿那身新衣服，嘴里哼着扬基歌，永远告别了家乡，登上马车，里面装着他的新兴趣，辗转四处。后来有人说在南部一个城市，他已经完全掌握这一行的决窍。他能轻松自如地走进笼子，嘴里嘟囔着"去他的"，很快就能制服最桀骜不驯的动物。他非常满意他的生活，老板们都认为他是巡回马戏团最大的亮点之一。

乔赛亚的老妻已经过世，但是他仍健在，身体健康，仍抽着十年前的那支烟斗，感到很心满意足。附近所有花园的活都是他一个人干，但是大家都说他对玛格丽特的花园格外卖力，因为别人的花园还没有她的一半漂亮。特鲁斯特太太老是说："有些人天生就很幸运。"而玛格丽特总是回答说："是的。"我们那个永不满足的朋友很少会去想——

"她自己内心的伤痛藏着不让别人知道。"

16. 猎手魅影

这是十二月的一个暴风雨之夜，这样的天气让农庄窗户透出的红色灯光给人格外的快慰，那感觉如同我们路过时瞥见炉旁围坐的人群，或者看到茶桌放着冒着热气的杯子和牛油酥，还有装满了金色蜂蜜的碟子，更不要说那些黄色的黄油球或者一大罐新鲜的牛奶了。

冬日的太阳，即使正午时分高挂蓝天也不会给人很多温暖，何况此刻已经落山一小时了。谷仓的房檐边上和树梢上吊着一串串冰柱，这些冰柱在正午明亮的阳光下闪闪发光，融化了的水珠一颗一颗地从上面滴落下来，使冰柱变得粗糙不平。

在山的背风坡，羊群和它们的幼崽紧紧地蜷缩在一起，希望风能对它们仁慈一些，因为夜晚实在太冷了！牛儿们挤在草垛旁边的畜棚里，最惬意的安排是有一些牛将它们的犄角倚靠在围栏上，时不时地偷吃一两口麦子。尽管那是陈年的或者已经糟朽的粮食了，但毫无疑问，对它们而言，这比那满院子都是的尚有余香的干草要甜美得多。不论是动物的本能还是人的理性都抵挡不住这种诱惑，越是得之不易甚或要冒风险才到手的东西越有吸引力。我不想讨论天性，不过没有这点天性，我们就变成懒汉啦！倘无此性，莉迪娅·希思的命运也许会和现在有着天壤之别。

一个寒冬的夜晚，我是说太阳落山一个小时后，狂风席卷了整个北面群山，它越过凋敝的树林，向南部的山坡吹去。天气还没有冷到令猫头鹰冻得发抖的地步，因为它周身都覆盖着厚厚的羽毛。

但是，它还是舒舒服服地缩进一个树桩里的洞中，一次也没有飞到山谷中去发出它那令人毛骨悚然的叫声。也许是今夜没有人在它神圣的领地里游荡，也许是没有月亮垂听它的抱怨，因为大团昏暗的铅灰色的乌云弥漫了整个天空。自从教堂塔楼上的钟敲了三下之后，雪一直像从筛子里筛下来一样落得很紧。有几个顽童在学校操场上玩耍，高高地抛起他们的帽子，高兴地拍起巴掌。也许他们应该有一辆雪橇，飞一般地从山上滑下去，或者把雪地中的小鸟从这儿赶到那儿。但是不必理会他们的感受是什么，从刚刚发出的喧闹声来看，他们是快乐的，因为这是一种新体验。积雪已经堆在了篱笆的顶上，堆在了树枝上。雪花打在旅人的脸上，他举步维艰地在风雪中跋涉，肩膀上扛着一根一头捆扎着行李的棍子，他的帽檐上也积了一层雪。看上去他已经走得非常疲倦了，虽然他还有很长的路要走，但他没有停下来的意思，他要一直走到终点才肯罢休。"这儿离苜蓿角还有多远？"他问旁边经过的一个男孩，男孩骑着没有配备马鞍的马，手里还擎着一个罐子，"您刚才是说苜蓿角吗，先生？"那个男孩露出一丝顽皮的神情说。那个赶路的人认可地点点头。男孩回答说："你才走了一半呢。"他用靴子的后跟磕了一下马，这马就继续向前跑，将雪花甩在疲惫的问路人的脸上。他有点泄气，一阵心酸，而后弯起腰身，尽量不让雪落到脸上，继续前行，最后走到一段称作乔纳森山的长坡，在山脚下的一棵大橡树下停下来。靠近树干的地上没有积雪，因为树枝上大量的黄色树叶挡住了落雪。在旅人头顶不高的地方钉着一块路标牌——白底黑字，他睁大眼睛，想方设法地想看清上面指示的方向，但是天色实在太暗了。他的前方看上去荒无人烟，道路两边都是茂密的树林，在路西的山坡上的树林边缘，他能看到一些旧篱笆，有的破了，有的倒了，还有一些影影绰绰的墓碑。就像我先前所描述的那样，这是一派孤独的景象，但是他太疲惫了，于是把包袱卷儿放在地上坐下来休息。

他听到不远处有驿车发出的辘辘声——在马蹄踏过桥的时候，那声音听起来多么空旷啊。驿车越来越近了，车灯发出的微弱的光芒已经可以看见了。来到近前，看清前面的两匹马是白色的，它们把马鬃甩得多欢呵，头也昂得高高的。虽然它们看上去很高兴也很有劲，但是很疲惫，需要稍事休息，恢复体力，好爬过前面的山坡。那马夫身上裹着水牛皮制成的长袍，他抖落皮袍上的雪后，拍了一两下巴掌，这样可以缓解冻麻的双手。他只逗留了一分钟而已，车里的乘客就已经不耐烦了，他们一个又一个地从窗户里探出头来，有几个声音同时问出了什么事，"放松点，"车夫说，"这是一座鬼山，我必须让我的马喘口气，这样它们才能尽快翻越这座山。"

"我感觉这树下有个鬼。"有一个乘客指着那棵橡树喊起来，是因为车灯照在那个路人身上，他坐在树下，白雪环绕。

"车夫，照看好邮包。"一个乘客说道。"我的行李都安全吗？"另一个人说。"快走，快走！"第三个人说，这四匹马的主人没有回答任何一个指令或者问题，只是轻轻地把马鞭打在一匹头马的肋下，马车突然往前蹿了一下，又往后坐了一点，缰绳便拉紧了，马队以平稳矫健的步伐开拔——那些乘客们对那个疲倦无辜的旅人进行了千百次的猜测："我怀疑他绝对是个醉汉。"一个人说道。"不对，不对，显而易见，他是一个歹人，"另一个人说，"要不然他怎么不说话？他肯定听到了我们在谈论他。""也许，"第三个人也插了嘴，"他已经死在了暴风雪中，也许他被人谋杀了，或者灵魂附体了，天知道？这是一座鬼山。车夫，你刚才不是说过这话吗？"发问的人把头伸出窗户，发出一阵满是怀疑的笑声。"可不要把俺们统统冻死！"坐在角落的一个身材魁梧的老人边扣上外套的纽扣边喊。"你不觉得开着窗户太冷了点吗，小姐？"一位穿着礼服大衣的小个子男士询问坐在他旁边的那位女士。"一点也不冷，先生，"她答道，"新鲜的空气让我感到愉快。""嗯，女士，"一位腿上放着一个包裹的老妇人说，"我真希望喜欢透气的已经吸够了新鲜空气。""您愿不愿意穿上我的斗篷？"一位穿着黄灰色外套、长相稳重的男士问道，"这样，您会满意，您也会满意。"他对两位女士点头示意。"不要让我的偏好对任何人造成不便。"这位年轻女士用非常甜美的声音说道，老妇人则默不作声地接过了斗篷。"我想即使关上窗户我们也会被冻个半死的。"第一个说话的人耸了耸肩说。"我在猜想到底发生过什么糟糕的事情让这座山起名为乔纳斯山？"一个瘦小的男子插了话，也许他故意要岔开话题。一位男士作了如下答复，他的脖子又红又长，头上戴的那顶笨重的帽子快要遮住他的眼睛了，还带着一块黄色手帕，手帕散发着浓重的鼻烟味道。

"我父亲刚到这乡下的时候，先生，大概是三十五年前啦，那时这里的路是你能找到的最颠簸不平的路：一路全都是些树桩，没有任何桥,从来都没平整过,你可以想想看,先生,就是这种条件。这片树林很是浓密,人们没有办法找到一条走出树林的路,你可以想象得到吧,那里面全都是些各种各样的野兽。我听父亲说,有一次,他还打死过一头熊,就是在辛吉斯老爷家的谷仓那个地方。""啊!的确如此!"一两个人插了话,尽管在这辆车里没有人知道是否有这么一个老爷或者是谷仓。"是的,"讲故事的人接着说道,"就在辛吉斯家谷仓所在的地方,我父亲射死了一头熊。我听他给麦克叔叔讲过这故事,而且好几次呢。""有可能的!"离他最近的那名听客礼貌地说。"是啊,我不止一次听他给麦克叔叔讲过,"那个手绢上散发着鼻烟味的男士继续说道,"就在上个星期尤妮斯到我们家的时候他还说起来过。""那个时候这路就叫乔纳森之路啦?"为了提醒他,又一个人问道。思路被带回来后,他接着说:"乔纳森·萨姆奈尔盖新房子的时候,他雇了很多帮手——他们中的绝大多数都是些野小子,但是乔纳森绝不输给他们中的任何一个人,我是听我父亲这么说的。有一次裁缝约翰到我们家给他量衣服时说过,还有一次我跟着他到爱尔兰人帕特里克家里买牛的时候,他和爱尔兰人帕特里克也说过这事儿。嗯,乔纳森想和他的人一起到树林里面打猎,所以九月的一天,一大早,他们就出发了,他们每两三个人组成一个分队,追赶他们找到的任何猎物,一直到太阳落山为止,他们事先约好了人数最多的一组连续开枪,这样的话散在四周的人可以集中到大的队伍中来,集合时能带多少猎物就带多少来。要点燃篝火,准备晚饭,完全像猎人一样度过夜晚。乔纳森呢,不顾其他人的劝阻,不断地脱离开他的那个分队,他转悠得越来越远,最后人们完全看不到他的影子了。晚上,信号一发出,一队队的人马陆续返回,乔纳森却没有回来。可以想象,大家相聚甚欢,很长一段时间内,没注意到乔纳森缺位。木头堆点起来了,晚饭也做好了,等了一些时间后,他们开着玩笑,开心地吃晚饭。人们在大树下的干叶子上铺好了斗篷和毯子,捕获的猎物摆得到处都是,有的挂在树枝上摇晃着。大家正准备躺下睡觉时,有人提出开枪发出另一个信号。信号发了,一分钟后听到了回应,有个人讲:'啊,不必担心乔纳森了。木头的余烬堆到一块,新鲜的鹿腰肉架在炭火上,这样他回来就能好好吃一顿了。'

"慢慢变小的欢笑声又大了起来,在黑暗中溅得很远的红色的火星还比不上笑声传得远。最后，牛排烤好了，烤过头了，火焰在灰烬中摇摆不定，但是乔纳森还没有回来。大家开始觉得是不是听错了刚才的回应信号。'我觉得那个声音不大像枪声。'一个人说，另外一个人也说：'我也觉得不像。'所以大家决定再开一枪。这次他们非常热切地仔细听起来，枪声一响就听到了清晰可辨的回复声，这次所有的人都声称这枪声是乔纳森的枪发出的。等了半个小时以后，他们就没那么肯定了。他们在谈论鬼船和鬼枪的传闻来打发时间，又用了半个小时，树林里响起第三次信号，紧接着，就像前几次那样，回复得很快。这一次大家一致认为，这压根就不是乔纳森的枪声，毫无疑问，他肯定被野人谋害了，那些野人开枪回复指望拖延人们的搜寻。这个问题很快激起了人们的勇敢精神，所有的人都收拾好家伙，准备搜寻传出枪声的那片树林。正当他们觉得找到了那个地方，要接近那个地方时，又放了一枪，让他们大吃一惊的是，回复的枪声听上去和以前一样遥远。有胆小的人建议回到营地去，甚至提议如果可能的话还是离开树林，但是剩余的人起誓说抛弃危难中的伙伴是可耻的。因为他们也许离他已经很近了，人们又开始了新一轮的搜寻，但是尽管搜寻持续了几个小时，还是没有接近那个发出神秘枪声的地方。

"快到午夜光景了，月亮又圆又亮，就在山脚下埋着那个老黑斯少校的地方，人们都累了，他们十分沮丧，也许还有些害怕，此时，他们刚好又转到刚才那条路上——整条路其实只是荒野中的一条小径而已。因为还能借着月光壮壮胆子，再加上确信乔纳森的所在，有个人这样说道：'小伙子们，快点儿，再打一枪算是告别的信号吧。''不，不，'有人回答道，'如果乔纳森不是要和我们恶作剧的话，你一枪打死我，快看那儿！'他指着一个人，那人在他们的前面不远处慢慢地走着，所有的人发誓说那就是乔纳森·萨姆奈尔。他走得很慢，好像带着极大的痛苦一样。'他看到我们了，'他们说，'好像又翻出什么新花样来耍咱们，咱们就假装没看到他。'就这样过了一会，他们跟着前面的那个人慢慢地走，但是终于他们对自己的速度有点不耐烦了，他们低声商量之后，决定超过他，但是在与他会合时不要显出任何惊讶的神色来，也不要让他察觉到他们一直在为他感到不安。他们认为只有这样，他才能品尝到大费周折却没有任何收获后的痛苦。'好啦，乔纳森，你难道不能稍微停下来等等我们吗？'有个人大声喊道。但是乔纳森肩膀上扛着枪，一言不发地像先前一样拖着痛苦的步伐前进，鉴于此种情况，人们加快了步伐，想尽快地超过他。尽管乔纳森离他们很近，甚至于可以清楚地看到他的枪和他外套的颜色，他们开始加快步伐，但是五分钟过去了，他们还是没能走得更近一些。看到这种情况，他们开始奔跑，五分钟后他们还是没能靠近他。后来，他们坐了下来，想借此迷惑他，但是经过半个小时的等待，人们看到那个神秘的人物静静地站在那里，和他们保持同样的距离。这可把他们吓了一大跳，他们又继续追赶，但是不论他们走得快还是慢，都不影响那个鬼魂，也许是乔纳森，也许是任何其他东西，从开始到回家的整个路途中都和他们保持同样的距离。在新房子对面的附近，也就是他们工作的地方，他们的注意力被奇怪的景象吸引住了，看到其中一个房间里竟然有明亮的灯光，他们再转过头看看，那鬼人再也看不见了。'打那以后也没有人，'讲故事的人说道，'乔纳森山就是这样得的名字。'"

"提莫希·萨姆奈尔先生和这个奇怪的人有任何关系吗？"那位喜欢新鲜空气的年轻女士问道。"一个兄弟而已！"一名男士回答道，说完他笑了起来，很显然他觉得自己的回答很风趣。"那个兄弟继承了房产吗？"年轻女士问道。那名男士说对此他不知情，但是那个提莫希住在乔纳森之家，其他人也都不敢住在那个闹鬼的房子里。他又接着说："提莫希有个儿子，不论从任何方面看，都和他的叔叔很相像。"

听到这些，她问那个有趣的乘客他能不能在提莫希·萨姆奈尔先生的房子那里下车。"不行，"他说，"我要在大卫叔叔家下车，但是我会和车夫说一声的。"他向窗外探出身去，对那个重要人物说了声："在蒂姆家停一下，别忘了。"他又接着说："你在大卫叔叔家放下我就行了。"重新坐下以后，他看了看，说："有一个人，在车后不远处，可能是乔纳森的鬼魂。他什么都知道。"大家都禁不住紧张起来。有一个毫不顾忌的年轻人喊道："哈，乔纳森·萨姆奈尔！是你还是你的鬼魂？"

"是我，我本人，"那人声称，"距离我下山进行那次著名的捕猎已经有很多年了。"

这时他们已经到达了山顶，乘客们当然有点心惊肉跳，他们对策马前进的皮鞭声已经不感到不忍心了，那些马匹几乎用尽全力奔跑着。大家的议论热火起来,一个人问要过多久才能到达苜蓿角,有的人问他们是不是可以在那里停下来吃晚餐,还有的人问多久他们才能到达下一站等等。但是那位年轻的女士一直保持缄默,她陷入沉思之中。现在车停了,那个拿着手绢上散发着鼻烟味的男士下了车。

"我希望大卫叔叔家的那些人见到他会很高兴。"那名刚才和鬼魂说话的年轻人说,在笑声还没有停息之前,马车又一次停了下来,车夫大声喊道:"车里有人到提莫希·萨姆奈尔家的吗?"听到一位女士低低的应答声,他跳下车来,用靴子扫开积雪,扶着她下了车,车夫们是很有骑士风度的。在打开的大门前,站着一位撑着雨伞的老人,手里提着一盏灯,他以一种老式的礼仪迎接她。雪依然下得很大,但是从门口到院落的小路已经被清扫得干干净净,房子的各个角落都亮着灯——楼上的一个房间让年轻的女士看了觉着不快。"好嘞!"车夫边说边把一个手提箱放进大门内,车辆继续前进,来接女士的老人边引路边随口问她是不是很冷、路上用了多久等等一些无关紧要的问题,只是表示善意的兴趣而已。

17. 莉迪娅·希思做客于萨姆奈尔家

提莫希·萨姆奈尔领着他的年轻客人走进一扇门,一进门便是一个看起来古色古香的客厅。深而宽阔的壁炉里,劈好的山核桃树枝混合着上面长满树瘤的枫树和榆树树枝熊熊燃烧,红色的火光映在对面的墙上,摇曳不定。在高高的壁炉架上一只钟表滴答滴答地走着,钟表顶上装饰着奇异的镀金人像,前下方以一幅有许多白色廊柱和红色窗子的大房子的绘画作为装饰,房前有三棵高大的绿树。

钟表的两边各贴了一幅用黑纸剪的人像,一个男性,一个女性:那位年轻的女子猜想后者一定代表已故的萨姆奈尔夫人,而前者是提莫希本人无疑。窗以下的那部分墙面贴了一层胡桃木,雕刻成壁炉状,门也是用同样的材料做的,并以同样的风格雕饰。地毯是有沉着色调方格图案的那一种,厅里其他家具也是只有在老式的乡下老房子里才能看到的那种暗色旧式图案的家具。但是纯白色的天花板以及纯白色的墙壁的其余部分,还有一盆盆花草、耶路撒冷樱桃树等,再加上壁炉里跳跃的暖烘烘的火光,使这间客厅并不显得格外昏暗沉闷。厅里的铜器和铁器已经被擦拭得几乎泛白,熠熠发亮,在莉迪娅坐在壁炉前等待茱迪丝和玛丽娅到来时,她甚至能看见在那上面映照出的自己的脸庞。茱迪丝和玛丽娅的父亲去叫她们过来,尚未回来。就在莉迪娅独自一人时,她先听见有人清除脚上的雪的跺脚声,再是敲隔壁房间门的敲门声,随后就是惊喜的叫声:"这难道是提莫希?上帝保佑你!我总算活到能见上你一面!"诸如此类的话。提莫希倒是没有格外惊奇,显然没有表示出特别的高兴,他说话的声调依然冷静沉着,不如她所期盼的声调高。新到者很快就离开刚进去的那间屋子,莉迪娅再也听不见他的声响了,女士们也随即出现在客厅。

茱迪丝是她们中间年长的一位,可能三十五岁左右,高个儿,微黑,健壮。她的眼睛黑亮,除去连丝缕花结都无法掩饰的缕缕银丝以外,她的头发有着与莉迪娅的头发一样的色调。她的鼻子是她面庞上的显著特征。她的前额和下颚向后倾斜,以至于额头、鼻子、下巴都构不成通常能看到的夹角。按她的身材论,她脚大手大。不难想象,她对人们赞许她的美丽从不抱多大期望。尽管如此,在她的神情和举止里仍然能很容易辨认出与她的出身相关的贵族气。毕竟提莫希·萨姆奈尔不仅是这里乡间最富有的人,而且他还可以把自己的身世追溯到比他的任何一个邻居更远的祖先,我甚至相信,比米德尔顿先生的身世还要远。玛丽娅比她的姐姐小十到十二岁,可以说与其姐有的一比,只是略显柔弱。她的头发黑褐色,没有一缕银丝,半卷着抚慰两个丰盈的、透着生命之欲望的脸颊,但仅仅是欲望而已。她没有姐姐茱迪丝的高个儿,也没有她那样结实的身材。她虽然算不上心直口快,但比姐姐随和、可人。

萨姆奈尔夫人去世多年,但是在世时,她一直是邻居的楷模:一顶帽子或一套裙装一经她穿便成为时尚,要是提莫希对美的判断不出错的话,她的美丽和高傲超过她的家族所有成员的总和。她在世时,他是她的忠实配偶,在她去世以后,他也没有对其他女人有丝毫倾心,即使聪明狡黠的寡妇们不停地以盈盈笑脸对他施以诱惑,他也从未动过心。

他要是在教堂里,他的朋友会告诉他坐在他周围的女人都是令人垂涎的对象。他如果因为暴风雨即将来临到草地去给黑佣人卡托些许需要的帮助,寡妇达特曼太太肯定会在窗口看见他,并且隔着一块地就远远地知道她的牛是否进到他的围栏里去了。他只要去城里，如果他乐意在车里让一个位置给斯柏克斯夫人的话，她肯定是要去的。在他城里的熟人里，有不止一位女士认为如果萨姆奈尔先生能让她们走出她们的家门造访他家，即便一两天，呼吸一下乡间纯净的空气，那都是个慈善之举。寡居的希思夫人也应该被算在这群女士之列。她总期望茱迪丝和玛丽娅到城里来时能把她家当成她们自己的家，她也常常让莉迪娅和她们住一个礼拜，这样她们就不感到有所犹豫、顾忌。尽管不太懂这方面的礼数，莉迪娅倒是乐于回访。希思夫人财富可观，不管她的初衷如何，都不是为图什么利。但如果说她有某种目的的话，那就是她也是萨姆奈尔先生的仰慕者，也许她动了什么念头，谁知道呢？

  乡下的女人肯定需要一些城里的朋友，不然的话她们如何了解眼下的时尚？就这样，希思夫人用心谱就了这台戏的前奏曲，各种铺垫也都作好了，这不，演出的号角正式在十二月的一个下午在她漂亮的大房子前吹响了。她告诉莉迪娅到人家要勤快，对人和善，特别是对萨姆奈尔先生更要如此，随后莉迪娅连同手提包和行李箱一起被送上车。

  现在让我们再回到客厅吧，那里有被留下的莉迪娅，她正和茱迪丝和玛丽娅坐在客厅里的壁炉前。她生在城里，习惯了那样的生活，尽管如此她一直对乡间生活有一种本能的热爱，此时她的心里已感到有一种难以遏制的、初见自由曙光的喜悦。她谈起这里的任何事都兴致勃勃，连暴风雪都成了让她由衷高兴的事。她一个人坐在熊熊的壁炉前，不时地在光亮的金属器皿上瞥一眼映照在上面的自己的面庞，她觉得她喜欢一直待在这儿。但是尽管她在这里感到十分高兴，并且愉快地谈论着这里的一切，关于一个诡异卧室的说法以及另一个更诱人的梦想一直萦绕在她的脑际。提莫希·萨姆奈尔先生真的有个儿子？如果果真如此，他叫什么名字？他长什么样？她不愿把他的长相想象成茱迪丝的样子。他有多大年纪？她不愿去猜想有可能他的年纪已经很大，她宁愿想象他比玛丽娅还年轻。她听到隔壁屋里正在准备午茶，很是高兴。可以见到他了，她想，或许还有新来的客人，她有一半把握新来的客人会是乔纳森叔叔。

  终于黑人女仆迪娜那张友善的面庞出现在半开的门口，向茱迪丝及其他女士们宣布午茶已准备就绪。莉迪娅的好奇心一下子活跃起来了，她将褐色的头发往后甩，笑着说至少她算一个，要品尝一下茶的浓香。她跟在高傲的茱迪丝身后，让人觉得很像阳光给乌云镶上金色的边：她是那样轻盈、善谈，满脸洋溢着源自内心的喜悦。玛丽娅不像她的姐姐那样傲慢，也不像她那样寡言，倒是更能从毫无拘束和谈笑自如的莉迪娅身上获得慰藉。但是小姑娘毫无做作的举止、笑谈中真诚的喜悦还是让莉迪娅感到有些吃惊。姊妹俩都注意到了莉迪娅的确受过良好教养，她出身古老而富有家族的事实不容怀疑。于是她做的许许多多事情都得以迁就，要是换了惠特菲尔德执事的女儿，或是特鲁斯特先生的女儿，或是汤普金斯的女儿，她们非得骂她不可。

茱迪丝小姐招呼大家上桌。对面坐着她的父亲，一副一丝不苟和傲气的神态，但具有让人不由得产生爱慕的气质。玛丽娅坐在桌子的一边，另一边是莉迪娅的椅子。其他人没有露面。

车上的那个人肯定搞错了，莉迪娅想。她转身问萨姆奈尔先生他是否知道这样一个人——她尽量给他描述那个人的样子，描绘他讲到他的亲戚朋友时的神态，仿佛大家都认识似的，甚至最后不忘记提醒大家他到"大卫叔叔家"那站下车。关于乔纳森山的故事，出于谨慎，她不想提，不过无意中还是提到了，说那个古怪的先生喋喋不休的当儿他们正往山上去。"我想大家都把那山丘叫乔纳森山。"她说，并环视了一下席上的所有人。

"是的，是的，他的确有点怪，我和他很熟。"萨姆奈尔先生回答道，口气和他往日相比有点急促，而且两姊妹中姐姐的脸上第一次出现了红晕（此后又多次出现）。

"我想他的确是诚实的。"莉迪娅继续说道。

"的确如此，的确如此，"萨姆奈尔先生说，"你说你们上山的途中他一直不停地说话，他到底给了你们什么提示呢？"

"哦，我几乎不懂他在说什么。"莉迪娅回答说。尽管她低着头，她的卷发还是不能遮住她脸上泛起的红晕，她完全清楚她是在撒谎。她很快定了一下神说："他告诉我们他的父亲是在哪儿射杀了一头熊，那是很久以前的事了，还有许多其他事。"说这些话时，她觉得是对她前面说的话作了一定的补救。

那天晚上，她无时不在寻思萨姆奈尔先生是否真的有个儿子，她觉得那个人说的不会有错，因为他似乎与萨姆奈尔很熟。还有，萨姆奈尔先生也说这人是个老实人。但如果真有这样一个年轻人，为什么在喝茶时没看见他呢？而且交谈中连提都没有提到过他？

莉迪娅正这样反复思索时，玛丽娅拿起小孩吃饭时用的胸巾，开始在上面缝花边。她忽然有了个主意：那个萨姆奈尔先生的儿子，玛丽娅的弟弟已结婚了，那个胸巾是给他的一个孩子做的。这是再自然不过的事了——她以前怎么就没有想到呢？为了证实一下这个想法，她装出对女红表示羡慕的样子说，"你没有弟弟或妹妹，对吗？"

玛丽娅笑笑说："我没有小弟弟，但我有一个大哥哥，这是给他的孩子做的。"

"啊，是的，是的，"莉迪娅回答道，"图案真好看！"过了一会儿，她说累了，便按着茱迪丝的指引回到自己的卧室。她现在觉得不如以前那样有兴致了，她也不知道是什么原因。她翻来覆去好久不能入睡，她在陌生的地方从来都睡不好觉。第二天一早，她又恢复了她那活泼快乐的天性，从一个房间跑到另一个房间，一会儿室内，一会儿户外，高兴得就像个孩子。她最终解决了那个关于兄弟的问题，至于那个陌生的客人，她几乎已经忘记了。

快到傍晚时，她偷偷溜出客厅，用斗篷和披肩把头包得严严实实，跟迪娜一起出去，去看她挤牛奶。积雪肯定有半英尺深，但那又怎样？已经有一条踩出的路通往奶牛舍，寒冷只不过将她的脸冻红了而已。当她发现已经来到有十一二头奶牛正在吃干草的奶牛棚时，她有点害怕，不过她勇敢地坦诚自己的恐惧，而且笑着告诉迪娜她所有想做的事情中，她最想做一个农夫的妻子。

迪娜真心地为之高兴，并发誓说她一定尽快把她的话告诉主人阿奇波尔德。

"请问他是谁？"莉迪娅问道。

"愿主祝福你，"女仆回答说，"他就是家里最棒的成员，你都没有听说过他？"

"哪家最棒的？"莉迪娅问。

"当然是老主人的家啦。"迪娜边说边挤牛奶，牛奶淌到锡桶底的声响使人听不清她说的话。

"噢，是啊，"莉迪娅说，"我想起我昨晚听玛丽娅说起过他。"

"她们跟你提他可真怪了，"迪娜说，"她们从不提及他的名字，就像他有和我一样的肤色似的，她们为他感到不光彩。"

"她无法回避那个，"莉迪娅说，"我问她给谁做胸巾，你也许看见她正在做那个胸巾，她告诉我她是为她哥哥的孩子做的。"

"哈哈哈……"迪娜大笑，她笑得几分钟都无法继续挤奶了，她真的笑作一团了。最后她还是竭力平静下来说："就算月球上的人有孩子，主人阿奇波尔德也不会有。"

"我不明白这是怎么回事。"莉迪娅说，但迪娜说她知道是怎么回事。那个胸巾是给主人威廉斯的孩子做的。威廉斯有好几个孩子，都住在萨姆奈尔村，而主人阿奇波尔德是个单身男子，就住在老屋。"不过即便你在这儿住一个月，你都见不到他，"迪娜补充说。莉迪娅自然要问为什么。"因为，"迪娜回答道，"她们为他感到脸上无光；他不修边幅，不像家里其他人；他喜欢在农场干活，赴约也不戴手套；更有甚者，他去年又得过天花，使他的容貌受损，她们因此更以他为耻了。"她继续说，"她们姐弟间无爱可言，因为他和她们互相看不上眼。"

"我倒想见见他，"莉迪娅说，"他不会和我们一起吃饭吗？"

"有这里的乡下邻居来访时，他们有时也会请他一起喝茶；但有像你这样的客人时，小姐，不会有人请他来出席，但我会在厨房里照顾他。"迪娜似乎为此感到庆幸。

"我该见见他。"莉迪娅若有所思地又说道。

"祝福你，孩子，"迪娜急切地说，"只要顺着那条巷子看去，拿着一杆枪，牵着几条狗的那个人就是他。"

莉迪娅朝迪娜指的方向望去，只能看到那人的轮廓，这时听到有人叫她的名字前，她一抬头就看见提莫希·萨姆奈尔先生已经站到她的面前。提莫希·萨姆奈尔说很为她担心，说着便急忙挽住她的手臂，领着她回去，一回去她就发现那两个姑娘明显惴惴不安。

她的确太轻率，满不在乎地让自己经受户外的恶劣天气，更不用说她所造成的惊恐。就像一个认错的好姑娘一样，她在壁炉旁坐下来，甘心忍受又一个无聊的傍晚。

茶后，有人提议玩桥牌，莉迪娅装作进入玩牌的状态，心里却想着要是阿奇波尔德而不是茱迪丝做她的对家该多好。回到卧室，她坐在壁炉旁，脑子里想的净是这个家的每一个人，更想到了阿奇波尔德，这时从隔壁房间传来的声音打断了她的思绪。连接两间屋子的门半掩着，她仔细听着，因为脑子里还是想着那诡异的房间，她无法完全听清楚里面到底讲些什么，但她不一会儿就确信屋子里讲话的是人：其中一个是坚定的男性的语气，这人完全有可能就是阿奇波尔德。和他讲话的人的语声断断续续、颤颤巍巍，表明年老体衰。听得出，他讲了狩猎、野营以及打架等的奇妙冒险经历。她对她的邻居不是幽灵而感到释然，又把思绪拉回到自己的事情上来，后来又回想起迪娜给她讲的所有事情，带着对乡下美好生活的想象，她们的说话声在她的耳边喃喃细语，伴她进入梦乡，她一直睡到第二天早晨阳光透过窗棂才起来。

两天过去了，莉迪娅没有见到也没有听到阿奇波尔德的任何事。她片刻不敢擅自离开客厅，唯恐让她的朋友们觉得她举止失当。她不敢蹦不敢跳，实际上她都不敢走动，除非有那样的实际需要。到了第三天，她实在无法继续忍耐那样的束缚，于是她向大家展示她按新的样式剪裁所有的衣物，她想萨姆奈尔家女人们也许会重新按最新的时尚改她们的衣裳样式；她还给她们讲她所了解的新发式；最后实在想不出别的表现勤快和和善的办法：与她们的交流受到礼数限制，而她天生不懂礼数。

她们大多时间都是在刺绣和做针线活，她们的脑子几乎都被那些事儿占据了，没有空与人说话，即使说话，也是冷冷的一两句，还充满着忧伤，表达的仅限于粗浅的感受而已。

萨姆奈尔先生是个考虑后果的人，所以不大说话，但是和他认为有同样身份的人在一起时，他却是个可亲而又健谈的人。但是他不愿和年轻女性闲聊，觉得那要耗费他大量时间，他是那种似乎老有许多事情要做可又没做的人。几乎每次晚上的聚会，他都习惯地说："茱迪丝，亲爱的，你是否可以让我把明天的早餐吃得比平时早一点？"茱迪丝对此的回答无一例外的是："我尽力而为吧，先生。"老先生便回答说："谢谢，我亲爱的。"然后起身，离席，睡觉。茱迪丝则举起一个小铃铛一摇，给迪娜发个命令。听到她十分熟悉的对话，迪娜常常会善意地大笑一通。

每逢快乐的一天，有时也有不太那么令人快乐的日子，萨姆奈尔先生会到毗邻的乡村去一趟。他到那里去的目的无人知晓，也从来没有人问过，知道他去那儿了就够了。

莉迪娅不免好奇，非要对他的目的搞个水落石出才能满足。于是有一天傍晚，在萨姆奈尔先生习惯性说完关于早餐的盼咐，然后说他要到邻村去的时候，她立即跑回厨房问迪娜萨姆奈尔先生到底为什么每天要去邻村。可是迪娜知道的，用她自己的口头禅说，并不必比月亮上的人知道得更多。据她回忆，二十几年前他在那里有些房产，但那些房产在萨姆奈尔夫人做了女主人后就变卖了。她还清楚地记得买那些房产的人为了感谢萨姆奈尔夫人爽快地签署了合约，还特意买了一双鞋送给她。她说她不会忘记这一点，因为那双鞋到现在还未穿过，萨姆奈尔先生每星期两次从橱柜里把那双鞋拿出来晒晒太阳，以此铭记他妻子的厚道。莉迪娅说过，萨姆奈尔先生在家时做的一件头等重要的事就是查看、包起、打开属于她妻子的所有物件。橱柜里上面一层归她使用，那里面通常展示着衣物、褪了色的丝带、帽子，曾经流行一时，眼下已风光不再，唯有让不感兴趣的人或笑话或怜悯的份儿，起码有一天莉迪娅偷看了一眼。真庆幸那天除了迪娜，再没有人看见她，她不仅大笑了一通，而且还说她会毫不犹豫地一把火烧了所有东西，除了那些保存尚完整的信物。有一封萨姆奈尔夫人五表妹的来信不要烧，信中讲她丈夫买了六件衬衣，还讲她正在服用印第安人治疗感冒发冷的灵丹妙药；她母亲的来信也不要烧，信中教她如何精心查看茱迪丝的牙齿长得如何或玛丽娅的哮喘病的护理，诸如此类的事。这些来信保管得不够精心，发黄发霉了，墨色已经褪成暗褐色。照料这些东西是很费时间的，这就解释了萨姆奈尔先生的时间为什么老不够用的原因。莉迪娅禁不住想，再没有哪一间屋子得到的光顾能够比这间塞满了装着那些旧物件的橱柜、衣柜的屋子更多。

　　让我们再回到厨房，莉迪娅正在那里给迪娜说起邻村，她打算到那儿去探个究竟。她甚至奢想可能是她两三天以来十分谨慎的行动使她获得了可以在厨房与迪娜小叙的特权，但是她错了。她的妄想被茱迪丝戴顶针的手指的轻轻敲门声（她戴了一枚金顶针）打断了。我忘记了她是以何种借口敲门的，反正是鸡毛蒜皮的事儿，那个高傲的女士说有事需要莉迪娅去客厅。"一会就来，"莉迪娅说，"我想学如何做这样的点心，迪娜恰好正在做。"

　　她真的想问问迪娜是否把她想当农夫妻子的话传了出去，她想知道卡托打算用他买回来的，现在靠墙放置的三大箩筐玉米做什么，但迪娜只是说一两句话无法说得清楚，刚讲到卡托和阿奇波尔德要在当天晚上进行一次脱玉米粒比赛，这时敲门声打断了她正讲的要如何帮助阿奇波尔德剥玉米的计谋。她的脸色一下变得木然，但听到迪娜低声说"不要紧，小姐，我有办法"，她又露出笑容。她转身回到客厅，继续给茱迪丝讲如何处理针脚。幸运总是眷顾勇敢者，她想。有一阵子她饶有兴致地干着针脚、十字针、复针之类的女红。时间一分钟一分钟的过去，迪娜还没有来，她开始觉得不如不来了。"在这儿再待下去毫无意义，"她想，"我永远见不到阿奇波尔德，至于这个家里的其他人，我永远不想和他们交朋友。"她一边点灯一边说她明天就回家去，待在她的卧室里，现在就作好准备以便有精神经受旅途之劳顿。

莉迪娅爱上了阿奇波尔德，不大可能，根本不可能。起初只是好奇心引起了一点兴趣，后来对他的特殊境况的了解只是加深了这种兴趣而已。她心地善良，把他看成一个被整个世界抛弃的人，更是被姐妹们的爱抛弃的人，因此甚至想象着帮他做点什么。要是她能够让他拉一车干草到城里，然后来她的母亲家吃一顿早餐，她将十分快乐。"他人很好，可以和他一起吃饭，"她说，"不然迪娜不会说他人好，因为她本人就是好人。"她一边玩味着孩子才有的幻想，一边把散放在桌子、椅子上的东西收拾到背包里。

当她忙着装东西的时候，迪娜回来说他们都在厨房剥玉米，玩得很开心，问她是否愿意下来和他们一起玩。

莉迪娅想：他们会想办法把我挤出去，没意思。便推说头痛，心情郁闷地回去睡觉了，心想阿奇波尔德那个名字有多难听。

提莫希·萨姆奈尔先生从邻郡回来时已是午夜时分，得知莉迪娅小姐提出明日一早就要回家，他感到十分惊讶，心里也有一份伤心。事情不该发展到这个地步，他坚信她原来是要多住些日子的，她执意要回去，肯定是他们在某些地方怠慢了她，不然就是她看到了他认为不该看到的一个家庭成员。这个假设为他了解到的莉迪娅曾经到过厨房和牛栏一两次的事实所证实。"好吧，我明天一早就去把这件事办妥。"他说。他从衣兜里拿出一封信，在信的背面用铅笔写了些毫无实际意义的符号。他回到卧室，嘴里嘟囔了一些关于阿奇波尔德和乔纳森大叔的话，大意是说他们最好还是住在森林里好——那里更适合他们。说真的，阿奇波尔德对他的父亲和姐姐们恪守的礼节毫不在乎，他更不修边幅。没有人对他感兴趣，因而他对自己的形象也不大在意，但最近几天里，他身上发生了奇妙的变化。他平生第一次和迪娜说，熨他的衬衣时再多用点心；他也不止一次把靴子拿到卡托处，让卡托给他的靴子搽鞋油；他还预约了理发师，在酒馆里把络腮胡修剪成整整齐齐的流行式样。他以前从未这样过，迪娜更是想象不出他能这样，用她的话说，不知道他到底着了什么魔。他从未见过莉迪娅，也没有可能见到她，因此可以说她与他的巨大变化似乎没有干系。

翌日清晨，树上的雪鸟还未啼叫，莉迪娅早已穿好了衣服，准备好回她的家。客厅壁炉里火光熊熊，她在火炉前坐下，有些不耐烦地等着早点。

她忽然有了一个想法——她要去厨房和迪娜谈谈，这样可以让时间过得快一点。迪娜一直对她很好。"我现在真的很伤心，"迪娜说，"你要离开我们了，这个家好久没有见到有你这样活泼开朗的人了。等天暖和起来，我们修整花园的时候，你一定要再来，你在这里等得再久，都见不到主人阿奇波尔德了。"

"这是为什么呢？"莉迪娅问道。"不过，"她又补充说，"我猜是因为他不想见我，不像我那么想见他。"

"他的确想见你，小姐，"迪娜说，"昨晚他穿着他最好的外套准备和你一起吃饭，这时傲气的茱迪丝披头散发地跑来说他看起来就像个雷公，还说如果是她，她宁愿远远地躲开人类——就那意思吧，"迪娜继续说，"意思是他应该躲着不见你，所以主人阿奇波尔德坐在这里难受了一个晚上，连晚饭都不吃了。但现在你见不到他的原因是，老主人今早上派他到政府办事去了。他现在应该在城里，因为搭乘的是到苜蓿角的第一班车"。

"这就是说他已经走了。他一定是个不可多得的人才。"莉迪娅若有所思地说。

迪娜说他的确是，又说："人都说他像他的叔叔乔纳森，但我不这样认为。"

"你见过他那位古怪的叔叔吗？"莉迪娅想起了那位陌生人的到来，以及那天晚上她所听到的怪诞故事。她还想问其他一些事，这时萨姆奈尔先生出现了，他一边很快地搓着手一边抱怨说莉迪娅不应该这样快就要走。他不想听解释。他已经安排好了很多郊游活动，肯定不会让人失望，除非她有更好的回城里去的理由。

迫于应对，莉迪娅只好想到什么就讲什么，她说她的衣物准备不足，所以不能在这儿待得很长，她下次乐意再接受他们的款待。"那你今天晚上就回来吧。"萨姆奈尔先生急切地说。年轻女士们脸上露出对此恳请赞许的神情。莉迪娅接受了萨姆奈尔先生的请求，并非出于遵从，而是不想再让人恳求。她不禁又加了句解释的话，说好像大家都不急着让她撤出厨房。不仅如此，他们向她保证她可以去这里的任何地方，包括谷仓、牛栏，只要她喜欢。

谈妥了她可以回去，回去拿了衣物就回来，于是大家像一家人一样坐下来吃松饼，喝咖啡。萨姆奈尔先生有要事去办，便马上和大家道别了。但走前一再重申他希望傍晚再见到莉迪娅，还得到她的允诺：绝不会让他失望。

他离开不久，一阵沉重的车轮声淹没了那只大钟表的滴答声，一直站在外面值班的卡托过来了，他接过莉迪娅的行李后，急忙出去挥手表示有乘客要上车。马车在门口陡然停住，行李放到上头，女士坐到了车里。莉迪娅从车窗向大家挥手道别，迪娜站在大门与堂屋之间，而卡托正靠着大门的栅栏，笑着表示对莉迪娅小姐的善意，更是表示对莉迪娅小姐的敬意，他做了个特别的道别仪式，将手横向一挥，吓跑了一只正在门柱上舒舒服服睡觉的猫。

"再要看到这个地方，肯定是很久以后的事了。"莉迪娅想。她注视着那幢房子，直到一个拐弯处，房子被一个树丛遮住为止。

"你那么出神地看的那个农场，"她身旁传来一个男性声音，"在夏天的时候更好看。"她抬头想看是谁在说话，可阳光照得她睁不开眼睛，她发现与她同行的乘客只有一位绅士，一副很帅气的样子，她觉得她以前肯定在什么地方见过他，或是见过长得像他的人。他那双没戴手套的手表明他是个农夫，莉迪娅想他一定就住在附近，便说："你好像很熟悉这里的景致。"陌生人听后答道："是的，"他从窗户把身子移开说，"噢，这不是欣赏这里景色的好时候。当远处的那片树林长出绿叶，果园里的果树花儿盛开，原野不再被大雪覆盖，那时的景致要比现在好多了。"

"你认识房子的主人吗？"莉迪娅问道。她的旅伴说有点熟识，还补充说："你也熟识，据我判断。"

谈话中提到萨姆奈尔先生，陌生人笑着问她是否知道萨姆奈尔先生常到邻郡去的事，他突然说了句："一个特别的家庭！"

"你认识那个年轻人吗？"莉迪娅问道，"他也特别吗？"

"噢，也许，"陌生人说，"我倒是有些喜欢他的特别之处。"

"我想我也是，"莉迪娅说，"说真的，我蛮认同他的特别之处。"

"你没有见到他吧？"问话者笑着问。

莉迪娅回答说没有见到。她重复了迪娜给她讲的一些事，最后说她非常想会会他，但他一早就被派去办公事，而且在她来访期间，他从未与家里其他人在一起。她还讲，大概她不会再来了，因而大大怀疑这辈子都不可能和阿奇波尔德先生认识。两个旅伴发现彼此都觉得对方很有趣，谈得很投机。飞快的车轮似乎也带动了他们的舌头，他们滔滔不绝地谈着，无拘无束，以至于在不算长的旅途结束时，两人都对自己的表现感到惊讶。

"就是说，"分手时年轻人说，"你很好奇，想见见这位阿奇波尔德先生？今天早晨我见过他，他说他晚上还坐这个班车回来。你既然受邀晚上还回来，若你愿意我会很高兴为你保留一个座位。"还没等莉迪亚说接受或谢绝，他便说："早安。"就下车走了。

希思夫人就在车门口等着，想问问她女儿这样出乎意料的回来的原因，但很快就又问起提莫希·萨姆奈尔先生。"是哪个乡巴佬扶你下车的？"她又问道。

莉迪亚脸上泛起红晕，她回答说她不认识那位绅士，她也不知道为什么，但她不愿意有人这样称呼他，她有点生母亲的气，当即决定下午就返回去。

"阿奇波尔德先生不会知道的，"她自语道，"我知道他也要坐那趟车回去，我倒不是为了那个原因才决定返回去的，事实上，我对他的回来并不期待。迪娜说过他有可能去一个礼拜，但我答应萨姆奈尔先生回去，我也不知道他有什么安排，我不能让他失望。"她以前所未有的细心挑选了一些衣物，认真梳理了一下她的卷发，然后就开始等车。

车按时到了，上面坐了八个乘客——只有一个座位空着。她早上结识的那位熟人也在车里，留给她的空位就在他的座位旁边。她看了看其他几个乘客，没有发现一个乘客的长相符合她想象中的阿奇波尔德的样子。她为她早上旅途中表现出的兴致感到有点不好意思，她不愿意以任何方式给他暗示什么，现在的她显得矜持得多，早上的她太随意了。那个陌生人长得很帅气，人很和气，她的举止没有因为拘泥礼节而有所收敛。这不是他的错。她是在生她自己的气，她早上和他交谈太随意了；又借故回了一趟家，又风急火燎地跑回来……车停在萨姆奈尔先生家门口，她好奇地看着，想知道到底哪位乘客会是阿奇波尔德。陌生人似乎注意到了这一点，因为在扶她下车时他微笑了一下："阿奇波尔德不在车里。"她回来后第三天，女士们受邀到苜蓿角参加一个晚宴，莉迪娅因冰雪消融时的寒冷天气而冻感冒了，她也不大愿意去，于是获准一个人留在家里。萨姆奈尔先生陪他的两个女儿去了。

她读书读到累了的时候，就到厨房去帮迪娜做甜点。

"照看一下烤炉，小姐，"迪娜说，"我去谷仓问卡托要三个鸡蛋去。"可莉迪娅自己立即去拿鸡蛋了。门大开着，大量雪水从屋顶流到窗台，再流到地上，地上到处是脱粒后的包谷棒子皮。卡托不在那里。听见上面脚手架上有人，她喊道："是你在那儿吗？"听见有人回答说"是的"，她又说："下来到这儿来，你正是我要找的人。"

"听您吩咐，小姐。"一个不算陌生的声音说道，只见那人顺着绳子溜下来，单腿跪在她脚前，莉迪娅这才认出那个人就是和她同乘一辆驿车的绅士。

那件事过去一年后的一天晚上，雪打在全克罗弗奴科最漂亮的一家人的窗户上，屋里两个人坐在壁炉前说话，从神情看他们该是丈夫和妻子。那女的一直在听男的讲故事，"可怜的老人啊！"听到结尾时那女的说，"他把这么好的农庄和这样漂亮的房子给了你，然后自己又回到荒野，在那里寂寞地死去！"

"那不是牺牲，"那位年轻男子回答说，"他很年轻的时候被野人掠去，学会了他们野蛮的生活方式，以至于文明对他一点诱惑都没有。讲到人们对他的轻蔑，那对他来说自然没有意义。而且在我们被遗忘以后，乔纳森山依然会永远保留对他的记忆。"

"我以前不认为你自私，"他的同伴说，她满眼泪水，似乎是对自己说的话感到羞耻，赶紧补充说，"他不知道有关魅影枪手和幽灵的事吗？"

"你也误解我，"年轻男子带着半责备的口吻说，"我曾竭力劝他和我共同拥有这个家，但他不愿意。我前面说过，他没有作任何牺牲，要是他留下，那才是牺牲。"她低下头去，直到她的卷发遮住了脸上的红晕，年轻男子一脸戏谑而又狡黠地微笑，他说："好啊，好啊，如果我是自私的，我正是你所想要的那个人，你已经告诉我你需要我这样的人。不然的话，莉迪娅·希思永远不会成为阿奇波尔德·萨姆奈尔的妻子。"

妻子把头发甩向后面，面带微笑，随即一个和解的吻印在了她的前额。她说："阿奇波尔德，多好听的名字！如果我真的告诉你你正是我想得到的男人，尽管那时十分盲目，时间已经证明我的选择并没有错。"

18. 克莱维尔一家

七月的太阳异常闷热，没有一丝风，干枯的树叶纹丝不动，云彩轻盈柔软，没有一点下雨的迹象，也没有鸟儿啾啾鸣唱让晒干草的人打起精神来。尽管我很愿意把农村出现的美好事物给予我下文要写的这些人，但我不是在写诗，因此不能随便说有这些东西的存在。这几个人中年龄最长的是克莱维尔先生，他身材消瘦，面容白皙，大约四十五岁。其他三个都是他的儿子，其中两个年轻人身材粗壮，一个十九岁，一个二十一岁；另一个大约再大两三岁，但是比其他两个消瘦得多。两个弟弟大卫和奥利弗正弯着腰，割着浓密的青草，边割边缓慢地向前移动。克莱维尔先生跟在后面，把割下的青草叉过来翻翻，以便尽快晾干。他的沙色长发从前额处一分为二，往后梳齐，此刻已经被汗浸湿了，一绺绺头发半卷着垂到脖子上。尽管周围热浪翻滚，他的穿着却始终如一，外面的衬衫里穿着一件红色法兰绒衬衫，这是他衣着中不可缺少的一件。他的马甲和裤子是黑色的毛料缝制的，脚穿厚重的长筒靴，头戴一顶宽边的黑毛料帽子，外面没穿外套。太阳已经晒到西面的山坡两三个小时了，但他们还一直卖力地干着活，大家都埋头苦干，没人说话。午后，克莱维尔先生抬头看看，发现一个割草人不见了，他丢下手中的耙子，从帽子里拿出一块红底小白点的丝绸手帕，擦擦脸和手，爬上干草垛，在田野中极目四望。一条深深的沟把这块田野一分为二，因此很大一部分都看不见。他是个脾气急躁的人，四处搜寻但是都没有看到目标，炯炯有神的蓝眼睛顿时燃起了怒火。他生气地把两个干活的儿子一一叫到跟前，讯问走掉的儿子的情况。

大卫抬手遮在眼睛上方，看着父亲，说："他说他的镰刀钝了，干不了活。"他父亲回答说："我认为最有可能的情况是他自己太钝了，没法干活。告诉他如果镰刀钝了，尽快把它磨好。他以为镰刀自己能磨好吗？"

大卫说："我不知道，先生。我只知道我的不会。"他弯下腰，继续干活。

克莱维尔先生停了一会，一脸疑惑。然后他整理了一下帽子里的手帕，手帕的一角耷在了左眼上。他朝着不远的低洼处一棵低矮的胡桃树走去。从斜坡方向看去，一下子就发现了那个开小差的儿子，四肢展开，正躺在一片高草丛中。他头枕着一只手，另一只手中拿着一根棍子，正用这跟棍子不停地把一条黑蛇卷起、松开，卷起、松开。蛇好像是他刚刚杀死的。

"是你吗，理查德？"父亲问道，语气中充满了愠怒。

"是的，爸爸。"这个偷懒的儿子说道，半坐起身来。他很惧怕他的父亲，但是又羞于流露出这种情感。于是他又重新躺了下去，继续玩他的游戏。克莱维尔先生继续说道："你就打算这样挣你的面包钱？如果这样，你连盐都挣不到！"理查德没有答话。而他的父亲又走近了几步，问："你为什么不干活？

'想发达的人必须五点起床，
已经发达的人可以睡到七点。'"

他总能说出这样睿智的格言来。理查德回答说他不舒服。克莱维尔先生怀疑地重复了一遍他说的话"不舒服"，又接着说："如果你生病了，先生（克莱维尔先生不高兴哪个孩子时，总是用这种语气），回家去拿一壶凉水到这儿来。先生，你觉得有力气做这件事吗？"

理查德一言未发，但是慢慢站起身来，遵照父亲的命令去做了。他对自己刚才的欺骗行为感到有点内疚，所以步履异常缓慢，仿佛走起路来都非常困难。他看见两个弟弟顶着强烈的阳光卖力地干活，扭过头看了看相反的方向，这时良心上感到深深的不安。他边走边想着为自己开脱，说自己的镰刀太钝了，没法割草，而且确实身体有些不适。他并没有自我欺骗，暗自下决心，等他把水带到地里之后，他会继续更加卖力地干活，一直割到晚上。

他的身体不适合干苦力活，而且他的确相信自己满腹才华。但是不如意的环境不断地把他的才华磨灭。实际上，他在学习上确实有些天分，仅仅做一名苦力确实很委屈，但是那点才华还不足以改变他的处境。

他读书总是很漫不经心，手边有些什么书就看什么书，很少能真正地欣赏。他并没有渊博的学识和智慧能透彻领悟事物的真谛，身边也没有人能鼓励他或与他有共同语言，也没有人能真正地给他指点迷津。诚然，他的母亲总尽可能掩盖他的缺点，对他身体的小毛病总喜欢夸大其词，他却装出有大毛病一般，这样能使他逃避那些他讨厌的苦力活，而且常常想方设法地逃避干活。有时候，良心的谴责和父亲的怒气会逼着他心不甘情不愿地去干活，但是内心不停地诅咒着，诅咒着那颗邪恶的星星把他变成了一个小丑和苦工，要在这人世间如此辛劳。

克莱维尔先生是个非常乐观、极具智慧又勤恳的农民。两个小儿子略显迟钝，人也乏味，但是都满足于现状而且很能干；而理查德，用他常说的话来说，简直就是他沉重的包袱。就像我笔下的这天，他本打算回去以后一直割草到晚上，他自言自语地说，就是要了他的命，他也要这么做。他内心对干活的不悦和恐惧并没有什么明显的缘由。他的胃口一直很好，睡眠充足，没有理由不干活。但是，这种感觉是真实的，只要没有办法逃避，他总会下定这样高尚的决心说就是要他的命，他也要干。

那只旧橡木水桶从井里提起，下面滴滴答答地滴着冰凉的井水。井水被倒入晶亮的锡皮桶里，满得快要溢出来了。他停了一下，他不清楚具体为什么。满是尘土的短小秸梗热浪滚滚，而低矮、枝繁叶茂的苹果树把清凉的树荫投在门旁的石路上，非常舒适宜人。不远处，在一个隔板搭的小棚子下，他的母亲正烘制葡萄干馅饼和姜饼蛋糕。她头上戴着顶帽子，带子松散着，腰间系着一条毛巾代替围裙用，粘得满是面粉。她看上去很热也很疲倦，但是始终很耐心。她看到理查德站在井边，水桶放在路旁，她微笑着朝他走去，问他是不是又生病了。

"没什么。"他说着，咧开嘴笑了笑，仿佛忍着剧痛一般。他嘴上这样说，其实却想让母亲明白他生病了。

"可怜的孩子，"她边说边把手放到他的额头上摸摸，"你有点发烧，你不能坐在这边的树荫下。你脸色不好，不能再到田地里干活了。"

"但是我必须把这水送去。"理查德说道,"我刚才停了一会儿,惹爸爸生气了。如果我不回去,他也许会气得把房子拆掉的。"

然而,当他母亲把椅子拿来,他还是坐了下去,对母亲说他脸色不好的话半信半疑。克莱维尔太太治疗百病都是使用同一个方子,不管是发热还是受伤,不管是烧伤还是关节炎,她使用的都是樟脑。很快,她就端来了一小碗樟脑。生病的年轻人远远地就闻到了樟脑的气味,连忙说自己好多了。听了此话,好心却做错事的母亲又去拿来了一块刚烤好的馅饼。馅饼香气扑鼻,他忍不住吃了起来。母亲让他在那里吃着,自己提着水到田地里去了。

"哟,多莉,你怎么来了?"克莱维尔先生大声嚷道,他扔下手中的耙子,疾步走上前去迎接妻子。她已经不堪重负,大汗淋漓了。

她详细地解释了一番,但是理查德生病的话语没有打动克莱维尔先生的心。他生平第一次说他妻子是个愚蠢的女人。尽管他觉得自己十分克制,语气很和善,但是听起来非常严厉。他让她回家去,再也不准在这样毒辣的太阳下到田地里来了。克莱维尔太太一句话也没说,把带来的馅饼连同咖啡壶装的水一起塞到丈夫手中。她并没有生气,但是"感情受到了伤害"。她一整天都忙个不停,来的时候,尽管又累又倦,但是满心期冀,内心曾以为他们会高兴,这也将给她带来极大的满足,但是现在她多么失望啊。当她转身离开时,大滴大滴的眼泪浸湿了由于长期劳作而红润全失的黄褐色脸颊。她全然没注意到栅栏里跑来的羊群,她的出现惊吓了它们,这些羊的羊角卷着倒垂在耳边,一只只紧挨着,顺着尘土飞扬的小路跑下去。她也没有看见不远处漂亮的鸽子,奶白色和浅褐色,翅膀和胸脯处显出金黄色或紫色,一只只浑圆肥胖,脑袋一顿一顿的,在她前面不远处走来走去。她的脚步逐渐靠近时,这些鸽子簌簌啦啦地振翅飞起,飞到常栖息的小棚子上去,排成长长的一排,不声不响。还有两头牛在古老的小桥旁的清泉边饮水。要是在平日,这是多么宁静祥和的画面啊,而现在没有任何意义。她继续往前走,越过一座小山丘,穿过一个大门,走过一棵细长的梨树,梨树圆锥形的树顶上站着一只孔雀,羽毛在阳光下显得格外漂亮、耀眼。她走到门廊下,站在苹果树树荫下。家也不是庇护所,不能为她排遣忧伤,而是一个劳作受苦的场所——这就是她当时的感觉。

理查德一手拿着樟脑瓶,另一只手拿着一本厚厚的书,坐在一张靠背椅子上，头挨着墙，一边看书一边打哈欠。一只棕色的老母鸡，羽毛凌乱，尾巴上系着一条红绒布（这是家庭主妇常用的一种方法，以防止母鸡到处下蛋），正在啄着刚才放馅饼的盘子里剩下的饼屑。旁边没有其他椅子，但是这个小伙子也没有把他坐的让给母亲。他压根就没有注意到她。后来她问他好些了吗，他咕咕哝哝地说了声不知道。这是实情，因为他根本没病，而且他确信自己跟她说过此事。

"你在看什么书？"过了一会儿，克莱维尔太太问他。

理查德没有回答，只是把书的背面给她看看，封面上画有一个风车装置，表面涂了一层东西，亮晶晶的。他非常清楚他母亲不会明白这是什么，就是她看到了也不知道那到底是什么。她没有再问下去。她觉得那书中全是智慧，她完全无法理解。她站起来，又去忙屋里的事情去了。

这时候，两个小儿子坐在干草垛的阴影处，吃着葡萄干馅饼，喝着壶里的凉水，而克莱维尔先生仍然忙着把割下来的草叉起来，擦成一长排绿色的草垄——他一点胃口也没有。热气慢慢散去，最后太阳西沉到一棵高大的橡树顶上，在干草地上投下长长的影子。克莱维尔太太在低矮的门廊下铺好桌布准备开饭。理查德放下手中的书，一脸的不屑，说他自己能写得比这好。

克莱维尔太太笑了，说："那当然了，你那到底是什么书？"

理查德又用手指了指风车，说："我给你看过了。"随后他离开了房间，自言自语地说了几句他生活的环境多么单调。他知道，父亲很快就要回家了，他要么装作身体已经全好了，正要去干活；要么继续装病，上床睡觉，这样可以避免一场风暴。他受到父亲的训诫之后知道，这场风暴迟早都会来临。

他骑上他那匹栗色的小马。他给他的马取名叫布斯菲勒斯，而家里其他人都叫它理查德的马。一会儿后，他出现在门前，让他母亲去提一桶水喂给他的马喝，一副厚颜无耻而又煞有介事的样子，对她说："如果老头子问我到哪里去了，你就告诉他我去耶路撒冷了。"

称呼"爸爸"，他觉得那样很幼稚。尽管有种种约束，他想了又想，采用了一个很讲究的称呼——"老头子"。他母亲显然很吃惊，但是她并没有责怪理查德，一方面是出于对理查德盲目的爱心，另一方面因为她害怕引起家庭纷争。直到现在，克莱维尔先生都还不知道他的长子脾气暴躁，行为不端。

布斯菲勒斯飞奔时扬起的烟尘刚散，克莱维尔先生就进了屋，又是生气又是难过。然而，他还是先去洗漱好准备吃饭。他的洗漱很简单，就是在立在井边的一只大桶中洗洗脸和手——这个大桶是一种家庭用的大盆，然后把红衬衫外面的棉布长衫的袖子放下来——这两只衣袖在他干活时总是被卷到胳膊肘以上，再把马甲的扣子扣上，把头发梳得整整齐齐。两个小儿子就是这样效仿他的。理查德觉得这种屋外的露天梳妆室太大，总是在自己房间里折腾自己的新创意。

克莱维尔太太默不作声地把清香的茶水倒好，始终眼睛也没有抬一下，但是这样没有用，内心的伤心很快就表现了出来。克莱维尔先生非常清楚，表现出少有的温柔。

"好了，多莉。"他说道，给她拉了一把很舒适的椅子。这椅子一直是他的专用，但是她摇摇头。不知所措的丈夫伸手拿来了鸡毛掸，她拿过来使劲地撑着苍蝇，没给自己留时间去享受端上桌的晚餐，只说自己头痛，一口饭都不想吃。克莱维尔先生说她太忙了。他决定等一忙完收割，就去找一个女佣来帮忙。克莱维尔太太的头越垂越低，好像在啜饮茶水，但是丈夫的软言细语很快就让她心软了。她突然离开了饭桌，回到自己的卧室，不由自主地流了一会儿眼泪后，想到这样对她丈夫有点苛刻了，便开始怨恨其生活的环境，最后只是责怪自己，因为她是个头脑简单、心肠很软的女人。她打开百叶窗，把一把扶手椅拉到了桌边，桌上放着报纸和《圣经》。她剪剪烛头，把房间收拾了一番，特别按照丈夫的心意收拾得舒舒服服。然后她走下楼，态度无比亲切和蔼。克莱维尔先生在渐浓的暮色中摸索着，由于没找到灯，他试着去摸灯，结果把茶具打翻了。

"是你吗，多莉？"他问道，看到她心情居然这么好，他感到很惊讶。她嘴里正哼着一支曲子——

"我能把我的名字念清楚，
　　向着天空中的琼宇。"

"是的，塞缪尔，是我。"她说。她哼到一半停了下来，把茶壶从桌子上拿到柜橱里去。克莱维尔先生阴郁的表情一下子也消散了，他用一只糖罐伴奏，也跟着唱了起来——

"我向所有的恐惧告别，
擦干我泪水滂沱的眼睛。"

曲子终了，他们谈了谈暖和的天气，谈谈他们的大丰收，谈谈邻居们，双方都很小心地避开提起内心深处的那个话题。

最后，克莱维尔先生说："真希望当初送理查德到铁匠铺去当学徒——'藏得好，容易找'，对吧，多莉？这孩子在哪儿？"

克莱维尔太太没有说他去耶路撒冷，只说她猜他很可能去给他的马打新马掌了。

"他是个坏孩子，多莉。"父亲说。

"不是坏，只是不走运罢了，"母亲说，"他好像做什么事情运气都不好。可怜的孩子，他干不了重活，但是他非常爱读书，我们是不是最好把他送去上学，塞缪尔？"

这个建议引起他们长时间的讨论。克莱维尔先生的看法跟他妻子的不太一样。"理查德，"他说，"并不喜欢钻研，恐怕他在知识领域也好不到哪里去。"

"可是，"母亲还是极力说，"如果他在一件事上做不好，也许另一件事能做好。我觉得我们应该给他一个机会。"这时她从衣柜里拿出两件新的红色法兰绒衬衫，放在丈夫的腿上，说："多么漂亮的红色啊。塞缪尔，你不觉得我们应该按照我说的那样来安排理查德吗？"

克莱维尔先生非常喜欢法兰绒衬衫——尤其是红色的法兰绒就更喜欢了。他摸着柔软的衣料，无比赞赏地拿起衣服，说："如果人们早知道红法兰绒的妙处，根本不需要治关节炎的药。'预防为主，治疗为辅'，多莉。"

"可是对于理查德，你打算怎么办？"克莱维尔太太说。"你比我明智。这些衬衫真漂亮，真是很漂亮。"

19. 学生哥

这次谈话后大约八九天的光景，理查德·克莱维尔一身文质彬彬的学生装束，赶往高级中学，他在那儿准备考大学。他拐着装满书的书包，还有两只装得满满的袋子横放在马鞍上，里面他妈妈塞满了考究的新衬衫和她亲手织的长筒袜，足够他这个学期用的。已经说好他每月探家一次，因为他此行的目的地榆木镇离家只有十英里路。确实他好像不大喜欢这样的安排,当他母亲泪水涟涟地恳求他不能一去不回,他却说如果不能旷课他就不回家,他根本不确定自己能回家,至少要等到他学完初级课程,但是她和父亲可以到榆木镇来看他,参加他的开学典礼和毕业典礼。走出一段路之后,他又心生疑虑。回头望去,他看到父亲靠在大门上望着他,他想起父亲的临别赠言:"只有傻瓜才讨厌读书。"他看到母亲依旧站在低矮的门廊下面,和他离开时一样。他的两个妹妹,玛莎和简,还是和玩"藏猫猫"时一样在大喊大叫,理查德离家她们并不在意,他从来不帮她们做一个玩具房子,总是弄死她们的宠物猫,还叫她们小傻瓜,就因为她们宁愿刷碗也不愿学语法,所以总的来说她们巴不得他离开。

大卫和奥利弗此刻肩上扛着斧子慢慢地走在林间小路上,对于他离家求学,他们一点依依不舍的感觉也没有。有理查德在家的确能分担他们的活计,但是微不足道,所以他离家求学就没什么值得流泪的了。回头望去,这一切他都看在眼里,心里真有点希望自己就留在家里,心甘情愿地为家尽自己那份力,希望会有任何似乎合理的回家的理由。但是没有什么理由——脚下的路是自己走出来的,眼前的情况就是这样,他无可奈何。尽管他已经二十三岁了,但除了和母亲一起串亲戚出去过一两天之外,他根本就没离开过家,一种凄凉的恋家的情绪油然而生,眼前的路延伸到一片茂密的山毛榉林中,家里的红砖房已经看不到了。他勒住缰绳,下马,坐在路边一根生着青苔的原木上,久久地陷入沉思,有时他觉得自己的想法还是很诚恳而有条理的。

"两个小姑娘正在玩耍,我想她们乐得见我离开。大卫和奥利弗现在估计已经伐倒了一棵树。我倒是不清楚是哪一棵,大概是今年春天长起来的那棵大枫树;也可能是那棵树皮有些层层剥离的山核桃树,我在树上捉过松鼠,简还因为我不肯把松鼠给她哭鼻子呢;要么就是玉米地里的那些山毛榉,他们很可能砍来备用的。让我想想,这些山毛榉才三英尺半高。爸爸此刻在干什么呢?(他心里并没把爸爸当做一家之长)我猜他在给妈妈读《圣经》,妈妈正在苹果树树荫下做面包。多好的女人啊!我真希望当初我答应她每月回家一次。我真希望当初她问我看什么的时候,我就告诉她在看《堂吉诃德》,而不该支使她去风车那儿。"

想到这里他灵机一动，也许有必须带的某本书或者某件衣物忘在家里了。他翻遍了自己的行李，就像找寻刚刚失踪了的宝贝一样，但是他白翻了一通，该带的都带了。此刻他有些不大情愿离去，就像一个一直以家为乐却被家抛弃了而无家可归的人。他重新收拾好自己随身带的东西，自己觉得随身带的东西又破有少。他从衣袋里拿出个小钱包，把里面装的钱倒出来，有几个硬币滚到他手里，他数了数，把钱又放了回去，叹了口气。"就是这样一片阴暗、密不透风的林子，"他说，"我可能一辈子就待在这里了。对别人来说我算什么？对这个世界来说我算什么？即使在家里也没人在意我。"停了一会儿，他又说道："唉，他们干吗要在意我呢？我从来没做过什么值得他们爱我的事情。我一直都无所事事，一直都是家里的负担。但我命该如此，我也没有办法。如果我有办法的话，我会好好做的。说我们可以创造环境，简直是谎言，是环境在创造我们。我现在不是贼或者杀人犯并不是我有什么优点，如果我接受了他们那样的训练和诱惑，我很可能也好不到哪儿去。我怎么可能知道我在不同环境中的表现呢？如果我当初就受到像父亲那样严厉的人的管教，整天去放牛，烧木头，挖沟，从来不看书或者从来没遇到过任何有品位的人，那么我很可能已经娶了多莉·汤普金斯那样的村姑——就像父亲一样——可能我就该那样。如果一切真的如此，我会比现在过得更糟吗？不！要好得多。别人的路我已经看得很清楚了，我自己总是打算干一番事业，但总是身不逢时。我现在宣布就此开始干一番事业，为什么不呢？软弱和犹豫，从此和我一刀两断。"在这一番自相矛盾不大光明的独白后，他站起身，一副坚决完成使命的样子，走上他的小红马，精神抖擞地向前方走去。

从那儿以后，我时常想，当初他要是能遇到某位和蔼而有眼光的朋友，能够透过他个性的弱点，看到潜在的高尚品质，他的任性和恣意妄为很可能就会得到遏制，他的弱点也很可能会转化为力量。当时我还太小，不懂这些，也不懂欣赏，不懂忍耐，对于自己的看法也非常错误和愚蠢，而现在一切都太晚了。我常常想起他，我非常了解他，我们都是小孩子时经常在夏日的午后一起坐在我家房前的大榆树的树荫下。那是很久以前的事了，我现在已经越过了人生的顶峰，此后的路一直向下，下到在暗处一直呻吟的死亡之河。我想起他的时候，我情愿相信的自己委婉的解释，觉得他真的是运气不佳。

就在悲伤和挣扎之间，懦弱和碌碌无为之中，我日渐老去，日益临近那个所在，那里有最柔和的气氛，最靓丽的喷泉，最动听的鸟鸣，还有已经铺好的裹尸布。那些早已来到这个新世界的灵魂使那灰色的早已尘封的记忆重又鲜活起来。我那些亲爱的儿时的玩伴又回到我身边，头上闪耀着纯美的光环，就像他们当初离去时一样。我最喜欢在这里遇到理查德，喜欢他那金色的卷发随风轻拂我额头的感觉。我们一起翻看图画书，有《公鸡罗宾》，还有另外一本，书名我记不起来了，那本书更大些，里面有一个比较严肃的人物，讲的是索尔、大卫和歌利亚等的故事以及

"哞哞叫着的牛沿着最直的路乱走，
此时以色列神灵的方舟在送腓力斯人回家"。

我们有的书并不多，但对我们来说是"充满魅力，常看常新的"。我们当时也不清楚别的孩子的书有没有我们多，所以很满足。

但是我不能留恋于此，就像波浪会在溺水的人头上合拢而后水面会和以前一样在阳光下泛起涟漪，今天的时光会覆盖我们昨天还在的地方。即使是对家人来说，短暂的离别后，我们再回来就会发现原来属于我们的位置变窄了或者已经有人取而代之，就不再有我们的位置了。

庄稼已经收割了，牲口都放在新修剪过的草地上——它们随意地跑来跑去，稍弱些的尽管吃饱了，仍然聚在一起吃一丛丛的新鲜的白三叶草。玉米还没有成熟。无论对人和牲口，都是一个好时候。克莱维尔先生已经从镇上回到家中，坐在门廊里看报纸。他累了，但是很风趣。累是因为他一路没有让那匹黑马拉车，是骑着它回来的。他说，如果它和汤姆一起拉车的话，它是头好牲口，所以考虑到它的倔脾气，除非有汤姆在才让它拉车，否则他一般都骑着它。他很风趣是因为自从理查德离家一切都很顺利。玛莎和简站在厨房桌子旁忙着收拾篮子里面从集市里买回来的东西，有褐色的纸包着的大包的糖和咖啡，还有一个用薄薄的白纸包的小包，可能是茶。她们闻到了包里芬芳的味道，大声说："噢，味道好极了！"接下来还有很多用蓝色纸包着的小方纸包，上面标签写着"上等姜"、"最好的调料"等等。她们急切地抓起来，让对方猜手里拿的是什么。无论猜对还是猜错，随之而来的笑声都一样开心。

大卫和奥利弗正在门前砍木头，只是为了消遣。他们整天都在树林里卖力地砍树，现在砍砍木头只是为了打发时间，等着把茶烧好。伐木可以强身健体，所以他们总是一心一意地去做。此刻克莱维尔太太，这个终日忙碌的家庭主妇在张罗着晚饭。雪白的桌布已经铺好，上面点缀着各种各样的好吃的——金黄的奶油，可口的面包，熟透了的黑莓，上面飘着银白色和金黄色的大罐的乳酪。没有给理查德留位置，而且玛莎和简已经升级住进了他空出来的房间。他留下来的东西都由母亲那双慈爱的手小心地放好，在这个家里母亲的慈爱可以包容她的孩子的任何过错。

大门的合叶发出"咯吱"的声音，趴在门旁的看门狗低吼了一声，接着是一声响亮的、挑战性的叫声，突然它停住了，然后蹲坐在路上，发出欢迎的声音；两个女孩放下手里的篮子跑到门口；大卫和奥利弗放下手里的斧子；克莱维尔先生摘下眼镜揉了揉眼睛，打量着门廊的拐角。

"噢，天啊，他衣锦还乡了。"两个女孩立刻叫起来。

"我想他已经完成学业了。"奥利弗说。两个男孩又砍起木头来。

"多莉，"克莱维尔先生望着厨房喊，"老天爷保佑我们，多莉，理查德回来了。"

"可能吗？"克莱维尔太太答道，"可怜的孩子，他肯定是病了，要不怎么才两个星期就回来了？"但是不管有病没病她都欢迎他回来。玛莎和简用怪怪的眼神看着他，她们似乎忍不住大笑起来，好像他很滑稽，所以她们没办法不笑似的。克莱维尔先生又看起了报纸，不过看的姿势很不自在，还皱着眉头，好像儿子的到来是出乎意料的，是不受欢迎的。克莱维尔太太独自迎上去，真诚中带有犹豫。可儿子就好像没看到她，眼睛盯着地上，牵着自己的布斯菲勒斯回到马厩。他父亲和妹妹们站在一边，两个兄弟站在另一边，但是他谁也没看，或者说谁也没看他一眼。由于他的归家，晚饭时间拖后了一些时间，但是他没有来，叫玛莎去喊他，回来时却带来没找到他的消息。听到这里，克莱维尔先生把自己的椅子拉向餐桌说道："丫头、小子，吃饭。"听他的语气一点不在乎理查德，克莱维尔太太不大情愿地开始给大家倒茶。

这顿晚饭尽管比平时要丰盛，但是大家都没心思享受，都静悄悄地把饭吃完。克莱维尔先生提了一壶温好的牛奶要去喂那些刚刚断奶的牛犊,走出了房子。克莱维尔太太把茶壶放到炉火旁,打发简和玛莎一起去,叮嘱她们仔细地找,看看能不能找到理查德,告诉他趁他爸爸不在马上到房子里来。两个女孩发现理查德在一个稻草堆上,但是他就是不肯进屋来,说他病了。后来直到夜幕降临,直到他确定全家人都要睡了,他妈妈亲自去才劝得动他。

他对自己的行为感到可耻和羞辱,和平时一样他还是用老办法来缓解自己内心的耻辱:他这次是走霉运了!老师们都是蠢货,他宁愿住在熏房里自己做饭也不住这样的地方,从来就没见过干净床单,枕头小得头睡在上面就痛——这样的条件让他根本没法学习。而且那些学生也是一群傻瓜,连豌豆都不认识,还自以为无所不知。鉴于这些情况和其他不值得重复的问题,他决定在家继续他的学业。他就没意识到自己为什么就不能在那里学得像在别处一样好,他妈妈也没意识到,于是定下来他的房间应该改造成书房,他不用离家就可以专心地读书了。玛莎和简很高兴她们有新房间住,还有她们会得到新娃娃的秘密承诺,所以答应不会去打扰他。克莱维尔太太尽其所能地在情绪不稳而恋家的孩子和他愤怒的父亲和兄弟之间调解。

"我说,塞缪尔,"她开口说,"理查德一直都有温馨的家和慈爱的父亲,给他提供了最好的条件。"克莱维尔太太说话是很有策略的。对于她这番恭维,克莱维尔先生确实有点飘飘然。他心里很受用,就说:"当然要尽可能给自己的家人提供好的条件了。"

"是的,你的确提供了,没有谁能否认,"她很及时地接过话来,"而且我觉得理查德现在已经明白过来了,从今往后会更珍惜自己有这么好的条件。"

克莱维尔先生说但愿如此。这可是令人振奋的,确立了这一点优势——但是我必须说,从对她公正的角度来讲,她当时没有想骗谁,只是希望一切都顺当些。她接着说:"我想对于我们任何人来说要离开家和陌生人相处,周围一切都是新的,和我们一直习惯的都不一样,面对这样的情况还能心满意足地待下去真的有点难为人。我肯定不想过理查德说的那样的生活。可怜的孩子!"

于是凭借克莱维尔太太的安排,还有理查德本人几天来孜孜不倦的实际行动,新的安排就自然而然地实施了,只是克莱维尔先生偶尔会把理查德叫做"病歪歪的学生"。玛莎和简被他惹恼的时候也会挖苦他:"嗨,你病歪歪地回家来,回来找妈妈吧!"

就这样他在家里住了两个星期,渐渐地开始厌烦了,觉得他的房间又小又孤单。他认为这不是学习的正确方式,身边没有老师,没有人鼓励他。他需要安慰,妈妈的面包和奶油虽然和以前一样可口,但是他吃起来也不觉得这样了。他不再尝试与这些和他远远不如他的人融洽相处;他的情绪捉摸不定,不大爱说话,人也变得很自私。看到周围人怡然自得的样子只会让他早已焦躁不安的心态更加恶化。他就一个钟头接一个钟头的一个人坐在自己的房间里,手里拿着书页不翻开,眼睛直勾勾地看着空空如也的墙壁或地板。他渴望做一名绅士,却不知该如何去做;想成为一个伟大的人,却没有精力通过实践去获得伟大。有时他臆想这大千世界没有适合他的位置,所以努力也是徒劳的;有时他就沉浸在自己天赋异禀的幻梦里,说不定什么时候机缘巧合就会让他成就一番宏图霸业。从此他走路就低着头,眼睛死盯着地面,就怕一不小心错过了他期待的宝藏;一点响动也会让他惊讶;他觉得神灵会来给他戴上皇冠,唉,可神从没来过。

一天下午他胳膊下夹了本书,用帽檐遮着眼睛,出了家门,可他不知道该去哪儿。四处游荡了一阵子之后,他就躺在路边一棵榆树树荫下的草地上,看着往来的路人。一会儿看见一个小贩弯腰背着一大袋东西路过,过了一会儿又看到一个赶车人吹着口哨坐在满载货物的大车边上。

"你好,克莱维尔先生!"一个充满幽默而又快活的嗓音对他说。抬起头,理查德看到了乡村医生红润的脸,他用手支起头,没有起身,没好气地回了一句。

"如果你有我一半的病人要治疗,"医生对他说,"你就没空为虚无缥缈的伤痛叹气了。想想我行医中所要面对的真正的苦难吧——悲伤、疾病、痛苦、死亡——死亡、痛苦、疾病、悲伤!"

"人终有一死,"理查德说,"是人生中最美妙的事了。我想我喜欢你的职业。"

"坐上来,"希尔顿医生说,边说边在自己赶的小马车上给理查德让出了身旁的地方,"今天我就带你去体验一下。今天我这一路行程相信你会有兴趣的。首先,我要去看一个断腿的男孩,很可能要截肢;接着去看一个已经无法自控的年轻人——为什么这么说呢?

他昨天想杀死自己的妹妹，德鲁塞拉，我确信今天得把他送到疯人院去。让我想一下：再接下来我要去看寡妇帕克斯顿——今年春天她被烧伤，就为了从火里抢出些家具，造成的烧伤已经无法治愈了，留下六个无助的孤儿听天由命，想想看吧，先生！快，上来，坐上来。"

理查德站起身来，拉了拉马甲，扶了扶领子，就上车了，但是还是有些幽怨地看着家里红色的房子。希尔顿医生看在眼里，拍了拍他的肩膀说："哎，克莱维尔医生，这样子可不行。"说完，两人放声大笑驾车而去。

20. 羊群犬祸

克莱维尔夫人对她丈夫说："你觉得理查德究竟出了什么事啦？"这是他离开的第三个早晨。克莱维尔先生在听到这个问题后仍继续吸着烟，又埋头读了好长时间报纸。但是他满脸愁容的太太又问了一遍："塞缪尔，你感觉理查德究竟出了什么事啦？"她继续叨咕着，理查德把所有东西都留在房间里，看样子他打算很快就会回来似的，一本书还摊放在桌子上，手表还挂在床头的钉子上。她看不出理查德随身带了什么东西，这似乎有点难以理解。克莱维尔先生丢下吸剩下的雪茄头，说道："等他衣服穿破旧了，饥肠辘辘的时候，他自然就会回来。多莉，我敢保证这一点。说不定他去了彼得舅舅家了。等星期六我去城里的时候，我要是看到彼得，而且我还记得这件事的话，我顺便问问他。但是他也可能并不在那里，或许他行踪不定呢。不要为他烦恼了，既然于事无补，不如顺其自然。"

"哦，我搞不懂，搞不懂，总是觉得这事儿怪怪的。"克莱维尔太太回答说。

"妈妈，怎么啦？发生什么事啦？"小女儿简跑过来，急切地问道，一脸的迷惑和焦急。

"没事，没事，小孩子家不要问那么多。"克莱维尔先生回答，又补充了一句："我们在说你哥哥理查德的事儿。"

这个回答对于小孩子来说太敷衍了事。简很想知道他们究竟在谈论什么，而不是指他们谈话的话题。但是简意识到不好再追问下去，也不好再说下去。她也就没有把她所了解的有关这个话题的一切和盘托出。实际上，她看到理查德和希尔顿医生一起驾车离开了。

父母是注定不可能长时间被蒙在鼓里的。这时候，一个小男孩突然气喘吁吁地跑过来。他满脸雀斑，满头红彤彤的头发用发夹扎得紧紧的，发梢向上翘着。他在惊慌失措中好不容易磕磕巴巴地把他这次跑来的缘由解释清楚。原来昨晚他父亲的十只羊被咬死了，他过来看看克莱维尔先生家的狗卡罗是否还在家里。

"嗯，是的，它一直待在家里，卡罗，快过来，卡罗，过来。"一只硕大的看家狗一边摇着尾巴，一边舔着自己的下颚，跑了过来。克莱维尔先生反复打量着这只狗，好像这只不说话的动物是受审的犯人一样。但这毫无意义，哪家主人会判定自家的狗有罪呢？

与此同时，邻居们正从四面八方急匆匆地赶到贝茨先生家。他家的羊群遭到残忍的屠杀，他们既充满好奇，同时又担心灾难会降临到他们头上。克莱维尔先生和身边的那个红发小男孩，还有其他人，正在匆匆忙忙地赶路。克莱维尔先生问道："你说损失了多少只羊？""十只。"小男孩回答说，"十只最棒的羊。昨天好多人愿意出二十美元的价格来买，爸爸都没有出手卖呢。"

"那你们怀疑是谁家的狗咬死羊的？"克莱维尔先生继续问道。

小男孩说："我们怀疑是一只长得很像卡罗的狗干的。今天早上我看到这样一只狗穿过我家的田地，向你家的方向跑去。不管怎么说，是一只大白狗干的。"

"绝对不可能是卡罗，我还从未听说过一只白狗咬死羊的事呢，这是不可能的。"克莱维尔先生没有继续询问下去。

在贝茨家的门口围站了六七个人，他们正在激烈地讨论着各种可能性。这个灾难可能是这样或那样的狗干的，同时一大群男孩子在一边围站成一圈，一个个都自信满满的样子，他们讨论得更为热闹。一个说："我打赌是皮特·希尔家的咆哮犬干的。"

"是啊，"另一个附和着，"就是它领头干的，不过我觉得能有六只狗帮它吧。"

"我知道一只狗干不成这事，"第一个发言的男孩说道，"不可能是我家的狗，不过如果证实它有罪的话，"他挺了挺胸接着说，"我情愿还人家一个公道。"

这几句表态引起一阵阵低声的赞叹。在场的每个男孩都希望他自己也这么说了，或者也能说上一段这般无私高尚的话语。但是没有用的，因为这种成功不可能在一天内接连发生两次。男孩们渐渐散开，加入到男人队伍中去。人群中最重要的人物是贝茨先生，他理所应当是核心人物。实际上，尽管如他所说，这十只羊他二十美元也不肯出手，但他几乎已经接受了损失十只羊的事实，因为这件事一下子提升了他的知名度。

贝茨夫人也处于兴奋的状态中，她此刻的心情是欢喜多于忧伤。她此时无法精力充沛地投入到日常家务活中，尽管这是她一向引以为豪的。她时不时地踱到门边，以各种理由走近蓄水池或是水井，以便能听到外面的谈论。她听到有人问："先生，你是否知道这是谁家的狗干的？"她丈夫回答说即使他有啥想法，也无济于事，因为像他这样的穷人，又怎么可能去指控一个富人养的狗呢。这时，她再也无法控制自己的愤怒，于是毫不含糊地冲着人群大声嚷道："我认为我们生活在一个自由的国度里。"这样的言辞再普通不过了，只是说没有特权阶级的存在，并没有暗含其他明确的意思。

"当然了，贝茨太太。"克莱维尔先生听到了这句话，出于礼貌而接过话来。

"但即使是我们生活在自由的国度里，如果我们不敢于直言不讳地讲出我们心中所想的，这又有什么意义呢？"

"这当然是我们的权力之一，难道你不敢说出你心中所想的事情？"克莱维尔先生一边说着，一边很迷惑地用手搔头发。不知怎么回事，他心里忐忑不安。

"不，我敢，"这个强健的小女人回答说，"但是有人不敢。"

"谁不敢？"克莱维尔先生马上问道。

"比如说贝茨。"她回答说。

"贝茨先生心里怎么想的？"

"他认为是一个有钱人家养的狗咬死了我们最好的羊，他家离这里并不太远。"

"你是说我家的狗干的？"克莱维尔先生说着，走近了一步，他湛蓝的眼睛突然流露出愤怒的神情。

"如果事实的确如此，你就要接受。我并没有说是你家的狗干的。"

"不是这样，你似乎不敢说出你心中所想，尽管刚才你还在宣扬这是一个自由的国家。我想知道你凭什么怀疑是我家的狗干的。"

"我的眼睛和耳朵就是最好的证据。我不知道在我们这样自由民主的国家里，这件事还需要别的证据吗？"

"你是说你亲眼看到我家的狗咬死了你家的羊吗？我记得你的孩子说羊是在夜间被咬死的。是这样吗？如果的确如此，你怎么碰巧看到了这一切呢？"

这时候，他们的谈话已经吸引了很多人的关注，而贝茨夫人很高兴能有此机会被他人所关注倾听，便继续解释她的理由根据："事情是这样的：估计是在午夜时分，我醒了过来，我也不知道怎么会醒来，因为我一向睡觉很死，除非我的某个孩子生病了，或是贝茨先生要去赶集，这种情况，我睡眠休息的时间很短。很快我抱起我的孩子萨蕊安出去随便走走。这听起来有点傻（贝茨夫人喜欢四处逛逛）。这个小家伙患了百日咳，这对我倒没什么，不过我很奇怪她是怎么感染上这病的，十有八九是在街道上被别人传染。我记得我曾经在马路上停下来和波莉·基特利聊了几句。我想买一种欧洲萝卜种子，而基特利家种的蔬菜一向是最好的。当时她怀里也抱着小宝宝，丽莎白·凡哈特，这个名字是以老人家凡哈特的名字命名的。据说老人家去世后大概会留给他们一大笔遗产。嗯，我搞不准当时是她家宝宝的头转向我家宝宝，还是她家宝宝的头转离我家宝宝，但是如果是她家宝宝的头转向我的宝宝，并且她的宝宝患有百日咳，那么我的孩子会轻而易举地被她的宝宝传染上这病的。"

"当然了，贝茨太太，"克莱维尔先生颇为和善地提醒说，"但别忘了我们在说羊的事。"

"我当然不会忘啦，我想在这个自由的国度里，我可以随意地谈点什么，而不会在我列举证据时因为多说或者少说一个字而被砍头吧。"

克莱维尔先生又重复了一次说："当然啦。"此刻他的微笑似乎已经升级成了大笑。这个健谈的小女人停了一下，接着又喋喋不休地说道："嗯，我说过萨蕊安患有百日咳，她病得不严重，咳嗽得也不厉害，贝茨先生认为她患病时间不长。其他那几个孩子也得了百日咳，每个孩子咳嗽得都十分严重，就像我以前看到患有百日咳病的孩子那样。我曾经看到有的孩子得了百日咳之后一直咳嗽不停，咳到脸都变红变紫了。但是自从他们百日咳好了之后，我晚上睡觉很少会被吵醒，除非我牙疼，或者是神经有问题，或者是大雨前担心我家的玉米要被水泡了。但昨晚我为什么碰巧醒过来，我也搞不懂。也许我做了个噩梦，但即使是这样，我也记不清梦的内容。不过，我隐约记得好像要把衣服摊放在小桃园的一角进行漂白，我似乎听到了狗叫，好像我家的狗在朝着邻居家们的狗叫个不停。"说到这儿，她瞥了一眼克莱维尔先生。"这些狗过来咬死了我们的羊。我家的狗在夜间对其他狗非常凶狠，尽管我家的狗在白天会对其他狗十分的温和。甚至在天刚擦黑的时候，我家的狗对其他狗也是非常友好。但是从午夜一直到天亮这段时间，我家的狗对其他狗就会很凶。"

这时候，贝茨先生显然有点局促不安。他溜进屋里，打了一个小孩几下，小孩子哇哇大叫起来。于是他能干的老婆的故事不得不匆匆地告一段落。这么冗长的讲述只不过是为了说明她似乎碰巧在灾难发生时醒了过来，除了她隐隐约约记得的梦境之外，她并没有根据做这样的推论。至于为什么她怀疑是克莱维尔先生家的狗，她并没有说。也许是因为克莱维尔先生家的土地多于她家的，并且克莱维尔太太有时候会穿一件特意请人定做的黑丝绸衣服。

贝茨太太发泄了自己内心的不满和怨恨后，回到屋里。这时，一个叫詹姆森的男士从人群中走出，踩在一块高高的木块上，开始发表他的演说。或许是由于他每次发言都是经过深思熟虑的，都很有影响力，也或许是由于他是这个小镇上最富有的土地所有者，所以他说话往往在邻居中很有威信。他说道："朋友们，邻居们，昨天晚上或是今天清晨，突然间，一场意想不到的大灾难降临到威廉姆·贝茨家，也把我们聚集在一起。（此刻，贝茨先生觉得损失得到了超额报偿，严肃地站在那里，有了庄严感）这使得我们每一个人都应该积极行动起来争取查明这次血淋淋行为的作俑者，来维护正义。不管是你家的狗，还是我家的狗（他做着手势来配合自己的演说），让惩罚来得迅速些、明确些。我个人愚见，有些事情，严惩等同于宽恕，这就是一个例子。在此我谦恭地提议，立即正式请希尔顿医生，让他来决定，让他凭借医疗手段来决定谁家的狗早上吃了羊肉。"詹姆森以询问的眼神看了一下敬仰他的人群，然后从大木块上走了下去。

男孩子们各个都主动要求跑去找医生。最后，詹姆森的建议毫无异议地得到了每个人的认可，男孩子们兴高采烈地出发了。

那时候苜蓿角村里只有一栋三层的砖楼，整个地区都称之为苜犄角酒店。舞台表演的大车会停留在这里，各种各样的广告宣传单也会张贴在这里，比如公开拍卖品、学校的辩论会、各种巡回演出，既有像森林里小孩乐队的表演，也有像德赖斯巴赫先生这样的驯狮马戏表演。村子里还有一家公立学校和一家私立学校，一家女帽商店，两个铁匠铺，两个教堂，五十多家旅店。最好的一户房子要属希尔顿医生的小木屋，整体是亮黄的颜色，门和百叶窗则配上绿色，门上装饰有两个锡制的标志。主要入口处前方地面上立有几根结实的柱子，上面配有铁链，为了便于拴马。一根柱子上倚靠有一种特殊的梯子，为了方便前来拔牙的人，或是来向医生咨询关于小孩子出牙的乡下女人。苜犄角酒店的位置几乎就在其正对面，这附近一带是小镇最繁华的地方。事实上向西一英里左右米德尔顿乡绅住的地方，或者是向北海伍德医生的住处，那里更加热闹繁华。贝茨夫妇住在村子边缘的一栋黑漆漆的小房子里。尽管他开垦的农场周围有很多更幽静、更合适居住的地点可以造房子，可他还是选择了这里。四周有一些马厩和机具店。他的妻子和女儿也许可以充分利用这里的上层社会。他的女儿充分地利用了这里的资源。贝茨太太以自己更经常待在家里且比其他人工作更努力而骄傲，她也为自己女儿成为她希望的淑女而欣喜。她自己是在无所事事中长大的，整天穿着漂亮的衣服，东家出西家进，随心所欲地扯闲话找乐子。

事实上，萨莉·贝茨是个很不错的姑娘，眼睛又黑又亮，红扑扑的脸颊十分圆润，一头卷发稠密光滑。按照贝茨太太的说法，她的身材十分完美，腰肢甚至比通常所认可的杨柳细腰还要纤细。她性情温和，和她聊天如沐春风。她最大的天赋在于可以逃避所有的苦难，迷惑住所有和她接触过的男子，无论年轻年长，无论高矮胖瘦。

希尔顿医生挎着背包，和跟在身边的学生刚一露面，萨莉就穿着考究的白色薄纱裙，头上戴着一圈假花饰品，出现在窗边。她把窗帘拉到一边，这样便可以看清克莱维尔医生的长相。她一直这样称呼他，尽管她很显然并不愿意让他同时看清她的相貌。

当他们走近时，"克莱维尔先生"，詹姆森先生说道，"你的长子理查德从父亲的庇护下走了出来，在神奇的医学领域里去谋求发展了？"

克莱维尔先生看上去既迷惑不解又有些惭愧，这是他第一次知晓理查德的行踪。迷惑使他忘记了作出任何回答。但是贝茨先生抓住这次机会说了很多恶毒的话，他说他认为克莱维尔先生不可能在孩子毕业时继续控制他们的生活。

克莱维尔先生先是大吃一惊，之后感到极度的羞耻。他既没有等着寻机扭转这种不利的局面，也没有询问理查德任何问题，而是选择突然抽身离开。贝茨先生继续说，说他希望克莱维尔医生的职业发展不要局限在现在的这个小区域里。理查德看上去有几分不修边幅，又有几分彬彬有礼，同他的父亲一样有些窘迫，他也没有想到会与父亲不期而遇。然而很快他就被萨莉明亮的眼睛和满头动感的卷发吸引住了。他已经完全被这个女孩迷人的动作、活泼的眼神所吸引，以至于忘记了他最初的尴尬不安。

这个女孩从窗户一点点向外探出身体，欢快地摆弄着卷发上的玫瑰花。突然起了一阵大风，风势远远超过平时的程度，吹落了她头上的花束，散落在离庞大人群不远的地方。理查德已经恢复了自己的敏捷，很快把花束送到了敞开着的窗户前。贝茨小姐的脸红扑扑的，鞠躬表示感谢。

理查德吃惊于自己以前从未注意到她的美丽。一个月后，一天早上，克莱维尔先生从苜蓿角办完事后，匆匆忙忙、跌跌撞撞地赶了回来。他得知好消息，而他早应该知道的，理查德和萨莉很快就要举行婚礼了。

"多莉，"克莱维尔先生坐在门廊上，一副筋疲力尽的样子，"多莉，把指甲花酒递给我。"

早应该提到的一件事是，所有被怀疑的犬科动物，在经过规定的严格检测后都体面地被宣判无罪。只有那只出名的看门狗例外，这只狗要是在守夜时受到其他狗的惊扰，它会比所有的狗都凶猛。

21. 愚蠢的婚姻

十一月的第一天到来了，绵长的秋雨结束了。小溪边和山坡上的绿草丛中曾经遍布的花儿，灰色的紫罗兰、深红色的福禄花和蓝色的风铃草，都枯萎死掉了。花叶凋零的季节已经过去。寒冷的北风吹散了整个十月都笼罩着蓝色天空的阴霾，空气清洌。

克莱维尔先生的谷仓装满了新晒好的干草，还有一捆捆金色的小麦和白色的裸麦。门边，一群长着斑纹的公牛、圆滚滚的棕色小母牛，还有刚长出角的欢闹的小牛，正在齐膝深的清香的稻草里走来走去。这一切看起来很美好——一派丰足的景象。玉米已收割，果园的水果也已采摘，辛苦劳作的人们都现出了丰收的喜悦。

　　在屋里，虽然壁炉的火正在熊熊燃烧，屋内却很静，出奇的安静，几乎令人感到不快。大多数时间，克莱维尔先生都坐在屋里，读着《圣经》或是报纸。他有时会给多莉读一条报纸上的新闻，或一则派或布丁的制作方法。她是一个没受过教育、头脑简单的女人。她从不关心理论的争辩和浮华的政治，对这些她丈夫却有着极大的兴趣。她勤劳而节俭，通常都在默默地做着她的活计，缝缝补补，整理屋子，准备饭菜。她的脚步不再似以前那般轻快，提到未来的次数也更少了，即使偶尔提起，也越来越不抱什么希望了。她已得到了教训，明了俗世愿望所具有的欺骗性，知道"悲伤头上的华冠就是记住那些快乐一些的事情"。那些曾使她那做母亲的欢欣鼓舞的预言，她那运气不佳的儿子没能实现，难怪她很悲伤，可怜的女人。

　　大卫和奥利弗从壁橱里取出了石板和教科书，开始在当地学校上课了。在壁橱里搁置了九个月之后，那些石板已落满灰尘，教科书也已发霉。他俩在这所学校上学已三个月了，而玛莎和简已在这里读一年了。这期间，如果遇到暴风雨或暴风雪的天气，她们便不能去上学，因为学校离家有一英里远，而她们既没有斗篷，也没有套鞋，轮不到她们有。

　　一天，阴云密布，狂风呼啸。和着窗户吱嘎作响的声音，蛐蛐儿们鸣叫着。克莱维尔先生边颤抖着往炉火旁靠，边说："多莉，恐怕我要得疟疾了，身上一阵阵的发冷，虽然今天穿了两件红法兰绒衬衣，可我好像还是暖不过来。"克莱维尔太太把樟脑拿给他，又把一块毯子披在他肩上，边做这些边说，她一整天都觉得好像有什么事情要发生。这时候，一声沉重的跺脚声和几声窸窣拖沓的脚步声吸引了他们的注意。

　　不过，让我先略提一下之前的事。流言这回成真了，在经历了一番调情和一些年轻人的多愁善感之后，理查德·克莱维尔与萨莉·贝茨被宣布为丈夫和妻子了。在那多愁善感之时，他们把对方看得比谁都好，只有在彼此之间才能找到爱与怜悯。一两周的迷恋之后，是一两周静下心来的平常日子，然后便有了无端的愤怒和不满，间或有一些刻薄的影射，再往后便是恶语相向和大吵大闹。

理查德受了萨莉的骗，萨莉也上了理查德的当。那个由甜蜜、温柔和美丽创造的奇迹，原来是一个游手好闲的长舌妇，爱钱胜过爱一切；那个英俊潇洒、很快就能发迹的医生，原来是世界上最爱挥霍、脾气最坏的恶棍。事实上，两个人都对，两个人又都错了，这种事情通常如此。他们先是听凭自己盲目而急切的冲动，随之而来的便是痛苦的反思，接着便会产生一系列的不幸。但凡他们肯听的话，这些不幸别人都早已给他们指出过。

这位少妇本来以为被大家称为有钱人的克莱维尔先生会一直供养着他的医生儿子，直到他开始了自己的事业。但是在这点上她想错了。不错，克莱维尔先生的土地确实值一大笔钱，但是这块地的产出只够勉强维持生活，这还得是辛苦劳作才行。他口袋里的钱从没超过五块，因为，正如克莱维尔太太所说，他是个很负责的养家的人，时不时地卖掉一头小公牛或一匹小马，或者一垛干草、几蒲式耳的燕麦，靠这些换来的钱，在支付了日常需要的糖呀、咖啡呀，还有千百样其他不起眼的东西之后，就所剩无几了。除此之外，大卫和奥利弗踏实勤奋，他们每过几天就得有些新衣服和新靴子，就像克莱维尔先生说的，不时还得有几个零钱花。而且，玛莎和简也得有些新帽子和新衣服，因为克莱维尔太太想让她们看起来跟别人差不多。她确信怀特执事家女儿们的裙子比她女儿们的多一倍。所以，考虑一下收入和需求，要说克莱维尔先生手头总是缺钱，也就毫不奇怪了。

然而，即使他手里有钱，他也不太愿意继续资助理查德了。他说，这五年来，除了吃住穿戴，他还给了他自立的时间。另外，他还给过他一匹马，给他钱的次数是给别的孩子的两倍，每次给的数目也是给别的孩子的两倍。而理查德一再让他生气，尤其是在这次婚姻上，没征询他的意见，也没经过他的同意，便娶了这个他怀有强烈偏见的女人。所以，考虑到这些，他不愿再向理查德敞开心扉，也就不令人感到惊讶了。虽然克莱维尔太太曾极力劝他，说他还未见过这位年轻的新娘，也没跟她说过话，新娘没准是完美的化身，能够帮助理查德在这个世界上安身立命，如果她能得到一些建议和鼓励，她就不会带来任何损害。然而这些都是徒劳，克莱维尔先生只说不愿见她。他知道这家人没文化，又很粗俗。他觉得乔·贝茨肯定不知道约翰·卡尔文是美国总统，而且很有可能他的女儿知道的更少——她是一个愚蠢、教养不当、只爱四处闲逛的人，还得他帮助她学会自助。

说到娶个妻子，理查德可从未想过要如何来养活她。他应该结婚，这是不争的事实，但他把婚后那些令人不快的柴米油盐统统抛到了脑后。更有甚者，他会卖掉他的爱马布斯菲勒斯来维持一段时间的生活，这是真的。马已经卖了，我提到的这个狂风呼啸的日子，正是他花光最后一分钱之后到来的一天。

自打结婚以后，理查德就表示要继续他的学习。大多数的时间里，他都坐在希尔顿医生那落满灰尘的小办公室里，把脚放在窗台或桌子上。不过，有时他也会改变一下这种一成不变的日子，卖上一盒药丸或一瓶止痛药，有时遇到儿童咳喘病的病例，或是轻微的烧伤或发热的情况，他也会拜会一下老师，请教专业问题。

有时他会在岳父家吃饭，有时在他母亲的配餐室吃，有时在宾馆吃，却从没付过账。萨莉仍然住在娘家，事实上是因为理查德养不起她，不过据她所言，是"因为母亲不想与她分开"。她那双白色的鞋已经穿坏了，白色的面纱也已污秽不堪。她父亲曾给她买过一两次新衣服，后来也开始觉得她该指望自己的丈夫了。他有好几天没来看她了，噢，她并没多想什么，她也不在乎什么，只是，她想要双鞋，也知道自己得提出这个合理的要求。她几乎再也无法出门了——这种状况她并不习惯。然而她的医生丈夫还是没来。她该怎么办？"哎哟，马上去问你丈夫，"她母亲说，"该是他养家的时候了。"萨莉也是这么想的，她也应该这么想。于是，穿上她那双前露脚趾后露脚跟的白色拖鞋，她动身了。风吹起了她的裙子，样子很难看。

到了办公室，她看到克莱维尔医生一副漫不经心的样子，穿着一件破旧油腻的大衣，坐在一个火热的炉子近旁，帽子耷拉下来遮住了眼睛，正在跟马夫倾诉自己的悲伤。马夫是一个黑人男孩，十四岁了，他们是在早先医生干得还不错的时候认识的，那时这个男孩被雇来做布斯菲勒斯的马夫。虽然那些日子早已远去，他俩偶尔仍会在酒肆或马厩旁相遇（理查德很喜欢马），这符合社会平等的观念。炉子散发出很多热量，热空气使得他们把门推开了一些，因此萨莉进去的时候，并没有打扰到两人的聊天。

"你为什么不离开她？如果我有这么个妻子，我就会离开。"她听到那男孩说。

"以老天的名义,我又能跑到哪里去呢?"医生回答道,努力用两根手指平衡着一瓶蓖麻油,"我是个傻瓜——我一辈子都是个傻瓜。"

萨莉虽然不太确定,但她隐约感到话题与她有关。她放开嗓门嚷道:"我真高兴你终于明白了——大家早都已经知道了。"

"明白什么了?"理查德说,一点也不显得惊讶。

"哎哟,明白了你是个傻瓜呀。你就不该有妻子——你不适合有。"

"我只希望你能明白得比我早一些。"理查德说。

"我也希望如此,"萨莉回答道,"以前我从没想到我会连双鞋也没的穿——你看看吧。"她把鞋一览无余地亮出来给他看。理查德没说话,她便接着说:"你想让我打赤脚吗,还是想让我帮别人洗衣服?"

"爱干什么干什么。你妈就是个不错的洗衣工,我想她会毫不费力地教你她这个行业的妙招。"

"对你妻子这样说话可真有你的。我相信我已经尽我所能了——真想死掉算了,那样就不会麻烦你了。"年轻的妻子哭了起来。理查德对自己刚才这样说话感到很抱歉,他还有些良知。这个年轻的女人也并不完全处于弱势。因此,在尴尬的沉默中坐了一会儿之后,他开口了:"我不知该怎么办,萨莉,跟你一样。我没钱,也没办法挣到钱。"

萨莉没有回答。他继续说:"你有什么建议吗?"

听到这句话,她啜泣起来,抽抽噎噎地说:"他们不想让我们回去了,我确定。如果我们能在哪找一间小房子,自己过日子,我就太高兴了。"

"跟一个连双鞋都买不起的人谈房子又有什么用呢?"

"那么,假如我们去你父亲那里住一段时间怎么样呢?"

"那又为什么呢——为了被赶出门外?"

"不,我们不会被赶出去的。我可以帮你妈干活,你也可以像现在一样努力地学习,学习之余再挣出你借住的钱。等他们烦我们了,你爸可以帮扶一下我们,这是他应该做的,我们就可以过自己的日子了。可能会有一些好事儿发生呢——谁知道呢?"

理查德觉得这些都在情理之中，但是真要这样去做，他却犹豫得很。但愿他的父亲在家，但是，一想到要出现在父亲面前，更糟的是，他妻子也在场，他就无法鼓起勇气这样做。然而，他别无选择，只好勉强遵从了妻子的建议。他们俩看上去垂头丧气、可怜兮兮的：理查德那曾经还算体面的黑衣服现在已破旧不堪，萨莉则穿着褪了色的新娘礼服——玫瑰色的丝质衣裙，还有那双残破的白色缎面拖鞋。

看到他们走了，贝茨太太倒是很高兴，因为她已经厌倦了"为这一家子当牛做马"。她不止一次地建议这对年轻人做点有用的事，这也是为了他们好，诸如此类云云。

可怜的理查德，他觉得自己就像个遭人鄙视的被弃者，将要回到那个曾经理直气壮地抛弃了他的家里乞求施舍。他试着劝自己，这就是命运，一切努力都是白费，他最好像个殉道者般认命得了。但这些劝解都是徒劳，没用的，谦卑、骄傲、不满、羞愧，种种情绪在他的内心激烈交战，他的心中充满了恶毒的想法。

路上，他们遇到了一个可怜的男孩，他的妈妈生病了。他衣衫褴褛，神情沮丧，一只胳膊用绷带绑着吊在胸前。他迟疑不决，怯怯地看着理查德，目光中充满探寻。理查德起初似乎没注意到他，然后猛然停下脚步，冷不防说："你想让我做什么？我什么也为你做不了！"

"希尔顿医生在家吗？"小男孩问。

"不在。就算在，他也救不了你妈妈。你最好尽快赶回去，因为很可能你还没到家她就死了。"

那孩子差点儿哭了出来，说："妈妈让我来，主要是为了我自己，不是为了她——你看我把自己伤成什么样了！"他伸出了他的手。

理查德打开绷带，检查了一下，说："两天之内就得截肢，然后你就什么都做不了了。你最好死掉算了。一个只有一只手的穷孤儿！唉，你会饿死的。"

听到这里，男孩放声大哭起来。虽然他不懂什么是截肢，可他隐约知道那是一件可怕的事情，而且也知道饿死是怎么一回事。

理查德接着说："你干什么了，把手伤成这样？我猜你肯定没干好事，你干的事足以把你送进州立监狱关你一辈子。"

"不，我没干坏事，"男孩说，"我只想生火，可是原木太大，我把一头搬上门口台阶的时候，另一头滑脱了，砸在了我的手上，就把手砸成你看到的这样了。"

"好吧，"理查德说，"我就知道是你不该干的事。穷人是不应该生火的，他们就该冻死，难道你不知道吗，小孩儿？"

"医生在开玩笑呢，小孩子，"萨莉说，语气温和，因为她是个女人，"你妈妈会好起来的，你的手也是。你们不该被冻死，别人也是。不过你最好走吧，给希尔顿医生留句话，让他一回来就去看看你妈妈。"听了这些话，小家伙破涕为笑，又忍不住抽泣，照她说的去做了。

他们继续往前走着，克莱维尔太太问："你为什么对那个可怜的小男孩说这些？"

"因为，"理查德说，"我的心中满是苦水，肯定会溢到什么地方。而且，这样想和这样说一样，都没好处。再说我也忍不住不那样想——也许你能做得更好一些。"

他的话被一阵脚步声打断了。一个老人从他们身边走过。他一把年纪了，身体虚弱，拄着一根藜杖，拼命向前走着。他以这个国家某些地方的人惯有的直率，跟这对儿年轻人打了声招呼。他看上去颇为慈祥，就仿佛他走过的路充满坎坷，而年轻人得需要鼓励和提醒才行。理查德脸上浮现出一丝难以言喻的讥讽。他说："如果我是你，灰头发老头，我会停下来搞些恶作剧。不过，也许这就是你的行当，我又跟着掺和什么？土都埋到脖子了，先生，你虚弱的身体怎能掌握得了命运？我还年轻，正是精力充沛的时候，人们是这样说，可我还是不是命运之魔的对手。"老人可能觉得这个年轻人有点儿不正常，同情地看了看他，便继续默然前行。

接下来的路上两人都没说话。到了家门口，理查德竭力做出一副自知会受到欢迎的样子，可是他的忧虑仍然难以掩饰。至于萨莉，当克莱维尔先生板着脸冷冷地跟她打了声招呼的时候，她的心中充满了疑虑，就连克莱维尔太太好心地打圆场，也没能驱散突然袭来的想家的感觉。每个人都尽量表现得自如一些，可是局促的感觉仍然难以消弭。第一个下午就这样别别扭扭地过去了。克莱维尔先生在埋头读着什么，或者假装在读。两个女人有一搭没一搭地聊着，也不过是表面文章，她们不友好的天性使她们难以体谅对方。理查德觉得找点儿活儿干能使自己感觉轻松点儿，再说也想避开父亲，于是便去砍柴了——以前他可从不愿干这活儿。直到下午茶的工夫他才回来，精疲力竭。由于从没在室外待这么长时间，他冻得浑身冰冷。

"这风刮得像是要下雪了，"克莱维尔先生走到窗前说，"你最好比平常早一点儿准备好下午茶，多莉，要不然医生和他太太就得摸黑走回家了。"

他是故意这样说，来羞辱他们的，因为他不知道他们是否要回家。他们也不知道，那天不知道，第二天还是不知道，第二天的第二天也还是不知道。不难想象，开头就如此不利，结局也不可能有多好。

这对儿年轻人不但帮不上什么忙，还不断惹来不便和麻烦。很快克莱维尔太太就不愿再充好人了，因为她再怎么努力也是白费。于是情形每况愈下。最终，年轻人和老人都烦透了彼此。一天早上，在一阵强烈的不满之后，萨莉戴上她的白色帽子，回了娘家。

22. 青年医生的生存之道

有一段时期，萨莉和她母亲住在一起，理查德和他的母亲住在一起，他们彼此不见面，只是偶尔捎个口信。这当然引发了左邻右舍的闲言碎语，这是克莱维尔夫人最为惧怕的事情。与此同时，女儿的降生瞬间强化了这对年轻夫妻的脆弱关系。

"你难道不认为，塞缪尔，"有一天早上克莱维尔夫人一边缝补着他的一件法兰绒衬衣一边说道，"难道你不认为老斑点牛已经过了壮年时期了吗？"

当我们对一件事不是特别感兴趣的时候，同意对方的观察结论会比表达完全不同的观点容易得多，于是，头也没有抬一下，克莱维尔先生简单地说道："我不太清楚，不过可能是这样的。"

沉默了几分钟后，克莱维尔夫人按照自己的思绪继续说道："你今天早上有没有注意到黑母马的表现？"

克莱维尔先生正埋头读一则关于范布伦的消息，没作回答。于是克莱维尔夫人继续说道："我从来没有看到过它表现得如此糟糕。戴维费了九牛二虎之力才让它动起来。最后总算动起来了，也全是汤姆出力拉套。看来我得瞧个好时机趁早把它卖了。你意下如何？"

"怎么回事？"克莱维尔先生说道，刚开始有点理解妻子跟他说的话。这当口看到她手里的活计，他补充道："多莉，我希望你缝的时候能够把从肘部到肩膀的那些线补好。我今天早上觉得有点犯风湿了。"

当然克莱维尔夫人觉得自己的方案不错，但要落实前，她尽量让她的想法得到充分领会。

"没用的，"克莱维尔先生说道，"那头斑点牛可比卖价值钱多了，至于那匹母马我还指望它帮我赶路呢。再说了，没有它，这农场我可没法维持下去。"

"为什么，塞缪尔？我看不出来对你而言怎么它就比别的牲口更有用，况且奥利弗想驯一匹小马，那将来这匹母马你就派不上什么用场了。"

"好吧，就算我忍心把它卖掉，那钱我也没什么用项。卖燕麦和干草的钱我就足够交税的了，再说我也舍不得打发我的牲畜。"

"我琢磨着要是理查德有点起色，能置办点家业，他和萨莉的关系会好起来。要是他们住在自己的房子里，再得到点支持，说不定会——谁知道呢？萨莉有张床、床头柜，还有六把椅子，如果我们再给他们补贴一点，他们会打理得很好。要是他们愿意尽力把日子过好，而我们没给任何支持的话，会是多么的遗憾啊。"

克莱维尔先生没有吭声，他露出使劲思索的样子。

"婴儿长得很不错，"克莱维尔夫人继续说道，与其说是对着克莱维尔先生说，还不如说替他说。"我昨天第一次去那里。我其实并不是很想去的，不过我正好路过，贝茨夫人正好在院子里，她一再坚持让我进去一下，我不好拒绝，你知道去那我不可能只待一小会儿，塞缪尔。我想如果这么做对他们有好处的话，也不会对我们有什么坏处，所以我就稍稍逗留了一会儿。"

这番道歉式的发言之后有一阵长长的停顿，似乎她丈夫也没想过要打破沉闷，给妻子一种不是很舒服的感觉。然而，不一会她就重新振作起来，把手放到补丁下面说："这样是不是又厚又暖和？他们想要你去，我告诉他们我会转告你，但是你有太多事情要做，我并不指望你会去，去了也帮不上什么忙。他们说要管宝宝叫多莉——一个很老式的名字了，我觉得他们不会喜欢的。"

"不妨叫她'傻蛋'可能会更好点。"克莱维尔先生说道。他的妻子听罢大笑说她也是这么想的，尽管她并不知道有什么好笑的，不过希望以某种方式让她的丈夫心情好一点，这么做多少起点作用，尽管看上去他似乎对这条讯息比对他妻子说的话更感兴趣。这次谈话后的一两周，有一天早上，克莱维尔先生拿着一对马蹄铁，把一条绳子系在奥利弗的小马驹的脖子上，准备出发前往苜蓿角。他走得很慢，因为这头小马不听话——一头长着乱鬃、长腿、长尾的栗色马，还没发育完全——克莱维尔先生使劲往后拉，一直把缰绳拉到了脖子边。

去铁匠家的路上要经过贝茨家，虽然他并没有转头朝那边看，还是透过窗户看到他的儿媳妇怀里抱着的宝宝。她看见他了，现在她的心对任何人都变得柔和起来，然后一种奇怪的、崭新的感觉油然而生，她叫住了他，请他进来一会看看小多莉。他犹豫了一小会儿，把小马驹系在门柱上，径直走进房间。又过了一会儿，他的孙女已经在他的怀里了。

一两个星期后，被奥利弗（他是一个顽固的政客，受他父亲的影响）唤作民主党人的栗色马，正经八百地在汤姆身边干活了，而黑母马和斑点牛已经不在克莱维尔先生家的家畜之列。理查德在老房子和村子之间购置了住所。他住的房子是一幢木质建筑，地方不大，然而给人感觉很体面很舒服的样子。正如贝茨夫人想的那样，地毯非常漂亮，窗帘很有品位，其他家具都很好，很实用。房子前面靠近门的地方装有一块写着"克莱维尔医生"的牌子，马厩里装满了理查德的新马驹所食用的干草和谷粒。他打算立刻开业。他想再学下去也没有什么用处，他知道的东西和希尔顿医生一样多，尽管他没有听过多少次讲演，也没有正规文凭，想要其他人相信他也不是一件容易的事情。然而，克莱维尔夫人和贝茨夫人提供了足以维持一个月消耗的一篮一篮的备品，这对年轻人开始在这个世上的独立生活。

理查德摇着摇篮，萨莉在做晚饭。当理查德给他的小马驹装上马鞍在附近溜达，装着很职业很全神贯注的样子的时候，又换成萨莉来摇摇篮。这样的事情持续了一段时间，但是到了月底，理查德的骑术还仅仅只是装样子而已。马厩里的干草很快就吃完了，储藏室里的面粉、肉、木材都需要补给，满怀希望和满意的事很快就变成了恐惧和焦虑。

理查德每天都来来回回于他父亲的家和他自己的家之间，拿回一篮篮的苹果或者土豆。每天玛莎和简都称呼他为克莱维尔医生，假装真诚地询问他病人的身体情况。有时问道："你想要多少？"他们通常会问几次，"价值一美元的东西或者少一点？"克莱维尔夫人会以一种斥责的方式说："行了，行了！"理查德则是因为觉得没面子保持沉默。

春去夏来，打理了一半的花园里长满了杂草，房间里生气的宝宝在摇篮里大哭，她那疲倦地、不耐烦地等待好时光到来的妈妈，变得对现状越来越不满，全然忘掉了她所享受的那些舒适时光，因为那种日子本身并不多。

有一天早晨（她一夜都没好好休息，照顾这个烦躁的小孩儿），起来的时候，她比平时更加疲倦、烦躁，没法准备早饭。灰暗的乌云笼罩着整个天空，没有丝毫气流吹动树叶，蜘蛛们在其中懒散地织着网，鸟儿发出无力的模糊的唧啾声，不是那种欢快的歌声，眼前雷声在遥远的地方轰鸣，发出沉重的隆隆声，暴雨快要来了。

萨莉说过她丈夫一两次，如果可能的话让他在下雨前砍一些木材来生火。但是他打着瞌睡，丝毫没有留意她说的话和提的建议。萨莉靠近了一点火炉，来来回回地摇晃着婴儿，悲观地、愠怒地看着窗外的暴雨。家里没有食物，没柴生火，也没有钱。彼此谁也再说不出善言、希冀与祝愿的话来维持他们心里很快将要消失殆尽的爱情。中午很快来临，天变得亮了点，雨几乎停了。

可怜的女子再也不能抑制她的悲伤和责备，再一次转向理查德，问他是否打算饿死她。

"那你想要我做什么？"他说，"在这么一个暴雨天出去祈求施舍？我没心情也没有希望——除了一个充满不满和责骂的老婆什么都没有。

　　'但愿我能死在你的前面！'"

她的眼泪流了下来，接着是更严厉的斥责，然后双方都说了些难听的话，再然后是闷闷不乐的沉默以及顽固的决定。快到日落的时候，怀里抱着宝宝，眼里满是泪水，萨莉冒着雨向娘家走去，留下理查德一个人在荒芜废弃的房子里——悲惨，十分的悲惨。

太阳下山了，雨一直下个不停，屋里屋外都是一片漆黑，理查德的心则是最漆黑的。他饿，尽管他几乎已经感觉不到饥饿了，却能觉得时间过得异常的慢，因为他烦透了自己，烦透了世界。整个一天他坐在那里双手抱胸，眼朝地面，几乎没有动过。最后他站了起来，不停地从房间这头踱到那头，开始一系列的沉思，有时候"如果我愿意的话我可能可以过得更好些"，一定以"如果我能的话我会做得更好"结尾。强烈的痛苦和喜悦的情感最终一定是使他感到精疲力竭，而年轻人心里的骚动最终屈服于绝望的平静。搜寻了几分钟后，他成功地找到了一支残留的牛油蜡烛，在烛光下，他阅读着令人伤心的查特顿的故事的悲惨结尾，但是他丝毫没有受到书中人物自杀后"有一个城里来的人来见他"的故事的鼓舞。他只是说死了比活着好，他的生命里似乎有一种邪恶的信号，只有来自墓地的树荫才能把它扫除；去死就等于把自己名字的回声留给这世界。于是漫漫长夜，他在黑暗和沉默中陷入苦苦沉思。

　　第二天早晨，憔悴、疲倦、饥肠辘辘，他回到父亲家，他母亲耐心地、亲切地听着他讲述老掉牙的故事：他的妻子残忍地抛弃了他，剥夺了他的孩子给他的安慰；事实上，从一开始她就是无情的，没远见的；这些年来她一直如此，她的所作所为可能最终让他心碎。他可怜兮兮、无助、绝望的样子让他的父亲也心软了，即使不给他安慰或者鼓励，起码克制住了责备的念头。理查德决定放弃他的职业，因为他既没有职业技能，又缺乏经营天赋。他决定回家来协助他兄弟打理农场。他的决定得到了赞同，于是民主党人和汤姆被套在了运货马车上，那些属于丈夫的物品和属于妻子的物品被分开。标牌拿了下来，尽管理查德小心地把它放在了他觉得既不会被自己又不会被别人看见的地方，但玛莎和简在玩那些孩子们所热衷的神秘搜寻时还是发现了它，有时把它钉在了他房间的门上，藏在附近的角落里等他回来，然后对他的惊讶和屈辱哈哈大笑。

　　理查德使劲干活，以此来证明自己还有用，但只几天工夫就故态复萌，又变得慵懒，万事不关心。有些时候他会坐在房间里，读他的那些老得不能再老的医学书，有时他会骑着他的小马驹在周围溜达，没有人知晓他为什么会这样，而且我猜他自己也不清楚。

　　与此同时，有谣言说贝茨先生要把他的房子卖了，搬到镇上去。谣言被贴在苜蓿角旅馆前面的告知所证实，通知也出现在了杂货店、墓地的篱笆上、克莱维尔先生家的门口，整个村子都有。

　　公告也出现在了一英里外惠特菲尔德执事家里，上面用打印的大写字母写道：贝茨先生家的房产将会于八月一日公开拍卖，包括以下财产：三头正处于产奶期的奶牛；一台搅乳器，大量的乳产品盛具以及一些家用陶器；两张来自于贝茨先生家自己养的鹅的鹅毛做的羽绒床，一个床头柜，一张早餐桌，六把椅子。此外还有两匹马、一台风选机、一把犁，各式各样的农用及家用器具，诸多杂品不便详陈。

据说贝茨夫人声称实在无法忍受与克莱维尔一家做邻里，于是，风选机、羽绒床、产奶的奶牛以及早餐桌最后只好草草处理了。贝茨一家人搬到了城里，开了一家供裁缝、小贩以及役童住的寄宿式公寓。萨莉主要负责接待客人，她母亲负责干活。孩子们从此被剥夺了他们早已习惯了的呼吸新鲜空气，进行自由、健康锻炼的权利；他们丢弃了简洁舒适的衣服，换上和别的孩子一样的穿着，贵得要命，式样时兴，却是既不耐穿又不舒服。他们的母亲觉得孩子们有了很大长进。结果就是，饱满的长着酒窝的两颊，还有红润的双臂、平滑的头发消失了，取而代之的是更加白皙纤细的肤色，宽大白色的灯笼裤，垂在背后的长长的辫子，故意在辫子尾部装饰上去的缎带。至于那些男孩，我无法描述那些纽扣、流苏以及装饰在他们身上的闪闪发亮的皮带。衣服似乎太紧身，样子也有点怪，他们也绝不会有以前穿着宽松的裤子在干草地里那样自在的感觉。城里的空气，还有疏忽的母亲都让婴儿不适应，任由她躺在摇椅的垫子上哭闹不停，要不就交给小保姆。保姆是个小姑娘，又小又弱，根本抱不动她。要么让别人抱来抱去，两码长的裙子拖到地上。多莉的名字没人叫了，改成了多拉。祸不单行，夏天还没过去，她瘦弱的双臂交叠，两脚摆直，送进了墓地。可怜的孩子，名字从未登记过，连墓碑上都没写名字。几许真诚的泪水，一段日子的真空，之后孩子裙边的白蕾丝重又引发了年轻母亲的悲伤。愿上天赐予这不为人知的小女孩以和平，天真地入睡，醒来时躺在救世主的怀抱，不需要惩罚肉体，洁净灵魂了。地狱之火不会降临给那些曾经听过这支动听的曲子的人——"让小孩子到我这里来，不要禁止他们[①]"她的倒霉鬼父亲永远不知道在日落的云彩下面，被人忽略的地下，有着

[①] 出自《新约圣经》马太福音19章14行。

小女孩的坟墓,她母亲也没有在上面种任何花草。

有时候我会惊讶于那些因为哀痛于孩子死亡而无法自拔的母亲们,她们忘记了孩子们因此得到了永恒的青春,她们忘掉了世界上到处充满着悲伤。自从撒旦挥舞着闪闪发亮的翅膀向下飞到地狱,宇宙中到处充斥着来自地狱回声的呻吟声。

迟早我们都会厌倦人世中的一切,垂涎于来自墓地的滴血的双脚以及破碎的心灵所带来的安慰,因为人生无不是善恶交错的。月桂树是靠着凋零痛苦的枝条而缠绕起来的,在漫卷了世世代代的火焰之下有着最急切的期盼的灰烬。绝望的浪涛不断冲击着希望的大本营,直到我们欣喜地拥抱我们周围的黑暗,住到下面的小房子里,至少在那里可以得到安息。没有让人烦心的梦打扰睡眠,不需要工作或等待,再也没什么让力量越来越弱的我们去面对我们害怕的厄运。白天逝去,又一次降临,日复一日,进入我们眼睑的不再是让人不舒服的光线。呜咽的春雨用花朵装点我们的墓头,秋天干枯的树叶飘落而下,冬天的白雪洒落在坟丘上面,如同盖住新逝者身上的床单,然而对于躺在里面的苍白的死者而言这一切毫无分别,因为坟墓里不用工作,不用心计,不用智慧,不用知识。对我来说,很多我热爱的人离开了我再也没有回来。孩提时代的金色卷发,长大以后黑色的、浓重的发辫以及年老时的细长银丝,都藏在寿衣褶皱里面再也看不到了。我不愿意唤醒他们任何一个,令其重新挑起生活的重担。如果他们还在的话,我的弱点或许会死死缠住他们的长处,我迟缓的脚步也会阻止他们实现雄心抱负,不会让他们为回报而奋斗。

23. 对比鲜明的访客

周六晚上了!一周的事务终于完成时谁会不感到欢欣鼓舞?尽管处理这些事务的过程中可能并未感到特别的悲伤或者焦虑。可以暂时放下心头的牵挂,轻松一下,自由地呼吸,不必再像平时那样瞻前顾后,患得患失。在城里,你可能会明显地知道一周的结束和安息日的到来。但在乡下,你必须用心感受。牛群被完全放开,可以在山上吃一整天的草;犁,或者任何农活,都会被搁置一边;宁静的气氛弥漫在整个村庄,不会被樵夫的斧子声或是农夫的歌声打破;村头肃穆的钟声响起,召唤大家来做礼拜。没有钟声齐鸣,没有交错的尖塔，没有华丽的圣坛，没有繁复的仪式，也没有花钱请来的唱诗班，昏暗的长廊上自然也不会响起训练有素的颤音——

"似乎上帝的耳朵也会被管风琴奏出的

些微带有稚气的赞美之音征服。"①

那些鸟儿的歌唱似乎不那么欢乐，它们的歌声如圣歌般从林中穿过。空中的风神预言般警示着灵魂，直至太阳在紫色的霞光中落下，苍白清冷的群星升上了碧空。

有时，乡下的安息日会变成出门访友的日子，但这并非对神的亵渎，因为通常这样做的只有那些工作日需要全力以赴投入工作的人，以及那些受到好友或兄弟的款待之后又与之分享了精神盛宴的人。没有装腔作势的炫耀，也没有任何消遣所需的忙乱嘈杂，但是客人们都会心甘情愿地伸出援手，尽可能地减少给主人带来的麻烦。女人们自然会睡在"精致考究而且用薰衣草熏过的"备用床上，而且下楼前会把床单铺平，房间收拾得井然有序，她们还会提供更多的帮助，经常是铺铺桌布，帮忙做一做只要稍加提示即可轻松完成的早餐，例如，是用白色手柄还是牛角手柄的刀叉，素白瓷器还是镀金瓷器，咖啡壶是用锡壶还是银白色合金的壶。这时，客人对于那些要用的白色手柄刀叉、镀金瓷器、银白色咖啡壶会非常熟悉。同时，男人们会去查看牛栏、工棚，还有谷仓，并根据自己看到的提出一些自家或是邻居应该如何改进的方法，同时用燕麦喂着马匹，或者把干草搬到羊群那里，或者去挤奶，"仅仅是因为他们宁愿做点事情而不是无所事事"，并且既不妨碍，也不打乱正常的秩序。要是有人知道约翰叔叔一家或是玛丽姑妈一家，或是别的什么人家要登门拜访，所有的准备工作都会在周六进行：喝住那些喜欢没头没脑地跑到屋子里来的小鸡；孩子们会非常勤快地搜遍干草堆、麦秸垛，有时候甚至冒险去草丛里摸一摸，看看母鸡有没有把蛋下在了鸡窝外面；做洗洗擦擦时会比平时更加卖力；要烤一个重磅蛋糕和一个布丁；日落时分全家人都会穿上节日盛装，面带微笑地等待重头戏上演，即"访问团"的到来。这样一次重大事件即将发生在克莱维尔先生家。一周的工作已经全部完成。大卫和奥利弗正训练他们的小马民主党人和鲁本学会稀奇古怪的戏法。克莱维尔先生读着

---

① 此处引用的是 John Greenleaf Whittier 的诗"Worship"。有改动。

《共和国》上的一篇政论文，而多莉在用理查德的小刀卷她的帽檐。玛莎和简似乎冷得发抖，但还是坐在大门口，急切地想要最先看到彼得叔叔一家人的到来。理查德漠不关心地，或者是感动地坐在自己的房间里，上上下下地拉着小提琴。尽管如此，彼得叔叔的来访仍将开启他生命中一个崭新的时代。

"哦，妈妈，妈妈，快来看这是不是他们，刚刚从山那边过来。"两个女孩子同时叫起来。克莱维尔太太一边起身从窗户里向外望，一边说："要是彼得叔叔的话，我们应该会先看到他的新马。不过，塞缪尔，无论如何你是不是最好出去把大门打开？"

"叫理查德去吧。"他答道。但是孩子们又冲了出去，说他们能开，因为他们以为这样的话来的人就会是彼得叔叔了。所以克莱维尔太太就说她觉得她们做的也不会比别人差，于是理查德就可以继续摆弄他的小提琴了。孩子们焦急地，甚至浑身颤抖地盯着。不久，白色车顶、绿色车身的小马车就出现在视线中了，彼得叔叔跟简姨妈并排坐在车上。马车很快就在跟前停了下来，两人笑着对孩子们点头，快步走在小石子路上，车轮的咯嗒咯嗒声向所有人宣布他们到了。克莱维尔太太戴着帽檐刚刚卷过的帽子，身穿熨烫平整的长裙，一只手拿着正在缝补的一只袜子——她从来不会闲着——走上前来表示欢迎，身旁跟着塞缪尔，他一步就跨了过来，一手拿着打开的《共和国》，一手拿着当做礼物的一把温莎椅。极为热情的握手伴随着对家中一切的友好问候，从孩子们到雇来的帮工比利，就连上了年纪的守门犬也没有落下。接下来就开始拆开各色各样的小礼物，装在纸盒里的、罐子里的、篮子里的——因为简姨妈从来不会空着手来——她总有些料定多莉会喜欢得不得了的东西：一些她正在吃的果酱，或者桃脯，这些生病的时候可是美味，或是她觉得孩子们可能会因为是简姨妈烤的而喜欢的刚刚出炉的长条面包，虽然多莉烤的要好吃得多得多。

简姨妈是个好女人，善良的言辞和行动就像泉水那样从她的心中自然地倾泻而出。她丝毫不懂得艺术与高雅社会的谄媚，对那些残酷无情、表里不一的欺骗行为一无所知，但是讨人喜欢的性情好过对规矩传统的顺从。简姨妈生活圈子里的每个人都非常愉快。她并不是我的简姨妈，正如戴尔叔叔不是我的戴尔叔叔一样，我们的确不那么亲近。如果她还在世，也一定已经饱经岁月的风霜，因为我猜从我记得她的时候她就已经四十岁了，那可是很久以前了。彼得叔叔现在安息在他以前经常干完活儿休息的那棵枫树的树荫下。他比妻子年长很多，甚至在婚礼上他的头发已经是白的了，但是她的情趣并未给他带来过什么不快，因为

"在清凉幽静的生命峡谷中，

他平凡地度过了自己的一生。"①

因此当生命的尽头到来时，他愉快地接受了。

"詹妮，保住家产，"他交代，"比利去照看农场：他知道我是怎么干的。我不喜欢用什么新式的犁或者耙。每三个月去看看克莱维尔一家，就像我还在你身边一样。不要难过，詹妮，现在吻我一下，让我睡去吧。"就这样，詹妮抚平他额前的灰白发丝，吻了他，一如二十年前炽热，他脸上浮起的笑容就那样永远留在了那里。但是我要讲的不是令人忧伤的生命的结束，甚至也不是之前他在世的那些岁月，我所要讲的只是影响了理查德命运的这一次到访。

太阳已经下山了，灯点起来了，餐桌也已经摆好。因为马厩要让给彼得叔叔的几匹马，民主党人跟鲁本就被赶到果园里去遛了，小提琴也静了下来。公路上的驿车引起了他们的注意，马车突然停下，有说话的声音，然后马车继续前行。很快门上响起了重重的敲门声，随着克莱维尔先生清楚的"进来"，走进来一位个头矮小、身材偏胖的妇人，帽子上垂下来的羽毛和身上裹着的皮草让人很难认出来是贝茨太太。克莱维尔先生冷淡又不失礼貌地问候了她，理查德则目瞪口呆，克莱维尔太太努力想要表现得热情，但显得神色不宁，紧张不安。

她应主人之请，摘下了帽子，脱掉了大衣，同时称自己是因为一件非常紧急的小事而来。"你们看，"她在简姨妈旁边坐下，接着说，"你们的理查德·克莱维尔娶的是我的女儿。她成为了他的好妻子，如果这世上有哪个女人能够成为一名好妻子的话。我这么说不是因为我是她的母亲，她是我的女儿，而是因为就算我不是她的母亲，她也不是我的女儿，我还是知道她是一个好妻子，就像我现在知道她是一个好妻子一样，而我的女儿被迫弃家而去全是因为他自己的邪恶本性。我还没有自负到认为自己的女儿是个天使，但是我

---

① 引自托马斯·格雷的一首挽诗，有改动。

的确认为就是天使也无法忍受他，正如我的女儿无法忍受他一样。一位天使领教了他的邪恶本性也会弃他而去的，就像我的女儿在目睹了他的邪恶本性之后不得不弃他而去。"克莱维尔感叹"傻瓜的嘴巴不会口干"，然后提出，不管她有什么事情，跟他说就是了。要不是克莱维尔先生打断她，真不知道她还要讲多长时间。

　　理查德已经躲开了，后面跟着的彼得叔叔对他念了《圣经》中一句绝妙的箴言：“永不放弃。”起初他说这根本没用，他的运气总是很糟，就算别人能应付得更好，他也希望如此，但他做不到。不过，慢慢地，他也一点一点地认可，开始鼓起勇气，心中升起了希望。

　　"我忘了，"贝茨太太对着克莱维尔先生说，"你是主人。我猜你希望我跪下来，向你请求能否允许我说句话。但是我可以告诉你，塞缪尔·克莱维尔，要是跪下来讨好你那就不是我寡妇贝茨了，绝不！寡妇贝茨还有那么多勇气，不像你，塞缪尔·克莱维尔，下跪，也不会讨好你，塞缪尔·克莱维尔——寡妇贝茨面对面地这样告诉你，塞缪尔·克莱维尔。"对，我们的老朋友现在是个寡妇。可怜的贝茨先生的小农场被卖掉以后他就失业了。诱惑来了，他屈服了。从前坚强独立的农夫退化成了一个软弱愚蠢的酒鬼，被自己的妻子和孩子赶出了家门，成了一个悲惨可怜无家可归的苦命人，不久就死了。

　　"能不能先喝点茶，吃几口饭，然后再谈事情？"克莱维尔太太问道。

　　但是贝茨太太自觉自己的寡居身份赋予了她某种尊严，并且非常喜欢提及她孤独无助的生活，因此她回答说寡妇贝茨宁愿不吃饭也要把要讲的话讲完，并且她孤身一人，若非如此，她绝不会对自己的敌人心存感激的。

　　"那就来吃饭吧，像一位女士那样，"克莱维尔先生说，"您从城里赶来，一定很饿了。我不会装成是您的朋友，但我也并非您的敌人。既然您在我的家里，就欢迎您来用餐，尽管我非常希望这是您最后一次来访。"

　　贝茨太太转了转她的黑色软帽，以更好地展示她帽子上红色的人造花，然后说她也希望这是最后一次登门拜访。她说这次来是要告诉克莱维尔先生一些对他非常有利的事情的，她不愿做对别人不利的事。但是当一个独身的寡妇牺牲自己的利益来为他做好事的时候，如果这个人没有接受好意的本事，她不知道自己是不是一定要牺牲自己的利益，强迫他接受自己的好意。

克莱维尔先生说如果她为了自己已经做出了这种牺牲，那么他感到很抱歉。但是如果她有任何对双方都有利的建议的话，他将洗耳恭听。

"你应该还记得我们那头黑色的奶牛吧？"贝茨太太说，并且重新坐了下来。

"它大部分时间都是在我的牧场里，所以我有理由记得。"

"你应该还有别的理由吧？"

"那就是那是一头又丑又老的牛，没人会不记得，还有它能像我一样把栅栏放下来。"

"是你像它——反正大家是这样说的。"

"那是什么话？我会把你的牛拉到我的牧场里？"

"众口不一——总有人说些你不爱听的话。"

克莱维尔先生的脸上闪着怒火，他说——

"直截了当地说重点，我不明白你的意思。"

"我说的就是重点——你可吓不住寡妇贝茨。"

"那你想说什么就说吧。"

"我已经尽可能地说清楚了，如果一个有钱人怨恨一个穷人，他就可能会把这个穷人的奶牛拉到自己的牧场里去，让它一直饿死，仅仅因为他是一个法律也管不了的有钱人，怨恨一个只是说了句话就被法律抓起来绞死的穷人。"

"啊，啊，我明白了，"克莱维尔先生说，她的一番话可笑得让他气不起来，"但是如果有人相信了您话里的意思，我看不出这是什么对我有利的事情。"

"我要是想把这个说出去，那就是对你不利了；如果我不说，那就是对你有利了。但是你觉得我会平白无故地就守口如瓶吗？"

"我只是个孤苦伶仃的可怜寡妇，而且我可能也不会像一位从书本上学习如何经营的律师经营自己生意那样经营我的生意。但是因为一件更重要的事情，我来了，以最快的速度，因为那头黑色的奶牛已经死了。可怜的家伙，不管它是用角挑开栅栏进到了你的牧场，还是它没有用角挑开栅栏进到了你的牧场，现在没什么区别了。鉴于它是以某种方式进到了你的牧场,并且因为这个原因死了,让我们的钱包里损失了将近二十美元。但是,正如我说的,那都无关紧要。"

"那是什么?"克莱维尔先生问。

"哦,"贝茨太太犹豫了片刻,说,"我的一个房客是位律师,很懂生意,也知道该怎么处理。他是从山的东边的一个城市来的,他说我女儿要离婚是易如反掌,他说的;他还说,他说这个案子一点儿也不费事,这是他的原话。"

"好吧。"克莱维尔先生说。贝茨太太接着说:"那位律师还说,他说要是这件事曝了光,他说,你会很丢面子。他还说,他说要是他自己,他说,他宁愿支付一千美元,他说,也不愿这件事曝光,他说。所以我就想来告诉你他的话,他说,因为他说他宁愿支付一千美元,他说,也不愿事情曝光。"

我不会过多地赘述这件贝茨太太拼命地在一点一点解释的重要事情。总之就是她的计划失败了,而且她怒气冲天地离开了那座房子,边走边说她"现在,完全相信,那头黑色的奶牛是得到了某种协助才进到了牧场里,而且那位律师说,他说离婚的过程一点儿也不难,他说的"。

尽管理查德躲在听不到以上谈话的地方,他也知道谈话的内容,并且对于简姨妈竟然听到了一切感到非常的丢脸。他恨不得从这世上消失。尽管叫了他一两次来吃晚餐,他还是磨磨蹭蹭不肯来,而是待在门廊上,装作是在观察天空中快速掠过的浮云,月亮和星星时而被云层遮住,时而又把所有的光辉洒向大地。

一股突如其来的悲伤之情突然掠过他的心头,将他本性中的冷漠和自私一扫而空,他渴望能够得到一个机会来做件好事或是说些善意的话语,以证明他并没有完全迷失。卡罗靠近他,用自己毛茸茸的身体蹭着他。"可怜的家伙!"理查德说,"快进来我给你拿点吃的。"

"狂风刮得像在下大雪,是吗?"简姨妈对理查德说,似乎对他的想法跟感受毫无知觉,"不过我们等你吃晚饭呢,所以别看那些云了。"

"是吗?"理查德说,"我不知道晚饭已经好了。"他牵上卡罗的颈圈,跟在简姨妈后面进了屋子。他一只手里拿着当晚餐的干面包,另一只手喂着狗。餐桌上非常丰盛，但是他没有胃口。例行公事后他回到了自己的房间里，从满是灰尘的橱柜里取出了那个老旧的棕色刚毛箱子。他换了一两根大头钉，又刷了刷箱子的表面，让它看起来尽可能的体面些，把克莱维尔医生的牌子用一张《共和国》仔细包起来，放在箱子的最下面。上面是小提琴，再上面是他衣柜里的那些衣物。箱子锁好后，他在窗边坐下，望着云层，思索着将来，直到天明。

24. 崭新的开端

安息日的夜晚四处寂静无声。当太阳收起最后一丝光芒，黄昏张开黑糊糊的翅膀，天上繁星点点时，年轻男女们都穿过碧绿的田地去乡下的礼拜堂听颂歌去了。

轰隆隆的车轮穿过长满草的小路，留下了深深的车辙，又在平坦的草地上顺利前行，几乎没有打破周围的寂静。牛群趴在篱笆下静静地反刍，光滑的脊背由于霜冻显得灰白，它们本能地时不时望望天，青烟从长满青苔的坡顶房舍上袅袅升起，狭窄老式的窗户上透出点点迎候的烛光，一根小小的蜡烛的烛光照得可真远啊！彼得叔叔和简姨妈马上就到家了，他们做客的感觉还不错，但是到家的感觉才是最愉快的。

可怜的理查德·克莱维尔，没人欢迎他来。当他坐在装满他所有家当的大箱子上时，他把脸别过去不看他的亲戚。他很难过，因为他打算试试看自己还有没有能力和男子汉气魄，尽管他自己清楚这两样他一样也没有了，至少他坚信自己的确很倒霉。

因为他对自己的处境非常恼怒，所以他会说"如果事情是这样或那样，情况可能就会不同了"等等。他认为，环境根本不听他的，上天已经决定了他的命运，所以他无助地坐在那里，打算听之任之了。我们自己是多么可悲的狡辩的人啊，我们的判断总会向着有利于我们的方面倾斜。在别人是罪过，在我们就是特权和机会。如果我们愿意，约束别人的神圣条规我们自己经常破坏，因为我们自己对自己保留着宽恕，却不让别人得到哪怕一点点的公正，所以我们有罪孽，在我们的一生做过很多坏事，留下很多悲伤和懊悔，即使到将死之时也不能停止。主啊，如果我们曾经使永恒之光有少许暗淡，请宽恕我们吧！面对人生所有的考验，在人性的弱点和诱惑下，还能提高精神修养是多么困难啊!

理查德很难过。我们不断地问自己：我们能否把命运从万能的神那里夺来放在自己手中呢？我们能让环境服从我们的意愿吗？我们能成为另外一个人吗？或者接受本能盲目的摆弄？有一个声音微弱而坚定，会在我们的内心责怪我们，比我们毫无意义的高调要高尚得多。会犯错的游手好闲的人啊，远离那些诱惑，工作吧，勤恳热情地工作吧，做你力所能及和应该做的工作，那么邪恶就会远去。计划再好，脑子再聪明，不干活是什么也做不好的。如果你遇到一块大石头，不能炸掉，不能打碎，不能从地下挖，不能从上面爬，也不能绕开走，那你就学习愚公移山吧，你会一点点地前进，每一步都会给下一步带来新的动力，直到你成功为止，即使"岁月染白眉毛"也不在乎。

经过了一段不长的旅行，马车停在一个红色的大门前，理查德更难过了。他必须不再想自己的心事，他必须面对一些新面孔，还要对别人的友善表达谢意。这一切让他很痛苦，他没有与自己的堂兄妹约瑟夫和汉娜说话，也没有听简姨妈绘声绘色地讲塞缪尔·克莱维尔叔叔的故事。她一边讲故事一边还忙着准备茶，挨个换黄油盘子，按原来的样子重新安排碗碟和调味汁的位置。理查德偷偷溜出屋子，独自坐在空场上，尽管外面非常寒冷而且不舒服。食槽、谷仓和干草堆的样子与家里的样子不同，大镰刀、小镰刀和锯扔在广场的一边很不合适。他爸爸都是把这些东西放在马棚的一个小房间里，彼得叔叔似乎还不够文雅。从广场尽头向南，能看见差不多离此有半英里远的迈德福德的小村落。一排排白色的房子掩映在绿树间，发出闪闪烁烁的光，一两个塔尖直插云霄，在如泻的月光下分外清楚。

那里有他努力的新天地。结果会怎样？他很久没有心思做任何事了，但是那个地方引起了他的兴趣，他希望现在已经是早晨了，他可以工作了，尽管除了在大门口的邮箱上钉上"克莱维尔医生"的牌子外他无事可做，因为从大路到彼得叔叔家有1/4英里，所以牌子必须挂在对着大路的门口。往北，是一片厚密的小树林，林子边还有些大大小小的空地和一些被烧得黑糊糊的残木，时不时还能看见一棵树，半数枝杈被旁边倒下来的树木折断压碎，映着冷冷的月光，在寒风中瑟瑟发抖。

在开阔地的中央有一个小木屋，烛光透过小小的正方形窗户显得很明亮，周围没有其他房子，理查德奇怪什么人会住在那里。他们之间只隔了一块小草地和一块空地。他想，可能是一户贫穷的移民或修路工。正在他这样想时，门开了，一个女性的身影出现在眼前，尽管他看得不是太清楚，但否定了他刚刚的想法。她双手环抱胸前，在那里站了一会儿——也许是心情好，也许在等什么人，理查德无法判断。理查德有点想穿过那片草地，看得清楚点，这时简姨妈来到门口，四处张望，大声说道："这孩子到底去哪儿了？"当她看到理查德时，说道："进来，你想冻死啊。"理查德进到屋内，饭吃得津津有味，过去一个月他都没讲过这么多话，也许他自己并不知道为什么会这样，很可能是不知道的。但是如果他刚刚没有看见月光下的那个女人，他心里就不会有这么激动的感觉。他一度想问问那房子的事，但是不知道为什么又犹豫了。最后，他决定侧面打听打听关于那个房子的事，于是他问道："你们北面的那个小树林挺浓密的。"

"是呀，"简姨妈说，然后又说起几天前邻居有个小孩儿丢了，半个村子的人都帮忙找。对此，理查德很好奇，他补充说："孩子在那里走丢应该不会找很久呀？我看见有几块空地直通小树林。"但是他像惯常一样又转移话题了，继续说如果他没弄错，林子里有个房子。简姨妈说他说的的确没错，那里是有座房子。

"看上去那房子荒废了。有人住在那儿吗？"理查德问。

简姨妈说没人住在那里，她特别强调"人"这个字，听到这里，年轻人们相视一笑。

"你喜欢月光下的村子吗？"彼得叔叔问。理查德的好奇心那晚还是没有得到满足。

他的房间在房子的最北边，睡觉前他拉下窗帘看着四周。烛光依然明亮，他看见下面的烟囱里火花喷溅，忽明忽闪，说明这火有人在照看。他睡着了，心里想着那个女人：她是老还是年轻？漂亮还是难看？当然结论是，那个女人既不老又不普通。

第二天早饭后，他说他发现北面的草地边有棵树，那棵树需要修剪，而同时他很乐意做这件事。

"还没到修剪树的时候。"彼得叔叔说。但是理查德坚持季节不是问题，事实上，他说现在正是好时候。几分钟后他穿越了那片草地，敏捷地修剪树枝，眼睛时不时瞄向那座神秘的房子。那房子门前全是玫瑰和紫丁花，墙上布满常春藤，窗上开满茉莉花。院子很破败，但没有黑糊糊的残木，有些树，那房子上面长着葡萄藤。蛇麻草、牵牛花，夏天就会变成碧绿的美景。现在，由于昨晚的雪，树上一片雪白。窗户的窗帘拉上了，除了烟以外，没有住人的痕迹，烟萦绕在屋顶，然后飘向长长的蓝色的山脊。

理查德在那里修剪树枝修了很长时间，但最后活还是干完了。看来他的计谋没有结果，因为他看到的只是增强了他的好奇心。他穿过湿漉漉的草地回了家，当听到彼得叔叔说"我看这树也没有更好看；你的脚湿了，手冰冷；更糟糕的是，你没看见村子里最漂亮的姑娘"时，理查德既气愤又失望。

理查德说他倒不在乎什么漂亮姑娘，然后闷闷不乐地坐在炉火边，全神贯注地看报纸。

一会儿，简姨妈来看她放在房子角落的陶坛子里的酵母，上面盖着桌布，结果酵母没有发起来，她就用一把铁勺子拍打起来，边拍边说："理查德，你昨晚问过林边的那座房子是吧？"

理查德说了个"是"，并没有抬头。她接着说道——

"住在那儿的那个年轻女人今天早晨来过了，就在你刚出门的时候她就来了。"

"啊。"理查德说道，因为他太生气了，所以说不出什么别的了。

"来看看我如何发酵母。"简姨妈大声说道，"我做的活很不错。我和凯蒂有很多话说。"

理查德想知道那个来访者的情况，例如她是叫凯蒂吗？她为什么一个人住？尽管他嘴上没问，心里却很想问。

"来，理查德，"彼得叔叔一边这样说，一边戴上他的连指手套，"我要去迈德福德。你不和我一块去吗？你知道，这个生意刚开始，我们顺便还可以把门牌钉好。"

但是理查德说他不想去，而且一整天闷闷不乐。

简姨妈一天都忙着干自己的活，似乎所有的活计都很顺利，除了酵母发得并不好，然而，她说她认为这样的话，炸面圈会更好吃。晚上炸面圈时，她依然确信自己的判断，她在一个蓝色的小盘子里放了两三个，让理查德尝尝，并且问他是否也认为这样更好吃。理查德也说味道真的好极了——值得这么长时间的等待。然后他感慨地说："有些人真有福气啊！"

"可不，"简姨妈说道，"有福气比有钱都好。"她又给了理查德一块蛋糕，告诉他拿着它暖和手，让他乖乖地去把那个门牌安好，也许很快这块"克莱维尔医生"的牌子就用得到了。没办法拒绝这一善意的要求，理查德一手拿着蛋糕，一手拿着门牌出去了。当他把门牌钉在门口的邮箱后，往一边踱了几步，吹起口哨，略带几分骄傲地看着门牌，好像看着自己的职业徽章。正当他看得认真时，一阵轻微的踏雪声引起了他的主意，他抬头一看，面前是一个很年轻也似乎很美丽的姑娘，她用头巾和披肩把自己围得很严实，所以他也不能确定她的长相。她一只手拿着一个小篮子，另一只手拿着两三本书。"一个学校的女学生，"理查德想，"我要看看她去哪间房子。"然后狠狠地敲了一下那个无辜的牌子，得意地看着自己的名字，心里想的是她是否看见他了，然后他斜倚在门上看着她的一举一动，目光定在那个有绿色百叶窗的房子前，心想那应该是她的家，她肯定不会住得太远，应该不会错。那些房子在路的东边，远离大路，排列在小树林的西边，周围有空地和小木屋，差不多在彼得叔叔家对面。一所、两所、三所，那个姑娘走过了好几所房子。现在理查德在想：这已经是我今天第二次看走眼了。只见那个姑娘推开树林边的门，穿过林地，向那个神秘的小木屋走去。他和她走在平行线上，沉思着她是否就是那个独居的凯蒂。他也往家的方向走去，但并没有忘记留意她是否停在那个小木屋门前，结果果然如此。他感到很快乐，甚至是得意洋洋。他已经看到了那个昨夜引起他好奇心的人，并且发现她完全就是自己心里想象的样子。他非常高兴地进了家门，在他拿起火堆上烧开的茶壶时，他说道："简姨妈，我已经钉好了门牌，而且我还看见凯蒂了。"

"是吗！"简姨妈边忙着泡茶，边问道，"你怎么认识凯蒂·艾伦的？"

"凯蒂·艾伦——很好听——是她的名字？"

"是住在小木屋的那个女人的名字，如果你看见的果真是她的话。但是，"简姨妈接着说，"她不是那么年轻了。"

最后这句话让理查德不怎么高兴，他回答说他认为她并不老，应该不过四十岁。"但是，"他接着说，"见鬼，她为什么一个人住？"

"说来话长，我要去挤奶了。"然后简姨妈拿起她的摇篮毯包紧了自己，出去了。小伙子待在火堆边，听着茶壶的咕噜声，陷入了沉思。他纳闷自己好像已经不像原来那么孤单和想家了。他认为这一切都是因为在简姨妈家；远处的村落很漂亮，小树林也很漂亮。他无论如何也不愿意离开这一切。这里宛如一幅美丽的画卷。

门口有动静：简姨妈这么快就回来了？很大一声的敲门声，像是用棍子敲的。理查德开开门，门口是个像机械工或体力劳动者的人，问克莱维尔医生在不在。理查德说他就是，心里油然升起一股职业的自豪感。陌生者说："我想请您去看看我的夫人，她牙疼得受不了。"他把手伸到嘴里，指着某颗牙给医生看，并且竭力告诉医生他们所采取的那些没有用的办法，例如抹芥末膏，还有吃醋泡的啤酒花，但是现在一切都白费，五分钟前，他夫人决定把牙拔掉。

丝毫没有流连温暖的炉火和晚餐，理查德出了门。他见到的这个病人是个脸色苍白有点紧张的女人，看上去就像她丈夫说的疼得受不了了。但是，她仍然坚持说宁可掉脑袋也不愿意医生碰她的牙，而且反复问拔牙会不会很疼。

"会有点疼，"理查德说，"拔牙不可能一点不疼，但是没有一个病人抱怨过我的技术。夫人，让我看看您的牙。"

由于心里有点底了，也由于害怕医生，那个女人张开了嘴。理查德迅速拿出工具把那颗坏牙拔了出来，当理查德把拔出来的牙给那个女人看时说："您看，拔牙不是那么可怕的事情，对吧，夫人？"

"如果把医生请来而你又不愿意拔牙，那你该多遗憾呀？"她丈夫说道。他轻拍着她的脸颊，说她是个小懦夫。

理查德猜他们结婚不会很久，所以他问道："你们在这里住很久了吗？"

"七年五个月零两天三个小时，对吧，夫人？"

"我确信我的确不知道。"女人说，脸微微发红。

"你当然知道，我们来的那天你在牧师面前发过誓的！"

"别说了！"那个女人说，"你怎么这么怪。"

"是吗？"她丈夫说，"让我看看那颗牙吧？"

理查德赶忙询问村里还有没有其他病人。

"当然了，医生，"那个年轻人说，"很多呢。她身体不好，"是说他的夫人。"自从我们到这里后，她就没有一天好的。"轻拍着他夫人的梳子，他接着说道："让这个新来的医生治你的病好吗？我想请他这么做，你看呢？"

因为理查德有本事那么神奇地拔了牙，最后他们都同意让他第二天早晨来继续他的专业治疗，直到那个女人康复——理查德表示很有自信可以让她恢复健康。

正如谚语所言：新笤帚扫得干净。这就是个好例子。一个可怜的女人病了七年却没有得到任何治疗，主要是由于她害怕以前住在村子里的医生。但是现在来了一个新医生，没人知道他的技术。她把这个医生是如何熟练地给她拔了牙的事告诉了所有邻居，还拍胸脯说，这世界上只有克莱维尔医生能治好她的病。

"不知道是不是真这么有本事！"一个人对另一个人说。

后来光顾理查德的人越来越多，好运道终于来了。且慢，晨曦的天空中仍有灾星高悬。

25．女教师

善恶之争在生活中永远不会消失，在俗世这"无家可归的荒漠"上，在目睹了恶行的奴役后，我们常常感到如果我们在这俗世消失，那该多好啊！但是在这可怕的阴影后是那神秘的死亡国度。死后的苦难可能比俗世的痛苦还要更严重。就这样，我们固守黑暗，向往光明，战战兢兢地活在俗世上，深怕拔出那些给我们稍许遮挡的荆棘，以免再也没有玫瑰花在那里开放。肉体的爱抑制了我们的祈祷。现实的影响深深刻在了我们的灵魂上。至于未来，"它飘游在无尽的雾霭之廊中，越远越模糊不清"。思想正确，行为坚定——这是多么不容易啊，甚至忠于自己的信念也往往不易——

　　　　"然而我们认为善良的行为
　　　　最终却变成邪恶的举动，
　　　　自然的悲苦，意念的罪孽，
　　　　疑虑的缺陷，血污的耻辱。"[①]

雪花悄悄洒落在屋顶，慢慢地屋檐和山墙都挂满了雪。人们只能看见石头烟囱上露出一点点的黑色。门前的地上没有植被，风也异常的繁忙，因为奇异的弧线、奇特的山峦和大大小小光秃秃的地

[①] 引自英国维多利亚时代诗人 Alred Tennyson（1809—1892）的"Oh Yet We Trust"。

面都能说明这一点。小兔子穿过这片白茫茫的原野，出没于林边，寻找可以吃的东西或者成为追踪它们到此的其他大动物的食物。玫瑰蔓垂到地上，树上的枝干挂满了白雪，偶尔，强风刮过，吹落一些积雪，让那枝干重新昂起头来。空地上的断株犹如美丽的雕刻，很多残株则如同厚厚的雪堆一般。

靠近林边，是一条被人踩出来的从小屋通往大路的小径。这是一个夜晚，一个阴沉沉的冬日的夜晚，透过雪地，透过挂满霜雪的藤蔓的掩映，烛光如豆。棕色的小鸟们"吱吱"地叫了一天，现在正在啄食小木屋里的姑娘撒给它们的面包屑，然后展开翅膀，抖落身上的雪花，飞回温暖的鸟巢里。一只红色的小脚躲在温暖的羽毛下，另一只脚紧抓住身下的枝条。橡树、枫树弯曲的树枝和白蜡树光滑的枝干在壁炉里堆得很高，炉火在熊熊燃烧，蟋蟀自顾自地唱着，穿过地板，来到对面的墙上。书页上的镀金字在书架上闪闪发亮，老式钟表的表面也闪着光，蓝色茶杯、精致的大盘子在碗柜里也亮闪闪的。房间很简陋，但是很安静，而且通红的炉火和凯蒂的笑容让屋子变得欢快起来，可是她眼中有着愁思。一小时前她还在桌旁做着缝补的活计，哼唱着无忧无虑的爱情小调。忽然歌声停止了，她默默沉思了一会儿。然后放下手中的活，翻开一本书读了起来，那书写的是一个不幸的牧童，来自鲜花满地的小田野，由于被一只无形的手召唤，离开了自己悉心照顾的羊群，"来到了一个不可视之地"。她的眼停留在那一页，没有再继续翻页。她是否在想那个可怜的牧童，并且采集花朵洒在她想象中的那个牧童的尸身上？或者她在想象中看见

    粗糙的荆棘是否扯掉羊毛
    从他那走失的羔羊们身上？

不，她心中愁闷所以脸上才有忧伤。穿过黑糊糊的树林，越过古老破败的教堂旁的小山，积雪覆盖在一个新坟上。坟前没有墓碑，因为墓的主人穷寡妇，只给那个今晚独自悲伤沉思的孤儿留下了勉强遮风避雨的陋室。当然，除了那座遮风避雨的小屋，还有她临终的祝福。她梳理了一下额前厚密的头发，一只瘦弱苍白的手托着面颊，看上去是由于悲痛和忧虑伤了元气，但是脸上带着沉着和镇静——她并没有在哀思死者。

忽然一阵强风刮来，火焰越蹿越高，门在吱嘎作响，心跳加快

使她的脸红扑扑的。自从那天白色的床单盖上了她母亲的棺材,她就习惯了沉默和黑暗,什么也不害怕了。为什么风会让她惊怕呢?也许她害怕的是一些单纯善良的邻居来这里,重复那个古老的故事——悲伤是多么的不对,或者死者现在是多么的好等等。无聊!无聊透顶!这些她都知道。但是知道这些那些悲伤的人就会少哭一点儿吗?她一点不害怕来的是简姨妈,因为她的哀悼不冒失,她从不说这些话,例如上帝的智慧对人类来说是多么不可及,或者对上帝的旨意提出质疑或表示悲痛是多么的叛逆等等。当然,她也歌颂神的美德,歌颂温暖的阳光、纯净的凉水、温暖的炉火——歌颂世界上所有的美好——然后用她自己的双手把这些美好带给她,使这个年轻的孤儿看见它们,感受到它们,使她坚强地做活计养活自己,并且心灵上得到平静。简姨妈是个真正会安慰别人的人。她从不撕开已经愈合的伤口,因为她从不谈及死者的美德,从不回顾死者面对困难时的坚毅,从不谈及在极度悲伤中应该表现出的顺从,从没有说到她们最后一次见面的谈话,也没有回顾过下葬时他们的表情,最后把这一切的一切归于上帝的意旨,劝那个可怜的孩子要顺从等等。她从不小心翼翼地避免谈到悲痛或死亡,但是她并没有使这些话题成为谈话的负担。她有时送来一碗甜牛奶,有时送一条面包或蛋糕,有时是最新的报纸,有时甚至是她新衣服的样品。这些小事不是没有意义的——它们体现了人类的关怀,使我们继续活在这世上,并且鼓励我们做好事回报他人。

在人生的道路上,有很多像简姨妈这样的好人。凯蒂害怕的并不是她,因为可以从她快步走向门口看得出,但对于她今晚的来访凯蒂似乎也高兴不起来。可惜只是风而已!没人敲门,凯蒂也没有听见脚步声,只能听见一伙人沿着大路行走的踩雪声。钟敲了起来,她没有回头看,而是心里默数点数。七点,只有七点。昨晚和前晚的这个时候已经过了七点。她站起身,把余烬重新堆好了,然后重新做自己的活计。天已经黑了很长时间,所以她认为时间已经很晚了也不奇怪。"我决定了,"她说,"就按照我的决定做了,他今晚来不来又有什么关系呢;如果他今晚来,那么这就是最后一次了。"她看了一眼钟,叹了口气,因为满怀着他今晚会出现的希望她才有如此的决心。咳,时间真慢!一会儿,一会儿,又一会儿!然而没有任何脚步声打破周围的寂静。她把手放在大腿上,紧盯着炉火,试图从通红的炉火中看见那些影像。但是没用——她什么也没有看到，没看到演奏竖琴的姑娘，没看见教堂和教堂上细长的灯塔，没看见老人领着孩子，没看见一条狗盯着水中优雅游走的两只鸭子的景象。尽管昨晚她看见了所有的一切，但是现在她只能看见燃烧的煤炭。又过了一分钟，她重新打开书，一页一页快速翻着，但是这样也没有用。对她来说，这些印满字的纸张就好像是空白页一样，不管书上写的是浪漫故事，还是历史，或者是荒唐的梦，情况都一样。很快她自己也意识到了这一点，她合上书，站起身，在屋子里来回地走，时不时地把脸贴近窗户，但是只能看到白雪覆盖的苍凉景象，然后她转回身，来来回回走得更焦急。钟又敲响了，现在是八点了。眼泪再也止不住了，顺着脸流了下来，直到她听到门口的铃声。很显然，这位访客很受欢迎，他轻敲了一下门，自己推门进来了，进门后，高兴地说："你今晚不愿意看到我吗？今晚炉火不够旺，欢迎也没有！"

凯蒂迅速转过身，这样一来心思都被人看穿了，但是和等待的痛苦相比，暴露自己的心思倒也无可厚非：你终于来了，很高兴你来了！

这些话并不是凯蒂想和理查德说的，因为读者们都知道她一整晚等的就是他，心里的话嘴上却不能说出来。他拥抱她，她没躲，他亲吻她，她也没说什么。

她在这个世界上孤苦无依，活计如此繁重，世界如此黑暗！但是理查德来了，她简陋的小屋成了天堂。在地区的学校教书多么愉快呀，孩子们很爱她，每天都会给她带来水果、鲜花，或者他们碰巧拥有的好东西。晚上回到家重燃炉火，坐在桌旁看书或干活，是多么高兴的事啊——因为理查德肯定会来，毕竟，这才是使生活完全不同的小秘密啊。

理查德近来很顺，顺得超乎期盼，人也变得友善起来。不仅如此，对更纯洁更高尚生活的追求在他心中也有了一席之地。他性格中所有好的方面都得到了发展，让他的笑容更加灿烂。他已经不再是过去那个自私、沮丧的理查德了，现在他心中充满了快乐与希望。当然，过去天性中的自私还有点残留在他性格中，而且他还坚守一个错误理念：他只能做现在他所做的事情。

也许是出于好奇，也许是排解心中的倦怠，使他第一次到那个小屋去拜访。很快他就发现,经常为做某件事找理由并不是一件容易事,尤其是当这件事一开始是出于感情而非理智时更是如此。"凯蒂今晚肯定很孤单,"他说,"您不这样认为吗,简姨妈?可能我也能去那里安慰安慰她。"

简姨妈天性善良单纯,说:"是呀,理查德,别待得太晚。"然后在她批准后,似乎加强了他去那里的念头,理查德就会边出门边说:"只要我们今晚快乐,明天的事明天再说。"然后他也会对自己说他正在做的事纯粹是出于乐善好施,并没有丝毫杂念。凯蒂本性忧郁,看到风凄惨地呼啸便会难过,阴天或雨天这些坏天气都会影响她的情绪,尤其是当她想到死去的母亲时,心情格外差,尽可能使她快乐的确成为理查德的一种职责。然后,又是满月时分,这时的夜晚是最寂寞的,比阴天和雨天还要糟糕。理查德睡不着也读不了书,他希望这时有病人来看病,就可以缓解他的寂寞,但是他不知道行不行。这时待在家里做什么也没有用。去村庄太远,凯蒂家正好住在对面,他认为他可以去她家待一会儿。他这样解释给自己听,并相信事实就是这样,可是如果他问问自己的心,他就会发现他愿意去那里的真正动机和目的。

约翰·吉平①所到之处,是因为他的马想去,当理查德·克莱维尔去那个小屋时,是他的心想去,他也根本没想过要遏制这样的想法。自我牺牲很难做到,相比较而言,攀越雪山,在沙漠上迎着太阳走,勇敢面对一千个敌人,做这些事只要有一点点希望,就比自我牺牲容易做。爱人类天性中美好的事物,或者希望自己所爱的人爱自己,是天性使然。

  谁能好奇地注视
  美人脸颊的光泽,
  而感受不到一颗火热的心?②

那些内心悲伤的吟游诗人由于没人愿意伸出双手接纳他们不得不到处流浪,他们是做不到的;那些地位卑微没名没姓的村民们也如此,不管他们对宫廷里常见的柔情多么麻木不仁,他们如何地只

---

① William Cowper 1782 年写的"The Diverting History of John Gilpin"中的主人公吉平出行坐骑失控,只好信马由缰。

② 引自拜伦的诗《恰尔德·哈罗德游记》。

想过与世无争的平静生活。

"我不能动心。"理查德说。但是如果他真的没动心，就不用这样对自己说了。当他最后再也不能自欺欺人时，他说："我自己受折磨就行了，我不会告诉她我爱她，也不会要求她爱我。"

他为什么要这样做呢？那是因为他那已经活动的心里清楚地知道：

"那是千般莫可名状的行为
平凡的词语根本无法说清
口不说，心却明了，
早已赢得她的芳心。"

理查德和凯蒂，他们俩坐在冬日的炉火旁。凯蒂很单纯，她说自己在这个世界上孤苦无依；理查德对她很好，在她知道理查德的心意前就已经爱上他了；现在她怎么能愿意重回以前孤苦的生活，甚至忍受比以前更孤单的寂寞呢？理查德是怎样安慰她的呢？他说："我们面前的世界就是如此，我们自己选择休憩的场所。我们的天性不是自己给自己的，人类天性中最强烈的冲动是否应该永远受压抑？如果是，那么谁会在此情况下得到好处——人抑或天使？两者皆不。即使我们压抑冲动，我们是不是就完成自己的职责了？我个人认为自我牺牲和严于律己并不是人的最高职责。当太阳出来时我们为什么非要在树荫下呢？又或星星满天时，我们就应该遮眼不看？或者我们身处俗世温暖的包围，却应该要让灵魂向往天堂永恒的庄严？我们是否要放弃清新纯净的喷泉，却选择喝苦涩发臭的池水？不！我们应该按你所说的分手，让我们心碎神伤，让我们不能享受我们本可以分享的事吗？难道我们不应该携手生活，帮助彼此？我们现在的关系比任何神圣的联系对我来说更重要。你在身边，我就可以坚强地面对生活中最大的不幸；没有你，我就很可怜很无助。"

哎，凯蒂无言以对，只有垂泪。简姨妈会怎么说？其他人会怎么说？她的心会责备自己吗？

"西部的山谷和这里一样郁郁葱葱，我们可以在那里安家，我们也可以在那里结交新朋友。没人见过我们，没人听说过我们，我们可以体面地生活，这样我们不会让自己名誉受损，也不会使上帝蒙羞。爱情的力量和纯洁不会伤害人，在爱情的力量下，我们是一体的，永不分开。如果我们分开了，世界将会变成荒原，我们这些可怜虫将会在黑暗里漂泊。"

我不知道理查德说的是否是真心话，但以我对他性格的了解，我认为他说的是真的。凯蒂不是小孩子，也不是脆弱的小动物，只是她饱尝过生活的贫穷、苦痛和艰辛，她的理智使她想逃跑。她原本打算悄悄离开，这让她非常难受，今晚理查德的话让她不再痛苦了，此时一点点的情感都会深深地感染她的心灵。

白蜡树光滑的树枝和橡树、枫树弯曲的枝干烧得红彤彤的，蟋蟀在灶台里歌唱，时不时有厚厚的积雪从树干上滑落，苍白孤冷的月亮高高地挂在天上。

在火炉余烬的映照下，一对恋人坐在一起，没人在意温暖的房子，没人聆听蟋蟀的歌唱，抬头仰望天上的明月，他们只是静静倾听彼此的心声。自从上次凯蒂数过之后，钟已经敲过好几次了，一只公鸡在简姨妈家旁边的老樱桃树下"喔喔"叫得很响亮，她家的烛光透过窗玻璃映射出来，回应着公鸡的叫声。

"谁说你与死亡一般强大不可抗，
爱情啊，你比死亡还要有力量。"

26．糖厂早春

冬季几乎接近尾声。山的北坡上还残留着东一片西一片的积雪，树木根部的青苔再次吐绿，丁香树的花苞渐渐隆起，野蔷薇红色的藤蔓也在春日中益发娇艳，小鸟们衔来蔷薇藤的嫩枝和片片绒毛或筑新巢或补旧巢，乡间的少女坐在窗边一边纺纱织麻一边哼唱：

"三月吹奏春颂，
新月渐渐盈满。
雏菊金色花蕊，
很快漫山遍野。"

克莱维尔先生已经在夏季到来之前收起了大衣，他白衬衫的袖子卷得高高的，露出了里面的红色衬衫，这会儿他正忙着在糖厂里干活。山上长满了树冠巨大的枫树，山脚下立着一个简陋的石头拱门，熊熊的火舌舔着六只巨大的锅炉的底部，锅中装满枫树汁液。烟囱里吐出红色的火苗，浓浓的白色蒸汽从沸腾的液体上蒸腾而起，又往南边飘散而去。

锅炉前是一座简易搭就的木屋，临火的一侧没有墙壁。地上整齐地铺着新割下来的麦秸，屋里只有一个木头长凳和一桶糖水。木屋是用牛眼树搭的，现在树干上发出了嫩芽。这些新枝生机勃勃，似乎是从仍然扎根于大地母亲的树干上长出来的。最新两期的《共和国》塞在墙上的缝里，这样克莱维尔先生坐下来休息的时候也能看点书。过度忙乱就是浪费，这是他的座右铭之一，所以他干重活儿时会偶尔停下来缓一缓。他就是这样知道了谁当选下一任总统的前途最为乐观，谁的原则跟他自己的最为相符，如何能使苍蝇不再成为牛群的烦恼，刚发明的犁的原理是什么，时不时还有治疗风湿的正确办法，说是既能用于预防又能用于治疗，尽管克莱维尔先生总是持否定意见，说这些东西都是骗人的，可是同时他又对红色法兰绒的好处赞不绝口。他言之凿凿地说他那些不看《共和国》的邻居们永远不可能知道到这些，更不要说更多其他东西了。

　　大卫和奥利弗用斧子砍树的声音从幽深的山谷密林中传来，为干活他们在距学校"荣誉奖"发榜日还差十天就把书收好放在老旧的橱柜里，一放就是六个月。大卫为此尤其感到难过，因为校长总是要学生们以他为当之无愧的榜样，向他学习坚韧不拔、持之以恒的精神，此外还经常在大家意见有分歧时叫他定何方正确。显然他对于获得头奖的期盼不是毫无根据的。但是，当父亲说"小伙子们，我认为，明天该是个不错的出糖日，而且，如果你们能来帮我的忙，我们就能有个不错的开始了"，那就意味着没有他说话的余地了。事实是，大卫不无难过地到谷仓里去搓那些还没有纺好的麻绳，他一边用手指和牙齿搓麻绳，一边想象着到底是约翰·哈特还是阿伯纳·伯茨获得了一等奖。他从未对别人说过不愿离开学校——但其实很不情愿，只是晚上回家的时候把书本用麻绳捆好带回了家。

　　每个人都说"大卫是个好孩子"，每个人都希望他永远这样性格温和，吃苦耐劳。结果，他得到的表扬倒不如只是偶尔做上一件好事收到的夸奖多。即使在她母亲的心里，理查德也是排在第一位的。

　　守门犬卡罗非常喜欢出糖的日子，跑到林子里转来转去，一会儿惊扰躲在叶子下面的一只兔子，一会儿又在某棵树下叫个不停，而安全地待在树顶上的松鼠正偷偷地往树下看。有时候玛莎和简会跟它玩，有时候她们撇下它在林子里逛，收集一些奇特的石头，或者把林子里四处躺着的朽木上的苔藓——金色、绿色或是棕色的剥下来，有时候她们也会挖一些长满了根须的根茎，然后用枯草扎成一捆一捆的，说成是萝卜之类的，等等。卡罗躺在火堆前而且没有睡觉的时候，会用鼻子紧贴着地面，看着那一簇火苗和消散在风中的白色蒸汽，林子里时而如严冬寒风凛冽，时而如四月微风拂面。

草场上那棵枯树顶上的乌鸦整日嘶叫着。连日的雨水让溪流中的水面上涨，从山谷一路潺潺而下。那里的紫罗兰还没有开出蓝色的花朵，但是已经长出了圆形锯齿状的叶子。山谷里山慈菇的斑纹叶片十分浓密，曼德拉草的粉白色新芽已经开始将周围的叶片向两旁推挤开去。很快雏菊就会开遍山的南坡，金色的水仙和紫色的花朵也会在家家户户的窗下随风起舞。

远处树林棕色的树冠上一片霞光。正是日落时分，水面上波光粼粼，高低错落的影子也都拉长了。玛莎、简跟卡罗还在林子里游荡，山谷中仍然听得到斧子伐木的声音，声音传到了远处的山坡又回荡到这里。在火上堆满了粗大的山胡桃树干，火堆中心通红的火焰十分猛烈。干完这个，克莱维尔先生一边尝着糖汁够不够甜，一边慢慢往家里走去，他想着事情，所以两手交叉背在身后，因为太累腰也有点弯。因为白天解冻地上的泥土软软的，但是随着日落又开始上冻，等他快走到家时，已经冻得很结实了——结实得连沿着小路奔出来迎接他的小母牛都没有留下蹄印，他在想自己好像有一点玉米穗可以给它吃，但是没有。他并没有停下来拍拍光滑的牛背，或者说："别挡着我的路，'宝贝'。"所以，小牛犊向两边甩着尾巴，使劲地伸着头和脖子，然后又向着对面的同伴垂了下来。

克莱维尔太太站在门口，手里端着一碗刚从搅乳器里盛出来的黄油。尽管也很累，她还是愉快地笑着——她从来不会累得笑不出来。她看着落日，说，"塞缪尔，我觉得我们明天出门天一定不错。"

"傍晚有霞光，清早有晨曦
明天一定是个好天气。"

克莱维尔先生答道。他拿起椅子上包装精美的包裹，坐下去，问那是什么。

正如他猜到的——是给理查德的小礼物——几双暖和的羊毛短袜，一个新手帕，一个领结，两三件衬衫。没人比他的母亲的手工更好了。

"真的，多莉，你做的东西都那么好，而这次我很高兴理查德没有辜负你的好意。但是我觉得他的成功是靠运气而不是靠他的脑子，因为这孩子干活从来不琢磨。"

克莱维尔太太看上去有些不快，神色中有些许责备，但她什么也没说，于是克莱维尔先生接着说："好吧，明天我们就会看到该看到的一切了。而且最好早点出门，对吧，多莉？"在得到了对这个提议的肯定答复之后，他就起身为这次计划好的到彼得叔叔家的拜访作准备去了。

27. 倒霉鬼的末日

轻便马车停在了门前，散发着沥青和稻草的味道。有一篮苹果，还有一些克莱维尔夫人挑选好，运输时要小心的一些别致的物件。红色的法兰绒衬衣和新裤子就挂在壁炉前，这样早晨穿的时候就会觉得暖和舒适。克莱维尔夫人认为她穿戴起来太艳、太时髦的帽子和裙子也放到了顺手就可以拿到的地方，她的帽子和裙子可是专门为参加特殊场合买的。

玛莎和简边走边笑，她俩一人身旁拖着一根长长的干芦苇，称之为马，这时一头毛管发亮的小母牛小跑到她们面前。小牛很生气的样子，看样子今晚不打算让人从它那挤出奶了。在她们身后不远，扛着大斧子走过来的是戴维和奥利弗，他们筋疲力尽，巴望着家里已经把晚饭准备好了。

"哦，玛莎，"简把她那根枯草靠在篱笆上，这就算作赶马入厩了，"哦，玛莎，"她说，"快看！好像有一个老妇人正朝我们家走来，她骑着一匹老白马，马鞍桥上挂着一个大篮子，她会是谁呢？她一定是一个小贩。"

玛莎抬头看了一眼，带着一脸的义愤从旁边跳过，赶紧去告诉她们的母亲简姨妈来了，而简管她叫小贩！

"天哪，是她简姨妈！"克莱维尔先生大声叫道。他一边帮助她把灯点亮，好像是在说"到底是什么风把你吹来了"。她的脸上充满慈祥的神情，看上去一点不像有人死了。于是他大胆地问了一句是不是家里一切都好，对于这个问题，简姨妈回答得很肯定，一边看着她的篮子一边回答道，据她所知家里没有人生病或者去世。克莱维尔先生很满意这个回答，牵着白马朝马房走去。而克莱维尔夫人不是这么想的，凭直觉，她觉得哪里不对劲，她很担忧理查德。

"他是病了还是死了，或者两者都不是？到底怎么了？"在简姨妈解开她的软帽之前她得知了事实真相。他消失了，没人知道他到哪里去了，大家都猜他带着村里的女教师一起走了。下面听到的事情让克莱维尔夫人觉得安慰了一点，诸如他现在过得如何如何好，治好了多少看过知名医生也使了各种招数都治不好的病人，他赚了多少钱，大家都认为他是如何的好等等。

他跑了，于是除了他母亲和简姨妈，大家只记得他的坏，没人记得他的好。克莱维尔先生说他早就料到会有这样的事情。晚饭后，克莱维尔说必须去一趟苜蓿角，给他的樟脑瓶罐灌满，尽管瓶子里现在还有一半的量不需要再加满。其实他只是想摆脱杂乱的思绪，仅此而已。他会发现这是很难做到的，可怜的人！尤其是他会碰到很多人，都能让他想起伤心事。若有所思地，克莱维尔先生走在渐趋暗淡的暮色中，伤心地思考着。他没有听见他身后咔嗒咔嗒的马蹄声，直到后面的骑马人赶上他，勒住马。这匹马浑身黑亮，粉红色的鼻子，脸上还有一条白斑。

"晚上好，可敬的邻居，"一个熟悉的声音说道，"我最近才得知一个让人心痛的事，和你紧密相关，不过和你大儿子理查德·克莱维尔医生关系更密切。就如同你猜想的那样，我非常厌恶没有丝毫顾虑和质疑就轻信证据，而且相应的对这些证据作出一些最苛刻的审查，力争真正反映客观事实。但是我热心地寻找缺陷的努力从一开始就遇到了明显的阻碍，事实如此。和我的那些报信人一样，我开始害怕起来，害怕所有繁杂的关系。和他有过几年交往，我已经不怎么记得到底是几年，那段时间他证明了自己是一个永远诚实、正直的老实人，可以用上这些词的最完整最充足的意思。因此克莱维尔邻居，我不愿认同那些如今普遍流行的说法，就是你的大儿子理查德·克莱维尔医生已经在米德福特村抛弃了他的医生职业，据报信人说这份职业获利颇丰。他秘密地在某个黑暗的时刻，也就是我们叫做夜晚的时分和一位漂亮的女士出走了——她简直是异乎寻常的聪明。过去几个月她一直受聘于一所小学教年轻的学生如何射击。可敬的邻居，请允许我表达对于这一让人悲伤但是有趣的事件的同情之心，也请代我表达对克莱维尔太太一贯的友谊、问候以及尊重。祝你有一个愉快的夜晚，我可敬的克莱维尔邻居。"詹姆森先生一提马缰绳，马很听话，向旁边一跃就跑起来。克莱维尔先生从口袋里拿出他的樟脑瓶，剧烈地摇晃着。

不过这仅仅是伤心事的开端。路过希尔顿医生家，克莱维尔先生想买一品脱最好的酒喝，也希望有一些稍微振奋的谈话。他发现医生出去了，坐在扶手椅上等他回来的是喜欢饶舌的贝茨夫人。她可能猜想希尔顿医生会告诉她她想要知道的一切。"毫无疑问，你可以如同希尔顿先生一样详细地告诉我我想知道的一切事情，因为和希尔顿医生所知道的我想知道的事情相比，你看上去更有可能知道我想知道的事情。"克莱维尔先生拿出他的樟脑瓶，重重地放在桌上，重到把它震成了碎片。贝茨夫人继续喋喋不休："覆水难收，樟脑瓶也不例外，与一些已经发生的事情相比，这只是一件小事而已，如果大家都说事情已经发生了，我猜你也知道事情是否像人们说的那样已经发生了，或者它们还未发生。"

"大家都怎么说的？"克莱维尔先生静静地问道。

"哎呀，他们说从米德福特村刚刚来了一个人，理查德一直住在那里，人们说这话是理查德说的，他说年轻的医生带着一个女教师逃跑了，他们说他是这么说的。但是，如果他认为是他抛弃了我的女儿的话，那么他错了，到周六我女儿离婚就两个星期了，所以他才是被抛弃的那一个。"

克莱维尔先生没有再买一个新的樟脑瓶，从此之后也没有听说他再用过樟脑油，他常常主张说苹果醋比它好很多。

他们很快意识到逃跑也无济于事，于是他们结了婚，理查德和他美丽悲伤的新娘生活在西部河岸边一间寂寞的小木屋里，他们都意识到他们最初这么做所带来的耻辱会一直紧追他们不放，他们也永远不可能再回去了。他们现在住的房子也仅仅是一个临时住所，除非理查德有时间沿着河岸去一个繁荣的村庄里寻找到一个更加舒适满意的地方。有一天带着这个任务出去，理查德遇到了突然到来的暴雨，附近没有可以避雨的地方，回到家之前他早已全身湿透。结果是他被在这个国家普遍流行的疾病所击倒，忽冷忽热，最终演变成最恶性的那种发烧。

年轻的妻子十分体贴、耐心地守在他身边，无微不至地照顾他，满足他的一切需要。但是尽管她做了所能做的一切，他并没有觉得好一点。此刻时间变得如此漫长和荒凉，没有朋友，也没有邻居过来给她一点建议或者帮助她一下。他病倒十天后，绝望向她袭来。那天小鸟无数次轻轻地飞到床头的窗户上，唱着欢快的歌声，和往常一样，凯蒂走向前去，想把它吓走。她不知道为什么，看到它的时候她觉得有点迷信的恐惧，她希望它不要再飞来了。

整个一天病人只是开口要水，日落时分，他看上去似乎苏醒了一点，抱怨说很疼，然后又说河流的噪音打扰了他，接下来，似乎有点彷徨，有点神志失常，他乞求凯蒂出去使他安静一点。希望能够迁就他所有的愿望，她假装出去了，坐在小木屋的门边。她看着日落，一个人独自流泪。太阳渐渐西沉直到消失不见，树荫越来越浓厚，直到小屋周围的森林完全黑暗。鸟儿已经不唱了，但是凯蒂一度听到过它的翅膀拍打玻璃窗的声音，大为不快。

淡淡的月亮奋力往上穿过树梢，成百上千只萤火虫沿着阴沉的河流发出一闪一闪的光芒——小河流在黑暗中不停地发出呻吟声，全然不顾那个将要死亡的人一直祈祷的那样安静下来。

"这如同斥责我的声音，"他说，"对此我无能为力。我是不是应该去责备统治我命运的灾星？我的河流，请你安静一点，让我睡一会！"但是河流的呻吟声一直在黑暗中穿梭。月亮越爬越高，月光穿过窗户，洒在地板上，洒在安静下来的熟睡者身上，他感受到了这片安宁，冰冷的月光、河流的呻吟声已经不再是困扰他的事了。

28. 两姐妹

多年前，在一个离苜蓿角不远的茅屋里，住着两个小姑娘。她们不漂亮，但是也不丑。她们是姐妹，彼此爱着对方，而且不止是爱。不过，与大家所想的不同的是，她们不是父母仅有的孩子。她们的性情并不完全一样，也许正是由于这个原因，她们才更加要好。从小，她们就连一天都没分开过。在树林里、果园中、小山上、草地上、学校里，她们总是形影不离。妹妹的名字叫艾丽，姐姐叫丽贝卡。艾丽性情温和而忧伤，即使在孩提时代也是如此。但是岁月的流逝及其剥落的沉甸甸的悲哀，使她的心情沉郁沮丧，以至于静静的忧郁常常袭来，蒙住了她生活中的阳光。她的镇静，源于清楚地领悟到了上帝为我们的忧郁安排好的意义重大的用途，但更多的是源于人类所能经历的最糟糕的感觉——对冷暖交替的漠不关心，对花开花谢的无动于衷。不过，我最好还是别妄加猜测。丽贝卡的性情少了几分梦幻和诗意，多了一些坚定和力量，活泼开朗，灵活变通。因此，妹妹常粘在她身上，像一棵藤缠绕在她年轻而健壮的树干上；或是倚在她身旁，像朵雏菊隐在大树树影的庇护中。

多年前，我曾千百次看到她们，胳膊挽着胳膊，浓密的黑发被风吹到了一处。我还记有一座小山，半山都长满了枫树。夏季来临的时候，她们常坐在山上，一个人在编织或缝纫——这个通常是艾丽，另一个则在读书，声音很大，因为她喜欢朗读。自从她会朗读开始，她就读得很好。有时，她会放下书，给她那充满崇拜和好奇的妹妹讲一些长长的故事，而妹妹也知道不要出声去打断她的沉思。有时，当她听到一些她觉得美丽动人的故事时，她深色的眼中会充满泪水。她常常半是哀伤半是自责地说："我永远也做不到你的一半那么好。"然后，姐姐会拂开妹妹额上的头发，一下下地亲吻她，说："亲爱的艾丽，你会成为一个诗人的。"这样便能哄她读一下头天晚上或上个安息日写下的诗句。姐妹俩是令人钦佩的，这毫无疑问。可是，爱及一种与生俱来的判断力超越了她们的其他优点。一如既往地，她们对自己和对方都很满意。迎着夕阳，她们穿过归途上的那片草地，一如从最神圣的歌声的灵感中走来。她们居住的房子是一个棕色的小农舍，周围没有任何诗意的事物，除了那棵苹果树。冬日里，树枝刮在墙上咯吱作响；夏日里，它会贴着窗户绽放花朵，结出果实。园子的篱笆旁长着几丛玫瑰，任由枝叶穿过篱笆，或爬到篱笆上。姐妹俩睡的房间比较低矮，屋顶下没有天花板。因此，她们常常醒来躺着，倾听落雨的声音——那么美妙的音乐。她们还会在云中构建城堡，让想象中的各色人物住在里面。她们会构想豪华的房间，墙上绘满了图画，天花板美轮美奂……

她们是两个奇怪的孩子，跟我遇到的其他孩子都不同，天赋禀异，极其敏感，却出身农家，几乎没受过良好教育。她们很早就开始感到不满，认为在她们的小世界之外还有一个世界，充满了阳光和欢乐。她们如饥似渴地读着所能得到的任何种类的书籍。她们离开家人，因为家里还有大大小小的其他孩子。她们谈论着，梦想着。

诚然，不上学的时候，她们得去干活儿。但是，每当早上的杂活儿做完后，她们会带着缝纫或编织活儿，来到果园里或草地上。

我常常会看到她们，或是在香甜的苜蓿地里坐在一棵漂亮的枫树的树影里，或是在小山坡上，或是在山脚下银光闪闪的小溪里，任由溪水冲刷着她们。溪边长着密密的柳树，长长垂下的绿色枝条，几乎触到了河面上。山谷里长满了蒲公英，花儿在纤细的花茎上绽放，当花儿枯萎、草叶凋零的时候，便会零落飘散，轻轻地飘向四方。还有许多别的花儿，娇嫩的小野花，有的漂亮，有的则十分普通，一如孩子们一般。我甚至不知道它们的名字，我没学过自然科学。但是我崇敬花神，单纯的崇敬与名字无关。牛儿散在四处啃食着青草，或是在凉爽的树荫里卧着，绵羊与羔羊在山间跳跃。所有这一切，共同组成了一幅静谧而美好的画面。

这个她们最喜欢来的地方，一边通向长满柳树的山谷，再往前便是一片狭长的树林，浓密而幽暗；另一边，在一丛丛的雪松和刺槐之下，便是我有时会提到的那片墓地，白色的墓石隐约可见，还有玛丽·维尔德明斯死去的那个小农舍。

"如果你活得比我长，亲爱的艾丽，"一天，在姐妹俩静默了许久之后，丽贝卡说，"别让他们把我埋在那里。"

泪水涌入了妹妹的眼里。她把胳膊搂在姐姐脖子上，说："你怎么说起这些呢？你永远不会死的。"

"为什么？"

"因为我爱你，"艾丽说，"我爱过的人都没有死的。"

丽贝卡脸上浮现出一丝苦笑。她抬起深色的眼睛，回答道："用不了多久，你就得去把那片墓地上的树枝分开的，艾丽，因为我肯定他们会把我埋在那里的。然后你就会在一块普通的小墓碑上读到'丽贝卡·哈德利，十五岁'，再过几个月吧，我也不知道到底是多长时间。不过，我会在十六岁之前死掉的，时间不会太长了。"她继续说下去，仿佛在自言自语："再过几个月我就十五岁了。"

"别再这样说了，"艾丽快要哭了，"我们回家吧，我要把妈妈给我做的新围裙送给你。"丽贝卡没有站起来。她的双手交叠着放在腿上，眼睛望着地面，仍然静静地坐在草地上。艾丽则在她身旁采着野花，做成花环挂在她的脖子上，或者一边将花编入她的发辫，一边闲聊着杂七杂八的事情，试图让姐姐忘记这世上还有死亡这么一件事。可是，为了忘却死亡而做出的努力反让这个恶魔待在记忆里挥之不去，仿佛一片乌云，不管她转向何方，总是横亘在她面前。

那一天过去了，然后又是一天，接下来又是一天。虽然姐妹俩再没谈论过死亡，但从那之后，她们的心中都有些压抑——意识中总是想着嘴上不能说的那件事。

在上学和放学的路上，她们总是会经过那一小片墓地。每当此时，艾丽总会在姐姐身旁紧走几步，并且会比平时更欢快、更大声地讲话。丽贝卡的面颊更丰满红润一些，脚步也更轻快。她的情绪通常都很高涨，可是，时不时地，她的心头也会笼上挥之不去的阴云——大致总是预言中确证的终极命运。艾丽的性情是压抑的，忧郁已经成了一种习惯。在这样的性情之下，却潜藏着一种能量，从没有人察觉到——多年来，她自己也未曾察觉。

一天傍晚，她们走在回家的路上。她们长长的影子投到了路的对面，清晰可见。她们慢慢地走着，谈论着学校的校长。猛然间，她们的聊天被打断了。

一群群的小孩子闹哄哄地从她们身旁走过。他们把盛午餐用的篮子扔到空中，脚下蹭起阵阵尘土，互相叫着绰号，因为他们很兴奋——学校放学比平时晚了一个钟头，所以他们各个都觉得自己有个重大战报要传递。他们互相追跑着，脸色通红，激动难耐，急着回家跟家里人说校长的坏话。

"老师干得不错呀。"威廉·马丁说。他是个粗野的孩子，总喜欢欺负弱小。"我真想让他再把我们留到这么晚一次，我倒要让他看看。"这样叫喊的同时，他在空中挥舞着结实的拳头，仿佛面对着一个不共戴天之敌。当他把拳头放下来的时候，突然又迅速拐出去，将一个安安静静的小男孩的帽子打掉了。小男孩的年龄只有他的一半儿大，吓坏了。完成这个壮举之后，威廉冲到了前面，扬起了一团尘埃，使那个小男孩看不到帽子被拿到哪里去了，他哭了起来。看到他哭了，威廉停了下来，冲他喊道："真是个好孩子！哭吧。有胆量你就光着头回家。等你回了家，看你丢了帽子，你爸会拿鞭子抽你的，到时候就有你好哭的了。"看到这一通话没有起到他似乎想达到的抚慰效果，他便跑到路的一边，爬到篱笆顶上，踮起脚尖站着，仿佛在穿过田野极目远眺。他说："是的，我告诉过你了，你爸已经听到你的声音了。我看见他正在砍一根桃树枝。现在他正在看那根树枝结不结实。现在他已经收起折刀了。现在他正以最快的速度朝这边跑呢——你最好安静点儿，你这爱哭鼻子的小孩儿，不然他会打死你的。"说完这些"好心的警告"之后,他越过一个站在旁边听着的小姑娘的头顶,从篱笆上跳了下来,喊道:"男孩儿们,林子里已经漆黑了,谁要跟我回去把校长那个老家伙揍一顿?看他还敢不敢把我们留得这么晚了!"

其实校长一点儿也不老,正相反,年轻得很——绝对不会超过二十五岁。可怜的家伙!他负责的这帮孩子们虽然够明智,但是很粗鲁,缺乏管教,没有礼貌,可以这么说:没一个愿意勤奋读书的。他们的学业进展缓慢,他们,特别是他们的父母,都把原因归结为校长的无能。在这个黄昏,人们对他的反感异常猛烈地爆发了。正如大多数学生所希望的那样,这将使他很快被赶走。

"咱们慢点儿走吧,"一个孩子说,"尽量晚一些,反正已经晚得不能再晚了。"

"我早就会算了,也早该放学回家了。"另一个孩子说,"我相信他自己不会算,这就是他放学总把我留下的原因。"

大多数孩子们都这样说,因为学校放学比平时晚了一点儿而愤愤不平。其实之所以晚了点儿,部分原因也在于他们自己不好好学习。不过,他们倒是希望自己不费力就让智慧跑到他们的理解力中。而且如果没能这样的话,那老师就肯定是个笨蛋。

丽贝卡和艾丽远远地走在孩子们的后面。她们也在谈论着校长,但话题完全不同。她们似乎停顿了一下,因为她们走到路边时,发现了那个小男孩的帽子,被风吹到了一片割过草的田野中间。然后,她们又聊了起来,比平时更诚挚,完全忘了天色已晚。

"我敢保证他病了,"艾丽说,"不应该怪他把我们多留了一会儿。他都不能来上课了,我知道的,他看起来面色那么苍白,还一直在不停地咳嗽。"

"我刚来的第一天,觉得他真丑,"她接着说,"你不觉得吗,丽贝卡?"

"丑!不,在我看来,他总是很英俊,说话的声音也像音乐一般。"

艾丽大笑起来。丽贝卡也为自己的失态感到脸红。她有点生气地说:"你笑什么?因为我不像你一样觉得校长丑吗?"

"噢,别生气,我什么也没笑。很多个下午,有时他的脸颊会发红,那时候我就觉得他还算挺好看的。今天放学前,当他朗读《圣经》的时候，他就挺好看的。而且，丽贝卡，他也觉得你很好看。"

"不，艾丽，你错了。没人觉得我好看，我自己也不觉得。"

她这样说的时候虽然有些悲哀，不过，她的脸上仍然现出一丝微笑，使她看上去真的很动人。这时艾丽接着说："今天我看到他写诗了。我假装问问题，走到他桌旁看看他写了什么。虽然没看到内容，但我确实看到诗的头上写着'致丽贝卡'。"

"世界上叫丽贝卡的多了，"姐姐说，"如果他真的在写一首诗的话，他很可能是写给某个朋友的。"

"也许是吧，因为你也是他的朋友呀。"

"好吧，艾丽，如果你非要这样的话，告诉你，我就会，比如说，把他编成一个故事的主人公，然后在最后一天的时候再去读它。不过，今天他跟你说了要你学法语之后，又跟你说什么了？"

"什么也没说，好像是这样。让我想想。噢，他问我多大了，然后说，'丽贝卡比你大两岁，是的，你必须得学法语'。他说的就这些。"

"我希望，艾丽，"姐妹俩默默地走了一小段路之后，丽贝卡说，"我希望我们能有双鞋子穿着去上学。"

"噢，多漂亮的一只狗呀！"艾丽喊道，一只非常漂亮的狗从她身旁走过，"真希望它是我的狗。"

"你真觉得它漂亮吗？"一个声音在她耳边响起。那声音一点儿也不粗鲁，反而是异常的亲切甜美，会让人本能地判断出是属于一个头脑聪明、举止文雅的人的。因为，在我看来，声音就如同相貌一样，能够表明一个人的品质。

姑娘的脸变成了深红色——她还从未如此地接近过一个在地位和教育上都如此明显地优越于她的人。于是，在一番犹豫和几近痛苦的尴尬之后，她回答道："是的，先生，我觉得它非常漂亮。"

也许是看出了她的迷茫，那位绅士尽力想要弥补，便继续轻松地跟她聊天，谈论着那些他自然地认为她很熟悉的事物——周围的乡邻、村民的性格、土地的肥沃程度，诸如此类。可怜的艾丽，她觉得她结结巴巴的，看上去笨拙不堪。意识到这些，只会让她觉得自己更像乡巴佬。对她知道的问题，如果她不在意自己在别人眼中的形象的话，她可能会回答得很好；可是现在她回答得不好，连正常情况下一半儿的机灵劲儿也没有。她希望他能明白，她懂的比她看上去懂的多,但她也同样希望他能走开,去与丽贝卡聊聊天儿,或做些别的什么事,简而言之,就是不要慢慢走着与她谈话。

姐姐没有加入到谈话中来。没有一个问题是特别问她的,有些想法她也表达不出来,所以她并不想说话。

然而,当陌生人说"你们老师叫什么名字?因为,照我猜,你们上过学"时,她满怀兴致地抬起头来。艾丽在犹豫着,仿佛这个问题是在问她,于是她便回答了。然后陌生人疑惑地接着说:
"好奇在不断增加,
他所懂的东西这小脑袋怎能装得下?"①

丽贝卡没有回答。那位绅士并没给她留下什么好印象。即便他补充说"我将很高兴与他结识",也无济于事。

丽贝卡说道:"他不可能不高兴的。"声调中或许带着一点讥讽。不管她有没有讥讽,显然陌生人认为是有的,因为他转向了艾丽,又回到了他们之前的聊天。他说:"我的小朋友,鉴于我想把帐篷扎在这里的山脚下,我很高兴能够听到关于这里的乡村和村民的如此精彩的描述。我们这么非正式地结识了,我认为,我们的相识将会,我希望,最终成为友谊。我们将成为友好的邻居,我相信。"他补充道,主要是对艾丽。由于不习惯这些客套,艾丽想不出该如何回应,只是望着田野那边,仿佛忽然沉浸在了自然界的美丽之中。她很少看到礼貌地点头,也不常听到"晚安,小姐们",而那位绅士正是这样说的,也是这样做的,然后便迈开大步,不一会儿就走远了,听不到她们的声音了。

有那么一会儿,姐妹俩谁也没说话。"我在想,"丽贝卡最终开口了,"我在想下午茶准备好了没有。"

"不知道,"艾丽回答,不久又加上一句,"我多希望我们能有双鞋呀。"

29. 威廉·马丁的懊悔

漫长而忧郁的夏日,阳光洒落在山林中,树木已经枝繁叶茂,

---

① 出自18世纪爱尔兰诗人奥立佛·戈德史密斯的诗作《乡村校长》("The Village Schoolmaster"),原文为:"And still the wonder grew, /That one small head could carry all he knew!"

早已退去了春天时的清新和光泽。酷热的天气禁锢了原本就很倦怠的风。小鸟们的唧啾声越来越不欢快。成群的黄蝴蝶在小溪河床上翩翩起舞。小溪不再泛出长长的银波，而是收拢在一处，成了一潭死水。收割已经结束，而玉米地里宽宽的叶子时不时地发出"沙沙"的声音，好像在告诉人们玉米熟了，寒冬即将来临。秋天还在恋恋不舍地炫耀其最后的美丽，花朵的根部开始泛黑，和田野里根茎泛着金色的小麦麦穗缠绕在一起，这是很早之前拾麦穗的人剩下来的，在丰收后的田野里闪闪发光。蜘蛛在苹果树枝间编织出一张轻盈的网，银光闪闪，悬挂了一天仍完好无损。现在是黄昏时分大雨来临前那段昏暗的时光。

学校正常运行着，再有两周就放假了。其间偶尔如遇先生身体不适，则会停课一天。每当这时候，威廉·马丁总是说："如果先生胆敢露面的话，我就用手指扭断他的脖子。"于是全校的学生便会把郁积在心里的所有怨恨一股脑地发泄在这个倒霉的年轻人身上。他毫无办法，又失道寡助，只好挣扎着逃回家装病。这些学生总喜欢给他弄出点麻烦，而且是很多不必要的烦恼和麻烦。有时候学生把他最喜欢的书藏起来，这样午休时，他本来可以躺在树荫下边咳嗽边思索的享受也被剥夺了，其实他们原本可以让他这样享受一下的；有时候他们很淘气地剪掉他那件破外套的扣子，这时候，总会招来一阵阵嬉笑声；有时候他们会故意打翻他的午餐盘，把所有的食物抖落在脏兮兮的地上。他们一直对他身体的孱弱或是无动于衷的反应开着没完没了的玩笑，有时候甚至搞些过火的恶作剧。

"祝您今天身体健康。"一天早上，艾丽·哈德利一边说着，一边把自己在上学路上采摘的一小束野花递给他。

他一向对泥土怀有深厚的感情，开心地笑着说："我感觉很好，十分舒服。"他极为欣赏地左右打量着这束花，又接着问："艾丽，这些花是你一个人采的吗？"如果他瞥她一眼的话，他就会知道不可能有其他答案。她是特意来听早上的课的。可以想象得出，她的脸颊此刻比以往任何时刻都要绯红。

那天，生命活力好像又重新注入他的体内。他谈论着下一学期、下一年的计划，他的学生们将会学到多少知识，他将以此为骄傲。他还告诉学生他将在这学期的最后一天送给他们他精心准备的小礼物，这些礼物会对他们的人生有益，对此他深信不疑。

"那么,"丽贝卡怯怯地抬起眼睛,说道:"你不打算回到你大山里的家了吧?""我的确有过这样的打算,"他说,"如果我身体状况越来越差的话。不过我不会的,这里空气凉爽,我会一点点好起来的。"一阵咳嗽打断了他的谈话。他又接着说:"或许我也该回去了。"他停了一会儿,又接着说:"如果我回去的话,我希望将会有一位比我更好的老师来教你们,但是你们不会遇到比我更喜爱你们的老师了。"他说,"因为你们每一个人对我而言都是非常可爱的。""我敢肯定,我们都非常爱你,"艾丽说,"是吧,丽贝卡?"但是丽贝卡并没有回答这个问题,而是接着问了一些有关语法课的问题。

校舍是一栋露天的木制建筑,四周种着树木,借以和马路隔离开。这里曾种过很多树木,但是没有一棵树能存活太长时间。有人指控威廉·马丁,说他知道的树木枯死的原因远远多于他坦白过的。学期初,这位可怜的先生原本无力做这样繁重的体力活,却辛辛苦苦劳动了一整天,在窗前种了些廉价的槐树和枫树。可这些树苗还未抽枝发芽,就很快枯萎了。后来一次,他看到威廉试图割开树干看看树木是否真的枯死时,他说:"我想,这里的土壤不适合种树木。""不对,先生,"比尔强忍着笑说道,"树木是可以在任何地方存活的。"他一边说着,一边跑开去告诉其他同学,他们的先生比他自己感觉的要愚笨得多得多,他的确是这样的。

离校舍不远的地方,也就是在马路的对面,生长着一片令人感到舒适的山毛榉小树林。男孩子们经常在那里打球,女孩子们则拿着废弃的板凳放在放倒的原木上玩跷跷板的游戏。先生中午也在这里看看书。他许诺送给他们礼物的那天,他像往常一样拿着本书,在一棵枝叶低垂的橡树下找了块舒服的位置,半躺在那里。他把艾丽送给他的花夹在书页之间。梦想尽管很朦胧,也很粗糙,但让人备受安慰,就像草地上的光影一样在他的内心深处颤动。"这些花,"他想,"去年寒冬时从根部开始枯萎,而整个又被冰雪所覆盖,冷风在它们的墓前为它们呻吟哀号。但是春回大地的时候,根部又抽枝发芽,绿汪汪的,在明媚的阳光下摇曳着花蕾和花朵,淡白色、金色、红色。也许大自然的精气又重新注入我的身体里,就像植物的汁液又输回到根部,这一滴滴同情的眼泪加上一张张灿烂的笑脸,融会在一起使我变得强壮健康。也许我应该,我确信我应该感到今天比以往几个月都舒服一些。"想到这儿,他坐起身,尝试抓住身旁一根绿绿的树枝来测试一下自己的力量。树根部还没有他的腰粗，树枝就更纤细了。他拽住树枝向下压。但是尽管他用尽了全身的力量，树枝也没有弯曲到他希望的那样。"我来帮你，"威廉·马丁说着冲了过来。树枝像根藤条一样弯了下来，但是他突然故意松开了手，树枝正好反弹在先生的脸上。先生向后踉跄了一下，然后手捂着脸，瘫倒在草地上，鲜血顺着他消瘦苍白的手指流了下来。

"先生，你受伤了？你受伤了？"这个小男孩惊叫着。这次，也是有生以来第一次，他吓坏了。"我不是有意的，我不是有意的。"他反复重复着这句话，好像是在为自己的良心开脱，找借口。

"哦，威廉，"先生终于开口了。他看着小男孩，或者努力想看着他，很难过地说："我看不见东西了，我眼前一片漆黑，但不要紧的。"他从小男孩的惊慌声和抽泣声中知道他吓坏了，又说："不要紧的。其实我早就看不到太远的距离了。把手给我，带我回校舍。"但是这个男孩无法面对自己犯下的大错，慌慌张张地跑开了。他很快又停下来，拔了些草，喂喂他之前数次以其为投掷目标的饥饿的猪群。然后他又看到阳光下有头奶牛，眼前遮了块木板，这是他一小时前绑在那里的。他跑了过去，解开木板，猛地丢在石头上。木板摔成了碎片。

"威廉，发生什么事啦？"丽贝卡·哈德利慢慢转过身问道。她当时正面对着校舍读书，因为干这样的事儿对于他来说一点儿也不奇怪。她看到了威廉脸上焦虑不安的神情和斑斑的泪痕。

"我没什么，"威廉从衣兜里拿出石笔，开始在栅栏上画着一道又一道直线，"但是先生病了，我猜他是病了，我说不清楚。"

"你凭什么认为他病了呢？"

"我不知道，"男孩子含糊不清地说，"我不知道是不是他。有个人躺在林里的一棵树下，我感觉他生病了。我不知道他是不是我们的先生，我也不知道他是不是病了。"

女孩合上书，疾步向他所指的方向走去。她试图游说男孩和她一起过去看看，但是没有成功。他把脸倚靠在栅栏上，目送女孩离开，然后转身坐在路边，抬起了满是灰尘的双手，来回审视着。他在想，如果一个男孩意外使一个人失明，他们是否会把他抓起来，关到监狱去。

"啊呀，先生，"当丽贝卡走近，发现先生的困境时，不禁失声大叫起来，"怎么了？怎么回事？亲爱的先生，你受了重伤啦。"她蹲下身来，把他杂乱的头发梳到脑后，用手绢给他擦了擦脸。"丽贝卡，亲爱的丽贝卡，"他终于开口说话了，并用手臂搂住她，把她拉到身边。她犹豫地退缩了一点，他的第一次也是最后一次拥抱使她有些忐忑不安。

他们心中埋藏了好久的思绪和感情，虽然此刻没有点破，但彼此都心领神会，虽说有点悲伤可最终找到了共鸣。一小时前，他们还不能表达出他们心中所想的，哪怕是一点点也不能，而现在可以非常镇定自若地说出来。希望之花现在已经化成冰冷苍白的灰烬。曾经绯红的脸颊上如今挂满泪滴。不幸的遭遇使得他们之间的障碍一扫而空，投入了爱的怀抱。

光线暗淡下来，就好比是个斗篷，遮得外部的视野黝黑一片，而内心深处的感知力加快了。之前些许悲伤的朦朦胧胧的感觉如今变得清晰无比，就像有时候我们能感受到地面下鼹鼠的忙碌。这个悲伤但又听天由命的年轻人听到了死亡的脚步声。他第一次有些叛逆的忧伤和激动平静之后，看上去比以往任何时候都高兴。太阳在晚霞的映衬下显得愈发硕大明亮，但是他镇定而又虔诚的灵魂在死亡的阴影中越来越大。

"生命对我来说是一场疲惫的旅行，"他说，"我一个人孤苦伶仃，没有任何美好的希望鼓舞我前行，前方的路漫长而又崎岖。现在，我遇到了你，丽贝卡，尽管你温柔的手仅仅在最后一刻为我开启了死亡之门，我还是很高兴，我会欣然地离去。"

丽贝卡还是个孩子，不过她的心智年龄要成熟得多。她清楚生命的快乐之花迟早会在严寒中凋零。当生命之花凋落时，尽管比预期来得沉重，来得要早，她也会松开手臂，放开自己所尊崇的人，将十字架放在下面。很难看到当玉米完全成熟时给人们带来的惊讶，但当原本可以结出更多果实的青色根茎将要被砍下的时候，我们只能无奈地拿着收割机来收割。

校舍前面的树木早已枯萎。学校已经停课十天了，看上去冷冷清清。当四匹灰白大马拉的马车咔嗒咔嗒路过时，再也没有一张张好奇的脸庞透过窗户向外张望。"威廉在家吗？"一个陌生的年轻人，勒马停在马丁先生家门口问道。他骑着的马光秃秃的，没有马鞍。威廉当时正在花园里收拾枯萎的豌豆秧。当他听到这询问时，颤抖着蜷缩在地上，悄悄地躲在藤蔓下面。他确信他将要被逮捕了。更令他惊慌失措的是，马丁太太当时正在大门口抖落桌布上的面包屑，顺口回答："嗯，是的，他在家里。"她把桌布叠好，然后左右看了看，大声喊道："威廉，威廉，威廉·马丁。"这喊声在远处不断地回响。马丁太太看到没有任何回应，于是就慢慢向这个男人走过去。比尔能听到他们的一些对话，但是弄不清楚谈话的具体内容。可他确信，他们提到先生怎样怎样了。此刻任何描述都是多余的，我们可以想象得出他内心饱受的煎熬。夜已经深了，马丁冒险偷偷溜出来，悄悄地爬向屋子。他在门口听了听，但是里面十分安静。"也许，"他暗想，"他们在屋里等着我呢。如果我现在进去，他们会马上抓住我，用绳子把我捆起来的。"于是，他又蹑手蹑脚地溜回到黑夜中。后来，他又爬了过来，用手指透过窗户上的一片碎玻璃的缝隙，轻轻地将窗帘拉向一边。他的妈妈坐在屋里，一边用一只脚摇着摇篮，一边在给他做新裤子。是要穿着这条裤子去蹲监狱吗？当然不是。也许他父亲将带着他参加史密斯先生的公开拍卖会。史密斯先生打算拍卖他家的犁、耙子、风扇机、羊群、六头奶牛，还有家里所有的家具，然后举家去威斯康星州。他多么希望自己也可以一道去啊。如果他只去参加拍卖会，那么蓝裤子又有什么其他目的？他可以让史密斯先生捎带上他，等到了那里，他可以说自己是威廉·史密斯，没有人会知道他弄伤了学校的先生。

想到这儿，威廉一下子打开了房门。他的妈妈问他到哪里去了，听到他说他一直就待在花园里拔豌豆秧，就又默默地继续干活。威廉此刻不敢问他心中急切想知道的事情，只好坐在地上，眼睛睁得大大的，看着蓝裤子的进展。每当妈妈说到小孩睡觉的时间了，他总是回答他也不知道为什么今晚就是不困。

最后，威廉怯怯地问："爸爸明天要去参加拍卖会吗？"妈妈有些抱怨地说她也不知道，然后好像自言自语地说："我倒是很想知道谁买走了羽绒铺盖。不过呢，说归说，做归做，我倒是不希望家里有张多余的床啊。"她叹了口气，然后把蓝裤子叠了起来。

"快点，快点，"她边说边严厉地看着眼睛还是睁得大大的威廉，"到小孩子上床睡觉的时间了。"她边说着，边揪着他的耳朵，把他推搡到房间门口。这个可怜的孩子，在床上辗转反侧了好久才睡着。第二天一早，他坐在木堆上，认真地观察父亲的一举一动，想看看他是否要去参加拍卖会,而他的母亲,腰上围了条毛巾当做围裙,走到门口叫他进去。他的蓝裤子已经做好,还有他那件最体面的衬衫,一同挂在火炉前的椅子上。他母亲指着新衣服,说:"去把手和脸好好洗干净,回来试试这身衣服。"他赶快去洗,但又听到母亲说:"你这个小子,不配穿这么好的衣服。"这时,他的心又沉了下来。他不知道这是对他长这么大的一个定论,还是就专指他这次犯的大错。被送到监狱的恐惧又重新笼罩在心头。他带着疑虑,按照吩咐去做了。当他穿戴一新后,他强迫自己待了一会儿,再一次擦干眼泪,然后走回到母亲面前。母亲让他戴上帽子去看看先生时,他的心又悬了起来。"为什么啊?"他问道,一下子瘫倒在椅子上。"我也不清楚为什么。因为你的先生疼痛中还派人找你过去,你这个调皮捣蛋的孩子。你啊,你根本不配过去看他。"男孩说他不想过去,但是根本没用,话说得很清楚,要么马上过去,要么挨一顿打。男孩磨蹭了一会儿,慢慢腾腾地出门了。

先生住的农舍孤零零的,又破又旧,门口的一大块草皮和一带林木将其和大路分了开来。附近有一家马拉的磨坊,一些周围邻居嫌几里路太远而不愿意去希尔叔叔家的磨坊,都到这里来磨面做饭。磨坊里枯燥乏味而又让人忧伤的隆隆声一刻都没有停止过。农舍四周的院子围有一圈木桩栏杆栅栏,还立有一根很结实的柱子。威廉·马丁赶到时,木桩上已经拴有三四匹马了。一个高高黑黑的女人,黑眼窝深陷,紫色的眼皮向下耷拉着,褐色的头发中夹杂着一根根灰色的发丝,从前额梳到脑后,脸上露出疲惫的神情。她正站在门口的石头小路上,搅制黄油。大门上的铰链吱吱嘎嘎地响着。她抬头看见他正犹豫不决,担心他是害怕门口的看门狗。那条狗正蹲伏在大门和房门之间,扬着前爪,狂吠不止。"进来啊,孩子,"她说,"进来吧,它不会伤害你的。"

她停下来一小会儿,拿起搅拌器,仔细打量着,看看黄油是否搅拌好了。然后,她带着几分疲倦、烦恼,还有几分温和、悲伤的表情,领着男孩穿过了一条宽敞幽暗的大厅。大厅的地面上铺着很多长条形的粗糙地毯。然后他们沿着一段陡峭的楼梯走了上去。楼梯的台阶是用岑木做的,洗刷得白灿灿的。在第一节楼梯的平台处,她停下来对战战兢兢的来访者低声说:"先生变化很大,我想你可能都认不出他了,他几乎遭受了所有可以想得出的痛苦。"她又接着说:"医生在他手臂上和脖子的后面敷了很多发疱药,一直折腾到半夜,但先生似乎不喜欢这么治疗,他一直在说这没用的。"她轻轻地打开门,走到床边,把先生那虚弱惨白的手从被单里拿出来,攥在自己手中,用一种鼓舞人心的欢快语气说:"这个小男孩过来看你啦。"

"我要喝水,给我点水喝。"病怏怏的先生说。

"不行,医生说了,你绝对不能喝水。等你病好了,我会打上满满一大罐泉水,就用那个上面刻有紫色玫瑰花的那个白色大水罐。那时你可以尽情喝个饱。"

"难道我现在不能喝点水吗?一小时后也不行吗?"他哀求着。但是那个女人已经离开,继续去搅拌她的黄油去了。

他强忍住了即将发出的呻吟声,喝了一口土坛子里的药茶水。那个土坛子上盖有一个碟子,就放在伸手能拿到的地方。然后他又恢复了病人惯有的笑容。房间的面积很大,天花板很低。屋里没有太多的家具,只有两三把未上漆的椅子,一张坏了一条腿的饭桌,还有一张核桃木写字台,一个小小的放大镜放在一个橡木做的框架里。屋里唯一的装饰品是一张悬挂着的苍白色的块状蛇皮,一根镶有灿烂羽毛的木杖,和一个深黄色丝绸做的针垫,看上去像个橘子。

纸糊的窗帘垂在窗台上,上面画有褐色的轮船和绿油油的树木,掺杂在一起,使房间呈现出一片黄昏的景象。床头的窗户微微敞开着,一股令人作呕的药味在屋内弥漫,一些小瓶子和纸片散落在壁炉架上。

先生已经要求所有的学生过来看看他,大部分学生都早于威廉先到了。他们有些害怕,有些沉默,坐着或是站在屋里,但尽可能地离床头远些。只有艾丽,倚靠在枕头上,手里攥着自己湿湿的长发,悲伤地、默默地为先生擦拭眉头间的汗水。她开始担心她所爱的人将要离去。

一只小鸟用翅膀不停地拍打着窗户上的玻璃,又飞进了屋内。小孩子们的注意力从恐惧中转移到追逐小鸟上,尽情地放声大笑。这熟悉的笑声使得先生脸上露出了笑容,但那笑容转瞬即逝。他说:"有一个人的声音我没有听到。"艾丽明白她的意思,说:"她今晚过来。""今晚,艾丽,"他说,"她今晚要赶过来,我活不到黎明了。"

很快,他要求抬高枕头,把眼前的遮光物拿开,因为他可以看到一点点。他把桌子上的包裹拿过来，打开包裹，里面装有很多小东西，上面系有镶金边的灿烂的带子。他把所有的孩子叫到身旁，说道："这些礼物是送给你们的，我可爱的小朋友们。我不能再教你们了，我要去一个很远很远的地方。这些礼物会使你们更加聪明睿智，远远超过我的智慧。你们都很爱我，我很难过我要离开你们。"他消瘦的手放在他们一个个的头上，为他们向上帝祈福，也为自己祈祷。屋外阳光并不灿烂。远处路上有迎接新娘的队伍匆匆赶过。一位疲惫至极的女人正坐在树荫下休息。幽暗的屋内，小孩子们哽咽着——向先生告别。

落日的余晖停留在东面小树林里的树枝上。疲倦的工人拖着沉重的脚步回家了。牛群被赶回到棚子和堆谷场上。忙碌的家庭主妇又开始了晚上的劳作。磨坊里"隆隆"的声音停下来了。

先生那栋黑漆漆的屋子敞着窗户，冷空气由此吹进吹出。窗下跪着一个心情沉重的小女孩，头发垂下遮住脸庞，她的嘴唇亲吻着死者的嘴唇。一个灵魂在敲打着通往平静的大门，渴望着新的生命之泉。

30. 格雷太太的两次造访

放眼人世间，人性的浪潮似乎永不衰退。当我们炕头的灯光照在不乏血色的脸和并无泪痕的眼上，当我们彼此之间形成的小圈子没有断裂，当在心与心之间回响的音乐没有被死亡的气息笼罩的时候，我们无法理解当熟悉的笑容渐渐消失时心灵所承受的痛苦和渴望，无法理解为何一座小小的坟丘会给所有相关的人带来阴影。如果有任何连快乐的圣油都无法治愈，即让生命变成空白而虚幻的永恒的悲哀，那么这就是让我们有生以来第一次被布裹紧仰躺着，狂野而热情地亲吻苍白而毫无声息的尘埃时降临的悲哀。主眷顾众生，永远保佑我们！请用您仁慈的臂膀拥抱那些背离阳光而寻求墓穴冰冷抚慰的痛苦的孩子们吧。

刺骨的寒风和光秃的树枝，亮闪闪的冰挂和反复无常的阳光，冬天所带来的这些都已经消失不见了。蓝色的鸟儿在筑巢，丁香花正萌发出新芽。在群山的北坡，在篱笆周围到处都是坚硬半融的积雪。羊毛刚刚开始卷曲的小羊跳过这些雪篱，啃吃嫩草。黄色的水仙花在农舍门旁绽放。菖蒲草从长长的枯草中伸出宽阔的绿色刀锋；

此时主妇们围裙里装满种子在菜园里播种新的菜畦。

丽贝卡和艾丽在树林里采野花。校舍的活动遮板打开了。学校来了一位新老师。"威廉你要去哪里？回来。现在放学了，你肩上扛着把铁锹打算把地挖穿啊。"威廉把头低下了点，一句话也没有说。马丁太太接着说，一副恨铁不成钢的样子："我真的奇怪了，有谁碰到过你这样的孩子？我一直试着让你变得和别的孩子一样，但是根本没有用，我已经没有什么耐心来教导你了。我会和你父亲讲，让他来管管你，看看一顿鞭子下去你会不会好点。我有没有和你讲过，你吃过早饭，喂过猪，去汤普金斯先生家，把奶油印模拿回家后，就直接去学校。你现在肩上扛着铁锹，我认为你自己都不清楚拿锹干什么用。"说着她走向威廉，抓住威廉的衣领用力地晃了一下，"难道你就这样来报答我和你父亲为你所做的一切吗？这法子不错，是吧？我本打算让你周六到镇里给自己买顶新草帽，可是现在你就扛着你的铁锹待在家里好了，你根本就不配有新帽子。现在去喂猪，然后去汤普金斯先生家把奶油印模带回家，再问问汤普金斯太太要不要换些鸡蛋。记住，别耽搁超过一个小时。"

威廉放下铁锹说他喂过猪了，汤普金斯先生家也去过了，他正准备去学校。

马丁太太说："这可能吗？"她的话远远算不上什么褒奖或鼓励，她接着又说："好啊，这可是你这辈子头回做对事，我想也会是你最后一回——去上学。"

威廉留恋地看了铁锹一眼，然后离开了，他心里想如果他长大了他就远走他乡，他母亲就再也听不到他的消息了。

就这样威廉一边闷闷不乐地想着心事，一边慢腾腾地朝着校舍走去。可还没等他走出多远，一位绅士驾着辆轻便马车就超过了他。拉车的是一匹毛色黑亮的骏马，绅士勒住马，亲切和蔼地说："小朋友上来坐一程吧。"从来没人这么和气地和威廉讲过话，所以威廉下意识地说了声"谢谢"就爬上了车。

一路上陌生的绅士给他讲了好多不同的事情，了解了他都学过什么，而且在不知不觉中传授给他其他他还不知道的知识，所以等马车停下来，他在校舍前下车的时候，他已经觉得自己俨然是个有些本事的孩子了。他心里想：我不在乎老师的好坏了，不管怎样，这个学期我要把地理和算术搞定,那位先生说我行,那我就真的行。

"天性聪明的少年,但是没有教好,没教好——遗憾哪。"陌生的绅士一边驾车一边在沉思。

丽贝卡和艾丽已经采了满怀的鲜花,此刻一起坐在一条长着青苔的小溪旁,清澈冰凉的溪水从青色的石板上缓缓流过。两个小姑娘一个忙着把鲜花编成花环,陶醉于美丽的鲜花和自己快乐的心情之中,另一个却把她采的鲜花晾在身旁的地上任其慢慢枯萎,自己双手抱膝,眼睛死盯着溪水,一言不发。小鸟们轻快地掠过枝条,围绕着郁郁葱葱的树林飞来飞去,在林间到处洒满了歌声和婉转的啁啾声,耕牛在山坡上来来回回地耕地,蜜蜂嗡嗡地飞出蜂房。就这样一整天她们俩就坐在这大自然甜美的音乐之中。渐渐地丽贝卡带着忧伤的笑容变成了嘴角快乐的笑意,因为身旁的艾丽一直不停地逗她开心。下礼拜她们要进城去了,她俩有生以来只去过城里一次,所以她们自然把这当成非常重要而有趣的事。她们会有新衣服、新帽子,还有一些其他东西,不过我不记得了。她们聊了很多关于什么款式和颜色的穿戴起来漂亮有魅力,还聊了穿上了新衣服该去哪里,都做点什么。太阳在西边的树梢边照耀着,这时她们站起来,顺着小路穿过起伏的草地,来到离家大约半里路的大道上,这条大道正对着孤零零的墓地。由于被墓地里某种声音所吸引,她们走近了些,但是她们发出的声响倒让那个人停止了动作,没有了动静,她们开始觉得可能是自己听错了,也许那只是树叶婆娑的声音。她们刚要离开,这时她们看到了威廉·马丁那张苍白的脸和黑黑的眼睛,他正靠着铁锹分开荆棘丛向外偷看。原来他正在填埋校长的坟呢。她们到家前,有一辆马车从身旁经过,就是早上威廉搭乘去学校的那辆,驾车的绅士用似曾相识的微笑向她们致以傍晚的问候。艾丽一时不知所措,一阵颤抖,手里有一半的花掉落了,丽贝卡却冷静地说:"这就是之前我们看到从学校方向过来的同一个人。"说话间她的心思飘回了过去。从看到他的第一刻起,艾丽的脑子里就对他产生了浓厚的兴趣,她一直在琢磨他是谁,是否就住在附近,正想着她们已经走到了家门口。

哈德利太太正从熏房里走出来,手里端着一盘子刚切下来的火腿,"丫头们过来,给我搭把手做晚饭。"艾丽靠近母亲急切地问:"谁来咱家了?"——家里有客登门可是件大事。

哈德利太太说是格雷太太来了,她接着说:"要是让格雷太太看到你们两个大姑娘都差不多成人了,手里还满是玩耍的东西,她会怎么想呢?把花都扔了,进屋来摆桌子。"就在此时窗子里出现了一顶白色棉布帽子,帽子上面有繁复的黑丝带装饰,帽子旁边还伸出一只有点枯黄的手,手上青筋暴露,这只手轻快有力地上下翻飞着,格雷太太可是个闲不住的人,无论是在家或者出门在外,从来都不肯闲坐着,总想着找点事做。她一刻也不敢忘记"魔鬼专找闲人使唤",并且反复念叨,尽管她这人性情连半点诗意都没有。

哈德利太太这个时候已经把晚饭安排好了,交代女孩子们去做了,自己拿起一双毛袜子,家里有好多双像这样袜面上有格子图案的毛袜子。她紧挨她的邻居坐下来,开始织自己的毛袜子之前,仔细端详了邻居手里织的东西。这是一件孩子用的围裙,是用带网眼的尿布做的,样式是哈德利太太从来没看到过的。哈德利太太非常羡慕地拿着这条围裙说:"快和我说说你是从哪儿弄来这么漂亮的图案的。"

邻居说:"你喜欢这图案吗?我想换换图案看起来会漂亮些,这个图案的来历是这样的:新搬到原来格雷海姆家房子的那家人派人到我家买了好多东西。他们到的第一个晚上就过来买了很多东西。汉姆斯塔德先生自己没过来,我想他这人大概很自以为是,但我知道我也不该这么说——很可能他在家里有事要忙——不管怎么说毕竟搬家是够忙的了。他打发一个黑人来,拿了一个大号的篮子,我一时也讲不清楚他都买了些什么。让我想想——他先是要买一整条面包——我觉得这很奇怪,但我觉得面包这东西我不能问人家要钱的。接着他又要了两磅黄油,一条火腿,十二个鸡蛋,一夸特牛奶,还有点从格雷那儿拿的小土豆,具体拿了多少我也不知道,但最奇怪的是,他拿了东西就直接放进一个爱尔兰式样的白色亚麻布药箱里。"格雷太太接着说这家人肯定很奢侈的,那个黑人从头到尾都没问过价,然后就拿出钱包付账,她开什么价就什么价,也不理睬她在一边表示像面包和牛奶这样的不值钱的东西她不想收钱了。

说着说着宾主双方都把围裙图案的事情忘到脑后去了。哈德利太太说:"我还不知道有新来的人家搬到格雷海姆家的房子里了。"

"这不太可能吧?他们到了有四五天了,你就没听说过吗?哦,我刚刚还看到汉姆斯塔德先生经过这里,连五分钟都不到——姑娘们，你们肯定见过他的。"

"就是那个驾着一匹黑马拉的马车路过的绅士吗？我见到他了——好像他就住在附近。"虽然说不清为什么，但是听说他的确住在附近艾丽就是很高兴。

格雷夫人接着说："不管怎样，我希望他们一家人别和我们这样的庄户人家有什么来往，人家都说，汉姆斯塔德夫人成天都穿戴齐整，除了看书什么都不做，甚至都不给自己的孩子喂奶。今天我来的路上就看到她在她家的菜园里，头上戴了顶软帽，那质地好得都可以赶集的时候戴了，再看看她那双手，雪白雪白的。"格雷太太最后说了句："唉，人哪，各有各的命呀！"似乎她的话就到此为止了，但是她又接着说起来："这也太怪了，一家人就使唤了三个女佣——一个丫头，一个奶妈，还有一个厨子，据说他们家把这三个人叫做佣人，天哪，这世道都变成啥样了！我和我男人说，我们就该像史密斯先生那样把家产都拍卖了，然后搬到一个新地方去，现在这里来了太多带着男仆、女仆，还有精美地毯和家具的城里人。"

可怜的格雷太太！她是个很守旧的女人，她先入为主的想法不会轻易地向现代的新观念屈服。她叹了口气，哈德利太太想转移她的注意力，于是说："你刚才说这个人叫什么来着？"

"我也不确定，"格雷太太说，"那个黑人叫他汉姆斯塔德，有人叫他汉普顿，但我自己觉得他应该叫海姆斯蒂德。"

丽贝卡这时正里里外外、忙上忙下地准备晚饭，没怎么在意这两个人在谈什么。她现在正想着校长，还有那个鬼鬼祟祟躲在树丛里填埋校长坟墓的威廉。但艾丽把两个人的话里关于那个奇怪的绅士的话听得一字不漏，她心里盘算着等她有了新衣服和新帽子，再去会会他。她心里想：因为如果我打扮得好我就会表现得更好，我可不想让他把我当一个单纯的村姑，像现在这样，可他又能怎么想呢？

就在这个时候，格雷太太缝好了她那件围裙，叠了起来，早就把她怎么得到这个图案的事忘记了。她兴高采烈地冲着小露西·哈德利拍着双手，小露西一整天就一个人待在她那个杂草丛游乐场里，现在刚回来。她离这位来客还有点距离就站住了，害羞地把手交叉在背后，仔细却并不粗鲁地打量着客人。格雷太太说："这是不是我家小姑娘呀？"露西不太习惯见生人，没有答话。她长长的睫毛垂下来，苍白的脸颊上露出淡淡的红晕，还是一言不发。

"你哑巴啦，"她母亲说，"跟格雷太太说你叫什么名字！"

格雷太太说："是的，她说不出来了——她的舌头给猫叼走了！可怜小姑娘，连名字都没有。"

"你这孩子，真给我丢人。"哈德利太太一边说着，一边用手抚平吹乱了的金色卷发。孩子用黑黑的小手擦了一把眼泪转过身去。她嘴唇颤抖着，她对大人的责备很敏感。格雷太太和蔼地把她揽过来，轻轻拍拍她的脸说："我刚才是讲故事呢，你有好听的名字，猫也没把你舌头叼走。"露西说"是的"，为了证明，她把舌头伸给格雷太太看，格雷太太高兴地说："这是个乖孩子，我就知道！"说着她把叠好的围裙打开拿给露西看，然后为了逗露西开心自己把围裙戴上了，露西本来忧郁的大眼睛现在闪动的都是快乐，她小鸟依人般地依偎着这位和善的妇人，格雷太太对自己有这样的福分颇为自得。

我把格雷太太称为和善的女人——她的确是这样的人，尽管有时不太明智。她身体靠向哈德利太太说："丽……"她声音很低，露西听不清楚名字其余的部分。哈德利太太又说："是不是还是对……的事闷闷不乐。"她这时又提起了另外一个名字，但是声音太低，露西还是什么也听不到。

哈德利太太笑着说小孩子的哀伤不会长久的，尽管两个姑娘都很爱她们的老师，但是她相信这种感情并不是真的爱情，所以她们不会一直就这样为他消沉下去。哈德利太太说得很真诚，毫无掩饰，所以她健谈的邻居又接着说："那么你难道就不知道某人在他死后还去上坟了嘛！"

"嗯，我知道的，这是她的自由。"

"那么你也知道某人给某人留下了份礼物，里面有一封信，内容谁也没看到过？"

"你要经常引用《圣经》吧——学生们人手一本不也是一样的用途吗？"

"嗯，我相信是这么回事，但不是每个学生都有一封信吧？"格雷太太说。

"写几句诫勉之言，再道个别——没别的。很遗憾外人有别的看法：丽贝卡知道了会很痛苦的。"

"你小点声，小点声！"格雷太太说，"有的时候小家伙耳朵尖。"说着转向露西说，"去吧，把你这件漂亮的新围裙给姐姐们看看吧。"

格雷太太于是又和哈德利太太说，现在大家都说丽贝卡和小学校长订过婚的，他们习惯在校舍旁边的树林幽会，他死后丽贝卡还去看他，哭得那个惨啊，校舍周围都听得到她的声音。现在看来，如果这一切都属实的话，其实也没什么大不了的。但是哈德利太太不这么看，她向来都是从最严苛的角度看事情的。何况，年轻人之间的彼此爱慕之情在村里喜欢飞短流长的人的嘴里又被添油加醋了。许多上了年纪的，甚至也包括一些中年人往往会犯的一个错误就是总是把年轻人之间单纯的乐趣看成不检点，把所有男女之间的情爱都看成恶事，他们忘记了自己也曾像他们现在说的那样年少轻狂，忘记了他们也有过各自不同的婚恋。哈德利太太此时此刻也犯了这个错误，她打定主意不能对这样无法无天的行为听之任之。作为女人，她正值壮年，做事果断，有着非常严格的道德观念，一向把孩子们喜欢幻想非常感性的性情当成很大的不幸，这种性情在现实中会更糟糕——是可耻的。孩子们在成长的过程中几乎没有从她这里得到任何鼓励。的确，她几乎没有觉察到孩子的存在。作为一个没有文化、普通而又很实际的妇女，她根本不懂什么是天赋或天赋有什么用处。她比邻居更谨慎，一点也没透露自己的想法或主意，但是在之后的一个礼拜里她反复在心里琢磨着这些事情。

现在家里年长的成员都在一起喝茶。太阳已经下山了，鸡都已经回窝了，艾丽和丽贝卡到牛棚去了，两个人在那里一边挤奶，一边和平时一样聊天：聊聊新搬来的邻居，聊聊格雷太太和她那些小道消息，聊聊进城，聊聊新衣服、新帽子。她们正忙着，露西穿着那件新围裙有点羞怯地走过来，眼神中有骄傲也有担心。丽贝卡装着没认出她，说："这是谁家的小姑娘啊？""我猜是约翰逊家的小姑娘，对，八成是。你好啊，小莎莉·约翰逊？"露西大笑起来，说她不叫莎莉，她叫露西。"哦，是的，我认出来了，"丽贝卡说着伸出手来，"是我们家的小露西穿了件新围裙。"

"你进城的时候会给我也弄一件这样的围裙吗？"露西用手抚摸着这件围裙，心里有说不出的羡慕。

可怜的小女孩！她长这么大从来没见过这样的围裙，从来也没拥有过，但她心里有种快乐的想法，因为丽贝卡说如果母亲同意她就会有一条。格雷太太要回家的时候这个孩子是够难过的,她必须和那件围裙告别了。

一个礼拜过去了,哈德利太太对她听到的消息只字不提,也没有流露出她对这些消息的讨厌。她对孩子们的态度总是非常内敛,冷冰冰的。母子之间没有什么知心话,没有什么玩笑,尽管孩子们都很爱她,但对她充满了敬畏,不敢和她沟通自己的喜怒哀乐。

星期六的早上,哈德利家门口停了一辆轻便的绿色的马车,拉车的是两匹膘肥体壮、皮毛发亮的栗色骏马。艾丽和丽贝卡穿着她们最好的印花布袍子,尽管她们没有手套,而且破旧已经不合脚的鞋已经遮不住她们的脚趾了,但当她们走出她们的房间,爬上马车坐在新铺的干净稻草上的时候,房间里面还是回荡着她们快乐的笑声。露西一双白嫩的小脚半陷在离车不远还挂着露珠的苜蓿草堆里,一双褐色的眼睛里半是期待半是眼泪,微张的嘴唇上露出一丝微笑,半卷的黄色发丝披散在脖子和肩膀上。她鼓起勇气说:"你们别忘了给我买围裙啊。"宽边礼帽遮掩了哈德利先生那张慈祥的面孔,他把缰绳从樱桃树枝上解了下来。

这时哈德利太太出现在门口,说:"等一下,丽贝卡今天不进城了。"她的语气低沉而平静,似乎在说一个普普通通的句子。丽贝卡感觉到了她的态度,二话没话,服从地下了车。

"母亲,我也留下吧。"艾丽颤抖着说。

"不,我的孩子,你要进城去,买身新衣服、新帽子,丽贝卡她不配有这样的待遇。"

这话听起来让人觉得似乎说话人有些委屈,好像她是出于重任在身才不得不如此。哈德利先生愣了一下,然后用手抚了抚自己灰白的头发,跨上自己的位置,一边把车赶起来,一边半带悲哀半带恼怒地问艾丽:"我不明白你妈到底怎么了?你姐姐到底惹什么乱子了?"露西坐在刚才站着的那个草堆上,一边拔草一边把草胡乱编成一根,眼泪静静地滴到她腿上。但是丽贝卡很平静,一言不发地换上了平日里干活的衣服干起平时的活来。午饭她没什么胃口,晚饭吃得更少,她忍着头痛不说,还一个人做着平时由她和艾丽两个人做的活。

天色入夜,她一边挤着牛奶,一边急切地听着路过的马车声,一辆又一辆马车驶过去了,但是直到门前的丁香花洒满了晨曦的时候才看到两匹栗色的骏马跑过来。

丽贝卡和艾丽分开了一天,这一天似乎出奇的长,她觉得现在非常需要别人的安慰和同情,所以她急切地跑到大门口就毫不奇怪了。但是艾丽不在车上。简姨妈一个人住着三间房子,做些缝纫活,劝说艾丽留下来,说给她做新衣服和新帽子,等她父亲下个礼拜去赶集的时候再一道回家。

月亮升起来了,又圆又大,月华如水,洒满小屋,窗棂和屋外的樱桃树把月光分割成许多格子和点点。露西在丽贝卡的怀里哭泣着进入了梦乡,不时发出一两声沉闷的喘息,打破丽贝卡身边的寂静。

这个睡不着的女孩一会儿一只手枕到头下,一会儿不安地翻翻身,最后筋疲力尽的她把枕头垫在身后整个人坐起来。月光静静地照进小屋——屋外的世界万籁俱寂,但女孩的身心无法平静。她想着独自在外离家很远的艾丽,在她看来她和艾丽彼此相隔的距离很远。她想起了小学校长和他的孤坟,她想起了自己。她就这样想啊,想啊,想啊,直到后来鸟儿已经在丁香花丛中飞舞鸣叫,已经发白的东方染上了猩红色,而她一夜无眠。

这个世界到处都是伤痕累累、满心凄苦的心灵;悲凉的呻吟随着阳光四处蔓延,哪怕是再欢快的笑声里也潜伏着呻吟;痛苦的枕头、无眠的房间遍布这个世界。既然蛇虫盘踞其间,这世上就没有不败的花朵;既然罪恶让这个世界坟冢遍布,天使白色的翅膀也为诅咒所遮蔽,我们就不再有安宁之日了。

我们如此孤立无援,所以我们需要和睦相处,要随时伸出爱心和援助的手给他人以鼓励,因为我们所要面临的黑暗和沉默不是一般的关心所能挽救的。我们面前有许多上帝广施恩德的范例,可是我们还是盲目固执地犯错!几滴苦涩的毒药就能毒害生命之泉,让其永远迟滞沉重。

艾丽走亲戚的一个礼拜过去了,她的新帽子做好了,新衣服也是漂亮的款式,所以看到带稻草坐垫的绿色马车和栗色马匹停在姨妈家整洁的房子前的时候她好开心。她快活地跑向父亲,问家里都好吧,但是父亲迎接她的笑容满是悲伤,声音满是抑制不住的忧郁:"丽贝卡病得不轻了。"

"哦,父亲!她真的病得很重吗?"艾丽问,心里一阵恐惧。

哈德利先生转过脸,努力用一种更欢快的语气说:"我希望她今晚能好点。坐好了，艾丽，我们尽快赶回家，她想见你，我可怜的姑娘！"艾丽系好她的新帽子，但现在已经没什么高兴的心情了，她把衣服叠起来放到一个干净的包袱里，很快坐到了车上自己的位置上。但是丽贝卡没有新衣服和新帽子，艾丽一直渴望的这些宝贝现在都一钱不值了。一路上她都在责备自己，如果她当时留在家里或者她当晚就回家的话……的确，她无可指责，但她心里的痛苦一点也不少。想到家里她有些迫不及待，可是她又有些害怕回到家里。

她看到一些工人在树林里伐木，边伐边吹口哨，看他们对她的伤心事既不知情也不在意，艾丽很委屈。一辆辆拉着衣着光鲜的人们进城去的马车从身旁驶过，艾丽满眼怨恨地望着他们。中午时分，他们驶过校舍。学校的门窗都敞开着，里面新来了位老师，就站在从前老师的位置上，孩子们在树林里嬉戏叫嚷，一切一如从前，就好像这里从未有人生病，从未有人死去一样。露西就等在家门口，她大大的忧郁的眼睛里没有眼泪，她还不懂什么是死亡，但一种莫名的恐惧让她感到非常压抑，而且家里人一直让她待在房子外面。汉姆斯塔德先生的马和马车停在院子里，但是房子里面似乎悄无声息，只看到格雷太太在窗旁缝着什么很白的东西。

艾丽和父亲都忍住没有向露西打听丽贝卡的情况，露西把两手交叉背在身后，好奇地看着艾丽的新帽子。哈德利先生开始把马从车辕上解下来，一路上急着赶路，马都累了，嘶鸣着要回马棚。艾丽犹豫地站在那里，一手拿着新衣服，一手拿着她的旧帽子。这时汉姆斯塔德先生一声不响地从房子里走出来和两个人握握手，接着从哈德利先生手里接过缰绳，然后低声告诉他们进去。父女二人照做了，父亲默默地用手背擦去眼泪，小姑娘却号啕大哭起来。格雷太太放下手里缝的东西——那是一顶棉布帽子，迎了上来，接过艾丽手里的衣服和帽子说："你过来看看她吧。"说着轻轻地打开门，父女二人跟着她来到了丽贝卡的房间。屋内的灯光昏暗，就在那张曾经憧憬过许多瑰丽梦想的窄床上躺着丽贝卡，她此刻已经无法再梦想了。艾丽亲吻着她苍白的嘴唇，但嘴唇上那平静的笑意并没有因这一吻而展开。她的手指原本深情地握着，但现在沉重冰冷地松开了。她的灵魂通过晨曦那白色之门去往那夜晚永远不会降临的世界。就在旧操场对面的墓地里有一块普普通通的墓碑石，上面镌刻着——

丽贝卡·哈德利
十五岁七个月零五天

31. 雨 天

  雨淅淅沥沥地下了整整一天一夜。傍晚时分，西方的云彩泛出一抹黄色，显示太阳的位置，但是阳光未能穿过厚厚的云层。所有的山谷都被灰蒙蒙的浓雾笼罩着，山头的雾气一片一片的，没有那么浓重，颜色也淡些，林中的雾则慵懒地从一个树枝爬过另一个树枝。时不时地会有鸟儿从叶间或其他藏身之处出来，落在栅栏顶端，拍打拍打翅膀，用喙理理胸前松散的羽毛，轻轻地喳喳叫几声。但是小雨始终下个不停，一会儿便淋湿了它们的羽毛，鸟儿无可奈何地飞走了，再也没有一丝声响。小鸡们三五成群地依偎在低矮的樱桃树下或黑醋栗丛里，有红色的、芦花的和棕色的，鸡胸脯上溅了些水花，亮闪闪的，它们都闭着眼睛站着，等待夜晚的来临。
  这个格外温和的秋天渐渐地接近尾声。严霜还未来临，园子四处的花儿花茎还未变黑，花上仍残留着即将凋落或是已经凋零的花朵，像木乃伊一样枯萎干瘪下去。漂亮的树叶是我们西部秋天最壮丽的景色，现在也正在慢慢凋零，尽失往日的美丽，飘然落去。几乎环绕着苜蓿角的那片黑色的森林地带总是云雾缭绕，而现在看上去也那么暗淡萧瑟。自从上一章中描述的事件后，又过了很多个春夏秋冬，附近的房舍和住宅又增加了很多。绵延起伏的草地延伸到天尽头，到处是毛儿又长又厚的绵羊、膘肥体壮的公牛、乳房低垂的母牛。这片土地尽是整齐的垄沟，盛产牛奶和羊毛。
  从艾丽出生的房屋现在可以看到五六座尖塔，但是从前在她的记忆中只有一座。她家里的财富和人口同步增长。旧宅保留了下来，她在那里度过了天真无邪的岁月，同时经历了很多艰难的时刻。如今，炉边满是紫蓟花，过去门廊处现在已经覆盖上厚厚的泥土。以前，夏天时门廊处开满了蓝色的牵牛花，遮住了炎炎烈日，红色的蜀葵随风摆动，金黄的太阳花朝西面伸展。过去花园的位置现在还有几棵苹果树和樱桃树，长久无人关注，更没有剪枝。过去蔷薇花爬上墙头，甚至一直攀爬到屋檐上，锯齿状的叶子、纤巧淡色的花儿使得整个房子都香气扑鼻；而今支离破碎，藤蔓交织在一起，半死不活。附近山坡上有一所新房子，虽然不是那么富丽堂皇，但是很坚固体面，里面住着哈德利家的遗留者，称其遗留者是因为这个家族圈子曾经是那么庞大，如今有些人流落他乡，有些人已经离开了世界。丽贝卡年轻漂亮，已经长得有了女人样，却又稚气未脱，正处在所谓"小溪汇入河流之际"。正是此时，无声的天使唤她而去，她用冰冷的小手把长长的卷发拉直，取出花朵饰物，系好放在手帕里，既没有叹息，也没有向下张望。还有露西——温柔可爱的露西，在这个世界上没活多久。她还没活到能了解世界上有怎样的苦难。当她的第九个夏天来临时，她黑亮深沉的眼睛失去了阳光，她的头一天比一天垂得低，好像金发上落的尘土越来越重，直到最后死亡的信使把她揽到怀中。春雨飘落，麦子的嫩叶渐渐变大，颜色变深。草场边翠绿柔软的水槽汇成缓缓的小溪流。成群的小羊来了，却没有那温顺的孩子做伴。

曾经有一个城里来的小女孩来看她，身穿白裙子。露西并不穷，只是身处乡野，衣服样式都很简单质朴。她最大的一个心愿是能有一件白衣裙，就像来看她的那个有钱的小客人穿的那样的。有时候，她鼓起勇气表达了她的愿望，但是受到一顿训斥，让她"最好是和乖乖女学"，吓得她再也不敢出声。终于白裙子穿上身，金色的卷发垂在上面，长裙一直盖过双脚，此时她已经对此毫无所知，也不会因为愿望得到了满足而会心微笑了。

她的母亲在诸多的操劳辛苦后也离世了。她墓石周围的草渐渐长得越来越浓密茂盛。她是个好女人，虽然在家教上过于严厉，但是如果她认为是她的责任，她总会从早到晚非常尽职尽责地去做，不是为了她自己，而是为了她的孩子。但是孩子减少两个，她的心都碎了，她的任务没有了，她无时无刻不在思念中度过，这种疯狂的思念迅速地耗尽了她的生命——只有在六翼天使在她的额头前收拢翅膀，使燃烧的烈焰冷却下来，这份狂热才消退。

其他孩子已经长大成人，纷纷离开家去挖掘新的兴趣，成立新的家庭。因此在这个新家里，艾丽现在是年龄最大的孩子了。她正值青春大好年华。妹妹们都迅速地长成了大姑娘，在她的眼中，她们都非常亲，但是仍然不能填补坟墓中的亲人在她心中的位置。照料幼小弟妹的重担落在她的肩上，她的性情生来忧郁，后来却习惯性地经常表现出忧伤、不满、痛苦的情绪。她的父亲是个好人，非常善良，但是他的习惯、思维和想法和上一辈是一样的。任何革新，不管有多好，都无法动摇他的意念，农作物的耕作、一日三餐的吃法、服饰的穿戴都是老一辈的样式。艾丽的衣服必须按照她母亲的样式去做，而且穿的时间也必须一样长。时代变迁了，但是在他眼中，先辈勤俭节约的好习惯即使在当前物质富足的年代也并没有任何不合适的。

在这个新家中，老式的细长家具看上去很别扭，光秃秃的地板要始终保持光洁白亮，要增加地毯或新椅子的想法是行不通的，要让仆人来做家务活，即使是苦力活，也绝不允许。哈德利先生说，纺纱织布已经废弃不做了，家里没什么活可做的。艾丽只受过一点点教育——比她所有的妹妹都要少，但是她天资聪颖，比其他孩子更胜一筹。只要一有机会她就会去读书，而且很善于思考。然而，二十五岁时，人们提到她时，只说她是个聪明的乡下姑娘。她很谦虚，甚至有点胆怯，生活离群索居。附近富裕时尚的社交活动对她来说没有任何吸引力，她也不曾做过任何努力去寻求认可。当想起她本可以有更高的地位，她会对约束她的环境不满，最终给她天生和善的性格增加了些许痛苦。

但是我还是先回到那个秋天和那场雨吧。

这是一个老式的装饰简单的房间，宽大的壁炉中木头在熊熊燃烧。壁炉前坐着两个人，大一点的是艾丽，她身穿一件朴素的印花棉布衫，棕色的头发非常顺滑，在前额处自然分开。前额由于忧郁操劳有些暗淡，但是没有皱纹。她一边缝制一件小孩子的衣服，一边听着坐在她旁边的佐伊读《马米昂》。佐伊很漂亮，比她的姐姐漂亮，比姐姐小将近十岁。两人肤色都有些黑。艾丽个子高挑修长些，而佐伊脸庞较圆，面色红润，她的脸色就像刚扬场过的麦子映着绯红色的落日所显出的颜色。她的黑发卷得很厉害，一缕缕垂到肩上，眼睛更黑，闪烁着笑意。她的衣服穿得比姐姐的时尚。在她的额头上看不出任何烦恼，家里平时也无须她做什么事情。

"好看！真的很好看！"佐伊赞叹道，同时放下手中的书，转向艾丽，"我多么喜欢看小说啊！"随后她站起身来，走到窗前说，"如果不是下雨，我真想出去，去借几本小说：夜越来越长了，这样的书可以帮助我们消磨时间。我很厌烦我们的这些旧书。但是至少两三天都出不去，瞧这雨下得多大！"

艾丽说："也许会云开雾散。"她的话语充满了希望，但是心中不这样想。"日落时分天空看起来很亮，但是我觉得就算不下雨，你也不敢贸然出去。"艾丽神情落寞地说，"我也不认识一个可以借书给我的人。"佐伊把门打开，眼睛急切地看着雨点。艾丽还在说着，"你呢，佐伊？"

"没有，我也不认识。"小姑娘说着，最初的那股强烈冲动一下子冷静下来。

从山上飞奔下来一挂单骑马车，欢跑的马蹄重重地落在雨水刚洗刷过的石头路面上，发出"嗒嗒"的响声，鼻孔呼出白色的热气在空中会成卷状。因为快到家了，马儿细长光滑的耳朵都向前支着。马车的窗帘关得紧紧的，孤寂的行人可以舒服地坐在干燥的马车里。艾丽此时坐在炉火边，满怀思绪，手里不停地做着针线活。她根本没听到车轮的响声，也没看到窗帘内的笑脸和熟悉的问候，她没听到一个声音说："是不是很羡慕我啊？"但是她看到佐伊神采奕奕的表情，听见她小声地笑着说："那当然啦。"

"当然什么？"艾丽问，放下手中的针线，抬头看看。"真冷啊！"佐伊说着，赶紧把门关上，走过来又回到座位上。她解释说她刚才在跟汉姆斯塔德先生说话。她觉得他大概刚从城里回来，回到他乡下的宅子里。读者可能还记得，他的宅子紧挨着哈德利的农场。"他是个多么令人愉快、多可爱的人哪。"佐伊继续对自己说，也对艾丽说，"我刚才已退缩的决心现在更强烈了，我有朝一日会向他借些书的。"

"哼！"艾丽说，神情忧郁而又若有所思地看着炉火。过了一会儿，她说："我觉得他只会对跟他交往的人才会屈尊帮忙。"

"如果我们不接受他的好意，他就没办法帮我们。"

"我根本没有机会拒绝他或者其他任何人的好意。"艾丽回答道，又是忧伤又是难过，手中的针线活放在腿上，她目光茫然地盯着火光。

佐伊快乐的情绪持续了一段时间，一会聊聊家里的事情，一会谈谈邻居正在做的事情，一会又说说她自己打算做的新衣服。"我想做一件很亮丽的衣服，"她说，"底色是橙色或者红色，用黑色的点点来点缀。"她笑着，自我陶醉，又看看艾丽，希望她赞同自己的品味。

艾丽也笑了，但是这是怎样的一个笑容啊！简直难以形容，那是嘲笑、爱怜、同情，这几种情绪兼而有之，但是她仍旧一言不发，真让人恼火。

"你老盯着那个方向做什么？"佐伊生气地问，很孩子气地撅着嘴。

"我不是在想让你高兴吗？佐伊，我没办法，我长得不好看。对我来说，我已经习惯了自己的平庸，但是你那么年轻，那么漂亮，我不能要求你像我一样容忍我的缺点——你看的肯定是另一个角度，亲爱的。"她开玩笑似的拍了拍妹妹的脸颊，又笑了。这一次和往常一样，仿佛佐伊真的像她想的那样看自己，仿佛她能忍受别人那样看自己。

佐伊的确看到的是另一面。她用一双棕色的手捂住自己的脸，眼泪默默地顺着手指流了下来。火光渐渐地使房间里的灯光暗淡，甚至有些可怕。西方天空中的那片黄云慢慢融入到夜色中。姐妹俩坐在炉火前，心情很郁闷，不畅快。

夜色渐浓，颇让人感到沮丧。风儿呜咽着吹过山冈，在树林里已经浸湿的浓密的树叶和长长的垄沟间穿梭而过。白天有时刮风，日落时分风向会转变，寒冷的东北方时常刮来大风，吹得厅堂的窗户呼呼作响，时而壁炉中的火焰也吹得贴到蓝色的炉壁上。

蟋蟀从温暖舒适的缝隙中钻了出来，从燃烧的原木尽头和硕大的壁炉的角落中传出它们的鸣叫声，与暴风雨呼应唱和。这时，这场暴风雨已经过去，地上形成了滂沱的急流，雨点轻轻地打在窗户玻璃上。一轮半月努力挤出云层，露出它暗淡阴郁的脸庞。不一会儿，大团大团的黑云集结在一起，又把它打退到黑暗中。雨又下了起来，如同所有的喷泉都被打破了一般。这真是一个寂寥孤独的夜晚。

长长的秋雨尽管让人的心情郁郁寡欢，但是同样让人宽慰，让人的心情舒缓下来，在晚上尤其如此。佐伊是个急性子，但是脾气并不真坏，此时不是生气，而是感到难过。她把炉中的余火拢到一堆，坐在靠近艾丽的地方，说："唉，要是我们有那样的书就好了。"听上去好像刚才没有哭过，没有发生任何气恼的事情一样。

"是啊，要是我们有就好了。"艾丽也说。两姐妹又陷入沉默中，时而听听榆木爆裂敲击墙壁的声音，时而听听紧贴着门槛蜷缩着的那条斑点狗的哀鸣声，它不愿屈服于暴雨的威力。

"这样的夜晚真让我伤心，"佐伊打破了沉默的场面，说道，"我又回想起童年，那时候，晚上我们那么多人都围坐在火堆旁，我们多快乐啊，根本听不到大雨落下的声音。今晚在坟墓中多凄凉啊。我几乎不忍心去想，冰冷潮湿的树叶落在静静的坟茔上，白色的高草丛被雨打得紧贴墓石。哦，艾丽，我希望我们都不要死，我们在这儿多快乐。"

"等你像我这么大，你就不这么想了，"艾丽伤感地笑了笑，说道，"走了的人再也不用操劳，不用受苦，而且也不会再死了。我觉得他们反倒很让人羡慕。这样的暴风雨夜晚对他们来说有什么呢？而你这个活着的人，年轻、健康、充满希望，倒被它弄得感伤不已。"

"如果我们有精彩的故事或是诗歌，我就大声朗读出来，这样我们就听不到暴雨的声音，也不会感到寂寞了。"佐伊站起身来，走到书桌前，使劲地在那堆少得可怜而内容糟糕的书堆里翻来翻去，但是她很清楚那些书名和质量。自然而然地，她空手而归，又回到了座位上，叹了口气，说："如果这雨停了，我就去拜访汉姆斯塔德先生，求他发善心借我些书看。"

看家狗一声低沉的叫声中断了她们的谈话，接着厨房前的石板路上传来了重重的脚步声，紧接着是一阵很响的敲门声。

佐伊跑过去开门，心中希望有点什么事情可以打破这种无聊的夜晚，却又害怕是路人或是亲密的朋友发生了不幸。一会儿，她回来了，满脸喜悦，手中拿着一个整齐的包裹和一张字条。她将字条对着火光去看上面的地址，字条的边缘反射着火光。她边看边说："你看我多走运，我觉得一定是我的美好希望施加了力量把这带给我的。汉姆斯塔德先生已经预感到我的愿望。刚才就是他的黑奴凯撒拿来了这包东西，好像是书，还有这个字条。"她点亮灯，把字条扔到艾丽的腿上让她读，呵呵地笑着说："我只认得学校老师的字迹。"

艾丽打开字条，读道：

"威拉德·希·汉姆斯塔德先生恳请能向哈德利小姐们表示其敬意，并奉上《黑夜与清晨》这部新小说聊以排遣无聊夜晚。这本书我本人觉得很有意思，你们的才学我早有耳闻，大胆期望此书能架起桥梁，消除鸿沟，增进邻里之间的情感，至少我认为一直存在的这种情感。基于此，我愿意随时听候你们的差遣……"

"柳树谷绅士怎么变得这么亲切？"艾丽说着，把字条又折起来。柳树谷是汉姆斯塔德先生农场的名字。

"我想他很乐意把我们当人看，"佐伊回答说，"就我而言，我看不出他在哪方面比我们强。艾丽，不是天上的星宿而是我们自己决定了我们是这样的谦卑。我们根本不必要这样与人隔绝地生活，这都是因为你傻乎乎的谦卑心理和不自信造成的。汉姆斯塔德先生的厅堂地板上铺着漂亮的地毯，而你没有，有什么关系呢？汉姆斯塔德先生有五百本书，而你只有五本，这又有什么关系？他吃饭使用银盘子而你没有，又有什么要紧？你何必认为你在学识上、在情感上、在一切社会给人划分界限的事情上低人一等？"

"你真是伶牙俐齿，"艾丽说，"在把你的想法付诸实践之前，我有一个小故事要讲给你听。"艾丽剪剪烛头，挑挑炭火，把新书连同字条放到一边，以她头脑中还不能称之为"故事"的事情为序，然后开始讲起来。（故事的内容如下一章所见）

32. 窘　境

"让我想想看——自打汉姆斯塔德先生第一次到我们这儿来迄今已经有十二三个年头了，我还清楚地记得我第一次见到他的情形。丽贝卡和我正在放学的路上，那时我们是打着光脚板儿的野孩子。他追上我们，我猜他是以他想象中的西部人所用的方式开始和我们交谈：先说到我们的校长，后来是村子、村子的自然风貌，还有村里那些人的脾性等等。在遇到他之前，我从来没有见过教养如此好，举止如此文雅，如此具有绅士风度的人。我还清楚地记得当时我打心眼里对我们的光脚板儿和我们粗陋的外表感到别扭。就连说起那些我知道的事情，也远不及平时在希尔先生或者戴尔叔叔那些熟悉的人面前表达得好。总而言之，在看到他之后我意识到完美的人是什么样的。

"有时候我看到他从我身后经过，有时候我看到他前往或者从村里返回，他总是忙于照应他的那些伙计，要把辛顿先生布满荆棘的农场改造成柳树谷是需要很多人手的。走近我们的时候，他总是面带微笑地打个招呼。有时我们能看到汉姆斯塔德夫人，她面容苍白，身材娇弱，从来不对我们微笑，或者看上去压根就没有看到我们。第一次认识她，或者说是我第一次见到她时，她的容貌十分标致，但是身体孱弱。她的衣服是用一种深色的料子做的。她走到院子或者花园的时候，总是用一块深红的披肩把自己裹起来。有谣传说她曾经继承了一笔遗产，但是由于丈夫在投资生意中失手，不仅损失了他自己的财产，还损失了她的大部分财产。他就是因为丧失了财产才搬到了我们这儿。财富的损失也使他们失去了在原来的城市的地位。

"而且，在我们这个小地方，你知道，比现在还厉害的是，在那个时候，像他们那样的人被我们认为是非常伟大的人物。许多人确实认为能和他们的保姆交上朋友就已经够好了，在和他们交往的过程中，便可以偶尔把客厅瞥上几眼，或者偷偷看到汉姆斯塔德夫人的帽子或浴衣的样式。其他人只敢轻叩厨房的门——把自己摆在和下等仆人一样的地位，只是为了能和别人说说他们曾经造访过汉姆斯塔德先生的家。

"那时这儿倒是有那么几家有钱人和时尚家庭，但不足以挽回这个地方相当没有教养的总体特征，这是事实，但是他们是例外，因此汉姆斯塔德夫人觉得我们比野蛮人好不到哪里去就不足为奇了。我认为，甚至可以宣称即使在那时，我们村子已是处于半文明状态了。但是她不能，也不愿意体面地将自己和邻居们放在同一个水平上，尽管她有时试着热情一些，但也顶多不过是和蔼点罢了，而且总是透着点屈尊纡贵的感觉。绝大多数的访客都很迟钝——于他们自己的快乐而言，迟钝并不是灾难，这迟钝虽然阻止他们了解交往双方的不对等，但经常和一位漂亮的女士一起品茶，至少对他们一方而言是愉快的事情。

"'汉姆斯塔德夫人是一位多么迷人的女士啊，'总有人对别人说，'你不知道你没有认识她是多大的损失啊。'尽管有人也如此恳求我们，尽管我们与汉姆斯塔德是近邻，但是没有人能说服我们去拜访她。植根于母亲脑子里的想法和植根于汉姆斯塔德夫人脑子里的想法一样坚定，认为城里人与乡下人的感情根本不可能有相通之处，实际上，她们不会注意到人性并没有边界，不管相互间思维圈子有多不同，但总有交结点。那时我还小，也不奇怪，汉姆斯塔德夫人习惯了有教养的优雅的举止，是看不到包藏在我粗朴的外表下面的聪颖的——要是还有点聪颖的话。既然我的才华没有外现，又怎么能够让她将我从我与生俱来的阶层、教养、生活方式中区分开来呢？的确，街坊四邻随便哪个修车工的女儿或者挤奶女工的条件和机会都比我强得多，但是即使如此我仍然对那无辜的冒犯者耿耿于怀。

"我现在觉得她称得上是一个善良、乐于助人的女人。丽贝卡生病期间，她来了，并没有大张旗鼓，还带来了很多精致的食品，表现出温情关爱，她的关爱当时恐怕没得到应有的敬意。有一次她带来了一些玫瑰蜜饯。我记得，家中有人评论：'毫无疑问她是想展示她那银杯。'我提到这个是想说属于奢侈品范围的物件会让人怎么想。汉姆斯塔德夫人这些善意的关心确实赢得了我对她的爱意，如果不是因为一次尴尬遭遇，我们倒有可能成为朋友。当丽贝卡去世后，我无法告诉你我有多么孤独，我的生活变得空荡荡的，当泥块压得她的棺木吱吱作响时，我从来没有像那样热切地祈祷过。我们以前总是在一起，现在我一个人活在这个世界里，无人同情。自此，我要一个人上学，一个人睡觉，到哪里都是一个人。在她的葬礼上，我穿着新衣服、新帽子和新拖鞋，我却一点都不高兴。

"一天晚上，我从学校回来，汉姆斯塔德先生从后面过来，车里只有他一个人，他要我和他一起乘车。我虽然得到了新拖鞋，但那不是为上学来回路上穿的。当然，因为降霜了，我的脚看上去红肿冰冷。汉姆斯塔德先生很让我丢面子地说我必须多关心自己的健康，不要忘记穿鞋。啊，我的天！没有穿鞋并不是我的错。他对我说话十分和蔼，到了墓地的时候，我说'让我在这儿下去'，因为我每次路过这里总要停一停的，他看上去感到很抱歉，坚持要送我回家，但是当我看到高高隆起的坟墓时，泪水再也没能忍住。他勒住马，抱我出来，打开车门的时候，他对我说：'别待太久，别哭了，我亲爱的小姑娘。'

"我想他一定想知道我为什么那么伤心，他的妻子至少是在同情我。在那之后一两天，她到家里来请我。我站在她面前的时候紧张得浑身瑟瑟发抖：在此之前，从来没有人提出过类似的要求。她邀请了五六个年轻女士一两天后和她一起品茶，她想让我成为其中一员。毫无疑问，这个小小的聚会是特意为我而设的。我那时还是个半大孩子，但是总是被别人完全当成孩子。我既不知道如何拒绝，也不知道该如何接受她的邀请，就结结巴巴地说了些如果可能的话我就去之类的话。随后，汉姆斯塔德夫人临走时对我说，她肯定我会去，而且她也肯定会等我。那些她已经邀请了的年轻女士是些吵吵嚷嚷、自信满满，而且毫无教养的人，我对她们略知一二，但一点都不喜欢。我虽然这样想，但是我觉得她是出于好心才邀请我。可是我要去拜访她的想法没有得到任何鼓励。当那一天来临的时候，我问道：'我应该穿什么衣服，妈妈？'她答道：'穿上去哪儿，孩子？'好像她从来没有想过我要去哪里似的。我解释了一下，她接着说：'如果你要去参加时髦聚会，我没什么可说的，但就怕你去丢人现眼。'我哭了一个小时，又待了一个小时，想着不如从这个世界消失。就在我戴上遮阳帽准备到丽贝卡坟上去的时候，家里人却告诉我汉姆斯塔德先生来接我了，如果我愿意的话就可以去。

"我仔细擦干眼泪，作好了准备。我懂一点打扮的方法，但只是知道皮毛而已，你可以想象，即使我精于此道的话，怎样打扮也都是一样的，因为我有限的衣橱里没有什么可替换的衣服。在出去之前，我照着挂在我房间一侧的小破镜子仔细打量了一下自己，虽然跟前没有人和我作对我不利的对比，我仍对自己大为不满。现在在这儿，我可以仔细描述我的整个长相。我那时正处在整个人生中最尴尬的转型期——我的手脚因为劳作和暴晒变得粗大还有些变形，又宽又大的手撑开了手套，手的上半部分裸露在外，我的双脚不习惯于鞋子的束缚，脚趾从我从城里带回来的那双秀气的拖鞋里伸出去老长老长。"

"噢，艾丽，对自己仁慈一点儿！"佐伊喊道，她不安地挪动着身子对姐姐说话，但是姐姐不仅不作任何响应，反而继续说道："长期粗心地暴晒已经毁了我的面容，它从来没有白嫩过，想想吧，我的衣服样式差，做工也差。这回，我穿了一件粗糙的棉布衣服，花色刺眼，没有披肩，没有领子，也没有缎带来冲淡这种效果。好在我指望着太阳帽可以进行弥补，它的价格抵得上我整套衣服，样式简洁大方，但是对我而言它太大了，也太过时髦了，它紫色的缎带和花朵不适合我淡橄榄色的脸。我脸上的泪痕清晰可见，这些苦涩的想法让我不能说任何话，做任何事，但是，我试着微笑，希望汉姆斯塔德先生不会像我自己看自己那样看待我。

"他那时并没有那样想。他对自己的外表不大在意，但是黑色的手套和优雅合身的灰色便装使他和我平时惯见的农夫们截然不同。那天天气晴朗，他也倾尽全力让我高兴。几乎每个人都感到愉快和荣幸,但是我极不愉快,也不感到荣幸。一到他家,我出发时的镇静顿时消失,一半原因是那个黑人男孩在照顾马匹,一半原因是汉姆斯塔德先生礼貌地领着我到了客厅,就好像我是什么了不起的名媛一样,穿着丝绸和皮毛制成的披风的汉姆斯塔德夫人正在客厅高兴地等我。

"那些女孩子已经到了——每个人都身着节日的盛装,要多高兴就有多高兴。我没有一丝像她们那样的喜悦之情,也不能加入到她们虽然活泼但无聊的氛围中去。我不希望和她们为伍,也不愿意被别人认为是她们一伙的。但我并不比她们强,口才也不行,我有什么权力让别人认为自己与众不同呢?当然没有。这我知道,我只是徒添自己的恼怒。我深为自己到这儿来感到愤慨,我更为自己的思想和感情被自己的乡土气息深深掩埋而生气。我完全可以表现得自然一些,说些我知道的事情就行了,但是假如我真的演了一个重要的角色,那也不过是上了一堂表演课而已,所演的角色实际上与我格格不入——绝大多数时间我都庄重地坐在那里,说些夸夸其谈的话,这既不是我的习惯,也不是教养所许可的。在上流社会的圈子里,所有你说的和做的都得循规蹈矩。

"汉姆斯塔德先生和那些女孩子开了玩笑之后,像一个普通的乡下人一样把外套扔到一边,出去干农活了。汉姆斯塔德夫人则尽了一个谦卑的女主人的份儿,做得如此之好,简直令人称羡。她以熟悉的口吻谈到了蛋奶沙司和布丁的做法,从事园艺活动的时间和方法,持家理财的最佳方式,还有许多她从未亲自做过也永远不会想着去做的事情。但是,我想,她是决心充分利用这最佳的机会,也确实试着制作了奶酪和黄油,并将自己和邻居放在同一个水平上。在这有纪念意义的时刻,她和孩子、保姆、厨娘以及没多少教养的农妇打成一片,好像我们生来自由平等是她信条中最高也是最无须质疑的真理。

"除了那些银器之外,苹果、苹果汁和坚果以真正的乡村的方式呈上来。姑娘们想她们给予主人的快乐和自己得到的一样多,她们却不知道,主人之所以取悦于她们完全是为了达到这种效果而装出来的。她们以这种自由、冷静的方式轻松地评价地毯、窗帘、半身像和他们视线以内的家具时的情形十分有趣。主人认为没有必要为款待我们而打开客厅,只把一个平常用作书房或茶室的套间用来作为这个小型聚会的场所。

"桌布被及时地铺上了,我们要趁着薄暮踏上回家的路,那些最能干最大方的女孩子帮忙收拾桌子,甚至还在厨房帮忙。总而言之,所有事情都进行得十分令人愉快。突然,从门口的碎石路上传来一阵吱吱呀呀的车声,引起了人们的注意。仅仅一瞥就足以说明这些新来的客人和我们不是同一个层次。对我而言,那些丝绸、皮毛、羽毛、缎带、黑色的细平布和灰色的披肩等等让我感到眼花缭乱,当他们快要进客厅时,我这才意识到自己穿的只是红色的印花布和白色棉布长筒袜,更觉得糟糕透顶。很明显,汉姆斯塔德夫人觉得处境尴尬。她本来可以游刃有余地分别处理好自己与不同层次的人的关系,但是放在一起,像油和水一样不能相容。

"汉姆斯塔德先生进来后,穿上了他的外套,在他经过我们这儿进入客厅时,他笑着说:'你们没有城里的朋友来打扰真是太幸运了,但是我必须对他们以礼相待。'之后他向我们鞠了个躬就出去了,又再鞠躬进了客厅。汉姆斯塔德夫人对她的客人说,她的女佣和孩子们正在进行周年庆贺,这符合农村的习惯,所以她必须时不时地忙一阵子,接着,又陪了我们一会儿。我们应该先喝茶,她颇为亲密地说,她的其他朋友除了面包、牛奶外什么都不要。就这样,女仆、厨房的女佣、孩子们和乡下的女孩坐在了一起。汉姆斯塔德夫人则一边在我们这儿尽主人的份儿,一边招呼她上流圈子的客人。

"很明显,喝完茶以后,我们这个小小的聚会就要散了,但是因为某些原因,我被邀请留了下来——也许我必须比其他人要走得更远一些。无论如何,我被邀请留了下来,我也确实留了下来,我觉得自己没有留下预期的印象,所以很高兴还有机会挽回些什么。不用说我这次败得很惨。混迹于一群时髦的受过教育的人之间,我显得分外突兀:我的脸从来没有像那天那样红过,我的手也从来没有像那天那样灰暗过,的确,我从来没有像那天那样,感到自己如此不雅,如此尴尬过,我憎恨自己,也憎恨整个世界。他们主要是谈论科学上的新发现,我仅仅知道他们也许在用希腊语交流。但是没有人注意到我,除了有时会看一下我,那时我恨不得从别人探究的眼神中不断缩小遁去。那眼神像是在问我一个问题:你到底为什么会到这儿来?的确有一位绅士问我是否进过城,问我是不是最喜欢牛奶或者是苹果汁。有时,汉姆斯塔德先生会回过头跟我说上几句话，可以说是关于我熟悉的事情，比如说我们家是不是有一个大型的牛奶厂，我会不会缝纫，我最喜欢学习还是玩耍等等。

"我无法尽述我遭受的所有屈辱和羞惭。我期冀自己在谷仓，在树林，在海底——除了那儿，哪儿都行。但是我怎样才得以脱身呢？我无法离开。我一直待在那里，直到那群人退回到走廊观看主人汉姆斯塔德家豢养的狗。那狗会做一些有趣的动作。我的机会来了，我这样想着，手里抓着我最好的那顶帽子，从偏门溜了出去。但是当身后的门关上之后我听到有人叫我：'哈德利小姐！哈德利小姐！'然而，我加快了步伐，并没有回头看。过了一会儿，汉姆斯塔德先生赶到了我的身边，说我这样一个人走回去不合适，他问我允不允许他和我一起走回家，或者他让凯撒和我一起走。

"我的眼睛里充满泪水，我的声音也在颤抖，我拒绝了他的客套，在夜色渐浓的夜晚，在暴风雨中，我独自一人走回了家。

"你也许会笑，但是那天我所受到的折磨实在是可怕，自打那以后，我再也没有进过汉姆斯塔德先生家的大门，甚至没有参加汉姆斯塔德夫人和小哈利的葬礼。你提到鲜艳的衣服，你建议到那里去拜访，这都令我十分敏感，让我立即想起当时所有的细节。"

雨早已不再敲打窗户，天空中乱云飞渡，月光在撕裂的云块边际闪烁，刺骨的北风呼啸而过。那些新书还没有被翻开过，佐伊把那张措辞有礼的便条扔到了壁炉的火里后，一言不发地点燃了夜灯，这对姐妹回到房间睡觉了——两人都不说话——两人都在回想那些苦涩的往事，无望地想着未来。在黑暗中默想的艾丽没有想到，不管是欢乐的冲击或是悲苦的重锤都无法探测到她的心灵深处，她也没有想到那些至今仍然清晰的景象竟会不知不觉地变得不那么重要了。

33. 派克斯夫人的派对

"骄傲首先能加强好感。"一位曾历经种种曲折心路历程的人士如此说，姑且不论此话是否适用于所有实例，这的确是一些特立独行之人的真实体验。艾丽·哈德利外表平静，内心却不乏果断、勇气，以及连她自己也从未意识到的傲气。汉姆斯塔德刚搬到首蓿角附近时，与他自己选择与之为邻的一般居民相比，他毫无疑问是高高在上的。这并非因为他天赋异禀，或是智力也许高于他的邻居们，而是因为他的禀赋均源于教育，又体现于他的风度翩翩、言谈优雅。

而其他人由于社会地位以及生活境遇所限,永远无法超出乡下人的智力水平。艾丽多年前就已经察觉他与那些自己熟知的人之间的差异。初相遇时她已意识到自己与他完全不属于同一阶层,每念及此,她便感到悲伤而又辛酸。

的确,她不得不承认,多么奇怪,他竟然会设法与他的邻居们交往并寻求认同。岁月流逝间她思想更加成熟,眼界日渐开阔,再无那些传统的狭隘偏见。于他而言,受过教育的思想所发出的光芒已经不足为奇,因此,如果现在艾丽不跳出她生于其中的乡村生活的追求和乐趣,从而去追寻能与自己相知相惜的灵魂,他又如何会尊敬自无知和迷信中透出的那一丝光亮,并且这一丝光亮还总是蒙上被牲畜的踩踏或车轮的驶过带起的尘土?奇怪的是他的思绪竟然如此自然地飘至新的方向,而他又对邻居们种种微不足道的计划产生了如此浓厚的兴趣,诸如开挖新渠、粉刷篱笆,或者设计乡间别墅等等。不过,这些行为丝毫未令他失去体面,他反而因此受到敬重,不但成了绅士的榜样,而且成了美德的典范,持续地影响着周围的人,使他们更加有教养,更加高尚。在几年间,主要在他的影响下,以往人口稀少、耕作不善的苜蓿角已经绿草如茵,处处可见灌木树篱围着的葡萄园、果园,公共场所有了醒目的高楼大厦。他自己的农场柳树谷的主人十几年前在此耕种时,周围遍是熏黑的树桩,杂草丛生,现在这里只见平坦的草场、精心修剪的树丛、风景秀丽的花园、弯弯曲曲的小路和灌木林,已经变得连主人都难以相认。他带着朋友们建造房屋,开垦土地,引得其他人纷纷效仿,如今无论是论品味还是实用,苜蓿角都拥有众多可以引以为荣的看点,其数目甚至可以与任何一座城市周边最为舒适的避暑胜地相媲美。它也完全有理由坦然接受任何针对其居民的总体智力水平和文明程度的最深入的调查。这些居民中,即使我们的老朋友米德尔顿先生跟海伍德医生,发现此地已有众多同道,也会很少想到要进城去交际了。事实上,村里也有众多年长者,他们卓越的天赋才能、骄人的学识,以及傲人的财富家产原该令他们得到比汉姆斯塔德先生更多的关注,可后者仍然最受众人垂青。他作为众人高雅与精致生活的倡导者享有盛名,因为同样出身的他的前任们各个为人自私,脱离大众;他的后任中则无人曾如他那样成为众望所归。汉姆斯塔德太太则从未受到过大众的如此宠爱,她的邻居们与她相处时从未感觉到轻松自在，尽管有时她们会假装如此。她对绿色小径的喜爱永远比不上铺砌的大街，她偏爱她所熟悉的毫无温情的礼貌举止胜过我们善良但不够文雅的好客之道。还没等她看到这里出现渐入佳境的变化，并不令她愉快的转变而导致的焦躁不安就消磨了她的生命。她甚至不愿自己的遗体将来与那些她去世时围在她身边的人安葬在一处，因此又被翻山越岭带回了她的家族墓地，在那里她优雅高贵地安息着。多年来，在上一章中提及的艾丽向妹妹讲述自己的回忆之前的一段时间，柳树谷的主人丧失了安慰与陪伴，那起初令他的新家备受艳羡。但是鳏居的他仍受大家爱戴，更有诸多佳人在他的葡萄园中采摘水果，在他的花园里采下一束束鲜花。不过，尽管光阴流转，他却从未屈就于时时包围他的款款美意。因此，他晚年送书给艾丽的做法应预示着与女人的密切关系，是大大出乎意料的果敢举动。

尽管已经四十五岁，他看起来仍然年轻，因为心态永远不老。褐色头发仍然富有光泽，并无任何其他颜色来泄露他的真实年龄，额头光滑没有皱纹，眼神明亮而不黯淡，笑容自然，毫不勉强，依然身材挺拔，相貌英俊，即使一个十六岁的少女也仍会为他动心。他的花园、乡间别墅以及书房是每个人无比羡慕的对象，艾丽也不例外，她频繁光顾苜蓿角，只是在经过柳树谷时，尤其当主人在家里时，她总表现出不是特别在意的样子。如果实在避无可避，只能表示认出对方了，但是会做得像是并不怎么认识他，即便略有所知，也不见得是对他的认可。

如果不是命运之神全然不顾我们的决心而安排了我们的结局，可能他们两人永远就这样过下去了。我说过"骄傲能加强好感"，也说过艾丽心中不乏傲气，也正是如此才使她没能带着更大的善意听进去众多诚实富有的追求者的求爱之语。心灵总要有所寄托，不是寄托于爱情，就是事业或者自尊。"他是个很不错的小伙子，"她总是这么说起一个又一个出于不同原因试图吸引她的注意的追求者，"不过他的青睐对我毫无意义。"因此时光飞逝，匆匆一瞥再也无法点燃少女心中幻想的火花，她也无须再以自尊为掩饰，以克制自己孩子般的任性固执。只是她心中仍密封着一个泉眼，几乎从未受到任何打扰。也许她已经意识到有那样一只手能够开启泉眼，故此才用那些过去的痛苦记忆筑成围栏封闭了自己。

我提到的那个夜晚之后又过了几日，此时人们心中被激起的涟漪已经逐渐平息下来。一天晚上，艾丽和佐伊正坐着阅读一部新的小说，敲门声响起，但是客人一进门，姐姐脸上的红润顿失，光泽退去，变成非常不满的表情。佐伊叫来人马丁先生，艾丽则喊他威廉。来人是一个高个子的年轻小伙子，给人犹似提起自己的小学校长时的那种感觉，他原本的笨拙却勉强装出悠闲和优雅，更加显得滑稽可笑。他对自己的父母几乎没什么感情，因此在被约束了多年后，一旦解放，就出来自己闯天下了，他如今是个工头，老板是这里最有钱的几个地主之一。他对自己的地位非常满意，从没想到过有些人竟会觉得他的前途还悬而未定，也从未料到还有些人认为他的身份必定限制了他与仆人们以及与他境遇相似的人群的交往。

他的老板为人温和，作风民主，对他平等相待，至少就能够允许威廉坐在同一张桌子上打牌聊天而言是这样，这一点成了威廉的一大优势，他充分地加以利用。他其实只是来送个信，可是迟迟不走，待了整个晚上，甚至已经站起身来打算离去，门也打开了，他又逗留了至少半个小时，反复地说着她们已经听烦了的话："两位小姐，你们一定要来，不然派克斯夫人跟我们大家都会很失望的。而且你们一旦来了一次，认路之后，一定要常来。你们可以直接穿过牧场过来——只要翻两道篱笆，过一条小溪——溪上有一根很粗的原木搭的桥，然后穿过玉米地过来，就能看到宅子了，最后过了草坪就到了。所以你们一定会常来的，对吗？派克斯夫人和我们大家看到你们能多出来参加社交活动都会很高兴的。你们一定一定记着要来啊。不过要是这次以后你们不来了，那周三晚上一定要来。我想我们一定会度过一个最美妙的夜晚的。"

起风了，几乎吹灭了灯，壁炉里的火苗借着风势蹿了出来，但是他对此视而不见，仍然不停地赘述着同样的话，直到姐妹两人再三保证她们接受了他传达的盛情邀请，最后只能指望自己的一言不发能让他识趣离开，小伙子最后终于走下了台阶。

"那么，"他的身影一消失，佐伊大笑道，"艾丽，我们要去吗？"

"我是不去的，"姐姐坐在壁炉前，隐在阴影里，一只手托着下颔，看起来不愿打破沉默。

佐伊兴致很高，部分是因为她所谓的马丁先生的好心，也因为邀请是来自派克斯夫人。"他们只招待几个朋友，而且还不是正式的宴会，派克斯夫人希望他们能光临她的寒舍。我想知道汉姆斯塔德先生会不会去？"她说，希望能够多少引起姐姐的一点兴趣。

"我不知道，"艾丽答道。那晚余下的时间里两人谁也没有再多讲一个字。

但是在派对之前的几天里，她们对期待中的派对大谈特谈，所有的利弊都经过了仔仔细细的斟酌，这次派对并不足以让她们为自己的享乐开脱，相反，倒像是她们生活得幸福还是悲惨要完全取决于这次派对了。而事实上，这件事的确对她们意义重大。

艾丽极力主张要送一封道歉的信去才合适，可佐伊的意见还是想去，所以她们什么也没做，直到最后她们要么就硬着头皮去参加，要么就失礼地始终保持沉默，不说去也不说不去。

"你打算穿什么？"艾丽问，这是那天的早晨。

"我不知道穿什么最好。"

艾丽说她没法替佐伊作决定，但是她自己没什么选的，会穿去年那件细布衣服。妹妹表示那件衣服本来就太素，现在又真的过时了。但是艾丽只是反复说她没什么选的，说如果她去，就一定会穿那条旧裙子，不过她更想待在家里，还说佐伊自己去就可以，不必顾及她。

"不不，你一定也要去，"佐伊坚持着，"如果你去了不开心，我以后再也不会要求你陪我去别的地方了。"

所以就这样，艾丽还是被说动了，不过说不上高兴也说不上满意。

太阳还没落山佐伊就已经一切就绪，她把晚上要干的活儿全丢给姐姐，自己坐在那里等着出发那一刻的到来。她穿着一条式样简洁的平纹细布裙子，尽管没戴什么饰物，但是黑色的鬈发让她看起来也十分动人。

七点整，威廉·马丁就已经驾着派克斯上校的小马车到了，又等了半个小时，等艾丽把茶点跟牛奶打点好，几个人就出发了。

"我更愿意跟别的任何人一起来。"艾丽说。进客厅之前，她又理了理头发，拉了拉过短的袖子，客厅里传来的欢声笑语令她不太舒服。"我就说我们该比别人来早点的，不然说什么我也不会就这样出现在大家面前，还是跟这个马丁一起，就像现在这样。再看看这条棕色的破裙子！唉，派克斯先生的女仆也比我看起来更像个淑女。

真希望我没来。无论如何我都不适合参加社交活动。"她站在那里，想着可能受到的痛苦煎熬，全身发抖。佐伊弯下腰把裙子拉低，使它显得长一点时，艾丽甚至觉得自己的眼泪落在了她的头顶。无奈中，佐伊只得说："亲爱的艾丽，你看起来很不错，而且可能根本没人会注意到威廉·马丁是跟我们一起的。不过就算有又怎样？如果我们的面子这么容易就丢了，那么这面子也不值一文。"

艾丽打量了一下自己，似乎自己被精灵变成了粗笨的样子，然后说她们没什么面子可丢的，接着两人都沉默下来。几个房间里都是灯火辉煌，人人衣着光鲜，有人在桌前打纸牌，三三两两的人群或坐或站，笑语喧哗，有人语气轻松愉快，有人腔调气势逼人。非常自然地，许多人的眼光都转向了刚进来的这几个人，可对于艾丽而言，似乎自己成了所有客人议论纷纷的对象。派克斯夫人走上前来叫道："亲爱的姑娘们！"她的话中透着熟人之间的亲切，只是艾丽和佐伊以前从未见识过不管是她还是在场其他人这样的做派，因此他们的镇定，即保持举止优雅的根本，一下全跑掉了，她们可从没觉得这么坐立不安，手足无措。

等到她们完全适应了装饰华丽的家具、灯光璀璨的吊灯，以及自己身处其中的优雅时尚的氛围时，威廉·马丁，或者大家嘴里叫的威廉，似乎仍丝毫无意要离开她们，还假装熟稔的样子，用半个房间的人都能听到的声音叫道，"汉姆斯塔德，这儿有两位你的邻居，你好像没看到啊。"这一下她们彻底感觉到既狼狈又难堪。

汉姆斯塔德走上前来鞠躬示意，他对两位女士表示了赞美，用词优雅而又简洁，同时表示恐怕他妨碍了女士们的闺房密语，就又回到房间的另一侧去了，并且很快就开始与一位六十岁的女士下起棋来。那位女士下棋时输了分，一边卖弄风情地向后甩着自己的卷发，尽管那卷发灰白稀疏，一边惊叫着说："噢，你真坏！""汉姆斯塔德先生，是真的吗？你真的自私地把柳树谷封锁起来了——不让别人光顾了？"

汉姆斯塔德声称此类谣言大大地冤枉了他，这一切绝非出自他的意愿，是两位女士经过的时候不但对他而且对柳树谷都不屑于瞧上一眼。"千真万确，"他补充道，手落在棋盘上，又转向佐伊，"而且我的小邻居可以在此作证。"佐伊此时已经跟着一位脸色红润、双手白皙的年轻绅士走到了一边，年轻人大谈人类的手足情同胞爱，大谈人性中趋向神性的一面，以及人类将很快回到天堂般的美好时光——他的高谈阔论佐伊并未领会多少。

可怜的艾丽现在完全被丢下了，因为佐伊一走开，威廉也不见了，她拘谨地坐在房间里最为昏暗的角落，两手交叠，没戴手套，脸上是一贯的凄惨表情，低头看着她简单梳理的发型，她与整个房间里欢乐的气氛如此不合，比平时显得更加姿色平庸。时不时地也真的有些好心的老先生停下手里的牌局，来跟她聊上几句——话题可能是怎样做最好吃的南瓜派，也可能是自制面包的诸多好处，或者柴火给人带来的温暖和美妙的感觉多么诱人。而佐伊愉快亲切的举止，也可能再加上她更加女性化的魅力，令许多人对她大献殷勤，所以这个晚上她兴高采烈，简直是喜出望外，以至于她把姐姐给抛在了脑后，她把一切都完全抛在了九霄云外，只顾着沉浸在派对上令她眼花缭乱的美景中。

宣布用茶点的时候，艾丽看着客人们纷纷离开客厅，直到只剩下自己留在房间里。这时汉姆斯塔德先生突然走了进来，然后，不管是否看到了她，很快地跟进来的时候一样突然退了出去，很显然他在找什么人。

这时，在餐桌那里艾丽没看到威廉好心地来做她的护花使者。尽管艾丽不引人注意，她还是发现自己的妹妹坐在桌子的另一端，一边对着笑容满面的、我前面提过的那个双手白皙的男子微笑，同时机智巧妙地应对着滔滔不绝的汉姆斯塔德先生，一头五十多年来一直用报纸和梳子调理的卷发几乎贴到他的脸上。

看到这一幕，艾丽不但恼怒气极，而且觉得辛酸，甚至对自己乃至世界仇恨起来。汉姆斯塔德先生又出现在昏暗的角落——可能是出于同情吧，她想——邀请她跟自己一起玩游戏。她对要玩的游戏一无所知，谢绝了邀请，表现得过度的冷淡和礼貌，但是男士非常坚决，她最后只好让步答应。但是她第一下掷出骰子时用力过大，几粒骰子噼里啪啦地滚过桌面，四散落在地上。她看到别人在笑，尽管很快就忍住了，于是她面颊由红变白，眼眶湿润。

片刻之后，她便在来时护送者的陪伴下悄然离开了，内心充满了敌视一切事物的情绪。她将佐伊一个人留在派对上，独自回了家，满心怨愤，忽而痛下决心，这决心出于愤怒而又淹没于满面泪痕。

443

34. 一个冬季的变迁

第二天艾丽和佐伊大谈前一晚的晚会。妹妹尽管发觉自己是派对上唯一一个着正装的人仍然心情愉快，而且她忍不住想如果艾丽不放任自己那愚蠢的敏感的话，本来她也能像自己那样快活的。毫无疑问，尽管不全对，但的确是这样，可这是艾丽的不幸而并非她的过失。她的才智先是陷于种种压制而得不到发展，之后经过她经年累月的努力，这其中从未有过任何外援，而且一半的努力都付诸东流，终于能够略微有所显露，却又因为同样的原因而无法为人所见。想到这样一个人，才智上等却又处处备受压制而整日满腹忧虑，我的确想不出会有任何人在任何情况下比她更加亟须慰藉。生气勃勃的泉水可能深藏地下，但是谁曾透过褐色的泥土、堆积的石块和丛生的杂草见到过它？谁会犹如珍视精美的珠宝中的黄金一般珍视原矿中的金砂？但是倘若才华，甚至天才，伴有明显奇怪的不雅或是笨拙，似乎就毫无希望了：有时目睹者可能会意识到才华的存在，却不会对其肃然起敬；又或者一个人可能与一个才智远远优于自己的人交往多年而从未想过对方会有任何非凡之处。这是因为智力最为超群的人通常表现的并非真实的自己，而是他们想象中的周围环境希望他们的样子。邻居家的约会、亲切流畅的言谈，都会令他们困惑或者约束自己，直到他们的语言再不足以表达他们的纷繁想法。

众多著名作者，倘无作品出版，将终日被误认为行为荒诞滑稽；而另外一些，因为语言能力所限，终生籍籍无名。

我所描写的年代的苜蓿角有几位女士，相貌美丽，谈吐活泼，人人赞其出色；艾丽·哈德利尽管姿色平平，籍籍无名，甚至遭人轻视，但是其灵魂极富创造力，这使她在本质上应当归属为更高层次。

伴着夕阳小酌，在山坡上迎风奔跑，或是兴奋地与鸟儿齐声高唱，都曾给艾丽带来最为甜美的享受。她还会体会到一种更为珍贵的奇妙感受，不是沉浸在自己的思绪和感受中，就是在梦幻的神秘国度中让思绪与诗人们一起飞翔。有时候她也会隐身于山谷中，草地如天鹅绒般柔软，流水淙淙，应和着她心中的旋律。她会将脸颊紧紧贴着芳香的泥土，整日陷入冥想，专注得远离了尘世的人烟与喧嚣……

一两周过去了，佐伊一反常态的开心兴奋；艾丽保持着惯常的平静，这种平静代表的如果不是绝望，就是无望。那位年轻的"改革家"已经发觉苜蓿角是一个绝对吸引人的地方，而且自从在派克斯上校家与两姐妹初次相见，他已经不止一次地用"好时候来了"的话开导她们，正如微笑掠过的眼神所泄露的，不管是出自对教会禧年大庆的期待，还是因为预见凡俗喜事，我不得而知，但是佐伊似乎从未如此快乐，满怀希望。此外，她眼界大开，许多东西对她也许并非毫无可能实现，而且又花不了什么大钱——她裙子的款式和行为举止都有了明显的改善。

"噢，艾丽，"一天，姐姐正在那张白色的松木桌子上用模子做面包，佐伊过去，说，"我有了个计划！""什么计划？"艾丽问，尽管自己没那么热衷，还是笑着，片刻之后又说，"你最近可越来越爱幻想了。"

佐伊的脸上掠过一丝红晕，吞吞吐吐地回答说她相信自己的计划是可行的，又接着解释说她一直在想艾丽很聪明，完全可以胜任教书，还说既然校舍空关着，现在就有一个好机会让她既可以发挥自己的才华为他人服务，又能为她们自己谋利。

"我没有受过足够的教育，"艾丽提出，"就算我有，也不是这种工作要求的那种教育，我那点微薄的知识都是在偶然的情况下获得的，我对什么了解得都不够彻底，而且我怀疑我这浅薄的学识是否能够利用上哪怕是一点点。"

但是佐伊继续鼓励她，所以犹豫了几天后，艾丽最终决定要试一试。连续数个夜晚，她坐在缝纫桌前，在烛光下复习地理、语法和拼写课本。尽管父亲一再问她为何这样浪费时间，她还是坚持下来了，而且这些课程完成后，还有两个非常严峻的考验等着她——从城里的某个她不敢去见的权威那里获得一张证书，以及之后拜访学校董事会的成员们，获得他们的一致同意。为了最后这件可怕的事，她在一个夜晚与家人的聊天中获得了些许的鼓励。

"父亲，你知道学校的董事会成员都是谁吗？"她一边倒茶一边说，一副漫不经心的样子。

"啊，知道，"哈德利先生回答道，"有一个是我们的邻居，汉姆斯塔德先生，我想，他对自己花园里的花的关注超过了对村子里孩子们的教育。"

"我觉得汉姆斯塔德先生对于邻里所作的贡献不比任何人少。"

艾丽说道，尽管要是别的什么人说些赞美之词，她很可能就会一言不发。

"哦，就我所知，他还算得上好人"，哈德利先生答，"他送给我一些葡萄藤和一两棵他从法国带来的树，不过他说话太快，我几乎听不懂，还有，他还有这么多出色的朋友，还有近来这样那样的事。"

哈德利先生很难确定这些事是如何对这位绅士产生不利的影响的，但是，这些事已经足够令他对他产生偏见了。

"其他董事们呢？"艾丽问。

"彼得斯先生跟詹姆森先生——不过，这个学校哪里吸引你了？"

艾丽说她原本就想过由自己任教，只是若没有父亲的同意，她可没有胆量迈出这样一大步，但是她十分确定凭借她可能提出的任何诚实的用以筹款的举措，一定能得到父亲的许可。哈德利先生对于自己女儿的能力深信不疑，只不过女儿的能力也仅限于在《圣经》上写上几句注释，至于女儿的能力是如何得来的他是一无所知，不过他认为这世上也没多少东西是她懂的或者她应该懂的。因此艾丽毫不意外地听到父亲说："主意不错，可能，到春天你就能挣够买上一两头奶牛的钱了。"后来更是认真地说："千万别买头有斑点的，艾丽，也别买牛角没长出来的。"他吃光了晚饭，看起来比平时还要津津有味。艾丽的希望受到了些微打击，她已经决心去找别的投资，而且她已经多次想象着那些她盼望已久的书本在她面前排列开来的场景了。

几天后，第一件令人恐惧的折磨已经过去了。艾丽也曾经因为惶恐而战栗，但目前为止她的努力都获得了成功，证书也带回了家，并且安全地放置在了《圣经》的书页中。

"我会去拜访彼得斯先生跟詹姆森先生的，"艾丽说，"而且可能根本无须去拜访汉姆斯塔德先生。"所以，在一个灰蒙蒙的早晨，她裹着披肩，戴着面纱，出门去找其他权威人士了。彼得斯先生家最近，因此她先去了那里，但是彼得斯先生本人在离他住宅最远的农场麦地的边上犁地。从不放过任何细节的彼得斯夫人说那块地已经有七年没有翻过了，以前那里的玉米长得可比她戴着一顶难看的高帽子的儿子约翰还高；玉米地里长的南瓜根本不用人打理也能长得很大，一个南瓜就能做一百个南瓜派。她还说，彼得斯先生犁地用的是几匹公马驹。经过了这样一番指点，清楚了要穿过几块地，如何绕开收割过的麦地，在哪里翻过篱笆，艾丽就上路了。

最后她终于到了，站在距彼得斯先生很近的地方，那位先生驾着马绕过田垄，靠在犁上听她讲话。

聊了几分钟后，艾丽就明白，膝下无子的彼得斯先生对学校毫无兴趣，也无意提供任何意见。不过他说他认为艾丽不会被难住的；而且孩子们大部分都年幼无知，一个女人完全可以把他们教好；不过有钱人是不会资助地区学校的；他建议艾丽向詹姆森求助，詹姆森喜欢做买卖，自己也有六个不大的孩子；最后他说他的小马驹们可不喜欢一直站着不动，就这样结束了谈话。

艾丽踩着刚刚犁开的犁沟，穿过了彼得斯先生身后的那块地，向詹姆森先生家走去。

詹姆森可是个有钱人，但生活十分俭朴，不管是住的房子本身还是周围的一切都十分落伍。艾丽走近时，能够看到孩子们款式过时的窄窄的短裙朝房子那边飘去。全家上上下下都不习惯见到陌生人，如果艾丽华丽的披肩颜色不是这么鲜亮，或者她的头上戴的不是软帽而是系了条手帕，他们也就不会如此瞠目结舌。从工棚下和别的什么地方跳出来的六条狗向艾丽冲了过来，并且齐声大叫，十分刺耳，一只老母鸡带着一群小鸡也扑棱着飞到她身上，用翅膀拍着她的脸，正在这个关键时候，詹姆森先生急忙赶来救场。他一只手拿着一本破旧不堪的书，另一只手拿着一根细软的树枝。他在狗群里辟出了一条路，并迅速而又果敢地抓住了那只发狂的母鸡。

詹姆森先生的业余时间都用来阅读法律方面的书籍，他手里拿的可能是一册黑石书店出的书，或者一沓表格。他比彼得斯先生对学校感兴趣，但是对于雇佣一个女人仍然犹豫不决。冬季就要到了，会有很多男孩子来上学，因此他担心她应付不了。不过无论如何，他也只是三位理事之一，下周他会在学校召集一次会议，他会通知她磋商后的结果。艾丽在得到了这样的一丝鼓励之后便动身往家走。

一周过去了，为了召开理事会议，校舍里暖意融融，灯火通明。当天晚上，艾丽与佐伊正坐在客厅里谈着可能的结果时吃惊地看到汉姆斯塔德先生走了进来，可是他今晚的举止与他一两周之前在派克斯上校家的样子是如此不同。他当时表现得含蓄而拘谨，令艾丽深刻地感受到了两人之间存在的鸿沟，可是这会儿那些含蓄拘谨都已不见踪影，他认可了他们之间的平等地位，又对她们的计划表现得饶有兴致，这些都令之前他们交往中笼罩着的难耐困窘烟消云散，故此他们的相处令每个人都更加愉快。汉姆斯塔德先生看起来也喜出望外，可以说他有了一个新发现，他谦逊低调的邻居不但与他旗鼓相当，甚至在许多方面比他更加得天独厚。

艾丽的学校在接下来的那个周一的早晨开学了。学校共收了十五个还是二十个你能想象出的最粗鲁无礼而又前途无望的顽童，他们带着各色各样的书本，各个都想着自己选择科目，还要按照自己的喜好来学习。但是恕我不能在这些细枝末节上花费笔墨——她所承担的责任对她并非难事，而且随着教学的展开这些事情于她而言变得日益轻松愉快。

从她书桌前的窗子望出去就是柳树谷，它的主人每天，几乎每个小时，都会出现在她的视线里；而且远不止如此，有时他还会到学校来——他看起来似乎是对孩子们很感兴趣，只是这种兴趣突飞猛涨，而且以前也绝对从未表现得如此浓厚。有时候汉姆斯塔德先生会逗留至放学时分，然后就会陪着艾丽走回家。起初只送艾丽到大门口，但偶尔天气寒冷，他就会进来与佐伊聊上几分钟，在炉火前取会儿暖，渐渐地几分钟的停留就延长至几个小时了。

世界在艾丽的眼中呈现出美好的面貌，原因无须我来解释。但是闪烁在她眼前的希望是摇曳不定的，有时眼前先是一片光明的胜景，然后暗淡模糊，几乎完全不见。我说的是，汉姆斯塔德先生常常到学校来，常常到哈德利先生家来，而且最后，尽管他从不言爱，他的举止可不再是一位普通朋友的表现。可是他几乎从未做过任何明确的表示，比如他跟艾丽要在什么地方有个小别墅，那么艾丽在建筑风格以及大小尺寸方面的品味就会被考虑进去，然后又会笑着问佐伊要是没有了他们她可怎么办；再例如，他把艾丽完全当做一个孩子，用一种保护人或者父亲般的语气说"亲爱的艾丽，要是你是我的女儿"诸如此类的话。可是接着可能一周或者两周过去，此间他既不到学校去也不到她们家里来，每每从门前路过时似乎完完全全没有意识到她们就在近旁。

每到此时，上课的时间就会显得乏味而又难熬，然而为了孩子们她们仍需备课，所以尽管家里黄昏至深夜这段时间十分难熬，却也使她们免于全然的枯燥沉闷。在这些夜晚，姐妹两人会坐在炉光里静默不语,渴望着听到令她们出乎意料的脚步声,直到夜色渐深,继续侧耳倾听或是心怀期待也毫无意义。然后她们会再次重复前一晚的谈话,直到最后,反复地说一定是发生了什么事让他无法前来,说他当然会再次出现,救她们于绝望中并且赋予她们希望,然后她们会伴着蟋蟀的鸣声入眠,只是醒来后新的守候会带来新的失望。就这样一个冬天消磨过去了,当青葱的春意悄然爬上枝头,新的烦恼和悔恨也随之而来了。

三月末的一个傍晚,她们坐在老地方,炉底埋着的树枝缓慢地燃烧着,不见火焰,窗户被抬起了一点,让新鲜空气进来——尽管大部分人家里还点着壁炉,天气还是正在回暖。门槛上响起了脚步声,她们很快地交换了眼神,同时感到自己在发抖,然后吃惊地感觉心猛地一沉——来访者是威廉·马丁先生。

佐伊并不那么失望,相反倒觉得兴奋,她试着做出高兴的样子,但是艾丽并未如此掩饰自己,她又回到窗前,望着窗外阴沉的夜幕缓缓降临。从她上一次见到汉姆斯塔德先生至今,或者从他表现出一丝与她相识的样子到现在,几周的时间已经过去了,因为她常常见到他从房前屋后路过,有时眼神与他的相遇,只是当时他的眼神冰冷,一如他看着那些不曾也无意有兴趣相识的人时的眼神。

艾丽眼前的世界看上去一片凄凉萧索。参差凌乱的云朵在空中飘舞,月亮时而在荒瘠的地面上笼上一层忧郁的轻纱。雨水已经淅淅沥沥了几天,纤细的秸秆开始顺着山谷中的积水涌出。紧贴窗户的下沿可以看到挺立的水仙阔阔的叶片、野蔷薇淡粉色的嫩芽,还有绵延至树林的田垄上绿色的麦苗。世界的欢快与悲伤取决于我们看待世界的心情,即使太阳高挂六月的碧空,这好时光也无法令艾丽的忧伤减少半分。

艾丽深深地沉浸在自己的思绪中,一开始一个字也没有听进去。最后威廉先生问她是否听说了什么消息,在得到了一个否定的答复后,他告诉她汉姆斯塔德先生已经卖掉了农场,很快就要返回自己的家乡——正如传闻所言,去结婚成家了。

现在艾丽知道曾经照射到她周围的希望的光芒破灭了。这位不请自来的客人已经毫无知觉地使自己变得讨厌可恶起来:她只想他走开,并且再不想见到他。他待了有一个世纪那么久!但是他终于走了,那些令她窒息的想法终于可以得以表达了。

佐伊看起来比自己感觉更乐观一些,她说:"想一想汉姆斯塔德先生这么突然地就处理掉柳树谷是不合情理的,就算那是真的,也有可能他既不是要离开苜蓿角,也不是要去结婚,因为那样他的一切行为不就背叛了他对你的爱情了吗?"

"但是他从未说过他爱我。"艾丽答道,仍然期冀着一些安慰。

"就是说了又有啥用?"

"见证——见证而已。"

又有多少最最真实的合约遭违背,只因为没有见证!

35. 故事结局

经历了几个星期的希望与忧惧的折磨,在清新的空气中,在明亮的月光下,我们能看到艾丽的身影,但她已经不再是孤单一人了。柳树谷已经出售,汉姆斯塔德先生就要离开了,但是秋天他就会回来,会看到那些小房子像他在时一样美丽。如果艾丽允许他写信给她,他即使不在也会从信里得到安慰。这是个多么崭新的世界!卸去生活的重担,她心里多么轻松啊!走过了长长一段路,他们俩停在了门口,久久不愿分别:他很明白这个姑娘和他一样快乐,因为他们心心相印,毫无疑问,这个姑娘对他很重要,然而——

寂静的夜色中两人默默无语,看上去由于某些原因两人神色凝重——但是否是同一原因我就不得而知了。"世界真美好。"最终艾丽说道,她的话与其说是表达内心感受,还不如说是打破沉寂更合适。"这里的确很美,"她的恋人(如果可以这样说的话)说道,"我愿意为你而死——现在正是时候。""不要这样,"艾丽回答道,"即使最痛苦的日子在我看来也是好日子,现在就更加美好了。如果你愿意为我死,为什么不为我好好活着?"

"为你而活!我必须和你说件事。"他神秘地说。

"什么事?"

"现在还不是时候,我打算过些日子告诉你,今晚你没有心理准备。"突然,他放下早就松开的手,转身走了。

"我什么时候能再见到你?"艾丽浑身打颤,半是急切半是犹豫地问道。

"很快,非常快,可能就是明晚,"他走回来平静地给了艾丽告别的一吻,感觉像是平常祝福的一吻。然后艾丽就孤零零地站在那里了——一副不安、不满的可怜样子。

第二天就这样过去了，接着又过去了几天、几个星期，汉姆斯塔德先生都没有来。这期间艾丽一直留意有关他的消息，没有一则让她宽慰的——有时听说他马上要离开，有时听说他早就走了，没有和她打过招呼。最后她确知他正打算走，听到这个消息时，她正和佐伊坐在广场上，透过浓密的树叶，路对面叮咚的流水声和夜莺哀婉的啼鸣不绝于耳，清晰可辨。

汉姆斯塔德先生在马丁先生的陪同下回来和大家告别。他没有找机会单独和艾丽说说话，也没打算要找这样的机会。看上去他想和艾丽说的话还没有和佐伊或马丁先生等人说的话多。事实上，他表现出他对大家一样都很看重。他谈到未来，谈到回来，谈到很盼望能再次见到他们，但是没有再和艾丽说起会为艾丽死或为艾丽活之类的话。分手时，他握着艾丽的手就像是握着马丁先生的手，看着艾丽难以遮掩的悲伤，只是说："夏天很快就会过去，我们很快就会再见。"马上又补充道，"那时你可能已经结婚了。"艾丽既没说是也没否认，接着尽可能平静地说了再见，就躲进了暗处。

佐伊没有安慰之语——她觉得那无异于让狂风平息，或者和绝望评理。

当一个人的信念被毁，希望化成泡影时，他的痛苦不是语言所能描述的。当我们拿着鲜花去坟上看望亲人时，天使会伸出双手从坟墓中将爱人接走——我们会听到甜美的声音："他们不在这里，他们去了天堂。"然而，当我们为人世的虚假而痛苦时，我们的心情都无所寄托，无论是在俗世还是在天堂。过去的就要让它过去，否则就没有未来。我们只能祈祷我们的心不再淌血，或者祈祷我们自己得到永恒的宁静，再也不会被俗世的嘲笑所刺激。人间并非处处是乐园，因此即使我们走在天堂葱郁的青山上，只要我们意识到自己的荒凉无伴，马上就会感觉到厌烦，即使有生命之泉浇灌，我们的嘴唇依然焦干。

日子就这样毫无意趣地过去了，由春到夏，由夏至秋。艾丽依然在学校里教书，忠诚地履行自己的职责，努力重建对生活的兴趣。在树荫下，靠近孩子玩耍的地方，我们能看见她若有所思地走来走去，或者倚着一个大树干，无精打采地拿着书，或者忘记带她的缝衣针。

十月份她的课程快结束了，她打起精神为接下来做什么作着打算——那一大堆书可以让她在漫长的冬日里获得安慰；还有，汉姆斯塔德先生要回来，她可不要像往常那样穿得那么土气和老气，好有一丝满足感。时光就这样过去了，终于学校放假了。还有些令人厌烦的琐事她和佐伊分着干完了，佐伊快要结婚了。

一个雾蒙蒙的下午，她和佐伊去了城里，买她们很久以前就说好要去买的东西。他们挑了新娘装和面纱，艾丽苦笑着说自己要买些黑的给自己。这时她看见了一辆色彩鲜艳的马车，车上是看上去笑不拢嘴的汉姆斯塔德先生，身边是一位优雅的女士，面容娇美，神情中带着傲气，还有几分悲天悯人。

可怜的艾丽原以为自己很坚强，但是直到那时她才知道自己的心里对汉姆斯塔德先生抱着多大的幻想。她该往何处去？她费尽辛劳换来的竟是这可怜的报偿？佐伊注意到她的神情，问她要买什么，她沉思了一会儿，说道："什么也不买。"然后她张开手，佐伊注意到那放着她全部家当的小钱包不见了。

冬日的风吹打着窗扉，艾丽独自坐在火炉旁，她已经习惯了别人的同情，现在同情都没有了，大自然把美景带走，只留下寒冷和枯萎给大地，她清楚地知道她只剩下自己了，在她身上她会发现她拥有的财富比她想象的要多得多。

环境，不论一开始我们如何悖逆它，总是会像潮水一样很快涌到我们面前，我们很难摆脱环境的曲曲折折，也很难置身事外，说什么如果可能、这样那样就好了等等的话，我觉得这就是天意的一个最美妙之处。当清晨透过晨曦露出脸来，在朝露中垂下深红色的长裙笑眯眯地看着我们时，我们恨不得时时都是早晨。但是当中午带来树荫，慵懒地在山顶眨眼，人们都在歇息时，泉水涔涔，井水凉凉，那真是个好时候，我们不能弄出一点声响来破坏它的宁静。当黄昏的霞光淹没在黑糊糊的丛林里，人们能看见满天繁星，月亮有时像个圆盘，有时像个圆环高挂在天空之中，这时似乎是一天中最美的时光，我们愿意对着黑影倾诉，或缩在自己的小屋里，让灰白的烟雾尽情缭绕。夜的世界深沉静穆。天空中的星系按着自己的轨道运行，投向地球的光线如同金梯，仿佛我们的思想可攀着它们去往天堂；团团黑云扫过天空，在地平线上堆起了黑黑的原野，有时彼此相靠，好像海面上那一排排的舰队齐头并进；风呼啸着吹过山峦，穿过原野，低吼着，哭诉着，晚上的时光真是好啊——适合思索，适合做梦，也适合安静地睡觉。

　　一年中的时光都是这样美妙。五月，树叶吐露嫩芽，花朵色彩灿烂，鸣鸟的歌唱让果园、牧场欢快无比，潺潺的溪水和争奇斗艳的花园让大地充满生机；六月，玫瑰怒放，蜜蜂飞舞，草原农场富裕丰饶，排排作物长得碧绿青翠，又高又壮；八月，果园果实成熟，谷物大获丰收；十月，树叶泛黄，树荫幽幽；十二月，漫天冰雪，用麻木的手指悠闲地吹奏乐曲——所有的季节都有自己的魅力。在夏日玫瑰爬满凉亭，或者在冬日手举火把时，我们都会快乐地说："神造万物，各按其时呈现美好。"我们围坐在火边，我们所敬畏的天使降临，带走了我们中的一员——抚摸过我们的双手，瀑布般飘洒在我们面前的美发都收敛入墓——我们看到坟墓的棱角，听到埋土时的隆隆声。由于极度的悲痛，我们痛哭流涕，难以停止。但是日子一天天过去，季节更替，慢慢地沉痛一点点逝去，阴影在眼前逐渐消失，我们又恢复了往日的快乐，又重新看到了世界的美好。圈子变小了，空荡荡的座位使我们想起逝者已去，我们还是一样有说有笑，最后会惊异于死者遍地。对往昔而言，我们都是叛徒！然而这也是最明智之举。为什么孩子们必须回顾那些我们已经无能为力的过去？为什么在将来成为现在或永恒之前，此时此刻不能成为我们人生中最美的时期呢？

　　我要写的就是平凡人生的故事，我写完了。至于艾丽的将来，关于自制和谦虚的用处，也无须再赘言了。她的额头满是忧伤；她忙着家务时尽量保持心里平静，但没人想象得到那内心流血的创痛，只有死亡才能完全平复这创痛。有时她受了落日余晖的启发，把思绪写成随意的韵文。而当她动人的描述搅起情感的喷泉时，没人会质疑那颗心及其情感赖以产生的生活。詹姆森先生时不时来看看她，告诉她没必要孤单地生活，还说他老婆觉得她是优秀的典范。威廉·马丁先生也来过，还三番五次发出邀请。尽管她对他们的善意敬谢不敏，但是她从来没有再到过教堂和墓地以外的地方。而当她经过柳树谷时，经常重复着英格兰阴郁的诗人的一行诗——诗行简单，含意深远——

　　　　伊人已陌路，
　　　　万事皆成空。

致　　谢

作为东华大学"英语文学文化研究中心"的一个项目，我们的翻译和研究工作有幸得到多方关注和支持。项目的完成与有关人士的大力支持是分不开的，特别是殷耀教授的关心和鼓励。同时本项目自始至终得到东华大学外语学院领导的关怀和鼎力支持。在此表示衷心感谢！

没有项目参与人员的密切配合和辛劳工作，本项目的完成是不可想象的。首先要感谢的是《苜蓿角》的所有翻译人员！大家利用业余时间进行翻译和校对，期间克服了很多困难。颜海璐和李盛两位在译文互校的组织、译名的统一和校对等方面做了大量工作。乔雪瑛、李盛、黄培希和高蕴华四位青年学者参与了分章写作，还协助将英文摘要翻译成中文，付出了额外的努力。对她们的工作在此表示特别感谢！

我的合作者 Dennis Berthold 教授一直是本项目的坚定支持者。感谢他在资料收集，绪论写作，英文篇章的组织和编辑方面的密切合作！

常耀信教授为本书撰写"序言"，并在"序言"中表现了奖掖后进的大家风范。感谢他的支持和鼓励！

感谢东北师范大学出版社对选题的认可以及社长吴长安先生的特别关照！

最后，感谢我的家人对我的事业的支持！

杨林贵